Close Enough to Perfect

Close Enough to Perfect

Close Enough to Perfect
By Terry Fowler

On a Clear Day
By Yvonne Lehman

Changing Seasons
By Colleen Reece & Renee Demarco

A Fairy-Tale Romance
By Melanie Panagiotopoulos

HeavenSent
FROM
Crossings

Close Enough to Perfect
Copyright © 2003 by Terry Fowler

On a Clear Day
Copyright © 2003 by Yvonne Lehman

Changing Seasons
Copyright © 2004 by Colleen Reece & Renee Demarco

A Fairy-Tale romance
Copyright © 2003 by Melanie Panagiotopoulos

This edition was especially created in 2007 for Crossings by Arrangement with Barbour Publishing, Inc.

Published by Crossings Book Club, 401 Franklin Avenue, Garden City, New York 11530

ISBN: 978-0-7394-8078-6

Printed in the United States of America

Close Enough to Perfect

Close Enough to Perfect

by Terry Fowler

1

$\mathcal{O}$he stood in semidarkness, engulfed by the deafening roar of fans calling for an encore. Tiny pinpoint flashes of light dotted the arena. These fans were not ready for their evening to end. Cowboy Jamboree didn't let them down.

When the band waved their way offstage for the last time, Genny Smith sighed with relief. She'd enjoyed the concert, but the late hour was catching up with her. Maybe she'd be able to nap on the trip home. Genny doubted that. After meeting the band, the busload of fans would be more exuberant than ever.

"Everyone move this way," the deejay instructed.

Genny could hardly believe she was going backstage. On a whim, she'd dialed the radio station's contest line, never expecting to win gold circle seats and a bus trip to see the CMA group of the year.

Stepping forward, she forced back a gasp at the discomfort that moved through her abdomen. Just as she suspected—eating a carton of Chinese take-out alone had been a mistake. She groaned when another twinge coursed through her.

"You're holding up the line," the guy behind her grumbled.

Doggedly, step by step, Genny forced herself to move. Surely it couldn't be that much farther. Another sharp pain cut through her. As much as she wanted to meet the band, she needed to be home in bed even more.

Each stabbing pain echoed her sister Sonya's sentiments. "Why anyone would subject themselves to a bus ride in the middle of winter to see some country group is beyond me." She'd tacked on "particularly a woman who's six months pregnant" to emphasize her point.

Maybe she should have listened, but Genny really wanted to see the concert. Her doctor gave her the go-ahead as long as she rested often, didn't take any chances, and wasn't alone. Technically, she wasn't alone. The bus bulged with revelers having the time of their lives.

Soon she would meet Stephen Camden, and then she would find a chair.

⁓❧

People blended together as Stephen listened to yet another fan's praise. Their manager's oft repeated instructions drummed in his head—Show just enough charm to convince them you're sincere. Flirt with the women, slap the men on the back, shake everyone's hand, give them an autograph, say thank you, and move on. The music gives them their money's worth. Anything more is icing on the cake. Ordinarily Stephen hated that philosophy, but tonight he longed for home.

Stephen credited his lingering dissatisfaction to Chuck Harper's visit that afternoon. He'd been less than welcoming when his housekeeper showed the man into his study.

"We've got a once-in-a-lifetime opportunity. I tried to call and kept getting the machine."

Stephen grimaced at Chuck's enthusiasm. "I didn't want to be bothered."

"Steve, Man, this is an honor that can't be refused."

"Some bigger name fall through?" he countered.

Chuck shrugged. "Maybe, but it's a chance to climb another rung on the success ladder. That doesn't hurt Cowboy Jamboree."

"We're tired. We just spent four weeks on the road. We only agreed to tonight's concert because it was close to home."

"That's the biz, Steve."

Stephen glanced at the television, the picture out of focus as he considered how tired he was of his lifestyle. "So you say. We're not programmed for continuous work."

"Steve, Man, what are you griping about? You've got the life men dream about. Nobody telling you what to do."

Other than you, he countered silently.

"No ties."

No one to love. Try another, Stephen thought grimly.

"Different women in every city."

Women who would do anything to be with a celebrity. No thanks. Every time Harper took advantage of another willing victim, Stephen prayed for the man and his family.

"Not to mention tons of money."

What good was money if you didn't have a chance to enjoy the things it bought? I can't hook my home behind the bus.

His lifestyle might be the manager's idea of perfection but it had a long way to go before it matched Stephen's. Right now, all he wanted was to sleep in his own bed and the crucial off time he needed to pre-pare himself for the next concert tour.

"At least you don't have to listen to a wife and kids nagging on the road."

The man doesn't know how blessed he is. I'd take a lovely, devoted wife and three children any day.

"The way I see it, the only thing a family is good for is a tax de-duction," Harper concluded.

That was an idea. If I can't enjoy the lifestyle my money affords me, a wife and family could. "I'd love some of those things you mentioned. Ties, a family to share my life, a reason to come home."

"Don't be so hard on me, Steve. We'll catch a break before the next gig. I promise."

Harper's promises were about as reliable as the man himself. Next time there would be even more reasons why the band couldn't afford to pass up another unplanned opportunity.

"What time do we leave?"

Harper literally beamed his satisfaction. Removing a planner from his expensive suit coat, he ripped out the page and jotted the informa-tion. Stephen flinched away from the slap on the back and crammed the paper into the pocket of his well-worn jeans.

In the entry hall, the manager nudged a canvas mailbag with his shoe. "We need to hire someone to take care of these."

No doubt the time had come to talk to the rest of the band. Single and tired, he could only imagine how the others felt.

Forcing himself back to the present, Stephen noted the woman.

Her fragile appearance bothered him as did the grimaces that touched her face. What was wrong with these people? She was obviously in trouble.

Of course, he'd long since stopped being surprised by the lack of compassion in others. These fans couldn't care less about one tiny, defenseless woman. He whispered up a quick prayer for her care.

He waved Kyle, the roadie who doubled as a bodyguard, off and stepped forward. "Hello, Beautiful." Stephen glanced at the backstage pass and saw her name was Genny. He had the distinct feeling he'd been punched in the stomach when her lips curved into a smile and her hand rested in his. She groaned, her knees buckling.

Stephen regarded the woman in his arms. He'd never had a fan faint before. This one was limp as an overcooked noodle and about as heavy. He sought her pulse and sighed with relief at the steady, if weak, beat.

"Somebody get a doctor," he called, looking around for a place to lay her down. People crowded the area and short of knocking the refreshments off the table, there didn't appear to be anywhere to put her. He swung her up into his arms.

"Steve, what are you doing?" Harper demanded.

"I'm not putting her on the floor."

"Don't be a fool. Leave her to the people she came with."

"Do you see anyone, Harper? Either help or get out of the way."

"She can sue us, Steve."

Obviously the man had never heard of the Good Samaritan. She needed someone and apparently he was the chosen one. "I accept complete responsibility. Will it jeopardize Kyle if he holds the door?"

The roadie cleared the way. "Where are you taking her?"

Cameras flashed all around them, and Stephen did his best to shield her. "To the bus."

"It's your skin," Harper called.

"Shout a little louder," Steve muttered. "There's a reporter over in the corner who didn't hear you." He whispered a prayer for forgiveness for his anger.

The long duster coat he wore on stage protected Stephen from the cold January night. The woman wore a dress that couldn't be all that warm and a long sweater. Where was her coat? Protectively, he tucked her closer.

Steve waited for Kyle to unlock the bus and carried her to the bed in the back. He reached for a throw and spread it over Genny. As the folds settled in place, her eyes fluttered open.

"Hello. Are you okay?"

She closed her eyes and opened them again. "I don't know."

He watched her closely. *Okay, God, I could use some help here.*

❧

She watched his thorough assessment and knew what he saw—mousy, shoulder-length brown hair badly in need of a trim, green eyes outlined by dark circles, and the swollen puffiness that distorted her entire body. Her largest dress fit snugly about her stomach and had seen better days. *What a mess he must think me.*

He looked younger than on his album covers, handsomer. His thick brown hair showed a liberal mixture of red highlights and nearly touched his shoulders. His shoulders strained against the long denim coat he wore, and his haunting gaze all but bored into her.

Her fascination lessened when her body reminded Genny of her dilemma. She rolled onto her side and found the position even more uncomfortable. She moved her hands protectively over her stomach.

"What's wrong?"

"I'm having sharp pains."

"A virus? Something you ate?"

Genny considered her gluttony. A number of foods hadn't agreed with her pregnancy.

"I hope it's not food poisoning," he said. "One of our guys said he'd never been so sick in his life."

She knew the feeling. She wanted to curl up and die but even that required too much effort right now.

"Can I get you some medicine? We have stuff in the first aid kit."

"I can't."

He settled on the edge of the bed, holding her hand in his. "Right. When's the baby due?"

Genny told him. "My doctor warned me to take things easy. I'm thirty-six years old." Why had she told him that? He wasn't interested in the facts of her pregnancy, nor the facts of her life for that matter.

❦

Stephen watched the apologetic smile disappear. "Are you here alone?"

Silence filled the room. Her fingers plucked at the throw. *Way to go, Man.* "Don't be afraid," he reassured. "I just thought that in your condition you shouldn't be alone. Where's your husband?" Stephen hesitated. "The baby's father."

She stared at him through uncomprehending eyes. "John?" Her voice sounded disembodied.

"Yes. John," he urged. "Where is he? How can we contact him?"

"He's gone."

The pinched whiteness of her face scared him. "Gone where?"

"I didn't know there would be a fire." Her voice caught suddenly, revealing a deep hurt within her. "If I hadn't told him to finish his work . . ."

The nightmare worsened. "I'm sorry." Stephen grabbed a tissue and wiped away the tears easing along her soft skin.

Despite her pregnancy, she was skin and bones. A strong urge to protect her pulled at Stephen. He continued to whisper words of comfort.

❦

Genny felt strengthened by Stephen's nearness.

The warm cocoon did nothing to block out the damp cold of the winter night or the whine of the gusting wind. The clouds released the rain that had threatened all day. Almost deafening, it pummeled the bus. Genny felt more than a little thankful she wasn't braving the elements. Feeling warm, she pushed the throw to the side.

Stephen pulled it back into place. "It's cold in here."

"Not to me."

"Even more reason. Do you have a fever?" He touched the back of his hand to her forehead.

Genny wiped perspiration from her face. "It's the pain. I splurged on Chinese food this afternoon. Maybe I just ate too much. Do you . . . ? Could we call a doctor?"

He jumped up. "Let me see what I can do. Wait, you have to tell me your last name."

"Genny Smith. Actually it's Genevieve," she admitted with an embarrassed smile.

"I like it."

"I never have."

He disappeared, and Genny tried and discarded every relaxation trick she knew. Not even the usually soporific tendencies of falling rain could induce sleep.

Nothing seemed capable of overpowering the nagging pains that plagued her. Surely they would go away after a good night's rest. Stubbornly, Genny snuggled under the blanket and squeezed her eyes shut.

❧

He beat a hasty retreat up the aisle of the bus and found Kyle in the driver's seat, staring glumly at the rain running in rivulets down the windshield.

The roadie looked almost relieved to see him. "Man, you won't believe the mess out there. Some idiot caused a pileup that's blocked all the outgoing lanes."

"Can we get out?"

"It's not going to happen for awhile. Can't find the group that brought her in either. We think they left her. You should take her back inside, Steve. You don't need the liability."

"She's not facing this alone."

Kyle shrugged, and his words echoed the manager's. "It's your neck."

When she called out to him, Stephen thought something about her voice didn't match the woman. She certainly wasn't beautiful, not like other women he knew. But her voice—now that was a promise of heaven. He could listen to her say his name again and again. And those eyes—huge and as green as a spring forest.

His next thought surprised him. *Oh, come on, Man. It's just wishful thinking on your part.*

Stephen found Genny sobbing softly, her face turned into the pillow. He reached for her hand. "We don't mean to upset you."

"You didn't. Pregnancy has made me more emotional. I cry at the drop of a hat."

Stephen grinned, entranced by the cadence of her voice. As a singer, he knew the voices that made the big bucks. "You have a fabulous voice. Do you sing along with the band when you hear us on the radio?"

Her strangled laughter produced the same lilting quality. "Please, my singing is your worst nightmare."

"You have a beautiful voice."

"They wouldn't even let me into the church choir."

He laughed. "Oh, come on. It can't be that bad. They let everybody sing in church."

"Why don't I regale you with . . . Ow," she grunted. "Noooo!"

"What? What is it?" he demanded anxiously.

"I think my water broke."

Tears flooded her eyes. Stephen whispered comforting remarks as he tucked a lock of her hair behind her ear. "Shush. Don't cry. Who's your doctor?"

"Rainer." She recited the number from memory.

Stephen raced up the aisle.

"What happened? Why is she screaming?"

Stephen forced himself to remain calm. "I think we're about to deliver a baby."

"I'm out of here. Vick just radioed to say the guys are ready to call it a night. I told him there was a traffic jam, but he says they're tired of the crowd and want to come on board."

"Tell them to come on. A couple of the guys have experience in the delivery room. And grab a cell phone."

"Man, are you crazy?"

Doubt filled Stephen. Was he taking unnecessary chances? Maybe. But if he didn't take care of her, who would? "Hang on, Kyle. It's going to be a rough ride."

"Hey, Man, I'm going to see if there are any paramedics in the building. Chances are they're all down at the accident scene."

"Do what you can. I'm going back to her."

⚬❧

Genny bit her lip as the pain tore through her. The doctor had said most first-time mothers were in labor for several hours, but he hadn't prepared her for this. Perhaps she should have read all the literature they gave her. She thought she had time. Some lesson in procrastination.

The silence weighed like a heavy blanket. Genny couldn't hear what they were saying this time. Where was the ambulance? Dr. Rainer had mentioned stopping early labor. Oh, why hadn't she listened? "Stephen?"

❧

Her cry reminded Stephen she had even more reason than he did to be afraid. "I'm here. Just relax, and tell me what you're feeling."

Genny grabbed his hand. "I'm not due for three months. I can't lose him. He's all I have."

He grew still at the whispered pleas. Stephen realized she was praying in earnest and joined in, sending up his own request. Stephen knew they shared the hope God would bring Genny and the baby safely through this frightening experience.

"Okay, now take a deep breath," he instructed.

Her fingers clutched his hand, her thumb rubbing idly against the callus from his guitar playing. "Dr. Rainer warned me. He's been warning me ever since . . ." Her voice cracked and strengthened. "I tried to take care of my baby. Honestly I did."

"I know, Honey. You did everything you could."

"I tried to eat right, and I stayed in bed until he said the crisis was past. My baby is all I have left."

He hugged her, and Genny's arms slipped about his neck, her head resting on his shoulder as her stomach fit itself to his side. The tremble of her pathetically thin shoulders wrenched his heart, and her suffering became his.

After a moment or so, he took Genny's face in his hands and looked deep into her eyes. "Stop now. This isn't helping. The guys will bring a cell phone, and we'll call your doctor. He can talk us through this."

"I've been so afraid," she said simply.

The whispered words grabbed at his heart. "I'm here now. We're not going to let anything happen to you or your baby."

"How are you doing?"

Her inquiry struck him as odd. "What do you mean?"

"Just wondering how you feel about this nightmare you've landed yourself smack in the middle of."

"I'm not thinking about me right now. You don't have any family?"

"A sister, Sonya."

"Why isn't she with you?"

"Her job demands all her time. I couldn't ask her to do more for me."

A distinct fuzziness crept in her voice as exhaustion took its toll. The quiet made Stephen wonder if she slept.

Couldn't ask for more. The words echoed in his head. Why should she have to ask? If she were his sister, he'd be there for her.

What would he do if this baby opted to make an immediate appearance? He glanced toward the door. Where were the guys with that cell phone?

Stephen knew the pain had worsened by her movements and the clutch of her hand. "Tell me what's happening."

"My baby's coming. Stephen," she began, pushing the request out with her next breath, "will you stay with me?"

"Of course I will."

"I mean if we get to the hospital."

"They won't let me."

"They'll think you're my coach."

Did she realize what she asked of him?

"Stephen, I'm scared. It's as though I have no control over my body. Over the pain."

"Yes, you do." Fear, mainly of failure, had been part of his life for years. Like him, Genny needed reassurance, help getting through this situation. And though he was scared of failing her, Stephen knew he had to give her his all.

Exhaustion showed in her voice. "In a minute."

A few minutes of uninterrupted quiet passed, and Stephen reflected on Genny's fear. Her baby was coming early, and she was stranded with strangers. She must be terrified.

"Stephen, I don't want to pressure you," she whispered.

He saw no reason why she should go through this alone— particularly if she needed him. Very few things had ever been asked of him in life, and this was something he could do. "If I can, I'll stay."

$$\textcircled{2}$$

*S*tephen paused, his gaze stopping on the isolette labeled Baby Boy Smith. He couldn't quite believe he had witnessed this child's birth. If the tiny baby wasn't proof enough, he had only to look down at the regulation surgical gown the hospital staff insisted he wear when visiting the nursery.

The previous hours were a blur. Once the entire band and crew became involved, Kyle recruited volunteers to find an ambulance and two band members remained, passing on information to Genny's doctor via the cell phone. Things went into fast motion after help arrived.

Stephen assumed Genny would forget about him, but she held on tightly. When the baby made its appearance, the EMT wrapped her son in a towel and placed him in Stephen's arms.

"He's so tiny," Genny whispered, her gaze following the baby's every movement. "And perfect."

Though weak, she enthused over his features, making Stephen count and admire miniature fingers and toes. Well, she hadn't actually forced him. From that shared moment the strangest feeling came over him, almost as if he should be passing cigars around.

That same feeling rushed through him now as the wrinkled scrap of humanity squalled in earnest. This tiny baby boy would provide so much love and joy to someone who needed it desperately. Stephen wiped moisture from his eyes, a sheepish smile touching his lips when the nurse closed one eyelid in a knowing wink.

He whispered a prayer of thanks. Born at least three months premature, with no doctor or hospital equipment to support him—God's hand was all over this miracle. The human side of him rated the baby's odds of survival as low. The believer knew God was in control.

The small baby, with skin so thin Stephen could see veins and arteries, made his presence known with a mewl of protest.

Genny amazed him. Despite the problems, she fought to give her child every chance. Stephen considered how she'd held on with all her might—right up to a couple of minutes ago when the doctor asked him to leave the room.

"How is my baby? Is everything all right?" she demanded.

Something in the man's expression warned Stephen the news wasn't good. His respect for the doctor increased measurably as he calmed Genny.

"How is my son? Is he okay?" she repeated.

"He's being taken care of. I'm more concerned with you."

With a nod, the doctor indicated Stephen should leave the room. After a couple of halting steps, he turned and looked at Genny. Her sad expression stopped him in his tracks. Walking back to the bed, Stephen reached for her hand. "I'll be back. I promise."

Stephen left the nursery window and paced the corridor outside the small waiting room, amazed and fascinated by the turn of events that had taken him from greeting a group of fans to witnessing the birth of a baby.

Harper was furious. The manager sent word to the bus driver that he wanted them on the road immediately. Instead, Stephen went to the hospital with a woman who made him feel the strangest things.

He really should leave. She didn't need him now. Stephen swept a hand through his hair and sighed. He couldn't do that to her. Okay, so maybe she was emotional, but he'd made a promise.

Hoping to catch his friend and fellow band member, Stephen found a pay phone and dialed Ray's cell number.

"Steve? Hold on. Hey, quiet down. Where are you?"

"Looks like I'll be tied up here for awhile."

"The guys won't appreciate a wild-goose chase."

Stephen felt torn. He owed the guys a lot more than he owed Genny Smith. But it went beyond debts. Genny made him feel needed. Something he hadn't felt in a long time.

Not even with the crowds. He gave a good concert in return for the money, but the experience no longer moved him.

"I'll charter a flight. Leave at the last possible moment."

"Why?" Ray asked.

Genny's vision lingered in Stephen's head. She had no one—only a tiny baby in an isolette. He needed to be there for her. *Crazy.* He shook his head to clear the fog. Stephen flexed his hand, felt the lingering soreness from Genny wrenching it with every contraction and said, "Because I'm needed."

"Okay, Buddy. See you when you get here."

"Thanks, Ray." He glanced up and saw the nurse pointing in his direction. "Gotta go."

He hung up and walked to the desk.

Genny's doctor appeared distracted as he fingered his stethoscope.

"How is she?"

"Are you a friend of hers?"

Stephen explained the events that had brought him to the hospital.

"I hoped you were a friend. I talked to her doctor. He said this woman has had too many shocks in the past few months."

"Will she be okay?"

"In time. She's had a high-risk pregnancy, aggravated by her age and the loss of her husband. Her doctor seemed surprised she survived a regular delivery. He planned cesarean."

A disconcerted smile crinkled the corners of Stephen's eyes. "Thanks for not sharing that a couple of hours ago."

"I don't know how, but you worked a miracle. That tiny boy wouldn't have survived if she'd been alone."

"Not me. God."

"Definitely. She's going to need all the support she can get. Her son will be in NICU for awhile."

"He's . . . ?" The words choked in Stephen's throat.

"No. No. He's stable right now, but Mrs. Smith will be upset, and it's not good for her or the baby. She'll blame herself, and nothing will change her mind until she accepts and deals with what's happened."

"I wondered . . . I sensed that she's . . . Well, how much more can she take?"

"I wish I knew. From what her doctor said, grief has taken its toll on her emotional and physical state."

Stephen knew without a doubt he wouldn't leave Genny without the support she needed. "I'd like to see her again."

"She's waiting for you."

Stephen pushed the door open and focused on the sleeping woman. In the shadowy light, her face rivaled the white of the sheets. She looked so small, defenseless. And yet, appearances could be deceiving. She had been strong and determined to bring her son, a baby barely as large as his hand, into the world.

Stephen prayed the determination would carry Genny through the turmoil ahead. He sat in the chair by the bed and waited.

"John?" Genny moaned as she woke, her eyes searching the room.

Stephen flashed her a reassuring smile. "Hi, Beautiful. How're you feeling?"

"Terrible," she admitted, groaning softly as she moved. The heavy lashes that shadowed her cheeks flew up. "Stephen? You're still here?"

"I promised."

"Do I really have a son?"

A big grin covered his face. "A very tiny baby boy."

"Is he all right?" Anxiety edged her voice.

Careful, Steve, he admonished. "I figure any baby tough enough to be born in an ambulance during a storm will grow to be a bear of a man."

"I couldn't have done it without you," she whispered.

He smoothed Genny's bangs from her forehead and found himself wishing he could drive the sadness from her eyes. "You did great, Genny. You were so brave."

"I was scared," she admitted, tears welling as she spoke the truth.

Brushing the moisture from her cheek, Stephen said, "Me too. What's his name?"

A slow smile crept over her face. "When we discussed names, John said if it was a boy, he wouldn't be a Junior. He hated the disbelieving stares when he told people his name was John Smith. He suggested Jonathan."

"And a girl?"

"Pocahontas."

Stephen laughed with Genny.

"Stephen?" she called drowsily.

He gave his support in the only way he knew how, wrapping her hand in both of his as his elbows rested on the bed. "Right here."

"Do you have a middle name? I'd like to name my son after you."

"It's Andrew, but don't you think you should name him after his father?"

"I'm going to name him Jonathan Andrew. That is, if you don't mind?" she said, almost anxiously.

"I'd be honored." The warmth of his smile echoed in the sincerity of his voice. He kissed her forehead. "Get some sleep."

"Did you see him again?" she asked, her voice barely audible from exhaustion.

"He's a beautiful boy."

"Does Sonya know?"

Sonya? The sister that couldn't be there, Stephen realized. "How do I contact her?"

Genny gave him the number, and Stephen dialed. "Is this Sonya Kelly? Yeah, I know it's late, but congratulations, Auntie. Mother and son are doing fine." Stephen squeezed Genny's hand and winked. "She's in the hospital here in Memphis."

"How stupid can one woman be?" Sonya demanded angrily. "I told her not to go on that bus tour. Who are you anyway?"

Her response shocked him. "A friend. We met at the concert." He shook his head when Genny reached for the phone. "Baby Jonathan was very unexpected."

Another long sigh preceded Sonya's next words. "Tell her I'll bring her things tomorrow."

Stephen replaced the receiver and shuddered. The feeling Genny needed someone strengthened tenfold. He didn't want to tell her what her sister said.

"She's not coming, is she?"

The tremble in her voice made him ache to gather Genny up in his arms and protect her from further hurt. "Not until tomorrow, but I'm here, and I'm not going anywhere."

Genny's hand found his jaw, her fingers stroking ever so softly over his face. "Thank you."

Stephen placed a gentle kiss in her palm. Something felt so right about being here with her. With that thought, he pulled back. "You need to rest."

She smiled. "I'm too excited. When are they going to bring Jonathan to me?"

Stephen found himself thankful for the low light in the room. "They'll probably let you know before too much longer." He changed the subject quickly. "Genny, I'll have to leave soon. We're performing in Atlanta tonight."

"Oh, Stephen, you'll be exhausted."

"I wouldn't have missed this for a million dollars."

"I love to hear you perform. Jonathan and I will always be your number one fans. We'll scream for your autograph."

Stephen grimaced. "Please don't. It's refreshing to be treated like a regular person."

"But you're not regular," Genny insisted. "You're a gifted man. I have all your CDs."

A smile lifted the corner of his mouth. Fans came in all shapes and sizes. "Thanks for buying them."

"Really, I love your music," she protested. "It's so . . . Oh, I'm no good with words."

Stephen thought she was. In fact, he enjoyed her praise more than any he'd received in a long time. "Enough talking. You have to rest," he ordered, tucking the sheet about her and kissing her lightly on the forehead. "Good night," he whispered, pleased by the steady breathing that indicated she slept.

$$\textbf{3}$$

enny came awake slowly, feeling disoriented as she tried to focus her gaze. A hand flew to her no longer pregnant form. She had a son. A slow smile crept over her face as the door opened to admit the doctor.

"Good morning, Mrs. Smith. How are you feeling?"

"Dr. Garner, where is my baby? Why didn't they bring him to me?"

His pat on the arm served more to irritate than console.

"Where is my baby?" she repeated, more insistently than before.

Sonya burst into the room and snapped, "What are you carrying on about now?"

"I want to see my baby." The words turned into a sob.

Sonya set a small suitcase on the end of the bed. "Oh, Genny, hush."

"They haven't bought him to me at all."

"In good time. First, we examine you, and then another doctor will talk to you about your baby."

Her gaze focused on the doctor. "Can't I feed him this morning?"

"I'm afraid not. He's in the neonatal care unit."

Genny crumpled, tears flooding her eyes as she pleaded with him. "He'll be all right, won't he?"

"Certainly. But we must be certain you're healthy enough to take your son home. You had a very difficult delivery, and if Mr. Camden hadn't been there, there's a good chance neither of you would have survived."

Stephen. She wished he were here now. All man, from the top of his head to the soles of the expensive cowboy boots, he made her feel safe and secure, happy even. She vaguely recalled him saying he had to be in Atlanta. "Did Stephen get off all right?"

"How should I know?" Sonya snapped. "Where did you find him anyway? He actually thought I'd drive up here last night."

Genny closed her eyes. Her only sister couldn't be bothered to drive a couple of hours to see her nephew.

"I've got to get to work. I'll get back when I can."

Sonya's words were cut off as the door closed behind her. Why couldn't Sonya understand? She hadn't even mentioned the baby.

She probably hadn't realized who Stephen was either. No doubt Sonya would have been there in record time if she'd known.

A thank-you note would never be enough for all he'd done. Perhaps she could repay him one day. Of course naming her son after him was high reward.

"Mrs. Smith," the doctor called impatiently.

"Sorry. What did you say?"

He scowled and continued, "I said a nurse will take you to the nursery to see your child. I . . ."

"Jonathan," she interrupted. "His name is Jonathan Andrew."

He nodded. "I want you to talk with Dr. Lee. Here he is now."

A stranger introduced himself and launched into a summary of Jonathan's case. "Your son is approximately twelve weeks premature, weighing in at 1563 grams." Noting her confusion, he gave the weight in pounds. "He's in what we classify the low birth weight group. Less than 2500 grams but more than 1500 grams, which is good since around 95 percent of those babies survive their newborn period with no future problems."

He droned on, his diagnosis almost too much to absorb. Certain words jumped out at Genny—Isolette. Sepsis workup. Infection. Antibiotics.

Dr. Garner stepped forward, his hand covering hers. "I know it's a lot to take in, but we have very high expectations for Jonathan. I'm sure Dr. Lee is more than happy to answer any questions you might have."

The other doctor nodded as Genny's eyes drifted from one to the other. "What will I do?"

"Just love him."

"You can't imagine how much," she responded softly.

In the nursery, Genny half listened as the nurse outlined the procedures for scrubbing and provided her with a gown to wear.

The nurse led her over to the isolette. "I'm Cindy. I take care of Jonathan during first shift."

Awestruck, Genny gazed at her son. "Isn't he beautiful? What do I do?"

"Put your hands through the portholes and touch him gently. Don't worry so much about the IV," Cindy instructed.

"I'll hurt him."

"It's okay. Really. He needs your touch, and you'll be surprised by how quickly he learns to recognize his mommy's voice."

Genny's hand trembled as she traced one finger along the diminutive arm.

"That's good. Relax," Cindy said.

"Why is he wearing the hat?"

"To retain body heat."

"What about the wires?"

"Monitor leads. See that machine? It shows his breathing and heartbeat. If it gets too high or low, an alarm goes off."

Genny smiled when Jonathan grasped her finger in his tiny hand. She glanced at the next incubator. "Where's her mother?"

"That little lady isn't as lucky as your Jonathan. Her mom's in a coma. Her father's military, and we're waiting for the Red Cross to get him here."

An alarm went off, and horror filled Genny. "What is that?" she demanded, her heart racing.

"The other baby's monitor. Spend a few minutes with Jonathan while I take care of her."

The thump of her heart barely slowed as Genny stared at the monitors attached to Jonathan's frail body. She had done this to him. She'd forced Jonathan to suffer for her weaknesses. A trail of tears chased each other down her cheeks.

"It's okay," Cindy whispered, rubbing Genny's back. "Let's get you back to your room. You can come anytime you want."

Once settled in bed, Genny gave vent to the overwhelming fear. Trembling encompassed her, and the tears flowed steadily. The telephone rang, and she groped for the receiver, brushing at her cheeks before she called hello.

"How are you feeling today?"

The undeniably male voice was unfamiliar at first. "Stephen? Oh, it's so good to hear your voice."

"Hold on a sec."

She could hear him speaking, almost angrily, to someone in the background. "I said I'll be there when I finish my call. Okay, I'm back. What were you saying?"

"Sounds like you're busy."

"Genny, don't hang up."

The urgency in his voice kept her on the line. "But you're busy."

He overrode her protests. "Tell me about Jonathan. How is he?"

"I don't know," she admitted. "He's so tiny. I can't hold him. There are all these wires. His doctor said something about an infection and antibiotics." Her guilt increased with each bit of information. "It's my fault, Stephen. I'm his mother, and he's suffering because of me."

"It's not. Genny, Honey, listen to me. Who's there with you?"

"No one. I'm okay."

A heavy sigh filled the receiver. "You're not. They expect you to grasp the significance of what's going on with your son after you've gone through a horrible ordeal."

"I have to. I'm all he has." Genny sniffed. "I painted this rosy picture of myself leaving the hospital with a healthy child. Now I'm going home alone. I don't even know how long he'll have to stay." She trailed off as the new worry occurred to her. "How will I get to the hospital?"

"Jonathan needs you more than that rosy-cheeked image ever did."

"What if I lose him?"

"We are not going to think that way."

We. With one word, Stephen made her feel protected. "You'll never know how frightened I was when I realized I was in labor."

"Not half as much as me. It certainly isn't an experience I'd care to try again anytime soon."

"I hope I didn't put you off becoming a father."

"Aren't I going to be an honorary uncle?" he asked. "Unofficially of course."

"Officially," Genny said. "If you give me an address, I'll send pictures."

"I'd take you up on a visit," he suggested.

"We'd love to see you."

"Soon then. Take care. And my best to Jonathan."

Genny turned off the phone. He'd soothed so many of her fears. Stephen was a special man. Not many people would put themselves out for a stranger.

And she was going to get a second chance to tell him so. Genny smiled as she drifted off to sleep.

❧

Stephen dug his wallet from his pocket. "Go on without me. I have another call to make."

"Just wrap it up quick and get downstairs," Harper ordered.

Stephen's frustration only made him angrier. How could her sister not be there to help? Such selfishness was mind-boggling.

Stephen had missed a friend's cry for help once, and it resulted in a senseless loss. He vowed it wouldn't happen again. One tiny baby boy wouldn't be all Genevieve Smith had.

Making the decision to help brought him great satisfaction. Maybe part of it was the need to reassure himself, but he suspected there was more to it than that.

Stephen thumbed through the papers in his wallet until he found his pastor's business card. Glancing at his watch, he dialed the home number. Hopefully Pastor Carl hadn't gone out.

"Hello, Carl. How are you?" he said when the preacher answered on the second ring.

"I'm fine, Stephen. And you? Are you in town?"

"Doing great. We're in Atlanta. I need to ask a favor. There's a young woman by the name of Genevieve Smith at the hospital. Her son was born prematurely, and she's really struggling. I wondered if you could go by and offer comfort? She and her son need our prayers."

"Genevieve Smith," the pastor repeated. "I'll visit her tomorrow."

"Thanks. It's a strange case. From what I know, her husband died recently. She has a sister, but the woman obviously isn't interested in helping out. Do you think some of our churchwomen might visit? I'd like to be there for her, but we're out of town for the next couple of days."

"I'll contact Mrs. Bellamy. She'll set the prayer chain into motion and round up volunteers. We'll take care of Mrs. Smith for you."

Stephen felt thankful that the minister didn't ask further questions. "I really appreciate this. I can't believe her sister could be so selfish."

"Let's not judge, Stephen. Perhaps circumstances make it unavoidable. Either way, we should pray for the sister as well."

"You'd think family would be more important."

"Most people take family for granted," Pastor Carl pointed out. "Have you thought about the matter we discussed?"

Stephen fiddled with the pens on the desktop. "All the time. I can't help but feel I'd be letting everyone down. Some of the guys have families. What would they do until they found a replacement?"

"You could continue until they find someone."

"I considered that. Perhaps I'm a coward."

"As always, pray for God's guidance, Stephen. He will light your path. Is Mrs. Smith a Christian?"

Stephen didn't know. They had spent hours together, and he honestly had no idea. "I hope so. She's going to need God's strength to get her past this hurdle. I'll see you in church the first Sunday I'm home."

"I'll look forward to seeing you. Meanwhile, we'll take care of Mrs. Smith for you."

Stephen thanked the pastor again and hung up. He was thankful, but something niggled at him. Some reason why he wasn't totally contented with the action he'd taken.

Stephen headed downstairs, stopping by the entrance as the truth hit him. He didn't want other people seeing to Genny's care. He wanted to take care of her.

4

$\mathcal{A}$t times, the experience of motherhood overwhelmed Genny, but she coped, forming an undeniable bond with her son. She examined him every visit, in awe of each perfect feature. At first, his tiny size worried her, but she soon learned to convert grams to ounces and began to ask questions. She stored away tidbits of information to share with Stephen.

Genny didn't find it strange that she would think of him. Every time someone from his church stopped by to check on her and Jonathan, to see if she needed anything, or to pray with her, she thanked God. Stephen called every day to offer support and reassurance. Mostly, he made her feel special, Genny admitted, glancing at the yellow roses he'd sent—her favorites.

She battled the strong temptation to share her burdens and found herself placing them in God's hands. Stephen's care and that of his congregation confirmed her faith that God would provide.

"Hello, Mrs. Smith. How are you feeling today?"

Genny missed the familiarity of her regular doctor but found Dr. Garner to be a pleasant substitute. "Fine."

The man flipped pages on her chart, pausing now and then to scribble on them. "You're doing remarkably well. I'm going to release you in the morning, but you have to promise to take things easy."

A knot formed in her stomach. "But what about Jonathan? Will Dr. Lee allow me to move him to Nashville?"

"He feels it's best that Jonathan stays here. I was able to extend your stay a few days, but we've run out of time. Have you checked into family quarters?"

Something else demanding money she didn't have. "I can stay in the waiting area."

"No," he said sharply. "You have to rest, Mrs. Smith."

"But my son needs me."

The doctor jammed his hand deep into the pocket of his white coat. "He needs you well and able to take care of him. Talk to your family. I'm sure you'll find a way."

Resigned, Genny called and left a message on Sonya's machine before making her way to the nursery. It was bedtime by the time Sonya got around to returning her call.

"I suppose you're wondering why I haven't been to see you?" Sonya went on about work and how there hadn't been a moment to spare.

"I'm being released in the morning," Genny said when Sonya paused for breath.

"You couldn't have picked a more inconvenient time to have a baby. What's the latest I can pick you up?"

"But I need to be here for Jonathan. Is there any way for me to stay?" Genny expected the sarcastic laughter.

"Just come home, Genny. The nursing staff can take care of the baby."

The baby. Why did Sonya never call Jonathan by name? "I'll be ready," Genny said, pushing the words past her tears. Life was so unfair. If only John were alive.

Early the next morning, Genny made a trip to the nursery before going back to her room to sign the discharge papers. When the volunteer wheeled her downstairs, Sonya loaded Genny and her things into the car and drove away without a backward glance.

As usual, the conversation quickly dwindled to silence. Genny wished Sonya would say something to take her mind off the separation. How would she survive without seeing Jonathan daily?

At the condo, Sonya parked and left the engine running. "Come on, Genny," she snapped, holding the door open. "I've got to go to work."

Genny fought back a wave of dizziness when Sonya rushed her up the walkway to the door.

Inside, Sonya swung the suitcase onto the armchair and sorted out a gown and robe. "Put these on while I get what you need." She disappeared up the stairs and returned with an armload of linens and a pillow. "Hopefully, I'll be home no later than six." Sonya checked the tiny diamond-crusted watch face. "Of course, I'm so far behind now I'll probably never catch up."

Disheartened, Genny sank down on the sofa. She supposed Sonya loved her, but there was a lot of their parents in her sister. Always on the go, much too busy for anyone but herself. Her sibling was the beautiful, self-sufficient one who never lacked for companionship.

They were complete opposites. Shy, skinny, almost mouse-like, Genny preferred to stay inside and read when Sonya was with her friends. They had been cruel to the little girl, telling her to get lost, to find her own friends. With no one to help build her self-esteem, keeping to herself became the solution. Some of the shyness disappeared with maturity, but for the most part she was still a loner who hated being alone.

Genny touched her cheek and realized she was indulging in yet another bout of depression. *Silly,* she berated, *drying her face. I will do better,* Genny vowed, going into the kitchen to prepare lunch.

Not that Sonya left much to prepare. Genny's search yielded half a glass of milk that surprisingly enough hadn't soured since the date was past that stamped on the carton. Scrambling the one egg and toasting the end slice of the bread loaf, she wondered if Sonya would make it home for dinner. Even then she'd probably be tired and want to order in.

Genny cleared the kitchen and went back into the living room to make her bed on the sofa. Tired, she dozed in a restless sleep, coming awake slowly upon realizing there was someone at the door.

Stephen flashed her a smile that set her heart to racing. "I woke you."

She became instantly alert, too surprised to do more than nod. The old, familiar warmth of security surrounded her as she recognized someone who cared. Genny took his arm. "Come in. When did you get back?"

She glanced at the sofa. The armchair held her suitcase and articles Sonya had thrown from her case. "Sorry," Genny exclaimed and started to move the linen.

Stephen looked pointedly toward the makeshift bed. "You were asleep? I should have phoned."

"You're always welcome," Genny emphasized. "How did you know where to find me?"

"Let's just say it doesn't hurt to be well-known."

Why was she so happy to see him? They were friends. At least she hoped so. "I'm surprised. I know you said soon but . . ."

"I got back earlier than expected. How are you feeling?"

"Fine." At his doubtful look, she laughed. "Well, as good as any woman who has just given birth is allowed to feel."

Stephen nodded. "Have you eaten?"

"Yes. I'd offer you something but I just bared the cupboards. Sonya's going to have to grocery shop. She'll hate that. She hasn't been since I came here to live."

"Did you have enough?"

"It'll hold me."

He frowned when her traitorous stomach rumbled in denial. "I bought you something." Stephen passed her a gift-wrapped package she hadn't seen earlier.

"You shouldn't have." Genny tore into the present. A sigh of pleasure slipped from her as she drew out a silky, crushproof dress in a gorgeous shade of green.

"I hope it fits. I told the saleswoman you barely weighed a hundred pounds, were about so high, and had just had a baby. She showed me this dress. Picking the color was easy. It's the same as your eyes."

"It's beautiful. But you shouldn't have."

Their gazes locked, tenderness growing in his eyes with his smile. "There's more. Under the dress."

The second item was a small T-shirt with the band's logo on the front and "Stephen's BIGGEST Fan" on the back.

"It's adorable," she exclaimed, leaning to hug him.

He held her until she pulled back. "Did you see Jonathan?"

"The nursery blinds were closed."

Genny sighed. "He's the most beautiful baby."

"You wouldn't be slightly prejudiced?"

"Maybe just a little," she agreed, stretching her arms wide to indicate how much.

Stephen chuckled. "Feel up to a ride to the hospital?"

She could think of nothing she wanted more, but it was a long trip. "It's too much trouble. You'd have to bring me back. Dr. Garner wants me to rest, but I can't think about anything but Jonathan. It's not fair."

He looked puzzled. "What's keeping you here?"

"Money. We are dependent on Sonya for everything."

"Why didn't you ask for my help?"

She looked him in the eye. "You've done so much."

"Let's go see Jonathan. And talk about this."

Genny looked down at the clothes she'd worn from the hospital. They were terribly wrinkled.

"Try the dress," he suggested. "Or is there something you'd rather wear?"

The meager contents of her wardrobe, including the shabby, secondhand collection that comprised her maternity wear, held nothing she cared to be seen in and nothing that would fit until her body returned to normal. Genny couldn't remember the last time she'd gone shopping. Sonya had bought the cheap maternity dresses, claiming she was sick of the robe Genny had lived in since the funeral.

"No, it would be a pleasure to wear something new."

Genny slipped into the bathroom and disposed of the wrinkled garment. A wave of dizziness hit when she slipped the dress over her head. She reached out, the palm of her hand hitting the door with a hollow thud.

"Genny?"

The door popped open, removing her prop. Stephen caught her. "Are you okay?"

"I overbalanced. Could you tie the sash for me?"

Genny's skin grew warmer as the vision of Stephen in the role of husband planted itself in her head. *Don't be ridiculous,* she admonished.

He helped her to the sofa. "Let me put the water container back in the refrigerator, and we'll go. Hope you don't mind. I was thirsty."

"Not at all. I should have asked. I'm a horrible hostess."

He seemed distracted when he returned. Eager to see Jonathan, Genny pushed her questions away. Seeing her son would put things in the proper light—remind her what was important.

5

She isn't coming back to this house until Jonathan is released from the hospital, Stephen decided as he helped Genny into his car. Accomplishing such a feat would take a miracle, but it had to be done.

Stephen felt guilty. He had not been completely honest with Genny. He'd flabbergasted everyone by walking out after the Texas concert. He hadn't been able to get Genny off his mind. Seeing her only reinforced his need to help.

He had no business nosing around, but a fridge stocked with nothing but ice water and condiments made him see red. Only Genny's bumping the door saved him from reacting angrily.

❧

"Something wrong?" Genny ventured only to receive a taciturn response. Bewildered, she rested her head against the seat and closed her eyes. First Sonya, now Stephen. No one ever seemed to have anything to say to her. What had happened? She'd been so glad to see him, almost frightened by the joy having him near brought.

He owed her nothing. She expected nothing. Loneliness made her so happy to see him. Soon she'd see Jonathan, talk to him, and just look until he fell asleep. She could hardly wait until they let her bring him home. He was hers to love, even if he couldn't talk or reassure her when the doubts were overwhelming.

"We're here."

She awoke to find they were at the hospital. When he opened the door, Genny moved quickly, dropping back with the wave of dizziness that swept over her.

Stephen kneeled before her, his hands warm as he chaffed her cold fingers. "I'll get a doctor."

She caught hold of his arms. "I'm fine."

He looked doubtful at best. "This can't be good. I'm going to talk to your doctor."

Genny's agitation increased when Stephen blocked her way. "I'm sorry I frightened you, but I have to see Jonathan now."

∾

Just who am I angry with? Stephen wondered as he escorted Genny inside. *Sonya for having to work? John for dying? Myself for not being able to do more?* He'd already done more than most men would do for a virtual stranger. Why? Because it was no less than Jesus expected of him? Maybe, but he suspected a deeper-seated reason.

"What time do you finish? There are a couple of things I need to handle, but I'd like to take you to dinner."

"I usually stay for an hour."

His hand rested protectively at the small of her back. In the elevator, a teenage girl studied him. "You're Stephen Camden," she exclaimed.

She dug around in a minute purse and checked her coat pockets. At her regret-filled sigh, Genny produced a slip of paper, and he scribbled his name.

"You made her day," Genny said after the doors closed behind them. The full benefit of her grin took Stephen by surprise. "She seemed surprised when you got off on the maternity floor. Let's hope this doesn't turn into some sort of tabloid nightmare. 'Country Maverick Fathers Child' or something like that."

Stephen frowned. "I hate it when people consider me public property. Is it so impossible that I have friends with babies?"

"It can't be helped. The handsome young bachelor image doesn't hurt your star status."

Star status. He only wanted to perform his music. Stephen eyed the hand Genny laid on his arm before he looked into her face.

"I happen to think you're great with your fans."

"It's hard, Genny. They're always watching, waiting for me to make the headlines. I wish I could say I've become used to something as simple as taking a walk with a woman being turned into an overnight sensation, but I haven't."

"I wouldn't either," she admitted.

Their steps quickened as they neared the nursery. Stephen gestured toward the closed blinds. "How am I supposed to see my biggest fan?"

"I'll arrange it."

❧

Genny entered the door marked Hospital Personnel Only. Once inside, her gaze shifted to Jonathan's isolette, and her breath slipped out in a thankful sigh. She had worried terribly about leaving him.

She explained the situation to the head nurse, and the woman agreed to her plan. Genny stepped to the door and gestured Stephen inside.

He shook his head. "I'll look through the glass."

"If that's what you want," Genny said, unable to hide her disappointment.

"I don't want to intrude."

"You could never do that."

❧

Stephen shrugged and followed Genny to the scrub area.

A few minutes later, he found himself fighting back jealousy when she smiled at another man.

"How's she doing today?"

"The same," he said softly. "Coming here helps."

Genny nodded and whispered to Stephen, "His wife's in a coma."

He watched over her shoulder as Genny touched Jonathan through the portholes. Mesmerized by her soft tone, he found himself unable to look away. She sparkled, her expression proud as she sought his opinion.

"He's growing." His reward was a delighted grin.

"You really think so?"

Upon recognizing the hope in Genny's expression, he became more cautious. "The scales will tell." Jonathan's crying saved the moment. "Even sooner if I get out of here. Enjoy yourself."

"Stephen, wait," Genny called. "You didn't touch him."

"I don't—"

"He doesn't bite." Genny slid one hand along Jonathan's arm.

Stephen smiled at Jonathan's response to his mother. "Spoiled already."

"I think he recognizes my touch. Come on. Say hello."

Their shoulders brushed as he moved beside Genny and slid his hand into the lower porthole. She laughed when Jonathan extended his legs, and Stephen jerked his hand back.

"It's okay. The nurses tell me premature babies benefit from touching. Still think he's beautiful?"

His head snapped up, their gazes locking. Jonathan's skin might be as wrinkled as that of an old man, ruddy in color, and covered in a fine layer of hair, but Stephen couldn't shake the feeling that wrapped itself about his heart as his gaze moved from mother to son and back. He nodded.

"Me too." Her gaze moved to the baby.

"I'll be back," he said.

"Stephen," Genny called. He looked at her. "You don't have to come back. I mean . . . Well, I know you're busy. You probably have a million things to do after being away."

He stripped off the gown and stuffed it into the container. "What if I want to, Gen?"

"We'd love to see you."

❧

She stretched her time with Jonathan as long as possible before relinquishing his care to the nurses. Genny slipped out the door and stood before the window comparing babies.

"Ready?"

Startled by Stephen's voice, she jumped. "Did you finish your errands?"

"They didn't take as long as I thought."

Stephen took her arm. The image of his hand landing as gently as a butterfly on a flower when he touched Jonathan came to her mind as they walked to his car.

"Where are we going?" she asked when he drove past the Nashville exit.

"My house. I asked Mrs. James to prepare dinner."

Stephen kept up a steady stream of conversation, urging Genny to talk about herself.

"Not fair. You already know everything about me."

He grinned. "I suppose I do have the advantage. Fear, or maybe pain, turns you into a talker."

"And what turns you into a talker?"

Genny found the answer was music as he said very little about himself and more about the band.

A large mailbox which appeared to have suffered from contact with someone's vehicle marked the turnoff. His house sat far off the road, down a winding driveway outlined with a white wooden fence.

Genny found the carefully renovated old brick home to be in stark contrast with the unlandscaped yard. Inside, the country place turned out to be her dream house. "Oh, Stephen, it's beautiful!" she cried, her head whirling as she tried to take it all in at once. All the trimmings, fireplaces, and French doors were improved rather than deleted.

"Thanks to my sister, Jane, the interior decorator. She relieved me of a chunk of my savings and convinced me it was the right thing. I am pleased with how it turned out. Only problem is I don't get to spend much time here."

Genny sighed. His beautiful home sat empty while she holed up in one bedroom at Sonya's condo. She supposed she should be thankful she had a roof over her head.

"Have a seat. I'll check on dinner."

Comfortable leather furniture had been grouped to take advantage of the gorgeous marble fireplace that served as the focal point of the living room.

"Ready to eat?" Stephen asked.

China, crystal, and gold flatware on a lace cloth gave the table a festive appearance. A huge, cut flower centerpiece adorned the table.

"Mrs. James prepared all my favorites," Stephen said as he seated her. "Hopefully, there's something on the menu you like."

Genny devoured every bite of the tender steak and fat baked potato dripping with butter, sour cream, and chives. "I was greedy."

"You were hungry," Stephen said.

She didn't deny the truth. Her meager lunch hadn't sustained her very long. "You're fortunate to have such a wonderful cook."

Stephen nodded. "Blessed. I tell her often. Let's go into the den."

She immediately recognized the den as "his" room. Stephen's stamp was everywhere. Packages covered the coffee table and floor. "You getting an early start on Christmas?"

"Would you believe me if I said yes?"

Genny noted the baby gift wrap and shook her head.

"Okay, it's an impromptu baby shower. The guys told their wives and girlfriends about Jonathan, and the next thing I knew, my house had become the depository. You can't send them back."

"Why would I want to?" Genny asked, her attention focused on a huge balloon filled with baby accessories.

"I thought maybe because the guys were strangers . . ."

Genny chuckled. "We became pretty intimate friends very quickly. And for the record, where my child is concerned, I have no pride. He needs things I can't afford to buy."

Confusion flashed across his face. "So why do you refuse my help?"

"Because you do too much."

"No more than I want to do. Is Sonya planning a shower?"

Genny shook her head. "She hates that sort of thing. Help me open the presents. Save the names," she cautioned. "I have to write thank-you notes."

Like kids, they dove into the pile of presents. Stephen opted to strip away the paper and pass the gifts to Genny. An explosion garnered a tiny scream followed by laughter when a balloon fragment landed in her lap.

He shrugged. "I tried to figure out how to open it."

"They thought of everything. Even preemie outfits for him to wear when he's released."

Stephen watched her refold the tiny garments. "Genny, have you ever thought God brought us together for a reason?"

Her gaze touched on him and then moved to the box she held. "I think God's deserted me."

"Losing your husband and having a premature child has been difficult, but God hasn't left you."

"Why wouldn't I think that, Stephen? All my life, I've tried to be good and look where it's gotten me. I'm a thirty-six-year-old mother with no way to support her child and no home for him when he leaves the hospital. I'm not even sure how much of the medical bills will be paid."

❧

Stephen prayed for answers. No doubt Christians suffered and most of the time their suffering turned them back to God. His own suffering enabled him to comfort others, but he believed all the praise and glory belonged to God. His belief assured him one day he would leave the worries of the world behind.

"I'm sorry. I shouldn't have said that," Genny said. "Everything seems so hopeless."

"What happened to your home?"

"Sonya sold it. No, it's not like that," Genny said at his surprised look. "I couldn't have survived without her help. After John died, I barely functioned. The house had to be sold to pay the debts."

What kind of help? Stephen wondered. "What about John's life insurance?"

"There wasn't any. I do try to thank God, and you've given me even more reason to be appreciative. Oh, look at this!" Genny cried, pulling the clown puppet over her hand and thumbing through the accompanying storybook. "I read to Jonathan before he was born."

"So what else do you like besides reading?"

"Cooking, decorating, and I adore gardening. I miss my yard more than my house. I couldn't keep my gorgeous plants when I moved to Sonya's."

"There's a greenhouse out back. I like to tinker there when I have time."

"What do you grow?" Genny asked, clearly excited that they shared a love of gardening.

"Not much of anything lately," Stephen said, smiling grimly. "I miss puttering around, getting my hands dirty. I grew the violets in the dining room."

"Ooh, they're my favorites," she exclaimed. "So delicate."

"And hard to grow. I love a challenge."

The discussion drifted on to other plant preferences, and Genny listened intently as Stephen outlined his plan to landscape his yard.

"I'll probably end up hiring someone to do the work. Genny, I've been thinking. . . . I'd like to make you an offer. For Jonathan's sake. You can say no if you want, but please think about it first." She nodded. "I'd like for you to use my guesthouse." He expected a refusal based solely on her expression.

"Stephen, you've done far too much already."

"Let me show you the place. Then consider the convenience factor. You're going to be miserable away from Jonathan."

"But I can't pay you," she protested.

"And I'm not asking you to. Let me get the key."

❧

Stunned, Genny stared after Stephen when he charged from the room. He couldn't know how much she appreciated the gifts. They'd provided every item she'd anguished over. And now Stephen wanted to provide her with a place to stay.

"Let's go take a look," he said, dangling the key ring from his finger.

They went through French doors into a garden badly in need of care.

"Sorry about this eyesore. The landscapers want me to work with them, and there's never time."

"It has great potential," Genny said, thinking of the tiny yard she'd turned into a beautiful garden. She had done all the designing and implementing herself, buying every bulb, plant, and tree in the area. She'd enjoyed every moment. Receiving the local gardening club's monthly award several times was just icing on the cake.

They approached a smaller version of the big house. In the distance, Genny could see other buildings. "Do you have acreage here?"

"About fifty." Stephen opened the door and flipped on the light. "This is the place I had in mind for you."

It was one large room, subtly divided into three areas—kitchen, bedroom, and sitting room. Her gaze was drawn to the small fireplace flanked by single French doors. "It's beautiful," Genny said.

"And if Jonathan gets released from the hospital but needs to stay in the area, you could use this room as a nursery," Stephen said, showing her a dressing room large enough for the baby's crib and furnishings, including a rocker. "You could leave the door open at night."

He's given this more than a little thought, Genny realized. "We don't need anything half as grand."

"It's here and it's empty. Don't say no when you really want to say yes so badly."

He spoke the truth. The few hours had seemed an eternity. How would she survive several days without seeing her son? And even then, she'd have to listen to Sonya's complaints about the toll calls to the hospital and the expense of Genny commuting to and from the hospital. It would be so reassuring to have Stephen so close—when he wasn't on the road.

Genny smiled at him. "I'll think about it. I promise. I do appreciate the offer and everything you've done for us."

He nodded. "We'd better get you home. I'm sure you've done more today than the doctor wanted."

She touched his arm. "I will consider your offer, Stephen."

"That's all I ask. I'm praying you'll make the right decision."

6

They returned to find Mrs. James had boxed and bagged all the gifts, and minutes later they were in the car headed to Nashville. The conversation was casual, comfortable, nothing like the tongue-tied efforts Genny expected.

She waited for Stephen to prod her into accepting his offer, but he said nothing. The urge to say yes was overwhelming, but she couldn't keep taking. While Sonya believed there was nothing wrong with taking advantage of things freely given, Genny disagreed. Taking advantage of people was wrong. Then again, she didn't think Stephen felt she was using him.

Back at the condo, Stephen carried the packages in. "I suppose you're sleeping on the sofa?"

"No stairs."

"What if I carried you up? You'd probably enjoy a shower."

Genny shook her head. "Then you'd have to come back tomorrow and bring me down and . . ."

"I've done too much already."

She touched his arm. "Don't be upset."

He stepped closer; watching her. "Think about my offer?"

"I am," Genny said. "You're much too generous, Stephen."

"I won't let you down."

His comment puzzled her. "You don't owe me anything."

"Pray about this, Genny. Don't make yourself miserable when there's no reason."

His earnestness touched her heart. She wanted Jonathan in his bassinet by her bed, not hours away. Genny nodded agreement, fighting back the tears that sprang to her eyes.

"I'm sorry. I shouldn't have reminded you," Stephen said. "How about a hug?"

Genny wrapped her arms about him and appreciated his comforting touch. She smiled at his admonition not to worry. The soft kiss caught her by surprise, but she didn't pull away.

"I'll tell the guys you love the baby stuff."

She stepped back. "Please do. I need their addresses. I'd like to send personal notes."

Stephen pulled out his wallet and thumbed through the cards. "Contact this office and tell them I gave you the number. They can help."

"You think they'll believe me?"

"Probably not." He turned the card over and jotted an address. "Send them to me. I'll see they're delivered."

"Thanks, Stephen."

"And here's my number. So you can reach me. Don't hesitate to call."

Genny's throat constricted and her eyes watered.

"Mrs. James says you need to gain weight. She put a few things in this basket. I'll stick them in the refrigerator."

She sighed. Any minute now, he'd probably give her his wallet and the shirt off his back. "I told you Sonya would take care of that."

He paused and looked at her. "Where is she, Genny?"

"At work."

"At ten o'clock at night?" His gray eyes sparkled like a flash of lightning in a summer thunderstorm. "Has she even called to check on you?"

Genny met his ravings with defense of her sister. "Sonya hoped to get home around six. It's a busy time for her. She said so when she brought me home today."

"And left you here. Did she even bother to check to see if there was anything for you to eat?"

"She didn't have time."

"Don't defend her," he snapped. "I saw the contents of your refrigerator. What time would you have eaten? Midnight? Tomorrow? No doubt you're having dizzy spells. You've got to be sensible, Genny, or you'll be back in the hospital. Maybe you should be anyway."

Her ire increased with his misunderstanding of the situation. "I'm doing the best I can."

She couldn't criticize Sonya. Not unless she wanted to risk making herself and her son homeless. "I have no money. What Sonya does for me out of the kindness of her heart is all I can expect."

His lips twisted in a cynical smile. "She doesn't have a heart."

Genny turned away.

Stephen touched her shoulder. His tone thawed. "I don't want to argue. I can't bear to think of you in this situation."

She stared deep into his eyes, seeing the things she'd imagined in her daydreams of him. Friendship had quickly turned into attraction on her part. His voice could soothe and excite at the same time. His presence reassured and pleased.

"Ever since I laid eyes on you, I've wanted to be with you. I think about you a thousand times a day, wondering how you and Jonathan are doing. The phone calls aren't enough."

Genny stared down at the floor.

"I'm sorry," Stephen whispered, cradling her chin with his fingertips.

"Sonya tries, Stephen. But she has a busy life."

"And I can't help but believe you need someone to look after you."

"I can take care of myself."

"Under ordinary circumstances, but there's nothing ordinary here. You don't have other relatives who can help?"

Genny shook her head, more tears coming to her eyes as she considered her solitude in the world.

"We'll find a way," Stephen said, pulling her into his arms.

She rested against his chest, feeling secure and safer than she had in quite some time.

He cupped her chin and pulled her face up to his.

She reacted in fear, wrenching herself from his arms. "No. Don't."

"Genny, don't run away."

"There's nothing about me that is even remotely like the women you associate with."

"Maybe that's why." He massaged the hand that rested between his larger ones. "There's never been a right woman for me. I think you could be."

"Don't be ridiculous. We shared something special. That memory is what you can't erase from your head."

"That memory has your face, your voice. Do you want me out of your life?"

Genny felt the stirrings of something more powerful than either of them but knew she couldn't take the risk. "We can't base a relationship on a memory."

"But we could base it on a friendship," Stephen said. He invaded her space again, and Genny didn't move away.

"Oh, Stephen, I don't know."

"What is it, Genny? Is it that you're not ready?"

Her legs threatened to give away. If only she could explain her confusion. The way things had been with her husband . . . her fears that she had been losing John before the baby . . .

"It's me," Genny admitted without further explanation, intent on escaping Stephen. She had to think. She couldn't explain. For the past months her life had run out of control. She'd be a fool to hope she could ever have anything with a man like Stephen Camden.

His world was as far from her own as the earth from the moon. But unlike the astronauts, she lacked the ability to explore new worlds. Her own, such as it was, had to be enough.

"Stephen," she whispered, reaching out to him.

"I don't want apologies."

"I don't want to hurt . . . ," she stuttered, staring deep into gray eyes that burned with emotion.

"Get some rest."

After he left, Genny sank down on the couch. Stephen wasn't fooled by her halfhearted refusals. He knew exactly what she needed. And although she knew she should be telling him no, Genny couldn't turn him away. She needed his caring—desperately.

Like other women, she'd appreciated Stephen Camden from afar. Now she knew a different side of the handsome singer, the real man.

Genny lifted her legs onto the sofa and covered them with the blanket. She would rest for a few minutes. The door opening woke her.

"What time is it?" she asked.

"Late," Sonya said. "Why is the lamp on?"

"I dozed off."

She flipped the switch, leaving the room in darkness. "Turn off the lights next time. Electricity is expensive."

"Sonya, do you have a minute? There's something I'd like to discuss with you."

"Can't it wait?" The sigh Sonya had perfected echoed in the room. "I suppose you'll obsess all night if I don't hear you out."

"I just wondered if there was something I could do at your office to earn some money."

"Do you honestly think I'd put my job on the line by recommending you?" Sonya scoffed.

"I want to support myself."

Sonya's sarcastic laugh filled the dark void. "The best you can hope for is minimum wage. That would hardly keep the baby in diapers, much less day care. You can't afford to work."

"It'll be a struggle, but I need a job."

A case snapped open, and the glow of the lighter lit Sonya's face. A red pinpoint light glowed, and the odor of tobacco smoke dominated the room. "You have no idea what a real struggle is."

Don't I? A real struggle was holding your temper in check while your only relative accused you of living in a fantasy world. Where was the fantasy? She was a woman with a child and no money, no prospects for a job, and definitely no supportive relatives.

She'd placed her faith in her husband, expecting him to provide for their future. Instead he had taken that future to the grave with him, leaving her impoverished and plagued with worry. For the first time in her life, Genny didn't know how to overcome adversity.

If she had to be dependent on the kindness of others, chances were she would be better off depending on someone who knew the meaning of the word. "Stephen offered me use of his guesthouse while Jonathan is in the hospital. I think maybe I'll take him up on his offer."

"What makes every man you come in contact with feel duty bound to protect you?"

"They don't," Genny objected.

"Hah. It can't be because you're a raving beauty." The light flashed on. Sonya hunted an ashtray and stubbed out the cigarette. "You say he offered you his guesthouse? When?"

"Tonight. He came to visit and took me to see Jonathan. Afterward, we went to his house for dinner."

"Just who is this guy?"

"Stephen Camden. He's the lead singer for Cowboy Jamboree."

Sonya's head snapped up. "You're kidding."

"Stephen rescued me when I went into labor. He's been a great friend."

"Why didn't you tell me this before?"

"You haven't exactly wanted to hear the story, Sonya."

"This is fantastic."

Genny recognized Sonya's enthusiasm for what it was. "I won't take advantage of his kindness."

"You owe me."

What about everything she and John had done for Sonya? Why was it their kindness account always seemed to be in the debit column? In the year before his death, John had spent more time doing chores for her sister than for her.

"I've pulled my weight around here, Sonya. I cleaned your house, did your laundry, shopped for food, and cooked meals when you could be bothered to come home to eat them."

"It's not taking advantage," Sonya cajoled, changing her tone. "We're family, sisters helping each other. All I want to do is drop by, get to know him a little better, and then sell him on my firm. Is that too much to ask?"

"It's not your firm," Genny argued. "You're a secretary. You can't sell anything."

"I don't plan to be a secretary forever," Sonya all but shouted. "I have my savings, and if I could lure a big group to the firm, I'd be on the fast track to the top."

"He's offered me his guesthouse."

"This solves a problem for you, doesn't it? Just remember that when the fantasy days are over and you come back to the real world, it's going to take a better-paying job to support the three of us. It would be smart if you helped me now so I could help you later. I'm going to bed."

Sonya moved up the stairs without saying good night.

Don't lose hope. You won't be a burden forever. Genny recited these words in her head. Sonya would see. She would find a means of supporting herself and Jonathan. As soon as the doctor released her and Jonathan was out of the hospital, she'd show Sonya just how well-grounded her world really was.

Genny stumbled to the bathroom in the dark, her heart stinging from Sonya's repeated put-downs. Tears streamed down her cheeks as she considered her financial situation. How could John have left them with nothing? They had discussed investments. She knew he'd made them. Had he lost the money and been too ashamed to tell her the truth?

One step at a time. For now, she needed to get her son out of the hospital. Then she would find a means of providing their own home. If it meant living in a studio apartment, she'd do that rather than feel like a burden to anyone.

At least she wasn't in debt. She'd paid all the funeral expenses, outstanding bills, and continued the health insurance premiums, which would pay a portion of Jonathan's astronomical medical bills. She and the baby weren't totally destitute—at least they had John's Social Security benefits.

Maybe she didn't have much more than her pride and her child, but they were enough.

7

*G*enny's agony increased overnight. Her longing to be with Jonathan overwhelmed her.

When the phone rang the following morning, she grabbed the kitchen extension. Genny experienced a fresh flow of tears at the sound of Stephen's voice.

"Gen? What's wrong?"

"It's . . . ," she began shakily, growing quiet as she fought for control. "Nothing," she managed finally. She did not sound the least convincing.

"Honey, tell me."

Genny wavered before she said, "Oh, Stephen, everything's awful. What am I going to do?"

"Has something happened? Is Jonathan okay?"

"Sonya and I talked about me getting a job. She says I can't earn enough to keep my son in diapers." A mighty sniff followed the words. "Why does she have to be so cruel?"

"Why are you worrying about this now?" he demanded. "You need to recover before you start thinking about the future."

Genny knew Stephen would never understand her need for independence until he fully understood the position she'd placed herself in. "I shouldn't be burdening you with my problems. I'm an awful imposition on your good nature."

"You never could be," he assured. "How's Jonathan?"

Genny went into raptures over her son, describing the little things the nurses had shared, laughing with Stephen as he teased her into a good humor once more.

"What if I pick you up and take you to the hospital? Would you like that?"

"Yes," Genny said. "Yes, I would. And Stephen," she began, finding the words hard to express, "if the offer is still open, I'd like to stay in your guesthouse for a couple of weeks. I can't bear not seeing Jonathan. It's like a part of me is lying in that nursery."

"The place is yours for as long as you need it. Now stop worrying. I'll help with your things when I get there."

"I'll be ready."

"Remember, no stairs," he cautioned.

"Okay," Genny said, hating the feeling of helplessness.

She replaced the receiver, finding herself in deep thought when Sonya came into the kitchen wearing an expensive, red power suit. Her sister's executive wardrobe went far beyond that of most secretaries.

"Who was on the phone?"

"Stephen. He's picking me up today."

"To visit the baby?"

Genny concentrated on pouring juice. "I'm moving into his guesthouse for two weeks."

"That's my girl," Sonya praised, her face breaking into a smile. "Let me know a good time to visit, and we'll have him eating out of our hands in no time."

Determination filled Genny. "I won't let you hurt him."

Sonya frowned and exclaimed, "Why would I want to hurt Stephen Camden?"

Because I know you. Sonya used people to achieve her goals. "You're my sister and I don't think Stephen would mind you visiting, but I'm not getting involved in your schemes."

"That's my job," Sonya said, radiating confidence. "And what a coup it will be." She all but danced out the door.

No doubt Sonya was certain she could do anything she set her mind to. In the looks department, her sibling netted everything Genny missed out on. Gorgeous blond hair, now twisted into a professional style for work, hung down her back in a golden waterfall when she released the constraints. Large blue eyes tempted men to look into her very soul. There were absolutely no comparisons between Sonya's curvaceous body and Genny's sparse frame. People always expressed disbelief that they were sisters.

The ones who bothered to look beyond the beautiful exterior generally got a good glimpse of Sonya's self-centeredness. No man had ever withstood Sonya's need to be the star of the relationship.

Now it was her job to ensure that Stephen didn't fall prey to Sonya's games. Her vow not to see him hurt was far more important to Genny than Sonya's lofty goals.

Genny spent the wait sorting through the mess in the living room, folding blankets, and repacking the small suitcase. She felt tempted to climb the stairs. She could pack and be downstairs before Stephen arrived. Maybe he'd think Sonya had packed her clothes. One foot touched the bottom tread just as the doorbell rang.

Feeling guilty, Genny opened the door and met his smile with one of her own. "You made the trip in record time."

He hugged her. "I've always had a heavy foot. Feeling better?"

Genny nodded, unable to get the words around the emotion clogging her throat.

"Let's get you packed. Mrs. James is airing the guesthouse and making the bed. Don't be surprised if she plans a special dinner by way of welcome."

"Stephen, please don't go out of your way. Letting me stay in the guesthouse is far too much."

He grinned and swung her up into his arms. "Nothing's too much for my friends," he insisted as they reached the landing. "Which room is yours?"

Genny indicated the smaller bedroom as he lowered her to her feet. His gaze moved about the tiny, furniture-packed space.

"It's crowded. These were the pieces I had to keep when I moved out of my house," Genny explained, attempting to shift the rocker so she could open the closet door.

"Do you want to take all of it to the guesthouse?"

"Oh no," Genny said. "Not for two weeks."

"Why do you insist on two weeks?" Stephen demanded, moving

the chair out of the way. "You have no idea how long Jonathan will be in the hospital."

He had no way of knowing how she felt about being dependent on others. "I'm hoping."

"Let's agree to play this by ear. Where's your suitcase?"

Stephen dragged the largest suitcase from the closet and laid it open on the bed. Genny slid her limited wardrobe along the closet railing. Only a couple of pieces were decent enough to be seen in public. She laid them over the back of the rocker and walked over to the dresser.

"Stephen, there's a robe on the back of the bathroom door. Would you get it for me?"

He returned with the faded terry cloth garment.

"On second thought . . . ," Genny said as she examined the tattered sash.

"Looks fine to me. I have this shirt the guys keep threatening to burn. I keep it hidden when I don't have it on."

He wasn't wearing the shirt today. Stephen looked very handsome in khaki slacks and a leather jacket over a button-down collar shirt.

Resigned, Genny folded the robe and tucked in into the case. It was the only one she had.

⁓&

As he watched, Stephen wondered how any woman survived with so few clothes. Granted, she didn't strike him as the most fashion-conscious woman around, but she needed more than a couple of changes of clothes.

"That should do it."

There was still room in the suitcase.

"What about Jonathan's clothes?"

"I should take a few things. Just in case."

Stephen left Genny packing her cosmetic items as he carried the suitcase to the car. I take more stuff than this on a two-day tour, he thought incredulously as he lifted it into the trunk.

Back inside, he ran up the stairs. "Okay, what else?"

"Just this." Genny held up a plastic shopping bag filled with her personal items.

"Okay, let's go." Stephen swung her up into his arms and descended the stairs. She wasn't much heavier than her luggage. "Where's your coat?" he asked, releasing his hold on her.

Genny indicated the heavy sweater. "I'd like to take the gifts. Let me get my purse, and I'm ready."

"You don't have anything heavier? It's cold out there."

"I'm not much of a coat person. The sweater's warm."

Probably because she doesn't own a coat, Stephen thought. "Okay, I'll put this in the car and start up the heater while you finish in here."

He started out the door, pausing when she called his name. "Is it okay if I leave your address and phone number for Sonya?"

Even though he wanted to separate Genny from her sister's hurtful ways, he knew he couldn't refuse. "Sure."

"Oh, I need the thank-you notes. They're upstairs in my nightstand."

"Top drawer?"

"Yes. The flowered box."

Stephen pulled the drawer open and hesitated at the stack of photographs of Genny's dead husband staring up at him. "Hey, Buddy, hope it's okay that I'm taking care of her for you," he whispered softly. The still photograph offered no clues.

"Okay, got them," he called down to Genny. "Do you want this photograph on the nightstand?"

"No, thanks."

She probably has a wallet-sized one, he thought. Stephen shrugged and made his way downstairs. He tucked the box in the bag. "Ready?"

Genny nodded and checked one last time to make certain she had the door key. "I always feel I've forgotten something."

"We can replace anything. I imagine the hospital is number one on your priority list?"

Genny smiled. "Only slightly ahead of thanking you."

❧

The trip seemed to take forever. After he parked, Genny all but floated to the nursery where the nurses welcomed her with smiles. They stayed a couple of hours before Stephen said, "I think maybe it's time for you to take a nap too."

"Just a couple minutes more," Genny said, caressing Jonathan's leg. "I missed him so much yesterday."

"He's a precious gift from heaven," Stephen agreed. "I'll wait for you in the lobby."

Genny thought about Stephen's words as she looked at her son. She did thank God for Jonathan's survival, but that didn't stop her from wondering why her tiny babe had to endure this.

Her life had never been perfect, but she tried to be a good person. Maybe it was time to look deeper. Suddenly Genny felt very tired. Stephen was right. She needed rest.

Stephen told her to pay attention to the route they took to his house. "You can drive this car to the hospital."

"Stephen! No!"

"Why not?" His expression resembled that of a disappointed child. "How did you plan to get there?"

"You've done much too much already."

"I'd like to do more," he said simply.

Leaning on Stephen Camden could easily become a habit. She couldn't let him get caught up in taking care of her. "I appreciate the offer, but I can get a taxi."

"Taxis are expensive."

"I'll go in the morning and spend the day."

Stephen shook his head. "You can't. The doctor doesn't want you at the hospital all the time."

"It's my problem. I'll work it out."

Genny tensed at his dissatisfied snort. "It isn't like you're putting me out. I won't be using the car. Wouldn't it be nice to drive yourself?"

"Dr. Garner doesn't want me driving."

"That's right," Stephen said. "Some of the guys said their wives couldn't drive right after the baby was born. Besides, with those dizzy spells, it probably isn't a good idea for you to be behind the wheel yet. At least let me arrange your transportation."

Genny shook her head in disbelief. "You're a stubborn, stubborn man."

"I like doing things for my friends."

"Well, this friend likes doing things for herself."

"But, Genny . . ."

"No, Stephen. I have to provide for my son."

He frowned. "I didn't realize you were so stubborn."

"I don't consider taking charge of my life as being stubborn."

Stephen parked and went around to Genny's side to help her out. "Let's get you inside. I'll get your stuff."

"Stop treating me like fragile china. I had a baby, not major surgery."

"I only want to help. It's cold out here, and that sweater is not all that thick," he protested.

"Fine. I'll sit on the couch like a good little girl. But you're only bringing my things inside, not unpacking or having them unpacked."

He threw his hands into the air and backed off. "Okay. Here's your key to the guesthouse. Let yourself in. I'll bring the luggage and get out of your hair."

"Stephen, I'm sorry," Genny said softly. "I don't mean to sound ungrateful, but you've got to let me do some things for myself."

Take it easy, Man, he cautioned. "I'm sorry too. Mrs. James can bring your dinner out here."

"I'll come over for dinner. If you don't mind," she said tentatively.

He nodded. Stephen placed her things in the bedroom area, told her to get some rest, and left. At home, he shut the door with a bit more force than necessary. Why wouldn't she let him take care of her? He didn't want to take over her life—just arrange transportation to the hospital.

She wasn't going to sit in the hospital waiting room all day. And she wasn't going to catch a bus or a cab. He picked up the phone and punched in the number.

"I need the name of the limo service we use here in town."

"Certainly, Mr. Camden. I'll get it for you."

The band's newest release came over the phone as she put him on hold.

"Steve, Man, what's up? You trying to impress some chick?"

Stephen groaned when Chuck's voice came over the phone. "Just making arrangements for a friend."

"Female, I bet. Anyone I know?"

"It's none of your business, Harper."

"Awfully protective, aren't you?"

Stephen's head filled with Chuck Harper's exploits to publicize the band. He wouldn't let him number Genny among that group. "It's people like you she needs protection from."

"I'm only doing my job."

"If you want to keep that job, you'll remember what I said."

Genny did a double take the following morning when she opened the door to the uniformed chauffeur intent on driving her to the hospital in a black stretch limousine.

"There must be some mistake."

"No, Ma'am. I'm Karen. Mr. Camden said to give you this."

She unfolded the paper and was struck by the bold slant of writing. *Genny,* she read, wondering if he had written the note or had told someone what to write.

> *I know what you said but the limo company has been instructed to take you to and from the hospital every day until Jonathan comes home. Please understand and do this for me. We'll be away for a few days. I'll call you soon.*
>
> Stephen

"I just started working with my dad today," the young woman said when Genny hesitated. "You wouldn't make me go back and tell him my first client refused to ride with me, would you?"

Genny smiled and shook her head. "Let me get my purse."

What was Stephen thinking? She rushed around gathering her

things. She locked the door and walked over to where Karen waited by the open car door. Feeling like royalty, Genny climbed inside.

"Just relax and leave everything to me, Mrs. Smith. There's fruit juice in the refrigerator. Mr. Camden thought you might prefer that."

The rich smell of expensive leather filled her nose as Genny wallowed in the luxurious seat. "Oh, Stephen, what have you done?" she whispered.

"Did you say something, Ma'am?"

Genny waved her off. The door closed, secluding her in privacy, and she explored the area. Every nook and cranny held a surprise. She marveled at the telephone, television, and other conveniences she'd never thought to see in a vehicle—especially the chilled crystal goblets in the refrigerator!

Several taxis a day wouldn't cost this much. She would tell him so the next opportunity she had.

8

everal days later, Genny lounged in the back of limo as if she'd been riding in them forever. Having transportation to and from the hospital was heavenly. Jonathan gained weight, and Dr. Lee felt encouraged. Genny shared the news with Stephen when he called, as he had done each night.

The first time, Genny confronted him about the limo. "I know you wanted to arrange transportation, but I never dreamed you'd go this far."

"It doesn't cost that much."

"Yeah, sure."

"No, really, these companies give us a good deal."

Genny wasn't convinced. "I don't know how I'll ever repay you."

"No need. I subscribe to the Second Corinthians 9:7 Scripture."

"What's that?" she asked curiously.

"The Bible reads, 'Each man should give what he has decided in his heart to give, not reluctantly or under compulsion, for God loves a cheerful giver.'

"Genny, one day, when you're able, you'll help someone in need. Meanwhile, get your strength back and bring Jonathan home so I can visit him without having to put my hands through portholes. I have nightmares about getting my hands stuck." With her laughter, he asked, "Can you do that for me?"

"Oh, Stephen," she whispered softly so he wouldn't hear, then answered, "Yes."

Genny concentrated on achieving the goal, following her doctor's advice to the letter and recovering from her pregnancy with no complications. Happiness coursed through her, particularly after spending time with her baby or talking with Stephen.

Sonya's question stayed on her mind, and Genny found she couldn't explain why men saw her as a little girl lost.

Genny never considered herself even remotely pretty. She was plain, a fact that made itself evident every time she looked into a mirror.

Granted, her mousy brown hair did have an attractive shine after a wash. But her face was a combination of sharp planes and angles, its shape a long thin heart with high cheeks and a sharp nose. She was short, with no physical allure. Her thin body had already thrust off the extra pregnancy weight, leaving no indication that she'd had a child. Forest green eyes were her only claim to beauty.

Guilt soared through her when she missed Stephen. She had no business thinking of another man so soon after John's death.

Still she felt delight when Stephen surprised her with an early morning visit. Feeling self-conscious in the tattered robe and looking less than her best, Genny invited him in. Her heart went out to him. He looked exhausted. "Would you like a cup of coffee?"

He nodded. Stephen sat on a stool, watching as she measured coffee into the coffee maker.

"Have you eaten?"

"We just got in."

She removed eggs and butter from the refrigerator and a frying pan from the cabinet. "How was the trip?"

"Hectic. Five cities in five days. Not to mention the recording session before that."

"When do you leave again?"

Stephen shrugged and yawned widely. "I don't even want to think about it."

"After breakfast, you need to go home and get some rest."

"Trying to get rid of me already?"

Genny nearly missed the teasing glint in his eye. "No!" she cried. "I'd love for you to stay, but you need sleep."

"I know. I wanted to let you know I was back and ask if I can take you to the hospital later."

"I'd like that."

After Stephen went home to rest, Genny dressed for her trip to the hospital. Karen arrived right on schedule.

Climbing inside, she greeted her new friend and said, "Stephen's home. He'll drive me to the hospital this afternoon."

The realization that her two weeks was half over marred her visit. Stephen would never hold her to the self-imposed deadline, but she felt obligated to honor her original plan.

It would be different if she were able to return the favor. Even at Sonya's she'd held on to her pride by keeping house.

"Oh, Jonathan," she whispered to the sleeping baby, "why do things have to be this way?"

Genny expected no answer. As the parent, the adult, she had the responsibility of seeing that this child had a good life. She would find a way, and until then, she would depend on the kindness of others to see them through.

"Hello, Genny."

She jumped, reaching to erase the trace of tears from her cheeks. "Dr. Lee. Hello."

"How's our boy doing today?"

"You tell me."

"I'm happy to say he's improving daily."

Genny waited while the doctor checked over Jonathan's chart and then spoke to the nurses. "Dr. Lee, do you have a minute?" she asked when he started out the door.

"Certainly."

"Do you . . . ? I mean, I know you can't really . . ." Just spit it out. "I need to know how long Jonathan will be in the hospital."

He shook his head. "In cases like this, it's day to day. Jonathan is developing, in this particular case outside the uterus, much as he would have done inside your body. He needs to mature and gain weight before I would even consider releasing him. What troubles you, Genny?"

"I've been staying with a friend here in Memphis," she explained. "I limited my stay to two weeks. I hoped . . ."

"No, we're looking at much longer. Would your friend object to extending your visit?"

"I can't intrude indefinitely."

"You certainly have a dilemma, one you need to work out as quickly as possible. Stressed mothers make irritable babies."

"So would it be better for me to go home and wait for his release?"

"No! Never!" Dr. Lee insisted. "What's best is that you're here with him. And that you find peace within yourself. Talk to your friend. You might be surprised by his response."

The doctor's words surprised her. How had he known her friend was a man? Had Stephen been in contact with the doctor? Surely not. Then again, she'd told the nurses they could update him on Jonathan's status.

Dr. Lee was right about the need to find peace within herself.

Stephen joined her for the second visit, and afterward insisted Genny stay for dinner. Preoccupied, she enjoyed yet another tasty meal and found herself ready to beat a hasty retreat. Coward, she chastised as she wished him good night.

"Don't be in such a hurry," he said. "Come with me. I want you to hear something I'm working on."

Genny followed Stephen into his den. Piles of sheet music hung over the edge of coffee table. His guitar leaned against the sofa.

"You've been writing? I thought you'd be too exhausted."

"Yeah. I felt inspired when I woke."

Genny reached for one of the pages and stopped. "May I?" He nodded. She read through the lyrics, surprised to find it was a Christmas hymn. "Is this song for the band?"

"We're planning a Christmas album."

"This is beautiful. When will it be recorded?"

"We worked on it some before the tour. I wanted to get the album out last year, but it didn't happen." He reached for his guitar and strummed a few cords.

Genny felt goose bumps rise on her arms as he sang the song. As always, the story of her Savior's birth moved her. The idea that God could love one so unworthy always amazed her.

"I already promised the guys we'll be home for Christmas this year. Harper isn't real happy."

Genny saw more in his expression than in the words he spoke. "What's wrong, Stephen?"

His sigh was heavy and burdensome. "I want to leave the band."

"Then do it." Genny lifted a hand to her mouth.

A tight smile flitted across his face. "I wish it were that simple."

"Why does it have to be difficult?"

"How do I throw away the security? My band members have families. I can't take away their livelihood. And it could mean I wouldn't have money to support myself or a family when the time comes. I feel like such a weak Christian."

"God provides, Stephen. I'm living proof of that. Where would I be if not for winning the ticket that brought you into my life? Would my son be alive if you hadn't taken us into your care? I don't see any reason why you can't sing the songs you dream of doing. Artists cross over all the time. You could too."

A slow smile creased his face. "You make me believe it's possible."

"God saw fit to give you talent, and life's too short not to do what you want."

"I've been working on the other music when I'm home. The guys look at me strangely when I mention I've been putting in a lot of writing time because I haven't produced much in the way of music for the band."

"They haven't seen these?"

"No. Harper's been on my case to write more songs, but my heart's not in it."

"Figure out how to make it work."

Stephen leaned back against the sofa. "What's happened to my faith that God will provide? I hate this power money has over my life. Years ago, before Christ came into my life, I loved the lifestyle. Now I despise everything about it. The concerts are okay but the drinking, profanity, and fighting in some of the small clubs overwhelm me. I want to stand on that stage and preach brotherly love, but I know they'd stone me if I tried. I know I should do it anyway," he admitted with a sigh.

"I jumped at the chance to do the Christmas hymns album. I'm more excited about this project than anything in a long while. Including the CMA Award."

"Sounds like you know what you want."

"I want to use my talent for God. I want my music to touch lives and share God's story."

"Then trust Him to make it possible."

Spouting off encouraging words of faith when in doubt herself made Genny feel like such a hypocrite.

"I know not to depend on myself, but humans are such strange creatures. We pray for guidance but more often than not wouldn't recognize the answer if it hit us over the head. I'm praying about this. Will you pray too?"

Would God even hear her prayers after so long? Genny nodded.

"What did Dr. Lee say about Jonathan today?"

"That he has no idea when they'll release him."

"Hallelujah. You're the answer to a prayer," he exclaimed. "Mrs. James is going on vacation, and I need a house sitter. You can stay, and I'll pay you."

Genny couldn't help but be suspicious.

"I know what you're thinking," Stephen said. "Sometimes I wonder why I bought a house. I never get to spend much time here. It would be a great help if you could stay. You can use my car. Mrs. James uses the car," Stephen said before she could object.

Genny gave up. "Okay. I won't fight you. I'll house-sit in exchange for the guesthouse and use of your car. I think I'm getting the better end of the deal."

"You obviously don't know how difficult it is to find house sitters. Even with the security system and such, I dread thinking of what would happen if I left the place empty."

No doubt the looters would steal him blind. "What about while I'm at the hospital?"

Stephen covered the wide yawn with his hand. "I'm more concerned about the house sitting empty."

"I'll take good care of your home."

"I don't doubt it." He yawned again.

"You're exhausted," Genny said.

"Let's just say I don't think I'll have any problems getting to sleep."

❧

Stephen insisted on seeing Genny to the guesthouse and returned home to toss and turn in his bed, his need for sleep overcome by the guilt feelings.

He'd given Mrs. James two extra weeks of vacation, and knowing he only wanted to help Genny, she'd accepted. At least now he could relax a bit.

The earlier conversation with Genny troubled Stephen. Was he thwarting his own desire to serve the Lord in song? It certainly seemed that way. He closed his eyes and prayed, "Blessed Father, I realize I'm fighting You for control of my life. Help me to release my worries into Your hands and guide me to accept and achieve Your plan for me. Bless Genny and baby Jonathan. Thank You for bringing them into my life. Amen."

9

The days passed, some quickly, and some as though they would never end. Genny felt even more confused. No matter how often she told herself guys like Stephen didn't fall for women like her, she couldn't forget her reaction to his presence. He filled her heart and soul, bringing more guilt when memories of John began to fade.

The battle of wills, Genny's attempts to curb Stephen's generosity overridden by his determination, seemed hopeless at times.

As planned, she reviewed the procedures of Stephen's house with Mrs. James before driving her to the airport. Every day, Genny checked the house, watered plants, dusted, and waited for Stephen's late-afternoon phone calls.

She looked forward to hearing from him and then berated herself for being so eager. Genny knew allowing herself to care would hurt even more when she did what she knew she must.

She waited as long as possible to call Sonya, fearful her plan would cause problems. Her suspicions Sonya had not forgotten were verified the moment she answered the phone.

"It certainly took you long enough to call. Is it a good time to visit?"

Genny twisted the telephone cord about her hand. "I'll be staying in Memphis for awhile longer."

"What about the meeting?" Sonya whined. "You promised."

"I told you I wouldn't abuse Stephen's kindness."

Another line rang, and Genny expected Sonya to say good-bye.

"Just hold on," she snapped.

Several minutes passed before she returned. "Look, Genny, you owe me this. I'll be there this weekend."

A shot of hurt spiraled through Genny. Not one word about her sister or nephew. They were only stepping-stones to the real prize. "I don't know if he'll be home."

"Then find out." The haughty demand carried a wealth of warning.

"I don't want to do this, Sonya. It reeks of deceit."

"Oh, please. It's business, plain and simple."

Somehow she would find a means of telling him what Sonya planned. "He checks in every day."

"Call the moment you hear," Sonya directed. "Tell him I'm coming for a visit."

Genny ended the conversation quickly. Allowing Sonya to coerce her had never been part of the plan. And she'd actually thought Sonya would forget if she delayed long enough. How could she be so naïve?

Stephen called later than usual to say they would be home Friday afternoon. "I thought we might run by the hospital and then go out to dinner."

"Sonya wants to come for a visit."

"The more the merrier. Want me to ask Ray along?"

"Are you sure?" *Idiot*, she chastised silently. *Tell Stephen the truth.*

"She's your sister." There was some hesitation before he admitted, "I'm not exactly endeared to her."

"There's a lot about Sonya you don't understand."

"How can you be so different?"

Maybe he'd understand if she explained Sonya might be less bitter if she had experienced love when she needed it most. But the past couldn't be rewritten and no matter how hard one fought to stop it from happening, it often affected the future.

"Stephen, you should know Sonya works for a PR firm in Nashville." There. It was out.

"That's nice."

"Did you hear what I said?"

"Sure. Sonya works for a PR firm."

"And that doesn't bother you?"

"Not particularly. I'm eager to get home."

He made it too easy. She hoped Stephen would realize what she was trying to tell him. "I can't wait for you to see Jonathan."

The conversation continued for a few more minutes before they said good night. Reluctantly, she dialed Sonya's condo, hoping to get the machine. *No such luck,* Genny thought glumly when Sonya answered on the third ring.

"It's about time you called. I turned down a dinner invitation and came straight home."

"Stephen just called. We're going to the hospital late Friday afternoon and then to dinner. He said to invite you along." A barrage of questions followed, most of which Genny couldn't answer.

"Do I need to give you a list?"

"I want no part in this."

"I'll meet you at the restaurant. I don't want to go to the hospital."

"But Sonya, you haven't seen Jonathan."

"You know how I hate hospitals."

"If that's what you want. See you Friday."

Sonya's attitude raised yet another important issue for Genny. What if something happened to her? Who would care for her baby?

On Friday, Genny spent the afternoon gardening. When the bus pulled up, Stephen jumped off and raced across the lawn, sweeping her into his arms and whirling her about.

Her love for the soil showed in the amount that clung to her old clothes. "You'll get dirty."

"I don't care."

He kissed her, and Genny's arms crept about his neck, and she kissed him back. The contact lasted for several heart-stopping seconds before catcalls from the bus forced her back to reality. She backed away.

"It's okay, Honey," Stephen said, taking her hand in his.

"Those clowns can't get out of the rain with directions."

He insisted Genny meet the guys and tugged her toward the bus. Her shyness was forgotten at their friendly reception.

They waved the bus off, and Stephen picked up his luggage.

Genny followed him to the house. "I'll change and meet you at the car. Sonya's going straight to the restaurant."

"Has she visited Jonathan yet?"

Genny shook her head. Afraid she would cry if they continued, she attempted escape.

"Wait. I have something for you."

She paused midflight, startled by the large box he placed in her arms. The beautifully wrapped package made a mockery of everything they had discussed.

Stephen tugged the artfully tied silk ribbon. Both watched it fall to the floor. A frown crept onto Genny's face when she recognized the logo on the box lid. He dropped the lid and folded back the tissue. Genny stared at the brilliant red suede.

"Take it out," he encouraged, doing it himself when she hesitated. He tossed the box onto the sofa and held the coat for her. "Slip your arm in." She did, surprised by how well it fit. "The color really suits you."

"You'll ruin it. I'm filthy."

"It'll clean."

She smoothed the sleeve of the fringed jacket and immediately fell in love. "It's beautiful but hardly practical. It must have cost the earth."

"You're worth every cent," Stephen said. "Wear it. For me."

"You can't buy me expensive presents."

"Actually I bought it for Jonathan. We can't have his mommy getting sick, can we?"

Their gazes locked.

"You know I have to wear it," Genny said, smiling sheepishly. "It's one of the most beautiful things I've ever seen."

Pleasure radiated across his face. "There's more." Tissue tumbled to the floor, and he held up a matching ankle-length skirt and blouse. "This is for taking such wonderful care of my home."

"For all you know, I robbed you blind and broke all your valuable art objects. Maybe I ran tours through here while you were away."

He laughed outright. "My riches extend to a tray of change on the dresser. I don't own any valuable art objects. The carpet's not worn or dirty, so I can rule out the tours. Just accept it as thanks for your help."

Thinking how she'd never had anything like this, Genny touched the soft material again. "Okay, but only because I don't want to embarrass you when we go out to dinner."

He looked surprised. "Why would you think that? Have I ever led you to believe I'm ashamed of you?"

"Well, no . . ."

"You could wear anything, and I'd never feel that way. Do you understand?" When she didn't respond, he continued, "I'm proud to be seen with you."

"You're a wonderful man. Too generous."

He chuckled at her words. "You had to get that in."

"I'll stop when you stop."

"Can't," Stephen said, shaking his head. "Get dressed, Woman. Meet me here at 4:30."

Genny raced home and into the shower. A few minutes later she combed tangles from her freshly washed hair. When it refused to be styled, Genny pulled it back with clasps. She reached for a bottle of foundation and smoothed the color on her face.

The suit fit as though made for her. Genny couldn't believe the difference in her appearance. Her self-confidence soared. Maybe clothes did make the woman.

She felt good enough to stand alongside her beautiful sister and not come up lacking. "God, forgive my vanity," Genny whispered, realizing the true reason had to do with her fears.

She wasn't suitable for Stephen, and yet she didn't want to give him up. Would he forget her existence when Sonya turned on the charm?

Stephen whistled when she stepped into the house. "You really do something for that outfit."

Genny curtsied slightly. "Thank you, but it's the other way around."

"No, it's definitely you. You're beautiful. Those clothes couldn't look better on a high-dollar fashion model."

"Please, Stephen, plain old me isn't used to such surprises and compliments."

"But I thought you liked surprises," he said as they reached the car.

He looked confused and Genny sighed. She had been sending the wrong signals—saying no and then becoming as excited as a child over his gifts. "I like surprises, but yours take my breath away. I need to psych myself up . . . to prepare for your world."

Stephen glanced at her and said, "That's ridiculous."

A wave of anger surged through Genny. "I don't think so."

"Why do you persist in believing our worlds are so different?"

"Because they are. Meeting you is the stuff of fantasies."

"Genny, my life has been one huge surprise since you and Jonathan came into it. Nothing I do for you can compete. You've given one disillusioned man hope for his future."

Her mouth dropped open, and he tapped her chin. "Ready to visit Jonathan?"

At the hospital, reporters waylaid them. Lights flashed, and Genny flinched at the onslaught. Stephen pushed a camera to the side, sliding an arm about her waist and turning her toward him.

A reporter stalked them like a hungry predator. "Mr. Camden, we got a tip that there's a mystery woman in your life. Is this her?" she demanded, swinging the mike toward Genny.

"No comment. Keep walking," he instructed softly.

"Maybe if I explain," Genny said.

"It doesn't help. They draw their own conclusions."

"I'll make them understand." Genny turned to the reporter and said, "It's thanks to Mr. Camden that my son is alive today."

A man shoved his way to the front. "So why did he bring you into his home?"

Memories of another time when reporters had no intention of listening assailed Genny. She had wanted to explain then, but they preferred to focus on the horror of the act rather than the grief of two young women.

Stephen stepped forward. "Come on, people, you're making the lady nervous. I've never asked your permission before but if you feel the need to approve my staff . . ."

"Staff?"

"Yes, Mrs. Smith is my assistant."

"Smith?" a reporter cried, disbelief coloring his words. "Come on, what are you hiding?"

"Do your homework," Stephen countered, quelling the man with one look.

"Why do you need an assistant?"

"Why do you need one?"

Genny envied him the ease with which he fielded their questions.

"Praise God, Cowboy Jamboree is becoming more popular by the day. Mrs. Smith will help me respond to the mailbags filling my entry hall. As for why she's living in my guesthouse," he said, emphasizing the word, "she works a flexible shift so she can spend time with her son. Any more questions?"

"You plan to chase her around the desk?"

"Do I look like a woman men chase around desks?" Genny's droll question garnered a few chuckles. She glanced at Stephen, wondering if he'd picked up on their incredulity.

"Sorry, Ma'am. Looks like a wild-goose chase. Sorry to bother you, Mr. Camden. Perhaps we can get together for a personal interview?"

"Contact Chuck Harper."

Stephen hurried Genny into the hospital.

"Why did you lie to them? What will they think when Jonathan and I go home?"

"It's a serious offer, Genny. You need a job. I need an assistant. I'm behind in my correspondence."

"You don't even know if I can type."

"Can you?"

"Well, yes, but . . ." He hadn't released his hold, and Genny felt winded by their rush down the hospital corridor. "You don't have to give me a job. I'll help you."

"Only if I pay you for your time."

"I'll think about it."

"Do that. Meanwhile, I'm going to chat with Mr. Harper. I warned him about the press."

"You can't be sure he did this."

Stephen's hold on her arm tightened. "You certainly can't be sure what he'll do or say next."

Inside the nursery, the media was forgotten when the nurse said Genny could hold Jonathan for the first time. Gowned, she held the infant as closely as possible, paying close attention to all the wires and tubes connected to him.

Stephen stood by her side, watching and smiling as she cooed words of love in a language only babies understood.

She glanced up. "Wish I had a camera. I'd love to show Sonya how he's grown."

Stephen glanced at the nurse. She nodded and returned a couple of minutes with an instant camera. "Hold him up."

Genny pulled Jonathan closer to her face and smiled. The woman laid the photo on the isolette before snapping another. "Mr. Camden, would you like to pose with them? I'm sure Mrs. Smith would like a picture for Jonathan's baby book."

"Can Stephen hold him?"

He shook his head and stepped back when the nurse said okay.

"It's not so hard," Genny prompted.

Stephen cradled the baby like a fine art object, concentration lines deepening along his brows and under his eyes. Genny adjusted his arm. "Don't worry. He won't break. Support his neck. You're doing great."

The time passed all too quickly. Tears came to her eyes when they returned Jonathan to the isolette.

"Won't be long before he's home," Stephen assured, stripping off the gown. "Are you hungry?"

"I could eat."

Traffic was comparatively light, but they were still a few minutes late. Genny experienced a moment of dread when he parked. The feeling she didn't belong made her tense when Stephen reached for her hand.

"What's wrong?"

"This place must be popular," she managed.

"Mitch does okay. You're going to like this restaurant. The building has never been renovated. He says you don't make changes when something works. Ready?"

Sonya sat just inside the door, chatting with Ray. The two seemed to be very comfortable. Genny wished she felt that same comfort.

"What happened to you two?" Sonya demanded.

"Genny got to hold Jonathan for the first time," Stephen said. "The hostess will show you to our table. I need to speak to Ray."

Genny wondered what was so important as they followed the waiter across the room.

"Thanks for the opportunity to talk with Ray. I think maybe he's interested—" Sonya interrupted herself as she touched the fringed sleeve of Genny's coat. "Where did this come from?"

"A gift from Stephen." Genny slipped the jacket off and glanced around. "Does this place have a coat rack?"

"By the door, but I wouldn't suggest you leave it there. It would develop legs before dinner is served."

Genny draped the coat over the back of her chair. When Sonya asked to try it on, she placed a protective hand on the jacket. "Not tonight."

"Looks like you've hit pay dirt."

"Sonya!"

"I like nice things too. He knows what suits you."

Before she could comment, Stephen came up and rested his hands on Genny's shoulders.

"Stephen, this is my sister, Sonya Kelly. Sonya, this is Stephen Camden."

Sonya reached out her hand and flashed him her flirtatious smile. "My pleasure. Ray introduced himself when I gave the hostess my name."

After they were seated and studying the menus, Stephen glanced at Genny. "Order anything you want. Your doctor said you should gain some weight so indulge yourself."

"Not the beanpole," Sonya said with a disparaging laugh. "She's disgusting. Genny can eat anything and never gain a pound."

"I'm not so sure that's a positive," Stephen said. "A few extra pounds would have made things easier for her with Jonathan."

Genny noted the way Sonya's eyebrows lifted at his protective words.

"Oh, that reminds me." Genny pulled her purse around and

retrieved the snapshots. "I want to show you how Jonathan's grown."

Sonya didn't bother to take them. Genny noted Ray's sympathetic look when he reached out. "Steve brags about how big he's getting." One by one, he flipped through the photos. "Mighty handsome boy, Genny. Here, Ms. Kelly, take a look at your nephew."

"Oh, call me Sonya, please." The pictures fell to the tabletop with barely a glance before she said, "Looks like he'll be in the hospital for awhile."

An uncomfortable silence followed the insensitive comment.

"He's improving every day," Genny whispered.

Stephen's hand covered hers on the tabletop. Once the orders were taken, Ray asked Sonya to dance.

"Not the nurturing sort, is she?" Stephen asked as the couple moved out of hearing range.

Genny picked up the pictures, a frown creasing her forehead. "I don't understand her aversion. He's not repulsive or anything. Why is she like that?"

"Honey, don't let Sonya upset you."

"I don't know what I expect from her. She never refers to him as anything but 'the baby' or my son. He's her nephew. Why doesn't she care? I would if he were her child."

"Could be she doesn't want to share center stage with Jonathan."

Genny twisted in her seat and glanced at the dance floor. Sonya flirted with Ray, oblivious to the hurt she had caused.

"Probably," she agreed with a slight shrug of her shoulders. "We need to discuss what you told the reporters."

The waiter's quick reappearance with their food was another perk of celebrity status.

"Not now we don't." Stephen said grace and took a bite of chicken. "Just like my grandma used to make."

Genny's brows shot up with her surprise. Of course, he had parents and grandparents. "Is she a great cook?"

"The best. Mom's idea of Southern-fried chicken is takeout," he said with an indulgent smile.

"Do your parents live in Memphis?" As soon as the words left her mouth, Genny wished she could draw them back. Questions begat questions. She wasn't ready to tell him the story of her life.

"They're in Houston. I can't wait to introduce you and Jonathan to them. What about yours?"

"Dead."

"I'm sorry."

"Sorry about what?" Sonya asked as Ray pulled out her chair.

"Genny told me about your parents."

"Did you . . ." Sonya stopped when Genny flashed her a warning glare. "Oh, never mind. It's old news."

"Excuse me, please," Genny said. "I need the ladies' room."

She returned to find Sonya wearing her coat.

"I was cold," Sonya said. "Stephen said it was okay."

Genny felt betrayed.

"What I said was it would be okay if you thought Genny wouldn't mind."

She experienced mixed emotions. Genny didn't want Sonya wearing her coat, but she didn't want to be selfish either. "It's okay. She's cold. Please be careful with it, Sonya."

No doubt she would hear from Sonya later, but the coat was hers. And she didn't want to share.

After a few initial false starts at conversation, dinner was consumed in silence. Not an impressive first meeting.

"I don't know about the rest of you, but I'm all for calling it a night," Stephen announced.

"But it's early," Sonya protested, sounding disappointed.

Sonya's nervous behavior didn't bode well. "Could we all go back to your place and visit? I wanted to spend time with Genny. Maybe see where she's living."

Genny almost screamed. Why couldn't Sonya leave well enough alone? Stephen wasn't stupid. He'd see right through her pitiful little act.

"Sure. You can follow us to the house."

Ray opted to head for home and wished them all good night. At the house, Sonya followed Stephen to the door with Genny bringing up the rear.

"I live in the guesthouse, Sonya. Let's go over there."

"Oh, but I want to see Steve's home." She wrapped her hand about his arm and smiled up at him. "You don't mind, do you?"

He didn't look too pleased. "Come in. I'll fix some coffee."

Sonya's gaze roamed about the beautifully decorated room. She waited until he left then said, "You've certainly done well for us."

"There's no us involved in this," Genny muttered, lowering her voice as she glanced toward the kitchen. "And cut the theatrics. You're being way too obvious."

"You'd better remember who's taking care of you and your brat," Sonya hissed. "I don't work all the time for pleasure."

Furious, Genny growled, "I thought you did. We're not destitute. We have John's Social Security, and I plan to work."

"Well, aren't we full of ourselves today?" Sonya's sarcasm strengthened as she continued. "You'd better watch that smart mouth. And I don't appreciate you making a fool out of me over that coat. You better hope it didn't hurt my plan."

Tears stung Genny's eyes. She was so tired of being afraid.

"I got a lead on a killer investment that's going to take all my savings. My budget won't stretch to cover your needs." Sonya drew a quick breath and continued. "I've considered what you can do and have a possible lead. One of the guys at work knows someone who needs a housekeeper. He thinks the couple would let you take the baby along—as long as he doesn't interrupt your work." Sonya shrugged as she worried over one of her perfectly manicured nails. "They're away all day anyway so they wouldn't know if you didn't tell them. And the good news is they want someone to start immediately." A little laugh escaped her. "They're so desperate for good help, they're planning to add on quarters for a housekeeper."

Tears flowed freely, as Genny fought back the sobs that rose in her throat. How could Sonya be so lacking in compassion? John repeatedly did favors for her sister. How could she repay them like this?

"She won't be needing your money," Stephen announced, slamming the coffee tray onto the side table and pulling Genny's trembling body into his arms. "It's okay, Baby."

"You misunderstood."

"I understand perfectly. I've never met anyone so heartless."

"I'm trying to help," Sonya said.

Anger sparked in the gray eyes. "You haven't taken care of Genny."

"I resent that."

"He doesn't mean it," Genny soothed, flashing him a warning frown.

"She should have been there for you."

"Genny knows I have to work to keep a roof over our heads. She's welcome to leave any time she feels she can do better."

They glared at each other, foes in a battle Genny felt powerless to stop. "She won't trouble you any longer. I'll take care of her and Jonathan."

"So Genny's going to become a kept woman," Sonya jibed. "Why doesn't that surprise me?"

Genny caught Stephen's arm when he took a step forward. "Genny has a job—with room and board. Your friends can build their housekeeper quarters for someone else."

"Why didn't you tell me?" Sonya demanded.

"Because it's none of your business," Stephen countered. "We haven't discussed the specifics yet. And you owe Genny an apology. That 'kept woman' comment was totally out of line."

"It doesn't matter," Genny said, silently pleading with Stephen to stop his tirade.

"She has no right to talk to you that way."

Sonya's expression spoke her opinion of his viewpoint.

Despair filled Genny. "Just stop!" she screamed. "I can't stand any more." She charged from the room.

What was he thinking? Genny felt a little crazed. Her life whirled like an out of control merry-go-round. Where would it all stop?

❧

"Well, isn't she a bundle of surprises?" Sonya exclaimed. "I never thought she had it in her."

"If you ever speak to her like that again, I'll make sure you regret it," Stephen said, abandoning all pretense.

"Don't threaten me. I know my sister. What happens when you tire of her? Don't expect me to pick up the pieces. Again."

"Like you have this time?" Stephen asked, his tone laced with heavy sarcasm. "No, Sonya, I don't think you know Genny at all."

$$\textcircled{10}$$

*H*eart pounding, Stephen burst into the guesthouse without knocking. He skidded to a halt before Genny. "I'm sorry."

She glared at him. "Just what are you trying to prove?"

"That you don't have to be dependent on that woman ever again. I'm offering independence, a job, and a place for you and your son to live without fear, without threats."

"What, Stephen? What can I possibly do to repay you? Do you have any idea what you're taking on?"

He hesitated. Should he just stay out of it? Leave her to make her own way? No. Jonathan wouldn't end up like Bobby.

The poignant story of his former band member's life tore at his heart. He hadn't listened to Bobby's cries for help. None of the guys wanted to baby-sit the barely twenty-one-year-old kid when he joined the band. They were too easygoing about his wild lifestyle, alcohol, and suspected drugs, only telling him to lay off when they should have insisted he get help.

Stephen's guilt had increased the night he packed Bobby's meager possessions and found the tattered sheet of paper in his friend's wallet. A letter from his mother dated a few days after his birth explaining why she had given him up.

Lack of money had been no excuse as far as Stephen was concerned. He blamed Bobby's mother, certain she could have found a way. But after meeting Genny, and witnessing her method of survival, he felt differently. Telling himself the two situations had nothing to do with each other didn't work. He wanted to help because he cared for Genny and her son. But he needed to do this—for Bobby.

"Let's just say I'm doing it for a friend. I've met a woman I like and respect." Her expression softened when he admitted, "I'm attracted to you. And I think you're attracted to me. But I'm on the road and you're here, struggling to support Jonathan, and I'm afraid circumstances will prevail. I can't help but worry. What would happen if you couldn't provide for Jonathan? If you had to put him in foster care?"

Genny's horrified expression told him losing Jonathan was something she hadn't considered. Stephen sat down and drew her into a hug. "You won't take money from me. Why not a job?"

"You've done so much. I don't want you to—"

"You think this is some trumped-up way of giving you money?" he interrupted. When she nodded, he insisted, "It's a real job. The fan mail is backing up while I'm on the road. If you don't believe me, come over to the house. I'll show you."

"I'm not a fast typist," Genny protested.

Her resolve is weakening. "We'll work out a plan."

"There's Jonathan. Once he's released, I can't take him to an office every day. Day care isn't a good choice either."

"You're putting up stumbling blocks. You can work here or at the house."

She stood and walked over to the fireplace. With her back to him, she said, "Oh, Stephen, I don't know."

"This isn't spur-of-the-moment, Genny. It's been on my mind during this last tour. I need someone and so do you. To put it simply, I like coming home to you and Jonathan."

Intense astonishment touched her pale face as she whirled to face him. "I don't think it's such a good idea for you to become more attached to us."

"We're single adults, Genny."

"I'm an older adult with a child."

"It's not an insurmountable number of years, and I love Jonathan. So where's the problem?"

❧

Genny felt stunned by Stephen's admitted attraction. "Just how involved are you planning on becoming in Jonathan's life?"

"As involved as you'll allow."

Genny lifted a photo from the mantel and studied her son.

"He may be a baby, but he's very aware of people around him. I'm worried he'll become too attached to you."

"Would that be so bad?"

It could be. Genny considered how much losing him would affect them both. "Maybe the years aren't such a big deal now," she argued. "But one day you'll want a child of your own. I see how you look at Jonathan. I know how important children are to a man. His children, not another man's."

Walking to where she stood, Stephen said, "For the first time in my life I'm thinking I'd like to be a father. But I'm not asking for anything more than a chance to spend time with you. Jonathan could use a man's influence in his life."

Back when she'd first married, Genny dreamed of the perfect family—happily married parents and two children. Reality took a radical turn with John's death.

"You'd be a wonderful father. So wonderful I can't let you get mixed up with my crazy life. There's a woman out there who can give you the special world you deserve." Her hand slipped to his cheek. "You won't find her if you don't look, and you can't look if you're with us."

"Let the future take care of itself." Stephen had used the same words only days before when he'd done his part to shape their future.

She felt so confused. She wanted his caring, but she needed her independence. Genny doubted she could have both. Stephen made her feel too safe and secure. "You don't understand," she protested.

"I do, Genny. Just don't feel guilty if the happiness you deserve comes quicker than expected."

"I'm not ready for a relationship, and I don't think you should wait until I am."

"I understand fear." Stephen retreated to the sofa and stared down at the hands that dangled between his parted thighs. The prolonged silence raised all kinds of doubts for Genny. He looked up, the gray eyes blazing with his inner fire. "More than you realize. Don't think I haven't been tempted to run the other way. But I can't. You draw me back. I can't leave again without knowing you're safe and secure. Hearing your sister tell you there's no money in her budget for your needs makes it even more urgent. I feel responsible for you already."

His words provoked her ire. "No one's responsible for me but me. Understand that, Stephen. No one. I won't be taken care of. I'm not the child."

"And I'm not the enemy. Take the job, Genny. We have all the time you need."

Her mind spun with her bewilderment. It would be too easy to accept. For Jonathan's sake. For her own. But what about Stephen? "It's not fair to you."

"Let me worry about myself. I know what makes me happy, and right now, I want to see you smile."

"And what about next week? The month after that?"

"I'm not into living for tomorrow, Genny. God tells me to take it one day at a time."

She stared at him, not really startled by his revelation. Admittedly, there was something between them—feelings stronger than friendship and her overwhelming guilt. Genny had never felt so torn. She had to keep John Smith's memory alive for his son. She owed him that much. Could she do that if she allowed her feelings for Stephen to grow? Did she have to face a future void of masculine attention in order to do that?

"What's going on here?"

Their attention turned to Sonya.

Sonya's gaze moved from one to the other. "You'd better think about this. You can't afford to be impulsive." She turned toward the door and then back. "You really need to get right on that housekeeper position. My friend doesn't think it will stay open very long."

Rebellion bubbled and overflowed as Genny understood the warning in Sonya's words. She refused to be manipulated any longer. She turned to Stephen, to the warmth in his gray gaze. If his eyes contained just a glimpse of the world he offered, they hinted at paradise.

His brow lifted, and he reached out to her. "Genny's going to accept my offer, aren't you, Genny?"

She took his hand. "Yes, Stephen."

Sonya shrugged. "I've got a long drive."

"Good-bye, Sonya."

The door slammed shut behind her. Stephen's arm slipped about Genny's shoulder. A deep sigh slid from her, and she wilted beneath his touch.

"Are you okay?"

Genny looked him in the eye. "I haven't been totally honest with you. Sonya has high aspirations—sees herself as an executive. She insisted that I help her."

"Help her how?"

"She wants to convince you to change PR firms. She's been on my case ever since she realized who you were, reminding me babies aren't cheap and saying if I expected her to help, we'd need a larger income. I'm sorry."

Stephen shrugged the words away. "Sonya plays on your insecurities. You don't need her anymore."

It sounded too wonderful to be true. She needed a break from Sonya. Some days she didn't think she could bear another threat or cruel comment. But what if Sonya's predictions came true? What would happen when Stephen wanted her and Jonathan out of his life?

"There's nothing I want as much as to regain control of my life, but I'm not sure I can swing it. Once I leave here, I have to consider how far the money will stretch."

Stephen pushed her chin up. "Genny, listen to me. I'm not turning you out in six weeks or six months. The place is yours for as long as you need it."

"You have a life, Stephen. How will you explain us to your friends?" Particularly the female ones. Genny didn't care for the surge of jealousy that spiraled through her at the thought of Stephen with other women.

"Why don't we cross that bridge when we get there? Mrs. James will appreciate your help taking care of the place."

Actually it's her house," he joked. "She spends more time here than me." The anguish in his voice made Genny ache. "There's a housekeeping fund. I'll authorize you to make withdrawals for groceries and miscellaneous expenses."

"I can pay for groceries and electricity. It's only fair."

"I prefer to cover room and board while you're house-sitting. After that, we'll work out an arrangement."

"Stephen, about the letters . . . I've never done any real office work."

"Just read the letters, answer those you can, and put aside the ones you feel you can't handle. As long as you don't book us anywhere or tell people where I live, I foresee no problems. If you want, I'll ask the other guys if they want you to handle their fan mail."

"I thought I would be answering mail for the whole band."

Stephen shook his head. "I can't speak for the whole group. Well, Gen, what do you think?"

What did she think? On one hand, it was as if she'd stumbled onto a pot of gold. She kept expecting to blink her eyes and find it had disappeared. On the other hand, she was afraid it would turn out to be fool's gold. Still, she recognized the job was ideal for her.

Stephen offered the opportunity to earn a salary and maybe even to relieve his burden in some small way. "When do I start?"

The corners of his eyes crinkled with his pleased smile. "Officially, you already have."

"What about the letters? I could start on those now if you show me what to do."

"You need to take it easy for awhile longer," he warned. "There's a lot of mail to sort through. We'll see how it goes before I ask the other guys. Of course, there would be a salary adjustment if you take on anyone else's mail."

"You're being more than generous."

Stephen took her hands in his. "You'd be doing more work."

She grew serious. "Please understand that I'm not unappreciative. I feel I'm taking advantage of your good nature."

Stephen shook his head. "I'm not doing anything I don't want to do. Remember that, Genny. Having you here has been good for me. You've motivated me to think about what God wants me to do with my life . . . from considering my career choices to dedicated prayer time. Whatever He intends, there's no question He'll provide as well. I'd better get out of here so you can get to bed. Don't worry. Okay?"

"You make it hard to do that. Particularly when you pulverize my every care with your solutions."

"I'm sorry about Sonya. Maybe she'll be more human now that her burden has been lightened."

Burden. No matter whose lips it came from, the word was as deadly as an untreated rattlesnake bite. Genny's eyelids dropped to hide her hurt.

Genevieve Smith had a goal too. One day she would be self-sufficient. No one's burden. No one's responsibility. And she intended to see that it came sooner than later.

11

_A_fter Stephen left, Genny found herself considering Sonya's little jab about making a career of being a housewife. It wasn't the first time she'd heard the words.

John's firm had been retained by her parents to renovate their house. With Sonya away at college, Genny had no competition for his attentions, and he quickly became a good friend, a confidant when times were difficult, and eventually the man she loved with all her heart. John knew where he was going, and at seventeen, she already she knew she wanted to go with him.

The job was partially completed when Sonya came home for Thanksgiving and her interest in the handsome contractor became obvious. When Genny told her she loved John, Sonya insisted he was too old for her. Genny met Sonya's threats to tell their parents with the firm resolve that they wouldn't change her mind. Sonya became even more determined, flaunting her beauty and flirting outrageously. Genny didn't doubt John felt flattered by Sonya's attention and prepared to fight for her love. But then Sonya returned to college.

When she chose to marry John, Sonya accused her of looking for a father figure. The ten-year age difference meant nothing to Genny. Still, John insisted they wait until she turned eighteen before he proposed officially.

The thought of how her parents rushed things along made Genny shudder. John had been supportive, moving her in with him and seeing to it that she took her finals and received her diploma. He insisted she have her own room until they were married. She found happiness in the haven of his home.

For more than seventeen years, she put everything into being

John Smith's wife. From the moment she accepted his proposal, housewife and mother had been her choice. John's ability to support them comfortably made the decision easy.

Genny knew she wanted it more because she'd never experienced a true family life. Her children would never know the loneliness of parents more involved with their careers than their children. John agreed it was important that their children have their mother home. Her efforts to make their home a happy place worked for years, until the perfection cracked about the edges when the family refused to arrive.

When John's behavior changed, she hoped it had more to do with the pressures of work than marital problems. He stayed on edge, and at times she felt every word he exchanged with her was snapped or growled. The least little thing pushed them toward arguments of major proportions.

Arguments she refused to participate in, always walking away until he was willing to talk reasonably. Secretly, she blamed herself for the changes.

And then her pregnancy changed everything. John's response was incredible. He became more loving and caring, responsive to her needs, and was home every night. When her doctor expressed concern about her age and health, she agreed to the battery of tests at John's urging. He insisted she focus on delivering a healthy child, and Genny reveled in his loving.

Her life took another unexpected turn with his death and the return of loneliness. Until she met Stephen. He forced her to confront her feelings. Genny cared deeply for him. If she admitted the truth, she loved him, but the feeling it was too soon tormented her.

But what could she do? Despair grasped Genny in its clutches, reminding her of times barely past. She fell to her knees and prayed aloud, "Father in heaven, thank You for all the miraculous gifts You bestow upon me daily. Thank You for the beautiful son You have given me. Please help him to grow and strengthen in Your love.

"Your lost child comes to You tonight seeking guidance. Confusion and hurt separated me from You. I don't want to ask why, but because I'm human I find myself doing exactly that. Now You've sent another wonderful man into my life, and I find myself at a loss as to how to deal with the situation. If You mean for Stephen to be part of our lives, help me accept and understand Your will. Amen."

Afterward, she stood and walked toward the bathroom. For the first time in weeks, she felt a sense of relief.

❧

Stephen returned to the house and went straight to the telephone. "I warned you about the reporters."

"What reporters?" Chuck Harper asked.

"The ones you sent."

"It wasn't me."

Stephen frowned. If it wasn't Chuck Harper, then how had they learned about Genny? How had they known to go to the hospital? A seed of suspicion planted itself. Only a few people knew their whereabouts, and Genny admitted to coercion by Sonya. Had they planned the incident? No, not Genny. She had told him about Sonya's plans.

"They'll be contacting you about an interview," Stephen said. "Find out who their source was."

"Sure. You plan to do the interview?" Chuck asked curiously.

"On my terms. With no reference to a mystery woman in my life," Stephen emphasized.

"What role is she playing?"

The man's question raised Stephen's resentment. He wished he understood why Chuck Harper set his teeth on edge. "It's not your concern."

"A lot of female fans like the fact that you're a single man," the manager reminded. "That makes it my concern."

Stephen sighed and muttered, "Genny's taking over my fan mail."

"Is that all she's taken over?"

The man never let anything drop. "She's a special woman," he admitted. "I care a lot for her and her son. I won't see either of them hurt."

After hanging up, Stephen went into the bedroom. He pulled a photo of Genny and Jonathan from his coat pocket and stared at the smiling twosome.

What a beautiful baby Jonathan was. Stephen felt a sudden long-ing to hold a child of his own, something he'd never experienced be-fore. Wives and kids were demanding, and he led a bachelor's life, following his career with unequaled desire for anything else.

He'd never felt any similar desire when holding his sister's babies. Why now?

∼❧

Stephen left for the next tour dates and honoring his insistence that she rest, Genny often reclined in bed or rested on the sofa as she sep-arated the contents of the mailbags.

Aware she should be happy, Genny found she fretted about every-thing. She wanted her baby home. She wanted her relationship with Sonya worked out. And she wanted to get some sort of perspective she could live with on her feelings for Stephen.

As she prepared for her checkup, Genny could almost recite what the doctor was going to say. She'd lost five sorely needed pounds, her face was gaunt, her cheekbones even more prominent. And what her doctor didn't say, Stephen was sure to add the moment he laid eyes on her.

She bundled into her coat and braved the dropping temperatures to race to the car. After allowing the engine to warm up, Genny turned the heat to high, rubbing her hands together to get the circulation go-ing. She'd opted to go to her regular gynecologist instead of the doctor who delivered Jonathan.

During the long drive, she debated going by Sonya's office after her visit. Would the visit cause another scene? For that matter, would Sonya even talk to her? She abhorred the idea of never speaking with her sister again. Family was important. She wanted Jonathan to know his aunt.

Dr. Rainer was enthusiastic about Jonathan's progress. "At this rate, he'll be a butterball before long. Now let's see how you're doing, young lady."

The 'young lady' brought a smile to her face. Genny wondered how old she would be before he stopped calling her that.

After the exam, Genny waited in his office, considering how much her life had changed since she last sat in the same chair. That day she'd asked about the trip that turned her life around. Her thoughts drifted to Stephen.

She wondered where he was, smiling as she considered she only had to check the schedule. Within hours they would chat on the phone. What would he say tonight?

Dr. Rainer closed the door. She jumped, a guilty smile curving her lips. "Why so fidgety, Genevieve?" He settled in the chair, his gaze on her chart. "You've lost too much weight, and you're anemic."

She squirmed, glad the man couldn't tell what was on her mind. "Everything's fine. In fact, I started work. I'm answering fan mail for Stephen Camden."

The doctor cocked an eyebrow. "The singer?"

"He's been wonderful," Genny enthused, tucking her hair behind her ear. "Stephen was there when Jonathan was born."

He nodded his satisfaction. "Glad you've met someone."

"We're only friends," Genny offered.

"Too bad. A good man would do you a world of good. You're perfectly healthy except for the anemia and needing to gain a few pounds. We can remedy that with good food and vitamins. And from the look on your face when you talk about this singer fellow, I'd say he could make you happy."

"It's not that sort of relationship," she objected.

"You're a young woman. You'll marry again. Probably give Jonathan a brother or sister."

His words hit her. "Is that really a possibility? I mean . . . Well, it took so long to conceive . . . And with Jonathan being premature, I thought . . ."

Dr. Rainer had no time for her stumbling words. "I don't see any problem."

Genny accepted the vitamin samples. Dr. Rainer had been her doctor forever. He'd done her physicals, counseled them on infertility, and cared for her during pregnancy. Now he seemed to think it logical she would have a relationship with another man. But not just any ordinary man—handsome, successful Stephen Camden.

In the car, her thoughts went to what he'd said. *Is he right about the possibility of my having another child? Could I still have the babies I've dreamed of?* A vision of Stephen with Jonathan popped into her head. He would make a great father. *With the right woman,* she warned herself.

But why couldn't that woman be me? Why do I persist in believing we can't have a future? Because Stephen is excitement personified while I am as tame as a toothless tiger, she thought with a wry smile.

Besides, the thought was ridiculous. The odds of finding herself the winner of a million-dollar sweepstakes were higher. All women had fantasies, and just because Stephen was helping hers along didn't mean he could ever love her.

She drove to Sonya's office. As much as Genny dreaded the confrontation, she knew she had to at least try.

Sonya was probably right. Stephen's interest would wane, and she'd be right back where she started. Genny brushed away a tear. She hated the uncertainty that tore at her. Why couldn't she accept God's promise that she need not worry about tomorrow?

Another secretary occupied the front desk and directed Genny to the conference room where Sonya assembled press packets. "Hello, Sonya."

"I wondered when you'd show up. Mr. High-and-mighty give you your walking papers?"

The fury in Sonya's tone surprised her. "I thought it would be a good idea if we talked. Things didn't go well the other night at Stephen's."

"Don't mention his name to me," Sonya snapped.

"Why can't you be happy for me?" Genny asked. "Aren't you the least bit thankful to him for all he's done to help me?"

Sonya slammed the handfuls of paper down on the conference table and shoved her long blond hair over her shoulder. "Genny, you don't even know the man."

"I know enough."

"He doesn't know you either. I bet you've never told him your disgusting little secret. Did you ever tell him exactly how our parents died?"

Genny forced herself to remain calm. "What's really bothering you, Sonya? Are you concerned that I could get hurt? Or that you didn't help me?"

"I gave you a lead on a job."

"The only job you considered me qualified for?"

Sonya glowered at her. "It's not like you have any other skills."

She registered the sarcasm. Sonya considered her ungrateful. "You know I can't leave Jonathan. Why are you so determined something bad is going to come from Stephen helping me?"

"Because I'm a lot wiser about the world." Sonya walked across the room and lifted a folder from the credenza. She flung it onto the table. "See for yourself."

Clippings flowed over the slick surface of the mahogany conference table. Genny caught one just before it floated off the table and laid the paper down without looking at it. "Why?"

"To prove he's no different from the others." Sonya quickly spread them about. "Look at the number of women. It's not all fun and games. People get hurt. It could be you."

Sonya considered her naïve. Maybe Genny didn't know a lot about Stephen, but she did know his intentions were honorable. Sonya's condemnation of every plan she made for her future played a huge role in her confusion. She didn't feel Sonya was being cautious. Nor did she want to accept that Sonya preferred her weak and at her mercy.

Genny pulled from the reserve of strength deep within her. She wasn't an idiot. The grief and problems since John's death made her look like one, and maybe it was taking her too long to get back to her feet, but she would stand tall again.

"I know everything I need to know about Stephen."

"You'd choose him over family?" Sonya asked, her fisted hands pressing into the back of a padded chair.

"If you force me to. I owe Stephen a lot, Sonya. He didn't have to do all he's done."

"And I did?"

Genny didn't flinch as she met Sonya's gaze straight on. "If the situations were reversed and your child was lying in the hospital, you wouldn't need to depend on the kindness of strangers. I'd be there for you."

Sonya bristled and roughly stuffed the papers back into the folder. "I've been there for you."

Genny shook her head. "You've shown your true feelings every step of the way. I took Stephen's job to take the burden off you. I don't want you to feel forced to take care of us when you obviously resent it so much. For some reason you pretend Jonathan is nonexistent. You never ask about him. You've never seen him. I'm not sure why, but it's your loss. My son is a beautiful child. You should know I confessed the truth to Stephen about your visit and my involvement."

"I told him, and I'll tell you," Sonya yelled. "After it's over, you'll come running back to me. You're too weak to stand on your own. Just remember my house is not a hotel. You and your baby won't be welcome there in the future."

Her words had the same effect as water on dying embers, outing the feeble flame that struggled to survive.

"I won't impose on you again." Like a diver cutting his air hose underwater, dread surged through her. *Please God, let it be so.*

"It's your funeral."

A picture of Stephen wrapped in a woman's arms taunted her from the tabletop. Genny didn't have to read the articles to learn of the band's wild antics. But instinct told her Stephen was a good man.

"Since you won't be returning, I'd appreciate you getting the rest of your stuff out of my house."

Sonya's caustic tone ate a hole in Genny's heart. "I'll take care of it this week and leave the key on the kitchen counter."

"It'll be wonderful not to feel so cramped."

"Forgive my intrusion on your wonderful life," Genny managed, masking her hurt with the same sarcasm Sonya showed.

"Oh, cut the theatrics, Genny. You can pretend everything is perfect but the truth of the matter is that your life is going to be a lot harder than you've ever imagined. How you think you'll work and tend to that sick kid is beyond me."

"The Lord will make a way." Genny realized she actually believed that.

"Yeah, like the Lord has ever done a lot for either of us," Sonya said. Laughter accompanied the disrespectful words. "I've got work to do."

Genny couldn't get out of the building fast enough. She raced to the car and climbed inside, breathing deeply as she fought back the tears. When would she ever learn? There was only one person in the entire world Sonya cared about—herself. Her sister shared that trait with their parents. They hadn't cared that they were destroying their children, and Sonya didn't care that she broke Genny's heart.

～✤～

That night, Stephen accepted the outcome of the meeting with an offer to help her move.

"I'd better get to work. My doctor's appointment put me behind."

"What did he say?" Stephen asked.

His not-so-casual question reminded her of the doctor's words. "I need to gain weight. He gave me vitamins and a prescription for iron tablets. Otherwise, I'm perfectly healthy."

She didn't tell him about the doctor's recommendation that she get on with her life, his suggestion that a good man would do her a world of good.

"Okay, I'll work on a truck."

"Thanks, Stephen," she whispered, once more reassured that she'd made the right choice.

"See you soon."

12

*S*tephen gestured to the two men standing behind him. "The guys volunteered to help."

Ray glanced at Kyle. "That's what he's calling it now."

"Hey, I only asked to borrow your truck," Stephen defended.

"And I go where my truck goes," Ray said. "Where do we start?"

"Why don't you and Kyle take the crib apart while I give Genny a hand with the other stuff?"

The two men shared a knowing look. "Good thing you bought your tools along," Ray told Kyle.

"I had an idea he'd pull something like this."

"Yeah, he can tear up a guitar, but he's dangerous with tools."

"Come on, guys, you're making me look bad here."

Genny moved to Stephen's side. "You didn't force them to help, did you?"

The men laughed.

"You can't make these guys do anything. They're the ones who in-sisted it wouldn't take as long with three sets of hands. By the way, this is Kyle. He's part of our road crew."

Genny shook his hand. "We've met before. I made you nervous."

Kyle grinned. "Good thing Steve was there. I was pretty useless."

"You pitched right in, just like today. Thank you both. Let me show you the crib."

Stephen caught her hand. "They can find it. Top of the stairs to the right. Big wooden thing with bars."

"You're such a comedian," Ray said, leading the way.

Stephen followed Genny into the kitchen. A box filled with baby items sat on the counter.

"Only a couple more things and I'll be done here," Genny said, reaching into the cabinet.

They worked quickly, and Genny wasn't surprised to find her meager collection of possessions barely filled half of Ray's truck bed. Paying their debts had been an honor thing for her. Almost every possession she owned, including the rings on her fingers, had been sold. The few salvaged pieces had more sentimental than financial value.

While checking to assure everything was packed, Stephen spotted some boxes in the back of the closet. "What about these?"

The cardboard containers held the things Genny had used to make her place a home. "My favorite cookbooks. Gardening books. Christmas ornaments. A couple of porcelain pieces my grandparents gave me. An afghan I knitted. I need to check on storage space."

"Why?" Stephen dragged them from the closet. "They'll give the guesthouse your personal touch. Make it more like home for you and Jonathan."

"I won't be there that long."

He glanced over his shoulder. "These things obviously mean something to you. Why not enjoy them?"

"You don't mind?"

Stephen hefted the closest one. "I want you to think of my home as yours. Understand?"

Genny nodded, and he left to carry the boxes downstairs. She vacuumed the carpet and checked one last time to make certain everything was the same as when Sonya said there was no other option but for Genny to live with her. Had it really been such a short time? It seemed more like a lifetime.

She no longer had to tolerate Sonya's abuse, and though she had no idea what the future held for her and Jonathan, Genny felt thrilled by the prospect of moving on with her life. The most frightening aspect was the developing relationship between her and Stephen.

He'd broken through her reserve and made her care about him. Though Stephen insisted the future would take care of itself, Genny's self-doubts made her question why he helped. Only time would provide the answer, but she realized something else. She loved having someone who cared, and if it were only days or weeks, she wasn't going to refuse his friendship.

"Genny, let's go," Stephen called. "Everything's loaded."

She hurried down the stairs, encountering air as she neared the bottom.

"Well, hello," Stephen exclaimed, surprise in his gray gaze when she landed against his chest. His arms secured her against his body, her feet dangling uselessly as Genny grabbed his shoulders to keep from falling.

"I missed the last stair."

Stephen's lips brushed hers and lingered before he pulled back and flashed her a teasing grin. "And here I thought you were really glad to see me."

Always. She almost spoke the word out loud. "I'm surprised I didn't knock the breath out of you."

He laughed and set her on the floor. "We need to concentrate on fattening you up. Either that or buy you lead-soled shoes to keep you from floating off."

"Good luck," Genny said as she pulled on her jacket. "My mother used to complain I was hopeless."

"You've never been any larger than now?"

"Well, if you recall a short time ago I resembled a baby whale, but you could say I've reverted to normal."

He smiled and dropped one eyelid in a way that made Genny's heart palpitate. "We'll soon have you so happy you'll have to work out at the gym."

"You can try." Genny worked the key around the ring and slipped it off. "I told Sonya I'd leave this on the counter." *Why don't I just tell him I can't go through with it?* Genny asked for the millionth time. *Surely he could understand her doubts. Their kisses could be a prelude to something bigger than the both of them.*

"You're not sure about this, are you?"

"Not completely," she answered truthfully. "I want to be close to Jonathan and earn my own way, but . . ."

"You don't want to interfere with my life," Stephen guessed.

"Yes . . . I mean, no . . . We don't want to stand in the way of your happiness."

"Think of this as your first steps toward independence."

"I can do that. If you allow me to work toward that goal."

Stephen kissed her forehead and rested an arm about her shoulders. "Okay, let's hit the road."

The guys had unloaded most of the stuff when they arrived at the house. "We can finish this if you want to go over to the hospital," Stephen said as he parked.

"If you don't mind. Just stack everything. I'll put it away when I get home."

He left the keys in the ignition. "Have fun. Oh, give this to Jonathan with my love." Stephen kissed her, and Genny sat there for a moment longer wondering how she would explain such a kiss to her infant son.

～❧

Two hours later, Genny returned home to find Stephen had done more than place her possessions in the guesthouse. The boxes sat in the various rooms, waiting to be put away.

He was in the process of taking a box of personal items into the bathroom. "I'll start the tub for you. I'm going to tackle the crib."

"You'll need help holding the pieces."

"Go," he said, pushing her toward the bathroom. "I can manage."

Relaxing in the warm water melted away the stresses of the day. Genny soaked, loath to move, even to soap herself. She could hear Stephen next door, and her lips twitched as he grumbled his way through the task he assigned himself.

He tapped on the door. "You've been in there long enough."

"Spoilsport," Genny murmured, using the hand spray to rinse bubbles from her body.

"I heard that. Get dressed and come over to the house for dinner."

～❧

Stephen glanced up when Genny entered the kitchen. Her skin was rosy-hued, strands of damp hair clung to her neck where it had slipped from the rubber band she'd worn all day, and she'd thrown on a pair of jeans and a shirt. She looked beautiful to him. Struck by the depth of his feelings for her, he sucked in a deep breath. "I finished the crib, but you should check it for sturdiness before you put Jonathan in."

"I'm sure you did fine," Genny said, joining him at the island. "What can I do to help?"

❧

Life settled into a routine. Genny kept the home fires burning while Stephen went out on tour again. He was due home that afternoon, which was a good thing. A surprise delivery of baby furniture and clothes—good quality, expensive things she could never afford on her salary—required an immediate discussion.

The dashboard clock caught her eye, and Genny panicked. Stephen would be home in less than two hours. She wanted to have dinner ready so she could get back to the correspondence after they talked.

The entire day had been behind schedule. She'd overslept, Dr. Lee had been late, and now this. Genny grabbed her purse and rushed toward the store. Walking the aisles reminded her of the times she'd done the same for John. She had planned special menus for every night. The well-thumbed cookbooks were the result of her refusal to settle for the ordinary. John's enthusiastic praise of her culinary skills had been embarrassing at times. Maybe food was the way to a man's heart, but she had no idea what Stephen liked.

Everything took longer than expected—a trainee cashier, un-priced items, even an accident delay on the trip home. Stephen arrived home to find her in a state. "I'll get dinner started. The groceries are all over the kitchen, and I have to work on the mail tonight. I haven't done any work today."

"Honey, it's okay." He slipped a hand behind her neck and pulled her forward, placing a kiss on her forehead.

Stephen sat down, using one booted foot to push at the back of the other. The worn leather boot refused to move. "Don't know why I wear these things."

"Let me." The shoe didn't budge with her ineffectual tugs.

"It's easier if you straddle my leg."

Stepping into place, Genny turned her back to him and grabbed the boot, jerking it free. The other shoe followed. Before she straightened up, Stephen toppled her into his lap, his breath warm against her neck as he whispered, "Thanks."

Genny stiffened and scrambled to the far end of the sofa. The situation was entirely too cozy.

"What's got you so uptight? Your boss isn't going to yell at you because you're running behind schedule, you know."

Gas logs burned in the fireplace between the kitchen and sitting room. The flames flickered with merry abandonment generating a warmth that combined with her own heat to make her more uncomfortable. "I know."

Stephen stretched his long legs before him and wriggled his stockinged feet. "Then what's wrong?"

"I'm not very practiced in relationship games."

Her reluctant admittance brought a smile to his face. "Is that what this is?"

The heat skyrocketed to her brain, her cheeks heating even more as Genny considered her naïveté. How could she even suggest anything more?

His fingers closed about her hand, bringing it to his lips. "Not that I'm adverse to playing games with you."

A warning flag shot up. The two of them couldn't be alone in a room for ten minutes before awareness overpowered them.

"I spent a lot of time thinking this last trip." He propped his hands behind his head, a contented smile on his face. "I figured out why I'm thirty and unmarried."

"You mean a reason other than the fact that you're gorgeous and popular with the women and have the lifestyle every man wants . . ." Genny broke off at his obvious enjoyment.

"Go on," he coaxed. "I love having my ego stroked as much as the next man."

A cranberry has nothing on me colorwise. Genny felt the blood rush upward. "You don't need it."

"Sure, I need to hear the woman I care about tell me I'm gorgeous. It's the only time the words really mean something."

"You've heard them before," she stammered.

"Not from a woman with impact."

"Impact?"

"I always knew the right woman would make me feel something. I never guessed it would be like driving my car into a brick wall." Stephen pounded his fist into his open hand. "Impact!"

He slid closer, bringing them together. "I've decided it's because I need an older woman. You."

Her view of the fire was replaced by Stephen's face as he kissed her.

Nervousness flooded through Genny. "Stephen?"

He sighed heavily. "I'm a grown man, Honey. I haven't been a little boy or an indecisive teenager in years. Once I make up make up my mind, it's full speed ahead."

"I know," Genny said, feeling unhappy with herself. Being with him contradicted every decision she'd made during his absence.

"You got something against May-December relationships?"

"December?" Genny sputtered. "I wouldn't go that far. I'm more of a late June, early July."

He chuckled at her indignant response. "I'm no spring chicken either."

Genny flashed him a derisive smile. "Yeah, you're getting older by the minute."

Stephen grinned. "All quality things improve with age."

Genny's hands went to his cheeks, holding him in place as she whispered, "I need you to be gloriously happy, Stephen. I don't want you to look back with regrets."

"I don't want to look back. I want to look ahead to the future. A future with you and Jonathan." Genny felt completely wretched. "Don't give me that look. Why don't we discuss it over a candlelit dinner?"

"No." She needed to get away before she did something really stupid. "I have to work tonight."

"Then we'll stay in. I don't want to go out anyway. Too cold."

"The letters . . . I'll go back to the guesthouse."

Stephen stood. "Stay. Keep me company while I cook. I'd like to hear what you think of my fan mail."

So much for putting distance between them. "And I'd like to know about all the baby stuff that arrived. Hundreds of dollars worth of things I can't afford."

First confusion and then determination highlighted his features. "I didn't."

Genny glared at him. "I'll buy the things Jonathan needs as soon as I can."

"Listen to me. I didn't do it. I told my parents about you and Jonathan. They think . . . Well, anyway, my sister was there, and she got excited about Jonathan. Said she had all this baby stuff taking up space, and the next thing I knew she planned to ship it to you. What could I say?"

Genny closed her eyes. "Don't tell me. You come from a long line of overly generous people."

He shrugged. "We can't help it. Besides, what's wrong with having the things he needs without having to buy them? You can save the money for more important stuff."

More important stuff, Genny thought with a pang. *Like getting out of his life.* "I'll get the letters."

Anything Stephen had to say was forgotten when one of the grocery bags toppled. Genny slipped out the door as he moved to retrieve the items.

Grabbing the stack of letters she needed help with, Genny settled at the island and found herself watching Stephen. He looked so comfortable in the kitchen. Stephen bent to look in the fridge, and she forced her attention to the letters.

"Stir-fry okay?" At her nod, he piled the makings on the countertop. His system was fascinating. The letters lay untouched as he wielded the knife with cheflike precision, cutting scraped carrots into precise, dime thin slices. He reached for a green pepper. "So, what about the letters?"

"Mostly like you said. Requests for autographed pictures, free tickets, and contributions. Does Ray get as much mail as you?"

"Probably more. He's more outgoing with the fans."

"More outgoing? I can't imagine that. I'd say the ladies really like you handsome, single guys."

"Harper will die when we get married."

Genny felt a sinking feeling in her stomach. "There's some of it, well, one letter that's . . ." She cleared her throat. "Rather personal."

Stephen glanced at her. "What did it say?"

She thumbed through the stack of envelopes, finding the pink one. Its heavy scent permeated the room.

He laid down the knife and wiped his hands before slipping the letter from the envelope. His nose wrinkled. "Think she buys this stuff by the gallon?"

Genny thought more along the lines of industrial-sized drums. "It's pretty strong."

He scanned it, laughing outright as he crushed the flowery stationery into a ball and aimed it at the trash can. As he caught sight of her expression, he cried, "You didn't . . . You think I'm interested in what she described?"

"It's none of my business."

"Let me assure you, my woman would never write me letters describing what we do in private. This woman is probably one of those people who sell those incredible lies to the tabloids." Disgust etched lines of disapproval on his unsmiling face.

"It's none of my business," she repeated.

Stephen took her face in his hands. "Have you heard anything I've said to you?"

Genny attempted to draw a reviving breath as she nodded slowly. Her heart had done flip-flops from the moment of his arrival, but nothing had changed. He was her friend, her employer, nothing more.

"Apparently I listen as well as you," she managed. "Sure, we're old enough to make our own decisions, mistakes even. But you've forgotten how having us around will change your life. I don't think it's such a good idea for me to live here."

His expression grew serious. "I thought we were past that."

"You deserve a spotlight woman. Not a plain-Jane."

"No, thanks." He looked as if the idea left a bad taste in his mouth. "You think people will wonder what I see in you?" She nodded agreement. "Let me tell you something, Genny. Some beauty doesn't go as deep as the skin. True beauty goes a lot deeper and lasts a lot longer. Think about that the next time you look in the mirror. You're too special to forget it."

Stephen walked out of the kitchen, and Genny fought the urge to call him back, to admit she didn't understand what was happening between them.

He returned, carrying a small box. "If you insist on gilding the lily, try this. Go on. Open it."

The beautifully wrapped package made a mockery of everything they had discussed.

"No." She pushed it back at him.

Stephen ripped away the paper. As Genny watched, he removed the lid. "Take it out," he encouraged, holding the ring box aloft when she made no move to do so. He popped the box lid open.

The emerald ring was the most beautiful thing she had ever seen.

"It's the same color as your eyes," Stephen said, tracing the stone with his finger. "I was walking down the street and saw it in a window. Ray thought it was hilarious that I had to go in and buy it."

She shook her head and tried to back away. "There are things you don't know."

He grasped her hands firmly. "I can't know if you won't tell me. I've listened to the protests, the arguments that I need someone you consider more suited. I'm not interested in a wife who's a vehicle for my career. I need a woman with a heart. With love to give. Those few years you argue about aren't important. Share your beauty with me, Genny. I need it badly."

Stephen pulled her into his arms. Genny wallowed in his tenderness, feeling no doubt the angels had truly been watching over her when they had sent him.

"Genny, what would you say if I asked you to marry me?"

13

T can't."

"Why? Because I'm a musician? Would you say yes if I had a nine-to-five job and reported home every night?"

Genny gasped. "No. Music's your life. Your wife should be young and beautiful, sophisticated enough to entertain the people you need to impress, an asset to your career. A woman who can give you children when you're ready for them."

"You seem to have everything figured out. There's only one problem. I love you. I am not looking for a beauty contestant to hang on my arm for the world to admire. You and Jonathan have become my family. When I'm away from you, I'm counting the moments until I'm home again."

"Please don't say that," Genny protested. As her feelings for him increased, it became more difficult to share the pathetic story of her life.

Heartfelt words poured from his mouth. "Do you have any idea what coming home to you means to me? It's like nothing I've ever known, and frankly I never want to be without it again."

"I thought you understood my need for independence."

"I'm not trying to take anything away from you."

"You're not making me reach for it either," she said, busily stacking the letters. "I can't even provide a home for my son. What kind of mother does that make me?"

"You're a wonderful mother."

"Not as long as I depend on others to provide my every need. How can I take care of Jonathan when I can't take care of myself?"

"If this is about money, I can place a lump sum in your account."

There was an audible sigh as she turned away from him. "Forget it, Stephen. You don't understand."

His hand rested on her shoulder. "I want to take care of you and Jonathan."

"Our relationship is too one-sided. You give and I take. That's not my style."

"But I love you."

Tormented by the confusing roller-coaster highs and lows of her emotions, Genny knew she had to confront this truthfully. "And I love you."

"Why do I have the feeling there's a 'but' to this?"

"Because I don't like feeling incompetent. I won't accept anyone feeling obligated to care for me or Jonathan. If you love me, you'll understand. I will control my destiny."

❧

Sleep was impossible. Stephen tossed aside the covers and left the bed. His mind raced with Genny's revelation. He'd learned more about her in that short discussion than in all the weeks he'd known her.

He walked to the French doors and stood watching the full moon, feeling the cold that made his warm breath fog the glass.

Did she resent the gifts? He liked doing special things for her and Jonathan. What other reason was there to work so hard? He gave a good percentage of his earnings to the ministry and had enough left over to live comfortably.

No doubt Genny had worked equally hard in her role as homemaker only to end up impoverished. Where did God fit into her plan to control her destiny? Did she honestly think she could depend on no one but herself?

Within hours, he would be on a bus headed for destinations that only took him out of her life. How could he gain Genny's trust when he stayed on the road so much?

Taking care of each other was mutual for a husband and wife. He would be as dependent on her as she was him. He couldn't be happy without the shared love and caring of the person who mattered most in the world to him.

A half hour ticked slowly by before Stephen gave up and went in search of sheet music for the song he needed to rehearse.

It wasn't in the file tray or on the desktop. He walked over to the table Genny used for work. Maybe I should have her organize my sheet music, he thought as he checked the neat area. He slid the center drawer open and stared down at the landscaping plan.

Eager eyes quickly assessed the drawing. It was his house, complete with a six-foot brick privacy fence and water feature, and so much more. So many of his ideas, thoughts he had never gotten around to putting on paper, were there.

Genny had taken the things they discussed the night they discovered a shared love of gardening and incorporated them into this plan to beautify his home. She had a gift.

The realization struck him. Quite possibly the answer to their dilemma. When he got back, he intended to prove how much he loved her. It was time for Genny to get on with her life, to be as happy as he knew she could be.

Stephen kneeled by the desk. "Father, I come to You with a request that You guide Genny and me to what You would have for us. I feel so happy when I'm with her, so confident she's the one. I know her life has not been easy. Help her realize she can't do it alone. Bring her back to Your loving arms. Amen."

Genny's lethargy tempted her to stay in bed the next morning. She only wanted to hide from the fervent desire to say yes to Stephen's proposal.

Without bothering to check, Genny knew the bus had left earlier, headed for points unknown. Already she missed him terribly. Her unrest disturbed Genny. For years she'd been happy as John's wife. Or had she?

Genny suspected her need to feel loved after the nightmarish way things turned out played an even bigger part in her happiness. Determination that her marriage not be like her parents' kept her going when times got hard.

What would be so different with Stephen? The question bounced around inside her head. He was the most wonderful man she'd ever known. She should be so happy. Instead uncertainties that refused to go away filled her.

His solution of putting money in her account bothered Genny. She knew he cared and only thought of her and Jonathan. If she needed tangible proof, all she had to do was look at the gifts he gave her. "Things," she whispered almost disdainfully. And just as suddenly Genny realized she only wanted his love.

The thought stayed with her throughout the day. Work, Jonathan, nothing took her mind off the truth. The phone rang late that night.

"Hi, Hon," Stephen said tentatively, sounding almost afraid she wouldn't talk to him.

Laughter filled the background. Who owns the high-pitched feminine one? Genny wondered. "Sounds like a party."

"The guys are giving Denise a hard time. How are you? And Jonathan?"

Denise Wilson, Genny realized, not liking the surge of jealousy. The beautiful singer accompanied them on the tour and opened for the band. "Fine."

"Can we talk about last night?"

She steeled herself for the dreaded confrontation. "I wasn't exactly myself."

"Yes, you were. You opened up to me about your needs. I couldn't sleep so I went into the study and found the landscaping plans."

Genny frowned. She had intended to bring them over to the guesthouse. "I wanted to surprise you."

"They're sensational. You put the dreams I had the first time I walked the property on paper. Things I've never told another living soul."

The design had incorporated most of her personal preferences. "It's not finished."

"I figured I'd have to hire a landscaping firm. When I saw your plan, I thought why not you? I know it's winter but you could collect plants, grow some in the greenhouse, and hire contractors to start the fence. You could have a reputable landscape design business going in no time."

Stephen couldn't know that for years she had dreamed of going into business for herself. She had landscaped the yard of her home, turning it into a veritable showplace.

After their discussion, Genny filled a number of solitary hours formulating the plan for his grounds. For fun. She never actually considered doing the work. "Reputable businesses require operating capital," Genny pointed out.

"I'd give you a loan. On paper, with interest and everything."

The woman's high-pitched giggle ran down Genny's spine like nails on a chalkboard. She wanted to scream when Denise distracted Stephen with her pleas to make them stop.

"You'd better get back to the fun and games."

"Ah, Gen, don't go. I waited all day to talk to you."

Just as she'd waited to hear his voice. Genny didn't want to doubt Stephen. No more than she had John. She knew nothing about Stephen's ability to resist a beautiful woman, but she couldn't hold a candle to Denise Wilson.

"We'll discuss this when you get home. Have fun."

"Genny, wait, please. Let me go to another room so we can talk."

Background chatter and then Stephen's yell for them to hang up sounded over the phone. "Okay, that's better. I'm not trying to push you into anything. Just offering options."

Genny giggled. "You making me an offer I can't refuse?"

Laughter relieved the tension. "I'd love to hear you say yes."

The giggle evolved into a sigh. "Oh, Stephen, every offer you make tempts me to the point where I don't even want to think about what the future holds. I can't allow that to happen."

"You're right."

His words shocked her. She blinked and waited for more.

"You need to consider the future with prayer. How's Jonathan today?"

Change the topic. That worked for her. "Wonderful as usual. His doctor says he'll release him soon if he continues to improve. I can't wait to get him home. I have plans to spoil him rotten."

"Sounds like he'll need a father figure to temper all that loving."

Genny shook her head at his obvious ploy. She changed the subject again. "You don't need to pay anyone to do the grounds work. Digging in the earth relaxes me. I've already been in your greenhouse. I planted several packets of seeds I found in a box in the pantry. I dug through the bulbs too. Some should have gone in before Christmas but there were a few that will bloom if I plant them now. I can do that if you tell me where you want them."

"Where ever you think best. I have no idea. I keep a lot of gardening catalogs on the bus and order things I like. A lot of stuff never gets planted. They rolled the sod in the front yard or I'd have weeds. There's stuff in the barn too. Statuary, yard doodads, a fountain."

Poor Stephen. His sacrifice was evident in his regret-filled tone. "Don't you ever get a vacation?"

"When I fight for time off. As a matter of fact, I told Chuck I'm taking a couple of weeks when they release Jonathan from the hospital."

A red flag popped up in Genny's head. Why would he choose Jonathan's release to take time off?

"I thought I could help you get settled in and spend a bit of time with my namesake. What do you think?"

What did she think? "If it's what you want."

"I can't think of anything I'd like better. I've got to go. The guys want to run through the new song again tonight. I'll talk to you tomorrow. Love you."

"Have a good session." Genny replaced the receiver, barely able to swallow past the lump in her throat. She loved Stephen Camden, more than she'd ever loved anyone, but the demon she fought was fear. Panic that she wouldn't be woman enough for the man of her dreams. And this time, it would be much more difficult to survive if she lost him.

The days dragged on. Stephen called several times but they avoided certain topics. Genny frequently made excuses to get off the phone, and by Friday, she felt edgy. Good news came in the form of Jonathan's imminent release from the hospital.

"When will you bring him home?" Stephen asked that night.

"His pediatrician is thinking next week. I'm excited but afraid. He's so tiny."

"Honey, you'll do great. You'll be able to make up for lost time. Jonathan's going to know so much love. How about I go with you to pick him up?"

"I'd like that."

There was satisfaction in his tone as he said, "So would I. And no more worrying. It causes wrinkles."

Genny laughed and agreed, "Something I can't afford at my great old age."

"You're not old."

"I'm on the downhill slide toward forty. Let's see how you feel in a few years when you start the trek."

"You've got Jonathan to keep you young, Beautiful."

Beautiful. Though she knew it wasn't true, the one word lifted her spirits immeasurably. "Bye, Stephen. Take care."

$$14$$

re you okay?" Stephen asked, surprised to find Genny wearing her robe when she opened the door. He glanced at his watch. It was Thursday. The day Jonathan came home. He'd caught a flight home so he could go to the hospital with her. "I was sure you'd be too excited to sleep."

Genny covered a yawn and gestured him inside. "Welcome home." She stumbled into the sitting area and dropped onto the sofa. Her head rested against the arm, traitorous eyes closing against her will.

"Genny?" Stephen called, shaking her. "What's wrong?"

"Tired," she said, her eyes closing again.

"Didn't you sleep last night?"

"When Jonathan would let me."

He leaned over her inert form. "Jonathan? Is he all right?" he demanded anxiously.

Her face came alive with the brilliant but sleepy smile. "He came home yesterday. I spent the night adjusting to motherhood. Those early morning feedings are a joy. I woke up every time he so much as moved in the bassinet. They told me it would be like that, but I never realized . . ." Another yawn escaped.

Stephen was disappointed. "But you said today."

"I wasn't going to say no when Dr. Lee said he could come home yesterday." Genny rose from the sofa and walked toward the kitchenette. "Coffee?"

He followed, climbing onto a bar stool.

In minutes, she had eggs sizzling and bread in the toaster. Somewhere along the way, she tuned the radio to a Christian station.

Angry cries filled the guesthouse. "That's my boy. He might just be the most vocal roomie I've ever had." Genny slapped the spatula into his hand. "Watch our breakfast."

Stephen smiled as she bustled away, all vestiges of her exhaustion gone. He took plates from the cabinet, removed the toast, and flipped the eggs.

She returned, cuddling the blanketed baby. "You feed Jonathan. I'll finish breakfast."

"You bet," Stephen agreed, abandoning the kitchen chores. Eagerness turned to hesitation when she placed the tiny bundle in his arms. He tried to give him back. "He's too little. I'd better cook."

Genny pulled Stephen's arm into place, tested the bottle, and helped him guide it into Jonathan's mouth. "He does all the work. Just in case." She placed a cloth diaper over his shoulder. "The fun job is burping him."

He liked the way Jonathan attacked the small bottle of formula. The domesticity of the scene pleased him—Genny, still in her favorite shabby bathrobe, making breakfast while he fed the baby. He could handle more mornings like this.

Too soon, she slid a plate of food on the table. "I'll take over. Eat before your food gets cold."

Food had never held less appeal. "He's almost finished. His eyes are closed, but watch his mouth when I try to take the bottle away."

Big blue eyes popped open when Genny removed the bottle. "I'll put him down and join you for breakfast."

Stephen shot to his feet. "I'll help."

He led the way, watching as she settled the baby in the crib. A colorful mobile that matched the cartoon characters on the bedding hung over the end of the crib. Stephen wound it up. Jonathan's eyes opened again. "A music lover already."

"Hand me that blanket."

She bundled Jonathan snugly.

"What are you doing? He can't move like that."

"We had an incident last night because I allowed him to get over-stimulated. I was ready to take him back. Trina said the doctor wouldn't have allowed me to bring him home if he hadn't thought I could handle it."

Stephen touched her cheek, trailing his fingertips over the soft skin. "I have no doubt that you can." He struggled to hide his yawn.

Genny kissed his cheek, lingering as she breathed the deliciously male scents she associated with Stephen. "Someone else needs a nap."

"The concert ended late, and I caught an early flight."

Genny's hand covered her mouth, her eyes widening with dismay. "Oh, Stephen, I'm sorry. I should have called."

"It's okay. You managed fine. I'm proud of you."

❧

Genny refused to allow Jonathan's homecoming to stand in the way of her work. She dressed and straightened the kitchen. Stephen's obvious disappointment touched her deeply.

As for feeding Jonathan, once he became comfortable, Stephen hadn't wanted to let go. What was his fascination with her son?

Genny resisted the temptation to stand over the crib and watch Jonathan sleep. She took the mail into the living room, setting a monitor on the nearby end table. Stopping only when the baby woke for feedings, she managed to get through a pile of fan mail.

Stephen reappeared that afternoon, refreshed and even more eager to lend a hand. "What can I do to help?"

Genny settled on the sofa. A fire burned on the grate, knocking the edge off their most recent cold snap.

He warmed his hands. "You think Jonathan's warm enough? It's raining. I wouldn't be surprised if it turns to ice."

"Rule of thumb is he's comfortable when we are. Besides, the heat's on."

"It's still chilly."

Droplets of water glistened on Stephen's hair. "You're cold because you just came in."

"So, how can I help?" he asked again.

"Jonathan will probably want his dinner shortly. Meanwhile, there are plenty of letters if you'd care to read a few."

He settled beside her, one long arm trailing along the back of the sofa. Genny glanced at him, noting the intensity of his gaze.

"So have you given any more consideration to what I asked before I left?" Her face felt frozen as she tried to smile and nod. "And did you notice I've behaved myself and haven't pushed?" Genny nodded again. "And wouldn't you say all good boys deserve a reward?" This time he didn't wait for an answer as he leaned over and kissed her.

At her whispered protest, Stephen pulled her into a hug. "Just let me hold you."

There in his arms, Genny forgot the doubts, the present, the past, the future.

The moment both realized the temptation they faced, they moved apart. Genny reclined at the opposite end of the sofa, encouraging him to talk about his trip. She shared a couple of requests she found particularly touching.

Jonathan's cries brought them to their feet. Together, they moved to the small nursery.

"Hello, Darling," she cooed. "Look, Stephen, he's smiling."

"I'll be right back."

Genny looked after him, surprised by his sudden desertion.

The camera in his hand explained Stephen's absence. "Hold him up."

"Wouldn't it be better if we were dressed for picture-taking?"

"You look beautiful," he said. "Now, show me those smiles."

The camera clicked time after time before he replaced the lens cap. He rewound the film and stuck the roll into his pocket. Genny popped a pacifier into Jonathan's mouth. "You know what you're doing with that."

Stephen returned the camera to its case. "It's a hobby. I've got albums of pictures from places I've visited. If you want, I'll find them for you."

"Yes, please. I'm an avid armchair traveler."

"I want you to keep this." He set the camera on the bed. "Start an album for Jonathan. I'll miss a lot of his growing up while I'm on tour so I'd like to have the pictures, or maybe I should get a video camera?"

She laid Jonathan on the changing table. "Don't you take it with you?"

"I have a couple."

"I'll try, but don't expect too much."

He moved closer and slipped a finger in Jonathan's hand. "I'll show your mommy some of the tips I've picked up so she gets great pictures of you for me."

"That would help." Genny pulled Jonathan's clothing back in place and lifted him to her shoulder. "You want to hold him?"

"You don't mind?"

Stephen seemed surprised by the offer. She commended herself on her remarkable restraint. She would make the sacrifice. After all, she would have many hours to cuddle her child. "If you baby-sit, I can finish the letters."

Jonathan rested on Stephen's knees, his blanket unwrapped as Stephen studied him like a proud parent. "You're a miracle, little guy. Did you know that?" He spoke softly to the baby. "Look at this tiny hand." He grinned broadly when Jonathan wrapped his silver-dollar-sized hand about his thumb. "That's some grip, Buddy. Want to arm wrestle?"

Genny smiled at Stephen's teasing. It was difficult to concentrate. She wanted to be part of the fun, not a bystander.

Genny stopped work frequently when Stephen insisted she see what Jonathan was doing. She finally gave up and joined them on the sofa. Once Jonathan had been fed and put to bed, Stephen suggested, "Why don't I fix us something? We can eat in front of the fire."

"I'll help."

Hunger or happiness gave her appetite the edge to consume her portion of the food they prepared. She leaned against the corner of the sofa.

Stephen eyed her speculatively and slid closer. "Why are you sitting all the way down there? Don't you trust yourself around me?"

Genny laughed and tapped his arm playfully. "Behave."

He shrugged and frowned. "I'm trying to be patient. You should know I'm not known for my patience."

"Duly noted," Genny said with a nod. "And you should know I rarely waver in the decision-making process as much as I have recently."

"Oh, I almost forgot," Stephen said. "Ray wants you to handle his mail. I told him what a relief it was not to have to deal with it. He says maybe I'll be able to find time for some of the things I'm always complaining I never have time to do."

The conversation turned to the activity of the week. Both were surprised to find the evening had slipped past.

"We should call it a night." Together they stacked plates on the tray. "I'll get you a refrigerator for the nursery tomorrow."

"A what?" Genny looked at him curiously. What on earth was he talking about?

"Refrigerator. One of those small ones. They don't take much room."

Genny found the extravagant gesture humorous. "It's twenty steps to the kitchen, Stephen."

"I don't want you stumbling about in the middle of the night."

"Why not a baby nurse to bring Jonathan to me in bed? I'm teasing!" Genny said before he could offer. "Did I ever tell you you're a sweet, sweet man?"

"Yes, but I don't mind hearing it again."

He kissed her good night. After he left, the night was pretty much a repeat of the one before, except that Genny lay awake a bit longer, thinking how much she enjoyed Stephen's company.

Jonathan's cries stirred her in the early hours. She flipped on the bedside lamp, and lifted her son from the bassinet. Detouring by the kitchen, she placed a bottle in the warmer, and carried him into the tiny nursery for a diaper change.

The baby refused to be contented. Had he experienced the same spells while in the hospital? She walked the small space in hopes of calming him down. She was beside herself when there was a knock on the door.

"Genny? Is everything okay?" Stephen asked when she let him in.

"I was in the study and saw the lights." Stephen smoothed a hand over Jonathan's head. "What's wrong with my little buddy? May I?"

She readily placed the bundled infant into his arms, feeling even more insecure that she couldn't comfort her son. Stephen headed for the nursery rocker.

"Poor baby." Genny knelt by the chair, her fingers smoothing the dark, thick curls. Stephen offered the bottle she attempted minutes before, and this time Jonathan ate.

"You want to feed him?"

She shook her head and leaned back on her heels to watch them together.

The clock John gave her for their tenth anniversary marked the passing of time with a little tune.

Jonathan lingered over the bottle, flailing his tiny fists in the air now and then. "You think he doesn't realize it's dark outside?"

"At least he stopped screaming. Why don't you sing him a lullaby? Heaven only knows, the poor babe isn't going to learn music appreciation from me," Genny prompted when Stephen balked.

Stephen tucked the infant against his shoulder and set the rocker in motion. One big hand softly caressed Jonathan's back. A big burp combined with the soft timbre of his voice, and they both grinned.

Genny sighed in pure delight as he finished the song. "That was beautiful," she whispered, trailing Stephen as he returned the sleeping infant to the bassinet. "Yours?"

"An original unpublished Camden." He pressed a warning finger to his lips when Jonathan stirred.

After checking the blanket and flipping the lamp off, Genny followed him into the kitchenette. "Why haven't you released it?"

"Some things are private."

Silence filled the room. Smothering a groan, Stephen stepped closer to Genny. "That didn't come out right. When I first started, I played in dives and beat the paths, hoping for success for the better part of ten years. I made a living but I was an unknown getting nowhere fast.

"I'd made up my mind to quit when Ray and the others wanted to form the band. Cowboy Jamboree caught on quickly, and we've managed to stay in the charts. Things changed after the CMA Horizon nomination. It's been a long hard pull, but I'd say it's been well worth the effort.

"But recently I've found the realization of one dream leaves room for another to take its place. I wrote that lullaby on our last road trip. For the child I'd like to consider my son. I promised not to push, but I want a family—you and Jonathan. Please give me some hope. Say you're considering my proposal."

Genny looked into his eyes, feeling the same yearning she saw in the stormy gray depths. "Yes, Stephen, I am. And I'm not taking the situation lightly," she admitted. "You hold a very special place in my heart."

Stephen gathered her into his arms and kissed her. "You are my heart," he whispered.

꙳

The same weary mother greeted Stephen early the next morning. "How about I take young Jonathan over to the house while you shower and dress?"

Genny yawned widely. Between Jonathan's feedings and their late-night chat, she'd been awake half the night. "Has it stopped raining?"

"Yeah, the sun's struggling to break through."

"Let me bundle him up and heat a bottle."

Genny showered and dressed in a pair of old jeans and a shirt. Even though Jonathan had been home only a couple of nights, the place seemed quiet in his absence. She eyed the bed for a moment longer, tempted to crawl back in and pull the covers over her head until she had an answer.

No sense hiding. Stephen wouldn't allow her to do it for long anyway. How she wished she could give him the answer he wanted, but she couldn't say yes. Not yet. Maybe never. And it wasn't fair to ask him to wait.

She stopped in his kitchen to pour herself a mug of coffee before following Stephen's voice to the study. At first, she thought he must be on the phone. Affection filled her as Genny found them in Stephen's recliner, Jonathan propped against his chest as he read aloud from the newspaper. "Can you believe that?"

Genny laughed out loud at Stephen's incredulous inquiry. "He has some pretty interesting reactions to the state of the world, don't you think?"

Stephen laughed as he glanced down at the baby. "Our Jonathan here is a man of few words. I thought you might have decided to sleep in."

"The brain's willing but my internal alarm went off. There's too much to do." Genny smoothed a loving hand over the baby's head. She glanced up and found herself startled by the open longing in Stephen's eyes. She couldn't get his late-night words off her mind. "I'm tired, but I need to get on those letters."

"You don't have to work all the time, Genny. Another day or so isn't going to make a difference."

"Tomorrow will bring a bring a new batch."

Stephen shrugged. "Keep the evening free. Ray's coming over, and we're going out."

"I can't," she protested.

"Sure you can. It's all arranged."

She stiffened at his assumption. "I don't appreciate having plans dropped on me after they're finalized."

"Nothing's changed, has it, Gen?"

How could he ask that? They had crossed the boundary to admitted love for each other, and there was no going back to the comfort of friendship. Doubts shafted through her like the sharp blade of a freshly honed knife. "Everything's changed, Stephen."

"I haven't. You're just as precious to me. My feelings have deepened, but they haven't changed. I'll work harder to prove it if you force me to, but I won't give up. As for the plans, this event came up, and I thought you might like to go with us. I knew you'd need a babysitter, so I asked the guys. Slay volunteered. Said Ronnie would help him."

Genny envisioned leaving her son alone with two strange men and immediately rejected the idea.

"Jonathan will love Ronnie. She's Slay's wife," Stephen explained, not giving Genny an opportunity to refuse.

"Ronnie? What kind of name is that?"

"Actually she's Veronica. Randy Slayman is our keyboard player."

"How many children do they have?" she asked suspiciously.

"They're expecting their first," he admitted with a sheepish grin. "They could use the experience."

"And you expect me to allow them to practice with my son?"

Stephen folded the paper and laid it aside. "They're intelligent, qualified adults. I think you like arguing with me."

Horror made her hands tremble to the point where she slopped coffee over the side of the mug as she set it on the table. "No."

"Genny? What is it? I was only teasing."

"I hate arguing. And I'm afraid to leave him. What if something happened? I'd never forgive myself."

"You can't be with him around-the-clock until he's off to college," Stephen reasoned. "We'd only be gone for three hours or so."

"I'll think about it."

"Do that. You're more than Jonathan's mom. Leaving him now and again will do you more good than you realize."

"Maybe." More than Jonathan's mom. Who was she? Daughter, sister, wife, widow, and mother. These were her roles in life. She didn't know how to be anyone else, particularly Stephen Camden's romantic interest. "I think I'll skip breakfast. I'm not really hungry."

"You're not a child."

"Interesting observation," Genny said. "Let me take Jonathan so you can finish your paper in peace."

"I'll bring him home after we cover the local news." He nodded toward the desk. "I noticed the photos. Did you need some signed?"

"It can wait. You should rest."

"Signing my name a couple hundred times isn't exactly strenuous work."

"Why don't you pursue some of those other interests you mentioned last night?"

A mischievous grin touched his face. "Because the interest I want to pursue isn't agreeable."

Genny's chest felt as if it would burst. She couldn't help but feel flattered by this man's attention.

"I promise to look and not touch," he said softly, the gray gaze holding hers. "For now."

The remainder of the day passed in a flash and by the time they finished an early dinner, Ray was at the door. Stephen showed him into the living room where Genny nervously awaited the arrival of the baby-sitters.

Ray sat beside her, admiring Jonathan. "Where are Ronnie and Slay? I thought they'd be here by now."

"He called about fifteen minutes ago," Stephen said. "They're on their way."

"What sort of benefit is this?" Genny asked Ray.

Stephen's hands rested on her shoulders. "Oh, no you don't. It's a surprise."

"Ray, tell me," she coaxed.

He glanced at Genny and then at Stephen. "Keep her guessing, Ray."

"Come on, guys. Tell me. Please."

"No way. You'll need your jacket. It's chilly out."

"Oh, it's at the cleaners," Genny said. "Jonathan spit up on me. I told you it wasn't practical. I guess I can't go."

"Hon, you're not getting off that easily. Let Ray hold Jonathan and come with me." When she hesitated, Stephen said, "Can't you see he's dying to get his hands on that boy?"

She settled her son in Ray's arms and watched to make sure he was comfortable. "I'll be right back."

Stephen pulled her to the hall coat closet. Genny watched as he rifled through the hangers.

"Aren't we going to be inside?"

He grinned and flashed her another "I'm not telling" look. She sighed her exasperation. He was much too good at this game.

Stephen pulled a coat from the closet. "Try this."

The fur-lined jacket was large but fit well enough. She pulled the lapels into place, breathing in the odor of fine leather. The sleeves fell over her hands when she dropped her arms to her sides.

Stephen adjusted the snaps on the cuffs to improve the fit. "Have you got gloves? A hat?"

"And a scarf," she added. "Cashmere. Sonya gave them to me last Christmas."

"A coat would have been better."

The aggrieved look she flashed him spoke volumes. The doorbell chimed, and Stephen reached to open the door, introducing the new arrivals to Genny.

Within minutes, Genny knew she could trust the Slaymans with her son. "He's been fed and is asleep. Chances are he won't wake. The doctor's number is on the desk by the phone." She glanced at Stephen and back to Ronnie. "Mr. Secretive here better give you the emergency number since he won't tell me where we're going."

"Slay has my cell number," Stephen said, dropping her scarf about her neck. "But he's not going to need it. Right, Slay?"

"Right, Steve," he agreed happily. "I hope you're wrong about Jonathan sleeping the entire time. We hoped for the opportunity to play with your little guy."

Fresh worries came at the thought of Jonathan's crying spells. "He was a preemie, so you have to be careful not to get him overexcited. If he starts to cry . . ."

"Don't worry, Genny," Ronnie assured. "My sister's baby was pre-mature." Ronnie smiled at her husband and balanced one hand on her extended stomach. "Slay thinks he can master the art in one evening of baby-sitting. Of course, I've told him I know it all. I'm the oldest of seven children and an experienced aunt. Go and enjoy the surprise."

With every step, Genny forced back the unease and allowed herself to be escorted to Ray's four-wheel drive vehicle. Stephen gave her a gentle boost into the high cab. She glanced at the stick shift and back at him.

"Looks like you'll have to sit in my lap."

Genny inched closer to Ray, latched the center seat belt, and cinched it up.

Grinning, Stephen latched his seat belt then dropped an arm about her shoulders, pulling her up against his chest. "Dance with the one who brung you," he murmured in her ear.

"Considering I have two dates," she emphasized, "that could be difficult."

The lights from an oncoming vehicle gave her a glimpse of his smile. "You're with me. Always."

"Tell me where we're going," she wheedled shamelessly.

"Wait and see," he persisted.

Her questions were answered with their arrival at the county fairgrounds. She had read about the benefit rodeo in the paper a couple of days before. "We can't go in there. You'll be mobbed."

Stephen slid from the cab and lifted his arms to catch her. "Sure we can."

Genny moved toward him, her gaze stopping on a mother and baby crossing the parking lot.

"He'll be okay, Honey," Stephen whispered, setting her on her feet and linking her fingers in his. "I promise. Do you think I'd let anything happen to Jonathan? I love him too."

They went through a private entrance, escaping the worst of the crowd. People were everywhere, and Genny's gaze darted about, certain they would be mobbed the moment someone recognized Stephen or Ray.

When no one seemed to notice, Genny decided she was being paranoid. Still she felt relieved when Stephen helped her into the roped-off bleachers facing the arena.

"I've never been to a rodeo before."

"You'll enjoy yourself," he promised, snapping her jacket and tucking the scarf closer about her neck. "Warm enough?"

"Yes, Daddy."

Stephen grinned and slipped an arm about her waist.

For the next couple of hours, Genny enjoyed herself tremendously. Stephen and Ray were introduced and spoke briefly on the importance of the fund-raiser, encouraging people to dig deeper in their pockets. Riders and mounts paraded around the arena as one event followed another.

Genny enjoyed the horsemanship of the barrel racers and the calf dogging, but the clowns' sidesplitting antics brought tears of mirth to her eyes.

One by one, horses charged from the chutes, their riders holding on with all their might as the horse bucked and twisted in its determination to eject them. One cowboy got his foot hung up in the wild mount's stirrup. Unable to watch, Genny gasped and buried her face in Stephen's chest.

He massaged her shoulder tenderly. "Don't worry, Love. These guys are tough. See, the pickup men got him."

Genny trembled with relief as the two men rode from the arena. The last rider won the purse, staying on for what Genny considered the longest seconds she'd ever lived through. A grin split the cowboy's face when he jumped to the ground and waved his hat in the air.

The loudspeaker came to life. "Ladies and gents, this unlucky cowboy drew the biggest, meanest bull this side of Texas. Let's hear it for Joe Kincaid riding Torture Time."

Animal and rider charged from the stall. The white hat was the first thing to go as the wily animal tossed his rider to and fro like a rag doll in a windstorm.

"Ouch," she muttered when he went down. The clowns rushed out to divert the bull's attention and the raging monster ran off. When the animal charged the fence in front of them, Genny shifted, sure she felt his powerful snort before he turned away.

"These guys are crazy," she whispered to Stephen.

"They're definitely braver than me. Had enough?" Stephen asked a few minutes later.

"I'm freezing," she admitted.

"Why didn't you say so?" He leaned over her to speak to Ray, and she stared at his expressive face, thinking how much she enjoyed looking at Stephen. Their eyes met, his eyebrows lifting. She smiled and dropped her gaze to her hands.

"Let's go." They slipped off the end of the bleachers and moved toward the exit.

"Hey, there's Stephen Camden and Ray Marshall," a woman yelled. Genny withdrew as the group converged on them.

A teenage girl thrust a piece of paper at Stephen. "Can I have your autograph?"

Genny watched as he charmed them with words and actions, jealousy sweeping over her when another woman attached herself to his arm. His warm smile set Genny's teeth on edge, and she stomped toward the truck, only to wait several minutes longer for Ray to unlock the door.

"Wow," he breathed, "that was some crowd. Poor Stephen hasn't gotten away yet."

"Maybe poor Stephen doesn't want to get away," Genny snapped, struggling unaided into the cab.

"He can't help it if the fans like him."

"I didn't say he could. Besides, I thought you were the more outgoing one," Genny snapped.

Stephen's broad smile reflected in the glow of the interior light as he dived into the truck. "Those fans were wilder than the rodeo cowboys," he declared. "Why did you disappear like that? I wanted to introduce you to the local fan club president."

"Please, those women only had eyes for you. Ray, will you turn the heat up? I'm freezing."

Stephen slipped an arm about her shoulders and drew her against his body. "It's only fair," he said when she squirmed in protest. "I kept you out in the cold for so long."

"What did you think of the rodeo?" Ray asked, filling the sudden lull in conversation.

"Maybe I could become a rodeo clown."

"Over my dead body," Stephen muttered.

"It could be arranged," Genny said as they faced off in the battle of wills. The house came into sight, effectively ending the argument.

"That looks like Sonya's car," Genny said, leaning forward for a closer look. "What's she doing here?"

"Why don't we find out?" Stephen suggested.

Lights blazed throughout the house. From the entrance hall, they heard copious weeping and Ronnie's agitated pleas. "Ms. Kelly, please calm down. You're frightening the baby."

Stephen hurried into the room, Genny on his heels. "What's going on here?"

Accusing eyes focused on Genny. "Where have you been?" Sonya demanded. "I needed you."

"The baby woke," Ronnie explained. "And then Ms. Kelly arrived. I haven't had time to feed him."

"Why don't you do it now?" Genny suggested, more than a little afraid Sonya would make a scene. "Where's Slay?"

"Making coffee."

"I'll help him," Ray volunteered.

Genny dropped onto the sofa beside her sister as the others left the room. Stephen remained nearby. "What on earth has happened?"

"My money," Sonya sobbed. "It's gone."

Genny gasped. "What?"

"I followed through on that tip I told you about. I lost everything."

Genny glanced at Stephen and back to Sonya as her arms slipped about her sister. "How could they take your money like that? Don't worry. Stephen will have his attorney check this out."

"How much?" Stephen asked.

"Twenty-five thousand." The words came out in a whimper.

Stephen emitted a shrill whistle.

"It's going to be okay," Genny said. "You've got your job."

Sonya sniffed. "There's no future for me there. I wanted to start my own firm."

Ray slid a tray onto the table and poured Sonya a cup of coffee.

"Genny, Slay and Ronnie probably could use a little help getting Jonathan settled," Stephen suggested.

His words prompted her to her feet. "How could that happen?" Genny asked as they walked into the kitchen. Slay held Jonathan.

"I see you got your wish," Genny said. "Ready to become a father?"

"More than ever."

"How was the rodeo?" Ronnie asked.

"It was fun. Thanks for making it possible."

"Our pleasure. We're sorry about the confusion. She arrived about a half hour ago. I tried to calm her down."

"I'm the one who's sorry," Genny said. "Sonya's high-strung."

"She kept talking about money. Is there anything we can do?" Slay asked.

Genny felt warmed by their concern. "Thanks. Stephen's checking into it for her."

Slay glanced down at the baby. "I think this little fellow is out for the count."

"He's such a sweetie," Ronnie added, touching Jonathan's head with loving fingers. "We want to take him home with us."

"Get your own," Stephen growled playfully.

Slay passed Jonathan to Genny and wrapped his arms about Ronnie. "We're working on it."

Everyone laughed. "We've got to get going," Slay said. "It's past Ronnie's bedtime."

The woman flashed her husband a loving look. "He's going to pamper me to death."

"What a lovely way to go," Genny said, swallowing hard as she realized that's exactly what Stephen was doing for her.

"I'll see them out and meet you in the study," Stephen said. "We need to talk."

Genny couldn't resist cuddling Jonathan. After verifying he was okay, she put him in his carrier, slipped off the jacket, and hung it in the closet before going in search of Stephen.

"You finally decided to come?" Stephen dropped the pen and stack of photos on the table. He took the carrier and placed Jonathan on the love seat.

"Can't this wait? I need to check on Sonya."

"Give me a couple of minutes. Please."

Genny sat on the sofa. "I'm not certain I want to hear this. Particularly if it's about my behavior. You didn't ask if I wanted to go to the rodeo. You didn't ask how I felt about Ronnie and Slay baby-sitting. Granted, everything worked out, but I prefer being asked."

"Point taken. What about that group of fans?"

"I felt . . . invisible."

Stephen rubbed a weary hand across his forehead. "I don't see other women. There's only one whose image haunts me, and I desire no one but her. You."

"I don't mean to hurt you, Stephen," Genny cried, dropping to her knees before him. She clutched his arms, forcing him to lift his face and look at her. "I never want to hurt you."

He searched her face, wariness filling his eyes. "John's dead,

Genny." He silenced her with fingers against her lips. "He wouldn't begrudge you your happiness. I can make you happy. Just don't fight me every step of the way."

"Stephen," she whispered as she faced the inevitable. She loved him. If she kept herself from this special man, she would never again find such a love.

Genny rested her head against his chest, closing her eyes as she listened to the steady thump of his heart. Why had he made her love him?

"I'm an idiot," he whispered. "No sensible man would take a beautiful woman to a rodeo on a cold winter night. Not to mention invite a friend along. I should have taken you someplace special."

She lifted her head and looked at him. "But I liked the rodeo. And I like Ray. And the Slaymans too."

"You need romance. I need to woo you. Pamper you."

One soft, slender arm followed her hand across his body as she wrapped it about him, her next words spoken from the heart. "You already spoil me sinfully."

"If you'll let me, I'll treasure you."

$\mathcal{G}$ enny needed to make a decision. Every time she saw the longing in his gaze, she felt like an ice cream cone in the hands of a deprived child. She'd never known anyone so free with compliments. Her self-esteem appreciated the boost.

"You know I've taken a couple of weeks off?"

Genny nodded. "I want to spend the time with you and Jonathan. I know Sonya needs you, but promise you won't let her hurt you again."

"She won't."

"Will you think about what I've said?"

"I've done nothing but think, Stephen," she admitted. "You need to think too." Genny's heart was breaking as she said the words. "You don't want to marry a thirty-six-year-old woman with another man's child."

He surged forward, meeting her stubborn resistance with his own. "Honey, if you believe that, you don't have a clue about what I need."

Genny picked up the baby carrier and moved into the living room. "Sonya, you can stay at the guesthouse with us. You're in no condition to drive home."

They said good night and crossed the backyard. After putting Jonathan to bed, Genny fixed cocoa and listened to Sonya rant about the situation. Her levels of anger were exhausting.

"Why don't we call it a night? I'm sure things will look better in the morning."

"I need something to sleep in," Sonya said, going to search through Genny's closet.

Genny removed a clean but worn nightgown from the dresser drawer. "You can use this."

Sonya's nose wrinkled with distaste. She glanced around the room. "This place is really nice." Genny didn't say anything. "Where were you tonight?"

"Stephen took me to a benefit rodeo."

Sonya tossed the nightgown on the bed and sat, coiling her long legs beneath her. "The man obviously has a thing for you. Look at all he does."

"Our relationship isn't about what he can give me."

"So you admit there is a relationship?"

A flicker of apprehension coursed through Genny. She didn't want to share the truth with Sonya. She couldn't bear to have something as beautiful as their love made dirty by Sonya's critical viewpoint.

"He's a good friend."

"I think he'd like to be more. If that's the case, you'd be a fool not to accept. Stephen Camden is quite a catch."

If only it were that simple. Just a matter of securing her future with no thought of how her action would affect their lives. Maybe she should stop being so conscience-stricken and go with her heart. No. Loving Stephen made her want his happiness more than she wanted her own.

Genny glanced toward the bassinet. Jonathan slept on, oblivious to the adult chatter.

"And as usual you're not sure," Sonya said with a shake of her head. "Don't you ever jump in and enjoy life?"

"I've prayed about it."

Sonya snorted. "Since when do you pray?"

When had she slipped back into the habit? It had been a gradual thing since coming to live near Stephen. She prayed for his safety, her child's healing, Sonya, and for her own guidance. She had conversations with God on a number of lonely nights, and He'd answered her prayers.

Genny felt out of sorts. Being around Sonya often made her feel that way. "Maybe if you'd sought God's counsel on your investment, you would still have the money."

"You know I don't believe in that stuff."

"It's not stuff, Sonya. You came in search of support, but you never had to leave home. Jesus wants to be your friend in times of trouble." Stephen had shared these truths with her when she felt confused.

"Yeah, sure."

"Psalm 46:1 says that God is our refuge and strength. If you show a little faith, He'll work miracles in your life."

"I'm going to take a shower."

For years, Genny had invited Sonya to church and tried to talk to her about God's love, and for all those years Sonya's response had been to ignore her.

"We'll have to share the bed. I'll take the side near the bassinet since Jonathan will probably wake during the night."

"I need my sleep."

Her attitude bothered Genny. She didn't want to share her bed with Sonya either. "You can have half the bed, the sofa, or the floor. Take your pick."

"The sofa."

"I'll get you a blanket," Genny said. I will not let you get under my skin, she vowed when Sonya disappeared into the bathroom.

❧

Sonya slept on the following morning as Genny dressed herself and Jonathan for the day. Unsure about Stephen's plans, Genny decided to play it by ear. After feeding Jonathan, she made the bed and started work.

Stretching luxuriously when she woke, Sonya threw her legs off the sofa. "What are you doing?"

"Working."

"I'm calling in sick," Sonya said, grinning slyly when Genny's eyebrows shot up in surprise. "I'm entitled."

"I want to hear more about this deal. I think you should have some legal recourse," Genny said.

"I need a bath."

Sonya spent over an hour in the bathroom and came out wearing the clothes from the previous evening.

"Why don't we go shopping this afternoon?" Sonya suggested over lunch. "You're earning money now," she coaxed at Genny's refusal. "Why not buy some new clothes?"

Genny didn't explain the reasons behind her need to save every dime. "I can't afford to throw money away."

"From the state of your wardrobe, I'd hardly call it a wasteful investment."

Unfortunately Sonya spoke the truth. Pregnancy had rearranged her body and her clothes fit differently now. "Maybe one outfit," Genny relented.

"For Stephen," Sonya said with a pleased smile. "A woman wants to look good for the man in her life. Just think how you could splurge if you were married. Imagine the gown you would have worn to the awards ceremony."

Her imagination barely stretched to the depth of her feelings for Stephen. Considering all the ways being the woman in his life would change hers frightened Genny.

"We can go after I drop these letters off at the office and pick up the mailbags."

Stephen insisted on keeping Jonathan for her. He promised to call his lawyer.

Still trying to catch her breath two hours later, Genny sorted through the racks in yet another store. She had no idea how many places they had visited nor how many pieces of clothing she had tried on at Sonya's insistence.

"You did remarkably well in losing the extra pounds," Sonya commented as Genny modeled the skintight dress.

Genny didn't care for the garment at all. "There's never been much shape to me."

Sonya sighed impatiently. "Take it off. It's not you either. Definitely the jeans. But you need a smaller size."

By the time they finished, Sonya had talked her into a new dress, a silk blouse, a pair of soft leather boots that were on sale, and the jeans. Satisfaction with her new clothes won out over practicality.

Genny tucked her bags in the trunk and went around to the passenger seat.

"You can wear them when Stephen takes you out."

They had never been on a real date. "I don't like leaving Jonathan."

"Don't be silly," Sonya snapped with familiar impatience. "It won't hurt to leave him with a sitter."

Genny looked out the car window. "That's what Stephen says." They couldn't understand her reluctance to be center stage. "I'm not comfortable in crowds."

"I don't think Stephen's ashamed of you."

"Sometimes I wish I were a sexy, younger woman."

Sonya's eyes drifted from the road. "Maybe you should let him decide what he needs. If it's you, all the better."

When they drove into the yard, Stephen carried the bundled baby out to greet them. "Hello, ladies," he called, focusing on Genny. "Miss me?"

No way would she admit how much. "Sonya kept me busy."

Stephen followed her around the car. "I hope you bought something special for tonight."

"What are you planning?"

"I want to get everyone together for dinner."

"Where?" she asked, swallowing the butterflies that stirred in her stomach.

"My place." Stephen followed them into the guesthouse.

Sonya disappeared into the bathroom with her purchases.

Genny flung her purse and bags on the bed. She took Jonathan from Stephen and carried him into the nursery. As she leaned over the side of the crib and whispered to the baby, Stephen's arms slipped about her waist.

"How are things between you and Sonya?" he asked softly.

Jonathan's eyes drifted closed, and she took Stephen's hand and led him from the room. "Sonya doesn't seem as upset. She offered to help finish the fan mail this morning, but never got around to it. Oh, I forgot the mailbags."

"I'll get them later."

They walked into the kitchen. "Chuck Harper introduced himself while we were at the office."

"What did he say?"

Genny thought he sounded suspicious. "Nothing much. He and Sonya seemed to hit it off right away. He said to tell you hello and that he'll be glad when the two weeks are up."

"Good old Chuck. Always hammering home his point."

Genny eyed him curiously. "Stephen, is it good for you to take time right now?"

He didn't look her in the eye. "We all need a vacation."

"Yes, but is it the best time for everyone? I mean . . . Well, I know you wanted to be here when Jonathan came home but what about the others?"

"No one's complaining, Gen. The guys are glad I put my foot down. I gave Harper sufficient warning, and the timing's perfect. Let me tell you what I have in mind for tonight. I thought we'd order a pizza and watch a movie. I have several I've never seen."

They were the kind of plans Genny could appreciate. "What about Sonya? Is she invited?"

"Three guests—you, Jonathan, and Sonya."

"Sounds wonderful." She hung her coat in the closet. "Did you talk with the attorney yet?"

"He's checking, but when I shared what you told me, he thought Sonya knew she was taking a big risk. He'd read about the stock and said it sounded iffy."

Genny frowned. "But surely she wouldn't gamble away that much money?"

"If she was eager to advance herself, she may have considered it a worthwhile risk."

"Oh, I hope not."

❧

It was a cozy evening. Stephen ordered the pizza and had the DVD queued up by the time they arrived at the house.

As soon as the movie started, Jonathan turned fretful. Genny attempted to pass him to Sonya so she could warm his bottle.

"He'll wrinkle my skirt," she demurred.

"I'll take him." Stephen made Jonathan comfortable.

Genny stopped just outside the doorway and glanced back. Stephen's behavior was so different from that first time. Jonathan's presence made no difference to him. He had become very comfortable with her son.

⁓❧

Sonya's day off stretched into three before she decided to go home. If her condo hadn't been big enough for them, the guesthouse had to feel less than cozy to Sonya.

Her determination to interfere with Genny's work came out in all sorts of petty ways. It was like having a second child demanding her time. Sonya repeatedly insisted they go shopping, and having fulfilled her wardrobe needs to the extent of her budget on their first outing, Genny refused. Sonya pouted.

Sonya continued to ignore Jonathan.

Genny insisted they not disturb Stephen, but he checked in frequently. When he detected Sonya's presence was affecting Genny, he suggested they do things together.

Slay and Ronnie baby-sat a second night for Stephen to take Genny and Sonya to an expensive restaurant.

Her sister seemed to have forgotten her feud with Stephen. Their parents had been socialites and evidently Sonya inherited every bit of their people skills. While Genny could be happy at a fast-food restaurant, Sonya was right in her element with the costly surroundings and unpriced menu.

They placed their drink orders, Genny and Stephen opting for iced tea. Sonya chose a mixed drink. After a third, she became almost giddy.

"I'm off to the little girl's room."

They watched her stagger away. "I'm sorry," Genny whispered.

He squeezed her hand. "You're not responsible for her behavior."

"I know, but you're doing this for me."

"Exactly. I'll tolerate Sonya for the opportunity to be with you." He laid his hand over hers. "How much longer does she plan to stay?"

"I felt certain she'd have gone back to work by now. I pray it's soon," Genny admitted.

"Look who I found," Sonya cried, dragging Chuck Harper toward their table. "I insisted he join us for a drink."

"You've had enough, Sonya," Genny warned.

Sonya giggled and said, "Would you believe she's the little sister?" Her behavior became even more excitable, her laughter almost raucous. "On second thought, I think she must be adopted. She doesn't act like anyone in our family."

Noting Genny's distress, Stephen motioned to the waiter. "Bring the lady a coffee, please."

"The lady wants another of these," Sonya said, waving the glass. When the liquid splashed at the waiter's feet, Sonya broke into hysterical laughter.

"The phones are ringing off the hook," Chuck said, taking the focus off Sonya.

"Let 'em ring," Stephen said.

The manager appeared none too happy. "So how's the time off going? You feeling relaxed?"

"Getting there."

Sonya wrapped her arm about Chuck's, sitting indecently close to him. "Let's don't talk business," she said, the telltale signs of too much drink showing in her voice. "How long have you and Stephen been friends?"

Genny noted Stephen's grimace.

"We've worked together for what," he glanced at Stephen, "five or six years?"

"Five." Stephen took a bite of his salmon.

Sonya flashed Chuck a brilliant smile. "I'm so glad I ran into you."

"You're certainly a bright spot in my day."

The waiter returned and set the coffee on the table. "Your party has arrived, Mr. Harper."

"Put this bill on my tab," he instructed the waiter as he pushed his chair from the table.

"Forget it, Harper. I'm treating these two lovely ladies."

"Oh, come on, Steve, you're my star performer."

"Yeah, Steve, he's just trying to be nice," Sonya defended.

Genny found Sonya's breathy words and behavior nauseating. Stephen was obviously uncomfortable, and Genny wished they'd stayed home.

"Fine," Stephen agreed reluctantly. "Thanks for the meal."

"Yes, thanks, Chuckie."

Chuck Harper grinned. "Good seeing you again, Mrs. Smith. I'll be in touch, Stephen. Sonya, drop by the office sometime. I'm always interested in another professional's ideas."

"Would you like to leave?" Genny asked Stephen.

"No," Sonya wailed. "I'm enjoying myself."

"Too much," he muttered. "You should know he's a married man."

"It's not like we're having an affair," Sonya said loudly.

Genny hazarded a guess that Sonya might jump at the opportunity if it were offered.

"Just as well," Stephen said. "You need to be careful where Chuck's concerned."

The nightmarish evening ended, and Genny insisted they go to the guesthouse when Sonya wanted to linger after Slay and Ronnie left.

"I'll talk to you tomorrow," Stephen called when she followed Sonya out the door. "I thought we might visit a nursery or two."

"Sounds good. Sleep tight and God bless."

He winked at her. "You too."

At the guesthouse, Sonya disappeared into the bathroom. She came out complaining of a headache, and Genny fought back the desire to share a few home truths with her. She took her turn in the bathroom instead. Jonathan's cries caught her attention, and Genny found Sonya fast asleep on the sofa.

Sonya disappeared for a couple of hours the following morning and came over to Stephen's when she returned.

"Genny, I'm heading home. Just need to pick up my things before I hit the road."

"I'll help." Hopefully she didn't sound too eager.

"Jonathan can stay with me if you girls want a few minutes alone."

In the guesthouse, Genny helped Sonya gather the items she'd slung over the small space.

"So what have you two been doing this morning?"

Genny looked at her. "Talking. Playing with Jonathan."

Sonya appeared to find the idea distasteful. "Is that all you ever do?"

"Stephen and I are friends."

"You're blind as a bat if you can't see that man's in love with you."

Sonya's interest in their relationship disturbed Genny. "So what are your plans?"

"Back to the office for now. Guess I'll have to concentrate on finding myself a wealthy man."

As Stephen suggested, they learned Sonya had known the chance she was taking. The money was gone, gambled on a less than sure bet.

Once Sonya left, they spent a lot of time together. When she said she had to work, Stephen would help with the mail. They lounged around home, watched movies, prepared meals together, planned the landscaping in further detail, and went to church.

Two weeks passed quickly and when the bus pulled away, Genny felt as if a part of her was on board.

16

*G*enny decided the best way to stop missing Stephen was to jump back into her routine as quickly as possible. She stopped by the office to drop off the mail and pick up the newest batch. Tracie, the receptionist, insisted on holding Jonathan while the bags were being unloaded and loaded.

"If the mail keeps up like that, they'll have to start delivering it to the house for you."

Genny nodded. "We really need to go."

"Don't be in such a rush," Tracie insisted. "The fans aren't that impatient. Besides, I need your help. We're planning something for Stephen's birthday. Any ideas?"

The casual question floored Genny. Even though they had discussed age, she didn't know his actual birth date. "When?"

"One month from today. He's turning thirty."

How was she supposed to make suggestions for his party when she hardly knew him? She knew so little about Stephen. Certainly not the date of his birth, the names of his parents or grandparents. None of the things she'd known about John before they married. The same went for Stephen. He knew nothing of her past. He might not want a life with her once he knew the truth.

Genny reached for the baby. "Can I get back to you?"

"Sure. We've got time. Bye-bye, Sweetie." Tracie waved to the baby.

She didn't have a clue as to how to organize a big birthday celebration. There had been no major birthday productions, generally dinner at home or in a restaurant with guests limited to Sonya or some of John's contractor buddies. A time or two the neighbors had been invited over for a barbecue.

Always the gifts were practical, new clothes or tools. She wanted to give Stephen something special. The lack of an idea troubled her.

He could buy anything he wanted. Actually there wasn't much he didn't already own. She selected and discarded ideas. The landscaping was out of the question. Her budget wouldn't allow for the purchase of shrubs and trees.

She put Jonathan to bed and straightened the sitting area. As she folded a knitted afghan over the sofa arm, an idea planted itself. What about a sweater? Stephen admired her work. She had time, and it would be an original, made with love.

As her enthusiasm grew, Genny spent hours looking for the perfect yarn for the pattern she selected. The specialty shop was her last hope.

"That's it!" Genny cried when the sales assistant showed her a silvery gray. "That's exactly what I want."

Genny paid the clerk and hurried to the grocery store next door. As always, she felt excited about the new project.

She picked up the items she needed and wheeled her cart into the checkout line and passed the time scanning tabloid headlines. They seemed more sensational than usual. *A thirty-pound baby? Who writes this stuff?* She read on, her gaze jerking back to a tiny photo in the lower left corner. It couldn't be.

"Come on, Lady, I don't have all day," the man behind her barked.

"Sorry." Genny grabbed the paper and shoved her cart forward. After the clerk scanned the price, she folded and stuffed it into her purse.

A few people were staring at her. Genny swiped her debit card, grabbed Jonathan's carrier, and hurried out the door. Her steps quickened when she heard someone behind her.

"Lady, you forgot your bag." The young man held the groceries she'd just purchased.

"Sorry. I mean, thanks."

At the car, Genny set the bag in the car and secured Jonathan's seat. Jerking the paper open, her fingers shook as she fumbled through the pages in search of the article. Her blood ran cold at the pictures of her with Stephen. And then the photos of her parents. She should have told him.

Somehow she managed to get herself, Jonathan, and the car home in one piece.

The answering machine light flashed in rapid succession, indicating a number of messages. Dread filled her as she hit the play button, and Stephen's voice floated into the room.

She jotted down the number, cringing at the coolness in his tone when he said he'd called for security.

Her feet dragged as she put the groceries away. First, she needed to read the article. Then she could talk to Stephen.

Dropping onto the sofa, Genny read the article. Just as she'd feared—her family history was the main thrust of the tabloid nightmare. Stephen was mentioned often, the facts skewed deceptively.

The phone rang. Genny reached for the cordless.

"Where have you been?"

Stephen. She closed her eyes and drew in a deep breath. "I stopped by the office to pick up the mail and did a little shopping."

"You've seen the rag, haven't you?"

Her heart raced. "Just now."

"Why, Genny? You had to know it would come out sooner or later."

"It never came up." The moment the words were out she wished them back.

"And you owe me nothing." Stephen's tone veered quickly to anger.

"I owe you everything," she countered. "I warned you there were things in my past. I didn't want you hurt."

His tone softened. "Don't worry about me. I need to know one thing. Did you release the information?"

Genny was horrified. "I would never do that. How could you even think it?"

"I don't." His agitation carried over the long distance. "You remember that day at the hospital? The reporters? I thought Chuck set them on us. He assures me he didn't, but if it wasn't him, then who?"

"It was public record nineteen years ago," Genny said. "Anyone could have dug it up. Maybe as background research on the woman in your life. I'm sorry, Stephen."

"I hope it's not too late to mitigate the damage," he said. "I'll see if the attorney thinks we should tell the story to a reputable magazine or just let it die a natural death."

"This isn't going to hurt you in any way, is it?"

"I was thinking of you and Jonathan. I don't want reporters hounding either of you. It's important that he lead a normal life."

Genny noted Stephen's controlled anger. No doubt his lips were compressed with the emotion. "Stephen, I'm really sorry."

"Don't be. Obviously, I haven't worked hard enough at earning your trust. I wish you'd realize your past isn't a good enough reason to give up on our future, but somehow you think it is."

"Trust had nothing to do with it, Stephen. I didn't tell you because I wanted to forget it ever happened."

"Trust has everything to do with it, Genny. You didn't trust me enough to tell the truth about your parents. You don't trust me enough to marry me. You don't trust me to take care of you and Jonathan."

"Stephen, it's not that—"

"Genny, it's obvious. It doesn't matter how I feel about you if I can't get past your doubts. Just let security deal with the press, because whether you believe it or not, we only have your best interests at heart."

A dial tone replaced his voice.

What had she done? "Oh, God, why did I have to hurt him so?" she sobbed in despair.

Why should she trust God? What had He done to make her life easier? Her parents hated each other. They'd destroyed each other. He'd sent John. They were having marital problems. He'd given them a child. Jonathan was premature and could have died. He'd sent Stephen. Sonya didn't want them in her home. He'd sent Stephen.

Could Stephen be the answer to an unspoken prayer? Hadn't God looked out for her even when she hadn't trusted Him fully?

Genny found herself running on adrenaline over the next hours.

When security recommended that she stay at Stephen's house, she agreed. She tried to occupy her time with the correspondence.

Stephen's words kept coming back to her. Did she want to spend the rest of her life trusting no one but herself?

The yarn lay on the desktop, tempting her to start work. She went into his closet and checked another sweater. Once there, she lingered, absorbing the scents she associated with Stephen. She missed him terribly.

"Mrs. Smith?"

"In here." She moved to the doorway.

"There's a Ronnie Slayman here to see you."

"Let her in."

Genny smiled at the woman's playful grimace when she followed the guard into the living room. "I feel like I've stumbled into Fort Knox," the willowy blond teased. "I've never seen so much security."

"Stephen's doing. For some reason he thinks more is better."

Ronnie grinned. "Isn't it?"

A smile crept over Genny's face. "Sometimes."

"Are you okay?"

"I've been better. What about you? How are mother and child?"

Ronnie rubbed a hand over her extended stomach. "Mother is getting impatient. Nine months never seemed so long."

Genny smiled. "Don't rush things. You'll be holding your baby before you know it."

"I can't say I won't mind not being pregnant," Ronnie admitted. "And it'll be wonderful to have this little part of Slay to keep me company when he's on the road. Coming home to loved ones is important to the guys. Their touring schedule is not what it's cracked up to be."

"I know Stephen gets very tired of traveling. Still, it would be a shame for them not to perform. They are so talented."

Ronnie studied Genny openly. "Slay says he's never seen Steve so happy."

Genny's eyes closed and she took a deep breath. "I can't tell you how that frightens me."

"Why?"

"Look at me, Ronnie. Do I look like Stephen's type?"

"Obviously Steve likes what he sees," Ronnie said. "Slay told me what happened. Stephen fired Harper on the spot. And not a moment too soon if you ask me. That man is a tyrant."

Following the woman's rapid-fire conversation took some doing on Genny's part. "Their manager? What did he have to do with this?"

"Steve warned him to leave you alone. When he learned Harper was involved in producing that trash, that was the end."

Genny blanched at Ronnie's words. The story of her life "trash"? Come to think of it, that seemed a fairly apt description. "But Stephen said Chuck Harper didn't have anything to do with the publicity."

"Well, he did."

Genny wandered to the window. Outside there was more activity than she would have considered her life warranted. She turned back to Ronnie. "How do you stand this fishbowl?"

"I don't. The guys do. I know Slay had a tough time getting used to the loss of privacy. They accept the fans and publicity, but that doesn't mean they wouldn't love to shut the door on that aspect of their lives. After the incident with Bobby, I thought the phones would never stop ringing."

"Bobby?"

Sadness touched Ronnie's face. "He was a member of the band. Bobby was a troubled kid. He overdosed on drugs. I think they all felt responsible. Stephen said they should have done more."

The revelation hit Genny like a 120-volt charge. Stephen hadn't been totally honest with her either. "What could they have done?"

"Exactly what they did. The kid was old enough to make his own decisions. Unfortunately, guilt and hindsight are powerful motivators. They need to understand it wasn't their fault. Learn to trust their instincts again."

And she had to learn to trust the man she loved too much to give up. "Ronnie, I need to ask a really big favor. Can you take care of Jonathan for a couple of days? I need to see Stephen."

17

*G*enny glanced out the plane window, wondering how Stephen would react to her arrival. This time she would do the surprising. It didn't matter that this little escapade nearly wiped out her savings. She was a woman with a purpose.

She almost surprised herself with the efficiency with which she handled this trip. Her faith that Ronnie would take good care of Jonathan helped. Leaving the plane with her carry-on, Genny caught a cab to the hotel.

Ray answered the phone when she called up to the room. "Steve just went out. He'll be furious he missed you."

They hadn't talked since Stephen accused her of not trusting him. "He won't miss me. I'm calling from the lobby."

"I'll be right down."

A broad grin covered Ray's face as he walked down the hallway from the elevator. "Stephen's doing a sound check. He's planning to leave for home right after the show. Where's Jonathan?"

"With Ronnie and that security army Stephen hired. So can you get a girl good seats at tonight's concert?"

"Not a concert. A gig at our favorite club. There's a table front row center. Right where Stephen can keep an eye on you."

Genny grinned. "Perfect. I need to change."

A twinkle surfaced deep in the man's eyes. "Something tells me Steve's life is never going to be the same again."

"No different than it's been since the first night we crossed paths."

Ray picked up her bag and led the way to the elevators. The doors closed, and Ray took advantage of the privacy. "Steve came very close to walking out, but after the mess with Harper he had to stay."

"I don't understand about Chuck Harper. What does he have to do with this?"

"The article was another of his publicity stunts. Steve fired him on the spot. Had security take him out."

"That's what Ronnie said. But Stephen said he told him he wasn't responsible. Who supplied the information?"

Ray clammed up, his bottomless well of information appearing to have run dry. Genny was immediately suspicious. What was he not telling her? "Let's catch up with Steve. He'll fill you in on the specifics."

"Do you think he'll forgive me for not telling him?"

"Stephen doesn't blame you, Genny. He knows you were just a child."

He gave her more credit than she deserved. "Not a child, Ray. I was seventeen. I married John a few months later. I thought if I pretended long enough it would go away. It hasn't."

"I can't say I blame you. I told Steve to take care in judging since he had no idea what you'd lived through." Ray unlocked the door and moved back to allow her inside. "That's Steve's room. You can change in there. Steve and I have the suite this time. We take turns so everybody gets a chance to feel invaded. It's where we gather to wind down after a show."

That explained the party in his room. "Will he come back to change?"

"He took his things with him. He has a 1:00 A.M. flight."

"When do we need to leave?"

"Twenty minutes ago. It's a miracle I came back."

As the cab pulled into the parking area of the club, Genny fought the feeling she didn't belong here. Part of her discomfort had to do with the location. In the past, a concert, a nice restaurant, or a dinner theater had been the extent of her entertainment search.

"What's wrong?"

She shrugged. "I'm scared."

"Don't be. Jerry's helped a lot of groups get their start. We try to get here at least once a year. Ready? It's almost time for us to go on."

Stephen was not in sight when Ray seated Genny at the large table before the stage.

"What would you like to drink?"

She told Ray, and he gestured for a waitress and gave the order. "Say a prayer for me," she whispered.

"I can't wait to see Steve's face when he catches sight of you." Ray winked and moved toward the stage.

The lights came up and with the first sounds of music, couples moved to the dance floor.

Genny's gaze zeroed in on Stephen. Their gazes locked.

She broke eye contact first, taking a sip of her soft drink when her throat became dry. As if drawn, Genny looked at him again. She stared deep into Stephen's eyes, smiled at his audacious wink, and toyed with her glass when she grew shy. Each time she looked up, Stephen turned up the wattage, the smoky gray eyes burning with love. Genny smiled, this time not looking away.

The mood changed, the lights dimming. Stephen pulled the microphone toward him. "This song is dedicated to my special lady."

He let go and swung his guitar around to strum the first chords of the romantic ballad. Genny blushed furiously when curious eyes turned her way. She had to get used to this—for Stephen.

All too soon it was over, and he said, "And now let's liven things up a little."

A group of dancers two-stepped around the floor.

"Let's dance."

The voice sounded in her ear, and Genny smelled the liquor on his breath before she looked up at the strange man. "No, thank you," she murmured, turning her attention back to the stage.

"Just one dance," he repeated, wobbling slightly as the alcohol slurred his persistent plea.

Genny sought Stephen's help. As if by magic a huge, burly man appeared at her table.

"This guy bothering you?"

"I'm sure he doesn't mean to," Genny allowed graciously.

"You heard the lady. Take a walk."

The man wandered off, and Genny turned to her rescuer with a heartfelt, "Thank you."

"My pleasure. Name's Jerry Todd."

"You're Stephen's friend," Genny exclaimed. "Ray told me about you."

"Then I'm surprised you're speaking to me." Jerry laughed at his joke. His laughter was as big as he was. "What's your poison?"

"Soda."

"Another teetotaler. I should have known. Let me order you a drink. No alcohol, I promise," he assured when she refused. Jerry caught a passing waitress and ordered.

The drink had the appearance of a glass of fruit juice. Genny took a sip and found the fruity flavor delicious. "It's not your usual," she admitted.

Jerry smiled. "It started as a joke. Cowboy Jamboree performed here the day their first song hit the charts. The bartender felt it reason to celebrate and improved Steve's usual orange juice. The C. J. Special caught on from there. Steve still does his without alcohol."

"Please have a seat, Mr. Todd," she invited. "I'm Genny."

"Jerry. Some crowd, huh? They can pack 'em in tighter than sardines. I'd have to build a bigger place if they were regulars."

"From what Ray said, they owe you a great deal."

"Steve and I pulled our stretch together in the military. When we came home, I invested my money in The Rodeo. At first Steve was my star act. Then the band formed, and they played here a lot too. He's paid me back many times with the good publicity he gives the club."

"I didn't know he was in the military," she said, glancing up as Stephen sang the last chorus and stepped back for Ray to sing the next number. His hair and forehead were damp with perspiration.

"How come we haven't seen you around here before?"

"Thanks to Stephen, I have an infant son who keeps me home."

His brows lifted. Genny realized her blunder and hurriedly explained Stephen's role in her son's birth.

Jerry's eyes crinkled merrily. "For a moment there, I thought my old buddy had been keeping secrets. What's his name?"

"Jonathan Andrew." Genny reached for the photograph she kept handy.

Jerry nodded appreciatively. "He's a fine boy."

"Thanks. I'm glad we got to meet. If you're ever in Memphis, you'll have to come for dinner one night when Stephen's home."

"It's a date. Just let me know when."

"Date?" Stephen repeated as he walked up behind her. "Trying to steal my girl, Jerry?"

"This one's only got eyes for you."

Stephen grinned and took the chair beside Genny's. "And I plan to keep it that way. Thanks for stepping in. I was about to come off that stage."

"I noticed. He won't bother her again. Jim likes a pretty face only as long as it likes him in return."

"I owe you one." Stephen's arm snaked about the back of her chair.

"Genny showed me a photo of her boy."

"Handsome little guy, don't you think?" Stephen bragged. "He's come a long way in such a short time, hasn't he, Sweetheart?"

Stunned by the pride in his voice, she nodded.

"Steve's one . . . uh, sweet guy himself, Genny," Jerry said, "but I suppose you know that already."

"More so every day."

A strange, faintly eager look flashed into Stephen's eyes. "Enough of this mutual admiration stuff. How about explaining why you're here."

"I think that's my cue to exit."

"Thanks for the rescue," she called as Jerry moved across the room.

"Any time."

"Genny, where are the security people?" Stephen demanded.

"Probably filing a missing person's report. I'm AWOL."

❧

Stephen ignored her droll comment. A knowing smile blossomed to fullness. "Having a good time?" he whispered against her ear.

"Wonderful."

"You shouldn't flirt with me like that. I hope the audience didn't notice when I stumbled over the words."

Genny studied the crowd.

"I see what you mean about these places," Genny said when a couple danced past, their bodies glued to each other. "Not exactly your church social."

Stephen's sigh warmed her ear. "Compared to some places we've performed, this place is tame. Just one more reason why I want out."

"I've been thinking about that."

"Oh no," Stephen groaned, his playful grimace bringing laughter.

"No, really, this is serious. You aren't the same struggling band you were all those years ago when you played in honky-tonks. People love and admire you, and if you let your light shine during interviews and record the hymns when you can, they'll know. And where is it written that you can't record a solo album if you want?"

"Nowhere that I know of," Stephen said, appearing to give the matter consideration. "So you're saying not to hide my light under a bushel, stay where I am, and be a witness the Lord would be proud of?"

Genny nodded. "I know you're not exactly happy, but what if it's where the Lord wants you?"

"I'd never thought of it that way."

"I'm praying for you too."

Stephen covered her hand with his, smiling broadly. "It's so wonderful to hear you say that. Have you made your peace with the Lord?"

"We've worked things out. You'd better go. They're motioning you onstage."

"Okay, but we have unfinished business. Oh, and don't you think maybe you should call the house and let them know where you are?"

"Ronnie will tell them."

❧

The concert ended late. Genny and Steve rode to the hotel in a cab. She had no idea where the others went when she and Stephen returned to the suite.

"Hello, Darling," he whispered. "I missed you."

Her arms went about his neck. "I had to come. Oh, Stephen, I'm so sorry."

"Why? What was so important it couldn't wait?"

"This," she whispered, kissing him again. "I had to tell you I love you. I couldn't bear you thinking I don't trust you."

"Oh, Gen. The situation caught me unaware. I should have known you'd tell me when the time was right. I felt disappointed because I wanted you to confide in me."

"I'm sorry about the way I've behaved, but I need to know why you want to marry me."

Stephen pulled away, grasping her hand in his and leading the way to the sofa. "I know you had the perfect relationship with your first husband and maybe we'll never come close . . ."

"We've surpassed anything John and I ever had," Genny admitted softly. "That's the most frightening aspect, knowing you're as close to perfect as anyone can get. I'm afraid I can't measure up."

"To what? I love you, Baby. That night we met, there was something so right about my being there. In the space of a few hours, I found I never wanted to leave you or Jonathan again." Genny gasped at his words. "You invaded my thoughts, filled my heart and mind. I crave your kindness and gentleness for myself. I'm not perfect, Genny. I never promise to be, but I do love you."

Tears slid down her cheeks. "That's not true. You're too perfect for me. You were so right about my not trusting in God. I kept seeing the things that happened in my life as His doing. I finally realized something good came out of every bad thing that happened."

"Then why won't you say yes to my proposal?"

"Because we don't know each other well enough yet." Genny swallowed the knot in her throat. "I'm sorry I didn't tell you the truth, but I'm ready to accept your love."

"Oh, Genny."

He moved to hug her, and she pushed him away with forceful determination. "Wait, I have to tell you about my parents. It's not a story I'm proud of. It's not even something I understand. John shielded me from the pain. I'm not going to let you do the same."

"I love you, Genny."

"I'll never be the woman you deserve."

"But you'll be the woman God intends for me. Perfection is the pinnacle we all strive for but rarely achieve. I want you to love me, with all my faults. I'm human with all the human failings you can name, but God forgives me when I sin, and I move forward in my efforts to be the man He would have me be. The only perfection I want to achieve is in going to heaven when I die and making our marriage last for at least fifty years or so."

"Oh, Stephen, I do love you. Almost too much if that's possible. My insecurities make me see the things you do as attempts to control my life. When Ronnie told me how you'd kicked yourself over Bobby's death, I understood why you had to help."

"It's important to be there for the people you love."

Genny tried to look at him but ended up looking at her hands, the emerald ring she'd placed on her finger that night. "Everything happened so quickly. I met you and my feelings escalated out of control. That made me more insecure. Maybe it's misplaced loyalty. I felt unfaithful to the memory of my son's father. I need to keep him alive for Jonathan. I thought I couldn't do that if I loved you. And I want to be more confident, at least a little pretty, for you."

"Sweetie, I like what I see. But even more, I like what I feel with I'm with you." He held her close for several minutes.

Genny lifted her head from his chest. "Who told the press my father killed my mother? Ray's fount of information dried up like a creek bed in a drought when I asked."

He seemed reluctant. "Sonya. Harper may have provided the gun, but she pulled the trigger. She went after the fast buck."

Genny twisted the ring about her finger. "She's like them. Everything in her world revolves around money and prestige. My parents would be alive today if they'd cared about anyone besides themselves."

Could I have changed things? She asked herself the same question every time she thought about that afternoon. "It was a couple of weeks before my high school graduation. I came home early and found my parents arguing. Their fights were always so violent. Almost deadly. There was no place to run."

"Was it different from before?"

She nodded. "They didn't know I was home." Stephen hugged her closer. "Mother screamed that she'd stayed long enough. She wanted the divorce Daddy had promised her all those years ago.

"Mother was cruel. She just kept hacking away at his pride, saying awful, hurtful things. She told him he was a lousy husband. Daddy slapped her. Her scream was the last thing I heard before I ran away. The police were there when I came home. Mother was dead. She'd hit her head on the stairs and broken her neck.

"The press had a field day. Mother was running for judge, and Daddy was a prominent doctor. Sonya was so unforgiving. She pitied Daddy's stupidity. Said he should have given Mother her divorce. She doubted they had ever loved each other."

Stephen dropped a kiss on her brow. "Was it always bad?"

"Just around Sonya and me. They were social creatures. Publicly, they tolerated each other. I'm sure people were convinced they loved one another."

"Honey, I'm sorry. I didn't realize how traumatic this was for you."

"That's not all," she continued. "It was ruled accidental, but Daddy couldn't handle what he'd done. His staff found him dead. They said it was a heart attack, but he had no medical history. The autopsy revealed he had injected himself with insulin. He tried to provide for us by leaving a large life insurance policy. It didn't pay because of the suicide.

"Sonya was angrier about the money than she was with Daddy for taking his own life. She missed our lavish lifestyle. She dropped out of college and took a job, claiming she needed to be there for me. I think she was too embarrassed to stay in school. I should have told you this before. Maybe if we'd taken time to know each other, I would have."

"I know everything I need to know about you. You're a special person. Don't you know that?"

"I've always needed someone to tell me. Until you, John was the only person who ever said he loved me."

"I don't expect you to be dependent on me."

"I can't be. I loved being a homemaker, but now I have a child. I need to be able to provide for him."

As the words left her lips, the truth struck Genny. She constantly spouted off about providing for Jonathan, but Stephen had provided the means. He'd provided her independence and she'd been too blind to see it. She misinterpreted his caring actions as charity when they were so much more.

"You want to be the perfect mother," Stephen said. "You think it's your fault that Jonathan was premature. Personally, I think it's remarkable you did as well as you did."

"Maybe you know me better than I know myself. I always tried to make up for my shortcomings by being the best wife I could be. When that was gone, I was pregnant and scared and forced to live a life I hated. Now I have to do things for myself, and you have to love me enough to let me."

"Honey, the only condition on my love is that you love me as much as I love you."

Genny found it too easy to get lost in the way he looked at her. "I'm too old for you."

"More experienced," Stephen whispered.

"Too insecure."

"Oh, really?" he asked more boldly. "Well, Genevieve Smith, you can be very secure about my love."

Silence filled the room as he kissed her thoroughly. Genny wrapped her arms about his neck and murmured, "I'm afraid I won't be woman enough to make you happy forever."

In his eyes, Genny saw the passion of loving. "If you can't, no one else ever will."

re you sure you want to do this?" Stephen asked.

"I have to confront Sonya. This vendetta has to stop."

"You want me to go with you?"

Genny slipped on her coat and smoothed her gloves into place. "I can handle this myself."

"Will you tell her we're getting married?"

"When I have to." At his pained expression, she said, "I don't plan to give her any news to impart to the press."

He nodded understanding. "Will you come to the house when you get back?"

"The moment I return."

Throughout the long drive, Genny struggled to come up with the right questions for Sonya. Only one that required an answer. Why?

The truth about what had happened with their parents was always in Genny's thoughts. If she had told them to stop, the ending might have been different.

She timed her arrival for when she could be certain Sonya was home. A light shone in the upstairs bedroom. Genny parked and went to the front door, listening to Sonya's loud muttering about late visitors as she came down the stairs.

"Well, well, to what do I owe the honor?" Sonya asked, grinning as she leaned against the doorjamb. "As if I don't already know. I don't suppose you ever got around to telling Stephen about your secret life."

Sonya couldn't know how hate-filled their mother's words had been, and yet the same mean-spirited behavior colored her words.

"It was an accident," Genny maintained in steadfast defense of her father.

"Bury your head in the sand. At least Stephen knows the truth now."

"Why?"

"They offered me good money for news on the lady Stephen's so desperate to protect. I think Chuck Harper was even more impressed after the 'scandal' came out." The way she used her fingers as quotation marks made Genny flinch. "He probably figured Stephen would dump you fast when he heard the news. It didn't happen though, did it?"

"Stephen understands."

"And Lucky Genny comes out on top again."

Sonya's voice carried in the clear evening air. Genny glanced around, uncomfortable airing their dirty laundry in public.

"Oh, for heaven's sake, come in," Sonya snapped, leaving the door wide open as she swept into the living room.

Genny followed, shutting the door behind her. Sonya had redecorated with new furniture, an Oriental rug, and expensive artwork. Were the ill-gotten gains the source of her decorating budget?

"What do you think?" she asked, whirling about happily. "I love it. I'm not ashamed to invite people over now."

There was nothing wrong with the old stuff. It couldn't have been more than a few months old. "I can't believe the levels you stoop to for a dollar."

"Oh, if you only knew."

Sonya's evil sneer disturbed Genny. "What have you done?"

"You really don't have a clue?"

"Sonya, so help me if you do one more thing to hurt Stephen or his career, I'll—"

"Pray for me?" Sonya laughed. "Grow up, Gen. You're as naïve as the day you were born. It's time you woke up. You never knew we were about to pull the plug on your safe, secure world. Didn't you ever wonder why there was no insurance? Why everything was in hock?"

"John was too young for insurance."

"John was an old man when you married him," Sonya said with heavy irony. "We were going away together when you messed things up with your news. That pregnancy was brilliant. He didn't want to hurt you. I said you'd survive."

"How, Sonya?" she demanded. "You weren't leaving me anything."

"John insisted you have the house and your car."

Genny thought back to how she had invested her share of the family estate into their business. Surely John experienced some degree of guilt over stealing from her.

"And enough money to survive on until you worked things out," Sonya added.

The money she'd used to pay his debts, Genny realized. The money from the sale of her home and car. At first, she'd been so angry, upset that he'd left her alone and then because of his failure to plan for their future. "He loved me."

"Of course he did. Your safe world was a haven for him too. He came to me for excitement."

"But you're my sister."

Genny shivered at Sonya's malicious smile.

"As children, when you had something I wanted, I took it. If I asked, you handed it over even quicker." Sonya spat the words at her. "I wanted John. Him and the almost five hundred thousand."

The pain almost overwhelmed her. "Don't you . . . Haven't you ever cared about me? My son?"

"That baby ruined my life."

"Because he prevented you from having someone who didn't belong to you in the first place?"

"I wanted a baby too. If John hadn't been so determined to finish that one last project, we would have been gone long before you told him you were pregnant."

"So why not tell me the truth then?"

"I loved him. I believed I would win. He kept promising we would tell you. I never should have left that summer. John didn't want me to go."

Genny looked puzzled.

"He didn't. He wanted a wife. A family. Said it would be over if I went back to college. I didn't want to give him up, but I wasn't housewife material either. I intrigued him, and I used it to my advantage. Your son could have just as easily been mine.

"And if I'd had any idea how much he wanted a child, I'd have made sure it happened," Sonya added. "All he talked about was the baby. He nagged. I threatened, and in the end he admitted he wanted his child more."

"Why tell me now?"

"Aren't you Christians always spouting off about how important the truth is?"

"Don't pretend righteousness, Sonya."

"Oh yes," she exclaimed, her blue eyes twinkling like jewels. "Nothing little Miss Perfect Genevieve ever did carried the same weight as Evil Sonya." Her resentful laugh ground out. "Bet you don't know the argument mother and father had that day started over me. I got into trouble, and mother was afraid my stupidity would hurt her career. Did you ever wonder why the idea of divorce didn't bother her? Because she had a bigger fish on the hook. I was at a friend's and saw her coming from her boyfriend's apartment. I wanted to confront her, but I stepped back inside and kept my mouth shut."

Secret lives. No wonder her parents led such a miserable existence. "So why are you angry with Stephen?"

"He doesn't like me," Sonya declared, slamming the pillow she held against the sofa. "I'm invisible to him."

Realization dawned. "It piques your pride that he's not interested in you?"

"Don't let your mockery of a marriage to John destroy the real thing you could have with Stephen. That man loves you. He plans to spend the rest of his days with one woman. You've got him wondering if you'll ever forget John. I figured the truth would make your decision easier. I won't lie and say I'm sorry, because I'd do it again."

"John didn't turn to you out of love," Genny said softly, confident she knew what drove her husband to Sonya.

"Don't be so sure of it, little sister."

"Did he talk? Did he mention the anxiety, the inadequacy, the unease?" Genny asked. "It was there. Every time another month passed."

"It wasn't his fault," Sonya defended. "You weren't fit to be his wife. He deserved better."

"Maybe," Genny agreed. The sting of the words brought back the doubts, her plans for a future with Stephen. "Maybe it's all true. But at least his son was more important to John than you."

"Touché, little sister. I wondered if you'd ever show any Kelly spunk. You're too kind and sensitive to be believed."

"It's part of me, Sonya. And it won't go away because two people I loved let me down. I defended you when no one else in the world would. Now I understand why I was the only one.

"I thought you needed love. That you were suffering because of the past. Our parents were so dedicated to their own needs they forgot they had children. Why should I think my sister would be any different? You're worse than they ever dared to be. You helped yourself to my husband, a husband who could set aside his cheating for the child I carried.

"And you made me feel like a burden," Genny accused. "Every time I mentioned money, all that time, knowing you'd stolen every cent from me . . ."

Sonya shrugged carelessly. "But you've landed on your feet. Why shouldn't I?"

"It's always you," Genny said, coming to her feet. Words, long bottled deep inside, surged to her lips. "Your selfish needs come first. Maybe I am a silly, insecure burden, but your derision and ridicule haven't destroyed me. I won't give you the opportunity to try again." Genny jerked the door open and started outside. She stopped to share her final words on the subject. "Consider the money you stole from my son payment for staying away from us forever."

"You'll forgive me," Sonya sneered. "You won't be able to help yourself."

"I already have," Genny said, taunting Sonya with the truth. "You're really bothered that a plain woman like myself found two men to love her.

"John played with you, but I wore his ring. He may have run to you for excitement, but he found peace with me. You should consider what you offer a man. Looks fade, and when they do, what will you have left?

"I love Stephen and he loves me," Genny announced confidently. "I intend to become a woman he's proud to have in his life. I may never be a beauty, but you're living proof that beauty is only skin-deep. The heart is where real beauty lies, and you don't possess one."

"You'll need me again."

"No." There was no doubt in Genny's vehement response. "I'll accept charity and live on the street if need be, but I'll never take anything from you again. Simply because you never give. You begrudge and expect homage for every gesture. Not once in your entire life have you shown charitable kindness or love. I hope you can be happy with yourself because unless you change, you'll never find anyone to love you. Men may put beauty up on a pedestal, but they want a heart when they seek love."

Genny walked out the door.

❧

The lights of home burned brightly, illuminating her way back to the man who loved her for herself. Anger didn't take away the lingering hurt. John was gone, but she had loved him, and knowing he planned to run away with Sonya intensified Genny's insecurities.

She could only wonder what kind of love she had shared with her child's father. A wry smile touched Genny's lips. She didn't want to feel satisfaction at destroying her sister's pleasure, but she was only human. The comment about his son being more important had hit the mark.

Stephen met her at the door. "How did it go? Everything okay?"

She swiped away the tears. "Just hold me."

Genny reveled in his loving embrace, knowing here was a man who considered her needs before his own. His hands soothed her back as he whispered gentle words of reassurance in her ear.

"Sonya told me she and John were going to run away together." Her voice cracked with pain as she added, "Jonathan was the reason he didn't go."

"Oh, Honey," he whispered, holding her closer. "I'm sorry."

"Me too. For many things. You saw the real Sonya. Maybe I did too, but I didn't want to believe the truth. She's all the family I have. I had no idea how much she resented me, how cruel she could be. She took great pleasure in telling me about John's infidelity. But she claims she told me so I'd see how much you love me."

"You still need her, Hon."

"I owe her. Sonya helped me realize I'm in danger of losing something more precious to me than I ever dreamed possible. I still have a lot of things to prove to myself, but no woman should reject the love of a man who loves her for herself.

"Remember I told you God uses us wherever we are. He made you my protector the night Jonathan was born. On the way home tonight, I thought about how short life is. I've wasted days refusing to accept what God intends for me. I want us to be married as soon as possible."

Stephen toned down his hurrah for the sake of the sleeping baby, but Genny knew he felt the same victory she did. Whatever life handed out, they would face it together, and the world would be a more wonderful place because two people believed in the miracle of God's love.

Epilogue

*G*enevieve Camden, stop arguing with me and breathe," Stephen instructed with mock severity, a glint of laughter in his gray eyes.

She touched his face. "What would your fans say if they could see you now?"

"I happen to think this outfit suits me perfectly. I'm considering auditioning for television's next heartthrob doctor role."

Genny snorted. "That color does nothing for you, and scrubs are hardly the attire of a well-loved singer noted for his romantic ballads. One who, I might add, should be at his awards ceremony."

"What could be more romantic than this? I'm exactly where I want to be," he said, bringing her hand to his lips. "Besides, I don't have a single female fan who would consider me hero material if I were there instead of here."

"You think they've forgiven you for marrying me?"

Stephen nodded agreement, his smile disappearing. Tension filled him when her eyes began to glaze over with the pain of another contraction.

Just as he had done with her every objection, Stephen used words to make Genny realize what God wanted for her. Even after admitting her love for him, she had her doubts she could be woman enough for him if she hadn't been for John. Stephen laughed outright at that, telling her he couldn't handle any more woman than her.

He pressed on about the landscaping business, forcing her to admit it was what she wanted and continued until she agreed to let him to finance the venture, all legal and with interest. She hoped to get several of Genny's Flower Gardens in the ground over the next year.

Of course it might be a bit difficult with a toddler and newborn in tow. That part of her plan had not changed. After God, her marriage and children were her first priorities.

She'd pushed Stephen into revealing his true feelings about Bobby, even to the point that he admitted his reasons for doing so much at first had been to make amends for the loss of his young friend. Genny believed Stephen when he said that changed when he fell in love with her.

And in that way of his, Stephen found a way around most of her arguments. Love made her putty in his hands, and he knew it, sweeping her off her feet before she could object to his plans.

Their wedding ceremony took place one Sunday morning after church services, a very low-key, informal occasion for friends and family. Genny met Stephen's family for the first time on the day of their wedding and immediately adored them. His mother claimed her as a daughter, and they visited often.

Fearful Sonya would sell the news to a tabloid, Genny hesitated over inviting her sister. Sonya kept their secret but didn't attend the ceremony.

She and Stephen, along with the entire congregation of their church, prayed for Sonya with the hope that she would one day submit to the will of her Lord and Savior. Genny prayed to make her peace with her sister.

Stephen was dedicated to protecting their privacy and keeping them out of the limelight. She forgave him for the one time he slipped up. Too excited to wait until he returned home to share the news, Genny and Jonathan flew to where the band was performing and went backstage. Stephen dragged them out onstage and introduced the loves of his life. The fans cheered with him when he shared their wonderful news.

Much to her dismay, Dr. Rainer had agreed she wasn't getting any younger.

She still felt the loneliness, particularly after waving good-bye to Stephen, but she never felt neglected. Genny never had the slightest doubt he would come home to them.

At fifteen months, Jonathan was a beautiful child. Together they watched him grow, and Stephen teased her mercilessly when his first word was Daddy. Of course that was only right since he pursued Stephen with steadfast determination, moving as fast as his tiny legs would carry him.

At times she thought they'd never have another private moment, her dear friend, Ronnie, whisked Jonathan away for a special play date.

Ronnie and Slay loved him, and Genny trusted them with the confidence of a woman who knew her friends would never allow her child to come to harm. She returned the favor, baby-sitting Randy Jr. when they needed time alone.

Stephen recorded his solo album. After many months, it remained at the top of the Christian music charts. Every time they received a piece of fan mail witnessing the blessings his music brought to believers and nonbelievers, Stephen said he had made the right decision.

She squeezed his hand as the pain encompassed her body. "Stephen!"

"I think this was where I came in," he joked, leaning to kiss her forehead. "Now focus and breathe."

"I told you I was too old," Genny said, panting with the contraction.

"You don't get pregnant and then decide you're too old. It's not the natural order of things."

"Natural order, indeed. If I didn't love you so much . . ."

He grinned and wiped her brow. "Well, Doc has assured me you're in perfect health. Better than some of his twenty-year-old patients. I think he's even more surprised that this baby isn't premature. Right, Doc?"

Dr. Rainer looked at him. "With your lifestyle, yes. Stephen, you really shouldn't argue with Genny right now."

"Right," Stephen agreed good-naturedly. "Did I tell you you're having a—"

"Baby," Genny supplied, tightening her hold on his hand.

"You don't have to break my fingers."

"I'll break more than that if you spoil my surprise."

"You said the S word," Stephen teased. "You must be delirious with pain."

"I suppose I'll never hear the end of it if I admit to liking your surprises."

"Nor see the end of them," he said with a quick kiss.

"Okay, you two. Let's get this over with. I want my dinner," Dr. Rainer called.

"Cruel." The word left Genny in a whispered cry as she followed his instruction.

Things sped up and in a matter of minutes, a perfectly healthy baby girl lay in Stephen's arms. "Her mother's eyes," he whispered.

"Her daddy's lungs," Genny added, marveling at the baby's lusty cries. The heart-rending tenderness with which Stephen stared down at his daughter brought tears to her eyes.

"I love you," Stephen said as he leaned to give Genny a glimpse of their child. "She's beautiful."

"What else would you expect of Stephanie Camden?"

"Other than perfection?" he suggested.

Genny smiled and lifted a hand to his face. Stephen had been right. Perfection was the pinnacle, but if their life together got any more perfect, she wasn't sure she'd survive it.

On a Clear Day

by Yvonne Lehman

With loving gratitude to Lori and Lisa for their invaluable comments on my work.

Jesus said to the people, "I am the light of the world. If you follow me, you won't be stumbling through the darkness, because you will have the light that leads to life."
JOHN 8:12 NLT

1

I can't have you working here anymore. I'm going to have to let you go."

Ellen Jonsen winced as a crash of thunder echoed through the mountains. Her glance darted to the window where hard rain pelted the small panes and blurred the landscape. A streak of lightning split the sky with the same tearing force Patsy Hatcher's words were having on Ellen's heart.

Ellen's gaze returned to the grim-faced director of the Little Tykes Preschool. "What did you say?"

Patsy opened a manila file that lay on the desk in front of her. "Ellen Jonsen" was written on the tab. Patsy drew out a piece of paper. "It's another complaint about your proselytizing."

"But I haven't—"

Patsy's uplifted hand stopped Ellen's words. "Did you, or did you not, invite Janice Sims and her daughter Judy to your church?"

Ellen had no reason to deny that. "Well, yes, after Missy told Judy about the Kid's Club and Judy said she'd like to go. I told Janice about the program. That's all."

Patsy tapped the folder. "That was done on these premises."

"And Janice complained?" That was unbelievable. She'd seemed interested.

"No, not Janice." Patsy's glare held accusation. "You were over-heard."

Overheard? That had to be one of the workers who often spouted her "tolerant" attitude. Tolerance—except for Christians. "You mean someone eavesdropped on my private conversation, then complained?"

"Your private conversations tend to be very public." Patsy's clipped tone stung. "This is not the first time, Ellen."

Ellen felt as if she'd suddenly become a little preschooler, being reprimanded for pushing a child and causing him to fall. "After you told me not to mention my faith, I stopped." That had been against her deepest feelings and against what the Lord expected of His followers.

"Oh, Ellen. Now tell the truth."

Ellen felt heat rise to her face. *Now I'm being accused of lying?*

Patsy didn't let up. This remarkable senior citizen, whom Ellen admired, had become her enemy. "You're always talking about what's going on at your church. You and Heather talk about Jesus as if He's your best friend. We all hear it. Even the children." Her shoulders straightened as she leaned back against her chair. "That's where I have to draw the line. We will not allow one person's religious beliefs to be taken as what we represent here." She leaned forward, her forearms resting on the folder. "We're not a church. We're a school."

Ellen felt as steady as the oak tree outside the window, whose branches swayed to and fro in the wind. Was there no getting through to this woman? She thought not, so why not speak her mind?

"Patsy, you all talk about the movies you see. The music you listen to. What you hear on TV. What's in the newspaper. Whatever is going on around you." She took a deep breath. "Why can't I talk about what's important to me?"

"Others hear when you talk about it to Heather, who is writing her master's thesis about this school. I'm aware that theses can be published as articles or books." Patsy stood.

Ellen wondered if she were having a nightmare. How could a person change so? This white-haired woman had represented a grandmotherly figure to her, had been her mentor in child care. Now, her tall slender presence loomed over her like a threat.

Patsy's lips formed a stern line. "The reputation of this school is at stake. I will not have it represented as a religious organization." She sighed. "Ellen, religion is not something you force on another person. It's private and personal. Especially around children."

Ellen gasped. "I would never—"

"Ah!" Patsy lifted a finger. "At lunchtime were you, or were you not, singing 'Jesus Loves Me' to Missy? And don't you think other children could hear that?"

"Missy was afraid of the storm, and I was comforting her. Patsy, she's my own child."

"Your own child?" Patsy scoffed. "That's not true, Ellen."

Accused of lying again.

Ellen swallowed hard. "It's true in the ways that count. In my heart."

If ever Ellen had heard a condescending tone, it was when Patsy walked around the desk and came close. "Maybe other things in your heart aren't true either, Ellen. Like your opinion of how everybody else can get to God."

~

I'm . . . fired!

Ellen repeated the statement to herself several times after Patsy left the office. Ellen sat alone, no longer aware of the storm outside. A great calm, like the calm at the center of a hurricane, enclosed her.

Patsy didn't want her to work a notice.

If she had quit, she'd be required to give a two-week notice.

Patsy didn't even want her to stay to tell the final story of the day. The children loved that. What would they think? What would the other workers think?

Ellen didn't have time to explain to anyone. Too numb for tears, she told herself she could handle this. But what would it do to Missy?

Missy had adjusted so well—had taken a sense of pride in Ellen's telling the stories.

Do I take Missy home now? She'll wonder why I'm not telling the story.

Should I say I'll be back for her later?

Should I let Missy continue in the preschool?

Ellen did not believe Patsy would ever mistreat Missy. She was not a terrible person. On the contrary, she was competent and well-organized. Ellen had never doubted Patsy's commitment to the welfare of those children. Patsy hired only the most capable, dedicated workers. They were wonderful. Heather would be there for awhile longer too. That was positive.

Numb from having been fired, Ellen wondered if this were some kind of nightmare. She walked from the office and down the hallway, glass windows along the outer wall on her right, being pounded by heavy rain.

Since her mom's unexpected death two years earlier, Ellen's emotions had stayed near the surface. And what had just happened was no small thing. She felt as if her world had collapsed again, bringing to mind the wall that had collapsed on her mom's car parked in a lot near the department store where she had worked. Mom wasn't the only one killed that day. Two workers on scaffolds and three other people in the car next to her mom's lost their lives as well. They'd gotten in their cars to go home. They'd never made it.

Struggling for control, Ellen stopped for a moment and placed her hand on the cool window pane.

Taking a deep breath, she gazed at the rivulets of water obscuring what lay beyond the windows. But the scenery was imprinted upon her mind. An immaculate green lawn spread out in front of the long white building on which cartoon characters had been painted. Atop the roof hung a huge sign announcing Little Tykes Preschool. The sign included wooden characters depicting little boys and girls. A girl with golden braids jumped rope. A dark-haired boy pulled a wagon in which two other children rode. A child held a teddy bear. A boy read a book.

The appearance of the school had attracted Ellen.

So had Patsy Hatcher, no stranger to hard work.

Ellen had been impressed with Patsy's reasons for having a school, rather than simply a day-care center. Patsy had been a principal at a primary school and saw firsthand that so many children weren't prepared to leave home and go off to a full day at school. Many were traumatized. She wanted to provide a means of preparation for children.

Many people whose advice Ellen had sought confirmed that Little Tykes had the best reputation around and advised that getting Missy into a program where she could relate to other children would be good for her.

Ellen had never doubted that God had led her to Little Tykes and the job that allowed her to spend the days with Missy, whose little life had been turned upside down.

Now, Ellen wondered if she had failed God. She'd messed up what had seemed like such a perfect solution to earning a living while having time to be involved with Missy. Had she really been so over-bearing about her faith? She didn't think so. But Patsy did.

God, don't let me fall apart right here. Give me strength and the kind of peace only You can give in the midst of trials.

She took a deep breath and turned to continue down the hall. On her left against the solid wall, red, orange, green, and yellow raincoats and umbrellas hung on pegs low enough for children to reach. Ellen passed the closed door with a big "2" on it, then a "3." Colorful baskets for the children formed a neat rainbow across the floor.

Ellen stood for a moment at the door with a big red "4" on it. Missy took pride in reading the numbers and finding her own room. The cold doorknob in Ellen's hand mimicked a spot in her heart. For two years, this had been a big part of her life.

I don't work here anymore.

A deep breath preceded her turning the knob, opening the door, and stepping inside the room onto the green carpet—the color of grass in the summertime. The big round smiley-face clock on the far wall indicated the time was 1:05 P.M. Five minutes past the time for the final story of the day.

There would be no story, except the one she'd tell Missy. And her dad. And Heather. And her friends. Patsy stood to one side, talking to Heather.

Some workers walked past with wet finger-painted pictures to be hung to dry on wooden racks in the hall. Others herded the little ones into the bathroom to wash their hands. Missy and several other children had already parked themselves on the floor, facing the chair where Ellen normally told the story that was in a picture book she'd hold up for them to see.

Patsy walked past without a glance.

Heather came over to the children. "Instead of a story today you're going to see a movie. *The Lion King.* Any of you seen that?"

Amid the clamor of children responding with arms lifted high, hands waving, "Yea's," and clapping, Ellen's gaze met Heather's questioning one.

Ellen gave a simple shake of her head. She retrieved her purse from a cabinet, then walked over to Missy and touched her shoulder. "Come on, Honey. We have to go."

Missy looked up, her blond curls bouncing against her cheeks as she spoke emphatically. "It's not time. We get to see *The Lion King.*"

Beginning to feel the full impact of the situation, Ellen blinked back the moisture threatening her eyes. Little children and workers looked her way. Was Patsy standing like a warden at the door?

"Come on. We have to go, Honey. I'll tell you why later. You can watch *The Lion King* at home."

Missy's voice and eyes pleaded. "I want to see it here."

"I'm sorry. Not today. Now come on."

Reluctantly, Missy rose to her feet. She glanced at a friend. "I have to go. Bye." She waved her little hand to some who looked at her.

The soundtrack marked the introduction to *The Lion King* and the dismissal of Ellen. She couldn't even say good-bye to the children. She looked around. Their attention focused on the TV. A few workers stared at Ellen and Missy.

Ellen could hardly believe Patsy would allow the children to watch a video. On very few occasions did they watch TV, then only an educational program. Normally, there would be interactive activities. Obviously, Patsy was quite upset.

At the doorway, lightening flashed and thunder crashed. Missy jumped, squealed, and wrapped her arms around Ellen's legs.

"Wow, that was a lot of potatoes rolling down the mountain. And the angels are taking a lot of pictures. See those flashes!"

Missy peered around her legs. "You said that's not really true."

"No," Ellen admitted. "But it's a good way to think about it."

Ellen closed the door behind them—closed the door to her livelihood and Missy's stability.

Hearing the door open, Ellen glanced over her shoulder. Heather came out. "Ellen, is something wrong?"

Missy detached herself from Ellen's legs and, in the relative quiet, walked over to the racks of newsprint, covered with wet finger paints.

Ellen mouthed the words, not wanting Missy to hear. "Patsy fired me."

"Fi—?" Heather stood with her mouth agape. "Why?"

"Tell you later." She took a deep breath, trying to suppress the mixture of emotions welling up inside, threatening to come forth like a cloudburst. "I'm too religious, so I've just been told."

Heather mouthed, "Ohhh." She raised an eyebrow. "I'll stay awhile and see what Patsy has to say, then I'll come over and you can tell me all about it."

Heather walked back into the classroom.

Missy wailed, holding out a painted finger. "It's still wet."

Ellen took a tissue from her purse and wiped the painted finger, then stuffed the tissue back into her purse. "Your painting will get even more wet and tear up if we take it out in the rain." She took Missy's yellow-and-green rain jacket and matching umbrella off the peg, then reached for her own red one.

She took Missy's papers out of her basket and her extra change of clothes required by the school.

"Come on, we'll have to hurry through the rain. We'll get your painting—" Her words stopped, before she added, "another time."

She'd almost said, "tomorrow."

But there would be no tomorrow here for Ellen.

Nor for Missy.

2

*T*he storm had moved farther away by the time Ellen pulled into the carport beside the long, brick, ranch-style home. She parked behind her dad's car and beside Miss Daisy's. The thunder was now a distant rumble, the lightning infrequent, the wind calmer, and the rain a mere drizzle.

The cloud cover, hanging over the neighborhood as if crying, gave Ellen an even more depressed feeling. Upon exiting the car, she could hear the TV in the living room. Ever since her mom had died, her dad always had it on, as if he couldn't bear the silence of an empty house.

"Take your jacket and shoes off in here, Missy. I'll take care of them in a little bit. Let's see if your clothes are wet."

Ellen slipped out of her own flats, suspecting they were ruined considering the puddles of water she'd waded through. The bottoms of her slacks were wet too. She'd deal with that later.

Ellen could hear Miss Daisy in the next room. "Well, hey, Missy," to which Missy replied, "Hey."

Above the sound of the TV news station, Ellen's dad asked what she was doing home so early.

"On't know," Missy said nonchalantly.

"On't know? What kind of talk is that?"

"On't know," Missy repeated and giggled. Ellen smiled. She'd have to work on Missy's diction, teach her to say clearly, "I don't know."

When she reached the doorway, Ellen's smile broadened as she observed the cozy sight. Her dad and Miss Daisy sat at a card table on which lay a jigsaw puzzle. Maybe Miss Daisy was getting her dad interested in something. He took off his eyeglasses, laid them on the table, and opened his arms to Missy.

"I know one thing. Your Pa-Pa needs a hug."

Missy ran over and threw her arms around his chest and made a contented sound as she hugged him tight. He kissed the top of her head. "Hey, you're all wet."

Missy moved back and pointed at his shirt. "You are too."

They both laughed, and he rumpled her already mussed curls.

"Don't they teach you anything at that school?" He tried to sound gruff, but he never fooled Ellen or Missy with the effort. The two of them knew his heart was mush where Missy was concerned.

"I painted a picture. I couldn't bring it 'cause it's still wet."

Ellen remained in the doorway, glorying in the easy camaraderie between that little girl and her Pa-Pa. "You're still wet too. Go to the bathroom." Ellen reminded her.

"Okay. Let me do one piece." She picked up a piece of puzzle and tried to force it into place.

"Missy! Mind your—" Ellen's dad paused and his brow creased.

Had he been about to say, "Mind your Mommy?"

His pause reminded Ellen of Patsy's saying, "That's not true."

He started again. "Mind your manners. Do what Ellen says."

As soon as Missy disappeared down the hallway, Ellen's dad moved his chair back from the card table. "Did the school dismiss early? I wouldn't be surprised if the electricity went off. It flickered here a few times."

Ellen didn't want to worry her dad. And she didn't want to go into details about being fired just yet. It would be common knowledge soon enough. At the moment, she felt the cruel sting of failure. "Dad, I need to talk to you about it."

Miss Daisy stood. "I was just thinking about what to do for supper. But like Jon said, we thought the electricity might go off, so he got out a puzzle."

Ellen saw the blush on Miss Daisy's cheeks. The older woman certainly didn't need to explain her actions to Ellen. If they wanted to bend their gray heads over a puzzle, that was their business. Dad paid Daisy to come in at her convenience and do light cleaning, some shopping, and cook supper on the days she came. Often, they'd have leftovers the following evening, order pizza, or go out. Sometimes on her days off, Daisy would bring over a casserole that she announced was simply too big for her. Ellen suspected Daisy cooked such meals especially for them since she lived alone.

Ellen walked over to the card table. "Looks interesting. Hey, I think this one might fit right there." She picked up a colorful piece to fit into a hot-air balloon. It didn't fit. She laid it back down. "I'm as good at this as Missy."

Even though the three of them laughed lightly, Ellen felt she just didn't fit into this puzzle of a life. She knew to look to the Lord with her problems, but more and more she realized her mom had been such a great source of stability and strength for her and for her dad. Mom had been gone for more than two years. And today was another reminder that things were going from bad to worse.

Daisy put her hand on Ellen's shoulder. Her soft gray eyes held a look of concern that Ellen had seen many times. No, she had not fooled this perceptive woman who was always ready to lend a helping hand. "Honey, let me take care of Missy. I'll get her changed. And I have a new book I brought over for her. I'll read it to her while you talk to your dad."

Ellen acknowledged Daisy's offer to help with a nod. "Thanks."

Watching Daisy proceed down the hallway, Ellen felt a rush of gratitude for her and a stab of regret that her own mom wasn't here to do those things. She turned to her dad, now standing. He nodded toward the kitchen door. "Let's have a cup of coffee."

He picked up the remote and switched off the TV.

Jon Jonsen used to say you could solve your problems over a good cup of coffee. He hadn't said that since Ellen's mom had died. But he did make a mean pot of coffee. That was one thing he didn't even let Daisy do. He didn't like store-bought coffee but preferred the kind that came monthly from a mail-order company. Flavors varied, and he'd spoiled Ellen with their aroma and taste. He was right. The taste was far superior to the supermarket packaged bricks of coffee.

Ellen savored the aroma, put in a dash of creamer, and took a sip. "Mmm, good."

She was ready to tell him the events of the day, but he spoke first. "Daisy was embarrassed."

"Embarrassed?"

He nodded. "Sometimes we sit down and work a puzzle together. Or talk. Or sit and watch a little TV. It's company, you know."

"I think that's great, Dad. You're the one who pays her wages. If you want her to relate to you, that's your business."

He set his cup down. "Not to her way of thinking. She doesn't want to give the wrong impression. She works for me. But we're friends. A few people have asked questions. You know, because she's a widow and I'm without your mom." He took a deep breath, then lifted his cup to his lips. After a swallow of coffee he said emphatically, "We're friends."

Ellen sometimes wondered if Daisy had ideas that went beyond friendship. She was a very nice Christian woman who had worked part-time for her dad for almost two years. Daisy and her husband had attended the same church as Ellen and her parents. Several years ago, Daisy's husband had died after a long illness. Ellen had been a high school student then and simply thought of Daisy as being an older woman. But now that Ellen's own mom had died, she began to have a different view of older people. Her mom was too young to die in her late fifties, and Daisy had just recently passed her sixty-second birthday.

Her dad had wanted someone to come in and help out. "I feel bad enough for your dropping out of college to take care of Missy. But I admire you for it," he'd said. "And your working in a place where you can still be with her all day. I just couldn't bear the thought of her being away from home that long, away from us, after all she's been through."

Now, Ellen had to tell her dad the situation had changed—drastically.

Her dad moved his empty cup aside. He held out his hands, and Ellen placed hers in his, feeling his strength and warmth. His voice held tenderness. "Tell me what's going on, Ellen."

She began. "I was fired."

He listened attentively as she related the episode with Patsy and smiled when she told of her inviting Judy and her mother to church. He nodded with a warm expression in his eyes when she told of singing "Jesus Loves Me" to Missy when the little girl had become frightened of the loud thunder.

When she finished, he squeezed her hands and gazed warmly at her. "I'm proud of you, Ellen."

"But Dad, I should have handled the situation differently. I could have called Judy's mother after work. I could have held Missy, rocked her gently, and hummed the song. She knows the words."

He shook his head. "You instinctively acted on your faith, Ellen. I can't fault you for that."

Ellen withdrew her hands and clasped them on her lap. "I don't know, Dad. It's only a few months until Missy will be in kindergarten. The school has been good for her. And for me. Now—"

She lifted her hands in an idle gesture. "Her life is disrupted again."

"That's not your problem, Ellen."

"Dad." She scoffed. "Of course it's my problem."

When he picked up his empty cup, Ellen thought his hands shook. His voice did not, however. "Maybe this happened for a reason, Ellen. You know I want you to get back in school. Heather's already working on her master's thesis, and you haven't even graduated from college."

"Dad, we've discussed this before. Missy's more important than college. A few months can be like a lifetime to a child."

With that unrelenting look on his face, he got up and headed for the coffee pot.

She turned in her chair, watching him pour. "I need to get a job, maybe with another day-care facility for the summer. Missy needs me with her."

He stood gazing out the window over the sink, holding onto the cup with both hands as if it might get away. "You don't need a job, Ellen. You've taken on too much responsibility already. Take the summer off. Get ready to return to college in the fall. This could very well be God's closing a door so you can walk through another one."

At the moment, Ellen's faith wasn't quite strong enough to take comfort in that comment. "Dad, I could register for college in the fall. But I still need to be with Missy this summer."

He set his cup down, turned his back on her momentarily, and held onto the countertop. Ellen wondered at the rise of his shoulders. Was he not taking her being fired as calmly as he'd seemed? Had he just said those things to help her feel better? Was he worried about Missy?

"Dad?"

He turned, facing her. His body looked stiff. His words were abrupt. "Get on with your life, Ellen. You're not her mother. Which reminds me. There's a note from Leanne in the mail."

Leanne—Missy's birth mother. Ellen sucked in her breath. She'd thought the storm was over, but she felt it churning in the pit of her stomach, and it seemed a cloudburst exploded in her chest. What had happened to that warmth and his sense of being proud of her?

His coffee untouched and his chin set in a stubborn way, her dad strode from the kitchen without looking at her.

His words echoed in her mind repeatedly: *You are not Missy's mother.*

Ellen wanted release from the storm inside her. But the confusion and hurt simply deepened as her world turned darker. The storm did not subside, nor did it allow release in the form of tears. She pushed it back and let it lie alongside her dream that her mother had not died. She wished she had not been fired and caused this additional burden on her dad and on Missy.

Ellen knew she'd be all right after the shock of being fired wore off. She'd talk to her dad at a more convenient time and try to get to the bottom of what he meant. If she was doing something wrong, she wanted to know.

Her gaze focused on the stack of mail and found the letter from Leanne. With a heavy heart, she pulled out a lovely card with flowers on the front and imprinted in big letters, "Thinking of You."

Dear Uncle Jon and Ellen,

Hope everyone is well. I'm great! I just got a bit part in a soap opera. That could lead to all sorts of things.

Give sweet Missy a big hug and kiss for me.

Love,
Leanne

P.S. I'm Carla Coatsworth in the soap Love's Sweet Promise. *I'll let you know when it airs.*

The salutation was almost longer than the message!

Ellen reprimanded herself immediately for feeling sarcastic. Maybe she was just jealous. Leanne had a job. Only nineteen years old, Leanne had broken into acting, something she'd wanted to do since childhood. Winning a local, then state, beauty contest had made a difference. She was a beautiful blond with blue eyes. Missy was the spitting image of her.

Ellen shivered. Leanne was not Carla. That was only a role she played. And three times today—first by Patsy, then her dad, and now Leanne—Ellen had been reminded that she was not Missy's mom. Ellen's mom and dad had adopted Missy, but Ellen had been like a mother to the child for the past two years. Did everyone else feel that Ellen was not Missy's mommy? That it was only a role she played?

3

$\mathcal{T}$'ll fix supper tonight," Ellen said when Daisy and Jon walked into the kitchen.

"I'll just go on then," Daisy replied. "The way that rain came down, I might have water coming in under the garage door."

"If you have water in your basement, call me, Daisy," Ellen's dad insisted. "I'll come over and help bail it out."

"That only happens about once a year, Jon, when so much rain falls so fast."

"Well, you let me know," he said. "And Daisy, Ellen losing her job doesn't affect yours in any way."

Ellen wondered what exactly was going on. She'd tried to be considerate by telling Daisy she could leave. Had her dad wanted Daisy to stay and cook supper?

Daisy turned to her and smiled sweetly. "Don't worry about your job, Honey. Remember, tests can become testimonies. I should know. I've been through enough of them."

Ellen nodded, returning the smile.

Daisy took her leave, and Ellen closed the back door behind her, wondering if she could ever be a walking testimony like Daisy was. She felt more like a false witness. Instead of gaining in maturity, she was obviously inept at everything she tried to do.

Neither Ellen nor her dad spoke as they heard Daisy's car leaving the driveway. Ellen turned to face him, wondering if she should try to communicate better. His comments about her job loss made her sense of failure that much greater.

The sound of knocking at the back door and the sudden pressure of the door being pushed against her back interrupted her thoughts. She hastily stepped back from the door.

Heather's face, surrounded by wheat-colored hair, peeked around the edge of the door. "Hey, what kind of welcome is this? You could at least use the deadlock instead of your body. I'm stronger than you, Girl."

Ellen was grateful for Heather's bubbly personality that had a way of bringing out positive responses in people. Dad laughed along with Ellen and invited Heather in out of the weather.

Missy ran into the kitchen just then, waving a video of *The Lion King*. She looked at Ellen. "You promised."

Ellen's dad put his hand on Missy's shoulder. "Don't you think you should speak to Heather?"

Missy looked at Heather, then up at the older man. "No. I spoke to her all day long."

He laughed. "Okay. I guess you have a point there." He lifted a little blond ringlet and let it fall back in place. "Let's you and me go watch *The Lion King* while these girls whip us up one fine supper."

Heather plopped down in a chair. "If that's an invitation, I accept, Mr. Jonsen."

Missy huffed and put her free hand on her hip. "He's not Mr. Jonsen. He's Pa-Pa."

With the heel of her hand, Heather pushed against her own forehead. "Oops. Sorry, Pa-Pa."

Missy ran on into the living room with the video.

Ellen's dad looked at the two friends. "I can hardly wait. I've only seen it two dozen times."

Heather laughed with him. "You're a good Pa-Pa."

He pushed his glasses further up on his nose. "Well, I hedge a little. I tell Missy I like to read the paper or a magazine while I watch TV. Never limit yourself to one thing."

"She lets you get by with that?"

"For the most part. She only tells me every minute or so that the good part's coming on, and I've just gotta watch." He headed for the living room.

"You're gonna cook, huh?" Heather questioned.

Ellen tried to make a joke of it. "This might be our last full-course meal for awhile, now that I'm out of work."

Her dad turned back and took a few steps toward Ellen and Heather. "Now, Ellen, don't go saying things like that. Some people might believe it, and you know little pitchers have big ears."

"I'll set her straight, Dad. I was joking."

"And understand this," he continued, "we don't have to worry about money, and you don't have to worry about a job, Ellen. What's mine is yours and that little girl's."

Ellen nodded. She spoke weakly. "Thanks, Dad."

After he left the room, Ellen shook her head and sighed. "I don't know what's wrong with him . . . or me."

Heather ignored the comment. A long lock of hair fell along her face. She pushed it behind her ear. "Where did that saying come from? Little pitchers have big ears?"

Ellen shrugged. "I don't know. Mom used to say it, and so did Grandma. I guess they used to have little pitchers. Maybe they called the handles 'ears.'"

Heather grinned. "Sounds more like a Little League baseball player to me."

"Does, doesn't it? Anyway, let me elaborate on what Dad said before you start thinking about working up a care package for us. Mom's insurance left plenty of money, and even the house is paid for."

Heather nodded. "That's a blessing."

"But it's not mine, Heather. It's Dad's. I've got to make my own way."

"You're doing more than that, Ellen, the way you take care of Missy."

"Oh, yeah! The way I take care of her is to lose my job, alienate my dad, appear to take over Daisy's job—"

"Oh, quit feeling sorry for yourself. Tell me what happened."

Is that what I'm doing? Feeling sorry for myself? I don't think so. It's all about Missy. But I need to quit dwelling on it and go forward. But where? And how?

Ellen walked over to the refrigerator, took out a package of frozen ground beef, and set it on the countertop near the microwave, getting ready to thaw it out. Suddenly, she looked at Heather. "Hey. This is supposed to be a joint effort. We're having Missy's favorite meal—spaghetti." She pointed to the refrigerator. "Dad said you and I were fixing supper. There's lettuce in there just waiting to be torn, tomatoes to dice, eggs to—"

Heather stood and gave a mock grumble. "Thought you'd never ask."

While they prepared the meal, Ellen told Heather what had transpired with Patsy.

Heather rinsed her hands after dicing tomatoes and wiped them on a paper towel. "There's got to be more to it, Ellen. You and I talked about things happening at church, and so you sang 'Jesus Loves Me' to Missy. That's not enough to be fired over. There's something wrong with Patsy."

Ellen gazed at Heather. "Everybody knows Patsy is perfect."

Heather nodded. "She's good at what she does, all right. And that's an important part of my thesis. But something's eating at her. Maybe she's under some kind of religious conviction."

"Yeah. Convicted that I'm not to work there anymore." Ellen sighed. "But even if that were true, Heather. She got rid of me. So there goes my witness—if I ever was one."

Heather lifted her finger. "Ah, ha! But I'm there. She can't fire me because she didn't hire me. She wants the publicity I can give Little Tykes. She wants to win that award for the best preschool in the nation."

The buzzer sounded, and Ellen turned off the heat from under the boiled eggs. "Well, do what you must. In the meantime, I have to do something about preschool for Missy and getting a job."

"A lot of children take the summers off from school and make it just fine. Missy probably wouldn't mind that. Your dad seems to take good care of her, and you can tell he loves her." She smiled. "He's a good man."

Ellen agreed. They didn't come any better. "But something's wrong with him, Heather. I think he just can't get over Mom's dying. He looks at Missy sometimes with sadness in his eyes and gets a distant look on his face. His mind is off somewhere on something else instead of on us, and when I get his attention, I have to repeat what I said."

"You don't think it might be anything serious, do you? Like . . . Alzheimer's?"

"No. It's not like he can't concentrate or can't remember. It's more like he just has something else on his mind. So, you see, I think Missy is better off at a day-care facility. But I don't know if she'd be happy there without me."

Heather sighed and shook her head. "Let me think."

She thought for a matter of about two seconds. "I know the perfect place. I'm including Ridgeway Conference Center's preschool in my thesis."

Ellen knew Heather's project involved comparing and reporting on various kinds of schools. "I didn't know they had a preschool."

"Oh yeah. And summer programs too, for children. And day care for conferees' children. I worked there a couple of summers. Remember?"

"You worked at the girls' camp, didn't you?"

"Yeah. But I know about all the other programs. They didn't have a preschool then, but they do now."

"One major drawback," Ellen said. "I can't give Patsy as a reference."

"Why not?" Heather looked determined. "Being fired for proselytizing should work in your favor at Ridgeway."

Ellen sighed. "I doubt Patsy would say that."

Heather nodded. "You're probably right. But that would impress the personnel manager, if he's the same one who hired me."

"Who's that?"

"Richard Williams. He was a neat guy." Heather looked as if she'd landed on the perfect solution to Ellen's dilemma. "So I'll be your reference. I've observed you at work. When I get through singing your praises, they'll probably make you director of that conference center." She frowned. "Well, not the director just yet. He's the one who gave permission for me to report on their preschool."

They both laughed. Ellen could always count on Heather as a blessing. She just might be a good reference since she'd worked at

Ridgeway, had permission to report on their preschool, and was a Christian. Her commendation of Ellen's qualifications might mean more to Ridgeway than Patsy's assessment. She could also use her pastor as a reference and maybe Daisy.

"And too," Heather said, "instead of watching *The Lion King,* Missy would learn about the King of kings."

That settled the matter for Ellen. "I'll call now. You know the telephone number of Ridgeway?"

Heather shook her head. "Don't remember. Where's your phone book?"

Within the next couple of minutes, Ellen was on the phone asking about getting an application. She hung up, smiling. "You want to thaw out this hamburger and start the spaghetti sauce while I run up there?"

"I know it's only a couple of miles away, El, but I'd suggest you drive."

"Ah," Ellen jested, "I knew I kept you around for something."

❧

"Not another one, MaryJo," Richard Williams groaned when his administrative assistant came into his office and slipped another application beneath the stack next to the folder he'd been perusing.

"It just came up from the front desk. But no more today, I promise."

He glanced over at her. "Don't make promises you can't keep. That baby can hear you, you know."

"Would I lie to my baby?" With a triumphant grin, she laid her hands on her stomach. "My doctor's appointment, remember? I'm leaving early."

He leaned back, releasing some of the tension in his shoulders from having bent over the application folders for most of the afternoon.

MaryJo placed her hand on a couple of folders at the corner of the desk. "These two cancelled because of the storm."

"Makes you wonder if they'd show up for work in a storm, doesn't it?" Richard said with a shake of his head.

MaryJo agreed. "This one—Ellen Jonsen—is either a duck, or eager for a job, to have come out in weather like this."

Richard agreed, then glanced over his shoulder to the windows behind him. "Looks like the worst is over. But you be careful out there."

MaryJo sighed and looked toward the ceiling. She spoke in monotone. "Yes, Sir. I'll drive home and have Ben drive me to the doctor. So, with a man in the driver's seat, I feel confident we'll be just fine."

Richard nodded. "That eases my mind some. He's the driver and you're the copilot. You're pretty good at telling men how to do their jobs."

"Is that a compliment?"

Richard pointed at himself and grimaced. "Would I do that?"

"Not often." She shook her head, but her eyes held warmth and her lips smiled.

He waved her off. "Hope all goes well."

She grew as serious as he. "Thanks."

His glance swept over her retreating form before he swivelled his chair toward the windows being pattered by the diminishing rain. He hardly noticed the rain. His thoughts were with MaryJo, Ben, and the baby due to make its appearance before long.

He'd appreciated MaryJo since she came to work for him five years ago, right out of secretarial school. He'd observed her grow up. Her plans changed; her conversations changed from movies she saw to where she and Ben went and where she and Ben would go on vacation. For months now, the conversation had been dominated by descriptions of how they were turning a bedroom into a nursery, surprise baby showers, doctor's appointments, and baby clothes. He'd learned that a certain kind of yelp from her office meant the baby had kicked again.

Richard rejoiced that a young couple was so in love and so obviously thrilled about starting a family. When Ben came around, he still talked about sports or movies, but he never failed to mention the baby.

As director of human resources, Richard had many opportunities to watch young people return to Ridgeway summer after summer and grow in work experience and faith. He believed that God, in His great mercy, had placed him in a position where he played a part, even if indirectly, in their spiritual growth.

He knew firsthand about irresponsible behavior that could irrevocably change the course of a person's life. Having gone to church all his life, he'd known right from wrong and as a child had even claimed Jesus as his Savior. Yet, he'd sinned. The consequences of his sin had resulted in his falling on his face, so to speak. Thankfully, he'd known where to turn for help and had fallen on his knees in repentance and committed his life to Christian service.

Some people spoke openly about their past sins and used that as a wonderful testimony to God's forgiveness and grace. Richard had never felt the need to do that, choosing instead to witness to his Christian faith by the way he now lived his life.

Suddenly, he slapped the arms of his chair. *Why am I sitting here, doing nothing?*

The weather—that was it. Dreary days had a way of seeping into his skin, getting under it.

He swivelled back to the desk and started to pick up the top folder. His fingers drummed against it, as if he had to allow one more pressing thought before returning to work.

He sighed. His position allowed him to see changes and growth in staff and conferees, but his own life was pretty much constant. And until now, that had been just the way he liked it.

$\mathcal{F}$riday morning, before nine o'clock, Ellen drove with Missy along the road that wound up and around Ridgeway's registration building. It loomed white and gleaming, four stories high. The blue sky was brushed with only a few white streaks of thin, washed-out clouds. The air smelled fresh, and everything looked clean from yesterday's drenching. Puddles of water still lay in holes and ditches. The ground remained soggy.

Ellen looked up on the mountainside to where work trucks were parked in front of a new hotel being built. The several-story structure dwarfed the small preschool below it. She parked in one of the spaces marked off at the side of the road. Parents with small children were exiting their cars. Bigger children ran from their cars over to the bridge. Some cars were leaving, others pulling in.

Ellen saw no cartoon characters, just a small sign identifying the building that looked like an adorable, storybook cottage. Missy had her door open and ran to the wooden bridge spanning the rushing waters of the swollen creek that ran alongside the road. She joined other children exclaiming, "Look. Baby ducks."

"Be careful now," Ellen called. "Don't lean over too far."

Missy put her arms on top of the wooden railing. She stood on tiptoes, peering over the railing at little speckled ducks following their mother down the creek and under the bridge. Ellen observed that the mother had her ducks in a row—something she couldn't say for herself.

Missy ran to the other side of the bridge to see them emerge. "Can I pet them?"

"They're moving too fast for that. Maybe later we can go to the lake and feed the ducks. I'll bet there are a lot of little ones there. But right now, let's see what this school is like. Okay?"

"Okay." Missy walked along with her as a couple of women smiled and spoke, while other parents tried to pry their children away from the bridge.

Ellen hung back with Missy on the porch that stretched across the front of the cottage and was surrounded by a white wooden banister. After the others went in, Ellen followed with Missy in hand. They stood in the foyer.

Smiling women with warmth in their eyes greeted the children, who rushed past them toward the play items designed to inspire eagerness for education. Most of the students gathered around a cage containing a calico cat. Others rushed to a huge plastic Noah's Ark and began matching animals, two by two, and placing them in the ark.

Yesterday, after handing in her application, Ellen had asked about the preschool and been given the name of the director, whom she called later in the evening. The director, Carol Freeman, invited Ellen and Missy to come and look it over.

After the children were in their rooms and the other parents had left, a woman held out her hand. "You must be Ellen," to which Ellen responded affirmatively. "And this is Missy."

The petite woman with a pleasant face surrounded by short curly hair smiled at Ellen, then devoted her attention to Missy. She knelt in front of Missy, who still held onto Ellen's hand. "Missy, I'm so glad you came to see us this morning. Would you like to take a look at Callie while I talk to your mommy?"

Mommy. While half-listening to Carol, Ellen realized that when she'd talked to the director on the phone, she'd said "I have a four-year-old, almost five . . . ," and Carol had assumed Missy was her child.

Carol was explaining that Callie was her cat that she brought to class every day and let spend some time in the classroom, although she played outside much of the time. "Could you do that while I talk with your mom?"

Missy nodded.

Carol must have caught the gleam in Missy's eyes. "Just don't put your fingers inside the cage. Callie likes to play and paw at the children, but she doesn't realize how sharp her claws are." Carol stood and called to a worker sitting at a small table, watching the children. "Jan, Missy would like to see Callie. Would you have her join in the activities while I talk to her mom?"

"Sure," Jan said, lightly touching Missy's back. "I have some other very interesting things to show you. Would you believe we can make it rain on Noah's ark?"

Missy snickered and looked up at Jan with excited eyes, her blond curls bouncing against her face as she shook her head.

Carol laughed. "The rain comes at the end of the day. The children love it. Serves a double purpose. We spray a little disinfectant soap on the ark and figures. It helps with keeping the plastic figures clean." Carol looked at Missy, who seemed eager to join the other children. "She'll be fine."

Ellen nodded and walked with Carol down a hallway and into a small office. There was barely room for the desk and an extra chair. Different from Patsy's big office. The room Missy had gone into was different too. It looked like many children's Sunday school classrooms, with pictures depicting Bible stories, including Jesus with little children at His knees and on His lap.

Ellen told Carol about being fired and the reason for the action.

"Little Tykes is reportedly one of the best in teaching children," Carol admitted. "Patsy Hatcher is known for being tops when it comes to running a preschool." Carol sighed. "But here, we stress the love of Jesus and how He wants us to live."

Ellen nodded. "Missy gets that at home and at church, but it would be wonderful if she could be here, where that is stressed as well. One can never get too much of a good thing."

Carol returned her smile. "Right. That can be said for most of us, I'm sure."

"Could you take Missy?"

Carol sat thoughtful for a moment, then looked across at Ellen. "You're in luck. Ooops, sorry. I forgot. Christians don't have luck. We have blessings." She grinned. "You're blessed. We had a cancellation at the first of the week, due to a family situation. The families on our waiting list had already placed their children elsewhere." She looked toward the door for a moment, then back at Ellen. "I don't see any reason why Missy wouldn't fit right in. But of course, when there are situations of not relating well, we deal with that."

"Missy's not shy."

Carol smiled. "I didn't think so. Oh, you need to know. Preschool dismisses at two. Then day-care workers come and stay with Ridgeway employees' children and a few other students until their parents get off work. All children must be picked up by five."

At least she had a place for Missy—in a Christian environment. But what about herself? Ellen took a deep breath, then plunged in. "Since I was fired, I'm looking for a job. Do you have any openings?"

A slow shake of Carol's head indicated to Ellen there were none.

"Your having worked at Little Tykes for almost two years speaks well of your abilities," Carol said, "as does the reason you were fired in relation to what we expect of our workers. We are to be vocal about Jesus and stress Christian principles."

Ellen needed some kind of confirmation of being worthwhile. Although she didn't feel she'd done anything that she deserved to be fired for, there was still the stigma of being fired from a job where you were responsible for children. Any secular day-care director would likely feel the same way as Patsy. And too, she'd felt Patsy was her friend. That was just another loss, piled onto the others.

"I wish I could hire you," Carol said, "but the same workers have been here for several years, and there's a waiting list for workers too." She shrugged a shoulder. "I don't know of anyone planning to leave, and although we could never have too many workers, I doubt that the personnel manager is hiring additional ones. We have a limit both on the number of children and of workers."

Ellen tried not to show her disappointment.

"Won't hurt to try, though," Carol said. "But I'm not the one who does the hiring. The director of human resources does get my approval and have me interview prospective workers."

Ellen understood. "I filled out an application yesterday."

Carol smiled. "I can show you around so you can see what all we do. You'll need to fill out some forms for Missy. I'm sure Little Tykes required medical records."

Ellen nodded. "They require a life-history of the children and the parents."

"Not a bad idea," Carol said. "If you'd like to leave Missy today, that would be fine, since she's been accustomed to being in school. Your little girl's a beauty."

My little girl. "Oh, I almost forgot. I guess I need to tell you this. Missy calls me Mommy. But she isn't my daughter."

Carol listened as Ellen related the relationship and the situation. "My parents adopted Missy. After Mom died two years ago, I've filled the role of mother. Missy calls me 'Mommy,' and I've allowed it. I'm her mom in every way except legally. Officially, she's my little sister."

When she finished, Carol stood and reached out her hand. "Ellen, I'm more impressed with you now than when you came in."

The compliment meant a lot to Ellen. But Patsy, then Ellen's dad, had reminded her she wasn't Missy's mom. Now Ellen had to admit it to Carol.

She had a sinking feeling. Was God forcing her to admit it to herself?

❧

Richard looked up and stretched his shoulders when MaryJo came into the office with a scrap of paper. "Carol, at the day care, sent a note to go in one of the files. She was impressed with this applicant."

"Okay, which one?"

"I put it at the bottom of the pile." MaryJo lifted the others. "Yes, here it is. Ellen Jonsen." She held it out.

Richard opened the folder and slipped the note inside. He appreciated additional background information on a prospective employee and valued others' opinions.

He scanned the information. Ellen Jonsen. Not a college student. Twenty-four years old. Had experience in a well-respected preschool.

Her name didn't ring a bell, but the reference person did: Heather Cannington.

"Somebody mentioned her at lunch the other day," Richard said. "Something about her writing an article on the preschool."

"Oh, is she the one? Martha mentioned that, but she didn't know who was doing the article. So, it's Heather."

"You know her?"

"Not really." MaryJo laughed. "Remember the incident with Jeff Blount a few years ago?"

"Right." No wonder that name had sounded so familiar. Richard began to nod. It was all coming back. He grinned. "They both denied anything serious between them."

MaryJo smiled. "You gave them the benefit of the doubt. So maybe that was true. As far as I recall, there was never any other problem with them."

"Right. And the next year Jeff came back, but she didn't."

MaryJo nodded. "She still has her maiden name." She reached for the file.

Richard held it out, then drew it back toward himself. "Just leave it on the desk. I'll take another look at it later on." In his quick scan, he'd noted that the applicant had indicated interest in day-care or children's programs and a willingness to work full time, part-time, permanent, or temporary. She'd consider any job. Sounded rather desperate, like she'd take anything.

There wasn't a "desperate" tab on any of the folders. However, that's how his mind registered a few applicants whose information crossed his desk. He'd much prefer thinking about the college students who likely would take a no with a grain of salt and think it was his loss by not hiring them. But the desperate ones touched his heart. Those were the ones he'd really like to help. But usually, he had to send word that he couldn't use them. He didn't say they lacked required skills but that usually was the reason.

Several times, he made notes on applications for MaryJo to deal with. "Can't use this one. This one is too young for the summer program this year, will consider for next summer. Have this one come in to talk to me. This one is a possibility for the new hotel."

He kept thinking about the "desperate" folder. The applicant wrote that her job at Little Tykes ended on Thursday. Apparently, she'd come directly to apply at Ridgeway. She'd come in the flooded streets when two other applicants had cancelled their interviews because of the storm.

Impressive.

He wouldn't need workers for several weeks for the new hotel. He could interview her, discover if he should keep the application on file for future reference and also determine if she was a candidate for hotel registration clerk, housekeeping, or the dining room.

He hoped he would never see prospective applicants as just names on paper. They were human beings trying to find their place in the world. As director of human resources, his responsibilities included helping them do just that.

His glance moved to the corner of his desk.

Ten minutes before MaryJo would leave for the day, he rang her office. "MaryJo, make an appointment for Ellen Johnson to come in for an interview toward the end of next week, please."

(5)

*T*hings were looking up.

And happening quickly.

The day after being fired from Little Tykes, Ellen had Missy enrolled in another preschool. This one was located in a Christian environment, no less.

Then late that same afternoon, Mr. Williams's administrative assistant had called, asking if she could come in for an interview the following Thursday afternoon at four o'clock.

Could she ever!

All week, Ellen couldn't help but feel positive about the situation.

But when Thursday arrived, she wasn't sure how to dress for the interview. Slacks had been fine for Little Tykes, considering one could expect the inevitable stains from fingerprints of myriad consistencies and textures, splashed finger paints, and grass or mud stains. She'd begun to wear her hair in an easy, simple ponytail. For the interview, she decided to let it fall in soft waves to her shoulders. The days of spring sunshine had already begun to bring out the golden highlights in her light brown hair.

She would look feminine, but conservative. She chose a pastel yellow sleeveless dress with a matching short-sleeved jacket. Two-inch heels instead of flats, small gold earrings, and a little more care with her makeup completed the transformation, although she preferred a more natural look. The few freckles across the bridge of her nose had long been an accepted part of her appearance, and she no longer tried to hide them as she had in high school days.

She looked herself over in a full-length mirror and felt pleased. Suddenly, she had an eerie thought. Suppose the personnel manager wanted to hire her full time? Would she still want to stay on after the summer, even after Missy started kindergarten?

Maybe she should work in the summer program instead of day care. That way she'd be free to go on to college or get a job. This was an issue she could talk about with Mr. Williams.

"Oh, you look so pretty," Daisy said when Ellen walked into the kitchen. The widow was putting the final touches on a casserole she was about to pop into the oven.

Ellen's dad sat at the table, munching on Daisy's famous molasses cookies and reading a fishing magazine. He looked Ellen over, then sighed as he laid the magazine on the table with a little more force than necessary. He spoke the same way. "You should be looking like a college girl, Ellen. Not somebody off to take some highfalutin job."

"Dad." Ellen felt like he'd let the air out of her confidence balloon. "We've been though this a dozen times, just in the past week."

He frowned. "You don't seem to be listening to me."

"Yes, I do. But I'm a grown woman. I have to start making my own way."

"You're not supposed to be a grown woman. You're a college-aged kid."

Fighting the emotion his comments evoked, she looked at her watch. "I have to go."

She stole a look at Daisy, who gave her a sweet, sympathetic look. The older woman mouthed, "You're okay," and smiled.

Ellen tried to get back into her good mood, but her dad had a way of spoiling it. Whatever had happened to that good-natured man who used to be her dad?

He'd said more than once that when Ellen's mom died two years ago, something had died inside him. Maybe he was right.

All Ellen knew was that she just couldn't do anything to please him anymore. And at a time when she needed him most, since her mom was no longer here, he remained distant.

Moments later, Ellen walked through one of the many glass doors at the front of the conference registration building. She turned to her left and ascended the curved stairs. At the top, she stepped onto the carpet of a long room surrounded by a wrought-iron railing. She looked down upon the lobby, decorated with cozy-looking furniture surrounded by potted plants and small trees. The tall glass windows, two stories high, revealed a spectacular display of mountainsides, coming alive with the look of spring.

Remembering the assistant's directions, she walked to her left again, pushed open one of the double doors, and made her way down a long hallway to an open door labeled "Richard Williams, Director of Human Resources."

Ellen stood for a moment and breathed a silent prayer for this interview to go well. This was Missy's fifth day at the preschool. She loved the activities and the teachers more each day. When Ellen had questioned her, she'd said she missed her old friends but had made new ones. She was eager to go each morning and see the cat and ducks. She'd begun to beg for a kitten of her own.

In a way, Ellen regretted not having thought of Ridgeway's preschool or day care in the first place.

Another failing of hers?

But then, it had worked well, her and Missy being at Little Tykes together. That had perhaps been best. She had thought it God's will. If so, was it now God's will that she be fired? Confusion rang dominant in her mind. She must put aside the idea of failure and walk into that office with confidence. Otherwise, she'd never be hired.

"Come on in," a female voice called.

Ellen realized she had been staring at the maroon carpet in the hallway. She looked ahead at a very pregnant woman who waddled across the floor, opened a file drawer, and slipped a folder into it. "I'm Ellen Jonsen."

"Hi. I'm MaryJo." She patted her protruding abdomen. "And this is Tyler. I can tell he's going to be a professional football kicker."

Ellen laughed with her. "Nice to meet . . . both of you."

MaryJo's outgoing manner and animated face put Ellen at ease. She sat in a chair that the assistant indicated. "Mr. Williams is kind of a stickler about time. At four, I'll let him know you're here."

Ellen glanced at the clock on the wall. Seven minutes to wait. At least she wasn't late for this "stickler about time."

Ellen needn't have worried about time crawling, however. After

MaryJo questioned whether she'd ever be able to walk across a room again without waddling from side-to-side, she began talking about her baby. She slowly lowered herself into the leather chair behind her desk and expelled a deep breath as if sitting down had been quite a chore. After that, Ellen learned all about baby Tyler.

❧

Richard Williams closed the "desperate" file after making notes about his impression of the applicant. Several items raised warning flags. But that's why a person in his position was needed—to weed through such things.

The wall clock indicated he had five minutes before the scheduled appointment. He expected punctuality but felt no need to give the impression he wanted employees on the job early. He could hear voices in the outer office, but a five minute wait would be best.

He turned the swivel chair to face the windows that revealed the panoramic view of mountainsides, lushly green. A week had passed since the big storm in the area. All looked bright on the horizon.

A sudden sense of restlessness assaulted him. It happened occasionally. Even a line of poetry trotted through his brain: *Spring is when a young man's fancy turns to love.* With a mental shake of his head and a wry grin, he reminded himself he wasn't a spring chicken anymore, at age thirty-four. And he'd redefined the definition of love eons ago.

Besides, spring was nearing its end. The rains, storms, and wind had subsided, bringing in the long-anticipated May flowers that would be followed by June's mild temperatures and the busy schedule at the conference center. Summer was knocking at the door.

Like a knock on his consciousness, his intercom sounded. "Mr. Williams. Your four o'clock appointment is here."

Richard turned toward the desk. "Send her in, please."

He touched the knot on his tie, although knowing it was still in place. It had nowhere else to go. That taken care of, he cleared his throat and was ready to stand when the hesitant applicant would enter as if she held the key to her future.

Richard felt first impressions were important. His brought surprise. In no way did this applicant appear desperate. Ellen Jonsen made a favorable impression as far as looks were concerned. The overall picture was of an attractive young woman, conservatively dressed, nice, nothing to detract, positively or negatively. He'd say . . . average. She looked to be in her mid-twenties, as typed on the application form.

He stood. "Miss Jonsen."

She nodded.

He reached his hand across his desk. "I'm Richard Williams."

They shook hands. "Please be seated."

She sat opposite him in one of the brown leather chairs with arms.

Upon closer look, he realized she wasn't exactly average. He watched as she pushed her light brown hair away from her face. She was quite pretty. Her eyes seemed to be a soft brown with a hint of gold, perhaps reflecting the sunlight shining outside the windows behind him.

She lowered her hand and grasped her purse as if someone might snatch it. That spoke of uncertainty. She looked across at him with concern in her eyes.

He wanted to set her mind at ease. She was certainly qualified to work in the preschool, day-care center, or in the children's summer programs.

But her reference was a coworker, not the director. He opened the folder in front of him. "I see your reference is Heather Cannington." He looked across at her. "A few years back, a young woman by that name worked here a couple of summers with the girl's camp."

"Yes, she did. Between high school and college, then after her first year of college."

"And she's working at Little Tykes now?"

"No, she's working on her master's thesis in child development and goes to the school quite often, doing research. She helps out too. Several times a week, for several months, she's observed my work."

Richard leaned back against his chair. "So Miss Cannington is going into child development?"

"No. She wants to write children's books. She thought a minor in

English lit and a major in child development would give her a good background."

"Mmmm. Impressive."

"So you . . . do remember her?" Miss Jonsen asked tentatively.

Richard laughed lightly. "Oh, I remember—" He stopped and covered what he was about to say with a clearing of his throat. Some things were confidential. And what he remembered had happened several years ago. "She was . . . interesting." He forced the smile from his face and turned his attention to the application.

This interview was not about Heather Cannington but about Miss Jonsen. And two questions loomed large in his mind. Why was she changing jobs, since this one paid no more than she had been making? And why was her letter of reference from a student doing research for her master's degree instead of from a coworker or the director?

The brief turn of her lips upward when he'd smiled at her indicated to him she wasn't really in a smiling mood.

He clasped his hands together, then rested them on top of her application. No need to rehash the obvious. She was twenty-four and had majored in communications at the area university.

"You didn't graduate from college?"

"No, I left midway through my senior year. Are you only considering college graduates?"

Richard felt on the defensive for a moment. "No, no. We have some summer employees who are just entering college in the fall. I was just curious."

She nodded but offered no explanation. He realized the issue was really none of his business. He leaned back against his leather swivel chair and let his hands rest on his pants legs. "Tell me, Miss Jonsen. If you were to leave this world and could come back as an animal, what animal would it be?"

Her eyes widened. Very expressive eyes. Sort of golden brown. Hazel, he supposed.

"Is this a quiz or something to see what I'd say to children about, um, animals?"

Apparently, she wasn't into playing games today. Except, this wasn't a game. He took it seriously. "No game. It's something I ask most applicants. How about playing along?" He'd just said it wasn't a game, yet he'd asked her to play along. What was happening to his professionalism? Just because it wasn't everyday such an attractive, appealing woman walked into his office. And he shouldn't be thinking that way. That's the last thing he needed . . . or wanted. "That's a question I ask those I feel are qualified for a position."

She stared. "Well, I really expect to go to heaven when I die, and I don't believe in reincarnation."

"I understand that. This is a make-believe situation. Just a fun question. Do you mind answering it?"

Suppose she refused? Would he ask her to leave? One thing was for sure—she didn't just go along with something because you asked. She weighed the pros and cons. That was good. Wasn't it?

"I suppose . . ." She spoke up just as he was about to change the subject. "I suppose I'd come back as a bird."

"Bird?"

"Not just any old bird. Like a vulture or anything." She sounded a little self-conscious. "Maybe . . . a finch. No, a canary. Yes." Her eyes brightened. "A canary."

"Why a canary?"

"They're pretty. Yellow."

You're far from yellow—well, her outfit was—but you are pretty. Trying to rein in his straying thoughts, he smiled and nodded at her, saying nothing.

"They fly." She waved her hand. "Just take off into the clear blue sky. That must be a wonderfully free feeling."

Ah, she wanted to be free. Of what? Of whom?

"Oh, and they sing. I don't have a great voice, but I'd love to just sing away as I suspect a canary does. Yes. I'd have to be a singing canary."

She seemed relaxed now. They were in sync. Asking the animal question generally put an applicant at ease. There was always a certain amount of tension, no matter how confident the applicant, since the final outcome rested with him.

"Oh, and I think it would be great to find pieces of colored Easter grass to weave into a nest. Then sit on little tiny eggs and sing until they hatch. And it would be fun being the early bird that gets the worm." She paused. "If . . . I were a canary."

Yes, the nesting instinct. Rearing children seemed to be most women's natural desire. Men's too, for that matter.

His intent had been to have her reveal something about her inner character and not just say something she thought a prospective employer wanted to hear.

"Mr. Williams," she said, "what animal would you be?"

6

*H*er question rendered Richard speechless for a moment. An applicant had never asked that during an interview. After he'd hired Jerry and they'd become friends, Jerry had asked. They'd discussed it and laughed about what kind of animal each might be.

Kidding, Richard had replied, "A louse," before answering Jerry's question seriously.

He believed Miss Jonsen was serious. Come to think about it, she had as much right to know the inner characteristics of people she might work with as those who did the hiring. He answered, "I think I'd be a lion." He raised his hand in a cautionary gesture. "Don't get me wrong. I don't roar a lot."

She laughed lightly, then smiled. A cute dimple punctuated her right cheek. "Why a lion?"

"Protective of my territory, I've been told." He looked at his wristwatch although the clock across from him was clearly visible. "Afraid we'll have to bypass delving into that."

He hoped he'd given the impression there wasn't time to answer. Although he had an inclination toward conversation with Miss Jonsen, he reminded himself of the purpose of their encounter. He looked at the application, although he knew its contents.

When he glanced up again, he asked, "Why did you leave your job, Miss Jonsen?"

Her dimple disappeared. "I was fired."

Her response caught him as off guard as her charisma had. "Fired?"

She nodded. "While on the property, I invited one of the mothers

210

to my church after her child had expressed interest in one of the church's programs. And I openly talked with another person about our mutual faith. Heather, to be exact. I didn't proselytize. We just enjoyed talking about the church, a faith question. It was as natural to me as talking about seeing a certain movie or TV program. I tried, but I can't pretend that God isn't a vital part of my life."

He listened intently as Miss Jonsen related the reasons behind her dismissal. His admiration and respect for her grew. "I see you're looking for full-time or summer work."

"I need full-time work. But I know you hire extra people here for the summer, and that would suit me while I try to find a full-time job in the fall, or I might return to college and get my degree."

"What was your major in college?"

She hesitated. "My plans changed. I was studying communications. I thought about being a TV news reporter, but I doubt there are many openings for that. Now, I'm thinking in terms of teaching kindergarten or first grade."

He could visualize her as a news reporter. She had a good speaking voice. Very articulate. He liked her looks and her uncompromising stance concerning her commitment to the Lord.

She'd be a great addition to the organization. Just one problem. Two actually. One, he had hired all the workers he needed. The preschool and day-care workers had been there for years, and he didn't know of anyone planning to leave. The children's summer program workers had been hired months ago. Many returned from having worked the previous year.

They could always use extra help, but there was the matter of the budget.

He'd wondered if she might consider housekeeping or dining-hall work. But after talking with her, he doubted she'd be interested. Although those positions didn't require skilled training, other than what the organization offered, she definitely was over-qualified.

"I'm sorry." He spread his hands. "We don't have any openings in day care or the summer children's program. Or in any department for which you're qualified."

He really was sorry. She'd been fired because of her faith. Now she turned to a Christian organization for acceptance. He regretted seeing the hope in her hazel eyes turn to disappointment. "Thank you anyway." She rose from the chair and turned away.

Maybe . . . he shouldn't have made the decision about what kind of job she would accept. "Miss Jonsen."

She stopped but didn't turn toward him when he called her name. "We do have other departments and the possibility of a different kind of position opening up in a few weeks. If you'd be interested—"

She turned, and he saw the light of hope spark her eyes. Her dimple returned. Yes, he believed she was . . . interested.

◦❧

Ellen knew her delight was showing. She couldn't stop smiling.

Richard Williams said, "I'll be out showing Miss Jonsen some of the buildings, MaryJo," and walked ahead to open the door leading into the hallway.

Ellen said, "Bye," to MaryJo, who lifted her eyebrows and made a sign with her thumb and index finger indicating to Ellen that MaryJo knew something she didn't. Likely, the boss didn't usually walk out with a prospective employee.

When Mr. Williams opened the door, then looked around at them, MaryJo took on an innocent look and waved.

Ellen tried to look serious as she passed in front of Mr. Williams. He closed the door behind them and led the way down the hallway. While he pointed out various offices, Ellen glanced at the corresponding names and titles on the closed doors.

In the back of her mind, however, she thought about this man wanting to be a lion.

What characteristics did a lion have? King of the jungle. Well, in reality a lion might be called king of the jungle, but the animal and the jungle belonged to God. The lion just watched over his own territory in a masterful way. Yes, that might fit Mr. Williams. He had the aura of a man in charge, one who knew his territory. But what did being "protective" of his territory mean? Don't invade it?

Somewhere she'd read that people saying they were a certain animal revealed something about their basic character—what they were, or sometimes what they were not but would like to be.

She had the impression Mr. Williams had lion characteristics. She could almost picture him like Mufasa in *The Lion King,* standing on a high rock overlooking his domain. Mr. Williams' position wasn't that high; however, he did have the aura of one who would elicit a second look.

Although he wasn't the most handsome man in the world—but then neither were most men on TV and in the movies who held such a distinction—she liked his looks. Nothing detracted, and she supposed her first impression was of a man in control, with dark hair, dark eyes, a conservative haircut, and wearing a conservative suit and tie. His shirt wasn't white though, but light blue.

She had the notion that the saying the eyes are the mirror of the soul held a lot of truth. She liked to watch a person's eyes as they talked. But during the interview, she got the distinct impression that Mr. William's dark eyes sought the same thing from her. His gaze seemed to penetrate her mind, as if he could read it.

That thought would have brought a blush if she were the blushing kind. She wouldn't want him to know she sat there analyzing him and considering him an attractive man. Not that it was wrong if the thoughts stopped there. Likely, a man who appeared to be in his mid-thirties was married or had someone special.

And she shouldn't be thinking that either. She was not looking for a man. She was looking for a job.

Almost before she realized it, they'd turned a corner, stepped into an elevator, and descended to the lobby where she'd come in.

Last week, she'd felt like the heavens were crying over her predicament. Today she felt as if a whole new world was opening up to her.

Mr. Williams paused for a moment in the spacious lobby, bright with sunlight from the tall windows. "We can sometimes use extra help with registration if there's a sudden increase in conferees," he was saying, as her glance swept up the staircase she had ascended earlier. Her gaze lifted higher to the top of the wooden-beamed cathedral ceiling with recessed lighting and great fans suspended from long golden chains.

"Miss Jonsen."

She returned her attention to him immediately.

"Shall we?" He moved to one of the glass doors with long panes separated by golden bars.

She stepped lively past the tall man. "Sorry. I was admiring the architecture. This building is beautiful. So are the others." She walked past him and onto the concrete porch. "The views are fantastic too."

He motioned down the long porch to his left, and she fell in step beside him as he asked, "Have you lived here long?"

"All my life," she admitted. "And I guess I take the mountains for granted to a certain extent. But never fully. It's always different. Each spring is like a new world." She liked the way he looked at her and smiled as if he knew what she meant. "And fall."

He nodded. "And summer. And winter."

"Exactly. And my being here is just another reminder of God's magnificent creation." She remembered the previous week's storm and how dismal everything had looked. One's outlook depended a lot on one's situation. But God's creation remained the same, even if one didn't appreciate it.

Mr. Williams must have sensed how she felt. He spoke of sitting in his office with his back to the view and how he could stare at it as it seemed to change daily. He laughed lightly. "I understand why I must sit facing a wall instead of the windows."

She laughed with him.

They walked down steps, up others, down a walkway, up steps again, onto another concrete porch, and into another building. "Rooms are in this building," he explained. "And also the cafeteria."

After walking down another long hallway, they entered the cafeteria, where he spoke to a couple of workers making coffee in huge urns. Then he led Ellen into a spacious dining room, filled with round tables that would seat six or eight. Only half the tables were spread with white tablecloths.

"We have a small conference in right now," Richard said. "Soon we'll be overflowing."

Ellen knew what he meant. The area was inundated with tens of thousands of people during tourist season. Would he offer her a job in the cafeteria?

As if she'd asked the question, he answered. "Right now we don't have any openings. But when the new hotel opens, and if we book additional conferences, we might need more help."

He led her out a back door, up more steps, past the bookstore, offices, gift shop, and up toward other buildings. "We use housekeepers in all the buildings, of course." He pointed out the various buildings that housed conferees.

"Up there is the new hotel," he said. "Do you think you'd be interested in a temporary, maybe even part-time job in the cafeteria or in housekeeping? Hey, we'd better move out of the middle of the street."

Ellen realized they'd come out the back way and were standing opposite the area where she drove to the preschool in the mornings. Parents were driving up. Others were already coming out with their children. She needed to answer his question. She couldn't honestly say she would like housekeeping or cafeteria work. But she could certainly accept that if nothing else were available. "That may be right for me at this time, since I'm thinking of returning to college in the fall."

"Would you like to see the hotel?" He laughed and added quickly, "When the traffic clears a little. It's not finished, but—"

She interrupted him with a shake of her head. "I would, but it's after four." She had picked up Missy at two all week, but today she'd received permission from Carol to leave Missy for day care. She saw a worker standing with Missy in the doorway. "I have to pick up Missy."

Before Ellen had time to explain, Missy saw her, broke away from the worker, and ran toward Ellen in spite of the worker calling her back. Ellen hurried across the street and toward the bridge to meet the little girl, afraid she might run out into the street.

"Mommy, Mommy!" Missy called.

Ellen laughed as Missy ran up, waving a bright yellow paper plate the size of a saucer while making a buzzing sound.

Bzzzzz. She turned the plate so a black triangle touched Ellen's arm. "You got stung."

Ellen pretended. "Ouch! Let me see that."

Missy held up the plate so she could see. "It has wings."

"I see." Ellen touched the translucent wings, made of waxed paper and taped onto the saucer. "That's a beautiful bee."

Suddenly, she realized that Richard Williams stood nearby, leaning back against the railing, watching them. Instinctively, she said what she'd normally say. "Now say hello to Mr. Williams." She glanced at Richard. "This is Missy. She's my—"

Being obedient, Missy said "Hello" before Ellen could complete her sentence, and Richard's action took Ellen by surprise. He knelt in front of Missy, balanced without his knees touching the floor of the bridge. How thoughtful that he'd stoop down to Missy's level.

"You wanna get stung by my bee?"

Richard laughed. "It would be an honor to be stung by such a fantastic bee."

"Bzzzz." She turned the bee so it stung his hand.

"Hey, he has eyes."

Missy's blond curls bounced with the nodding of her head. Little flecks of sunlight danced in her blue eyes. "I colored them."

"Very nice. And it's very nice to meet such a pretty little girl, Missy. You have dimples, like your mom."

Missy corrected him. "She just has one. I have two."

"So I see," he said. His fingers touched the bridge to help with balance, then he stood.

Ellen realized how at ease he was with Missy. Did he have children? Not wearing a wedding ring didn't always mean a man wasn't married.

Missy tugged on Ellen's skirt. "Can we get some honey? Bees make honey."

"We'll talk later, Missy." She turned to Richard. "I can take Missy home and come back if you want me to see the hotel, or—"

He was shaking his head before she got halfway through the sentence. He looked around, acknowledging a couple of workers and a parent. His glance fell upon Missy, now exchanging bee stings with a little boy. He lifted his arm and looked at his watch, then back at her. "Well, I need to get back. My administrative assistant will be in touch. Thanks for your interest."

She nodded. "Thank you."

She wanted to tell him this could be an answer to prayer. She wanted to hug him right then and there for making it probable for her to have a job and for Missy to be in such a wonderful preschool that she loved already. She extended her hand.

He took her hand and released it almost as soon as he touched it. Nope, a hug wouldn't have done.

Heather had said, "He's a neat guy." Ellen agreed. She did get the feeling that he had a territory she mustn't invade. He was friendly, nice, but had an air of being in his own realm. She was very much aware that he was in charge, that he would make the decision of whether to hire her.

"It's been nice meeting you, Miss Jonsen."

She detected a slight pause before he hastily added, "You have a beautiful little girl there."

Suddenly, it dawned on her how this looked. She was a "Miss." But a child called her "Mommy."

$\mathcal{E}$llen gazed after Richard Williams as he hastened down the road and strode across the concrete walk.

She loved Missy calling her "Mommy" instead of Ellen. She would not try to explain that away. It would be like a mother denying her own child. She couldn't call out to Richard Williams that she was not Missy's mommy, and she definitely could not say such a thing in front of Missy. She'd rather lose out on the job than hurt that child in any way.

"Come on, Missy. We need to go."

On the way home, Missy chattered away about what she'd done that day. Ellen listened, but at the same time, her thoughts drifted elsewhere.

She'd never forget when Missy had first called her "Mommy." It all began when Missy was three. The little girl had always called Ellen "Eh-wen," but then their mother died. Dad hadn't felt comfortable taking complete responsibility for a three year old. After seeking advice from her dad, friends, acquaintances, and the pastor, Ellen had finished the semester at the university, then hadn't registered for additional classes.

Her dad had encouraged to continue her education. "I'm grieving too, Dad," she'd said. "I'm sure it's in a different way than you. But I don't want to study. I just lost my mother. So has Missy. My school work doesn't hold the importance it held before Mom died."

He'd said they'd talk about it later. He hadn't protested during the next months, as Ellen took over the household chores and the primary care of Missy. "I love doing this, Dad," she'd said many times.

He'd nodded and turned away. But not before she saw the moisture in his eyes. Almost daily he told her that he appreciated all she did.

Most days at some point, Missy would go from room to room, calling for and trying to find her mommy. When she cried for Mommy, Ellen was there. When she awoke from a dream or nightmare and called for Mommy, Ellen hurried to her. When she fell and wailed, "I want my mommy," Ellen consoled her. At times, Ellen let Missy sleep with her. Ellen understood. She had her own dreams about her mom, and a hollow spot was in her heart that nothing could fill. Mom had been a vital part of her life. Ellen felt Missy was handling the loss better than she and Dad.

They'd told the little girl often that Mom was in heaven with Jesus. They'd painted a beautiful word picture of heaven. "Can I go?" Missy had asked, her eyes wide with excitement.

"No, Darling. God wants us here until He's ready for us to die. God decides when He wants us to be in heaven."

Her little lips pouted. "I want to see Mommy."

"I know, Honey. Tell you what. Let's look at the scrapbooks and pictures. We will remember the good times we had with Mommy."

Ellen had hugged Missy. "I'll be your mommy."

She hadn't meant that Missy should call her that, but from that point on, Missy had started calling Ellen "Mommy." A few times, Ellen had explained, "I'm Ellen. Your mommy is in heaven."

Missy had looked at her with big blue eyes. She accepted whatever Ellen told her. But the next day at school, Missy had said, "Mommy, look what I did." And Ellen had stopped trying to convince Missy to call her "Ellen."

And now nothing would make Ellen call Richard Williams and explain the situation.

❧

Richard marched across campus, feeling the heat, not only of the bright afternoon sun, but from his quick stride and his frustration. He removed his suit coat and tossed it onto his shoulder.

Miss Jonsen had a child. One she hadn't bothered to mention.

Closer to the buildings, he strode along the concrete passage in the shade of the overhanging branches of oaks and maples. He wondered if he had overlooked something on her application.

He returned to the office. MaryJo had already gone. He went to his desk and looked at the application form. There were squares into which one could mark married, single, divorced, widowed. Under marital status, Miss Jonsen had checked "Single."

Had she been in such a rush on the day she filled out the application that she'd neglected to respond to all the questions? He saw the note from Carol. It seemed likely that Carol would have written the note after talking with Miss Jonsen about enrolling Missy in day care, rather than only talking with her about a possible job.

Why hadn't she mentioned her child? Having seen Miss Jonsen with the little girl, he had no doubt of the love between them.

If she'd never married, she possibly wouldn't feel comfortable talking about that.

He could understand that. Some things were best buried in the past. And he wasn't thinking only of Miss Jonsen. Things in his past were better left behind him.

However, those thoughts served no productive purpose, so he busied himself with jotting down some ideas he had about the new hotel dedication to be discussed at the next meeting of department heads.

Glancing at Miss Jonsen's folder that he'd laid aside, he told himself once again that while he could wonder, his place was not to judge.

8

On Saturday morning, Ellen awoke at her usual early morning hour. Her dad almost always made whatever she and Missy wanted for breakfast. He'd done that when she was growing up, but he'd steered clear of household chores. Now, Daisy did most of those.

Saturdays were Ellen's time to catch up on all the things she couldn't get to during the week. Having a little girl around meant there was always laundry to do. Also, that was her only day for getting a haircut, buying personal items, and doing something fun with Missy.

Normally, she slept in for about thirty minutes or just lay in bed enjoying a short period of time before starting her hectic day of taking care of necessities and spending quality time with Missy. Often on Saturday, Missy came in to Ellen's bedroom, and they'd read books together in bed or watch a cartoon.

Ellen had too much on her mind to just lie there this morning. Besides, the smell of bacon frying in the pan and the voices of her Dad and Missy beckoned her into the kitchen.

Yawning, she walked into the kitchen and pushed her hair away from her face. "Mornin', Sugar Foot," she said to Missy. "Hi, Dad. Smells great."

Her dad returned the greeting. "The water's boiling for eggs. You want two?"

"That's great."

Missy looked up from the Barbie doll she was dressing. "Why you call me Sugar Foot?"

"Because you're so sweet."

"My foot is sweet?"

Ellen and her dad laughed.

"Sure."

"Just one of them?"

"No. I guess I could call you Sugar Feet."

Missy giggled. "You can call me Barbie."

Her dad brought the bacon to the table. Both Ellen and Missy reached for a piece.

He stood for a moment, and Ellen looked up, chomping on the bacon.

He said, "I'm taking Miss Sugar Feet Barbie here to that new Disney movie this afternoon."

Missy cried, "Ohhh," and rushed over and hugged him around the waist. "You're the bestest Pa-Pa in the world."

He patted the top of head. "You'd better tend to your Barbie and let me get back to the stove, or I'll be the worst cook in the world." The affection in his eyes, looking at Missy, touched Ellen's heart. They both needed that little girl so much.

Ellen swallowed the bite of bacon. "A movie sounds great. What time, so I can be ready?"

Her dad took an incredible length of time before answering. "Um, Miss Daisy's going with us."

"Oh." Ellen started to say, "The more the merrier," but something about the way he looked at her before turning away and walking to the stove gave her the impression she wasn't invited.

She talked to his back. "If you'd like, I can have supper ready when you get home."

He stirred the boiling eggs that didn't need to be stirred. "We'll just go to the cafeteria. Missy would like that."

Several questions popped into Ellen's head. Was she losing her mind, or was everybody turning against her? Was she doing nothing right anymore? Had she begun to take everything too personally?

"Well." She tried to sound cheerful. "Don't let her eat too much popcorn and candy."

He looked over his shoulder and peered above his eyeglasses. "I think I can handle this. I raised you, didn't I?"

Was this one of those kidding times . . . or was he reprimanding her? *Don't be paranoid, Ellen,* she cautioned herself. *Take it as playful bantering.* "Yeah. Mom always said that." She laughed lightly. "But I loved that candy and popcorn. I'm glad you didn't listen." She tried to mean that, although there was more information around nowadays about too many sweets than when she was growing up. And moms seemed more cautious than dads about such things anyway.

But I'm not a mom . . . so everyone tells me.

❧

When Dad left with Missy to pick up Miss Daisy, the last thing he said to Ellen was, "Go out tonight. Have a good time."

Ellen stared after him. Go out? Where? With whom? The idea of "going out" hadn't crossed her mind since her mother had died. Her college-girl persona had died with her mother, and a mature outlook on life had been born.

Although she missed her mom, she had dwelt more on what Missy had lost. Ellen had years and memories. Missy had just begun to know the mom who adopted her. Ellen had tried to take her mom's place. Had wanted to.

And now, she was being constantly harangued by implications that she hadn't . . . or shouldn't.

Ellen went into the bathroom to straighten up. She smiled and shook her head to see the wreck one little girl could make of a room just by taking a bath. She dried off a couple of toys and put them on the corner shelf, returned the soap to its dish, and wrung out the washcloth and hung it over a towel rack. She rinsed the tub with the showerhead, put the bath mat on the side of the tub, then wiped up splotches of water with the towel that had been tossed carelessly on the floor.

That done, she looked at the now-neat bathroom. A child took a lot of time and effort. Sometimes it seemed there was never enough time to keep up with the needs nor to give Missy all the attention she deserved.

Ellen felt tears smart her eyes. The house was silent. No TV. No little child. Just Ellen and her thoughts. She felt her mother's absence keenly.

No way would she trade that little girl of hers for something so meaningless as a clean bathroom, a silent house, a joyless life.

She needed to talk to someone.

After putting in a load of laundry, she called Heather, then made dinner reservations at the Chinese restaurant.

❧

"I know I've been a hard pill to swallow this past week, Heather." Ellen sat across from her friend at the restaurant. "You should be home studying."

Heather objected. "I need a diversion from all that required reading and studying. And you know, as much as I wanted the two of us to be roommates, I don't know if I would get through this master's deal if we were together all the time."

"Well, now, that's a fine howdy-do."

Heather laughed. "It's a compliment. We'd be out doing the town or yak-yakking all the time. The way it is, I'm either in class or holed up in my room at home, frying my brain. Oops! With required reading, I'm talking about."

They both leaned back as the waitress brought their menus and put glasses of water on the table.

"Oh, by the way," Ellen said after they had ordered. "Richard Williams is still the director of human resources at Ridgeway. He remembered you."

Heather grinned. "Well, haven't you realized I'm unforgettable?"

Ellen laughed lightly. "Actually, he implied that. He started to say something about you and got a weird look on his face like he was trying not to laugh. He definitely remembered something about you."

Heather cried out. "Oh, no!" She placed her hand over her mouth and looked around. A couple at a nearby table looked back curiously. She leaned toward Ellen and spoke in a lower tone. "I'm so sorry, Ellen. Maybe I shouldn't have been your reference after all. I didn't think he'd remember *that!*"

Ellen was puzzled. "What?"

"I told you about it. Jeff and I went for a hike and got lost."

"Oh yeah." Ellen cast her a teasing look. "You two were lost overnight, as I remember."

"Well, believe me, we held hands during that all-night trek. Good thing it was a clear night, although the forest was pretty dark at times. Anyway, Jeff called and had somebody from Ridgeway come and pick us up. Mr. Williams wanted to see us right away. After all, Jeff was a wilderness guide. He's not supposed to get lost. I think Mr. Williams was trying to find out if we were really lost or just took a hike for indiscreet reasons."

"Well, which was it?"

"Really, Ellen. What a question. Don't you know the answer?"

"Sure. Indiscreet reasons. You were crazy about Jeff."

Heather scoffed. "Now those dark patches of forest were interesting. But neither of us were crazy enough to deliberately spend the night in a snake- and bear-infested forest."

Ellen laughed. "You've lived an exciting life at times, that's for sure."

"Wait 'til you hear what I did to Patsy." Heather's gaze lifted to the ceiling and back again to Ellen. "I can't believe I did it."

"Oh, Heather. You didn't talk about me, did you?"

"Not directly. I didn't even go back for a week. I knew I had to have a cooling off period or I'd give her a piece of my mind. The worst piece, I might add."

Ellen smiled at her friend. She appreciated her loyalty. "It's not worth fighting over."

"She defended firing you, although I didn't attack her. I didn't accuse her of a thing. But the last thing I said to her was that Jesus loves her."

Ellen's mouth dropped open. She didn't know whether to commend or reprimand Heather. "That's the last thing she'd want to hear."

"I know. At first, I wanted to say something to get back at her. But I refrained. Since you and I were both open about being Christians, I knew I mustn't do or say anything to make Patsy have more to hold against Christianity. I didn't plan to say that, but when I did, the strangest thing happened. She became quite serious. I mean it. I really like Patsy. She's a good person and to be admired. She runs a great school."

Ellen agreed with that. "You think she thought you meant it?"

Heather shook her head. "Probably not. She fired you for singing 'Jesus Loves Me.' She could have thought I was being disrespectful."

The waitress set their food before them. They bowed their heads, and Ellen said grace. As soon as she finished and they'd both taste-tested and approved their food, Heather insisted Ellen tell all about the interview.

Between bites, Ellen told Heather how well things went until Mr. Williams met Missy. "I didn't even mention Missy during the interview. I didn't want him to think I was trying to push my way into a job by enrolling Missy in the preschool."

"Didn't you do that at Little Tykes?"

"Not really. Patsy was sympathetic about our situation with Mom dying and my needing to find a place for Missy, and I mentioned I'd be looking for a job. She initiated the conversation from there. She asked me to tell the story that first day, then I was a volunteer for quite awhile before she hired me. I didn't expect that. I don't want someone to give me a job out of sympathy, and I don't want it to look like I'm trying to manipulate my way into a job."

"But what's it going to look like if you don't explain about Missy? I mean, you said she called you Mommy."

Ellen took a deep breath and let it out. "It's going to look like I have a child who I didn't mention."

Heather nodded in agreement.

"Heather, there was a place on the application where one could list the names of children and ages. I am at such a loss in what to do anymore. I didn't have to do that with Patsy. She knew my situation and that I was Missy's sister. I didn't put it on the Ridgeway application because legally Missy isn't my daughter. To put her down would look like she's my dependant or that I have sole responsibility for her, which would affect my working hours. That's not how it is. Dad can drive Missy where she needs to go. Or even Daisy." She made a helpless gesture with her hands.

"Ellen, do you think you should clarify the situation with Mr. Williams? How will he look at this? You didn't mention that you had a child. But a child called you Mommy?"

226

"Heather, I wish you wouldn't ask questions—just tell me what to do."

"I don't know what to do anymore than you, Ellen. I just wonder how it might affect him. How would it affect you?"

Ellen could answer that with immediacy. "Adversely."

"Maybe you should clarify it with him."

Ellen sighed. "You know, it's just the title 'Mommy' that causes any problem. Patsy called me a liar. Dad reminded me I'm not Missy's mom. I wish Dad would let me adopt her."

"Have you asked him?"

"No. The time never seems right. I didn't know for awhile if I could or should try and be Missy's mom. But I do know now. I wanted to wait until Dad got over Mom's dying. But Heather, he seems to be getting deeper into some kind of depression. There's something wrong. It's like he resents my mothering Missy, when he had appreciated it until recently."

"Talk to him."

Ellen nodded. "I'll have to. Even though he's not very receptive to anything I do or say nowadays."

❧

Jon Jonsen had to drive by his house when taking Daisy home. He glanced at his carport and stated the obvious, "Ellen's car isn't there. I guess she took my advice and went out for the evening."

That's what he'd encouraged her to do, but it made him uneasy. He understood it all too well. He was uneasy when Ellen took over the role of mother to Missy, and he was uneasy at the thought of his taking over full responsibility.

"She needs to get out once in awhile, Jon."

After driving a few blocks farther, he pulled into Daisy's driveway. "Missy still asleep?"

Daisy looked back. "Dead to the world."

Jon switched off the engine. He could talk to Daisy. She'd been through losing a husband and understood how devastating that could be. At the same time, he wondered if it was easier for a woman. They could do so many things. "I've put too much responsibility on Ellen. It was easy to do after Mary died. Ellen just picked up with Missy where Mary left off. I don't know how to do that, Daisy."

She patted his hand. "You do fine, Jon. You two love each other. That's the important thing."

There was no denying that. "But Daisy. I have this heart valve thing that slows me down. The docs say it won't kill me if I take it easy. I'm not up to running after a little girl. And what happens in her teen years? I'm afraid I'm not the best person for her."

"You're a great Pa-Pa."

He nodded. "Yes, but not the dad she needs."

"There's Ellen. And she'll marry someday."

Jon sighed. "That's what worries me, Daisy. She doesn't go anywhere to meet anybody. And the field is now limited since she's taken on the care of Missy. It's just not right to let her do it."

He wished Daisy would contradict him. Or that his own mind could contradict him. But Daisy just sat there, squeezed his hand, and looked out at the darkening sky.

That was something he didn't like and did like about Daisy. She didn't tell him what to do when he needed somebody to do that. But he did like the fact they could just sit in comfortable silence.

"You never can tell how life's going to turn out," he said after a long moment. "Mary and I looked forward to my retirement from the post office. She was going to quit work too. Of course, we couldn't foresee that accident."

He continued reminiscing. "We were going to buy a camper and make payments on that. Take Missy with us and travel. See America." He scoffed. "I don't have to worry about money now. Life insurance took care of that. The house is paid off. I have a savings account, and nothing to spend it on."

Oh, he knew a lot of good could be done with that money, but he just had no sense of motivation in particular. He needed his heart to be in anything he did, and he felt like his heart had lost its capacity to feel. He touched his chest with his left hand. "I have a big rock where my heart used to be. Maybe it was buried along with Mary."

"I know how you feel." Daisy moved her hand away from his and onto her lap. "But the heart is an amazing thing, Jon. It has all those arteries and veins. And just imagine when one's heart isn't working right, they can go in there and clean out those arteries that keep the blood from flowing right. And think of all those bypass surgeries they do. They don't take the heart out. They just clean up what's messy or make a new path. The heart can handle a lot of redoing and be about as good as new."

"I was talking about emotions, Daisy."

"Well, so was I, Jon."

She smiled sweetly, said "Bye," and got out of the car.

Jon stared after her until she disappeared into her house and shut the door. His fingers tapped on the steering wheel. Sometimes that woman said the strangest things.

$$\mathcal{9}$$

*F*irst thing Monday morning, Richard spied Ellen Jonsen's folder on his desk. Whatever her personal situation, the fact remained that she needed a job. More than that, her child needed her mother to have a job. Now he understood why she wanted a job immediately and was willing to take anything, full time, part-time, or temporary. How difficult it must be to say, "I have a child, but I've never been married." She might think he'd stand in judgment of her.

Did he?

Most definitely!

He had very strong opinions about such matters. He greatly admired any single woman trying to support her child.

"Where should I file this one?" MaryJo asked upon seeing the folder still lying on the corner of his desk.

"This is a tough one, MaryJo. Apparently, she really needs a job and quickly. I can't use her in the preschool or day care. The summer program is set unless someone cancels, but we can't count on that. I think she'd probably take a housekeeping or cafeteria job, but I doubt she'd stay any length of time. It's not a good practice to hire someone you believe won't stay. Anyway, I can't use her there for a few weeks yet."

MaryJo grimaced. "Yeah. Too bad. I really liked her. I mean, getting fired for talking about your faith. Now that's something."

He thought so too. It spoke well of her. And it was often the failures people have that turn them in the right direction. MaryJo took his silence as not being able to offer a job to Ellen Jonsen. She picked the file up and headed for her office.

Richard prayed about his job. He wanted everyone working at Ridgeway to be in the will of God. He wanted his own life and work to be in God's will. He needed God's wisdom to make decisions, and none were too trivial to pray about.

He hadn't felt a peace about Miss Jonsen. That hadn't happened since the situation with a dining-room worker who told him she had breast cancer and would be taking treatments but needed to work and wanted to work as long as she could. He'd struggled with that. He'd known too many people taking those treatments who grew tired and weak. Would he be helping or hindering her by allowing her to continue working? Finally, he'd told her she could work as long as she was able.

That had turned out to be a wonderful blessing to everyone around her. When she became weak, the cashier exchanged jobs with her. Everyone who knew her situation, admired and respected her. She was a prime example of a woman of faith, ready to leave this world if God so chose, but determined to face each day with faith and joy.

He'd detected some of that kind of strength in Ellen Jonsen.

He wished he could help in some way. If he hadn't seen her child, he likely wouldn't feel so strongly about this.

God, let her find the right job. One You have picked out for her.

Determined to let it go, he turned to the papers on his desk.

He looked up when MaryJo returned to his desk. "I had a thought," she said.

He grinned. "Commendable."

She gave him a mock-mean look. "Really. I'm going to be out of the office for only three weeks after the baby's born." She tapped the folder. "You suppose she could fill in for me?"

Richard hadn't considered that. "You know we talked about calling the temporary secretarial service when you're ready to leave."

She shrugged a shoulder. "We didn't tell them that."

For some strange reason, this began to feel right. Miss Jonsen had said if she got temporary work, she might return to college in the fall. He nodded. "That could work to her advantage—and ours."

MaryJo opened the folder and looked at the application. "She has more skills than I had when I started the job. And it's not likely that the temp service has someone experienced in conference work."

He felt good about this. "Okay, let's give her a try. I'm not trying to rush you, but do you have any idea when you'll be leaving?"

"Yeah." She laughed. "As soon as I can be replaced. It's getting harder and harder to roll myself out of the bed every morning and waddle around here."

"All right. Call Miss Jonsen and see when she can come in. We'll give her and us a week to see how things go."

Richard stared at the door, even after MaryJo had gone into her office and closed it behind her.

Workers at Ridgeway were involved in God's work daily. What better place could there be for a young single mom?

His answer came in the form of a sense of peace.

❧

Ellen didn't want to go to the unemployment office just yet. She hoped she would be hired at Ridgeway for housekeeping or dining room at least for the summer. It might be a couple of weeks yet, but that would give her time to take care of household chores, some deep spring cleaning, take quilts and comforters to the cleaners, do any mending on hers and Missy's clothes. Missy had been experiencing a growth spurt lately and could use some new clothes. She was constantly growing out of her shoes.

After returning from taking Missy to preschool, Ellen encountered Daisy in the kitchen, washing breakfast dishes. Ellen's dad sat on the back deck, reading the morning paper. She pulled out a wrought-iron chair and sat next to him. She spoke softly, so Daisy wouldn't hear. "Dad, Daisy doesn't need to come while I'm not working."

He did not keep his voice low. "Ellen, I can't do that to Daisy. She is my housekeeper and cook. This job helps me and her. Now, do you really think it's fair to put her out of a job just because you lost yours?"

"Well, no, Dad. Not when you put it that way. I just thought maybe she'd like a break. And I can take care of things here."

He sounded as distant as his gaze that swept beyond her to the distant mountains. "I have a better idea. Why don't you go on a vacation? Or even take some summer courses at the university, or something. Ellen, you can go anywhere. I'll foot the bill."

He doesn't want me around anymore. No, don't go there, Ellen. Look at the positive side of what he's saying.

She took a deep breath and spoke as calmly as her emotions would allow. "You know, Dad, that may be a good idea. Missy doesn't have to be in preschool all the time." Ellen didn't think it a good idea to take Missy out of preschool when she was just getting adjusted to the change from Little Tykes. And how could she take a job and say she had to go on vacation first? But she wanted a right relationship with her dad. "Where would you like to go, Dad?"

The way he stared at his paper that she knew he wasn't reading said more than she wanted to believe. Then he said it in words. "No, Ellen. That's not what I mean. Oh, we can all take a vacation before Missy starts kindergarten if we want to. But what I mean is, while you're out of a job, why don't you go somewhere and have fun? Take Heather. Like I said, I'll foot the bill."

He wants me out of here. Why?

She didn't trust her voice, so she simply stood and laid her hand on his shoulder. He still didn't look at her. She dared say only one word. "Thanks."

The call couldn't have come at a better time. Ellen had just splashed cold water on her face after shedding hot tears. Her heart and mind had called out to her mom. Things would be so different had her mom not died. That had changed everything—and her dad most of all. While she longed for comfort and assurance in his arms, she received only condemnation and a feeling that he didn't love her anymore. Did he want her to move out?

Lord, where are You in this? Are You leading? I feel like a lost sheep in need of a Shepherd.

After a deep breath, she tried a cheerful, "Hello."

"Ellen? This is MaryJo at Ridgeway."

Ellen held her breath for a moment. Was this a yes or no or what?

She released a grateful breath when MaryJo asked if she'd like to come in the next morning, on a trial basis, with the possibility of replacing MaryJo while she was on maternity leave.

As MaryJo talked, Ellen's eyes clouded, this time with tears of gratitude. God heard her prayers after all. He was answering. And this was only Monday morning. She'd lost her job on Thursday. Missy had started to school on Friday, she'd been interviewed the following Thursday, and now she had the prospect of a job that excited her even more than working at a hotel or in a cafeteria. She'd be working right next to someone who seemed to be what Heather had described as a "neat" guy—Richard Williams.

🙵

On Tuesday as Richard approached MaryJo's office at nine, he heard voices. When he got to the doorway, he saw MaryJo and Ellen. They stopped their conversation and looked at him as he walked into the office and said, "Good morning."

"Oh, good morning," Ellen Jonsen replied, her words accompanied by a spark in her golden brown eyes and a dimple in her cheek that indicated she was quite pleased. "Thank you so much for this opportunity, Mr. Williams."

"My pleasure," he said. "We'll see how it goes this week and take it from there."

"Yes, Sir."

"MaryJo can fill you in on the basic requirements of the job. If you feel this job suits you, then come into my office before lunchtime, we'll talk, and I'll have you fill out the official forms."

She nodded. As he headed for his office, Richard heard MaryJo begin her instructions. "Let me show you what we have to enter on the computer. That will take up most of your time and concentration."

Richard entered his office and closed the door to give them more privacy. He'd thought of answering the phone himself, then thought better of it. That's something Miss Jonsen needed to learn too, regardless of how busy she might get.

Close to noon, she tapped on his door and spoke softly. "Mr. Williams. Would you like me to come in now?"

"Yes, that would be fine."

Although he wasn't sure he would have thought of her for this job without MaryJo's prodding, he felt good about the decision. He needed to feel that his job was a mission, with purpose.

MaryJo stood back at her desk, holding up her hand, forming an A-OK sign. She was a good judge of character. He'd come to appreciate the insight of a good assistant.

He had no doubt that Ellen Jonsen would do her best.

How good that was would be determined by the end of the week.

"I really appreciate this," Ellen said, even before she sat in the chair across from him, toward which he gestured.

Her eyes held a softness and warmth, full of appreciation. He smiled. Anyone liked to be appreciated.

"How's the instruction going?" he asked. "Is this something you feel you can handle and would like?"

He wondered if her hesitation meant he had asked too many questions at one time or if she had reservations. "I know it would take time for me to catch on to everything. MaryJo's a whiz."

Richard nodded. "True, but she had to learn. She's been here five years."

Ellen's dimple appeared, despite the wariness in her eyes. "I think the job is fascinating. Right now I feel overwhelmed, just because I don't know the routine. But MaryJo has a calendar of events, times, and schedules."

"We all have such calendars," Richard said. "Certain conferences and programs are basically the same during the summer, our prime season. Then, of course, we book new conferences, plan programs, and have to work closely with conference leaders and Ridgeway staff. Our summer youth staff is constantly changing since we employ a lot of college students. They graduate and go on to their careers. We plan some conferences. We assist organizations who plan their own."

Ellen was nodding. "MaryJo has written out so much for me. She's going to write more. I have a feeling much of my time will be taken up reading her notes."

"No one expects you to know everything right away. If you did, my job would be in danger." He hoped his words would dispel any concerns she had. "We all had to learn. And we're still learning. This is a place of both constants and change."

He heard her shaky intake of breath before she spoke. "Mr. Williams, if you think I can fill in for MaryJo, I'll do my best. I'll be honest; it is overwhelming. But I really want to try."

"Part of my job is to guide my assistant," he said. "If you can follow instructions, we should be fine. Of course, you can ask about what you don't know. And too, our volunteers will be trickling in soon. They're invaluable."

He talked to her about the business side of things, such as salary. She would not be entitled to benefits because of her temporary status. He wondered if she had any kind of insurance. He knew that children had periodic and unexpected visits to doctors.

She filled out the necessary forms for withholding taxes and signed the temporary job form that included the rest-of-the-week trial-basis clause.

She handed it to him. "Is that all?"

"Yes, thank you."

She stood. "MaryJo said to tell you we're going to lunch, if that's all right. She wants to start introducing me to the buildings and staff."

He nodded. "That's perfectly all right."

She returned his smile, then left the office.

Richard felt good about this situation. He swivelled around and stared at the old faithful mountainsides, now lushly green. Yes, God had a will for those who believed in Him. And it could be interesting sometimes, watching God work in His mysterious ways.

10

$\mathcal{E}$llen squealed to Heather over the phone. "I got the job! I mean, at least I signed the contract that says I will be temporarily employed if I do okay during this week's trial basis. There's so much to learn, but I really want this job."

By the time she told her dad, she'd calmed down, cautious of his reaction.

Daisy had stayed for supper, during which Missy filled them in about the frog she'd made at preschool, complete with the ribbit-ribbits. Then Ellen told them all about the job.

"Goody, goody," Missy said. "You'll be working close to my school."

"That's right. I could pop in there anytime."

Everyone seemed excited for her. That is, until after Missy left the table to play with her frog. Daisy poured coffee.

The inquisition from her dad began almost immediately. "So, you have to prove yourself before the job is really yours?" he asked.

"Yes, Dad, but I know I can learn how to do the job."

"I have no doubt of that, Ellen. How long does this job last?

"For three weeks after MaryJo has her baby."

He sighed like she was a tremendous disappointment. "Then you'll go into housekeeping or cafeteria work, huh?"

On the defensive, Ellen shot back. "Dad, do you have something against housekeepers?"

He paused, glanced quickly at Daisy, and said, "Not if they're middle-aged women."

Daisy laughed. "He's lucky he didn't say 'old.'"

Ellen and Daisy laughed. Ellen's dad grinned, but he wasn't about to let this go. "I do have something against my college-aged daughter being a housekeeper instead of going to school."

Oh, not again! "Dad, I will register for the fall."

He blew on his coffee, then took a sip, peering over his eyeglasses. "And your boss? You like him?"

Ellen couldn't help but smile. "Very much. He's so nice."

"Is he single?"

Ellen glanced at Daisy, who grinned. They both knew what he was getting at. "Dad, MaryJo said he's never been married."

"How old is he?"

"I'd say mid-thirties."

"Something wrong with him?"

She really couldn't think of a thing wrong with him. "I don't think so, Dad. Just a confirmed bachelor."

Her dad nodded. "I was one of those until I was in my thirties. Then along came your mom. That 'confirmed' changed to 'eligible' right quick."

Ellen saw the shadow cross his face as he whispered, "We had a good life. I miss that." He looked down at his food and moved it around on his plate with his fork.

Daisy broke the silence. "Jon, I'm ready for you to plow my garden if you still want to. Won't be long 'til planting time."

The food suddenly seemed tasteless to Ellen as she watched her dad seem to drift off into another world. Daisy kept talking about planting cool-weather crops first, like spinach. Her dad's moodiness wasn't good for her, and it certainly wasn't good for Missy.

After supper, while her dad watched the news on TV in the living room and Missy played on the swing set in the fenced-in backyard, Ellen helped Daisy with supper dishes. Maybe she could offer some advice.

"Daisy, do you think Dad is regressing?"

"Re—?" She looked at Ellen as if she were the one who had lost her mind. "What do you mean, Honey?"

"I don't know if he just can't get over Mom's dying or what. But he seems so different lately. And he's always at me to enroll in college."

Daisy talked as she scrubbed at spots on the table, invisible to Ellen. "You're under his roof, Ellen. My advice is do as he asks."

That wasn't what Ellen expected. *Under his roof?*

The implication made Ellen feel the same as she had so often lately when talking to her dad. Maybe he wanted her to move out.

Daisy walked closer to Ellen, glanced at the living-room doorway, then spoke in a low tone. "Now I'm not saying he would make you move out, but you need to consider the possibility." She lifted her hands in a surrender gesture. "Now I'm not saying he would. But he is your dad."

That left no doubt in Ellen's mind about whose side Daisy was on, if one were taking sides.

Maybe Daisy could offer some advice in another area.

"Sometimes I feel he doesn't . . ." Ellen's voice broke as she tried to say it. "Doesn't love me anymore."

"Oh, now, Honey, don't ever think that. Sometimes children don't understand when parents are using tough love."

Ellen wanted to scream that she wasn't a child. She was a twenty-four-year old adult taking on the responsibility of a mom. But it wouldn't do any good to say that to Daisy. Nor to her dad, who would simply say, "You're not Missy's mom."

Daisy touched Ellen's arm. "Your dad has loved you for twenty-four years. That hasn't changed, except to grow deeper and stronger."

Ellen attempted a smile. But if her dad still loved her, tough or otherwise, then why didn't she feel it?

❧

Ellen felt great on the job from the time she stepped into MaryJo's office each morning for the rest of the week. In addition to MaryJo's notes, Ellen took some of her own. She realized that a lot of the job did not require initiative on her part but rather responses to upcoming events. She attended a staff meeting and took notes on an event being planned. She answered the phone and learned to check the calendar and the computer for pertinent information.

MaryJo often asked Richard questions about events. He, in turn, informed her of things that needed attention. On Thursday afternoon, MaryJo helped at the registration desk for a conference. After watching for awhile, Ellen registered conferees while MaryJo looked on.

"You don't have to do this often," MaryJo said, "but sometimes an emergency occurs and a worker can't be here. We pitch in wherever needed, whenever possible."

Ellen liked that spirit of cooperation.

And as much as she loved children, she discovered she also loved relating to adults for a change. She realized she'd never related in exactly this way before. She'd been a college student with studies primarily on her mind, then had the responsibilities of caring for a little girl. She believed Missy's welfare must come first and that meant more to her than any job. But she did enjoy being a part of the workplace and feeling that she was making a contribution to a worthwhile organization.

On Friday, Richard asked MaryJo to have lunch with him. Ellen had a strong feeling he wanted to ask MaryJo's opinion of her ability to handle the job for a few weeks. Ellen stayed in the office.

For an hour, Ellen told herself not to be nervous. She'd made no terrible boo-boos during the week that she knew of. MaryJo had been a good teacher. She had a lot to learn, but she'd proved herself capable of learning.

MaryJo returned alone.

Ellen whispered. "Is he coming in?"

"He who?"

"MaryJo, don't tease me. I know you guys had to be discussing me."

"Right. But he likes to be the one to break the news—good or bad."

"And you can't tell me if it's good or bad."

If anyone ever had a "happy face," it was MaryJo. Ellen thought if the news were bad, she'd see sympathy or regret in MaryJo's expression. Now MaryJo turned away.

Ellen decided she would not look at Mr. Williams when he came back into the office. If he called her in and said he didn't think she was right for the job, she wouldn't ask "Why not?" She wouldn't cry. She wouldn't beg. She wouldn't run out the door—or the window!

Or would she?

She felt like a downpour was about to happen just thinking about not fitting in here. She loved it. She liked relating to MaryJo each day on an adult level.

"I've gotta run down the hall a minute," Ellen said after another hour had passed. She grimaced. "Nerves."

MaryJo nodded.

Walking briskly toward the door, Ellen looked back over her shoulder at MaryJo. That was just long enough to hear a yelp of "Ho oh!" from the doorway. She turned to find herself eye-to-tie with Richard Williams. She looked up.

All she could think of in that moment of eternity, about two inches away from him and staring up into his face, was that his eyes held an expression of . . . was that mischief?

"Hey," he said, raising his arms in an "I surrender" position. He held a waxed-paper-wrapped bouquet of flowers in each hand. "I always bring flowers to my administrative assistants, temporary or not, but you don't have to fight me for them."

She heard MaryJo's burst of laughter, but her mind was registering his saying "my assistants," plural. Did that mean she was definitely hired?

Oh, she could hug him! She squelched the urge.

He handed a bouquet of red roses to Ellen. "Welcome aboard. That is, if you take the job."

She could cry. Instead, she said, "Yes," and thanked him. He handed the other bouquet to MaryJo.

"For me?" MaryJo smelled the roses. "Whatever did I do to deserve this, Richard?"

"Nothing at all," he said, as if he meant it. "I'm teaching that son of yours a lesson. If there are two women in an office, never dare to bring flowers to only one."

MaryJo nodded vigorously. "You're very smart, Richard."

He laughed. "I know. That's why I'm the boss."

MaryJo looked at Ellen and mouthed, "He thinks."

Ellen was surprised at his bringing flowers. All week, things had been business-like between them.

"Is there a vase?" she asked.

"Why don't we take them home, since it's the weekend." MaryJo looked at Ellen. "I think you can handle things without me, Ellen. The doctor said I need to stay off my feet. This close, I don't want anything to go wrong. Richard may not know the answers, but you can call me at home if you need me."

He picked up her bouquet. "I'll just take these back."

MaryJo grabbed for them. "Oh, no, you don't."

Laughing, he returned the bouquet to the desk. "By the way," he said, "to celebrate MaryJo's departure and your staying, Ellen, I'm throwing an impromptu cookout at my house tomorrow. Come around four or five. I have a pool. You might like to swim."

"Uh oh," MaryJo said. "That 'impromptu' means BYOF!" She looked askance at Ellen and mumbled, "Bring your own food."

"MaryJo, that's not true. I'm providing the meat—steaks, hamburgers, hot dogs."

"And we just bring the accessories."

"That's all."

Ellen liked the friendly bantering between the two. He glanced from MaryJo to Ellen, the light of humor still dancing in his dark eyes. "MaryJo can give you directions to my place."

"Thank you, Mr. Williams. For . . . everything."

He smiled, and she felt like he had truly given her everything.

"You're welcome," he said. "And feel free to bring a friend. There will be some couples and some singles. And if the word gets around, some party crashers."

She laughed with him. "Thank you."

"Bring Missy if you like. My friend Jerry will likely come and bring his son, Jacob. He and Missy look about the same age. He may even be in her class at preschool."

"I've heard the name," Ellen said. She didn't, however, know which child was Jacob.

After he went into his office and closed the door, Ellen laid her roses on MaryJo's desk. "I know you said he was generous and had a sense of humor, but that's the first I've seen of it."

"He's very serious-minded on the job. I've kind of caught on when he's in the joking mood. Ellen, he's really a great guy."

"I guess so, if he always gives his new employees roses."

"This is news to me." MaryJo's eyebrows moved upward. "I don't remember any flowers when I came to work here. I get a feeling he's not at all sad that I'm leaving." She grinned as if expecting a reply from Ellen.

Ellen headed for the door. "Gotta go. Nerves."

While she arranged the roses in a vase, Ellen told her dad about the cookout.

"That's nice," he said. "You can leave Missy with me."

"But Dad, other children will be there. She'd love it. Mr. Williams said I could bring a friend. It's fine if you want to go with me."

"Ellen, I'm Missy's dad. She calls you Mom. You're my daughter. How's that going to look? We have to go through all those explanations, if anybody dares ask."

Is that what had been bothering him? Ellen had never thought of it in that way. "Dad, I can easily say she's my sister. Missy knows she's adopted and that I'm her sister. She just wants to call me Mommy. Maybe I was wrong to let her do that. But when she lost Mom, she transferred that title to me. It just seemed right at the time."

"Yes," he agreed. "To me too. But now . . ." He shook his head. "I'm re-thinking the whole situation. I think some changes need to be made."

"So do I, Dad. I don't know if this is the time to say it, and . . . it's nothing against you. But would you consider letting me adopt Missy?"

He stared as if she'd struck him. Couldn't he just say no without looking as if she'd committed a crime?

Finally he spoke. "That's not at all what I have in mind, Ellen."

She hugged her arms to herself, feeling a chill.

Her dad turned and walked away.

What did he have in mind?

Saturday morning, Jon went to Daisy's and began tilling her garden spot. He paused and wiped sweat from his brow on his sleeve as she brought out two glasses of lemonade. They sat in wooden chairs on the back deck. He told her about the cookout.

"Now, Jon. It's a beautiful day. It's Saturday. How could you think Missy shouldn't go to that cookout?"

"I don't know what to do anymore. What's best. What's right. I pray. I try to listen, but . . . I don't know. That job has made a huge difference in Ellen. Kind of like a lightbulb was turned on inside her. She loves the job. She likes her boss. And that's good. Ellen should be thinking of herself. Her own future, instead of only Missy."

"She can't, Jon. She took Mary's place with that little girl."

"I know. But none of us could foresee how this would play out." He had already told Daisy much of the story. Mary's niece, Leanne, at age fourteen had become pregnant. Neither she nor her mom could care for the baby properly, and they had planned to put it up for adoption. Mary took Missy to keep her from being adopted by strangers. She thought Leanne might change her mind after she grew up a little.

"Mary and I fell in love with Missy but considered ourselves foster-grandparents. Then Leanne went back to school, got into activities, got the lead part in the school play. A year passed. Leanne's mom said Leanne was getting on with her life and something had do be done legally. Mary wanted to adopt her," Jon said. "She was part of our family. I went along with it. Our grandchildren called us Ma-Ma and Pa-Pa. Before we adopted Missy, that seemed the best title for us. After the adoption, I thought it best for her to continue calling me Pa-Pa. Mary began to call herself Mommy to Missy."

He sighed. "Is Ellen right and am I wrong? Oh, I know we're responsible for that little girl, and I love her with all my heart. But am I right for her?"

"Jon, that child loves you."

"I know. I'm her Pa-Pa. I'm even more of a Pa-Pa to her than to my grandchildren since we adopted her. But suppose Ellen wasn't in the picture? What then? I mean, Mary took care of little girl things. I wouldn't know if Missy needs a haircut or how to make a ponytail or when she should or shouldn't get her ears pierced and things like that."

"But Ellen is here."

"Suppose she wasn't? Would you be willing to take on that kind of responsibility day-after-day, day-in and day-out?"

He thought she'd never answer. He didn't seem to be getting through to anybody nowadays. Finally, she looked him in the eye with that composed expression of hers.

"Jon, you have to find your own answers to how you will live your life. And about Missy."

He scoffed. "Daisy, God's supposed to speak through people. You're a big one on prayer. I thought He might've told you something."

She got that huffy look as she straightened her shoulders and scooted her chair back from the table. "Jon, God tells me my answers. Not yours."

She lifted her lemonade to her lips as he mumbled, "Thanks a lot!"

Well, that got him nowhere. He'd try again. "Ellen should be out finding herself a husband instead of being a mom."

Daisy answered quickly. "She loves that child as much as you, Jon."

"I know. But it's not fair to her. If Ellen wasn't around, what kind of dad would I be? Just me and Missy? Am I best for her? I'm not very exciting."

The next thing he knew, Daisy reached across the table and laid her hand on his. She spoke in that soft way of hers. "Now, Jon, don't put yourself down that way. 'Exciting' depends upon one's definition, I suppose."

Daisy got up and took their empty glasses into the house.

Jon went back to his plowing, trying to figure out Daisy's unexpected "exciting" response.

Richard couldn't have ordered a better day for a cookout. Who could ask for more than a day in the mid-seventies, a cool breeze, and a clear sky, accompanied by his spectacular view?

Maybe one thing—it would be nice if Ellen showed up, since he'd planned this primarily for her and MaryJo.

Just as he was about to give up on Ellen's coming, he saw a little tow-headed girl in shorts and shirt, with a tote bag over her arm, run around the side of his chalet. She stopped, stood with her hands on her hips, apparently surveying her surroundings through her sunglasses that had some kind of female figure on the rims. Looked like one of those Barbie-type dolls. He smiled. She was a little beauty.

And her mom's nothing to sneeze at, he thought as Ellen came up behind Missy. He shook away that thought. Yes, she looked quite nice in denim jeans and a green T-shirt.

Then he realized someone was with her. Richard stepped away from the grill and walked toward them. "Welcome," he said. "Hello, Missy. You look like a swimmer to me."

She sighed heavily. "Yes." She looked toward the pool. "If it's not too deep."

"It's deep," he said. "But right over there are floats, life jackets, and boards you can hold onto."

She smiled. "Okay."

"Hold it!" Ellen's words stopped Missy as soon as she turned toward the equipment. "You wait for me. We've already talked about this."

Missy sighed again and turned toward the pool, watching the activity.

"Mr. Williams, this is my friend, Heather—"

Heather interrupted. "Oh, Richard and I have met before."

He laughed with her. "Yes, Miss Cannington. I believe we have." He really hadn't remembered what Heather had looked like, except he'd thought of her as a rather gangly teenager. She'd grown into a lovely young woman.

"Oh," she said. "I slaved over a hot stove all day cooking these potato chips."

He recognized the store-bought brand. "Thank you. Here, put them on the table. I don't use bowls. Just open the bag."

Ellen set down her dish and lifted the edge of the foil. "I did cook these."

"Brownies?" They must still be warm. He could smell the chocolate.

"With walnuts," she said. She looked up at him. Her cheek dimpled. Her eyes looked green.

He reached over and pinched off a big chunk. "I have to test these. Make sure they're okay."

"Well?" she queried.

Well what? Oh, the test. For a minute there he forgot anything but realizing she stood there, gazing at him with brown eyes touched by the golden glow of a sunny summer day.

"Oh. Can't tell. I'll have to try again."

Her dimple appeared. "You're the boss."

He corrected her. "Only in the office."

"In that case . . ." She pushed the corner of the foil down just as his fingers reached for another bite. "Dessert later," she said playfully, as if she were speaking to Missy.

He liked this relaxed Ellen. In the office, she'd been reserved. But then, that's what cookouts were for—to make friends and influence people. "Here," he said, "I want you to meet Jerry."

She turned around to where he gestured.

Jerry, Ridgeway's graphic artist, had tied a short beach robe around his waist and had just walked up. He stood near Heather and Missy. His curly auburn hair looked like a rust-colored mop that hadn't been wrung out. Pool water dripped down his face. "I'm Jerry," he said in greeting, "and this is my son, Jacob."

Missy nodded. "He's in my school."

Jerry took over from there. "I'm the official lifeguard," he told them. "But first, let's go meet everybody."

Richard returned to the grill and lifted the huge lid. The hot dogs were ready. Hamburgers and steaks had a way to go yet. Placing the hot dogs in the warming bin, he smiled, observing his guests. MaryJo sat on the edge of the pool with her feet in the water, while Ben swam side-by-side with Ken, the youth pastor at the church Richard attended. Ken's girlfriend hadn't been able to come.

Leon and Sue, good friends who were a few years older than he and managed the bookstore, sat in lounge chairs. They had teenagers at home and said they just wanted to sit, observe, and relax. Near them lounged Jerry's administrative assistant and her husband. They'd recently welcomed their first grandchild into the world.

Jerry took Ellen, Heather, and Missy around and introduced them, then fitted Missy and Jacob with life jackets and got them into the pool. After speaking to everyone, Ellen pulled up a chair near MaryJo at the poolside, talked to her, and watched the children. Soon, Ken swam over and talked with her.

After they all sat down to eat, Richard observed Heather's outgoing personality, like Jerry's. Heather told about getting lost overnight with Jeff when she was a teenager, and they all laughed. She talked about her master's thesis that included research at Little Tykes and inclusion of the Ridgeway preschool.

Ellen had no problem relating to everyone, but she did have to divide her attention between them and her daughter. Missy and Jacob had chosen to sit at a picnic table apart from the others at the long table.

He could understand how Ellen and Heather would be friends. They said they'd known each other since grade school. Heather had been a cheerleader, outgoing. Ellen had been the president of the student body, more academic.

Heather's taking courses in child development in order to learn more about the children's books she wanted to write was impressive. She laughed and said, "I picked a thesis that Miss Academia could help me with. I'd never have gotten this far without Ellen. Never learned how to study. Tell them your formula, El."

"Six steps," Ellen said, counting them off on her fingers. "Sit down, shut up, read, take notes, reason them through, and apply them to memory."

Heather sighed. "She's a tough taskmaster."

They all laughed. Ellen shook her head. "Don't let her fool you. You have to have brains and apply them to get through college and into a master's program.

"Did you go to UNCA too, Ellen?" Ken asked.

"I did, but I dropped out in my senior year to take care of Missy."

"I'm sorry I didn't have a permanent position to offer." Richard tried to manipulate the conversation without prying. "I'm sure it's quite expensive raising a child."

Heather spoke up quickly. "Oh, Ellen's not the financial support for her sister."

Ken spoke up. "Missy's your sister?"

Richard noticed that Ellen didn't quite meet anyone's eyes. She looked very uncomfortable.

Heather answered for her. "Now there's something to be praised," she said. "After her mom died, Ellen has taken care of her little sister like she was her own child."

Little sister?

Richard stared at Ellen a moment longer. As if feeling his stare, her gaze locked with his. Then she looked toward Missy.

Missy had said, "Mommy."

Heather said, "Sister." And that she'd lost her mom. Did she still have her dad? Obviously, she'd put her own future on hold for her little sister.

The more he knew of Ellen Jonsen, the more Richard admired her.

And the more a nagging uneasiness began to grow deep within himself.

❧

Ellen hadn't had a crush on a guy since high school. She liked the academic type, like the gorgeous boy who'd edited the school paper and played a saxophone in the band. Not that she had a crush now, but that came to mind when Mr. Williams brought out his drums and Jerry his guitar.

She could almost forget thinking about Mr. Williams as her boss. She could easily see him just as a man she really liked. He and Jerry sang a silly song and taught it to them all. Heather suggested they sing a popular Christian song and pulled Ellen in on it.

Her alto and Heather's soprano blended well with Richard's and Jerry's voices, accompanied by the drums and guitar. Then Heather sang a song with a mock nasal country sound. Everyone loved it.

All had their turn at singing. Some attempts caused hands to be placed over ears. Missy and Jacob had joined in, complete with clapping.

"I can sing 'Froggie Went a Courtin',' " Missy said. "Pa-Pa sings it to me a lot."

She sang the two verses that she knew, bobbing her head when she emphasized the "uh-huh, uh-huh" part.

"One more time!" Richard said. "And we'll all sing the 'uh-huh's. Lead us, Missy."

She shook her head, becoming suddenly shy.

"I'll sing it with you." He started, "Frrrrr . . . roggy . . . ," and looked at Missy who glanced away from him as if to say he'd ruin it. He continued, then she began to sing along with him.

Richard gestured with his hands, as if pulling them all toward him. They all joined in with the "uh-huh, uh-huh's" along with a few "ribbits."

At the end, while everyone followed with laughter and applause, Richard put his arm around Missy's shoulder and pulled her gently to his side. She looked up at him with her big blue eyes. Ellen thought the way they related indicated a mutual liking. How wonderful if Missy could have a dad like Richard.

Immediately, she felt she'd done a disservice to her own dad. But she hadn't meant to think of it that way. Her dad was the most wonderful man alive. She loved him more than any man in the world. And she'd always admired and respected him. He had no major flaws. He had his human imperfections, but who didn't?

Her dad didn't have the energy, or the inclination, to be the kind of active dad that he'd been to Ellen. And his desire to do so had waned in the past couple of years. That was understandable. Missy had been her mom's major responsibility before she died, not his.

Ellen observed that Missy left Richard's brief embrace and ran off with Jacob and Rachel, who hopped up and walked along the top of the rock wall several feet high that surrounded the patio. However, strangely, the world around her seemed to have faded into the background while she stared into Richard's eyes. How long had she stared before he turned to another guest?

Before long, some of the guests were leaving. Jerry was supervising Missy and Jacob throwing a rubber ball back and forth, near the pool.

Next thing Ellen knew, Heather brought her a cup of coffee and sat beside her.

"Imagine. You and I without a man and right here are three eligible bachelors."

Ellen remembered what her dad had said about eligible and confirmed. "Maybe they're confirmed."

Heather scoffed. "That means he's tenacious about remaining a bachelor. But you know another saying—he runs, until she catches him."

"Who's trying to catch anybody?"

Heather bumped her shoulder against Ellen, almost making her coffee spill. "Ellen, this is me. We're red-blooded American girls, and there's nothing we'd like better than to find Mr. Right."

Ellen sighed. "Does he exist?"

"Well, these ain't bad. But at the moment, I'm knee deep in a master's thesis. Can't handle a man."

"Well, I'm waist deep in a child. So I know what you mean."

Heather burst into laugher. "Yeah. Means we don't have anyone head over heels about us."

Ellen agreed. But she didn't want to spoil a good working relationship by letting her mind take off on some fantasy trip. Richard Williams was her boss, a confirmed bachelor who'd hired her to fill in for a few weeks. How eligible was anybody anyway? "I don't know Jerry's situation, and I heard Ken has a girlfriend. And Mr. Williams and I," she emphasized, "are not even on a first-name basis."

She looked around. "We'd better go. We're almost the last ones left."

Just then, she felt someone sit on the bench beside her.

The surprise of it made her heart beat faster.

Heather said, "I'll get Missy." She ran off.

Ellen glanced over at Richard. "Thank you so much, Mr. Williams, for inviting me. Missy had a great time." She laughed lightly. "So did I."

"I'm glad. But let's get one thing straight. Here, I'm just Richard. You may have noticed that when we're not conducting business, even in the office, MaryJo calls me Richard. May I call you Ellen?"

"Oh, please do," she said, feeling a rush of excitement like a high school girl when the saxophone player just says, "Hi." She really had been out of circulation for a long time.

She looked down from his smile and at her coffee cup. Heather's words—"Mr. Right"—rang in her ears, along with a delicious thought.

Richard and I are on a first-name basis.

*W*hen Richard arrived in Ellen's office at nine, she was talking on the telephone.

"Yes, I will give Mr. Williams the message. Good-bye." She hung up and sounded very professional as she looked at the note she'd taken and explained to him, "Daniel Smith's mother called. Due to circumstances beyond their control, Daniel will arrive here a day later than scheduled."

Richard nodded, watching the becoming color rise to her cheeks. "And what do you plan to do with that information?"

"I just told my boss," she said, then grimaced as if she might have said something wrong. To reassure her all was fine, he nodded and smiled.

"And too," she said, her dimple showing, "I will put a note in his file, and I will contact the summer staff director's office." She gazed at him with her eyes wide, waiting for approval.

"Very efficiently handled." He saw the disappointment in her face when he added, "You've done only one thing wrong this morning. We begin our day with a little informality. So let's start over. Good morning, Ellen."

"Good morning."

He cupped his ear with his hand, and she added, "Richard."

That's the first time he'd heard her say his first name. He'd only meant to be friendly and put her at ease. Instead, the tentative way she softly said his name, in almost a whisper, touched something deep inside him and elicited that uneasiness again.

But he had neither the time nor inclination to explore why he had reacted in that way. Work awaited. "First on the agenda," he said, "we should tour the new hotel. I'd like for you to be a tour guide at the dedication."

"Tour guide?" She looked doubtful. "I get lost going from the cafeteria to the bookstore."

"It's only a tour of the hotel. So if you'll put the phone on answering machine, we can go."

After they walked out a back door of the administration building and across the concrete pathways, he noticed her gaze moved to the day-care center, as if wanting to see Missy. "At the cookout, Heather mentioned your mom dying. I'm sorry."

"Thank you," she said softly.

"Do you have a dad?"

"Yes, Missy and I live with him." She briefly mentioned the accident that killed her mom. She talked of her parents' having adopted Missy at birth.

He already knew Ellen was special. But this was even more remarkable. She loved Missy like a daughter although they were not blood-related. With all the negativity in the world, how wonderful to be reminded of the goodness in some people.

She asked about his parents.

"They live in Raleigh," he said. "My dad has an accounting business. They both work there. They come here for conferences occasionally."

They reached the covered entry, bordered by newly planted blooming flowers, lush green plants, and bushes. The hotel rose four-stories high and was surrounded by exquisite mountain views.

"It smells so clean and new," Ellen said upon entering the hallway with offices on each side and a spacious area in the center where hallways were located to the left and right. Long windows formed the wall across from them, exposing the panoramic view of one mountainside after another.

More beautiful, however, was the young woman beside him, taking in the grandeur of a newly built structure. He led the way to the auditorium, where more than two hundred chairs, each with its own desk that could be raised or lowered to the side, faced the glass window that reached from the floor to the high-beamed ceiling.

"All the latest equipment," Richard pointed out as they went into classrooms and saw panels with switches, computerized buttons, and electrical sockets set flush with the wall. "State-of-the-art technology," he said.

He showed her the board room.

"Impressive," she said, touching the polished wooden table surrounded by twelve high-backed leather chairs. She drew in her breath and walked over to a painting. "He Lives," she said, reading the title of the painting of Peter and Andrew. "That's . . ." She paused as if searching for the right word and then said, "Awesome."

Richard agreed. The look on the disciples' faces as they gazed at something not shown in the painting, but likely the Christ Himself, held pure awe.

They rode the elevator to the upper floors, walked across the brown-and-beige carpet, bordered by a darker brown strip on each side, and explored VIP rooms, fellowship rooms, and banquet rooms.

When Richard finished the tour, he said, "Okay. Now it's your turn. Give me a tour."

As he followed her, he listened to her and watched her look at him with little golden flecks of mischief in her eyes as she performed her serious mission. He could see she liked a challenge. When she returned to the painting, her expression changed to reverent appreciation.

"Oh," she exclaimed when they returned to auditorium. "I remember there are two hundred chairs in here, but I forgot how many guest rooms there are."

"One hundred twenty," he said. "But all that will be written out on the programs given to everyone."

She gave him a now-you-tell-me look that made him laugh. Working around Ellen was going to be easy—and difficult.

On Tuesday morning, MaryJo's husband burst into the office. "Guess what! Guess what!"

Richard almost ran into Ellen's office, then stopped and laughed. "Ben, I can't imagine. As if that euphoric look on your face says nothing. Not to mention what you're waving around in your hand.

Ben laughed. "I think you guessed it. Tyler has arrived!" He pulled out two pieces of bubble gum wrapped in blue paper from the bag he held. He handed a piece to Ellen and one to Richard. "It was hard on me," he said, "but MaryJo's fine. Tyler weighs eight pounds, six ounces, is twenty-two and one-half inches long, and has terrific lungs."

After Ben left to deliver more bubble gum and spread the news to others, realization struck Ellen. This meant her job would end in three weeks. Her quick glance at Richard revealed he wasn't smiling either. Did he think the same thing? Did it matter? Was he looking forward to MaryJo's return? He looked down and fingered the bubble gum.

Three weeks.

The idea of working in housekeeping or the cafeteria had lost all appeal since she'd been working with Richard. She'd been totally happy with the job and felt she'd done well. Now a creepy, desolate feeling washed over her. She tried to shake it.

"Richard." She hesitated. Two weeks ago he was Mr. Williams. Now the name Richard rolled off her tongue without hesitation. And she liked the way he said her name. How could she ever like another job? But she mustn't think that. She hoped her voice didn't betray how her emotions were trembling. Uncanny how one's outer demeanor could reveal what lay beneath the surface. "I'll go see MaryJo after work. Want me to tell her hello for you or anything?"

Whatever emotion had caused his frown vanished. He chuckled, stuck his bubble gum into his pocket, walked over and balanced his hands against the edge of her desk, and leaned toward her. He made his face look grim, but his eyes were smiling. "Are you trying to tell me I should send flowers or something?"

MaryJo had told Ellen she would need to remind Richard about special events that weren't directly business related. He tended to forget some of those. This might be one of those times. She jested with him, as MaryJo had done. "That would be nice, Richard," she said playfully. "She is your administrative assistant."

After a moment's hesitation, he said, "She was. She will be. But for the present . . . you is."

She couldn't help but laugh. "I is?"

"That's what I said, and I'm the boss. I might add I'm very pleased with you. With your work," he said, with a look that warmed her heart.

She couldn't look away. "I like this job."

He nodded and looked as if he were about to say something more when the door opened and Jerry walked in, holding out a piece of gum in the palm of his hand.

Jerry must have wondered what Richard was doing, leaning over her desk. Ellen saw his quick glance from one to the other as Richard straightened. Jerry gestured toward Ellen's piece of gum. "I see the happy father has been here too."

"Right. How's it going, Jer?" Richard asked.

"Great. My boy's turning five this weekend." He pulled an envelope from his pocket and handed it to Ellen. "I told him he could invite a few friends and we'd go to putt-putt. He wanted to invite Missy. And of course," he added, "parents, guardians are always welcome."

"Thanks," Ellen said. "That sounds really nice. Missy loves putt-putt."

She and Jerry smiled at each other. When she glanced at Richard, he wasn't smiling. His expression was thoughtful as he glanced from her to Jerry.

Could it be possible?

Her heartbeat speeded up.

No. Richard couldn't be jealous.

❧

During the rest of the week and into the next, Ellen had little time to either think of Richard or see him. Everyone worked frantically making sure all was ready for the dedication on Friday. Besides that was the usual work of staff meetings, a couple of small conferences that came and went, new bookings, and the never-ending telephone and e-mail messages.

Along with the work came some volunteers, and Ellen began to understand why she'd heard over and over that Ridgeway couldn't do without them. An older couple, who had worked with MaryJo and

Richard for a couple of summers, returned, and Ellen found them invaluable, not only in working, but in knowing what to do when she was uncertain.

Ellen liked dressing nicely every day instead of wearing jeans or slacks and her hair in a ponytail as she had at Little Tykes. For the dedication, she bought a new white summer suit to wear with a black shell and adorable black and white speckled high heels. She even put her hair back in a twist to give herself a more mature look. She liked feeling like a woman, involved in things, instead of a college-aged dropout.

She didn't know if Richard was really taken aback or if he were just kidding like that. But he looked and sounded serious when he came to work and said, "Everybody's going to be looking at you instead of the hotel. You look beautiful." His smile touched her heart.

"You look nice too," she said. His suit looked more formal than what he wore in the office, and his tie looked like silk against his white shirt. He always looked good to her. She suspected she thought of him too often, but she was so grateful for his giving her this job that was changing her life. She tried to remember that is was God who made all things possible, and she thanked Him.

At ten o'clock, Richard said she might want to go on to the hotel and be ready if people came earlier than ten-thirty, the time printed on the invitation. She already knew what kind of guests to expect. All the staff were invited, along with people who had some connection with Ridgeway, like local officials and pastors, including Ken and his girlfriend. Even Heather had been invited. They assumed that was because of her writing the article about the preschool.

Heather was in Ellen's first group of eight people that she led through the hotel. She felt even more at ease after the first tour. Like other staffers serving as tour guides, she led her group to a refreshment table, then took several more groups on the tour until time for the dedication service.

Following the welcome by the general manager, a woman gave a testimony about the meaning, purpose, and spiritual success of the center. The president of Christian resources gave the dedication message. That was followed by a solo, "Find Us Faithful," sung by the summer camps director. A final prayer was offered, then the guests were dismissed for lunch.

Since Ellen wore a name tag identifying her as a tour guide, several people stopped her to ask questions about the building or to express their feelings about the center—all favorable.

She was among the last to enter the dining room, and the elegance and beauty of it almost took her breath away. She'd seen the room, but not when it was decorated. Tables were set with gleaming dishes on white squares of cloth over maroon table coverings. Tall cloth napkins stood by each plate near glasses of tea and water. In the center of each table was an arrangement of multi-colored flowers. Tables sat on the same brown, beige, and maroon carpet. The brown-and-gold patterned, high-backed, padded chairs blended with the earth colors, and the gold drapes with their looped valances lent an elegant aura.

Then Ellen spied Heather, standing and waving. She'd saved her a seat at a table with some of the staff. Heather sat next to an older volunteer couple. Ellen's seat was next to Helen and Joe, a couple who had worked at Ridgeway after retirement. Across the way sat Jerry by an empty seat. Ellen thought she knew who would sit next to Jerry, and she was right. Richard soon came and occupied the seat.

Ellen was grateful Heather had come. Her friend could distract her from looking across into Richard's eyes. Ellen and the others talked about the elegant dessert at each place. Each dessert plate held a round pastry, filled with vanilla pudding, and seated on red raspberry sauce. Pastry sprinkled with powdered sugar formed wings, while another piece of curved pastry formed the long graceful neck of a swan. A small purple lily adorned each plate.

After the invocation, a young man came to the table and introduced himself as Tony, the server for the table. He looked elegant in his white shirt, maroon vest, black tie, and black pants. He served the table with finesse. From the apple-nut-greens salad on a vinaigrette base to the Chicken Oscar plate that included steamed shredded carrots, broccoli, and a flower of toasted mashed potatoes, everything looked and tasted marvelous. The hot rolls were light and flaky.

Joe, a former pilot spoke up. "Helen and I met at the center in the dining room where we worked when we were college students."

Helen, a lovely lady with a wonderful personality added, "We shared our first kiss here."

That began talk about how many people had met at the center and married.

"We have prayer brigade now," Jerry said.

Heather questioned that. "That wasn't here when I worked here."

Richard explained. "No, it's been in effect a couple of years. We built the new prayer garden, then discovered some of the college students went there late at night when they were supposed to be in their rooms—and they didn't go for prayer. So the prayer brigade sneaks up there, taking their big water guns, and douses any unauthorized visitors good."

They all laughed. "But wait 'til you hear this," Jerry said. "This old man came stomping into the general manager's office one morning, telling his story. He and his wife had been sprayed with water while they were on their knees praying. The brigade assumed it was young people. In the dark, they couldn't tell."

Ellen loved the stories. She hadn't seriously thought about meeting someone at Ridgeway and sharing a kiss with him, but the idea certainly held appeal. Rather than yield to the temptation of looking into Richard's eyes, she shared glances and laughs with Heather.

She reminded herself that Richard seemed to like her, but he'd given no indication their relationship might be anything more than that of employer-employee and perhaps friends. Then with a sinking feeling in her stomach, she remembered all this was going to end in a week.

❦

The workload had doubled after public schools let out for the school year and the summer programs began. Summer staff, mainly college students, inundated the campus. Lodges were filled to capacity with conferees.

Three weeks had passed since Tyler's birth.

On Friday, every time the phone rang, someone opened her office door, or Richard stepped into her office, Ellen expected to hear that this would be her last day—that MaryJo would return on Monday.

Perhaps she'd still be needed. How could MaryJo keep up with all the work after just having a baby?

The nearer to closing time the hands on the clock moved, the more fidgety Ellen became. She reprimanded herself when the thought occurred to her that maybe MaryJo wasn't able to return to work just yet. Ellen didn't want to go job-hunting again. In a way, it would have been best not to have worked here at all than have to leave—

The door opened. MaryJo came in with little Tyler in her arms. All thought of herself vanished as Ellen looked upon the faces of that precious baby and his radiant mom.

After the ooohs and aaahs and catching up on what had been going on in their lives, Ellen called Richard on the intercom. "MaryJo and Tyler are here to see you, Richard."

"Be right there."

Ellen detected the most wistful look in Richard's eyes, although he refused to hold the baby. But he made weird clucking sounds at the baby, who apparently found that delightful. Tyler resembled his mother, with his animated face and dark eyes. He cooed, gurgled, and slobbered, to everyone's delight. Especially MaryJo's.

She suddenly became serious. "I need to talk to you Richard."

"You want to come in the office?"

"I don't mind if Ellen hears me. She will have to know anyway."

Know? Of course. She wants her job back.

"Could I hold Tyler?" Ellen asked. Maybe MaryJo could talk more freely if Ellen held the baby.

"Oh, sure." She put the baby in Ellen's arms. That felt so wonderful. Ellen would love to have a baby of her own someday.

"It's this, Richard. And I hope you're not going to hate me," MaryJo began.

"No more than usual, I'm sure," he said and looked at her like he wanted her to respond to his jesting.

She did, with a grin and sideways glance at Ellen. She looked at Richard again, took a deep breath, and plunged in. "I can't come back to work."

He stared at her with a blank expression.

"There's just no way I can leave this baby." She gestured toward Tyler. "Now tell me, could you do that?"

He shrugged. "Um, well. Somebody has to pay the bills."

"Ben has a job. He can pay the bills. We figured up how much money we can save by having only one car and my not having to wear nice clothes every day. I can plan meals instead of throwing stuff together or getting fast food."

Richard surrendered. "I understand."

"Besides," she continued, as if he hadn't really understood, "if you bring a child into this world, then aren't you responsible for taking care of him?"

"I agree with you one hundred percent," he said.

MaryJo looked at Ellen with an apologetic expression. "Oh, I don't mean they're not supposed to go to preschool or a good day care when they get a little age on them. That's good for them too—learn things, associate with other children. But this is a baby!"

"You're kidding," Richard said. "Let me take another look."

He walked over to Ellen and Tyler, then faced MaryJo again. "I think you may be right."

"Oh, Richard." She lightly slapped his arm.

"Seriously, MaryJo," he said. "I can't fault you for this decision. I think you're right, and I respect you for it. But you're sure?"

"I am. I'll miss everybody, but I know this is right. I can't leave my baby, not even with my mom."

She reached out to Richard and they hugged—something Ellen had wanted to do a couple of times. Well, maybe more than a couple.

MaryJo stepped back with tears in her eyes. "You're a good man, Richard. I've loved working with you."

After MaryJo and Tyler left, Richard stood in Ellen's office for a moment. Would he ask her to make this temporary job a permanent one?

After a long moment, he spoke. "Ellen," he said. "Are you planning to return to college in the fall?"

After Missy went to bed and a commercial came on, Ellen talked to her dad. Just as she feared, her elation was squelched when she told him that Richard had asked her to stay on. And she had agreed.

"Just for the summer?"

"No, Dad. Permanently. As long as I want to stay or as long as he wants me to."

She knew when he switched off the TV, she was about to get a lecture.

"So this means no college. No career. No goals for the future except working for that man. This is what you want to do for the rest of your life? When you could go anywhere in the world and prepare for any career? You'd rather stay with that man you claim is only your boss."

Ellen moved to the edge of the couch and turned to face him more directly. "Dad, how many times do I have to say this? I can't go off somewhere and prepare for a career as if Missy doesn't exist. She does exist. My responsibility is right here. My first priority is Missy."

"You're wrong." He spoke forcefully. Ellen blinked as if he'd struck her. "Missy is not your responsibility. She's mine."

This was not the man she'd known all her life. Was he jealous of her taking over with Missy? Did he want to be the little girl's sole support and caregiver? "Dad, I don't understand."

"Ellen, you've been forced into the mother role. For the past two years, I've let you take over all the responsibilities."

"I wanted it, Dad. She is my sister."

This seemed the perfect time for Ellen to say what she'd wanted to say for a long time. She reached over and enclosed his hand in hers. "Dad, let me adopt her."

"Ellen. She needs young parents."

"I'm young," she reminded him.

"But," he added, "you're single."

"I'll marry," Ellen said, knowing the only real prospect she had was hope. "Someday."

"I hope so, Ellen. But then what? You expect your husband to move in here? Can I turn over my daughter to some man I don't even know? Maybe your husband wouldn't want a ready-made family."

Ellen spoke quickly. "Then I wouldn't want him."

"Ah, Ellen. It's not that easy. Not when you find someone who makes your blood run fast. I felt that every time I looked at your mother."

"Now, Dad. I've heard you two argue, or as you called it, disagree."

"Well, like I said." He grinned with a twinkle in his eye. "She could make my blood boil."

They shared a laugh. For a moment, "Dad before Mom died" surfaced.

Then he became reminiscent. "But it was never dull. We loved each other. Respected each other. Liked each other."

Sadness clouded his face. "Ellen. Everything looked different when your mother was alive. I just don't have the energy to be a full-time dad again without Mary." He took a long breath. "I've even mentioned this to Daisy."

"Daisy?" Ellen moved her hands away, and her dad's hand lay limply on his pants leg. She wasn't sure where this was going. "Are . . . you thinking of her . . . taking care of Missy full time?"

He grimaced as though his thoughts were painful. "I've considered all possibilities, Ellen. But she's close to my age. After you raise little ones and they grow up, you think, 'Been there, done that.' Sounds terrible, doesn't it?"

"No, Dad. It sounds real. Is that what's been eating at you?"

He nodded. "What do we do when you marry? How do we divide that child?"

The answer seemed perfectly clear to Ellen. "Let me adopt her. I'll be her mom. You'll still be her Pa-Pa."

He stood and blinked away the emotion she knew he was trying hard to conceal. She'd seen her dad cry no more than a couple of times in her life. He looked close to it now. "That sounds like the perfect solution, Ellen. But my conscience won't let me allow that without considering other possibilities. You'll marry one of these days. If you adopt Missy, what kind of man would be her dad?"

How ridiculous could he get? "Dad, what kind of man do you think I'd marry?"

"The right kind, I hope. But Ellen, you don't even have any prospects, do you?"

How could she answer such a thing? Prospects? "I have no one asking to marry me, if that's what you mean."

"Exactly. Frankly, I would need to approve any man I would turn my daughter over to." He shook his head as if this were a hopeless situation. She could hardly believe what he said next. "I talked to Leanne today."

"You called her?"

"I asked her to visit. I want her to see Missy."

That left Ellen speechless.

"Don't look so shocked, Ellen. I've been telling you. You're not Missy's mom. Before it's too late, I need to consider what Mary and I discussed when we took Missy in as a baby. Maybe she and her birth mom need each other now."

Ellen didn't think anything could upset her more than being without her mother. But her dad's words absolutely floored her.

"Dad, you can't be serious. You can't uproot Missy from the only home she's ever known."

"Ellen, this breaks my heart. But I'm trying to put that child's needs ahead of my own. And, Honey, you're my child too. I have to do what I think is best for you."

Ellen saw the heartache in his eyes. She also saw his resoluteness.

He gave Ellen a long, sad look. Then with a crumpled face he turned and walked from the room. That's how it was. He never argued or discussed issues for long when disagreements arose. He stated his opinion and as far as he was concerned, that meant his opinion was written in stone.

He was dead serious.

13

*A*ll weekend, Ellen functioned like she had after she was told her mom died. The news hadn't seemed real. Not even when all the funeral plans were being made or when she was sitting at the service. She'd been fine.

Several days after the funeral, however, the reality of Ellen's loss had overwhelmed her. She'd turned up the music on the radio and gone into the shower. Her wails of "No, no, no" accompanied the tears that washed her face. After that, she'd cried with Heather and alone, several times.

Now, facing the possible loss of Missy, she kept telling herself this was no situation for grief. Her dad wouldn't take Missy from her. He wouldn't do it to Missy.

She understood her dad's reasoning. From his point of view, it sounded right. Ellen had to ask herself if she wanted Missy for her own sake. Was Missy filling the void left by her mom's death? Was she being selfish, wanting Missy? Was Leanne the best one for Missy?

Dad was right too about something being done as soon as possible, if it were to be done. Leanne was Missy's birth mother.

Ellen decided to simply pray harder for her Dad to come to his senses. He would. He wanted her to revert to being a young, single college girl with career or marriage on her mind. She couldn't turn back time. She'd have to convince him of that. Maybe enlist Daisy, Heather, the pastor—anybody she could think of—to get through to him.

At work on Monday, Ellen managed to control her emotions until near closing time. But she had to answer the question of why she had told Richard she would stay on with this job. Had her decision been based on being near Missy? Or had it been based on the possibility of being near Richard Williams?

She had agreed for both reasons, she told herself. But the floodgates opened, and the liquid heartache spilled out.

The phone rang while she was in the bathroom trying to repair her face. She let the answering machine pick up. When she came out, the door between her office and Richard's was open. He must have wondered where she had gone. Whenever she left the office, she'd tell him where she was going, or simply say, "If you don't need me, I'll be back in a jif," and he'd acknowledge that, usually with an "Okay."

Their eyes met. She'd just stopped crying. Then it started again. She hurried to her desk and pulled out another tissue and began to swipe at the tears.

"Ellen?" He came and stood in the doorway.

"I'm fine. Just . . . emotional. I'm . . . sorry."

"Sorry," he said in a teasing voice. "You're sorry you agreed to keep this job?"

She laughed lightly at his attempt at joking, but the waterworks wouldn't turn off. She owed him some kind of explanation for crying. She walked past her desk and came to stand near him. "It's my family situation. Dad thinks I will get married and wonders what will happen to Missy then. I want to adopt her. I don't think he's going to let me."

He reached out and held her arm. "Ellen, I know how much you and Missy mean to each other. I think she belongs with you." His expression was pained. "But then, I'm partial."

Ellen gazed at him. Partial? He had special feelings for them? For her?

Their gaze held. She felt the strength of his hand on her arm. Was that a special caring in his eyes? Maybe it was a reflection of her own longing—not his. Her own fantasies—not his. But she knew he was a caring man.

He let go of her arm, an action she took as meaning she'd invaded his space.

"I'm sorry. I shouldn't have burdened you with my problems. I'm okay." She turned, but not before her tears began to bathe her face. Oh, how she hated being such an emotional wreck.

Before she reached her desk, he turned her to face him. He placed his hands on her shoulders. He was so close and spoke softly. "You're not okay. If I have any authority at all around here, you'll come into my office and talk to me."

Authority had nothing to do with it. She wanted to respond to his caring attitude. And she owed him some kind of explanation for falling apart on the job. She sniffed. "I have to pick up Missy."

"Can someone else do that?"

She nodded. There were plenty of people to do that. Her dad. Daisy. Heather if she was home. All her friends, neighbors, and church members were eager to help. Her dad could hire two-dozen nannies. Who needed Ellen?

"You don't want her to see you like this, do you?"

She shook her head.

"It's almost closing time. Let's go up to my house and talk. Can I call someone for you?"

"I will."

He moved his hands away, but she still felt the warmth of them, along with the caring look in his eyes. She was glad when Daisy answered instead of her dad. She'd break down again if she had to speak to him just now.

Daisy said she or Jon would pick up Missy.

"I'm going to be here for awhile, Daisy. Don't wait supper on me."

"Okay, Honey. Don't worry about anything here."

"Thanks. I won't. Bye."

She hung up. No, she didn't need to worry about anything at home. They'd manage fine without her.

"Working late, huh?" Jon said to Daisy when she told him either he or she needed to pick up Missy.

Daisy shrugged a shoulder. "She didn't say 'working,' Jon."

He grinned. "Maybe things are looking up."

"Now, Jon . . ."

He frowned. "Don't contradict me, Woman. Maybe she's coming

around to my way of thinking. I know she believes she has to raise Missy. I know how she feels. But I have to try and push her away from that, so she can live her own life without feeling guilty about it. This has to be my doing. You understand?"

"I understand what you're saying, Jon. But I'm not sure if you're right. If she has to give up Missy, it will break her heart."

"Yes, I know. But people can get over a broken heart if they have the right person to help them. You know what I mean?"

"Not exactly, Jon. You'll have to spell it out for me."

He turned to walk away, grumbling, "Obviously, I'm not a very good speller."

Ellen wanted to drive her own car farther up the mountain to Richard's house rather than have him drive her back down to the center. She arrived before he did and sat in the car on the concrete drive near the front of his house. The driveway was bordered by a rock wall about four feet high, back from which grew rhododendron that had to be several years old. They mingled with a forest of maple, oak, and dogwood trees. He had no flowerbeds, but azalea bushes that had already lost their blossoms edged the house. High on the deck was one splotch of bright color—a hanging basket laden with multicolored petunias.

She got out when Richard drove up.

"Supper," he said, climbing out of his car. "Straight from the Ridgeway kitchen."

So that's what had taken him so long. He held two carryout boxes. She followed him up to the deck at the second level. He held the boxes out to her. "If you'll take these out back, I'll go through the house and get silverware and something to drink."

Ellen knew the deck wrapped completely around the chalet. It would be nice sitting on the deck looking out on the fantastic view. She hadn't paid much attention, however, until she reached the back and realized the sky was overcast. The pool water lay still, reflecting the gray of the clouds that obscured the view of the mountains.

They ate, talked about such trivial things as the hot sultry day, and were thankful for a light breeze making the humidity bearable. Richard spoke of the float that Ridgeway was making under Jerry's supervision for the upcoming Fourth of July parade.

Talking to Richard was easy. He was a friend.

As Ellen finished the spice cake, she realized her tears had dried completely. Her fears had been put at the back of her mind. She recalled her dad saying it wouldn't be easy giving up someone she cared about if he didn't want a ready-made family. For a moment, she understood what he meant.

But she wasn't faced with such a choice.

Richard hadn't indicated an interest in anything beyond friendship. And if he were to do so, she didn't think that she would have to worry about his attitude toward Missy. Richard liked children.

Suppose, just suppose, her dad did something unthinkable and gave Missy back to Leanne. Although it would break her heart, she could imagine leaning on Richard, as she had leaned on Heather after the loss of her mother.

All her thoughts returned to the issue at hand, however, after Richard threw away their boxes and brought out coffee for them both. They turned their chairs toward the view, still obscured.

"I shouldn't burden you," she said.

"No burden," he said. "Even if all I can do is listen, I'm willing."

That's what she'd come here for, wasn't it? What else? She fought back the answer. "Dad is Missy's legal parent. He says my raising Missy is unfair to me because I should get my education, get married, have children of my own." She sighed. "If he does something foolish like trying to give her back to Leanne, her birth mother, I'd want to take it to court."

Even as she said it, she faced the absurdity of that. "But how could I fight my own dad? How could I even hope to win a court case against Missy's legal dad and her birth mother?"

Observing the thoughtful expression on his face, Ellen waited for his response. Finally, he spoke in a low tone, as if to himself. "Ellen, how could Leanne give up her own daughter?"

She told him about Leanne's situation. "She was only fourteen when she became pregnant. Her mom was divorced, had a job, and couldn't care for the baby. Mom and Dad agreed to keep Missy for awhile to make sure she and her mom were making the right decision. After a year, they decided they still couldn't care properly for Missy."

"Ellen," he said. "Couldn't your dad be doing the same thing? Making a sacrifice for the good of both his children?"

That's not what she wanted to hear. "It's not right," she protested. She stood, set her cup on the table, then walked over and stood with her back against a post that ran from the railing to the roof over the deck.

"Ellen, I'm not saying it's right. I'm just trying to make you see his point of view. This sounds to me like his decision is based on love for Missy and on what he thinks is best for you."

"He's wrong. Oh, Richard, he is so wrong." Then the moisture fell, not from the clouds, but from her eyes.

Richard jumped up. "Ellen, I'm not saying he's right. I'm just saying understand him so you can talk to him."

She felt his hands on her shoulders. Saw the concern in his blurry countenance, heard it in his voice. "I know you love that child like she's your own. She loves you." His voice became a whisper, and he softly spoke her name. "Ellen."

Richard was holding her. Consoling her. Wiping away her tears.

"If my dad makes me lose Missy, then I'll be losing my dad too. Oh, this is so hard." The tears started again.

"I know, Ellen. I know."

She felt his heartbeat. Or was it her own?

She looked up at him. His words didn't sound like a trite, repeated phrase. His face was so close. His expression so full of caring. He really seemed to know. "You've lost someone, haven't you, Richard?"

His arms around her stiffened. Finally he laughed, without humor. "We're discussing you tonight, Ellen. Not me."

Would they ever discuss him? Or was he so protective of his inner self that one dared not intrude?

Yes, the lion in him was showing again.

❧

Richard realized his wayward hand had caressed Ellen's back as he held her. Even now, as she looked up at him with questioning eyes, her face was so close to his, lifted to his own—how easy it would be . . . how easy . . .

He became aware of himself as a man holding a woman, a soft, warm, appealing woman. For an instant, the moment had become something other than a boss consoling his employee, a man consoling a woman. He wanted to give in to the growing feelings in his heart and pursue a relationship with her. But that included revealing things that he'd tried to put behind him. How much did a person have to reveal about the past?

Acceptance had not come easy for him. He'd given that situation from his past to God but kept taking it back. He'd lost respect for himself. He didn't want to lose Ellen's respect.

He moved back, lest she detect the increase in his heart rate. *Get hold of yourself, Richard. You know better than to let this happen.*

Had Ellen wondered about his hasty retreat? She turned and held onto the railing. No, her mind wasn't on him at all. His shouldn't have been on her. He sat in his chair, forcing his thoughts back to the issue at hand.

Richard believed if he had been married, had a child, and the child's mom died, he would not even consider giving up the child. Yet if he were a grandfather and the situation was like Jon Jonsen's, he might think like him. Mr. Jonsen's attitude seemed totally unselfish. As did the action of Missy's birth mother when she was fourteen.

But Richard also knew he would want his birth child. He believed that would be best—whether the child came to him at age four or fourteen.

He also agreed that the ideal for Missy or any child was two loving parents. But this was not an ideal world. And after seeing Ellen's grief at the prospect of losing Missy, he could honestly say, "Ellen, I believe you and Missy love each other as much as any parent and child could."

She faced him then, smiled through her tears, and managed a weak, "Thank you for saying that."

He almost said that if God wanted her and Missy to be together, then they would. But he couldn't say that with complete confidence. Sometimes people got themselves into situations contrary to the will of God. They had to live with the consequences. Everything was not the way God preferred it.

"We'll pray, Ellen. For God's will in this situation." That was the best he could do.

She nodded. "Somehow, I have to convince Dad that Missy and I belong together."

Yes, he thought. *But how?*

*E*llen asked me if I'd ever lost anyone," Richard said to Jerry a few days later at lunch in the cafeteria. "I couldn't tell her, Jerry. I've never told anyone but you. I think I would have exploded if I hadn't had you to talk to. I couldn't even do that until after you lost Amy."

"I have a book that might help you, Richard. A book on grieving."

"Grieving? Jerry, why a book on grieving? I think Ellen is handling her mother's death quite well. She understands her emotional fragility. Remembering at odd times. She's talked about that."

Jerry was nodding. "Yes, Richard. She's open and honest about her feelings. About losing her mother and now about possibly losing Missy. But this book is not for her, Richard. It's for you."

"I'm not grieving."

Jerry was relentless. "I think you are."

Richard scoffed. "Jerry, you can't grieve over someone who's never been yours."

"Sure you can. People can grieve over losing a job, failing a test, breaking a leg, anything. And your situation is bigger than that." Jerry's eyes misted over. "Amy had a miscarriage before Jacob. You've seen how MaryJo and Ben acted when they were expecting. Well, Amy and I were just as excited. And when she miscarried, we grieved. I don't know how to measure grief, but it was just as real as when I lost Amy. Will you read the book? Consider what I'm saying."

Richard had known it for years, but it was impressed upon him again that Jerry was more than a friend. He was Richard's only confidant. They'd helped each other reason through and pray through some of life's most difficult situations, both bitter and sweet.

Richard promised to take a look at the book.

❧

The next day, the door was open between Richard's and Ellen's offices when Jerry walked in with a book in his hand, the title in plain view while he talked with Ellen.

"Here's the book I mentioned," Jerry said, when Richard walked in.

"Thanks." Richard quickly changed the subject, lest Ellen ask about the book. "How's the float coming along?"

"We're still working on it," Jerry said. "That's one reason I stopped by. You two come down and see. It's almost finished."

"It better be," Richard quipped. "Tomorrow's the Fourth." He looked over and winked at Ellen.

Ellen's expression questioned Richard, who grinned and then looked at Jerry. "You go on. We'll be there shortly."

After Jerry left, Richard went into his office and put the book in a desk drawer. He returned to Ellen's office and pushed the buttons that switched the phone to the answering machine. Then he took her hand in his. "Come on. Break time."

She rose, laughing with him. He let go of her hand, and they walked to the site of the center's Fourth of July float that would be driven in the downtown parade. Richard spied Jerry and some of the staff and summer college students working on the float.

Jerry noticed the new arrivals just then and called out, "Ellen, you know the preschool and day-care children will ride on the float, don't you?"

Ellen nodded. "Missy is so excited about it. Hey, let me do something. At least one thing."

"Sure, come on over. You too, Richard."

They went over. Jerry had each of them screw in one of the battery-operated candles that would surround the float. "Now you can say you helped."

Aware of his standing there, laughing and associating with Ellen and Jerry, two people so valuable to him in many ways, Richard felt blessed. Soon, however, he had to say, "Ellen, we'd better get back to work."

Walking back to the office on a beautiful summer day, Richard was aware of the bright sunshine that turned Ellen's hair to a light golden brown. She often looked at him, her cheek dimpling, in a way that made him think she thought him special.

Sometimes around her, he felt as mature as a high school kid. He thought of the late evening when the singles' group had come to his house and gone swimming. Jerry had commented, "No disrespect intended, but she's easy on the eyes."

"Who?" Richard pretended innocence.

"Your administrative assistant."

Richard knew how she looked. It was common knowledge that men were attracted to women. He saw her five days a week at work. He liked the way she looked. He'd learned how to handle physical attraction and not be disrespectful by harboring lustful thoughts.

But what he had a problem with was her more impressive qualities. Those were the thoughts that lingered. How could one pray, "God, help me not have such beautiful thoughts about this person?"

To make it worse, he thought he saw in her eyes the willingness to go beyond friendship.

What was he going to do about those thoughts before they turned into an irrevocable condition of the heart? She had brought something wonderful into his life by her commitment to the Lord and to her little sister. She had confided in him. She apparently looked to him as a mature man with possible answers to some of life's problems.

He was pretty good at that—except when it came to his own problems.

But he wanted to help her.

Then he had an idea that might help him put an end to his growing feelings for her and help several people at the same time. It could also influence Ellen's dad to reconsider doing anything too hastily.

He'd prayed about all aspects of the situation—within the office and out. Then he recalled a story about a person who had asked a pastor, "Why doesn't God do something about the poverty in the world?"

The pastor had replied, "That's what he put you here for."

Okay, then, perhaps it was time for Richard Williams to put feet to his prayers. Right after the Fourth, he would do . . . something.

✒

Ellen and Heather stood on the sidewalk downtown and watched the parade go by. There wasn't much to it compared with what the TV showed. But each year it grew more patriotic. Just about everybody waved a flag. Onlookers weren't just observers anymore, but participants.

"Oh, I need to talk to Patsy. Come on." Heather began walking farther down the sidewalk.

Ellen had dreaded it, but she knew it was inevitable that she and Patsy would run into each other at some point. Might as well get the encounter over with.

Patsy looked startled when Heather walked up beside her and said, "Hi, Mrs. Hatcher."

She glanced over. "Good afternoon, Heather. Hello, Ellen."

Ellen could think no other response but, "Hello," and a brief smile that she hoped didn't look fake. Much as she might have found it difficult to believe at the time, she had become glad that Patsy had fired her. That action had led to so much good for both Ellen and Missy. Ellen kept her eyes fixed on the floats.

"I believe the parade's a little bigger this year," Patsy said.

"I don't think I saw it last year," Heather replied. "I thought I might see you here. I wanted to tell you I got an E-mail this morning from the magazine. The editor loves the article about Little Tykes. I'll send you half the money when I get the check."

"No, no." Patsy shook her head. "You wrote an excellent article that will be wonderful publicity for the school. You keep the money. You've earned it. I don't need it."

"Thank you," Heather said.

Ellen was reminded that Patsy was a good person. She would continue to pray for her.

"Oh, there's Missy." Heather waved with her arm above her head.

Missy waved and shouted. "Hi, Mommy! Hi, Heather! Hi, Mrs. Hatcher!" Her voice carried over the camp director singing, "My Country, 'Tis of Thee," and Richard playing the drums for accompaniment.

The float's skirt was white with red hearts and gold stars. Printed in blue letters were the words, "Jesus Is the Light of the World." The battery-operated candles glowed around the edge of the floor of the float. The children waved Christian flags.

Ellen pretended to not hear Heather pointing out that the drummer was Ellen's new boss and Patsy's response that she was glad things were working out well for Ellen and Missy.

"Oh, your float looks great," Heather said to Patsy as the Little Tykes float began to move by.

Ellen agreed the float looked beautiful, decorated with numerous cartoon characters. Little Tykes Preschool children and workers sat on it. Ellen and Missy had been with them last year. Missy, a year younger then, had sat close to Ellen, perhaps for a sense of security. This year, the brave little girl expressed her independence without Ellen right beside her.

As soon as the last float passed by, Patsy said good-bye to Heather and Ellen. "I feel a chill. I think I'll go on. I don't want to get caught in all the traffic. Have a good day."

"You too," Ellen and Heather replied.

Ellen's gaze followed Patsy, walking swiftly along Main Street to the parking lot that belonged to a friend of hers who was a shop owner and always let Patsy park there. Ellen looked at the big sign at the bank that gave the temperature of eighty-seven degrees. Patsy felt a chill? Maybe it was just nerves. Ellen had felt a little uncomfortable herself when she and Heather first walked up to Patsy.

"Oh, no," Ellen exclaimed suddenly, seeing Patsy falling. The woman tried to brace herself. Her hands seemed to give way, and her head stuck the concrete sidewalk.

"Mrs. Hatcher." Heather was one of the first to reach Patsy.

Almost immediately, an EMT was at the injured woman's side. Soon an ambulance arrived.

Patsy was saying, "I'm all right. I'm all right."

The EMT said, "Ma'am, you'll be fine, but it looks like you have a broken arm. You have anyone who can ride with you?"

Nobody spoke, including Patsy. Ellen knew the woman had no relatives in the area. Her dad had already planned to pick up Missy after the parade. "Can I ride with you?" Ellen asked.

On the stretcher, Patsy's eyes squeezed shut, as if she were in pain. Heather rode in back with Patsy, and Ellen rode in front with the driver, who sounded the siren as the ambulance headed for the hospital in Asheville.

Later, they learned that Patsy had a broken arm. The doctors wanted to keep her overnight for observation since she had also suffered a head injury.

Ellen had already called Daisy so that she might either come and get her and Heather or watch Missy while her dad came.

"I'll stay in touch with the hospital," Heather said later on the way home. "I'll keep you informed about Patsy."

❧

The next morning at work, Ellen told Richard about Patsy.

"You're remarkable, Ellen," he said. "She's the one who fired you, isn't she?"

Ellen smiled, not holding back her joy. "That turned out to be a great blessing."

"Good," he said, but the way he avoided her gaze by looking down at the floor made her wonder if she were too transparent. Then he looked up and asked, "Are you busy tomorrow night?"

If she hadn't been sitting in the chair behind her desk, Ellen thought she would have fallen. Was he asking her for a date? She suddenly realized she hadn't dated in two years.

"Could you be at the Eclectic at six o'clock?"

The Eclectic! That was one of the two nicer places in Ridgeway. Expensive too.

"Yes," she said, all the while thinking she'd have little more than an hour after work to get ready for what could be one of the most important days of her life.

"I've asked Jerry if he will talk to you. I think he could help you with this problem with your dad, since Jerry's a single parent. He's also lost his wife, and you might find it helpful if he talks to your dad."

Ellen stared at a letter on her desk while nodding slightly, avoiding Richard's eyes. He wasn't asking her for a date. He was trying to help her with a bigger problem. She had to get her mind back on track. It had wandered way too far.

She wanted to say that she could talk to Jerry anywhere. Why the Eclectic? She felt like shouting, "Is it Dutch treat?"

Oh dear. Ellen, control yourself. He's trying to help you with the most important matter in your life. Appreciate it. "Why talk there?" she managed to say.

"The atmosphere," Richard said. "And I would like to treat my friend and my employee to a nice dinner. The reservation is in my name. You know how to get there?"

"Yes, I've eaten there." She didn't add, "Once."

"Great." He turned and strode back into his office. She thought his face had flushed. Had he known she'd assumed he was asking her for a date when he'd asked if she were busy?

Well, he couldn't really know her thoughts.

She'd committed to this "date" before she knew the circumstances. How could she bow out gracefully?

Especially when Richard was trying to be a friend.

"Maybe Richard is going to show up," Heather said that evening, rummaging through Ellen's closet for the right outfit.

"I don't know. I wasn't about to ask. Even if he does, I'm going to feel . . . funny."

"Funny? With two handsome men? Well, give me one."

"Oh, go with me!"

Heather shook her head. "No, I'll just wait for your leftovers."

Ellen shook her head and tried to be jolly. They decided she should wear her beige silk dress, gold earrings, and heels. Not too dressy, but not as conservative as what she wore in the office.

Just in case Richard showed up.

She warned herself to stop thinking like that. Again, this was not a date. It was simply a helpful gesture from her boss.

❧

Ellen sat at the table in the Eclectic, looking at the card on the golden disk in front of her that sat on a lace tablecloth. She opened it and read:

> *In appreciation for my most efficient administrative assistant.*
>
> *Richard*

Hey! And it wasn't even officially Administrative Assistant Appreciation Day.

Maybe Richard did intend to join them. He might have thought it would look strange, picking her up as if this were a date, then meeting Jerry.

Smiling, she closed the card, tucked it away in her purse, and looked around at the European decor. The flicker of candlelight from each table emitted a warm glow. A classical pianist accompanied a young woman who stood back in the shadows, softly singing love songs. How could anyone not succumb to such a romantic setting?

She held her breath when she realized the waitress was escorting a man toward her. Not Richard, but Jerry.

They spoke to each other, but he hesitated before sitting. Ellen returned Jerry's uncomfortable smile and refused to look at him again. She kept her attention fixed on the waitress.

In the unromantic silence, the waitress asked, "Would you like something to drink?"

"No!" they said in unison.

The waitress stepped back. "I'll bring your menus."

"Is Richard coming?" Ellen asked.

"I don't think he planned to, Ellen. He told me he would like for me to talk with you about your situation with your dad and Missy. He really thinks I might be able to help. But—" He cleared his throat. "I know how it looks with his having us meet here." He raised his hand. "Don't explode. It's kind of funny."

Ellen looked away. Real funny! She was dressed in a way she hoped would make Richard find her attractive, sitting across from Jerry who wore a knit shirt and casual slacks. No tie. But that's not what mattered.

"Oh, Ellen. I don't mean it's funny being with you. It's funny what Richard is doing. Oh, foot! Maybe it's not funny."

She looked at him then, and rather than cry, she laughed. Jerry plainly saw this as a setup. She had to blink away the moisture of anger, hurt, disappointment, confusion, frustration, embarrassment— every vile emotion one could have.

"Why would he try and be a matchmaker? Doesn't he think we could do this on our own if we wanted?"

He shrugged a shoulder. "Well, you gotta understand him."

Ellen nodded. "I think I'm understanding him loud and clear."

Jerry grimaced. "Well, Ellen. I suspect he wanted to take you out and got cold feet. He did tell me he thought we should talk about your situation. He also told me he'd made reservations here for six o'clock for my birthday, which is Sunday by the way, in case you want to get me a present. Kidding."

She smiled. So, the world was full of jokers! And this joke was on her. Foolish, foolish girl! "He doesn't strike me as one to have cold feet."

Jerry grew serious. "In the area of serious personal relations, he does."

That was hard to believe. "Why?"

He shook his head and smiled sadly. "Sorry, I can't betray a confidence."

Now that piqued her interest. "But there's something? I saw you give him that book on grief. Is he grieving over something or some-one?" That might explain Richard's actions when she had asked if he had ever lost anyone. Was he dealing with something too difficult to discuss?

Jerry simply grimaced and looked around as the waitress came.

"Would you like to know what the special of the house is tonight?" she asked.

Jerry looked at Ellen, who wondered if she should say she'd rather just go. But he smiled and said, "Sure."

Ellen suspected it would be cooked goose.

$$\text{15}$$

an-fried trout. Herbed mashed potatoes. Steamed broccoli. House salad." The waitress handed them the menus and walked way.

"I'm sorry, Ellen," Jerry said.

"It's nice of Richard to do this—I guess," Ellen said.

Jerry took a deep breath, held it for quite a long moment, then exhaled. "I know how it looks, Ellen. And I don't know how to say this, without insulting you, but I didn't put him up to this. I haven't implied anything that might cause him to do this."

He seemed so sincere and uncomfortable, Ellen believed him. "Well, neither have I," she said. "I mean, I've said I thought you were a nice person. That's the extent of it. I mean I might have said, 'You're the greatest,' or something. That I liked you."

"And I admit I've said . . . let's see . . . what were the exact words?" He looked toward the darkened ceiling, then at her again. "That he was fortunate to have found you at the time MaryJo was leaving. He said you were very capable, efficient, and dedicated."

Jerry sighed and shook his head. "Confession time. I also said you were attractive." He spread his hands. "But believe me, I didn't mean a thing disrespectful." He gulped. "Maybe he took me wrong. However, why shouldn't two nice, attractive—whoa, you didn't say I was attractive though, did you?"

Ellen laughed. "I'll say it, Jerry. You're . . . there's nothing wrong with you."

"Okay." He laughed. "Why shouldn't two nice, attractive single people have dinner together?" He grinned. "Especially when it's paid for. Richard said this is on his credit card."

285

Ellen was grateful the room was dim. Maybe he couldn't see her cheeks, which she felt must surely be flaming. Not just with embarrassment, but with a sense of chagrin that anyone would do something like this to her.

"I believe you," she said. "I'm sorry to say this, but rumor has it that you're not interested in dating."

A sadness crossed his face. "That's true. It's not that I can't accept my wife's death. But I won't burden you with my life story."

"It would not be a burden, Jerry. I've had losses of my own. But, if this is too uncomfortable, we can leave."

He remained silent for what seemed an eternity, looking down at the round gold plate in front of him. Finally, he looked up. His eyes were warm. "I've known Richard for several years now. He's a confirmed bachelor, but he loves the idea of family. He means well. But I don't like surprise dates. I think he did it because he likes us both. He thought we'd hit it off." Jerry held his head. "Oh, man. I'm making a mess of this."

"No, no, you're not. I understand. Well, I don't exactly understand Richard's reasoning. But I understand what you mean." She leaned back. "Shall we go?"

He looked sheepish. "Pan-fried trout sounds really good to me. I'm a fisherman. Or rather I used to be. Too busy for that most of the time, with work and Jacob." He sighed heavily. "Maybe if we have a meal together we can get back to being comfortable with each other."

Ellen nodded. Pan-fried trout sounded good to her too, but she didn't want to give the impression she and Jerry had a lot in common. She opened the menu. Many of the entrees looked equally good. She chose the chicken cordon bleu.

They both ordered coffee to keep them busy while waiting.

"So," Ellen said, after the waitress took their menus. "You said you're a fisherman." She laughed lightly. "Or used to be."

By the time the waitress brought their coffee and wheeled over the house salad, on which both accepted fresh black pepper from a pepper mill, they were engrossed in conversation about the area streams and rivers liked by fishermen.

Jerry paused. "Shall we say grace?"

Ellen nodded.

They bowed their heads. Jerry thanked God for Richard's friendship, for the opportunity to make new friends, and for the food.

Ellen knew Jerry was attempting to put everything in perspective. At the "Amen," he opened his eyes and smiled, then continued the conversation where they had left off. "I like the river, but Jacob prefers the streams he can wade in and toss the line, whether or not he's catching any fish."

"I never took to fishing very much," Ellen admitted. "But Dad loves it, and so does Missy. He doesn't go much anymore either."

By the time the entrée arrived, she'd told Jerry about her mom's death, her dad's sadness and ongoing grief, and her concern about Missy.

"I know our ultimate purpose in life is to serve the Lord, but we have our human responsibilities. A man's identity is wrapped up in his job, Ellen. His reason for going to work every day is for his family, taking care of his wife. Amy was my reason for waking up in the morning, for going to work. I can teach Jacob about men's work—the trash, the yard, sports. But when it comes to the tenderness, the emotional side of things, I feel totally inadequate. I can understand how your dad feels. I would like to talk to him. He could likely be helpful to me."

At the end of the meal, they discussed dessert. "We don't want Richard to get off easy, do we?" Jerry asked.

Ellen laughed. "No way."

Each ordered blueberries flambeau and delighted in the waitress preparing the concoction at their table. They, and patrons near them, laughed when the contents of the pan flamed up right at their table.

"Ellen," Jerry said after a couple of bites. "Maybe we should give this a trial run and see what happens. Wouldn't want to hurt Richard's feelings, would we?

Yes, she would!

But that was anger and hurt thinking. That isn't what she wanted at all. Had anyone but Richard done this, she would think it clever. She blinked away the emotion. Her gaze met Jerry's.

"For Richard's sake," he said, with a knowing look in his eyes. "And yours."

She swallowed a big lump of ice cream and waited for the headache matching her heartache.

Looked like she and Jerry understood each other. And who knew what might come of it?

They even sat through another cup of coffee.

❧

Ellen arrived home a little past nine o'clock. Missy was already in bed asleep.

Daisy and her dad were watching TV.

"Have a good time, Dear?" Daisy asked, rising from her chair.

Ellen could answer that truthfully. "I sure did. Jerry is a great guy."

"Jerry?" She gave Ellen a "what's going on" look. "I thought you were having dinner with Richard. Was it a double date?"

"No. Just me and Jerry."

Her dad even turned off the TV. "You sure you didn't go out with Richard? That boss of yours?"

"No, Dad." She raised her hand to her chest. "Did I say, 'Richard'? I had dinner with Jerry. You know, the one who had the birthday party that Missy and I went to. Oh, and he likes to fish."

"What kind? Deep sea?"

Ellen laughed. "No, Dad. The same kind you like—fishing the streams for rainbow trout."

Her dad pursed his lips and nodded. "He sounds okay so far."

"Don't leave on my account, Daisy," she said as Daisy walked toward the kitchen. "I'm beat. Going to bed."

"I need to go home and do that too," Daisy said. "Good night, Jon."

"Night." He switched off the TV and looked at Ellen. "I'm glad you had a good time, Honey."

She nodded, went over, and bent for his hug. She kissed him on the cheek and for a meaningful moment he held her arms. "I love you, Dad."

"I love you too."

Ellen went to her room, telling herself she hadn't lied about Richard and Jerry. One just didn't need to tell everybody, everything, every time.

It had been her own wishful thinking that Richard might be personally interested in her. Maybe he had been. But he was a confirmed bachelor. She knew he liked children, but maybe a thirty-five-year-old bachelor was like her dad had said, not interested in taking on a ready-made family.

Or maybe he just didn't like her . . . romantically.

During that night, Ellen cried. She reminded herself of what she'd felt when she'd heard of girls going back to guys who were no good for them or becoming weeping willows when they were jilted or returned to abusers saying something as foolish as, "But I love him."

Love!

She understood it now.

She knew she wouldn't stand for abuse, she wouldn't chase a guy who ran the other way, she wouldn't accept a man who wasn't good for her. But the other part—the feelings—she wasn't entirely in control of. Feelings and actions, she reminded herself, were two different things, and she was in control of her actions.

Should she quit her job if feelings got in the way? She'd seen old movies where secretaries stayed with their bosses for decades, pining away for them, giving their lives to someone they couldn't have.

She wouldn't be that way.

But she couldn't quit her job just now. Not with this situation with her dad about Missy.

She shouldn't quit anyway because Richard set her up with Jerry. He apparently thought he was honoring his employee and friend with a special dinner. Neat idea, huh? He must think a lot of her to set her up with his best friend. She'd have to thank him.

But at the moment, she would just cry him out of her system.

Thank you, God, that tomorrow is Saturday. I'll wear cucumber slices on my puffy eyes all weekend.

❦

"My pleasure," Richard said Monday morning after Ellen thanked him for the dinner at the Eclectic, but she seemed different. Friendly as ever, but somehow reserved.

Then Jerry stopped by, smiling from ear to ear. He walked into Richard's office, talking about what a great friend Richard was to think of a dinner, with a date no less, for his birthday. Very creative.

When he left Richard's office, Jerry kept the door open, and Richard watched him lean over Ellen's desk and talk to her, like Richard had done at times. On second glance, not exactly like he'd done. Richard hadn't leaned over quite that far, with quite that silly look on his face, and he didn't think Ellen had smiled up into his face like that.

Richard drew in a deep breath.

That was good, wasn't it? What he wanted, wasn't it?

What better thing could happen for two of the finest people he knew than to get together? This might help Ellen's dad think twice about not letting Ellen adopt Missy. If she and Jerry married, she'd be a mom to Jacob. It would be foolish not to let her be a mom to Missy.

Awhile passed before Richard realized Jerry had turned toward him. "Hey," he called, waving his hand in circles like people do when they imply you don't really see or hear them. "So long."

Richard forced a laugh and pointed to some papers on his desk and made circles at his head, meaning he had been deep in thought about his work. "See ya," Richard said.

Jerry and Ellen said final good-byes, then Jerry left.

Richard sat staring at his desk for a long moment before he got up and closed his office door.

❧

Quite often, Richard and Jerry ran into each other at lunchtime in the dining hall. Feeling restless, Richard decided not to wait until Ellen returned from lunch. Sometimes she had errands to run and was a little late. She'd be back soon. He went to the dining hall and filled his plate from the serving line and walked into the dining room, searching for someone he might sit with. He saw Jerry and Ellen.

Never before had he been reluctant to sit with friends or coworkers. But they seemed to be having such a good time, eating, talking, laughing. Yes, he'd been right. Those two hit it off. He'd done well, getting them together.

Just as Richard started to sit at another table, Jerry looked his way and motioned for him to come over. He shouldn't be reluctant. After all, Jerry was his best friend.

He sat.

"Uh oh," Ellen said. "My boss is here. I'd better get back to work."

"Nothing pressing," Richard said.

She smiled. "I'm finished. I do need to get back to work. Don't want to take advantage of my boss's good nature."

Good nature, my foot. Perhaps it didn't show, but Richard knew his attitude lately had been anything but good.

"Before you leave, Ellen," Jerry said. "What were you saying about fishing?"

"Dad says if you want to go Saturday, he'd like to fish the Swannanoa River. Jacob can stay with me and play with Missy. So, are we on for Saturday?"

"You bet. Looking forward to it."

Richard ate his lunch, although he had no idea how it tasted. At least he could use the excuse of eating for not talking. Jerry had finished his lunch. As Jerry talked, Richard made a comment or two, but his mind was seeing a replay of the MaryJo incident. This time the picture was Jerry and Ellen. They'd marry. Everyday he would see Ellen. And when they started their family, she'd grow more beautiful every day. They'd have Jacob and Missy and a newborn.

Richard Williams had instigated the whole thing.

They would thank him . . . profusely.

He'd been overjoyed for MaryJo and Ben.

Why wasn't he feeling that about Ellen and Jerry?

"I want to thank you again for getting me and Ellen together," Jerry said. "I would never have made a move toward her." He laughed. "There for awhile I thought you might be interested in her."

"Me?" Richard almost choked on his food. He glanced down.

Fish! Good. "Think I swallowed a bone." He took a sip of water, then looked over at his friend. "You know I'm a confirmed bachelor."

"Right." Jerry sat there grinning as if he knew a huge secret. Richard supposed he did. Now that he was seeing Ellen, he'd know much more about her than her boss.

16

*E*llen had been thinking about Patsy's situation for several days. On Saturday morning, once her dad and Jerry left to go fishing, she made pancakes for Missy and Jacob. After they discarded their paper plates and she'd wiped the syrup from the table, she asked if they'd like to make cards for a sick woman who had a broken arm and head injury.

The children loved the idea. She'd half-hoped they might say they'd rather watch cartoons, a video, play outside, or even play with Barbies. No such luck. They jumped at the chance. When Ellen said the injured person was Mrs. Hatcher, Missy's little mouth drooped. "Ooooh," she said. "Can we give her flowers?"

"Wonderful idea."

The children made cards from construction paper, markers, and smiley-face stickers that Ellen had saved from an advertisement that had come in the mail. While watching them, Ellen wondered if she should call first.

No, she couldn't chance Patsy saying no.

Heather had said she was more troubled by Patsy's mental outlook than by her physical problems.

"See my card?" Missy smiled, and her blue eyes danced.

Missy had drawn an eye, a heart, and a big U. She put flowers, ranging in color from bright yellow to black, all over the paper.

"Oh, it's beautiful."

Seeing that Jacob was still working on his, Missy said quickly. "I'm not finished. How do you spell "Jesus"?

Ellen told her.

Missy added, "Jesus, heart, U."

Oh dear, maybe this wasn't such a good idea after all.

No, she wouldn't back down. This was a message from Missy. And it was true.

Jacob drew something closely resembling a stick figure with an arm that had squiggly lines going through several places on it. "That's where it's broke." He looked at Ellen for approval.

She gave it, then at his request spelled out "Get well" for him. It looked fine, even though it read "Get mell." She didn't correct him. At a time like this, it really was the thought that counted.

Patsy had a nice brick home in an older residential section of town. As she drove the children to Patsy's address, Ellen warned them that if Patsy wasn't home they would just leave the flowers and cards at the entry. However, she rang the doorbell and after several seconds, Patsy opened the door.

They both looked at each other in silence.

Patsy looked older. Although her hair looked neat, every strand was not in place. She looked pale and thinner than normal. How could she cook, with only a left hand?

A long strip of dark stitches ran across the side of her black, blue, and yellow-green forehead, halfway between her eyebrows and hairline. Dark circles lined her eyes. She wore a loose blouse over slacks. Her right arm, with a cast to the elbow, lay in a sling that draped around her neck.

Would she invite them in?

"Missy and Jacob made cards for you."

Yes, that did it. Patsy would never be rude to a child. "Well, come in," she said softly and smiled at the children. They all stepped into the foyer, and Ellen closed the door behind them. "Now let me see those cards," Patsy said.

Ellen saw Patsy's lips tighten as she looked at Missy's card.

"They designed the cards themselves," Ellen said.

Patsy's quick glance seemed to hold a tinge of amusement. Of course, Patsy would know the children made the cards. But Ellen didn't want Patsy to think she'd prompted the "Jesus loves you" as a reminder of her having been fired.

God, let me not offend her, but let her know I really care.

Patsy praised the children for such thoughtfulness and creativity. "Let's put these in the family room," she said. "Then we'll go into the kitchen and see what kind of surprise we might find for you."

In the family room, she had the children stand their cards up on the desk where several others lay. Two potted plants sat on the desk. "Can we stand these cards up too?" Missy asked.

Patsy said that would be nice.

She led them into the kitchen. "If you'll look under the sink, you'll find some vases."

Ellen found them. She put water in one and arranged the colorful bouquet, then placed it on a small table beneath a window.

"They're beautiful. Thank you so much." Patsy said.

The children were eyeing a plate of brownies. "A neighbor brought those over," Patsy said. "Would you like some?"

The children readily agreed, and Patsy had Ellen tear off a couple of paper towels for them to place their brownies on. Even that small chore would be difficult to do with just one good hand. Ellen felt strange, but good, that Patsy was letting her, even telling her, to get glasses and pour milk for the children. She told them to stay at the table while eating their brownies, then invited Ellen into the sitting room.

Patsy offered Ellen an easy chair, then sat down on the couch, where she leaned back against a pillow. She sighed heavily. "I've never been sick. Now, I feel so . . . helpless."

Helpless? Patsy?

Well, yes, Ellen could see that a vital woman in control of her life and her business would feel terribly helpless under these circumstances.

"I understand a little of how you feel, Patsy. I felt that way when I lost Mom and thought of Missy being without her. That changed my whole life."

"I could empathize to a certain extent, Ellen. I was sorry." She took a deep breath. Ellen had to fight the moisture threatening her eyes when she saw tears in Patsy's eyes. That woman never allowed anyone to see a sign of weakness. She was a very organized, controlled individual with a successful business. And a most difficult business—that of teaching and training little active, energetic children.

"But," Patsy said after a long silent moment. "It's coming closer. My parents, who have always been healthy as horses, are having problems. Mom's memory lapses have become too obvious to be ignored. She's going this week to be tested for dementia. I can't even be there to help right now."

Ellen said softly, "I'm sorry."

She prayed silently as Patsy spoke distantly. "Since Mom's problems began developing, Dad's had difficulty with his breathing."

Knowing Patsy needed to talk to someone, Ellen listened carefully. She almost missed Patsy's near-whisper. "Dad's afraid of hospitals."

Ellen decided to speak. "Well, it's not the most pleasant place."

Patsy looked at her then. "No."

Ellen got a strong feeling Patsy was afraid of hospitals . . . or something. "Can I help in any way? Patsy, I would love to. I had people help me after Mom died. I appreciate that, and it's something I really want to do, if there's any way."

Patsy spread her unbroken hand. "There's nothing anybody can do. I've even been diagnosed with osteoporosis."

Ellen feared saying the wrong thing. "There's medication for that, isn't there?"

Patsy nodded. "Yes, but I've had this for a long time. It was described as mild. Now it's advanced to moderate." She tried to laugh, but the sound came out more like a cry. "I could end up with a hump on my back."

"Maybe not."

Patsy gazed at Ellen for a long moment, then repeated. "Maybe not."

Patsy changed the conversation to Ellen's job. She sounded really interested and pleased for Ellen that things were going well for her and Missy at Ridgeway.

Then Patsy expressed her worries about Little Tykes. "You know Rose, my codirector. She can fill in my job well. My secretary knows how to get things done and consult with me when needed. Even so, I still worry."

Patsy paused, then reached over and touched Ellen's hand. "I want you to know I'm sorry I fired you. If you ever want to come back to Little Tykes, you may."

"Thank you." Ellen felt like Patsy looked as if she'd cry. She thought they were both glad the children came in just then. Ellen said they needed to leave. "But first, we need to make sure the kitchen is clean."

Ellen cleaned up the table and eyed the brownies.

"Why don't you have a brownie, Ellen?" Patsy said.

She did.

When they were ready to leave, the children ran out into the immaculately trimmed lawn and looked at the flower bed. Patsy said, "Ellen, will you . . ." She cleared her throat. "Keep us in your prayers?"

"Yes."

Patsy nodded. "I knew that." She glanced toward the children. "Without asking."

❧

Richard marveled at the light in Ellen's eyes the next day at the office when she told him about going to see Mrs. Hatcher and the favorable response she'd received.

"I called her on Sunday and told her I would be bringing dinner tonight. Of course she protested, then said that would be nice."

"She's the one who fired you, right?"

Ellen nodded. "I think she's never really needed anyone before. If she goes to church, I guess they're not bringing in food. Maybe her friends don't realize how incapacitated one can be with a broken arm."

"Hey, you can get supper from the dining hall any time and take it to her."

"Thanks, Richard. Daisy cooks three nights a week, Dad two, and I do weekends." She laughed. "That's why we eat out on Sunday. But it's no trouble cooking a little extra."

"I understand that. But it might be good to let her know other people care. Our singles group could take dinner at least one night a week. I grill a mean steak, remember?"

She smiled. Richard always noticed the way her dimple dented her cheek in such a delightful way.

"Oh, and I wanted to ask you if this would be possible," she added. "Could I take my lunch hour and breaks at one o'clock, to tell the story at Little Tykes, then come back?"

"Yes, Ellen. You may."

"Thank you." She looked relieved. "Patsy needs to know that I forgive her for firing me. She's been open about having made a mistake in doing so. She's asked me to come back, but I don't feel that's right for me. I took that job primarily for Missy's benefit. Things have changed. But if any of my work isn't finished by Fridays, I'll come in on Saturdays."

Richard stood. "Deal." He extended his hand.

She placed her warm soft one in his.

He shouldn't have done that. He wanted to hold her hand longer, to tell her what a wonderful person he thought her to be. He wanted to encourage her. He wanted to—

He let go of her hand and kept the smile pasted on his face, but he looked down at the desk as he sat down in his chair. "Well, I'll let you get back to work. You're doing a great job, Ellen." He tried to sound like a professional boss. Strictly business. He didn't have a friendly personality like Jerry did. Particularly around Ellen, Richard felt he had become a stiff, withdrawn, self-absorbed man.

But not without good reason.

Richard told himself to keep his mind off personal matters and on spiritual ones. "You know, Ellen," he said as she turned toward her office, "this is an example of why we need to let people know where we stand with the Lord. They may reject us, but they know where to turn in time of need. My mom had a neighbor who didn't want to discuss the Lord. But when her sister was diagnosed with brain cancer, she asked Mom to pray for her."

Ellen nodded. "I guess it's true, God works in mysterious ways."

After she went back to her office, Richard considered the mysterious ways God was working in Ellen's life. Ellen was becoming more confident in her work, in herself, with him. When she first came to work, he'd sensed she wanted to be efficient for him. Now it seemed she wanted to be efficient for the job, as it should be. She even had Patsy Hatcher's offer for her job back if she wanted it.

But he missed the way Ellen used to look at him . . . before Jerry. He felt she was separating herself from him. Before, she'd been reluctant to ask to leave a little early. Now she boldly asked so she could help out the woman who'd fired her.

As if feeling his eyes on her, Ellen looked up from her desk, then stood. "Be back in a jif," she said.

After she left her office he stared at her empty chair.

He missed her.

He had gotten an administrative assistant who replaced MaryJo.

Was there one who could replace Ellen if she went back to work at Little Tykes?

He drew in a shaky breath.

He should be happy. He no longer had to worry about any deep feelings for Ellen. He didn't have to worry about having to reveal his past or give up his personal freedom.

Freedom? He laughed inwardly. The brick wall he'd built around himself hadn't crumbled. It was intact. It was his prison. A great loneliness enveloped him.

He'd done himself a great favor.

He'd done his friend Jerry a tremendous favor.

His ploy . . . had worked.

*E*llen stayed busy. She felt good about Patsy's letting others help her. She liked the work hours too and not having idle time when thoughts of Richard Williams could surface in her mind—just her work. He obviously felt nothing toward her other than as an employer and friend. He'd set her up with Jerry. She should jump at this chance with Jerry. Men like that were rare, she felt sure.

She liked Jerry. He was a wonderful man. A terrific father. A dedicated Christian. But she did not have those special feelings about him. She didn't know how to describe those feelings, but it was something like being in kindergarten and there being one special boy who made her want to please him, to sit near him, and even have him hold her hand.

In college, she'd dated and always asked, "Could I spend my life with him, wake up in the morning lying in the bed beside him?" The answer had always been no. And for the past two years, there hadn't been time or inclination to date. She really hadn't had opportunity to meet any new guys. Suddenly, this summer she'd met two: Richard and Jerry.

Richard wasn't even a consideration if Jerry was right in labeling Richard a confirmed bachelor. Why? Had he just never found the right woman? He had the opportunity to meet many women all the time through conferences and summer programs.

She and Jerry had become close friends. She'd invited him to her home. His son and Missy played well together, a fact that gave the adults a break for a few minutes at a time—at least until someone needed to soothe a hurt, settle a quarrel, put in a video, fix something to eat or drink, or answer two-dozen questions while wiping up a spill.

Jerry and her dad liked to talk. Jerry liked the influence Ellen had on his son. Jerry and Ellen discussed parenting. Did counting to three really work? Spanking? Time out? Being a parent wasn't something that came naturally. He, at least, had to really work at it.

Ellen knew her dad needed to see that she wasn't devoting all her life to Missy. She had activities and people in her life. Her life was full.

She knew Jerry was a wonderful man. There was nothing to detract from him. A woman would be blessed to have a husband like Jerry. *Like* Jerry. Not Jerry himself. He wasn't for her. She wished he were. She wished she wanted to fall into his arms and get that warm, fuzzy feeling she'd heard about. She didn't. To consider that almost seemed to betray their friendship.

❧

Jon liked the idea of Ellen and Jerry together. However, Jerry seemed to spend more time with him than with Ellen. But the children did have to be supervised, and Ellen enjoyed doing that.

He liked Jerry and would enjoy being a grandparent to Jacob." He mentioned it to Jerry one day while they were fishing.

"That sounds ideal, Jon," Jerry said. "There's just one problem. Ellen and I are not in love with each other."

"Well, what's stopping you from falling in love?"

"I don't know. I think it's called the heart."

Jon looked sideways at Jerry. "What's wrong with you fellas?"

Jerry laughed uncomfortably. "Good question. As far as I can see, there's nothing wrong with Ellen. Any man would be blessed to get her. But Jon, she's not interested in me beyond friendship."

Jon tromped down the stream in his waders and cast the line far out from him. He shook his head. Then he looked over his shoulder and shouted, "It's that boss of hers."

Jerry shrugged. "I can't say. She hasn't told me anything like that."

She hadn't said it in words to Jon either. But it had been in her eyes, in her voice when she'd talked about him before she started up with Jerry. When she spoke of Jerry, her eyes just held warmth. When she spoke of her boss, they held a wistfulness.

Things being so unsettled with Ellen seemed to confirm for Jon that no, it wasn't God's will for Ellen to adopt Missy.

᠅

Richard opened his office door after lunch and couldn't believe Ellen and Jerry stood there, embracing. He stared. They broke apart and stared at him, then Ellen sat down as if nothing had happened. Jerry followed when Richard said to him, "Would you come in here, please?"

Jerry walked past him, then Richard shut the door . . . firmly.

Jerry sat in a chair as if nothing was amiss. Trying to control his emotions, Richard paced. "That is not the kind of behavior I tolerate, and you know it."

Jerry sighed. "Can I say something?"

Richard stopped pacing and faced him. "What?"

But he didn't give Jerry time to speak. "That you're sorry? It won't happen again? Forgive you? Forget it?" He shook his head. "Jerry, we don't operate that way here. You know I've sent young people home for any hint of intimacy with each other. Adults have to set the example."

He couldn't believe he heard right when Jerry said, "I'm resigning."

"What?"

"I'm resigning."

Richard shook his head, then put his hand to his forehead. He went over and braced his hands on the window sill and stared out the window. Finally, he went behind the desk and sat. "No, Jerry. I'm wrong here. I made too much of this. Forgive me."

"I'm not angry, Richard. You're right in what you said. And I know what Ellen and I did was perfectly innocent. But I'm resigning."

"Jer—we've been friends for years."

Jerry smiled. "We still are."

"Then why would you let my foolish rantings cause you to leave? Of all people, you know I'm not perfect. And Jerry, my taking out my frustrations on you isn't nearly as bad as some things I've confessed to you. You know how stupid I can be at times."

"Look at me, Richard."

Richard finally fell silent and looked at his friend.

"Do I look mad?"

"Quite the contrary." Richard didn't understand the look on Jerry's face. "Frankly, your expression is annoying."

"Well, I wasn't born to be the most handsome man around, but that's no reason to insult me."

Richard couldn't help but grin and shake his head at his friend of many years. Jerry had often joked about women chasing Richard because they thought him good-looking. But Richard knew his own reserved personality didn't appeal to others the way Jerry's warmth and openness did. "I'm aware you know how to behave in public, Jer. I was off-base. Sometimes things just pile up."

"I know that, Richard. I can't even count the times I've lashed out at you and the world and God after Amy died. You're the one I took my anger out on and sometimes in a way that I made you the object of that anger."

"I understood that, Jerry."

Jerry nodded. "And I understand this."

Richard stared at the knowing eyes of his friend. Knowing, or accusing? Jerry couldn't possibly understand what lay at the bottom of his anger. "Okay, then you forgive me?"

"Sure," Jerry said. "I forgave you before you said it."

"Great. And I forgive you for not resigning. Now, you'd better get back to work before I fire you."

They both laughed.

But Jerry continued to sit. "Richard. My resignation has nothing to do with what went on out there or your reaction. Jacob is starting public school in the fall. He needs his grandparents, and they need him. I have decided to go back to my own hometown. I'm ready to live now, Richard. I've lived only for Jacob since Amy died."

They talked for awhile longer, then Jerry rose to leave. Richard again apologized for his outburst. "I don't know what's wrong with me."

Jerry said, "Don't you, Richard? I think it's time we both got over our losses. Ellen taught me that. Her dad taught me that. I think I can move on now. Be ready to relate to a woman in a more personal way if God has that in mind. I never thought I could. Now I do."

He spoke emphatically. "Richard, it's time we both let go of the past."

Jerry didn't close the door when he left Richard's office. Richard watched as Jerry placed his hands on the edge of Ellen's desk and leaned toward her.

Ellen listened attentively to the words that Richard couldn't make out. She smiled and nodded. Jerry smiled and reached over to clasp her hand.

Richard didn't have to hear what was said. He could read the body language. It spoke as loudly as words—perhaps more loudly. He turned toward the window, hoping his face would cool before either Jerry or Ellen might walk into his office.

His eyes lifted toward the opaque white sky. Isn't this where he was supposed to say, "Thank You, Lord"? Isn't this what he wanted when he threw Jerry and Ellen together? Didn't he hope those two deserving people would become a family and then two little children could have two loving parents?

He'd heard the saying, "Be careful what you want. You might get it."

Be happy for them, Richard. This is a good thing. You accomplished something good. They would have found each other without you. But you did play apart. It's your doing . . .

Well, fine . . .

Accept it!

Richard was disgusted with himself. He had no business letting emotion get the better of him this way. He was a matter-of-fact man. Man, yes! Not a kid. He needed to act mature. Be mature.

Determined to obey his mind, which he'd often lost confidence in, he swivelled around again and there stood Jerry, with that unreadable silly expression again. Is that what's called the love expression?

Next, Jerry would probably tell him that he and Ellen were to be married. He'd ask Richard to be the best man.

Best man?

What a joke. *You're the best man, Jer. I'm the worst.*

❧

As usual, July was particularly busy. The center was filled with one big conference after another. Richard had little time for personal pleasure. Jerry was busy getting ready to move as well as taking care of his increased workload that occurred every July as he designed more and bigger brochures for conferences and continued work on the coming year's catalogues.

Richard spent more time in the office with Ellen, as they worked closely together on preparations for the final candlelight service for summer staff.

"All the staff is expected to attend," Richard said. "We like to make this an unforgettable experience." He hoped she might give him a clue if she would be here. Jerry was leaving the day of the service. Neither of them had been as open with each other since Jerry and Ellen had become close.

Now, Ellen just nodded that she understood.

"Also," Richard said. "You can start organizing the list for making appointments at colleges for my recruitment of summer staff. That will begin in the fall after school starts." He watched her making notes. "Are you planning to return to school this fall?"

She glanced up at him and back at her notepad. "I'm not sure yet."

"You'll let me know?"

He wanted to know if she and Jerry were serious. Or if she was going leave him and return to school. But she gave no clue.

"Sure I'll let you know," she said. The phone rang, and she turned to answer it. Richard returned to his office.

He regretted that Ellen had moved away from him emotionally. But he had no one to blame but himself. He'd pushed her away. He should have been honest with her from the beginning. But then, that might require being honest with himself.

Now, he must get back to the way things were before Ellen came into his life.

Back to business . . . as usual.

$\mathcal{E}$llen still loved her job but wondered about the wisdom of working so closely with Richard. Her feelings for him were growing stronger, rather than weaker. She honestly didn't know what to do about work or school. She kept praying for a sign.

In the meantime, she counted her blessings, knowing they were numerous, and she had little choice but to stay busy. She rarely saw Heather, who was over her head in finishing her thesis and studying for the pass-fail comps she'd have to take in a few months.

One Friday evening in mid-July, Ellen took supper to Patsy and sat across the table from her, drinking a cup of coffee.

"You're looking good, Patsy," Ellen could honestly say. The bruises had vanished, the stitches had been removed, and the red streak was fading. She'd gained some weight back.

"Thank you," she said, "but Ellen, what's bothering you? You're not your old cheerful self."

Ellen didn't want to share her feelings about Richard with anyone. She needed to stay focused on the more pressing issue. She knew Patsy cared about Missy.

"Dad has invited Leanne, Missy's birth mother, to come and visit. That bothers me. What if Leanne wants Missy now?"

Patsy listened intently to all Ellen said about the matter. "Ellen, I can't say what is best. But the Lord knows. I could tell you were devastated when I fired you. But God worked that for good, didn't He?"

Ellen nodded. Even if there could never be a relationship with Richard beyond friendship, she wasn't sorry for having known him.

He was a wonderful man, who considered his job a service for the Lord. But what did Patsy know about the workings of the Lord?

"You're surprised, Ellen," Patsy said, as if she'd read Ellen's mind. "Let me explain. When I was principal of the primary school, I had to be so careful to avoid offending someone of another faith. But things have gotten so out-of-hand, Ellen. Everyone can be open about their faith except Christians."

Ellen knew how that felt. It had happened to her at Little Tykes.

"Yes, I do believe in God," Patsy continued. "One would have to be an idiot to think this world came from a big bang, and a human being was once a fish in the ocean. I mean, where'd the stuff come from to bang and where'd that single cell come from? It just happened?" she scoffed.

Ellen smiled.

Patsy's voice lowered, as if trying to keep from startling Ellen further. "I even believe Jesus is the Son of God. I was jealous of your openness about your personal relationship with Him. I'd become conditioned to saying that's private. What I really was saying is that my faith wasn't top priority."

Ellen saw a tear roll from the corner of Patsy's eye and got up to get a tissue. This was so unlike the woman. She never cried to anyone.

"I couldn't have children. I wanted that more than anything. My husband wanted a family. I was jealous. You lost your mother, but you had a beautiful child. I love children."

"You're good with children, Patsy. They love you."

Patsy nodded. "I've decided to quit blaming God because I was barren." She took in a deep breath, then exhaled. "Firing you was a mean thing."

"Patsy, I forgive you. Maybe you need to rest. We can talk about this—"

Patsy was shaking her head. "Please, I need to say this."

"Okay."

"Firing you turned out to be one of the best things that could have happened to me. My conscience wouldn't let me be. Or maybe more accurately, God wouldn't let me be."

Ellen reached over and squeezed her hand. "Then I think I served my purpose—or God's—in working for you for two years."

Patsy smiled. "I've decided I should let the world and the children know that I am a Christian. I know that some of them don't go to church, because they talk about where they went over the weekend. I need to be open about my beliefs. Not force it on any child, but let it be what I believe and leave it up to the parents what to do with that information. Forgive me, but at the time, I said to myself, 'What does that young, uneducated whippersnapper Ellen know about life and raising children?'"

"I do forgive you. And I don't know a lot about raising children. I have to learn as I go."

"We all do," Patsy admitted. "I wanted to hurt you by saying you're not a mother. But you are. You have a mother's heart, a mother's instinct toward Missy."

Ellen replied, "Like you've had with hundreds of children, thousands really."

"It's what I like to believe," Patsy said. "And don't you forget, you have a job at Little Tykes, if you ever want it."

❧

Ellen could go back to Little Tykes. She'd liked it there.

She liked the job at Ridgeway, even if she could never be more than friends with Richard. It was a worthwhile job working with an organization whose purpose was to attract people to the Lord Jesus Christ and strengthen their faith.

She could easily have fallen in love with Richard. Now that she'd been forced to take a few steps backward and analyze her feelings, her deeper desires surfaced. If Richard wasn't the man God had chosen for her, or she was not the woman He'd chosen for Richard, then God had someone else in mind for her—she hoped. If not, she could devote her life to making a difference in the lives of others, as Richard had apparently done.

Just raising Missy in the admonition of the Lord had been a full-time, most rewarding project. She smiled at the thought.

She was still smiling when she opened the kitchen door, saw the stack of mail on the table, and opened the letter from New York addressed to Ellen and Jon Jonsen.

Dear Uncle Jon and Ellen,
  Thanks loads for inviting me to visit.
  I can fly down as soon as there's a break in my soap story. You know, they jump from one thing to another, and others on the soap have the leading story at times. Right now, it's mine. So, I'll let you know.

  Love,
  Leanne

P.S. I have a man in my life finally. Hector Myers, known as Rock Samson *on* Love's Sweet Promise. *He's the one with the muscles.*

Ellen had ceased to smile. She remembered her dad being concerned about what kind of man would raise Missy. What more could one want than a rock with muscles! She told herself not to be sarcastic. More seriously, she wondered what all her dad had said to Leanne.

She asked him after Missy went to bed.

"Ellen, I've agonized over this. I've been reluctant to consider changing our situation. Missy is my daughter. I've asked Daisy if she would help me raise her. She doesn't feel up to taking her on as a full-time responsibility any more than I do. It's not that I don't want to. I'm just not the best person for her."

Ellen felt the frustration welling up in her again. "And you don't think I am."

"Oh, Ellen. I know you are. That's not the problem. And Jerry has helped me see that a single parent can do a great job with a child. You've proved it for the most part during the past two years. But I am not convinced it's best for you."

"It's what I want, Dad."

He sighed. "I know. But this decision is mine to make, not yours. I have to live with giving my little girl to someone else. I want to do the right thing for everyone, and what that right thing is simply isn't clear to me yet."

Ellen began to understand that her dad's struggles were not against her or her ability to be a mom. "Dad, I'm sorry I haven't been more sympathetic."

But she couldn't bear to think of Missy leaving them. "Dad, you're great with Missy. Can we just leave everything like it is? If I ever do marry, I'd still be part of Missy's life. Let's just not make any hasty decisions."

He was nodding, but the look on his face didn't reflect agreement. "I've struggled with this for a long time, Ellen. In all good conscience, I have to give Leanne the opportunity to settle this once and for all. I know it's settled legally, but if that girl changes her mind and wants Missy, then it can cause all kinds of trouble for us. It's different since your mom died. I've seen situations on TV and read in the news about parents showing up later in a child's life and gaining custody. I don't want to chance that."

"I understand that, Dad. But you're forcing the issue. Leanne has seen pictures of Missy, and she's never indicated she wants her."

"She's nineteen now, Ellen. And her letter made it sound like she is thinking of serious relationships. She's not a fourteen-year-old girl anymore." His eyes became teary. "This breaks my heart, Ellen."

Tears stung Ellen's eyes as well. She hadn't seen her dad cry since her mom died. She began to realize how he agonized over the situation. She began to see the situation from his point of view. Her dad didn't think her a terrible mom. He just wanted to do the right thing for both his daughters.

He opened his arms to Ellen, and she fell into them. They hugged each other more tightly than they had in a long time.

◦৶

Richard helped with the planning for the going-away luncheon the department heads would have for Jerry on his last day at Ridgeway, but he still wanted to do something special with Jerry apart from that. Before he decided what to do, Jerry came up to him after church.

"Let's have lunch together, Richard. Jacob's going home with his friend Chris for the afternoon."

Richard wanted to spend time with his friend, but he hoped he wouldn't end up hearing all about the growing relationship between Jerry and Ellen. They were two of the most wonderful people he knew, and already he felt the loss of them both.

Since the two men ate daily at the Ridgeway cafeteria, they opted for the Fish Camp, where they could be waited on. They sat in a booth by a window with a view of a deep green boxwood hedge bordering the parking lot and beyond that the main road with the mountains in the background.

Richard knew Jerry liked the mountains. "Think you can adjust to being away from here?"

Jerry scoffed. "You're my best friend. I plan to come back and visit often."

Richard felt uneasy, thinking of Jerry and Ellen in his home as a married couple. "You're always welcome. But it would be a little strange to have you at my home with a wife."

Jerry stared at him the entire time the waitress set their plates in front of them. As soon as she moved away, Jerry said, "A wife? Does that mean you have someone else in mind to set me up with?"

Richard stared at him. "Uh . . . let's pray." He quickly added, "You pray."

Jerry asked God's blessing on the food, then looked across at Richard with a dumbfounded expression. "I should have prayed for your sanity, Richard."

"What do you mean?" Richard unwrapped his silverware from the cloth napkin.

"I mean, there's nothing beyond friendship between me and Ellen. I knew you were just trying to back away, like you've always done when it seems you or a woman might start getting serious."

Richard poised his fork over the fish. "You know me too well."

"Fortunately." Jerry picked up a fried shrimp, dipped it in sauce, and took a bite. After a moment, he spoke. "If either Ellen or I didn't care about you, then that situation might have been ideal. We like each other, Richard. But I'm your friend. You and Ellen will have to deal with what you are to each other."

Richard took a bite of his fried oysters. "Good," he said, while chewing, wondering if Jerry would believe his pleasure was because of the food.

He didn't. "Richard, it's time you dealt with your problem and let it go. Ellen and her dad are the kind of people who can understand what you've been through."

"I've dealt with it." Richard poked his oysters with his fork. "I think Ellen likes me and respects me. But why should I tell her something that's going to make her lose respect for me? I mean, look at her. She's gorgeous, makes all the right decisions. How could she accept my past?"

"Oh, Richard. You just don't know. She has her faults."

Richard straightened. "What faults?"

Jerry put his fork down and laid his hand on the table near his plate. He began to tap on the table with his index finger. "She does that when she's thinking or agitated."

Richard stared at him. "You're kidding."

"Nope." Jerry picked up his fork and started eating again.

"Jerry. That's nothing. I'm a drummer, remember."

Jerry looked across at him quickly and with food in his mouth said, "Well. That sounds like a match made in heaven to me."

Richard finished his meal, thinking it was the best he'd eaten in a long time.

❧

On Monday, Ellen felt the pressure of constant activities at work. All departments cooperated in dealing with conferences, big and small, which created a constant flow of people coming and going. Richard had said July would be the most hectic month, and she'd discovered that was an understatement. Besides daily business, there was the planning for the final candlelight service for the summer staff around the lake.

She and Richard hardly had time to acknowledge each other's presence, until he said, "It mustn't rain on closing night. You put in an order for a clear sky."

She laughed. That felt good. There hadn't been either time or inclination for much laughter. Also she was working on setting up his recruitment appointments.

After lunch, she was needed for a couple of hours to help with registering conferees.

"Your dad called," Richard said when she got back to the office.

She returned the call and slumped into her desk chair when her father asked if she could pick up Leanne from the airport. Her flight would arrive at 4:14. Daisy was cooking dinner for them all. He'd already gotten Missy from preschool. "Do you mind?" he asked.

"Hold on," she said. "Let me ask."

"I know it's our busiest time," she said as she walked into Richard's office. She told him why she needed to leave within thirty minutes.

"You may leave now, if that helps," he said. "Come back in after you hang up with your dad."

Minutes later, she went back into his office and stood beside his desk, looking out the window.

"We haven't talked for awhile, Ellen, about the situation with your dad and Missy. I just wanted you to know I care, and I've been praying about it."

"Thanks." She tried to force down the flood of emotion she feared might erupt. "I appreciate that. I'm beginning to understand my dad, although I still think he's wrong. What do you think? Should he even consider bringing Leanne into this?"

Richard rose from his chair and went over and closed the door. He stared at the floor as he paced a few steps. "Ellen, it seems to me that a child who has had one loving home for over four years, shouldn't be uprooted. At the same time, I can sympathize with parents who might want their child, even if they haven't seen the child in over four years. At the same time, I know what this is doing to you. I know."

The way he said it made her believe he really understood. "Richard, do you know firsthand about these types of situations?"

Suddenly, she felt like a curtain closed between them. He took a step, as if to walk away from her. She saw the rise of his shoulders. Then he turned toward her again. His dark eyes seemed filled with pain. After releasing a deep breath he said, "Ellen, I can empathize to a certain extent. There is something I would like to tell you. It's a situation that comes between us, totally because of me. Right now, I would like to tell you. Maybe that's because you have to leave and there isn't time."

"I wish you could confide in me," she said sincerely.

He nodded. "I would like to. In another sense, it's something I don't like facing over and over. It's done. It's unchangeable, but it haunts me." He shrugged. "But you don't need the burden of my confession. You have your own problems."

"Oh, Richard. Maybe I can't solve your problems. But it's meant so much to me when you've listened about how I hurt when I think of Missy being taken from me. I can't handle my concerns by myself. It helps just to talk about it and get another's opinion."

"I know," he said. "I've talked with Jerry. That was hard, but in a way it was a release. If ever there's one in whom I could confide, Ellen, it would be you. I have been praying about this and will continue to until I feel peace about disclosing something this personal that happened in my past."

"The past is forgiven," she said. "It's over."

"Yes," he said. "But think of it this way. If your cousin thinks she made a mistake for giving up her child, she could be forgiven. But there are still issues to be dealt with and decisions to be made. A beautiful child's future must be decided. I wish I had the answer. But I'm sorry. I can't be objective about this situation. If Missy were yours, and you were the one who had given her up, do you suppose you would not have thought of her, wanted her, even if you had done the right thing at age fourteen?"

Ellen hadn't wanted to look at it that way. "Oh, Richard. You're right. I wish you weren't. I can see that my desires may be selfish."

He shook his head. "No. I think your desires are based on having become Missy's mom in every way except having given birth to her."

"But I need to think of other people too. Leanne's only nineteen. I wasn't very mature at nineteen. But I'm sure her situation at fourteen matured her in many ways. Just as my mom's death and my home situation matured me."

Richard nodded. "I understand. These jolts in life have a way of making us face ourselves in a different, more mature way and realize how much we need God to be in our lives, not just on the periphery."

Ellen knew Richard had a great strength within him. She was so quick to tell whomever would listen about her problems. She wished Richard would confide in her. At the same time, she admired his maturity in trying to be sure that he should share his burden.

She didn't think about what happened next. She just went over to Richard, and when she came close, he opened his arms to her, like her dad had done. The embrace felt like friends consoling friends.

After a long moment, he released her. His lips brushed hers for the briefest moment, then he held her at arm's length. "Ellen," he said. "As much as I would like it to be different, I know what is between us must come to a stop unless I can be honest with you about myself. Now you'd better leave, or you'll be late."

She nodded.

Richard did care for her. But what terrible thing had he done that so disturbed him?

～❧

On the way to the airport, Ellen gave herself a good lecture. She began to see that her motives in wanting Missy to be hers had been based on what she believed was right and good. But she hadn't considered the distress all this had caused her dad.

Ellen had agonized over possibly losing Missy. She hadn't considered that Leanne might have agonized over having given up Missy.

And she had been more concerned about her own situation than about picking up on the distress in Richard's life.

"I'm trying, God. I'm giving it to You," she said aloud while speeding along the interstate. At least she said the words, even if her heart still held on. She wanted Missy. She believed Missy needed her more than anyone. Well, no, she needed her Pa-Pa too. Ellen began to realize her dad was going through the same kind of agony as she.

She recognized beautiful Leanne immediately, although she hadn't seen her in more than four years. She'd seen the younger girl in photos and a couple of times on the TV soap opera.

They hugged.

Ellen began to realize that Leanne was more nervous than she.

"You think I'm awful, don't you?" Leanne said as soon as they were settled in the car.

That surprised Ellen. "Why would I think that?"

She could barely hear Leanne, who spoke softly when she said, "Because I gave up my own baby."

"No," was all Ellen could say for a moment. She focused on the road in front of the airport and on making her turns before pulling out onto the main road. Again, it struck her how she had not considered others' feelings the way she should. Her mom and dad had sent pictures of Missy to Leanne. Ellen had never written a letter to Leanne or acknowledged that Leanne's heart might be broken by her sacrifice.

Ellen began to talk honestly and listen attentively to this young girl who had lost what had become most precious to Ellen. Finally, Leanne said she always thought she'd done the right thing.

"But I've lived a life of pretense," she said. "In high school, I went to ball games, acted in all the plays, and pretended I was just another teenager." She shook her head.

Ellen glanced over and saw the tears on Leanne's cheek.

"I know," Leanne said after taking a tissue and dabbing at her eyes, "that Uncle Jon wants me to take Missy now."

"Oh no," Ellen said quickly. Then she stopped to think how to say this without imposing her own desires. "He just wants you to have the opportunity. He thinks you should see her and settle this once and for all."

"We did that when Missy was born," Leanne said.

"I know, Leanne. But our situation changed. Dad thinks yours may have also. But I want you to know that I am selfish enough to want Missy as my own. I feel like she's my own."

"I do too," Leanne said. "Your dad has written about how you took over after Aunt Mary died. You're in the same position I was in when I gave her up."

"Not really." Ellen paused as she turned onto the interstate. "You were younger. Didn't want a lasting relationship with Missy's dad. You said you weren't ready. Leanne, I am ready. Missy was my little sister for two years. For the past two years, she has been my daughter."

"Do you think maybe you're trying to fill the void of losing your mom?"

"No." Ellen could answer that without hesitation. "Nothing can fill the void left by my mom's death. And to be honest, I don't need Missy in my life to be fulfilled."

Ellen had to stop and let her throat clear before she could go on. The emotion was just too great. She tried again. Her chest hurt. "If you take her, I would be devastated. In my heart, she is my child. But I also love her enough to accept giving her to you, if that's what you and Dad decide is best."

Leanne sat silent for a long moment. Then she took a deep breath and spoke again. "I don't know how I will feel when I see Missy for the first time."

❧

When they arrived home, Leanne embraced her uncle Jon. Ellen then introduced her to Daisy and Missy.

"Missy, this is my cousin, Leanne."

"Hey, My-cuz-in."

They all laughed. Ellen explained that "My-cuz-in" wasn't Leanne's name. She was a relative, like an aunt or uncle.

Missy's eyes brightened. "Oh, yes. I have two cousins. They're in . . . Where are they, Mommy?"

Ellen dared not look at Leanne to see her reaction to Missy calling her Mommy. "Bret and Rita are in Arkansas."

"Yeah. Arkansas."

Leanne smiled. "You're adorable."

Missy took on her sassy attitude. "I'm Missy."

"An adorable Missy."

"And you're My-cuz-in." She giggled.

They sat down to supper, and Missy did what she loved doing when allowed—talk constantly. She told about her school, fishing, friends, and church. Ellen watched Leanne for reactions. She could tell Leanne loved Missy from the moment she saw her, and her wonder at the little girl seemed to grow.

Ellen also noticed that Leanne ate very little of her supper. Was it because of inner turmoil or was she simply watching her calories?

After supper, Leanne leaned back in her chair. "My flight goes out tonight at nine-thirty. Uncle Jon, could I talk with you?"

"Let's walk," he said.

Ellen and Daisy cleaned up the kitchen, while Missy dressed her Barbies for Leanne to see when she returned from her walk.

After they came back and Missy showed her Barbies, Dad said, "Missy, let's let Ellen and Leanne talk awhile. You, me, and Daisy can get some lemonade and go outside to the swing set. What do you say?"

"Oh, neat!"

"By that response," Ellen said, "you'd think this was her first time on the swing set instead of it being something she plays with several times a day."

Ellen dreaded the wistful look in Leanne's eyes as her gaze followed the gray-haired man and little tow-headed girl as they walked out into the backyard.

"You guys have done a great job with her," Leanne said. She sighed. "I talked to Hector about it. His career is just taking off like mine. He doesn't think marriage is best at this time, much less taking on the responsibility of a child. I don't even have mom to help me. She's tied up with her work and her own life. Like you said, Uncle Jon is trying to do the right thing. I think he has all along, Ellen, and so have you."

Ellen held her breath. Was Leanne saying what Ellen hoped she was saying?

"I'm so glad you want her, Ellen. You or your dad, either one. When he called me, I thought he wanted me to take her. But in my line of work, raising a child would be difficult. Especially a child who doesn't know me."

"Do you think," Leanne said, tears filling her eyes, "someday you could let her know about me? That I . . . loved her?"

Ellen breathed a sigh of relief and a thankful prayer. "Yes, we can do that."

(19)

*f everyone lit just one little candle, what a bright world this
would be.*

The line of that song ran through Ellen's mind as she
stood in the last row of hundreds of people, each holding a candle,
gathered around the lake at the boys' camp. This service marked the
end of the summer season.

It might mark the end of her summer season too. So much had
happened—losing and regaining a relationship with Patsy, fearing losing Missy but coming to an understanding with her dad, not really
losing Richard because he'd never been hers. The past week had been
too busy for confidences, other than her briefly telling him that she
and her dad were seriously talking now about Missy's future without
Leanne being an issue. Richard had been pleased, but he hadn't confided in her about himself.

The song leader led the group in the season's theme song, "Jesus is
the Light of the World."

I can do all things with Christ's help. The verse ran through Ellen's
mind. She'd lived without her mom. Her dad had said he wouldn't try
to force Ellen into a relationship or a career but would just let her
make her own decisions.

What did God have for her? The words of the song rang through
the night. She couldn't help the emotion that welled up in her. She felt
God's peace, but at the same time, her heart was filled with thoughts
of her mom; Leanne, who didn't have her child with her; and Richard
with whatever secret he harbored. She turned and stepped away from
the crowd gathered around the lake.

She was startled to see Richard. Apparently, he'd been standing back from the crowd, behind her. She looked up at him, knowing her eyes were moist. She couldn't speak.

He reached out his hand. "Could I talk with you, Ellen?"

Unable to find words, she nodded and put her hand in his.

They walked together along the shadowed path, where moonlight filtered down through the overhanging tree limbs.

❧

Richard knew he could only tell Ellen in the dark. He wished he could be telling her he loved her and wanted to spend the rest of his life with her and Missy. But a night that might have been romantic was instead a night to face the consequences of his past. This would put an end to his own longing that could never be fulfilled.

Jerry had always said Richard got cold feet when anything more serious than friendship threatened to develop between him and a woman. Now his feet felt like ice!

But as they walked along the path toward the picnic area, Richard knew if he didn't face this now, he never would. The sound of singing faded in the background, replaced by the flow of babbling water in the creek.

Now that he'd decided to talk, he knew no other way than to just say it. "Ellen, my withdrawal from close personal relations began with four words spoken by my girlfriend when we were in college. She said, 'I've had an abortion.'" He admitted what hurt so much. "Because of my callousness, she did that. She wanted me to love her. And I made it clear I didn't want a baby. Before I even had a chance for the news of her pregnancy to sink in, she had the abortion. But her choice was my fault. I had told her that I loved her, but my reaction to her pregnancy showed anything but love. I didn't tell her to have an abortion. But I caused her to make that choice by my attitude."

❧

Ellen felt Richard's sorrow as he walked over and slumped down on the seat of a picnic table. She sat beside him. "Did you ask God to forgive you?"

"Over and over," he said.

"And how many times does it take before He forgives you?"

A scoffing, laughing sound emerged from his throat. "Well. Come on, Ellen."

"I mean it, Richard. How much begging do you have to do before God forgives you?"

"You know the answer to that."

She spoke softly. "I would like to hear you say it."

He sighed heavily. "Of course He has."

Richard's face was in shadows. She could hear the anguish in his voice. "Because of me, my own baby . . . was murdered."

Ellen didn't know how she could reply to that. He believed abortion was murder. His baby had been aborted. "But you didn't do it. And God will forgive your girlfriend if she asks."

"I believe that," he said. "But she did it because of my reluctance to admit or take responsibility. I could have said I'd marry her. Or that I would take care of the baby. My parents would have done that. Just like your parents wanted to take Missy. Mine would have helped in any way. But I was irresponsible."

He took a deep breath, and his next words sounded shaky. "I'm responsible for the murder of my own flesh and blood."

Silence. Crickets. Frogs. The rushing water a background for what? To Richard, was it all a condemnation?

Jesus came to give living water—forgiveness.

"Richard, I've sinned too. I've done the usual things teens get into, and in college I went further than high school days in many areas. Even today, I speed on the interstate. I lose my temper. I have thoughts I shouldn't have and sometimes entertain them instead of getting rid of them. Right after Patsy fired me, I hated her for what she was doing to me and Missy, how she had disrupted the routine we'd seemed to be settling into after Mom died."

He scoffed. "Ellen. That's nothing compared with what I've done. What I have to live with."

"Isn't it?" She felt herself becoming angry. "Did Jesus die only for the people who speed or steal a twenty-dollar bill or curse?"

"Come on."

"No, Richard. He died for every sin, or none at all. I can't say a person gets forgiven for speeding, but not for . . ." She hated the word but knew he had said it. Taking a deep breath, she continued. "Not for murder. Do you believe people in prison can be forgiven for murder?"

"Yes," Richard answered. "If they're truly repentant and proclaim the Lord Jesus as their Savior and change their ways. Ellen, I've known these things all my life. I could answer any of the basic Bible questions that you could ask me."

"Oh, it's just you who can't be forgiven then?"

"Okay, Ellen. You want me to say it. Yes, God forgave me. But I can't forgive myself. I try. No, I don't go around thinking about it. But it's like my heartbeat. It's a part of me."

"And you're trying to punish yourself by never getting married. Never having a child."

"I want those things, Ellen. I just can't see anyone respecting me after knowing this about me. I've never told anyone except Jerry."

"Why are you telling me?"

"Because I care for you and every day that caring grows deeper. I want to be near you, around you. And I have to do something to make you go away from me. I wouldn't have to tell you if you married Jerry, but you didn't. I wouldn't have to tell you if MaryJo returned, but she didn't. And it's ridiculous to fire you and get someone else now that you know the job. I feel I owe you an explanation for my actions, although I have to face the fact that you can never respect me again, that there's no chance for the two of us together."

No chance? Her heart beat fast at the prospect of every chance. But at the moment, this conversation was not about her. Richard was confiding in her, like a friend would do. She must keep her focus on that.

"Richard, what would you say to one of your college staff in this situation?"

"I would tell them to accept God's forgiveness, forgive themselves, and go on with life. I know those things. I don't listen to my own counsel." He turned his hand over and held hers. "Now that I've told you, I realize even more that the problem lies within myself. I remember the last time I saw Colleen, we were in a screaming match. She was telling me what she thought of me, which wasn't much, and I was blaming her and killing her heart with my words."

"Richard, have you forgiven Colleen for killing your baby?"

He shook his head. "I've tried."

Ellen laid her hand on his shoulder. "I hope you find it in your heart to forgive her."

Richard nodded. "I have to find a way to let go of this, so I can go on with my life."

"Richard," she said softly. "I respect you for admitting this. I can see how hard that is for you. I just want you to know that I think you're a wonderful man."

❧

Richard awoke in the middle of the night with Colleen on his mind. He also thought of Mark Freedlan. Mark had been a friend of his at the university. Now he was a college professor there. They hadn't kept in touch, but Richard received a form letter from the university each year about alumni gatherings which Richard had ignored.

Early in the morning, although having no idea what time Mark might leave home for the university or how far from it he lived, Richard called the university. He drummed his fingers on the countertop while listening to numerous computerized responses until he realized that this was exactly what callers got when they called Ridgeway, unless they knew the number of a person in a particular department.

Finally, he managed to reach a person who connected him to Dr. Freedlan's voice phone. Richard left his name and number.

That evening, Mark called, excited to hear from him.

"We'll have to get together one of these days and talk over old times," Mark said. Richard heard children and activity in the background. Mark said he had married and they had two young children.

They got to talking about some of their old friends and acquaintances. Mark mentioned a girl he'd dated who married a guy they both knew.

"Any idea whatever happened to Colleen?" Richard asked.

"Colleen?" Mark hesitated for a moment. "Oh, yeah. You dated her for awhile, didn't you? She's a doctor at Mission Hospital, here in this city. Still single, last I knew. She's come to a few of our alumni meetings. Something I can't say for everybody I know."

Richard laughed with him and talked awhile longer. They both promised to drop in on each other if they were in their respective areas.

Richard knew he had enough information.

The following morning, he asked and received permission from the director to take a couple day's leave to handle a personal matter. It would be a four-hour drive. He told Ellen where he was going.

She'd nodded, but her expression seemed to ask what he felt inside—where would this lead?

❧

While Richard was away from the office, Ellen continued preparations for the fall term. But as she worked, she kept wondering if Richard had found his college sweetheart. Would she be married? Would she still be in love with Richard? And he with her? Would they renew their relationship?

If that's what was needed for Richard to forgive himself and to allow a woman in his life to bring fulfillment and children, then she wanted that for him. Yes, even as it broke her heart to think of it, she loved him enough to want what was best.

Ellen shook her head. The truth was she wanted her own will to be done. Richard Williams was in her heart and mind. She wanted him to love her and for them to build a life together.

Even as she wanted that, she prayed as she knew she must. *Dear God, Thy will be done.*

20

*E*llen was all nerves on Saturday night while waiting for Richard to pick her up. He'd called the night before to let her know he was back, then had asked if she would have dinner with him at the Eclectic. He drove to her house, came inside, and met her dad.

Ellen hoped her dad wouldn't say anything too personal to Richard. He'd already said to her, "He's the one you've been interested in all along. Right?"

"He's my boss and my friend," she'd said.

Her dad had nodded. "And one of those confirmed bachelor guys." He'd laughed then.

When he met Richard, however, he said nothing to embarrass her.

Ellen and Richard made small talk on the way to the restaurant. They talked about the work at Ridgeway while he was gone, how things were going for her with her dad, and even the weather. Ellen longed to question him about Colleen but decided to be patient.

After they were seated, Ellen thought how different this was from when she'd sat in this same restaurant with Jerry. Soft candlelight and music set the stage for her and the man she loved. Richard looked more peaceful than ever before. Was it because of Colleen? Had they renewed their relationship?

After their order came, Richard began to talk about the trip. "I talked with Colleen," he said. "She forgave me years ago. She said that tragic event caused her to give her life to the Lord and seek a profession in pediatrics, where she can help little children through their illnesses. She teaches a class of young girls in Sunday school."

Seeing his enthusiasm, she had to ask, "Are you still in love with her?"

"No," he said, putting down his fork. "Colleen is a wonderful Christian woman, but she's not the woman I love." He paused, reached across the table, and captured her hand with both of his.

"There's only one woman in the world I love and want to spend the rest of my life with," he said softly.

Ellen looked down at her plate, not able to bear the tenderness in his gaze as he studied her face.

"Please look at me," he whispered.

Feeling unexpectedly shy, she looked up at him.

"Ellen Jonsen," he said quietly, "I'm in love with you."

"Oh, Richard. I love you too."

Tenderly, he caressed her hand. "I don't know if I can finish this dinner. I'm eager to hold a woman in my arms without that terrible anguish of holding back."

She gave him a warning look but smiled. "Well, I don't know about that."

He laughed and shook his head. "I mean holding back my awful secret. I know for now I must settle for a hug and kiss . . . until marriage."

"Marriage?" She could hardly believe that after so many months of being so reserved, he was ready to make such a commitment.

"Ellen, when I think of us together, and I do often, I want to spend the rest of my life with you."

Ellen thought her heart would burst with joy as she and Richard spent the remainder of the meal revealing how they had come to recognize their love for each other. But before the evening ended with a prolonged kiss at Ellen's doorstep, the couple had also agreed on the importance of Richard spending more time with both Ellen's dad and with Missy.

"Your dad can't consider me as a prospective father for Missy until he knows me better," Richard stated. "And even if he agrees to let us adopt that little girl, we can't do something that will create so many changes in her life until I spend more time with her and she can get used to the idea."

Over the next few weeks, Richard visited Ellen's family many times. Miss Daisy often joined them. After several visits, Richard took Ellen's father aside and told him of his past, then asked if he could approve of him as a son-in-law and a prospective dad for Missy.

"Well, I think this is something Ellen and Daisy should hear," Jon said.

Jon told Missy to play with her Barbies for awhile. The adults gathered around the kitchen table.

Richard had no idea what might ensue. He watched Jon look around at each one, then focus on Richard. "I have no problem with you as a son-in-law. Or with Ellen as Missy's mom."

Richard glanced at Ellen and saw the joy in her eyes. Then Jon focused on Richard again. "However, Missy will have to make a transition from here to your house. That may need to be done slowly. Of course, I don't have any reason to change her room. It's not likely Daisy will have any more children."

"Jon!"

He ignored Daisy's outburst and continued. "Missy can live at both places." He addressed Richard. "You'll need a transition period too. Get used to having a little girl around." He looked over the top of his eyeglasses and spoke ominously. "The biggest transition is having a big girl around."

Richard grinned. "Looking forward to it."

"Yes, I know the feeling. It's happened twice in my life."

"Twice?" Ellen questioned. She'd never heard that.

"Yep. With your mother. Now Daisy."

"Dad! You and Daisy . . . ?

"If I can talk her into it, we'll get us a motor home and tour the U-S of A."

Daisy tugged on his shirt sleeve. "Um, Jon. Would you let me drive some of the time? I just don't like the way you tailgate."

"Sure." He gave her a sidelong look. "Might as well be in the driver's seat as to sit over there beside me telling me how to do it." He grinned and winked at Ellen and Richard.

Daisy sighed heavily. "It's about time I got through to him. He thinks he's going to talk me into it. Men! He has no idea I've been here for two years not because I like to clean his house and cook. He'll learn. I like to watch TV and work jigsaw puzzles as much as he does."

"I make up my own mind about things, Woman," Jon said.

Daisy looked toward the ceiling, then sat there grinning.

"There is one more thing," Richard said. "How Missy feels will play a big part in this."

Ellen stood. "I'll get her."

After Missy came in, holding her Barbie, Richard asked, "How would you feel about my being your daddy?"

"I have a Pa-Pa." she said. "I want to stay with Mommy and Pa-Pa."

Richard felt his heart stop. This wasn't going to work after all.

"Well, I was thinking of marrying your mommy. She'd still be your mommy. Your Pa-Pa would still be your Pa-Pa, but you would live with your mommy and me."

Missy glanced around at each of them. Then she looked up at Richard with her big blue eyes shining like he'd given her the world.

She looked at Ellen. "She would still be my mommy?" She pointed to Jon. "You would be my Pa-Pa? She looked at Richard. "And you would be my daddy?"

He nodded. "That's right."

Her cheeks dimpled, and she said, "Okay. Now can I go play?"

Epilogue

*T*he wedding ceremony had been beautiful, and at last the pastor declared, "I now pronounce you husband and wife. You may kiss the bride."

Ellen faced Richard, looking up at him with her heartfelt love shining in her eyes. As much as he wanted to whisk her away and kiss her in private, he had something else he must do first. "Not just yet," he whispered to Ellen.

He motioned Missy to come over from the spot where she stood as a flower girl, then he got on his knees in front of her. "I promise, Missy, to be your dad. I will be to you the best dad I know how."

Richard reached for her left hand and held it in his left one. Then he reached into the pocket of his tux and drew out a small gold band. "With this ring, I promise to love and cherish you as long as we both shall live."

He slipped the ring on the finger next to her little pinkie.

Her face looked as if the sun had risen inside her. She threw her arms around his neck and hugged him. Then she kissed his cheek. "I love you, Daddy."

"And I love you, Missy."

"Oh," she said, "now can I go to your moon with you?"

❧

Richard and Ellen had decided on a two-day "moon," as Missy called their honeymoon, in the bridal suite at the Grove Park Inn. They had the rest of their lives to be together. Both were eager to make every day a honeymoon and begin their lives as parents to Missy.

There was no more beautiful place than western North Carolina, they agreed as they drove on the parkway toward the inn and stopped at an overlook.

"Missy would love this," Richard said.

"Stop worrying, Richard. Missy will look forward to the huge teddy bear you promised her. She'll get over being disappointed about not coming on the honeymoon with us. And she'll understand it in about ten years or so."

Richard grimaced. "In the meantime, I have to live with her. Try and keep two women happy."

Ellen grinned. "Two or more."

He drew her close. "The more the merrier. I can picture you now. That yellow canary singing to the little ones."

She nodded. "While daddy goes out and gets worms."

He laughed. "I'm the lion, remember." He grew serious. "You and Missy and your dad, Daisy too, are part of my territory now, Ellen." He took a deep breath and exhaled. "I don't want to keep bringing it up, but let me say this. I'll probably think of my past many times— particularly if and when you get pregnant. But it's not like an albatross around my neck anymore. It's a fact. One I accept. One I forgive myself for. I know it wasn't intentional, although it involved my own selfishness."

"It also involved your fear, Richard. You were a young man with dreams. With plans and goals. You saw that tumbling down. You saw yourself as a failure before you even got started."

"Dreams change."

"Yes, Richard. I didn't dream of you." She grinned. "Until after I met you. And now I feel my dreams are coming true. Spending my life with you, finding the mate God intended for me. That's more important than a job."

"I'm glad to hear you say that. I'll quit my job, and we'll live on love."

Ellen poked him on the arm lightly with her fist. He drew her to him, held her tightly, and kissed her. When they broke away, he kept his arm around her waist.

The pastor had pronounced that Ellen was his "to have and to hold" from that moment forward. Richard was holding her . . . in his heart.

Ellen looked up at him and said gently, "Richard, you don't want to keep talking about it, but don't you think your little baby is in heaven with God and Jesus, clapping her hands that you're no longer worrying about her?"

He inhaled deeply. "I like that picture. Before, I've thought of her wanting to ask me why I didn't want her. Why I didn't let her have a life on earth." He glanced around quickly, surprised. "Do you realize you said her?"

"I don't know why," Ellen said. "I just pictured a little girl. Maybe because of Missy."

Richard smiled. "I've always thought of her as a girl. You've done so much for me, Ellen. I believe God brought you to me for many reasons."

"Well, if I've done my job, I'll leave." She turned to walk away.

Richard caught her arm, and she didn't resist when he brought her back to him. "Oh no, you don't. It will take you a lifetime to straighten me out."

"I welcome the challenge," she said and snuggled closer to him. This was the beginning of their life together.

"Let's just stand here a moment and enjoy God's great creation."

Ellen looked out over the miles and miles of lush green forests. How far she had come from that stormy day when her life was at such a low point. How true that God's mysterious ways could take one from the valleys of life and set them on the mountaintops.

And today was particularly awe-inspiring. Sometimes clouds or fog obscured the view. Not today.

"It's so clear," Ellen said.

"And for the first time, in a long time," Richard said. "I feel clear-headed."

She looked up at him. "You know what they say about a clear day?"

"Yes." Richard glanced up at the blue sky, imagining a happy little girl with curls bouncing as she danced and sang and clapped her hands. Then he thought of one entrusted to him to nurture, along with her beautiful mother. He drew Ellen close.

"Yes. On a clear day, you can see forever."

Changing Seasons

by Colleen L. Reece and

Renee DeMarco

For all those who are still waiting for love.

Prologue

Alderdale, Oregon—mid-August

The clump of solid footsteps, the rustle of skirts, and the heavy scent of perfume heralded the first two guests to arrive at Bill Carr's wedding in the small church his family had attended for several generations.

Harriet Taylor—tall, spare, and gimlet-eyed—led the way down the center aisle, leaving her middle-aged daughter a few paces behind, as usual. Harriet's diagonally striped dress gave her all the charm of a black-and-white barber pole. She surveyed the quiet, dimly lit chapel with satisfaction and boomed, "No one here yet. Good. I do like to be first and have my choice of seats." When she reached the reserved area in the front, she ruthlessly tore free the guarding ribbon. "Come, Amelia. We'll sit here. After all, I *am* Bill Carr's third cousin twice removed."

"Yes, Mama." Amelia's subdued voice and demeanor blended with the pale blue outfit Harriet had deemed suitable for one who had lost her husband a year earlier. Amelia's thin shoulders drooped as she preceded Harriet into the pew, the second row from the front. "Shouldn't we sit at the far end, so latecomers can get in more easily?" she timidly asked.

"Nonsense! If people can't arrive on time, it isn't my fault," Harriet snapped.

Amelia's "Yes, Mama" was barely audible.

Harriet planted herself by her daughter, next to the aisle. She peered at the altar and sniffed. "I s'pose Emily brought the flowers from her garden. It's just like her." She scowled at the lovely late-summer roses that tastefully decorated the dimly lighted chapel, drowsing in the afternoon sun. "Seems like she could have forked out for a professional job. After all, Bill *is* her only nephew."

She paused, then pounced on a new topic with both large feet. "I wonder what Emily will do with Bill married and Danielle off to college next week?" When her daughter said nothing, Harriet went on as if there had been no break in her monologue. "You have to hand it to Emily for doing her duty," she offered grudgingly, not bothering to quiet her voice an iota. "I wonder what she'll wear. It's too warm for her old black suit." Harriet sighed as if the weight of the world rested on her sharp-bladed shoulders.

"Maybe she'll wear her lavender crepe," Amelia said. "She looks real nice in it."

"Nice!" Harriet's unladylike snort condemned the garment as being unthinkable. "It's at least five years old and doesn't have an ounce of style." She added condescendingly, "I know the Carrs have had expenses for years, what with all the trouble and such, but a woman owes it to herself to keep from being dowdy. Especially if she ever wants to catch a man." She straightened in the pew and turned to face Amelia. "That's just what Emily needs, you know. A husband. She's going to die an old maid if she keeps on the way she is, just like that aunt of hers, Carolyn Sheffield."

Harriet set her lips in a grim line. "Well, I for one am *not* going to let that happen. One old maid in the family is embarrassing enough, much less two. Carolyn is years beyond help, but I plan to see Emily Carr married off, sure as my name is Harriet Taylor. Or if I can't, it certainly won't be from a lack of trying!"

Amelia's voice rose. "But what more can you do, Mama? You've already sent every Alderdale bachelor and widower from forty to seventy calling. And what good did it do? All Emily did was smile and tell them her family needed her."

"She doesn't have that excuse any longer," Harriet gloated. "Besides, I know just the person to save Emily from a life of loneliness." She quivered with excitement. "Herman Dobbs—our very own cousin-in-law."

Amelia gasped. "*Herman Dobbs?* He's only thirty-five, ten years younger than Emily!"

Harriet tossed her head. "So much the better. Herman has always been weak, and ever since his waif of a wife died, leaving him with those five children to raise, he's been at his wits' end. It won't be easy for Emily. He doesn't have much in the way of modern conveniences, but she can get by. She's had a lot of practice at doing without. After all, it's not like beggars can be choosers," she added sanctimoniously.

"Shh. People are starting to come in," Amelia warned.

Harriet had the final say. "Mark my words, Amelia. Emily Carr is going to marry Herman Dobbs and be as happy as you and dear Porter were until he died. Herman will do whatever it takes to get himself a wife who will mind the children. He's coming as soon as he possibly can." She leaned back, closed her eyes, and smiled, obviously feeling proud of doing right by "poor Emily."

Her reverie was interrupted by Carolyn Sheffield's voice. "Well, if it isn't Harriet Taylor, spreading warm rays of sunshine, like usual."

With a low moan, Amelia slid as far down in her seat as possible without completely disappearing under the pew in front of them.

Harriet whirled toward the center aisle, indignation deeply etched in every crevice of her thin face. Her mouth flopped open and closed like a brook trout out of water.

Emily Carr, gowned in the scorned lavender crepe, stood silently beside her hopping-mad aunt. Twin spots of scarlet stained her lightly lined face. Although she towered over her stylish sixty-nine-year-old companion, she did not dwarf Carolyn, who was anchored at Harriet's right hand like a 105-pound angel of vengeance.

Harriet Taylor's silence spoke louder than words. Emily could be intimidated; Carolyn could not. Harriet had learned from bitter experience how formidable Emily's aunt could be—especially when it came to her beloved niece.

Now Carolyn's blue eyes looked as if they had been chipped from glaciers. Her voice dripped ice when she said in tones guaranteed to reach all those near enough to have heard Harriet's machinations, "Thank you for your—*concern*, Ms. Taylor. Neither my niece nor I need your matrimonial services." She grasped Emily's arm and led her up to the front row.

"Don't pay any attention to her," Carolyn furiously whispered after they were seated. "Harriet Taylor has always considered herself chief understudy to God. I don't know how she dares set herself up as an authority on marriage! Everyone in Alderdale knows her own marriage was a disaster. Poor Amelia, hitched to Mama Taylor's personally selected 'dear Porter' all those years."

"It's so humiliating," Emily said as her fingers clenched the lavender dress. "She didn't even spare my clothes!" Her fingers stilled. "Bill asked me to wear this."

"You look good and so does the chapel. Bill will love it. Now forget Harriet Taylor and enjoy the wedding," her no-nonsense aunt crisply advised. "*I* intend to." She resettled herself in her seat, raised her chin, and crossed her arms in the way that always made Emily smile.

It worked. By the time Bill followed the minister out of a side room and gave Emily a crooked I-love-you grin, Harriet Taylor and her plotting might as well have been dead and buried in the Pacific Ocean.

~❧~

Not so for Carolyn. Her mind running double track between the wedding and Harriet Taylor, Carolyn squared her shoulders and clenched her jaw. Good thing she had canceled an important business appointment and driven down from Seattle this morning. The more she thought about the incident, the angrier she grew. At least her years of experience as a professional paralegal had taught her the value of concealing her feelings. What Emily needed was support, not a display of rage. Besides, it was illegal for a sixty-nine-year-old woman to leave her seat and throttle a meddler, especially in the middle of her great-nephew's wedding.

Snatches of the overheard conversation sizzled red-hot in Carolyn's brain. What business was it of Harriet Taylor's—or anyone else's for that matter—if she and Emily stayed single, got married, or joined the circus? Clenching her hands until her well-cared-for nails bit into the palms, Carolyn breathed deeply, glad her niece was absorbed in the service. *Just let Harriet bring on her Herman Dobbs and see* what I do to both of them. On the other hand, Emily has managed to send Harriet's motley group of suitors packing.

So what if Herman Dobbs is already hurrying to Alderdale, seeking a drudge for himself and his five children? Why be concerned? Despite Harriet Taylor and her meddling, that drudge is not going to be Miss Emily Ann Carr.

Carolyn sternly repressed a chuckle at a new thought, a paraphrase of the odious Harriet Taylor, "Mark my words. Sure as my name is Carolyn Sheffield, I, for one, am not going to let that happen."

Part 1: Emily

1

*A*pproximately fifty miles southwest of Portland, Oregon, the winds of change crested the Coast Range. They gathered momentum with every mile. When they reached Alderdale—the small town that looked as if it had been lifted from a Norman Rockwell painting and set down in the Oregon forest—the breezes shooed away lingering wisps of fog and gleefully moved on. The inhabitants of Alderdale were left to enjoy a perfect day.

From her seat near an open window in the inner office of the Gerard & Son law firm, Alderdale's largest because of the "& Son," Emily Carr breathed in the fresh air, then watched swaying tree branches slowly return to their usual position. Would she also slowly settle back into her usual position? *Never,* she vowed. She unclenched tightly-clasped fingers, glad the elder Gerard had been called away for a few moments. It gave her time to try and assimilate what she'd just learned. The winds of change that still blew through Gerard & Son's office, sparked hope.

Snatches of a poem Emily learned as a young girl came to mind. The poem described a road that lured the adventurous west, east, south, and north. While most roads led homeward, this road encouraged readers to "leave gray miles behind" and travel "in quest of that one beauty God put me here to find."

"West, east, south, and north," Emily softly repeated. She bowed her head and closed her eyes. Visions of cities and seas, mountains and valleys, burning desert sands and icy glaciers kaleidoscoped through her mind. Her heart pounded. Had the long-delayed "someday," for which her longing heart clung to during all the gray miles her sensible shoes had traveled, really come?

"Heavenly Father, my roads so far all have led homeward. Have You really opened a way for me to seek Your beauty? If so, what is the beauty I am to find?"

Her answer was a burst of song from a bird in the large maple tree just outside the office window. Emily opened her eyes and located the soloist: a little brown bird that clung to the highest swaying branch. How amazing for glorious music to spring from just a tiny bunch of feathers! Emily smiled in empathy with the plain little songster. She also had no fine feathers—just a heart filled with songs yet to be sung.

I wonder what Aunt Carolyn will say about my good news?

The unspoken words brought a familiar twinge. Emily loved and admired her only aunt but always felt awed by her presence. *Why?* she wondered for the thousandth time. It certainly wasn't size. Emily's nervousness fled and a chuckle broke the silence. She towered over Carolyn Sheffield by a good six inches and outweighed her plain-speaking aunt by twenty-five pounds.

Perhaps it was the age difference—the fact go-getter Carolyn was twenty-four when Emily was born, well on her way toward making a mark in her chosen career. She hadn't had much time for Emily or her brother Davey, born five years after Emily, although they always recognized that she was fond of them.

"If things had been different, I might have been more like her," Emily mused. She sighed and shook her head. Life had marked out vastly different paths for each of them. Their only similarity was in sacrificing their chances for love and giving themselves to a purpose instead. *Carolyn's sacrifice was from choice,* a little voice whispered in Emily's soul. *Yours was out of necessity.*

Emily impatiently squelched the inner voice. No use reliving her childish determination to "take care of Dad and Davey" after her mother died when Emily was ten. Or the long, weary years of her father's invalidism, which required all of Emily's faith and strength to care for him after his logging accident.

Pain too deep for tears stabbed at her heart and she unseeingly stared into the early summer day. "Why, God?" she said. "Mama. Daddy. Davey." *David*, she reminded herself. The name *Davey* belonged to the child her beloved brother had once been, to a happier time with the little brother she'd cared for and played with. It didn't fit the stony-faced man who, after the departure of his dissatisfied wife, pleaded with his sister to care for his small children. Neither did it fit the forty-year-old Captain David Carr, who had given his life for his country while serving in the Middle East, leaving his children fatherless.

Emily forced her mind away from the past when Isaiah Gerard, senior member of the firm, reappeared and strode to the worn office chair his wife had long since given up threatening to abolish. He sank his ample, white-haired bulk into its depths. His keen dark eyes twinkled. "Emily Ann Carr, if anyone deserves to fall into good fortune, it is you." He waxed eloquent on a subject obviously dear to his heart. "When I think of you being tied down for . . . how long has it been?"

Emily struggled to regain her composure. In three decades, no one except Isaiah had ever called her Emily Ann. It made her feel like a young girl—the girl that life had jealously kept her from being. "Thirty-five years." She paused. "My family needed me." She proudly raised her head. "I don't regret it."

Isaiah grunted. "You wouldn't, being you." He fumbled for a handkerchief in his rumpled jacket and loudly blew his nose. "Back to business. Who would have thought, after all this time, that what was considered worthless stock in your daddy's friend's mine would prove valuable?"

He didn't wait for an answer but gestured toward the open window that framed an incomparable view of a bald eagle ascribing circles in the blue sky. "So, what are you going to do now that you're free as that fella?"

Emily felt a tingle of new life and opening vistas stir within her like fluttering wings. "I had no idea why you asked me to stop by. We've always had to live frugally. Now . . ."

"You won't be rich, but there's enough to keep you comfortable, no matter what the economy does," Isaiah promised. He cocked his shaggy head to one side. "Emily Ann, can't you think of *anything* you want to do?"

The wings took flight. A cry, born from her years of restrictions, burst out, magnified by Harriet Taylor's critical comments on the way she dressed. "Yes. I will throw away every piece of 'sensible' clothing I own and go shopping in Portland!"

Isaiah Gerard looked at Emily as if she had taken leave of her senses. Perhaps she had. If she'd had time to think, it was *not* the answer she'd have given. The utter look of shock on Isaiah's face accomplished what Harriet's careless remark had started weeks earlier. Emily felt gales of laughter rise within her. She clutched the arms of her chair and let it pour into the room. Laughter, absent for too much of her life. Laughter, coming when tears would not. Cleansing, healing laughter that changed to tears.

Isaiah handed her a box of tissues and let her cry.

At last the storm subsided. Emily gulped, blew her nose, and stammered, "Forgive me. I . . ."

"No apologies, Emily Ann. Best thing in the world for you," the old lawyer told her gruffly. He pointed to a door that she knew from previous visits led directly into a private washroom. "Go mop your face. Then we'll talk."

She choked back a final sob and did his bidding, splashing cold water into her face again and again. When she raised her head and caught sight of herself in the washroom mirror, she gasped. A blue sparkle had replaced her tears. The peace of one who has fought a good fight and conquered had subtracted years from her countenance. Even the few glints of silver in her disarrayed brown hair shone like tiny mountain streams threading their way to the valleys below. Gratefulness flooded her body. "Thank You, God," she whispered.

Emily opened the washroom door, switched off the light, squared her shoulders, and walked out of the shadows into the sunlit office.

$\mathcal{T}$o the inhabitants of Alderdale, the Emily Ann Carr who left the law firm of Gerard & Son looked no different from the well-known woman who had walked the tree-lined streets earlier that day.

Emily knew better. Although she smiled, nodded to acquaintances, and returned pleasant greetings, her heart kept time with the music in her soul. Music punctuated with the sweet sounds of loosening shackles and breaking chains.

The perfect day shimmered around Emily, as rich with hope as a rainbow after a storm. She pinched her arm to make sure it wasn't just a lovely dream, a fleeting moment that would soon be overcome by reality. The sharp nip of her fingers reassured her. The music of freedom gloriously proclaimed the joyous news that her long-awaited "someday" had arrived.

Someday. How she had clung to its promise through all the years of fulfilling her vow to "take care of Daddy and Davey." Someday she would be able to think of herself. Someday wonderful things would happen. Someday her prayers and dreams would come true. Psalm 37:4 had become her watchword in the darkest hours: "Delight thyself also in the LORD; and He shall give thee the desires of thine heart." So she gladly served, trusted her heavenly Father . . . and waited.

Emily wanted to skip, to shout, to laugh. She nobly restrained herself. Such behavior would set the local gossips, especially Harriet Taylor, buzzing like a swarm of angry hornets. A chuckle escaped in spite of her determination to act as usual. She muffled it in a spotless handkerchief and turned in at the gate of the old Carr place.

How shabby it looked, the two-story white house built when

Alderdale first came into existence! A pang went through Emily. In her great-grandparents' day, it had been one of the finest homes in town. Now it reminded her of an ancient, but well-loved, family dog—cherished because of long association, not beauty. Or a dowager in faded finery, gathering her skirts around her in an attempt to maintain dignity. Even though Emily had been able to keep up major repairs, the house badly needed painting, and a new roof would do wonders for its appearance.

She slowly walked up the path leading from the picket fence to the wide covered porch. Pink, red, yellow, and white roses clambered up the porch posts and perfumed the air with memories. She dropped into the porch swing that had hung there since she was a child. Sister Feline, the black-and-white cat Danielle—Emily's niece—had found as a kitten and mischievously named because her markings resembled a nun's habit, curled up in Emily's lap. "We'll pronounce it *Feh-leen*," Danielle had gleefully announced. "It's more elegant than Fe-line, and still means 'cat.'"

Emily smiled at the memory. Shabby or not, this was home. "Even if I decide to travel, I'll keep the house," Emily told her cat. "I can afford to fix it up. That way I'll always have a place to come home to when I grow tired of wandering." Sister Feline's gravelly purr gave no argument.

Emily started the porch swing gently rocking. The motion, combined with the cat's companionship, calmed her as nothing else could have done. She bowed her head. "Heavenly Father, it's the strangest feeling. The past is over, but the future is so uncertain, it's almost frightening. I'm like the old woman traveling on the king's highway who wondered if she were really herself, and if not, who she could be. I certainly don't feel like myself."

Her thoughts trailed off and she closed her eyes. A jumble of memories and things to consider immediately assailed her, clamoring for her attention. The habit of years when she could only find stolen moments for reflection also plagued her, along with the feeling that she needed to be up and doing something. Anything.

She finally realized what was bothering her. "I need time to think," she told Sister Feline. "I have to make the transition from the person I was, to the one I will be." She drew in a deep breath. "There is only one way." Setting the cat on the porch floor, Emily opened the screen door. The narrow hall—with its staircase to the upper-level living room on one side, dining room and kitchen on the other—felt cool after being outdoors. It was cool and fragrant from furniture polish and the bouquet of roses Emily had picked and placed on the hall table just before receiving the summons to the law office. That seemed an eternity ago, not just a few earth-shaking hours.

After consuming a cup of herbal tea and a sandwich at the round dining-room table that had hosted countless family gatherings, Emily went to her bedroom. A well-fed Sister Feline followed. Emily turned the key of the foot locker in her large closet and removed a great stack of notebooks. "These aren't for you," she warned the cat, whose reaching paw and inquisitive nose indicated a tendency to investigate. Sister Feline meowed and trailed Emily to the living room. With no lap invitation forthcoming from her mistress, who was seated on the worn but comfortable couch amidst a clutter of notebooks, the cat plumped down on the hearth rug and began to groom herself.

No one but Emily and God knew the "Secret of the Notebooks." She had named them that at age ten, when she first began filling the pages in a desperate attempt to hide her grief from her father and little brother, lest it make them feel even worse. The books were not diaries—neat little blank volumes offering a few lines on which to record daily events— but fat journals. From the time her mother died, Emily poured her innermost soul into her writing. Joy and sorrow. Letters to God when she could not put the prayers of her heart into words. Feelings of comfort and peace that never failed to follow such entries. All these were mingled with stories she wrote to amuse young Davey. Thirty-five years, starting with pencil recordings in composition books that gave way to neat ink entries in bound blank journals. A review of her life to date.

"I haven't read these journals in years." Emily whispered so quietly that Sister Feline only flicked an ear in her direction and went on washing. "I know it won't be easy, but it's necessary to reconcile with the past before I can move into the future." She opened the first notebook and began to read. Tears came unbidden with the first childishly formed words:

My Journal
by Emily Ann Carr, age 10

Mama went to heaven today. I feel sad.

The words on the page blurred. A scene swept into Emily's mind, a scene as vivid as the day her mother died. Mama's long illness had stolen her strength, but it hadn't diminished her faith and loving spirit. Emily could almost feel her mother's transparent hand on hers when she said, "Emily Ann, I want you to know what a comfort you are to me. You are Daddy's and my own beloved daughter." Her eyes sparkled as they hadn't done in a long time. "You are also a wonderful sister to little Davey. I've seen the way he follows you like a shadow."

A smile softened the sharp planes of her thin face. "Knowing he and Daddy will still have you when I'm gone brings me peace. You have learned your lessons well, my child. Young as you are, you're already a better cook and housekeeper than most of the women and girls in Alderdale. I am very proud of you."

Emily didn't fully understand what her mother meant at the time. Long years passed before she recognized the truth. Mama hadn't been laying the burden of looking after father and brother on Emily's slim shoulders. She had been offering the only consolation she had left to give—pride in her daughter, a memory to lighten the pain of parting. She never dreamed her praise would unknowingly light a candle of resolve in Emily's childish heart: *Daddy and Davey need me. I will take care of them.*

The memories rushed on.

Davey asking, "Mama, will you forget me?"

Mama, smiling through her tears. "I could never forget my little boy, or Daddy, or Emily Ann. Be a good boy, Davey. Do what Daddy and sister tell you. Grow up to be a strong man who loves God. Someday we will all be together again. Now, give me a hug and a kiss, and go out under the big tree. You, too, Emily Ann."

Mama's hug and whisper, "Always remember the peace you gave me."

Davey's grubby hand in Emily's as they sat beneath the tree by the fence.

Daddy, coming from the house with his arms outstretched. Emily knew Mama had gone to heaven even before he had told them.

Finally, the memory of tightening her arms around her father and little brother, silently repeating her vow: *Daddy and Davey need me. I will take care of them.*

Emily dropped the notebook to her lap. Scorching tears fell. How well she remembered that long-ago day and the bewildering weeks that followed!

She continued reading. The meager journal entries, as if the writer had no time or heart for writing, bore mute witness to the loss of the beloved mother. Occasional golden sentences stood out like shafts of light in the family's dark world. Davey's finding a buttercup and laughing when Emily held it under her chin so that it made her skin look yellow. Davey's sixth birthday.

Again Emily had to stop. She felt a chuckle rise in her throat. She had reminded her father it was Davey's birthday. He brought a cake mix and birthday candles from the store. Davey said it was the "bestest cake in the whole world," even though the frosting stayed runny. It made her father laugh, the first time in months.

It was a long while before Emily could take up the notebook and go on. The turning of dog-eared, yellowed pages whispered down the long path from the past and into the silent room. Sister Feline yawned, curled into a ball, and relaxed into sleep.

A succession of much-later entries followed. Emily skimmed them, sometimes rereading certain passages. Now and then, she paused to unfold time-worn, creased pieces of paper tucked between the pages: poetry and quotations. She hadn't remembered how strong her childhood dreams were all those years ago.

Someday I will write wonderful stories and see faraway lands. Someday I will buy Davey things he doesn't ask for. He knows it would make Daddy feel bad that we can't afford them.

Someday I will do things for others. Daddy says I already

*have—for him and Davey. Mama, if you can see me, you
know I'm taking care of them.*

Emily paused to marvel at the child she had been. Even though
the confident expectation dwindled a bit, and a degree of resignation
crept into the journal entries as the years passed, the shining hope for
"someday" continued.

Emily returned to her task. She relived the tragic logging accident
that left her father an invalid and more dependent on her than ever.
Unwilling to dwell on the shattering time period, Emily laid the journal aside and moved to another. She lingered over some of the entries
from her early teen years. A tender smile curled her lips.

*I am so excited! I've been promoted to the Advanced
Language Arts class! I'm the youngest person in class and will
have to work hard to keep up. I don't mind.*

*Some of my classmates don't act very pleased at having
me with them. One boy is really nice, though. He is two years
older than I am and has dark hair, a wide smile, and twinkling
dark eyes. His name is Nathan Hamilton. I looked his name up
in a book that tells about names. Nathan means "gift."*

*Our teacher, Mrs. Sorenson, had us write an essay.
Nathan said his dream is to be a writer. I've never told anyone,
but that's what I want to be, too. I wish the stories I write and
tell Davey were as good as Nathan's stories. At least I'm a
good speller. Nathan isn't. He's always asking me how to spell
"atavistic" or "precocious," or some other big word Mrs.
Sorenson says is pretentious.*

*Nathan is polite, but he doesn't pay much attention to
girls. He's too busy writing and studying and playing sports.*

*He always acts like he appreciates it when I help him. His
dark eyes laugh. Well, not really. Mrs. Sorenson keeps
reminding us that eyes can't laugh or fall to the ground, or do
any of those things some books say they do. She tells us to say
"gaze," as in, "Her gaze fell to the ground," but it doesn't sound
right to say "His dark gaze laughs."*

Nathan is the only one except Mr. Gerard, the lawyer (and he doesn't count), who calls me "Em'ly Ann," as if both names run together. I feel like a different person when Nathan whispers, "Em'ly Ann, how do you spell 'atrocious'? My a-t-r-o-s-h-u-s doesn't look right." Then he grins.

Nathan is always quoting from Walden, *by Henry David Thoreau: "If a man does not keep pace with his companions perhaps it is because he hears a different drummer. Let him step to the music which he hears, however measured or far away." It sends chills chasing up and down my spine.*

Nathan hears that music, the beat of a different drum. I can tell by the way he speaks the words and the way his eyes glisten. I hear it, too.

Someday I will be free to follow the different drumbeat. I wonder if either of us will ever become an author. I am going to try. I want to write stories that will help to make the world a better place. Is it unrealistic to hope they will be published? No one from Alderdale has ever been published, except in the local newspaper.

I know it won't be easy. Matthew 22:14 says, "For many are called, but few are chosen." Will Nathan be chosen? Will I?

A plaintive "meow" from Sister Feline bridged the gap between junior high days and the present. Emily roused to discover that dusk lurked just outside the windows. Lengthening shadows surrounded her. Still under the spell cast by her mental journey to the past, Emily laid aside the journal and made room on her lap for the cat. She switched on a nearby lamp, leaving the rest of the living room in partial darkness.

Whatever happened to Nathan Hamilton? Did he ever think of the shy girl who used to help him with his spelling? More important, had he been able to fulfill *his* dream? At the end of the school term, he and his family had moved. Not even Harriet Taylor had been able to ferret out their whereabouts.

Emily sighed. For years she had searched *Books in Print*. No Nathan or Nate Hamilton was ever listed. Evidently his boyhood dream had been derailed, as hers had been. He would be forty-seven now. If Nathan had carried through with his plans, surely he would be published. Emily sadly shook her head. What a waste. Even the strict, impossible-to-please language arts teacher had admitted Nathan had talent. Mrs. Sorenson had been harder on Nathan and Emily than on anyone else in the class. On the rare occasions when she praised their work, they exchanged glances of delight.

On the last day of school, their teacher had called them aside and announced in her usual brusque manner, "You both have writing ability. That's why I pushed you. I've done all I can. Now what you do with your God-given talent is out of my hands."

If only Mrs. Sorenson had stayed in Alderdale, instead of transferring to another school at the end of the term, Emily thought while preparing for bed. In spite of all the obligations to Daddy and Davey, perhaps things would have been different.

If only Nathan had stayed in Alderdale, her heart whispered, *perhaps things would have been even more different.*

Emily felt hot color flood her face. The "Secret of the Notebooks" wasn't the only buried secret in her life. All through the years, whenever she thought of the mate she felt God intended her to have, a crystal-clear image rose from her heart to her mind. Tall and strong, straight as a mountain fir, as filled with joy as the streams that laughed their way to the sea, her "someday" love was simply a grown-up edition of Nathan Hamilton.

$$3$$

*T*ired without being sleepy, Emily propped herself up in bed in the pale green and white bedroom that had been hers since childhood. The walls could use a fresh coat of paint; now they could have it.

Emily smiled and continued reading her journals. The digital clock on her bookcase headboard showed 4:30 before she finished the last one. Sister Feline lay curled at the foot of the bed. *Is she dreaming dreams of her own?* Emily wondered.

A cool breeze stirred the simple white window curtains, then danced across the quiet room, out the open door, and into the upstairs hall. An early-rising bird caroled a single, day-welcoming note. It began a chorus in the trees outside the window.

A searching sunbeam discovered and touched Emily's face. She felt as if she had returned from a very long journey. Her life events, so faithfully and poignantly recorded in her journals, fell into formation and again marched through her mind:

Her injured father's long illness and his unwillingness to allow anyone except his daughter to care for him, even though it meant Emily could not attend college.

The continuing need to stretch a disability income to meet the needs of three people.

Mr. Carr's prideful refusal to accept offers of help from his wife's sister, Carolyn Sheffield.

His death many years later.

The expectation of release from duty and the opportunity for Emily to have a life of her own.

The desertion of her military brother, David Carr, and his two small children, Bill and Danielle, by his wife.

The further postponement of Emily's dream in order to help where needed.

The death, somewhere in the Middle East, of the brother she loved.

The task of comforting David's grieving children as Emily had once comforted Davey.

The humiliation of being called an old maid.

Harriet Taylor's never-ending stream of impossible suitors.

Emily's admiration for Aunt Carolyn, busily making a mark in her chosen career.

Emily's reward when Bill and Danielle credited her with their honors and success.

The sacrifices of education, fashionable clothing, travel, *even love*, for the sake of the children who thought of her as their real mother.

The years she served as a caregiver—until Bill married and Danielle won a full scholarship to a prestigious eastern university.

A quiet house with only Sister Feline for company.

Finally, the stunning revelation—not yet fully registered in her mind—that opened the way for Emily to do all the things she'd dreamed of doing . . . for what felt like forever.

Would they include love? Emily turned off her bed light and pondered, while the walls of her room gathered color from the coming day. So many journal entries had to do with her desire for love. Not just love of family and God, but the love of a good man, one to whom she could joyously repeat the timeless words Ruth spoke to her mother-in-law, Naomi, in the Bible: "Intreat me not to leave thee, or to return from following after thee: for whither thou goest, I will go; and where thou lodgest, I will lodge: thy people shall be my people, and thy God my God."

For a single moment, Emily's strong faith faltered. "Lord, what if I am too old for love?" she whispered into her line-dried pillowcase. Then, "No! I've waited all these years. I can't bear living the rest of my life alone, the target of Harriet Taylor's cruel taunts and everlasting matchmaking."

Emily's protest awakened Sister Feline. She leaped from the bed and disappeared out the open bedroom door in a streak of black and white.

Filled with rebellion at the possible loss of her most treasured dream, Emily ignored the abrupt departure and stared out the window into the blue heavens. "I'm neither Cinderella nor Sleeping Beauty, Lord, but now that I'm free, surely love will come. I don't want a knight in shining armor. Or a prince on a white horse. Just someone who serves You, and who will love, honor, and cherish me."

Exhausted more by her emotions than the sleepless night, Emily closed her eyes and waited for peace to steal into her troubled heart and mind. Halfway between sleep and awareness, visions of Nathan Hamilton's twinkling dark eyes, wide grin, and fondness for many-syllable words, swirled through Emily's mind. Her last waking thought was: *Nathan will never know how intensely I shared his love for writing—just that Mrs. Sorenson said I had talent. He will never know the joy and brightness he brought into my dull life. I wish . . .* Sleep claimed her before she could finish her thought.

❧

Emily Ann Carr awakened on a morning that Alderdale considered just another in a series of late summer days. She knew the day began a new era for her. A favorite Scripture, Psalm 118:24, came to mind: "This is the day which the LORD hath made; we will rejoice and be glad in it."

Emily was far too happy to contain her feelings. She sang the praise song taken from the ancient Scripture, ably accompanied by Sister Feline's rumbling alto purr. After breakfast, she whipped through her morning chores and prepared to go out.

A goodly sum of money lay in the bottom of her plain purse. The largest balance she'd ever possessed fattened her normally lean checkbook. Emily quickly concealed a few "egg basket" bills inside her clothing, recalling a story about Grandmother Sheffield. When Aunt

Carolyn was a child, her mother lost her handbag while shopping in Portland. "What are we going to do?" a worried Carolyn asked.

"Now, don't you concern yourself," Grandmother Sheffield admonished. "I don't carry all my eggs in one basket." She led the way to an empty restroom nearby, where she unfastened the garter holding up her long cotton sock and removed a ten-dollar bill. From then on, the Sheffield family motto was, "Don't carry all your eggs in one basket."

"I wonder if Aunt Carolyn still stashes cash." Emily laughed. She found it hard to imagine anyone attempting to steal anything from Ms. Carolyn Sheffield! Aunt Carolyn marched through life with a don't-mess-with-me-or-else stride that gave an impression of added height. When necessary, her blue eyes could don an icy stare, a stare guaranteed to humble her adversaries.

Emily closed her front and screen doors and set off on foot for the downtown bus station. The desire to skip her way down Main Street that had pestered her the day before, returned. Even those in the early autumn of their lives should pay tribute to good fortune. Emily allowed herself one childish skip, under the guise of avoiding a rough spot in the sidewalk. A smile started in her heart. It crept up and erupted into a laugh. What fun to have a secret in a town where secrets didn't remain secrets for long.

"Not so this time," she gloated. "Isaiah Gerard is as closemouthed as a razor clam. Even Harriet Taylor won't be able to pry anything out of him."

"Emily Carr, you look like the cat that gobbled the canary," a familiar voice accused. "What are you mumbling about?"

Speak of the devil, and her horns appear. Emily silently chastised herself for the uncharacteristically uncharitable thought and said amiably, "Hello, Harriet. It certainly is a nice day."

Harriet barely glanced at the sunny sky before turning back to Emily. Avid curiosity shone in her searching gaze, and she looked more like a barber pole than ever in the red-and-white striped dress that hung loosely on her angular frame. "So, what did Isaiah Gerard want? I hear he called you in."

"I really can't say," Emily said, using the ploy she'd discovered worked well with nosy people. It allowed her to remain truthful without explaining whether she couldn't say because she didn't know, or because she wasn't at liberty to divulge information.

Harriet's mouth flew open, but no words fell out.

Emily took advantage of her tormentor's speechlessness and remarked, "I really have to be running along if I'm to catch the bus. Do have a pleasant day."

She made her escape, followed by an indignant gasp and Harriet's comment, "Well, I never! What's gotten into you, Emily Carr?"

Gleeful at her adroit handling of her long-time tormentor, Emily hurried away before Harriet could gather her wits and ask where she was going and why.

~❧

The bus ride from Alderdale to Portland gave Emily a little over an hour to make a list. The shopping mall she and Danielle patronized on their trips to the city had a variety of department stores. Several offered quality clothing at reasonable prices. Despite Isaiah Gerard's assurance that she need never scrimp again, Emily did not intend to go overboard in assembling her new wardrobe.

It was a spree to remember. Emily selected clothing to satisfy her beauty-starved soul. Modest and well-cut, nothing outlandish. She bypassed dark and serviceable garments, concentrating on soft blues, greens, rose, cream, and white. Even the house dresses she chose were bright and pretty. A navy suit she admired came with a gorgeous scarlet scarf. Should she . . . ? Well, why not? If Harriet Taylor could dress herself in red-striped dresses, surely Emily Carr could add pizzazz with a red silk scarf.

On her way to the cashier, a tastefully displayed dress caught her attention. A lavender dress cut along the same lines as the tired gown Emily now wore. But what a difference! The beautifully tailored garment boasted a lace collar and impeccable workmanship. The desire to own it surged through Emily. What better way to silently rebuke Harriet Taylor for her unkind comments than by showing up at church wearing an exquisite replica of the dress Harriet had scorned.

The dress fit perfectly, but was far more costly than any of the others Emily had chosen. *Take it,* she fiercely told herself. *You deserve this dress and everything else you're buying.* She slipped into her old dress and carried the lavender dress to the cashier.

"Do you want these shipped?" the saleswoman asked.

"All but this one." Emily pointed to her final selection. "I need shoes to go with it."

It didn't take long to find a pair of soft gray shoes that complemented the dress. Emily treated herself to chicken salad and a tall, cool glass of lemonade in a quiet tea room, then purchased a leather-bound journal before catching the bus to Alderdale.

❧

Sunday dawned bright and clear. Emily ate breakfast, fed her cat, and put on the lavender dress. She peered into her mirror. What a difference new clothing made! She looked and felt years younger. She walked to church and quietly entered. Harriet Taylor and her daughter, Amelia, stood just inside the door. Amelia's plain face blossomed into a smile that made her almost pretty. Harriet's did not. Her disbelieving expression was worth every penny Emily had invested in the lavender dress!

Following several announcements and the usual songfest, the minister said, "Our text this morning is Mark 2:21: 'No man also seweth a piece of new cloth on an old garment. . . .'"

A choking sound from Harriet's direction nearly proved Emily's undoing. Was the choosing of that particular Scripture pure coincidence? Or did God have a sense of humor the size of the highest peak in the Coast Range? It took all of Emily's self-control to maintain proper decorum and force her mind back to the sermon.

Late that afternoon, while Sister Feline drowsed on a sunny windowsill, Emily opened the journal she had purchased as a symbol of new beginnings. She dated the first page with the date she'd gone to see Isaiah Gerard, then recorded the events of the past few days. She finished her entry with:

> *Perhaps it was wrong of me to get so much enjoyment from the shock on Harriet Taylor's face. It's just that . . .*

Emily's pen faltered. The memory of the befuddled woman's countenance floated between her and her journal. She brushed it aside and quickly wrote:

> *Lord, none of this good fortune is my doing. Help me*
> *remember it is a gift from You. Thank You.*

❧

By the end of the week, Harriet's, "Well, I never! What's gotten into Emily Carr?" had spread through Alderdale like a river in flood. Harriet repeated it so often and to so many people, Isaiah Gerard sourly stated the day of the Town Crier hadn't passed.

Speculation about Emily's new clothes reached fever pitch. They weren't Carolyn Sheffield's castoffs, everyone agreed. They were obviously new. Besides, the two women could never wear the same size.

Emily kept her own counsel. The news of her change in circumstances would eventually become public knowledge. At least Herman Dobbs hadn't yet shown up. According to the local grapevine, his youngest child had broken his arm. Emily pitied the boy but thanked God for the postponement of an unpleasant, Harriet Taylor–inspired interview. With prayer and trepidation, she took a bold step toward doing something entirely for herself, something she had longed to do ever since she made up stories to entertain her little brother. She enrolled in a hands-on writing class at a nearby Christian college. She knew it wouldn't be easy. She dreaded having to read her work before strangers even more now than she had in the Advanced Language Arts class.

To Emily's great relief, the instructor announced at the first class, "I have few rules, but they are to be strictly observed. Constructive criticism is always welcome. Negative comments will not be tolerated." He outlined the contents of the course and ended with, "There is no better way to perfect our writing than by reading the work of authors we admire. Your next assignment is to choose a contemporary novel, preferably one you have read more than once, and write a letter to the author. Tell him or her how and why the book spoke to you."

He scowled. "Please, people, spare me the platitudes and generalities. Go beyond the obvious and look for hidden treasure. Try to crawl inside the author's skin and see what motivation led to the title you choose. Then write your letter. It doesn't matter whether you receive an answer. Some of you won't. What counts is your having identified the elements of good writing and how they have been applied."

Emily drove home in a state of near panic. Had signing up for the class been a terrible mistake? Who was she to write such a letter? "Stop it," she ordered herself. "Remember what Henry Ford said? 'Obstacles are those frightful things you see when you take your eyes off your goal.'" The admonition brought comfort. Long before she reached Alderdale, Emily had mentally inventoried her bookshelves and chosen a book and author. Her light burned into the early morning hours as she reread a title that had made a difference in her life.

The next day, Herman Dobbs and his five stair-step children appeared on her doorstep. He pushed his way into the hall and wasted no time in speaking his piece. "Miss Emily, it's been brought to my attention that you are no longer tied down and that you are interested in having a home and family of your own. I'm here today to offer you my hand and my heart." A huge paw slapped the middle of his chest. "We can either live here, or . . ."

"Pardon me, Mr. Dobbs," Emily interrupted in an icy voice worthy even of Aunt Carolyn. "You have been grossly misinformed concerning my circumstances. I am not interested in receiving either your hand or your heart."

The stolid man blinked. "You refuse to take pity on these five motherless children?" he demanded, pointing at the cluster of urchins balefully eyeing Emily from outside the screen door. If their expressions accurately indicated their feelings about having Emily Carr as a new mother, they were even less eager than she for her to assume such a role!

Herman Dobbs wasn't through. He pointed a fat finger at her and demanded, "How can a good Christian woman such as you are said to be, fail to have mercy on a poor, lonely man trying to raise five motherless children?"

The whole scene was so like a scene from an old-time melodrama,

Emily struggled to keep from laughing, in spite of her indignation. She had dealt with previous matrimonial candidates according to their varied approaches, but never had she encountered the effrontery Herman Dobbs displayed! She disciplined the beginnings of a smile that might convey to him that she was weakening, then primly said, "God has not put it into my heart to care for either you or your motherless children, Mr. Dobbs. Good day."

She shooed the protesting man onto the porch, went inside, and locked her door, to the tune of loud thumps and Herman calling, "Beggars can't afford to be choosers, Miss Carr. I will call again!" He sounded so much like his cousin-in-law, Harriet, that Emily felt like going upstairs and dumping a bucket of water down on his conceited head.

A few days later, news of her inheritance leaked out. According to hearsay, the amount ranged between $25,000 and $2,000,000. "Let 'em think what they wish," Isaiah Gerard advised Emily when she dropped by his office. "They will, anyway. I don't know who got the information, but I suspect one of our phone conversations was overheard."

Emily sighed. "I've already begun receiving letters begging for money."

The lawyer shook his shaggy white head. "Don't let it get you down, Em'ly Ann. 'This, too, shall pass.'" His eyes twinkled.

She laughed in spite of her annoyance. "The sooner, the better!"

Emily wasn't laughing when she got home. Five screaming Dobbs children swarmed through her yard. Harriet Taylor and Herman Dobbs, who had obviously been hanging around waiting for Emily to change her mind, were parked on the Carr front porch. They must have hot-footed it to the Carr home the moment news of Emily's inheritance reached their greedy ears.

"Dear Emily," Harriet gushed, "we are *so* happy for you! Is it really true you are now the richest person in town?"

Emily brushed past her. "You'll have to excuse me, Harriet. I have a headache." She opened the screen door, barely missing Herman Dobbs's nose.

She *did* have a headache. Seven of them, in fact, cluttering up her front porch, her yard—and if Harriet Taylor could manage it, the rest of Emily Ann Carr's life.

4

*N*athan Hamilton, a.k.a. *N. Alexander*—his first initial and middle name—dropped the pen he'd been using to proof his latest novel and flexed cramped fingers. Just a few pages to go. Good. *The Overcomer* was his most satisfying project to date. It had also been his most challenging. The army of loyal fans who had flocked to buy *The Seeker* a year earlier had sent sales sky-rocketing, placing the title at the top of both Christian and secular best-seller lists. Readers and reviewers demanded a sequel.

Would *The Overcomer* find an equally responsive audience? God grant that it would. Nate's protagonist represented all who meet life's bitterness in their search for peace in a chaotic world. People needed to be reminded of the simple truth Jesus promised in John 14:1, as Nate's overcomer had done: "Do not let your hearts be troubled. Trust in God; trust also in me."

With a prayer that the book would be instrumental in bringing peace, if only to the hearts of individuals, Nate picked up his pen, impatient to finish and get outside into the fresh September morning. He yawned and glanced through the window of the apartment he'd inhabited for the past several months. Except for the persistent sunlight making tunnels in San Francisco's early-morning fog, his accommodations were similar to dozens of others he'd had. New York, Toronto, Mexico City, Tokyo—none was ever a home, simply a place to research, write with few interruptions, and revise until Nate knew it was time to let go and submit his manuscript.

He chuckled, remembering the question invariably asked during interviews the world around. "Tell us, Mr. Alexander. What is your finest novel?"

His quick reply, "My next," always brought a wave of surprise and the need to explain. "Authors should strive to make every project better than the last. 'Just as good as' isn't acceptable."

Nathan stretched to his full height and went back to his job. A few minor comments, a protest against an editorial change that lessened the impact of what he wanted to express, and *The Overcomer* was finished. The bone-weary author knew he was too keyed-up to sleep. He needed physical exercise to counterbalance the stimulus of reliving the just-proofed book, so he ran through a list of possible places to spend the day.

Nate had long since developed the habit of talking to himself. He'd found the sound of his voice was better than too much silence. Now he told his growling stomach, "Fisherman's Wharf first. Seafood chowder, sourdough bread, coleslaw, and salty air are just what I need." He grabbed a windbreaker, opted for the stairs rather than the elevator, and headed down to the street. A pang went through him. Too bad he didn't have someone with whom to enjoy this incomparable day. Someone to join him on the cable cars, explore Chinatown, or visit Golden Gate Park.

"The motto 'He travels fastest who travels alone' isn't as wonderful as people think," Nate complained. He thought of the struggling years he'd spent trying to break into the Christian fiction market, long before the genre exploded into its present popularity. It had been necessary to follow assignments wherever they took him. Things didn't change much with his first successful title, despite his being hounded by publishers and the public clamoring for more books.

"According to the press, people envy me because I've remained single and able to roam the world," Nate muttered. "Easy enough for them to say, when they have families to go home to. They have no idea what my life is like. I'm forty-seven years old and tired of being a workaholic for the sake of the literary world." *Or to compensate for the lack of a companion,* he mentally added.

He thought of the eligible girls and women he had known, often introduced to him by matchmaking friends. None had impressed him enough to share more than an occasional dinner. Long experience had taught him that they were more interested in N. Alexander—sometimes likened by critics to John Grisham—than in Nate as a man.

During the past several months, Nathan had recognized a growing dissatisfaction with his life and himself. He'd chalked it up to fatigue and identifying so closely with the hero of *The Overcomer*. Now the prospect of continuing on the writing and speaking merry-go-round that had whirled him from deadline to deadline was repugnant. He broke into a long lope, trying to outrun his restlessness. It dogged his steps closer than a shadow and brought him to a monumental decision just as he reached Fisherman's Wharf. Summer was over; autumn and winter lay ahead. Now that *The Overcomer* was finished, he would refuse to give in to his publisher's and editor's pleas for more.

"I need to be among people who demand nothing of me," he decided. "First, I have to make it clear I am *not* going to start another novel until I'm good and ready, whether it's January or June or a year from now." The promise of freedom mingled with the breeze off the bay. It reminded Nate of distant school days, when the school bell heralding the beginning of vacation sounded. He couldn't remember when he had felt so exhilarated. Now all he had to do was to decide where he would go in order to find the companionship he craved.

His answer wasn't long in coming. When he reached his hotel, he discovered an invitation from an old college friend. Their class was having a long-overdue reunion, a weekend house party at the home of a classmate whose wise investments had kept him affluent even in these shaky times. Could Nathan come?

Nate sent his acceptance the same day. He also called his editor and broke the news of his impending sabbatical. The phone line reverberated with protest, but Nate held firm. "I have to get away. Yes, I have ideas for other novels. . . . No, I am *not* going to start one anytime soon. . . . If I don't back off, I'll burn out." He hung up the phone, feeling good about himself. The next few months would counteract the effect of the sacrifices he had made for far too long.

Laughter and good cheer abounded at the house party. It was great to knit together the years between college and the present. However, it didn't lessen Nate's awareness that while he supposedly had it all, there was still an emptiness inside him. Not even old acquaintances and half-forgotten friendships could fill it.

~&

At his former roommate's insistence, Nate signed up for a cruise planned as a follow-up to the house party. To his dismay, however, reminiscences soon began to bore him. He stole away to a quiet spot on the deck as often as he could without being discourteous. He loved the rolling waves that stretched to the distant horizon. They reminded him of Rudyard Kipling's "The Explorer."

Nate's pulse quickened, the same way it had when Mrs. Sorenson, his junior high language arts teacher, first read the poem in class. Although written in 1898, it challenged Nate and set him afire to someday write words that would touch others as deeply as Kipling touched him; to encourage them to listen for God's "everlasting Whisper," and to follow wherever it might lead.

> *"There's no sense in going further—it's the edge of*
> *cultivation,"*
> *So they said, and I believed it—broke my land and sowed*
> *my crop—*
> *Built my barns and strung my fences in the little border*
> *station*
> *Tucked away below the foothills where the trails run out*
> *and stop:*
> *Till a voice, as bad as Conscience, rang interminable*
> *changes*
> *On one everlasting Whisper day and night repeated—so:*
> *"Something hidden. Go and find it. Go and look behind the*
> *Ranges—*
> *"Something lost behind the Ranges. Lost and waiting for*
> *you. Go!"*

Nate and his classmates had sat spellbound, transported by Mrs. Sorenson's dramatic voice to a faraway country where the explorer's ponies froze to death, where terror and despair threatened to overcome him and drive him into madness. Yet through it all, he heard God's "everlasting Whisper," and refused to turn back. How Nate and the others rejoiced when the explorer found food, water, and a land rich with ore, wood, cattle, and "coal and iron at your doors." Then came the thrilling conclusion.

> God took care to hide that country till He judged His people ready,
> Then He chose me for His Whisper, and I've found it, and it's yours!
> Yes, your "Never-never country"—yes, your "edge of cultivation"
> And "no sense in going further"—till I crossed the range to see.
> God forgive me! No, I didn't. It's God's present to our nation.
> Anybody might have found it, but—His Whisper came to Me!

Nate considered the magnificent words second only to the Bible in literary value. Now he stood at the rail of the ship, watching the far horizon. For many years he had "looked behind the ranges." He had sought and accomplished much. Why did he feel this sense of loss, of having missed something hidden and waiting? Was the "everlasting Whisper" beckoning him? He had to know. During the rest of the cruise, Nate spent a great deal of time in soul-searching. A trusted friend who had mentored him early in his career came to mind, and Nate had the conviction that he should go to him.

∿

Back on land, Nate tracked down his mentor's Denver address, called, and made an appointment. His heart leaped when the plane neared the city after crossing gigantic mountain ranges. Was this where he would find the missing piece?

The atmosphere of the wood-paneled living room in his friend's home encouraged him. A few insightful questions on the part of Nate's host loosed dammed-up floodwaters. Nate talked without interruption for almost two hours. Then he waited.

At last his friend said, "Nathan, You know God. You love Him and write about Him. You are helping change lives with the talent He has given You. Yet from what you have told me, it seems you may be robbing our Master. How long has it been since you put aside your writing *for* Him in order to spend time *with* Him?"

The truth hit Nate like a Greyhound bus. He bowed his head and stared at the hands that had typed millions of words about God, but seldom stilled longer than a few minutes in prayer. "I don't know."

"Is it possible you have made a god of your writing?" the other inquired.

Silence fell into the room like a cloud descending to earth. A minute passed. Two. Five. Nate stood and shook his mentor's hand. "Thank you."

"Godspeed, boy." The old farewell. The old blessing.

Nate stumbled from his mentor's home filled with determination. He returned to San Francisco and stored everything except the clothing and personal effects he planned to take with him. With a farewell wave, he drove through Nevada and into the mountains of Idaho and Montana, then across the Canadian border. He traveled under his own name. N. Alexander had no place in this odyssey into a world far from publicity blitzes and book-signing tours. He chose modest motels instead of luxury accommodations and never once switched on his laptop computer. He felt each mile of his journey moving him closer to the unknown goal that still eluded him.

In Vancouver, B.C., Nate had noticed a brightly colored brochure touting the city of Victoria, one of the few places he'd never visited. He immediately set out for Victoria. Its old-world charm claimed him from the moment he drove off the ferry. He explored the length and breadth of Vancouver Island. Some of the small towns reminded him of Alderdale. Butchart Gardens kindled a spark with their beauty and history. Someone's dream had changed an ugly quarry into an exquisite masterpiece, just as God's dreams transformed ugliness into beauty.

Nate visited Butchart Gardens again and again. The burning desire to write returned. Not another novel, although he had material enough for several. Nathan watched a tiny hummingbird probe a nearby honeysuckle blossom for nectar. The sight solidified his longing. "I want to write my life story," he said, "to dig into the past and find all it has to offer. It won't be for publication. Just for me, a search for the boy who began to slip away at my first success." He lapsed into silence, wishing for simpler days, simpler ways. "Is it true you can't ever go home again, as Thomas Wolfe says?" He wished he could. Fame had come at a high cost: Passing years had touched his dark hair with silver and stolen some of the laughter from his midnight-black eyes.

The hummingbird moved on, just as Nate had moved on so many times. He set his jaw. Not this time. He would lease a place that overlooked the water and was equipped for housekeeping. There he would begin writing his memoirs.

Nate miraculously found just what he wanted that same afternoon. The furnished cottage felt like home. The harbor view from the living room was incomparable. Half-forgotten memories pounded at the door of Nate's mind and demanded admittance while he shopped for groceries. He didn't stop to unpack his clothes; he just put away his food and unearthed his laptop. The *click-click* of his fingers on the keyboard resembled the sound of hail on a metal roof.

A clock on a nearby public building chimed twelve before Nate stopped typing. He hit Spell Check, stretched, and laughed. Years before he owned a computer, he'd had his own personal spell-checker: a brown-haired girl promoted to his Advanced Language Arts class in junior high school. *Where was Emily Ann Carr now?* he wondered. He never used Spell Check without remembering her.

"My spelling is no better than it was then," he admitted. "That girl sure was a big help. I never found a copy editor who could spell as well as Em'ly Ann. Her eyes always shone when I read what I considered were masterpieces. Too bad we moved away from Alderdale. I'd have liked getting better acquainted with her."

He stared out the window at the lights blossoming in the harbor. Emily Ann's writing had been unique. It had been difficult for her to read in class. No wonder, the way some of their fellow students treated her. "Probably jealous of her talent," Nate surmised. His thoughts rushed on. Had life given her the opportunity to develop her budding skills? Probably not. He'd never seen her byline anywhere.

Nate sighed. He'd never know. A second thought followed. Even if she read N. Alexander's books, Emily Ann would have no reason to suspect the author was the boy she used to help with his spelling. She wouldn't know the far-reaching effects of her help and encouragement The idea depressed him. He shut off his computer and went to bed.

The next morning, Nathan continued his task. He found himself savoring his return to childhood. Word pictures of frosty waterfalls and forest glades crept into his story. He'd never before appreciated how deeply Alderdale had influenced his writing. Things had been so different then. Right was right, wrong was wrong, and never the twain should meet. Nate's books always upheld good over evil. Now the re-living of his early years strengthened his early exposure to the simplicity of Jesus' teachings and brought him closer to his heavenly Father.

❧

One day the fan mail forwarded by Nate's publisher included a letter with *Emily Ann Carr* written in the upper left corner of the envelope above an Alderdale, Oregon, address. Nate stared. Why would his long-ago friend write to him after all these years? Perhaps it was a different Emily Ann Carr. If not, the girl he once knew evidently hadn't married. Why not? If she had stayed as sweet and pretty as when she was a girl, any man would be proud and blessed to have her for his wife.

Any man? Nathan nodded. Any man, including him, if he wanted a wife. He grunted. It was uncanny to hear from her when she'd so recently been on his mind. The next moment, his delight over the unopened letter gave way to common sense. The letter was addressed to Mr. N. Alexander.

"What did you expect?" Nate rebuked himself. "No way could Em'ly Ann connect us. It would be nice to see her again. She may be a mother and grandmother and have kept her maiden name." He shook his head and sighed. It was probably better to remember her as she used to be, rather than risk the disillusionment that often comes from renewing old friendships.

The letter was exactly what Nate would have expected. Emily Ann explained her writing assignment and went on to relate how *The Seeker* had inspired her. She focused on several points that Nate felt represented the essence of the book well. She ended by writing:

> *Whether this book wins awards, as some of your other titles have, isn't nearly as important as the encouragement it offers to those bound by the "everydayness" of life, as well as by major obstacles.*
>
> *I am sure many readers will be blessed by the example your courageous hero set. Yet if I were the only one,* The Seeker *still needed to be written.*

Nate had never felt more humble. Gratitude mingled with the knowledge that Emily Ann's letter had taken him another step nearer to finding what he sought. The wish to learn more about her grew. Why not correspond with her, but as N. Alexander? He would soon learn whether she remained as delightful as the young girl who encouraged him in his dreams. Mischief surged through him. "I'll plant hints to my identity with occasional misspellings and see how long it takes for her to catch on," he decided.

Nate grinned in anticipation, feeling younger than January and more lighthearted than he'd been in years.

$\mathcal{F}$rom the time Emily Carr was big enough to toddle to the mailbox, she considered it one of the most exciting places in her small world. Rain or shine, she seldom missed waiting for the mail carrier. He often teased her and adapted the U.S. Postal Service's motto into, *"Neither snow, nor rain, nor heat, nor gloom of night stays Miss Emily from meeting me at her mailbox."*

"You bring wonderful things," she replied, hugging the day's mail.

He never failed to raise a bushy eyebrow and say, "Mostly advertisements."

Emily always politely nodded, but she could never resist telling him, "They are such *wonderful* advertisements!" Their little joke continued until he retired years later.

Emily's joy of getting the mail never faded. She loved the anticipation that sped through her just before she opened the box. She always hesitated with one hand on the latch, savoring the moment. What lurked inside? A letter from Aunt Carolyn? A Sears & Roebuck or Montgomery Ward "wish book," filled with promise? How many happy hours Emily and Davey had spent making lists and selecting all the things they would have "someday." As an adult, Emily marveled over their joy. Both had always known the treasures described wouldn't be theirs, at least not for a long, long time.

Years passed. The mailbox delivered other treasures. Emily vicariously lived Davey's experiences at church camp, financed by a newspaper route that roused him from sleep before dawn. If a tear dropped to the boyish scribbling, she made certain no one ever saw it except God. Emily would erase all signs of wishing she could be enjoying camp with her brother before reading the letter to their father.

Changes came for Davey. They did not come for Emily. School and being the woman of the family took time and hard work. After Davey went to college, letters signed "David" marked the passing of boy into man. Marriage, the birth of Bill and Danielle, and the departure of David's wife followed. Because of David's military career, Emily became both mother and father to the children. Life continued, with the mailbox containing "Dear Aunt Emily" letters from a second generation of church camps.

When David was sent to the Middle East, Emily had a hard time getting to the mailbox before young Bill and Danielle. Overseas letters were infrequent. The three "home-front soldiers," as David called them, read the few letters that did come, until they were ragged.

One day a letter addressed only to Emily arrived. It amply rewarded her for the long stay-at-home years and gave her the courage to continue her task. David wrote:

> *You will never know what it has meant to me to know you are carrying on, while I am half a world away trying to prevent individuals who lust for power from destroying America and the world. The knowledge that my children are being trained as we were gives me peace of mind. Thank you.*
>
> *Emily Ann, if I'm not permitted to return to Alderdale, take heart. We will meet again. I am more confident of this than ever. I've felt the Spirit of God working in my life, and have taken Romans 8:38–39 for my watchword. "For I am convinced that neither death nor life, neither angels nor demons, neither the present nor the future, nor any powers, neither height nor depth, nor anything else in all creation, will be able to separate us from the love of God, that is in Christ Jesus our Lord."* Now I add, nor from each other.

For the first time in years the letter was signed: *"Your Davey."*

Emily folded the pages and slowly returned them to their envelope. That evening, she read the latter half of the letter to Bill and Danielle, carefully omitting her brother's special message to her. Danielle scooted closer to Emily. Bill said, "I'm glad Dad wrote like that, just in case . . ." He strode from the room, chin up, shoulders squared, a replica of his courageous pilot father.

That was David's last letter.

~&~

With Bill married and relocated to Arizona, his letters helped fill the mailbox and Emily's empty heart. So did Danielle's. Hers were filled with a jumble of excitement, homesickness, and reflections on how different Boston and the university she was attending were from Alderdale. When she learned Emily had signed up for a writing course, she sent a letter via Federal Express that contained only two words: "Go, girl!" Emily grinned, but she appreciated her niece's approval and support.

The more practical Bill responded by phone. "You've never wanted a computer, but you need one if you're going to be a world-famous author. Now that you can afford it, get yourself good equipment and take a computer class. Get rid of the old typewriter Danielle and I left there. I know a guy who'll give you a good deal on a computer, and he'd be happy to get you set up."

"Computer? World-famous author?" Emily laughed into the phone. "You must be joking."

"No way. You'll have Internet access for market and other research, plus e-mail, which means we can keep in touch with Danielle and each other more frequently. It's cheaper than phone calls and easier than writing letters. C'mon, Aunt Emily, be a sport."

She signed up for a computer class at a nearby community center the following day. Emily also gave Bill a go-ahead to contact his friend. By the end of the week they had converted a small, unused room that overlooked her tree-filled backyard, into an office. She began her new class, heartened by her nephew's phone calls. His "You can do it!" spurred her on. So did the patient teacher who never made her students feel stupid when they asked questions.

Even Emily's exciting classes couldn't overcome the disappointment about her unanswered letter to N. Alexander. Her instructor read it aloud in class, considerately omitting her name. Emily's classmates' comments were as positive as the large red "A" it earned for clarity, brevity, and sincerity. It gave her courage to polish a long-dormant children's story, take a deep breath, and read it in class. The story earned praise and excellent suggestions for improvement from both the instructor and fellow students.

Emily hadn't really expected a personal reply from her favorite author, but anyone so famous as N. Alexander surely had a secretary to answer fan mail. It seemed strange that she hadn't received so much as a printed acknowledgment.

Late one afternoon, Emily fled home for refuge after another un-avoidable and especially unpleasant encounter with Herman Dobbs. The stolid man had persisted in walking down Main Street with her, then waiting for her outside the library. Emily shuddered to think how Alderdale would jump to conclusions. She told Herman pointblank, "I don't care to walk with you. Good-bye."

It did no good. He simply smirked and said, "I can bide my time." It took all of Emily's Christian charity to keep from telling him to go chase himself.

For once, even checking the mail held no appeal. She jerked open her mailbox. Empty. Either the carrier was late or she had received no mail. Emily walked into the house and burst out to Sister Feline, "I'm beginning to feel like a prisoner in my own town! There must be a Dobbs child spying on me from behind every tree. Otherwise, how would that father of theirs know every time I leave the house?"

She took Sister Feline's plaintive "meow" for agreement and rushed on. "One of these days . . ." The sound of the mail truck cut off her dire threat. Instead of rushing outside, she watched from the window. The carrier was putting an envelope in her box. Good. A let-ter from Bill or Danielle would do wonders in taking her mind off Herman Dobbs. She hurried outside and opened her mailbox.

The envelope lay address-side down. Long, white, and fat, it little resembled the envelopes Bill and Danielle sent. Emily turned it over and peered at the return address. Her spirits shot from the depths to the heights. It was from the publisher that presented N. Alexander's books to his salivating public!

"They must have stuffed it with brochures of upcoming titles,"

Emily reflected. Too keyed up to wait until she was back inside, she ripped off the stamped end and gasped. There were no brochures. Just several closely typed pages.

"I see you have an official-looking letter, Miss Carr." Herman Dobbs's grating voice jarred Emily from her absorption. "If it's about your inheritance, I'd be glad to help. I have a lot of experience with legal issues."

Resenting being interrupted and cheated of her initial pleasure in the letter, she glared into the man's snooping face. "My correspondence is none of your concern whatsoever," she told him. "Furthermore, if I see you near my mailbox again, I will report you to the U.S. Postal Service for interference."

The man's mouth dropped open. "I-I wasn't . . ."

"Well, see that you don't," Emily snapped. She turned and forced herself to walk up the path to her porch without looking back. The dull tread of Herman's clodhopper boots on the gravel outside her fence proclaimed his more-than-welcome departure.

Good heavens, where did that come from? she wondered. There was no law preventing Herman Dobbs from standing near her mailbox.

Emily's jangled nerves were not conducive to enjoying her much-anticipated letter. She forced herself to drink a cup of tea and make a casserole for supper before settling down on the couch with Sister Feline curled up close beside her.

> *Dear Miss Carr,*
>
> *I apologize for not having answered your letter sooner. I have been traveling, and it only caught up with me today—in beautiful Victoria on Vancouvre Island. You'll never know how glad I am that you signed up for the writing class and chose me for your first assignment. I've been going through a frustrating time in my life and career, I needed to hear exactly what you had to say.*

Astonished, Emily reread the words. This was no routine acknowledgment, but a highly personal letter from the author! Her fingers shook, and she read on.

*For some time I have sensed a growing discontent with my
life, a feeling of something missing. I pushed it aside until I met
the deadline for The Overcomer, which you'll be pleased to
learn is a sequel to The Seeker. I believe it is the best work I
have done.*

Emily paused again. How wonderful to have such a book to look
forward to reading! She eagerly returned to the letter. N. Alexander
shared how his old mentor helped him realize he had allowed his
writing to overshadow his personal relationship with his heavenly Father. He told how his sojourn to "Vancouvre" Island and Butchart Gardens gave him a whole new closeness with God.

Emily smiled at the spelling of Vancouver. Evidently, Mr. Alexander hadn't used Spell Check. Memories of Nathan Hamilton returned.
His face was as clear in her mind as it had been more than thirty years
ago. How they'd shared the joy of being praised by Mrs. Sorenson
when one of them wrote a story that pleased her!

There was more, much more, before N. Alexander ended his letter.

*Is this your first writing class? How is it going? Have you
been interested in writing for a long time, or is it a new
pursuit? If all your work is as interesting and well-written as
your letter, you certainly should pursue the writing craft. I
hope you will write to me again at my Victoria address below. I
can't begin to express how your comments lifted me up at a
time I most needed to hear exactly what you wrote.*

Never in her wildest imagination had Emily dreamed she would
receive such a personal letter from an author, especially one she
deeply admired. It left her overwhelmed with gratitude. It wasn't so
much that Mr. Alexander had taken the time to write. What touched
her most were the words: "If all your work is as interesting and well-
written as your letter, you certainly should pursue the writing craft."
They danced through her mind, bringing confirmation that the falter-
ing steps she had taken were in the right direction.

That night Emily prayed long and earnestly about her future. She finished by saying, "Lord, this day has been a roller-coaster ride. From Herman Dobbs to N. Alexander—what a leap! It seems it would be rude not to answer Mr. Alexander's letter. He must be sincere about wanting me to respond or he wouldn't have asked all those questions."

She fell asleep in the middle of her "amen." She awoke clear-headed. She would wait a week before she responded to Mr. Alexander's letter. That way, there was no danger she would appear forward.

⤔

Emily received an answer to her second letter—it was filled with more questions—by return mail. Then she received another. And another. She realized she was beginning to look forward to the renowned author's letters far too much and laid down the law. "Emily Ann Carr, stop acting like a schoolgirl with her first crush," she chastised. "Stop this racing to the mailbox, your heart pounding like a sprinter after a hundred-yard dash. Have your manless years, broken only by wannabe suitors the caliber of Herman Dobbs, made you desperate? The only thing that can come from this is heartache. N. Alexander will tire of corresponding and go back to the world in which he belongs. A world in which you can never be a part."

Emily's scolding was to no avail. She rebelliously wrote in her journal:

> *So what if it happens that way? He will never know how I feel, and I may never again have anything so wonderful happen to me. Mr. Alexander has never hinted at anything more than sharing his thoughts and feelings in our letters, but he's given me a touch of the romance I've longed for. One day he will go away, just as Nathan Hamilton did—but I will still have my memories.*

Her burst of independence should have settled the question. It didn't. In desperation, she called Aunt Carolyn and asked her advice, carefully omitting her own growing feelings. "Should I continue writing to Mr. Alexander?"

"Go ahead. Anyone who writes the way he does isn't likely to wind up on the Most Wanted list," was her forthright aunt's half-serious reply.

Emily hung up, laughed until tears came, and began writing another letter.

6

ate Alexander riffled through his just-delivered letters and impatiently tossed them aside. For the past ten days he'd eagerly awaited the mail, only to be as bitterly disappointed as a child who reaches into a cookie jar and finds it empty. There had been plenty of time for Emily Ann Carr to answer his letter, even considering possible delays due to his being in Victoria.

"Seems like she could at least answer," he grumped. "The Em'ly Ann I knew would have." Unwilling to stay inside with only his disgruntled self for company, Nate caught up a warm jacket and the keys to his car. At least the weather was cooperating. Fall had fallen. Literally. Golden maple leaves and the red of sumac punctuated the landscape. Another visit to Butchart Gardens would help restore his spirits. In spite of an early morning frost that had increased the color spectrum of the leaves, hardy roses and a multitude of perennials continued to bloom.

The western sun was flinging a lingering good night to the island when Nate drove away from his temporary home. In all his travels, he had seldom seen sunsets comparable to those in Victoria. No artist or photographer could ever capture the panorama of red, gold, orange, and cerise, spreading over the water to mantle the land with a rosy glow. The first star broadcast a light signal for hosts of its comrades to appear. A full moon crept up over the horizon and promised a spectacular drive.

"I wish . . ." Nate sighed. Even though his time in Victoria had brought the presence of the Master more deeply into his life, how wonderful it would be to have a companion, especially at times like this. A world that caught at one's throat with its beauty was meant to be shared. No wonder God had said in Genesis, "It is not good for man to be alone. I will make a helper suitable for him."

Nate had never felt the need of a helper enough to consider praying about it.

Until now.

Ever since that fateful morning in San Francisco, the feeling that he stood on the precipice of change had lurked in the back of Nate's mind. His old mentor's counsel had turned his thoughts toward God. So far, his odyssey had proved satisfying, although he recognized he still had far to go to find the "something lost and hidden" waiting behind the ranges of his future.

Will part of it be love and marriage? he wondered, while purple dusk crouched on the horizon before fleeing from the approaching night. He uneasily shifted position in his seat. After years of flying solo, could he change his thinking from "me" to "we" and be a good husband?

Nate laughed in derision at the thought of what kind of husband he would make, with no prospects of a wife in sight. "Hmm. I wonder what Em'ly Ann would think of such a preposterous idea?"

As if you'd tell her, his conscience jeered.

Laughter died as suddenly as it had been born. "It looks like I'll never have the chance to tell her that or anything else," Nate said. A pang went through him. He wouldn't have believed how much contentment could come from sharing his struggles, as he had done in the letter that hadn't been answered. He would never have risked writing it if he hadn't known her years ago.

"The problem is, Em'ly Ann doesn't have a clue I'm anyone except an author she admires. Having a total stranger write the way I did may have offended her."

Nate mulled it over until he reached Butchart Gardens. The lights of San Francisco reflecting in the bay were no more impressive than the scene that lay before him. Artificial lighting paled by comparison to the fully risen moon. A slight breeze harvested perfume from hundreds of drowsy roses.

Nate sauntered through the gardens, then climbed to a high point where he could be alone with the night. He listened to the song of fountains and waterfalls until his hands and face chilled and the desire for companionship drove him back among strangers—strangers who would offer occasional smiles and greetings. As N. Alexander, he'd grown tired of the multitude that surrounded and drained him with their demands. Like other authors who shot from obscurity to fame after long years of slow but steady growth, he'd been besieged by those asking him to speak, teach, and mentor.

"I spent a lot of time and energy learning I couldn't be all things to all people," Nate said quietly, his voice tinged with regret. "It's nice to be incognito for a time. Mr. A. Nonymous in person."

Nice, but lonely. Right?

"Right." Held captive by the night and his ambivalence, Nate drove home and headed for his computer. Writing normally freed him from daily irritations. It also often brought answers to his most perplexing questions when the characters he created faced similar situations. Now he decided, "If I can't find what I need in the present, I'll look for it in the past."

Hours later, Nate yawned, switched off the computer, and went to bed. His journey into yesterday had succeeded in replacing his gloom with hope. A new day lay waiting just beyond the horizon. Would it bring a letter from Alderdale?

～❧～

Nate was not disappointed the next day. He read the new letter twice: the first time for content, the second for enjoyment. He marveled at Emily Ann's ability to paint with words. Her description of Alderdale made him long to drop everything and rush back to the small-town way of life he'd almost forgotten still existed.

He shook his head. "No. It's too soon. One good thing, though: Em'ly Ann sure sounds like the girl I knew in junior high. The value of her writing is in its simplicity. She must remember Mrs. Sorenson telling the class, especially me, 'Less is more. Don't attack readers with bursts of adjectives and adverbs.' Em'ly Ann always could make one word say what she wanted."

Nate chuckled. "I can't go home yet, but I can keep writing letters loaded with questions. It will keep Em'ly Ann corresponding, even if only to be polite!"

❧

During the rest of the fall and early winter, letters flew like carrier pigeons between Oregon and Victoria, B.C. With every letter, Emily continued to fight a losing battle with her unruly heart. All the telling herself she was behaving foolishly didn't stop her traitorous heart from hammering or prevent warm color from rushing to her face when she read her messages. She wrote in her journal:

> *What I am feeling is probably hero worship, nothing more.*
> *Gaggles of silly women fall in love with well-known authors.*
> *I've always despised their foolishness. Now I'm dangerously*
> *close to joining their ranks!*
> *All I know about romance is what I've read in books and*
> *through daydreams about a boy who has long since forgotten*
> *me. I should be ashamed of myself for trying to find more in*
> *Mr. Alexander's letters than what is there.*

Isn't there more? Unsophisticated as she was in matters of the heart, the growing affection in N. Alexander's letters seemed obvious. Emily continued writing.

> *He evidently sees worth in my writing and is kind enough*
> *to encourage me. He's never asked how old I am. That shows*
> *he has no interest in me except as a correspondent while he is*
> *far away from his friends.*

She snapped the journal shut and scooped up Sister Feline from a nearby chair. "Enough acting like a moonstruck schoolgirl," she firmly told her cat, feeling she had won this skirmish—but aware the war between common sense and long-suppressed hopes raged on, fueled by every letter from Victoria, misspellings and all.

A few days later, the sharp ring of Emily's doorbell interrupted her inadequate attempts to send an e-mail attachment to Bill. She made a face and didn't answer.

The ringing persisted, followed by a voice calling, "Miss Emily? Are you home?"

Emily glanced out the window. The local florist's delivery van was parked by her gate. She gave thanks that it wasn't Elmer Dobbs or Harriet Taylor and hurried to the door, Sister Feline at her heels. "Sorry. I've been trying to conquer e-mail."

"Good for you." The florist, who had served the town's needs for decades, held an enormous arrangement of roses, carnations, and decorative ferns. A handful of blue forget-me-nots nestled in the center.

Emily gasped. "My goodness! That's not a bouquet; it's an entire garden!"

"Would you like me to carry this inside? The crystal vase is pretty heavy."

"Please put it on the hall table, if you would." She held the screen door open.

"Sure. There's no card. It was ordered anonymously." He set the flowers down. "Someone sure admires you, Miss Emily. But then, everyone does," the florist added. "Good luck tracking down the sender." He touched his forehead in an old-fashioned salute of respect and whistled his way back to the delivery van.

No card? Someone admires me? Indignation flooded through Emily. "Is this another attempt by Herman Dobbs to ingratiate himself?" she demanded of Sister Feline. Doubt crept in. Surely the rude man wouldn't spend so much money on his wife-finding campaign—not even to obtain a mother for his children.

Oh, yeah? a warning voice mocked. *The cost of the flowers is a pittance compared with the vast fortune he and Harriet think you inherited. If Herman Dobbs sent the flowers, he will consider it an investment in his future.*

The thought was so repulsive, Emily reached for the bouquet, fully intending to throw it into the street. When her unwelcome suitor passed by, he'd see what she thought of his tactics. Common sense prevailed. "He may not have sent it," Emily told her cat. "I can't imagine Herman Dobbs, or even Harriet Taylor, being subtle enough to include the forget-me-nots. Neither seems the anonymous-acts-of-kindness type. Even if they were, it's been years since anyone sent me flowers. My last were from Aunt Carolyn, when I graduated from high school. Why deprive myself of the pleasure they will bring?" She buried her nose in the fragrant bouquet. "Besides, they aren't Herman Dobbs's flowers. They were originally God's. Now they're mine." Sister Feline rubbed against Emily's ankles and began to purr.

꩜

A week later, Emily Ann found a package in her mailbox. The return address was a specialty bookstore in Portland. Strange. She'd never ordered anything from them. It must be a mistake. On the other hand, it could be one of those promotional advertisements, where companies send out books in hopes of gaining customers by hooking them with the first title of a new series.

This was not the case. Safe in her living room, hidden from possible prying eyes, Emily opened her package. To her amazement, it was a beautiful, leather-bound edition of *Little Women*. The name *Emily Ann Carr* was engraved in gold on the cover.

She couldn't believe it. Who would send her such a gift, and for no apparent reason? Christmas was weeks away; her birthday long since past. This couldn't be Herman Dobbs's doing. Even if he were to send a book, he had no way of knowing *Little Women* was one of Emily's all-time favorites. Neither did Harriet.

Emily felt a blush start at the neckline of her modest blue house dress and creep upward. Was it possible that . . . ? She shook her head. "If Mr. Alexander were kind enough to send me a book, it would be one of his titles that we discussed. We've never talked about Louisa May Alcott's work and how much I like her writing." She ran her fingers over the golden letters of her name and told her omnipresent cat, "Now we have two mysteries. I never did find out who sent the flowers, just who didn't. If Herman Dobbs were responsible, he'd try to move heaven and earth to make sure I and everyone else in Alderdale knew it!"

Sister Feline cocked her head to one side and looked wise.

Encouraged by N. Alexander's praise for her interesting letters, Emily Ann dug out a few children's stories she'd made up for her brother and, later, for his children. Their quality surprised her. Even those written when she was quite young had a certain charm and appeal. She diligently polished them, using all the skills her eager mind was absorbing in her writing class.

"You may wish to try submitting them," her instructor told her.

Emily shook her head. "I'm not that confident yet." She didn't explain she wouldn't get to that stage until Mr. Alexander had seen a story. She definitely wasn't ready for *that,* even though he'd invited her to send samples of her writing.

Emily Ann continued to spend a great deal of time in prayer concerning her deepening attraction for her "by mail" friend. At last she "dumped it all in God's lap," as she told Sister Feline, and was rewarded with the peace she badly needed.

Three hundred miles north of Alderdale, autumn flew south with the wild geese. Stark, leafless branches warned that winter lingered just around the corner. The feeling he needed to return to Oregon before he could finish his memoirs haunted Nathan Hamilton day and night. So did the knowledge that letters were a poor substitute for love.

The advantage of knowing with whom he was corresponding had served him well. On paper, Emily Ann was the same girl he'd known long ago, only more mature.

One wild afternoon, when rain pelted Nate's cottage, he knelt beside his bed and surrendered himself to his growing feelings. "Thank You for leading me here, God," he prayed. "I've found what I was missing for so long: a more personal relationship with You. I also feel Em'ly Ann may be the companion I need and Your answer to my loneliness. Am I the right husband for her? N. Alexander already has her friendship and admiration. Will it grow into love for plain old Nate Hamilton?"

There was only one way to find out. Just before Christmas, Nate wrote a letter designed to play on Emily Ann Carr's sympathies and put him back into her life.

7

*E*arly one nippy autumn morning, Emily received a call from Isaiah Gerard.

"I need to see you," he said brusquely. "As soon as you can get here."

The lawyer sounded so unlike himself, an alarm bell went off in Emily's mind. "Right away. Does this have anything to do with my inheritance?"

"It has everything to do with your inheritance," Isaiah snapped. "I'll tell you more when I see you." He broke the connection.

Emily stared at the silent phone and slowly replaced it in its cradle. Never before had her friend spoken to her in such a manner. There must be something terribly wrong or the usually unflappable Isaiah Gerard wouldn't have hung up without the courtesy of a goodbye! With a quick prayer for strength, Emily hurried to change from nightgown and robe into warm clothing. She hastily donned her navy suit and arranged the scarlet scarf with nervous fingers.

Her shadow, Sister Feline, extended a paw toward Emily's pantyhose and meowed indignantly when her owner pushed her away. Emily barely heard her. She rushed downstairs and out the door, leaving her cat complaining in the hall.

Main Street lay mercifully empty, except for a few parked vehicles with heavily frosted tops and windshields. Emily Ann traversed its length in record time. Her cheeks burned with cold when she reached the law offices of Gerard & Son.

Isaiah's warm welcome contrasted sharply with the way he had sounded on the phone. *Surely there couldn't be too much wrong,* Emily thought.

"Sit down, sit down," the white-haired attorney boomed. "Hmm. You are certainly looking well. You must have walked. Your cheeks are brighter than your scarf." His eyes twinkled. "You should wear red more often, Em'ly Ann. It makes you look young."

Emily felt a flutter of pleasure at his compliment. "Thank you. I feel young. It's all I can do to keep from skipping up and down the streets."

Isaiah threw his head back and laughed heartily. "That I'd like to see." An instant later, a frown appeared and spread. He picked up a pen from his desk and dropped a bombshell. "What's this I hear about you getting married?"

Emily felt hot color surge into her face. Mr. Gerard *couldn't* know she'd thought a lot about marriage lately. She had never confessed her growing desire for a companion except in prayer and to Sister Feline. "Wh-who told you that?"

Isaiah's face set in an expression of stern disapproval. "So it's true? Em'ly Ann Carr, I'm disappointed in you. You are far too good for Herman Dobbs. Furthermore—"

"Herman Dobbs!" It came out as a strangled whisper.

"Yes, Herman Dobbs. I worked late last night, and he slouched in here trying to get information concerning the size of your inheritance." Isaiah mimicked his visitor to a tone. "'As Emily Carr's intended, I have the right to know how things stand.'" Isaiah scowled and bent his pen so hard, it snapped in two.

Emily tried to collect her scattered wits. She couldn't believe even Herman Dobbs would go so far! "What did you tell him?" she faltered.

Isaiah scowled. "I asked him to leave. He muttered and sputtered and threatened to have my license revoked; for what, I don't know. About that time my son walked in. He threw Herman out. You aren't *really* going to marry that lout, are you, Em'ly Ann?"

"Marry, him! I can't get rid of him!" She sat bolt upright in her chair. "Herman Dobbs, ably abetted by Harriet Taylor, is making my life a nightmare. He squeezes past people at church so he can sit next to me. He insists on walking with me when I go downtown. Lately, he's been strolling past my place and waving at the house. Anyone who sees him is sure to think I'm returning his greetings." Tears of frustration crowded behind her eyelids. Emily held her eyes open wide to keep them from falling.

Her attorney grunted. "It figures." He paused, then leaned forward with his usual kindly look. "Too bad there's no law against extreme annoyance." Isaiah shrugged his shoulders expressively. "Of course, persuasion is my business. Tell you what, I'll call Dobbs in and give him something to think about." A gleam of mischief danced in the attorney's eyes. "I can be quite firm on occasion."

The blatant understatement tickled Emily's funny bone. Isaiah Gerard's cross-examination of lying witnesses was legendary in the state of Oregon. Emily grinned. He could be quite firm, all right! A half-hour later, she left the office feeling freer than she'd been since Harriet Taylor imported her obnoxious cousin-in-law. Her euphoria didn't last long, though; Harriet lay in wait.

"I am . . . so glad . . . I caught you!" Harriet panted between words. She had obviously spotted her prey while Emily talked with Isaiah on the steps of the law office and had run to catch up with her. "Is there anything new concerning your inheritance?"

Emily limited her reply to, "Good morning, Harriet. It's another nice day."

"Not so nice for some," the other woman said. "Dear Herman is heartbroken and distraught at the way you are treating him. How can a good Christian woman like you refuse to take pity on him and his children in their hour of need?"

Hour of need? Harriet sounded like a low-budget soap-opera character.

Emily stifled her mirth. "I'm sorry, Harriet. I've said everything I care to say on the subject of Mr. Dobbs.

"Tell me, though," Emily continued. "How are things going for the community Thanksgiving dinner? You're in charge this year, aren't you?"

The ploy to sidetrack her adversary worked. Harriet bridled with pleasure. "Yes. It's going to be the best dinner ever." She launched into a detailed, glowing description of decorations, menu, and planned entertainment.

For the first time, Emily saw past Harriet's meddling to the woman's deep-seated need to be appreciated by more than her daughter Amelia. If Harriet had been blessed with grandchildren, perhaps it wouldn't have been necessary for her to seek attention by interfering in the lives of others. Pity temporarily erased Emily's annoyance and softened her voice. "It sounds wonderful. What would you like me to bring?"

"Pumpkin pies. Three, if you will. You make the best pies in Alderdale."

Emily felt her lips twitch. No one could turn a compliment into a flat statement of fact like Harriet Taylor. A few minutes later they parted, with no further discussion of Herman Dobbs's state of mind and heart.

When Emily arrived home, she checked her mailbox and gave it a surreptitious pat. It continued to provide moments of delicious anticipation, but so had her entry into the world of e-mail. Once she'd mastered its intricacies, it offered the same feeling of being on the brink of wonderful things that her faithful mailbox had provided since childhood. Emily held her breath each time she hit Get New Mail, wondering how many messages waited for her. She hadn't yet confessed to N. Alexander that she had e-mail. Messages displayed on a screen might not seem as exciting as those that came in fat white envelopes.

"How much I've changed in the past few months," Emily murmured. "Even Mr. Gerard said so." The same thrill she'd felt in his office inched through her. "So he thinks red makes me look young and that I should wear it more often. Maybe I will."

The desire for another shopping trip seized her. Most of her earlier purchases were more suitable to summer and fall than the cold season lurking just out of sight. Winter had already laid a gentle hand on the higher hills, leaving a frosting of white that foreshadowed more to come. Snow shovels were prominently displayed amidst the Thanksgiving and Christmas decorations in some of the stores on Main Street.

For the rejuvenated Emily Carr, to think was to act. The following morning found her back at the mall in Portland, reveling in the variety of warm clothing available. She selected skirts and slacks, then chose pretty sweaters to mix and match with their darker colors. A turquoise skirt and twin sweater set joined the pile to be purchased. So did a fisherman's knit sweater, something she'd always longed to own.

Emily turned toward the cashier, experiencing a moment of déjà vu. Except this time, the mannequin wore a holly berry red dress instead of a navy blue suit and scarlet scarf.

I want that dress.

Had she spoken aloud? Emily glanced both ways. No one was paying any attention to her. The dour faces of ultraconservative ancestors came to mind. Their forbidding expressions clearly indicated what *they* thought of such apparel.

Was she going to let long-dead ancestors dictate to her? No. Emily steadied her voice and said, "I'd like to try on the red dress, please."

"It will look lovely with your brown-and-silver hair," the saleswoman told her.

Emily dismissed the comment as part of the woman's sales technique, until she put on the dress. Its soft folds fell about her as if it had been expertly fashioned for her by a couture. *What would Mr. Alexander think if he saw me now?* Emily wondered. The blush that sprang to her mirrored reflection rivaled the dress in color and tipped the scales. Even though there was little chance she would ever meet N. Alexander, Emily left the store with a jaunty step—and the dress. She'd leave it in her closet until Christmas. It would give her more time to get used to the idea of wearing it. Her newly purchased turquoise skirt and sweater set would do nicely for Thanksgiving.

The bus ride back to Alderdale gave Emily time to reflect on the pleasure she'd felt at the thought of N. Alexander seeing her wearing the exquisite dress. It also reminded her of the silken threads binding her closer to the author with every letter. Doubt crept in. Even though she'd turned her feelings over to God, shouldn't she be making an attempt to regain control over her usual, composed self?

A startling idea came. Perhaps instead of writing off the possibility of a meeting with her correspondent, she should initiate one. It wouldn't be hard. Aunt Carolyn had suggested several times, "If you ever want to meet your boyfriend in person, but don't feel comfortable asking him to visit you in Alderdale, come stay with me. We'll invite him here where you'll both be on neutral ground."

"Thanks, but he isn't my boyfriend, and even if he were, I don't have that much courage," Emily always responded.

Aunt Carolyn invariably sounded skeptical. "Why not? He's been interested enough in you to correspond, hasn't he? If you want something, go for it. Just give me fair warning if you decide to come."

Now her aunt's advice pounded in Emily's brain. It hammered at her all during the successful Thanksgiving dinner, even though Herman Dobbs's baleful gaze reproached her from across the tastefully decorated church fellowship hall, and his five children glowered. Emily Ann didn't know what Mr. Gerard had said to Herman, but it had been enough to make him back off. For how long, Emily didn't know. His biding-my-time expression made her shudder, and the realization that Alderdale still considered her far wealthier than she'd ever be, boded no good for her while Herman Dobbs hung around.

Shortly before Christmas, a pathetic-sounding letter arrived from Canada. N. Alexander praised Emily for her description of the Thanksgiving dinner and those who attended; she had pointedly excluded all mention of Herman Dobbs and his brood! Then he said:

> My mouth watered when you described the turkey, stuffing, pumpkin pies, and all the rest. It reminded me of the "olden days," when parents and grandparents, nieces, nephews, and always a few strays gathered around a table groaning with the weight of good food. Things have certainly changed.
>
> Canada celebrates Thanksgiving in October instead of November. The restaurant where I ate dinner wasn't bad, but it was a far cry from home cooking.
>
> You mentioned your niece and nephew won't be home for Christmas. Do you have any special plans?
>
> I'm great with a microwave and can opener, but not much of a regular cook. I haven't made friends here, only

acquaintances. I don't want to impose on them, so I suppose I'll look for a place that will serve a reasonable facsimile of a Christmas dinner. I can't say I look forward to it. Celebrating the birth of Christ all by myself isn't my idea of the way things should be.

Emily didn't know how to respond. She called Aunt Carolyn immediately and read the letter over the phone.

Carolyn snorted. "I've heard some pretty broad hints in my time, but this beats them all. Give me his address. I'll invite him to come to Seattle for the holidays and have Christmas dinner with us."

A few days later, Emily received an e-mail from her aunt. It was crisp, blunt, and exactly like Carolyn. "The glue on my envelope barely had time to dry before your friend's acceptance arrived!"

When Nathan Hamilton first came up with the idea of appealing to Emily Ann Carr with a "far-from-home-and-family" plea, he also firmly decided to return to Alderdale, regardless of the outcome of the meeting he felt sure would take place. The thrill of "going home" made him feel more like a boy than ever. Love was not just for the young but for those of any age who believed in it and sought it. By the time Carolyn Sheffield's invitation arrived, Nate was "chomping at the bit and raring to go," to use the vernacular of a western story he wrote when he was in junior high. Mrs. Sorenson had torn it up, saying it wasn't worthy of his talent. It wasn't. Even Emily Ann had struggled to keep from laughing when he read it in class.

Packed and ready, Nate faced an obstacle that loomed larger with every passing hour. He paced the floor and considered his problem. "Shall I write and confess who I really am, or wait until I meet Em'ly Ann in Seattle? If I tell her ahead of time, she may not come. If I wait, she will know I finagled the Christmas invitation under false pretenses. Can I convince her that what started as a joke has brought me great happiness? She's never given any indication of picking up on the clues I planted. How will she feel when she learns I've been deceiving her?"

During his long sabbatical, Nate had well learned the importance of turning to God in everything, not just before making major decisions, although this could certainly be considered one. After a great deal of prayer, he muttered, "The old cliché 'Desperate times call for desperate measures' is right on target." Grinning broadly, he ignored his laptop and picked up pen and paper.

❧

Nathan's letter arrived at the Carr home while Emily was packing. She had just lovingly wrapped her new red dress in tissue paper when the mail arrived. She stared at the handwritten envelope, remembering the day she finally accepted as fact that she truly loved her by-mail friend. Her passionate desire to ensure that Mr. Alexander would never again face another lonely holiday had prevailed, shouting down all her objections. Still she doubted. Was meeting N. Alexander God's will or her own scheme? Even if he one day returned her love, what place could a nobody like Emily Ann Carr have in his world?

Emily walked into the house and tore open the envelope with shaking fingers. A picture and letter fell out. The letter was short and to the point.

Dear Emily Ann,
You are in for a surprise. I hope it makes you happy. It does me.
N. Alexander

Emily reread the cryptic message. "How odd. He never calls me Emily Ann." She picked up the picture and stared. A laughing woman stared back from her position between two smiling men. Although the snapshot had evidently been taken from a distance, the beauty of the woman's face could not be denied. Nor could the fact that both men's arms lay across her shoulders. Or the look of joy in all three faces.

Emily turned the snapshot over, hoping to discover which man was her correspondent. There was no identification. "What does this picture have to do with Mr. Alexander's surprise?" she asked Sister Feline.

The cat gave her an unblinking stare.

Emily examined the photograph again. She racked her brain for a logical answer. It came with sickening force, sharp as a heavy stone launched by a strong hand: Mr. Alexander must be bringing a fiancée. He had never mentioned a woman in his letters, but it was difficult to believe there were none in his life. Perhaps someone dear to him was part of the reason he had fled to Victoria. Perhaps they had quarreled and finally resolved their differences. Perhaps . . .

"So what did you expect?" Emily told herself. "That he would fall in love with you? He, a celebrated author? You, a woman beginning the autumn of her life?"

Yes, her heart responded. *That's exactly what I hoped would happen.*

Panicky and on the verge of calling Aunt Carolyn to cancel her visit, Emily turned to her well-read Bible. It fell open to Proverbs 3, and her gaze dropped to verse 6, which she had previously highlighted: "In all thy ways acknowledge him, and he shall direct thy paths."

She laid the Bible aside. For better or worse—and if what she suspected came to pass, it would definitely be worse—she had to go. N. Alexander must never know how much she cherished his friendship. Or to what extent she had hoped it would someday turn to mutual love.

8

On Christmas Eve morning, Emily Carr clasped her hands in the lap of her navy blue suit and stared out the window of the jetliner, still parked on the Portland tarmac, and thought about the short flight to Seattle. Her heart felt so heavy, she wondered how the plane could lift off and stay in the air long enough to reach their destination. The only bright spots in her world were the brilliant sunshine and the fact that misery over the upcoming ordeal superseded her fear of flying for the first time.

The plane swooshed down the runway and lifted off. The hum of excited conversation and eager faces of those homeward bound surrounded Emily. They made her feel worse than ever. She turned away from them and focused on the retreating landscape below.

I wish I were home. Christmas with only my cat for company would be better than this. Better for her, too.

Emily felt the start of a smile. Spoiled because her mistress was never away from home overnight, Sister Feline had gone into her carrier docilely enough, but threw a cat fit when delivered to the Gerard home. Her black-and-white fur puffed in outrage until she looked twice her normal size. Emily fervently hoped Isaiah and his wife wouldn't regret their cat-sitting offer!

"We'll be arriving at SeaTac International airport shortly," the pilot announced. "Please stay in your seats and fasten your seat belts. We hope you have a pleasant trip."

Emily Ann obeyed his directions and braced herself. Would Mr. Alexander's fiancée be as lovely in person as she was in the hazy photograph? Would she be at the airport? The plane circled and began its descent. Emily riveted her gaze on the earth rushing up to meet her. A psalm that often comforted her when she felt she couldn't go on, came to mind. *"The LORD is my strength and my shield. . . ."* She squared her shoulders, lifted her chin, and prepared to meet one of the hardest trials of her life.

❧

Nate Hamilton arrived in Seattle the morning of December 23. He immediately contacted Ms. Carolyn Sheffield. "If you are free for dinner tonight, I'd like to take you out," he offered.

She wasted no time in accepting. "Fine. Did you fly or drive?"

Her direct response was catching. "I drove." Nate didn't add that before he saw her, he intended to exchange his faithful vehicle for the SUV he'd been considering for some time.

"Good. Pick me up at seven. You obviously have my address."

Nate received the distinct impression she was about to hang up. "Do you have a preference in restaurants? We probably need a reservation."

"If seafood is acceptable to you, I'll contact Ivar's Salmon House."

Nate raised an eyebrow in amusement. Evidently Ms. Carolyn Sheffield was one independent lady. "Thanks. It sounds good. I'll see you at seven." He hung up, wondering if his plan to admit his true identity, in hopes of enlisting her support, was really such a good idea. His hostess-to-be sounded formidable. He grinned. It would take more than a formidable aunt to keep him from winning Emily Ann Carr. If, of course, Emily was willing to be won. He quickly pushed the thought aside.

The afternoon that Nate had expected to drag by until time to meet Carolyn Sheffield, actually flew past in the sights and sounds of the celebrating city. Beautifully decorated streets and stores and laughing shoppers. Joyous music by sidewalk carolers and loudspeakers. Bells being rung by those who cheerfully donated time to don Santa Claus suits and man a multitude of Salvation Army kettles that would help provide for the needy. Tantalizing aromas from dozens of ethnic restaurants, reminding passers-by of the rich cultural diversity of the "City on the Sound."

Nate thoroughly enjoyed it all. After selecting, purchasing, and taking possession of a dark red SUV, he hurried back to his hotel and dressed as carefully as if he were being presented an award. He had a feeling nothing would get by his dinner date.

He was right. Instead of saying "hello" or "good evening" when she opened the front door of her home and allowed him to step into the tastefully decorated foyer, she bluntly inquired, "Just why did you ask me to dinner, Mr. Alexander?"

Nate felt impaled by her steely gaze. "N. Alexander is actually my pen name," he blurted out. "My real name is Nathan Alexander Hamilton. I went to school with Em'ly Ann."

Carolyn Sheffield looked at him with intelligent blue eyes. She said nothing, but Nate recognized that she was sizing him up with the scrutiny of a father whose sixteen-year-old daughter was going on her first date. "And she doesn't know."

Nate met her gaze unflinchingly. "No. It started as a joke. It isn't a joke now. God and Em'ly Ann willing, I intend to court and marry her."

A twinkle crept into Carolyn Sheffield's eyes, as unexpected as a party hat on top of snowcapped Mount Rainier. "So, did you come for my blessing?"

Nate suddenly found himself liking the straight-speaking, diminutive woman. "No, but now that I've met you, I'd like to have it."

A quick smile did wonders to warm her stern face. "I'm not the best person to ask about courting and marrying. I strongly suggest you have this discussion with my niece."

"I intend to. May I accompany you to the airport to meet Em'ly Ann's plane?"

"You can do better than that." She scowled. "Our law offices have been a madhouse lately. Deadlines galore. I need to go in tomorrow morning, long enough to make sure everything's in order before the holidays." The twinkle returned to her eyes. "Besides, if you plan to tell Emily who you are as bluntly as you told me, you don't need a third-party witness."

Nate couldn't help laughing, although his heartbeat quickened at the thought of meeting Emily alone—except, of course, for a multitude of other incoming passengers and their waiting families. He held out his hand. "Thank you, Ms. Sheffield. If all goes well, I hope to someday call you Aunt Carolyn."

The older woman reverted to her usual pseudocynical self. "Perhaps you should break the news to Emily before you count that chicken. . . . Now tell me, are we standing here all night, or are we going to eat? I'm starving!"

Two hours later, following an excellent dinner, Nate dropped Carolyn Sheffield off at her home. "Has Em'ly Ann changed much?" he inquired before leaving. "Will I recognize her?"

"You'll recognize her" was Carolyn Sheffield's enigmatic reply. "Thank you for dinner. Goodnight." She closed the door with resounding finality.

Nate chuckled all the way back to his hotel. If there were more women like Carolyn Sheffield, the world would be a better, more forthright place!

⚓

The next morning dawned clear and special—a perfect Seattle winter day. Mount Rainier reigned over the city like a benevolent monarch. Puget Sound shimmered with golden, dancing motes of light. The cries of seagulls joined with the deeper tones of ferryboats plying their trade between the city and nearby islands. Nate Hamilton drove to the airport in a world filled with sunlight and holiday spirit. He found a space in the parking garage and hurried to the terminal. Too bad he couldn't watch Emily Ann's plane come in. Since the tragic events of September 11, 2001, only bona fide passengers could go beyond the security-check stations.

The flight was on time. Nate headed for the baggage-claim area. Carolyn Sheffield had told him to meet Emily there. It felt like an eternity before a trickle of passengers became a steady stream waiting for their baggage. The stream dwindled to a trickle. It ceased. Nate's spirits sank. Had Emily Ann decided not to come?

A few minutes later, a slim woman in a navy blue suit and fetching red scarf appeared. A few silver threads enhanced her brown hair.

Her blue eyes looked enormous and a bit frightened as she scanned the baggage area.

Relief flooded through Nate. Except for being more attractively dressed than she used to be in junior high, Emily Ann Carr was simply a grown-up version of his long-lost friend. He should have known she would be the same sweet girl, only older.

❦

Emily Carr gripped her carry-on bag and scanned the baggage area. Where was Aunt Carolyn? She had to be there. Aunt Carolyn was never late for anything. Had she been held up in holiday traffic? If so, she would arrive fuming. Well, there was nothing for Emily to do but claim her suitcase and wait. Emily glanced right again, then left. Still no sign of her aunt.

A tall, handsome man with dark, silver-edged hair stared at her from across the room. Emily wrinkled her forehead, wondering who he resembled. She didn't know anyone in Seattle but her aunt. Yet his twinkling dark eyes stirred memories and reminded Emily of something pleasant. She glanced at him again, wishing Aunt Carolyn would come. The man was coming her way. What if he spoke to her? Emily took a deep breath. If the man bothered her, she could always summon security.

A final stride brought the stranger to within a few feet of the suitcase Emily had retrieved and parked at her feet. She looked up, prepared to freeze him with a glare, call for help, or both.

The stranger held out a strong hand. His gaze never left Emily's face. When she merely stared at him, he asked in a deep voice, "Don't you know me, Em'ly Ann? You used to." A mischievous look crept into the dark eyes. A smile spread across his face. "Can you still spell *atrocious* and *pretentious?* I never did learn."

Childhood scenes replaced the present: A schoolroom. A shy girl promoted to an Advanced Language Arts class. A friendly boy who turned to her for help.

"Nathan?" she whispered. "Nathan Hamilton?"

He raised his hand. "Present."

She blinked and tried to collect her wits. "This *is* a coincidence! What are you doing here?"

"Meeting you. Your Aunt Carolyn had to go into her office for a short time. I said I'd be happy to pick you up."

His irresistible grin plucked at Emily's heartstrings. She shook her head. Why should this chance meeting with a childhood friend leave her breathless? "How do you know Aunt Carolyn?" she demanded. "Where is Mr. Alexander?"

All traces of mirth left Nate's face. A wistful expression crept into his eyes. "Right here, Em'ly Ann—come to spend Christmas with you."

Emily felt more confused than ever. Her head spun. Had Aunt Carolyn secretly arranged for Nathan to join them, in an effort to spare Emily's feelings when she met Mr. Alexander's fiancée? If so, how had she been able to track him down? How would she even know about Nathan Hamilton? Emily had never shared her girlish admiration. "I–I don't understand," she stammered.

"It's really quite simple, Em'ly Ann. I write and publish as N. Alexander." Nate gathered up her luggage and laughed. "That's the surprise I mentioned in my letter. I'm amazed you never caught on, after all the misspellings I put in my letters for clues."

"*You're N. Alexander?* That's your surprise?" Emily went from despair to joy. "I thought he was—you were—bringing a fiancée. You know, the woman in the picture." The next instant she'd have given her inheritance to recall the words. Her face scorched with embarrassment. Nate was sure to laugh. When he did, she would march to the nearest ticket counter, obtain the earliest reservation possible, and fly back to Oregon where she belonged.

Nate looked puzzled, but at least he didn't laugh. "Fiancée?" Understanding crept into his dark eyes. "I sent the picture to see if you by chance would recognize me after all these years. The couple in the snapshot are my publisher and his wife."

Publisher and wife? Emily's knees threatened to give way in relief.

Nate took her hand and quietly said, "There has never been a fiancée, Em'ly Ann. Sometimes I've wondered why. Now I know." His smile curled into Emily's heart the way Sister Feline curled into her lap: warm, comforting, and filled with the promise that this Christmas would be a holiday to remember.

"We need to go. We don't want to keep your aunt waiting," Nate reminded.

"Does she know who you really are?"

"I told her last night."

Emily burned with curiosity to hear Aunt Carolyn's response, but decided not to ask. Mischief danced in Nate's face, and Emily wasn't sure she could handle her aunt's reaction on top of the shock she had just sustained.

❧

Christmas Eve and Christmas Day were perfect—from the midnight church service to the wonderful dinner Carolyn provided. Emily wore her new red dress on both occasions. She basked in the frank approval she saw in Nathan's eyes. Aunt Carolyn tactfully arranged their schedule so as to allow Nate and Emily Ann time alone. They discovered they had even more in common than what their correspondence had revealed. The love rooted in mutual admiration from junior high days and nurtured through their letters, burst into full bloom, as pure and beautiful as the ivory poinsettias decorating Carolyn Sheffield's lovely living room.

Their idyll ended far too soon. To Nate's dismay, he received a summons from his New York publisher. Changes in world conditions required significant revisions to *The Overcomer*. An urgent personal meeting was mandatory.

Nate wasn't happy about his impending trip. "I'll come to Alderdale as soon as I can," he promised. "I wanted to drive you home. We have a lot of years to recapture."

"It's probably just as well," Emily told him. A ripple of laughter escaped. "Harriet Taylor might have a heart attack if I came home from Aunt Carolyn's place with a man. Especially when that man is N. Alexander!"

"Always just Nathan or Nate to you," he reminded. His tender expression and farewell kiss made Emily feel young again. She flew home hugging her precious secret so close, the most prying Alderdale gaze could not ferret it out. There would be time enough for an announcement when Nathan came.

9

A series of complications conspired to keep Nate in New York. Several frustrating weeks passed before he could return. He resented the delays. "Em'ly Ann and I have already spent too much time apart," he brooded. "I want to get this job done and head back to Alderdale." He contrasted his quiet time in Victoria with the rush and hurry of New York City, and shook his head. New York was a wonderful place to visit, but he longed for the Pacific Northwest's green meadows, towering trees, and singing streams.

❧

While Nate restlessly lingered in New York, excitement descended on Alderdale. A widowed missionary arrived to hold a series of meetings in the church. His first glimpse of Harriet Taylor's quiet daughter Amelia evidently stirred a heart that had been lonely far too long, helping him to see Amelia's potential to be his perfect helpmate. Within days, he had won Amelia's love.

Harriet Taylor swelled with pride that her daughter was marrying such a dedicated Christian man, a man who outshone "dear Porter" on all counts. Her pride soon turned to horror. The "dedicated Christian man" not only planned to take Amelia out of Alderdale, but spirit her into overseas mission service in some faraway land!

Harriet flew into a rage that resounded throughout Alderdale. "No daughter of mine is going to spend the rest of her life taking care of heathens in some God-forsaken country," she proclaimed loud and long. "There are plenty of heathens right here in Oregon who need missionaries."

Meek Amelia evidently didn't care to wait and inherit the earth. When Harriet continued to oppose her daughter's marriage, Amelia straightened her backbone and eloped, leaving Harriet aghast—and alone. Some folks said it served her right. Emily felt sorry for her.

The shock of the elopement didn't lessen until Nathan Hamilton, a.k.a. N. Alexander, arrived and placed a diamond solitaire on Emily Carr's ring finger. The expression in his eyes when he knelt in the best marriage proposal tradition and said, "I love you second only to our Master, Em'ly Ann. Will you marry me?" more than compensated for all her years of waiting for "someday."

She threw her arms around him and whispered, "I will" through happy tears, but she couldn't resist adding, "I'll do the invitations. We want to make sure they are spelled right!" Their betrothal kiss was flavored with laughter.

Tongues wagged about the engagement, but in a kindly manner. Most of the townsfolk were happy for Emily. Isaiah Gerard remembered Nathan as a boy. He and his wife promptly installed Nate in their spare room, telling him to "make himself at home" until the wedding.

No one could figure it out, but for some inexplicable reason, Emily's engagement helped restore Harriet Taylor's shaken self-confidence. She immediately sent Herman Dobbs and his children home and began dropping hints that the engagement came about as a result of her efforts on behalf of "dear Emily." Isaiah Gerard rolled his eyes and snorted.

Nate Hamilton found Harriet's antics hilarious. He had developed strong feelings for the gossipy, close-knit little town and had received Sister Feline's acceptance. At their first meeting, she sniffed Nate and promptly climbed into his lap.

⤙

Nate decided there was no better place than Alderdale to settle and complete his memoirs. He and Emily Ann could travel yet always have a home base. He secretly planned to have her old home restored while they were on their honeymoon. Emily Ann had been too busy with fall classes and falling in love to begin remodeling.

"Do we have to wait until May to get married?" he implored.

Emily hesitated. "I suppose not, if that's what you want."

The slight hesitancy in her voice made Nate add, "On the other hand, it might be fun to be sweethearts for a few months before we become man and wife."

Emily's radiant face more than repaid his sacrifice.

One afternoon while writing a particularly memorable experience, Nate's laptop froze up. "Great. By the time I take it somewhere for repairs, I'll have lost my train of thought," he grumped. He quickly called Emily Ann. "May I use your computer, if you aren't?"

"Of course. I'm going grocery shopping." The lilt in her voice made Nate smile.

A short time later, he watched her swing down the walk to her gate, happiness evident in every step. He turned to boot up the computer and switch on the printer. A printout lay in the tray. A title, "The Watch Cat," followed by Emily's byline, caught his attention. Sister Feline's blank stare from a nearby chair made Nate feel like a thief, but temptation proved irresistible. So did the story. Every word moved it forward. Nate's memories fled out the open window. He quickly typed the story on a blank document, printed out a copy, and deleted all evidence of his crime. "Stop making me feel guilty," he told the watching Sister Feline. "It's for Em'ly Ann's own good. She hasn't had the courage to show me her stories, so she obviously hasn't submitted them anywhere." He chortled. "Unless I'm badly mistaken, Em'ly Ann Carr is in for a surprise."

The cat slit her eyes, bounded from the chair, and marched out of the room. Nate was left with the distinct feeling Sister Feline wanted no part of his petty larceny!

❧

Spring danced into Alderdale, following a few halfhearted snow flurries that swirled in the air and moved on. Purple and gold crocus cir-

cled the big tree that had stood by the Carrs' front gate for generations. Emily confessed to Nathan, "I planted the crocus in our school
colors as a sign of loyalty. How fanciful I was in those days!"

His eyes twinkled. "I hope you haven't changed."

She just laughed.

Spring came early to Emily Ann. Days of delight piled on top of
each other. The alders, from which the town took its name, clothed
their naked limbs with new leaves. Pussy willows discarded their
winter-brown coats in favor of soft, silvery jackets. On a long tramp
through the woods, Nate cut a great mass of branches for the table in
Emily's hall. "They're enough to 'warm the cockles of your heart,' as
Mother used to say," he told her.

She smiled up at him. "My mother said that, too." How good to
have someone who understood her upbringing, the way of life that
was all she'd ever known—and her love for hometown basketball. Her
brother David had been too busy for sports, but Nathan Hamilton had
played on the junior high team. Emily's girlish heart thrilled with
pride over his success, even though she wasn't able to attend many
games.

It was a different story when Bill and Danielle reached high school
age. Both loved the sport and made the starting teams in their junior
and senior years. Like many small towns, basketball was king during
the winter months. No NBA team was more loyally supported than
Alderdale's high school teams. Win or lose, the townspeople turned
out for both home and away games. Even Harriet Taylor always went
to the district finals that determined which teams would go to the
state tournament. "They are really the only games that count," she'd
been heard to say. No amount of explaining a team wouldn't be in the
finals without a good season could change her mind.

Emily reveled in the games. All the pent-up longing of not being
able to attend regularly during her high school years made her a faithful fan. She cheered with joy and groaned with despair, depending on
which team scored. The looks of triumph Bill and Danielle sent to her
in the bleachers brought contentment, and the knowledge she was living up to the trust her brother had placed in her.

Now the basketball games took on an added dimension. Entering the gymnasium on Nathan Hamilton's strong arm made up for Emily's years of seeing couples together while she walked alone. Even knowing she was the target of speculation couldn't dim her joy. It sparkled brighter than the diamond in her engagement ring. Her cup of happiness threatened to run over.

One evening Nate reached for her hand and, under cover of the high school band's lively rendition of "Stars and Stripes Forever," whispered, "Em'ly Ann, I'm so glad we decided to wait until May to get married. Not many people are able to reclaim lost opportunities. I never had a high school sweetheart. All this makes me feel like a teenager again, only better. I'm glad God allowed us to find love later in life. No adolescent romance could compare with what we share."

Emily felt flags of color spring to her face. She squeezed his hand and nodded, too filled with emotion to speak. That night, under the watchful gaze of Sister Feline, she wrote in her journal:

> *Forgive me, Lord, but all this still seems unreal at times.*
> *Most unreal of all is realizing You must have been planning*
> *this all the time I waited for "someday."*

She fell asleep smiling.

❧

After their initial telephone congratulations, Bill and Danielle kept Emily's e-mail busy with further comments. Danielle enthused:

> *It is so romantic! I don't want to wait more than twenty*
> *years to get married, but if it were to someone like N.*
> *Alexander—woops, Nathan Hamilton—it might not be so bad!*
> *I hate to ask, Aunt Emily, but would you be broken-hearted if I*
> *don't fly home for the wedding? My course load is so heavy this*
> *quarter, I really need the time for study. Besides, that*
> *wonderful man of yours promised he would bring you to see*
> *me here at the university when you come back to the East*
> *Coast on your honeymoon. What do you think?*

Emily wrote back:

> *I think it is romantic, too. Don't worry about not making it*
> *for the wedding. We plan to keep it simple, although it will be*
> *in the church and I'll wear a white dress. Nathan likes me in*
> *white.*

The irrepressible Danielle shot back another message.

> *I certainly hope he likes you in other colors, as well!*

Nate laughed when Emily read him her niece's comment. "I love you in any color." His eyes twinkled. "Especially in that red dress you wore at Christmas. Oh, and the lavender dress with the lace collar. You wore it to church last Sunday."

Emily suppressed a telltale gasp. Someday she would confess to Nathan the unworthy reason she'd purchased the lavender dress. Not now. It meant opening freshly healed wounds, something Emily didn't want to do in the midst of their joy.

Bill sent a different type of e-mail message in response to Emily's request that he either be Nathan's best man or serve in place of Emily's father and give her away.

"Sorry, Aunt Emily. If Mr. Hamilton wants me for his best man, I'll be happy to serve. But if you think I'm going to give you away, forget it. I'll be happy to walk you down the aisle, although it seems more appropriate for Isaiah Gerard to do that. No way am I giving my Aunt Emily away to anyone!" Bill added a postscript:

> *In other words, your fiancé can be part of our family, but*
> *he can't take you away from Danielle and me.*

Nate grinned, picked up the phone, and got Bill on the line. He mimicked Bill's ultimatum. "No way am I going to take Em'ly Ann away from anyone. If I didn't love her to distraction, which I do, I'd be tempted to marry her just to get a nephew and niece. I don't have a single, solitary living relative. You're stuck with me, Bill. By the way, can I count on your being my best man?"

He held out the phone so Emily could hear Bill's laugh, followed by a hearty, "Sure. If you can put up with Danielle and me, we can put up with you! What do you want us to call you?" He laughed again. "It sounds like there are plenty of choices."

"Nate works for me." Nathan cradled the phone. His dark eyes shone with mischief. "Having those two for relatives is going to be great. We'll get along fine. They remind me a lot of the way I used to be." He grinned.

"And still are?" Emily challenged.

The grin widened. "I'm working on it. Say, what do you think of Bill's idea about Isaiah Gerard? I didn't say anything earlier, but he has dropped a couple of broad hints."

"They couldn't be as obvious as the hints in a certain letter I received before Christmas," she teased. When a gleam came into Nathan's eyes, she hastily added, "Not that I minded. Let's go ask Isaiah. His wife volunteered to play the organ."

The gleam deepened. "We could ask Harriet Taylor to sing," Nate suggested. "Maybe your other fiancé would like to come. Isaiah told me about him."

Emily refused to be baited. "He's long gone, thank goodness." She shuddered. "If I thought Herman Dobbs would show up at our wedding, I'd insist we elope!"

Nate put his arms around her and rested his chin on top of her head. "I doubt that will be necessary. Isaiah says he hasn't seen 'hide nor hair of him' for weeks."

He spoke too soon. After making highly satisfactory wedding arrangements with the Gerards, Nathan and Emily Ann came face to face with her nemesis in the middle of Main Street. His five children surrounded him, and Harriet Taylor was heading toward them with the flat-footed grace of a racing turtle. Heads turned. Emily wanted to sink through the pavement with embarrassment.

Harriet's voice preceded her down the street. "What are you doing here, Herman?" she demanded. "If I've told you once, I've told you a dozen times. It isn't proper for you to be bothering Emily, now that she's promised to Mr. Alexander."

Emily could hardly believe what she was hearing. Harriet Taylor, championing her in front of the listening town?

Herman gave his cousin-in-law a black look. "Mr. Alexander, is it! Don't make me laugh. Underneath that fancy name is plain old Nate Hamilton."

Nate gave him a sunny smile. "That's right. How are you, Mr. Dobbs?"

"Mister nothing. Herman is good enough for me, not like some folks who go sashaying around under an alias."

Alias! Was Herman Dobbs so dumb he didn't know what a pen name was? Emily struggled not to laugh. With Herman in this mood, things could turn ugly.

The wannabe suitor's face contorted into a sneer. "Just 'cause you're some fancy book writer doesn't give you the right to steal my woman. I'm as good a man as you are any day. What do you have that I don't?"

Emily's heart skipped a beat. She felt the muscles of Nathan's arm tense, then relax. The twinkle she loved sprang into his eyes.

Please, God, let his sense of humor get us out of this humiliating mess.

Nate pulled himself to full height and smiled. "I have Em'ly Ann," he said quietly. The next moment, his jaw set. His eyes flashed, but not with fun. The only time Emily had ever seen him like this was more than thirty years earlier. Nathan had caught the school bully picking on a smaller child. Emily Ann had held her breath then, just as she did now.

Nathan's ringing voice dripped icicles. It could be heard the length of Main Street. "Get this, Dobbs. Em'ly Ann has never been 'your woman.' She never will be. If you ever again show up at her home, I'll see that you're arrested for trespassing!"

Herman Dobbs and his children left town the same day.

❧

On Valentine's Day, Emily received several gifts from Nathan. First, the largest heart-shaped box of chocolates she'd ever seen, complete with an old-fashioned paper lace frill and an enormous satin bow. Emily had to shoo Sister Feline away to keep her from chewing on the decorations.

Next came flowers. Emily felt her mouth drop open when Nathan slipped outside and returned with a duplicate of the bouquet she had labeled a "complete garden" months earlier. Mirth bubbled up inside her and she blurted out, "I nearly threw the other bouquet into the street. I thought they had come from Herman Dobbs!"

"You did?" Nate stared at her. "What stopped you?"

Emily wiped away tears. "I decided they were originally God's flowers, and once delivered, they were mine." She breathed in the bouquet's fragrance and continued. "I also wondered if he sent me a copy of *Little Women* but decided it wasn't logical."

"Did it look like this?" Nate lifted the beribboned cover from a box. A leather-bound edition of *Little Men* had *Emily Ann Carr* engraved in gold letters on it.

Her heart thumped, and she reverently lifted the book from its box. "So it was you all the time! How did you know Louisa May Alcott is one of my favorite authors?"

Nate looked sly. "I remember a lot of things from Mrs. Sorenson's class." It was the only explanation he would give.

When Emily reluctantly laid aside her presents, Nate said, "I have one more gift for you, except you don't get the best part of it yet." He handed her a single page on letterhead from his publishing company.

Dear Mr. Alexander,

Thank you for submitting Ms. Emily Carr's story, The Watch Cat. We are as impressed with her work as you obviously are. Does Ms. Carr have other animal stories? If so, we would like to see them as soon as possible. Should we find them as well-written and entertaining as this sample story, we can certainly find a place for them on our children's book list. Thanks again.

"I don't understand," Emily faltered. "How did they get my story?"

Nate dug the toe of a well-polished shoe into the carpet and looked shamefaced. He resembled a small boy caught in mischief.

"The day I used your computer, I found a copy printed out." He told how he read it, then rekeyed it back into her computer and made a second copy before deleting the story. "Sister Feline made me feel guilty," he admitted with a quick glance at the cat. "She walked out. I interpreted that as a refusal to condone my misdemeanor."

Sister Feline yawned and looked bored.

Nate grimaced and told Emily Ann, "I was afraid you'd never get around to showing me your stories. I also knew you didn't have the self-confidence to submit them. I considered waiting until our wedding day to give you the letter, but we can't stall the publisher until we get home from our honeymoon. He wants your stories now."

Emily wrapped her arms around him. "I never dreamed the autumn of my life would be the best season of all," she whispered.

"Our winter will be even better," Nathan promised.

February bowed out with the Alderdale basketball team losing at the district tournament but vowing to win the following year. In early March, Emily found the old saying "The course of true love never runs smooth," couldn't be more true. Just when everything seemed perfect, a mixed blessing arrived. Reviewers were heralding Nathan's upcoming novel, *The Overcomer,* as his finest. He received a flood of invitations to speak.

Emily was torn between pride in the man she loved and wishing she could have a little more time for him to be "just hers." While she admired "N. Alexander," Nate Hamilton was the boy who captured her heart and kept it. What price would fame demand of them? Qualms concerning her ability to be the wife of someone in the limelight increased when Nathan reluctantly agreed to be the keynote speaker at a Portland convention, where he was to be honored.

"You'll go with me, of course," he told her. A wide grin reminded her of the boy still lurking inside him. "I can hardly wait to have you in the center of the front row."

Emily cringed at the idea. She, appear in front of hundreds of people who had come to see N. Alexander? She opened her lips to refuse but was silenced by Nathan's wistful remark: "I used to envy those who had someone they loved sitting in the audience."

That evening, Emily wrote in her journal:

> *Galatians 5 says longsuffering is a fruit of the spirit, Lord. I'm sure Paul didn't mean what I'm feeling, but please, help me make it through this ordeal.*

Despite her prayer and the confidence inspired by the red dress that Nate insisted she wear, Emily trembled when he seated her in the front row of the large hall then walked to the stage with the convention chairman. Only a few feet of space separated her from her fiancé, yet every glowing word of the introduction made Emily aware of a great gulf widening between them. A quick glance around brought no reassurance. The crowd had not come to see her beloved Nathan, but one of the leading Christian authors in the world. Who was Emily Ann Carr to try and become part of his life? She could almost hear his fans say, "With a world filled with women from which to choose, why on earth did N. Alexander marry such a nobody?"

$$\left(\begin{array}{c}10\end{array}\right)$$

$\mathcal{N}$. Alexander stepped to the microphone and waited for the audience's enthusiastic reaction to the convention chairman's introduction to subside. Yet it was Nathan Hamilton, not N. Alexander, who looked down into the face of his beloved. He saw the shadow in her expressive blue eyes, the way her gloved fingers interlaced. In a heartbeat, he recognized her distress—and the cause. Long accustomed to the glare of publicity, he'd never considered what this first public appearance with him would mean to Emily. She looked so fragile and vulnerable, he wanted to leave the speaker's platform and go reassure her.

He couldn't do it. In fairness to the crowd that had gathered to hear him speak, he must carry out his part of the program.

When there's no way out, there's always a way up.

Nate mentally cheered. Of course! It wouldn't be hard, either. He had given up speaking from notes years ago. No one knew what he had planned to say. He felt a grin begin and held up his hand for silence. The applause ceased. A final cheer echoed and died. Nathan began to speak.

"I'm not going to tell about the years of struggle I experienced before God opened doors for success. I'm not going to review previous books or preview *The Overcomer,* which will be published in a few months. You can go to the Internet and read all that on my publisher's Web site." He chuckled. "Our publicist does it better than I do anyway!"

Laughter rippled through the audience, a sure sign all were with him.

Nate waited, gaze directed at Emily Ann, who had leaned forward in her seat. Her eyes no longer held a shadow. A tentative smile rested on her lips. Nathan reluctantly tore his attention away from her and swept the audience with a glance.

"Remember when stories began 'Once upon a time' and ended with 'they lived happily ever after'? I'd like to share such a story with you. Once upon a time in a small Oregon town named Alderdale, a boy in a junior high school Advanced Language Arts class dreamed of one day becoming an author. The boy and his classmates had two things of immeasurable value: their teacher and a young girl who had been put in their class because of her intelligence and writing ability. I'm sorry to say it, but we didn't appreciate either Mrs. Sorenson or the newcomer as much as we should have."

Nate sent a quick look at Emily. The blaze of happiness in her eyes and the flare of red in her cheeks made her more beautiful than he had ever seen her. He thanked God that she was here with him and would be for the rest of their lives.

Emily Ann has always been with you, a small voice reminded, *waiting to break free from her chrysalis and into your life like a gorgeous butterfly.*

Exhilarated by the prospect of those years ahead, Nathan went on. "The Bible tells us it is good to confess our sins." He leaned forward and said in a stage whisper, "Don't tell anyone, but I am a terrible speller. I always have been. Two factors made things even worse when I was in school. First, this was BSC—Before Spell Check. Second, and contrary to good writing rules, if I could find a big word, I used it." The audience gasped, then broke into a group laugh.

Nate couldn't remember a time when he'd enjoyed giving a presentation more. "My young classmate saved my skin. If there were words she couldn't spell, they probably weren't in the dictionary." Remembrance stole into his voice. "She also encouraged me more than she, or I, knew at the time. Although she was too shy to say much in words, her eyes lighted up when I read what I considered to be masterpieces in class. Her expression silently shouted, 'You can do it. I believe in you.'"

The silence of the crowd paid homage to the girl in Nathan's story. He cleared his throat and continued. "My family and I left Alderdale at the end of that school term, but I never forgot my faithful friend." He chuckled. "Especially when I hit Spell Check!"

A swell of understanding rose and fell. When it ended, Nathan changed from lighthearted to a serious tone. He outlined his feeling that God was beckoning him to something in addition to writing. "Kipling called it God's 'everlasting Whisper,' the call that comes to those who listen," he explained.

The audience sat spellbound as he related how he began an odyssey to discover what was hidden, lost, and waiting. "I decided to write my memoirs, to reach deep into my past and find the boy buried deep under layers of years and success. I also sought God with my whole heart and listened for His whisper. I felt His presence in my life stronger than I'd experienced in years."

Nate paused, reached into his pocket, and unfolded a crumpled page. He looked down at Emily, whose eyes opened wide. "A letter concerning *The Seeker* helped give my life and search perspective. It ended with these words: 'Whether this book wins awards, as some of your other titles have done, isn't nearly as important as the encouragement it offers to those bound by life's "everydayness," as well as by major obstacles.

" 'I am sure many readers will be blessed by the example your courageous hero set. Yet if I were the only one, *The Seeker* still needed to be written.' "

Nathan paused and waited for the obstruction in his throat to clear. When he could speak coherently again, he quietly said, "The letter came from a woman I hadn't seen in more than thirty years. She had no idea N. Alexander was the boy she'd helped with his spelling in junior high!"

The audience straightened, as if jolted by his words. Some started to clap, but Nathan raised his hand for silence and resumed his narrative. "I decided to learn more about the writer. I began to correspond with her, always as N. Alexander. There had been no time for love in my life and travels, but as the weeks passed, I came to care deeply for my new correspondent. She still didn't know who I was."

He smiled down at the center of the front row of seats. "I won't go into the details of our first meeting. It's enough to say that my memoirs will have a 'happily ever after' ending." He left the platform, marched to the front row, and escorted his fiancée to the microphone. "I am proud to announce that my childhood sweetheart, although I didn't recognize she was that until recently, has agreed to become my wife. I give you Em'ly Ann Carr, the love of my life and a blessing from my heavenly Father."

❧

It felt like an eternity to Emily Ann before the standing ovation ended. Nate kept her hand in his and laughingly answered or fended off questions from the audience. Emily tried to concentrate but failed miserably. All she could think about was the look of love in Nathan's shining dark eyes and the high tribute he had publicly given her. She would never again need to feel unworthy. She was acceptable in Nathan's sight—and God's. It was all that mattered.

The crowning moment of the event came unexpectedly and after Nate received his award. The crowd had dispersed, except for a few stragglers expressing congratulations.

"Well done, Nathan. I knew you could succeed if you tried hard enough," a familiar voice said. "Hello, Emily. It looks like the Spell Check on Nate's computer is being replaced."

They turned toward a beaming white-haired lady. Emily gave a happy cry. "Mrs. Sorenson!"

"None other." Their old teacher's laugh took Emily Ann back to the classroom. "I see you haven't forgotten *The Explorer*," she told Nate. "If you had used it in your N. Alexander books, I'd have suspected who you really were. I'm proud of you." She turned to Emily. "What about you? Were you able to continue writing?"

She shook her head. "Mostly journals."

"Don't be modest, Em'ly Ann," Nathan objected. "My publisher is impressed with a children's story she recently revised. It may become the core story of a book."

"What wonderful news!" Mrs. Sorenson exclaimed. "By the way, am I invited to your wedding?"

"If you promise not to critique it," he teased. They parted in a wave of excitement and with the knowledge that they would meet again soon.

❧

April came to Alderdale. March storms were replaced by gentler, rain-filled breezes that kissed blooming trees and flowers. Emily Carr found herself repeating Song of Solomon 2:11–12: "For, lo, the winter is past, the rain is over and gone; the flowers appear on the earth; the time of the singing of birds is come, and the voice of the turtle [dove] is heard in our land."

Nathan always responded with the last sentence of the next verse: "Arise, my love, my fair one, and come away," followed by a mischievous grin.

With each passing day, Emily and Nathan's love deepened. With each passing day, Emily Ann gave thanks to God for the wonder Nate brought into her life. A simple walk beside a brook or through a meadow became an adventure. The first time Sister Feline accompanied them, curled around Nathan's neck like a black-and-white muffler, Emily Ann laughed until her sides ached. The cat purred and looked smug. From then on, she trotted to the door and meowed every time Emily put on a jacket.

Emily had always loved the woods. She had sought refuge from heartache in their depths countless times. Now the thrill of sharing a place she cherished with the man she loved enhanced every turn of the trail.

"Even though there are a lot of changes, it still feels the same," Nathan said one afternoon, when the forest's invitation to explore proved too alluring and took him from his memoirs. "I knew I missed it, but I didn't realize how much until I came back. Does that make sense?"

"Yes." Emily felt herself blush. "That's the way it was when you came back into my life." She adjusted the crown of leaves he had made and placed on her head. "I just didn't want to admit it for fear you wouldn't . . ." Her voice trailed off.

"I understand." Nate's eyes glowed with tenderness. "I'm glad that's all behind us." He put a kiss in her palm, closed her fingers over it, then curled her hand in his. "Let's never have any secrets between us, all right?"

"Right." She smiled, feeling happiness rise from the toes of her sturdy walking shoes to the leafy crown.

Nate completed his memoirs near the end of April. Emily Ann proofed them. She marveled at the high place he had given her and secretly prayed, *Lord, please help me become what Nathan thinks I already am.* Her children's stories were finished and submitted. Emily alternated between believing Nate's prediction that they would be published and feeling he was prejudiced.

May 1 crept into Emily's pale green and white bedroom on silent feet. She awakened troubled. Not with feelings of inferiority, thank goodness, but a more practical dilemma. Only two weeks remained before the wedding, and she still hadn't found a satisfactory wedding present for Nathan. When she timidly asked him what he wanted, he smirked and said, "You!" Her persistent inquiries as to what he really wanted brought the same unhelpful answer. He had relented and told her his gift was to restore the old home. What could she offer him in return?

A daring thought came. *Give Nathan a part of yourself. The thing only you, God, and Sister Feline know exists: your journals.*

Emily immediately rejected the idea. "I can't," she whispered, so low, Sister Feline didn't stir from her slumbers at the foot of the bed. "It would make me too vulnerable."

Nothing else you possess is so fitting.

The silent reminder haunted her day and night. A week before the wedding, Emily packed her journals in chronological order, put a bow on the large box, and quietly gave her innermost self to Nathan one sunny afternoon. Then she fled. From the shelter of a curtain, she watched him walk down the rose-strewn path to her gate, carrying the heavy box. For the first time since she was ten years old, she had no journal in which to write, or the incentive to start a new one. Had she made a terrible, irrevocable mistake?

The memory of Nathan's face that day in the woods when he said, "Let's never have any secrets between us, all right?" shimmered in

Emily's tear-filled eyes. She hadn't been thinking of the journals then, just the joy of being loved.

Peace came softly. Yet anticipation and dread for the moment when she would face her fiancé, knowing he was aware of every secret corner of her life, mingled. Evening fell. She and Sister Feline sought out the porch swing, half-hidden by the clusters of roses climbing the porch posts.

Ringing footsteps heralded Nathan's approach. Emily felt powerless to rise and go to him, as she normally did. The gate opened. He walked up the path, up the steps. An expression of humility, awe, and yearning blended with inexpressible love. "My dear Em'ly Ann." He held out his arms, obviously unable to say more.

She unceremoniously dumped her cat onto the porch floor. She barely heard Sister Feline's infuriated "Meowrr!" Straight as a homing pigeon, Emily Ann flew into Nathan's waiting arms.

❦

The clump of solid footsteps, the rustle of skirts, and the heavy scent of perfume heralded the first guest to arrive at Emily Carr's wedding in the small church her family had attended for several generations.

Harriet Taylor—tall, spare, and gimlet-eyed—marched down the center aisle and surveyed the quiet, dimly lit chapel with satisfaction. No one here yet. Good. She did like to be first and have her choice of seats. She reached the reserved area in the front and ruthlessly tore free the guarding ribbon. After all, she *was* Emily Carr's second cousin twice removed.

❦

Carolyn Sheffield observed Harriet's entrance from the one-way window of the cry room at the back of the chapel. She remembered the altercation at Bill's wedding and grimaced, but behind Emily Ann's back. No unpleasant memory should mar her niece's wedding day. Besides, Harriet without Amelia seemed pathetic.

"So much for having a small wedding," Carolyn told Emily.

"I know." Emily Ann's face shone like one of the flowers in her bridal bouquet, a smaller replica of the others Nathan had given her. "I couldn't draw the line." She paused. "Aunt Carolyn, you don't feel bad about not giving me away, do you? Isaiah Gerard really wanted to do it."

"*I?*" Carolyn sniffed. "You'll never catch *me* walking down a church aisle in a wedding."

"Never say never," Emily teased. "Look at me."

"I've got you by a good twenty years," her aunt reminded. "Are you ready? It's almost time." She surveyed her niece with satisfaction. "That white silk and the circlet of flowers with the short veil are perfect."

"I hope Nathan thinks so." Emily fingered the rich folds of her skirt.

"He will." Carolyn checked her watch. "Isaiah is waiting for you, and it's time for me to go be seated." Her fingers pressed Emily's. Affection softened her voice. "You look lovely. Your mother would be so proud." She slipped out before Emily could reply, leaving the door open.

Emily watched her aunt take Bill's arm and walk to the front row. Her throat tightened. If only Mother could be here today. Mother and Father and David. Their precious faces passed through Emily's mind in a kaleidoscope of memories. She was thankful that nothing could dim those memories.

Isaiah Gerard's soft, "Em'ly Ann?" recalled her to the present. This day must not be spoiled by looking back. "Remember Lot's wife," Emily told herself. She laughed, stepped from the cry room, and firmly closed the door behind her.

The fragrance of candles and roses greeted Emily—roses from Emily's garden, lovingly arranged by the churchwomen. A beaming Isaiah Gerard offered his arm. The wedding march began. Approving faces—even Harriet Taylor's—turned toward Emily. Mrs. Sorenson caught her attention and slowly winked. Emily took a deep, tremulous breath. Her *someday* had really come. Or was it all just a lovely dream, a dream from which Sister Feline's cool nose and reaching paw would awaken her? The need for reassurance made Emily's lace-clad fingers tremble on Isaiah Gerard's strong arm.

Did he sense what she was feeling? Perhaps, for he patted her hand with his free one, then whispered so low that no one but she and God could hear, "Don't be nervous, Em'ly Ann. Look at Nate."

She raised her head and gazed at the tall, handsome man waiting for her at the altar. A quick mist blurred her vision but could not dim the blaze of love and admiration in Nathan Hamilton's unguarded dark eyes. His look of mingled pride and humility swept lingering doubts away forever. The wedding was real and the love she and Nate shared would be theirs for as long as they both should live. Emily Ann tightened her grasp on Isaiah's arm and proudly stepped forward to meet her *someday*.

Three things about Emily's wedding registered more deeply than all the rest. First, Nathan's ringing, "I, Nathan, take thee, Em'ly Ann." Next, the irrepressible mischief in his eyes when he slipped a gold band on her ring finger. Finally, an incident following the simple reception in the fellowship hall that she and Nathan had chosen over some elaborate affair.

"Don't forget to throw your bouquet," Nate told her when they reached the sidewalk in front of the church.

"I hate to give it up, even though you had it reproduced in silk," she said with regret; but she obediently turned. Arm high, she gave her flowers a mighty fling.

The bouquet sailed high over the heads of those gathered, as if ignoring the bevy of eager, reaching hands in order to seek out a more worthy recipient. It landed in a pair of arms automatically flung up in self-protection against the flowery missile.

Carolyn Sheffield's arms.

Silence gave way to cheers. Nate hurried Emily into his waiting car. "Now's our chance to get away." He laughed uproariously. "I suspect this is the first time your aunt has ever been shocked speechless. Did you see her face?"

Emily Ann burst into giggles. "That's not all I saw!" Tears of mirth streamed. "Harriet Taylor stared at Aunt Carolyn as if she'd received a sign from heaven." Emily wiped her eyes. "I hope she doesn't start plotting to marry off Aunt Carolyn!"

"Carolyn Sheffield can take care of herself," Nathan reminded. He put the car in gear and grinned across at Emily in the endearing way that made him so boyish and beloved. "Time to start our honeymoon, Em'ly Ann." Laughter twinkled in his dark eyes. "Just one thing. How do you spell *stupendous, exhilarating,* and *worth waiting for?*"

Part 2: Carolyn

⑪

*A*nticipation buzzed through the Seattle law firm of Jensen, Cook, and Franz like power lines against a high wind. Carolyn Sheffield was not immune. Fifty years at the firm and she still felt the Bonus Day butterflies. August 1 was a day that rivaled Christmas in the minds of the 152 firm employees.

Carolyn chided herself. Fifty years of August firsts at the firm, and she was still acting as if it were her first prom.

She knew the routine by heart. Mr. Jensen would gather all the partners in the boardroom. The firm's annual profits would be unveiled. Then each partner would leave with an envelope. Not just any envelope: The Envelope. Each employee would pretend not to look as it passed office door after office door. But the secret held within was too powerful. Invariably, eyes would be drawn upward. They had to look. As if looking would reveal contents. Hushed whispers speculated. Fifteen thousand dollars, twenty thousand—could it be thirty thousand dollars? Finally, the opening and grand announcement. The Bonus amount each employee would receive, and greater still, the Employee of the Year.

"Employee of the Year," Carolyn murmured in hushed tones, as if saying it too loudly would detract from the reverence of the title. Sixty-nine years of life, and she still had seen no greater honor. Past winners were treated like royalty. Whispers of awe and respect followed them.

Carolyn sighed. "Winning that honor would make me the happiest woman in the world. I don't suppose You'd like to help out on this one?" she whispered with a heavenward glance.

The jarring ring of the fax jolted her out of her blissful daydream. "You silly old woman," she said, shaking her head. "A grown professional paralegal dreaming like a schoolgirl."

Forcing her mind back to reality, she tackled the large pile of papers next to her with gusto. She had work to get done, and daydreaming was not going to make the pile go away. The red numerals on the clock teased her. "One second, two seconds, three seconds," each flash of the dots seemed to say.

This is ridiculous, she decided, turning the clock toward the wall. *Clocks cannot speak—and two o'clock will get here a lot faster if I don't count the seconds.*

The day droned mercilessly on. Carolyn unsuccessfully tried to find ways to concentrate on something other than the magical hour. But the Kelly brief, the Lyons motion, and the summons and complaint on Baker fell short of the mark. After three hours of semisustained effort, she managed to make a small dent in the pile, but not without a number of forays into the land of daydreams.

"Carolyn, are you feeling all right?" Her coworker Anna's question pierced her reverie.

"Oh," she replied, looking down at her wringing hands. "It's just a little carpal tunnel syndrome. It will be fine."

"I'm amazed you can still work twelve- to fourteen-hour days." Anna shook her head in disbelief. "Not to mention training all of us youngsters to be acceptable paralegals and attorneys. You know you're the only reason half of the attorneys here keep their jobs. If you weren't walking behind them cleaning up their messes and preparing their briefs, they'd be sunk. I guess that's why you get paid the big bucks. In fact, if I were choosing, without a doubt you'd be the Employee of the Year."

Carolyn looked at the girl. "Well, you know, I just do my job," she mumbled, not exactly sure how to deal with such complimentary statements.

"Anna's right, you know." Bryant, an associate fresh out of law school, peeked his head around the corner. "We attorneys couldn't do without you; you know more law than the lot of us combined. Besides, what would we do without you telling us how wrinkled our shirts and how atrocious our manners are? You've got *my* vote for Employee of the Year, too."

Carolyn warily looked over her nose at the black-haired charmer and suppressed a grin. "Don't you believe for a second, Mr. Black, that I don't know the game you're playing. I've been around too many years to fall for your line. Your brief is still due on my desk by Friday, and I still do not get your coffee."

Bryant smiled and lifted the five-foot-two-inch, 105-pound object of his teasing off the ground in a boyish hug. "Ah, Carolyn, if I could only find a woman like you my age, I'd be married in a second."

"Bryant married? Now that's a scary thought," Mr. Jensen's administrative assistant Evelyn teased, coming around the corner.

"Hi, Ev." Carolyn smiled. "What are you doing slumming in our department? Don't suppose you want to share any leaks about what's going on behind the conference room's closed doors."

"Carolyn." Evelyn leaned in. "You and I have been here longer than most. You know I would share anything I know with you, but that meeting is as closed as Fort Knox. Jensen even types the agenda himself, on one of those old typewriters. All I know is, I was sent to come get you."

Carolyn's eyebrows furrowed. "Whatever for?"

"I have no idea, unless . . . well, you know the rumors."

"What rumors, Ev?" Bewilderment resounded in her voice. "What on earth are you talking about?"

"Oh, come on, Carolyn, you know you're a shoo-in for Employee of the Year. Everybody knows."

Could it be true? Following Evelyn down the hall, Carolyn felt the blood rushing to her face, coursing with the possibility. *After all this time?*

Memories of the past fifty years came flooding into her mind. Long hours spent at the office. Night and weekend activities sacrificed for pending deadlines. Canceled dates. Broken romances, victims of her desire to be a "working woman." Friendships ruined by lack of time.

Looking back, Carolyn marveled. She had **given up** so much.

Everything, really. Fun. Friendship. A love life. *Love*. The word made her stop short. Experience had taught her that its synonym was *heart-break*. She was terminally single and glad of it, she reassured herself. *So much gone*, she mused, *but in pursuit of what?*

My career, my dream, she answered quickly. *And now*—she paused, letting the reality soak in—*now I will receive my reward. Carolyn Sheffield, Employee of the Year. It has a nice ring to it.*

"Thank you, Lord," she whispered, surprised at how foreign the words sounded. Could it have been that long since she had prayed? "You really didn't forget me."

The conference-room doors were open when Evelyn and Carolyn arrived. Carolyn caught Evelyn's smile and thumbs-up as she stepped through the marbled doors.

Seated at the head of the table was Mr. Jensen, flanked by rows of dark, expensively-suited attorneys. "Welcome, Carolyn." His gravelly voice echoed in the marbled chamber. "Please sit."

Carolyn gingerly sat on the edge of the velvet chair he indicated. How exactly was one supposed to look when given such an honor, she wondered. Surprised? Elated? Deserving? Cool as a cucumber? Classy? That was it. She would be classy.

Pulling herself out of her internal debate, she caught only part of what Mr. Jensen was saying.

"And so, Ms. Sheffield, we felt we had no choice but to take this course of action. You have served this firm well. We will miss you."

"I'm sorry," Carolyn queried. "Miss me? I don't understand."

"Like I said, our profit earnings came back at a record low this year. A breakdown of the figures shows the revenues from the firm's Personal Injury section failed to cover its costs for the second year in a row. We have no choice but to dissolve the entire section. We won't be doing any more PIs. The existing cases will be farmed out to the other departments to wrap up. Given your longevity, we thought you should be the first to know. I'm sorry, but this is good-bye."

Carolyn blanched. The blood rushed from her face, leaving an expressionless pallor. Numb, she looked around the table at those with whom she had worked. None would meet her gaze. Her legs suddenly seemed like stiff boards. The wooden feeling moved upward.

She stood, aware of only one thing in the room: the door. She had to get to the door. Staring straight ahead, Carolyn walked stiffly out the door, down the corridor, and out into the atypical gray August Seattle day.

$\bigodot$
12

Carolyn Sheffield glared at the face staring back at her from the beveled mirror in her foyer. "Who took my features and gave them to this old woman?" she half-sarcastically remarked.

Moving closer, she examined the lines marking the edges of her face. "Laugh lines," as her ever-optimistic friend Ruth Welch referred to them. Only, unlike Ruth's, the grooves etched in Carolyn's face didn't even hint of a smile, much less a laugh. "Old age breeds character," Carolyn reminded, but failed to convince, herself. "Old age breeds loneliness and ruin" had a much truer ring.

She pulled herself away from the mirror and slumped down in the burgundy Queen Anne chair standing guard in her home's vaulted entryway. Only a few months ago, she had treasured the sun's rays that flooded the foyer through the skylight and glass-paneled doors. Now the autumn light not only revealed every flaw in her sixty-nine-year-old face but also mocked the darkness that permeated her from head to toe. In search of a place more in keeping with her mood, she headed for the living-room sofa, planted herself face down, and covered her head with the throw pillow. Even there, the thoughts she'd been trying to escape since her lay off two months ago pelted her like icy chunks of hail. *Alone. Old. Worthless. Unemployed.* It didn't matter what politically correct term Jensen, Franz, or whoever else tried to attach—it all boiled down to the same ugly truth. She had been fired! More than fifty years of her life had been devoted to her profession, and it was over. The sacrifices! Sleep. Vacations. Friends. Love. For nothing. How could God let this happen? Wasn't He supposed to care about her?

The incessant ringing of the doorbell brought a welcome interruption from the company of her own morbid thoughts. *Now, who would have nothing better to do than visit this sorry old woman today?* It was a bit refreshing to know that even her negative alter ego parried in sarcasm. Perhaps the old spitfire Carolyn was down there someplace. *But where?* Carolyn asked herself as she slowly went to greet her semi-welcome caller.

Her hand barely touched the knob before a whirlwind of energy that rivaled the sunlight blew through the door.

"Carolyn, dear, how are you today?" Ruth's arms stretched around her childhood friend in an embrace as warm as fresh cinnamon buns. Just a shade over five-feet-three-inches tall, Ruth's frame softened in all the places Carolyn's angled. Her spunky energy was fueled by a heart that worked on overdrive and a spirit to match. Even long-term acquaintances marveled at the life-long friendship between the two unlikely comrades. Sarcasm and guile were as foreign to Ruth as the high-powered legal career her friend Carolyn had chosen. Ruth's life had been devoted to her family. After her husband, Jim, passed away a decade earlier, she had thrown herself full-time into the charitable work that came so naturally to her. Yet despite their differences, the bond these women forged was unbreakable.

Carolyn avoided her friend's question. "Lemonade or soda?"

"Lemonade, please. Oh, and we have so much to talk over. How about wrestling us up a couple of cookies?" Ruth's concerned gaze wandered over Carolyn's disappearing figure. She remained silent. Years of friendship had taught Ruth the fruitlessness of mothering Carolyn.

Returning with the refreshments, Carolyn seated herself next to Ruth. "Now who are you saving in the world *this* week?"

"I wish I could say you. Carolyn, I'm so worried about you." Ruth's eyes filled with tears. "You have to get out."

Glancing over Carolyn's shoulder to the assortment of delivery and take-out boxes on the kitchen counter, Ruth continued with an uncharacteristic boldness. "From the looks of things, I'd guess it's been at least a week since you've left your house. You're wearing the same ensemble you had on when I saw you last week. And don't forget, honey, I have seen that walk-in closet of yours. I know it isn't because you have a lack of clothing options."

Ruth paused, taking a deep breath. "Carolyn, in the sixty years I've known you I have *never* seen your hair out of place." She ran her hand through her own wayward white locks. Eyes twinkling, she lowered her voice in mock horror. "The style you are sporting today wouldn't even qualify as disheveled. Today your hair looks worse than *mine!*"

Despite her best efforts to be angry at Ruth's interference, Carolyn couldn't help but chuckle. "Well, Ruth, if what you say is true about my hair, I must be in terrible trouble. Worse than yours? It can't be. The horror. The *horror.*"

As the two friends shared a laugh, Carolyn noted how foreign it felt. Had it been that long since she'd laughed aloud? The thought unnerved her a bit. Perhaps there was something to Ruth's concern. Not that she'd ever admit it to her friend, but she had noticed her clothes were hanging loosely on her five-foot-two-inch frame. She hadn't had a lot of impetus to do her hair or choose her clothes lately, either. Carolyn pulled herself away from her reverie and joined Ruth midsentence.

". . . so I thought you would be able to come out with me and celebrate."

"Celebrate? I'm sorry, Ruth; celebrate what again?"

"The Hospital Guild is going to have a fund-raiser for the cancer unit. They are giving me some kind of award for the work I've done with the Guild. Please come. You can support me, and maybe there will be some nice older gentlemen there. . . ."

Carolyn snorted. "Nice older gentlemen. Please. You are talking to the wrong woman. Remember, I'm terminally single and proud of it. I need another bad experience with a man right now about as much as I need a kick in the head. I've told you before, and I'll keep telling you—I don't want to double date, even with you. I certainly don't want to single date. Right now I hate the idea of dates so much, I wouldn't even eat one."

"Now, Carolyn," Ruth gently responded, ignoring her friend's tirade. "How are you going to meet a nice man like your niece Emily did, if you won't even be in the same room with one?" With a wink Ruth added, "I think there are some wonderful older Christian men out there who are just waiting for two almost-seventy-year-old mature and beautiful women to knock their socks off. It might as well be us."

Carolyn rolled her eyes and shook her head. "As usual, my friend, you are ever the optimist. Emily found a wonderful man, that's true; but she's more than twenty years younger than we are, and she was extremely lucky. I'm afraid she pulled the needle out and left us the haystack. I don't know about you, but I have absolutely no interest in hay. And I certainly have no interest in knocking anyone's foot coverings off. I will, however, accompany you to the Guild's fund-raiser."

Carolyn stopped, then teasingly added, "That is, if I can find anything my newly appointed fashion critic will deem suitable for me to wear. *And* if I can get this disheveled mop on my head in order."

Ruth smiled at her friend. "I don't care if you stay in that outfit and don't touch your hair until the fund-raiser night; as long as you are there by my side, I will be thrilled."

As she headed out Carolyn's front door, Ruth smiled and yelled over her shoulder, "But if you want to attract one of those nice men, you might consider a comb and a good launder of those clothes!"

❧

Carolyn glanced in the mirror and brushed down a stray silver-tinged auburn lock before heading out of her bathroom. Not perfect, but presentable. At least more presentable than she had managed in the last couple of months. She had almost called Ruth to back out of attending the fund-raiser, but she couldn't bear to hurt her friend. The familiar sound of Ruth's VW Bug's horn beckoned from the curb. Carolyn hastily grabbed her shawl and headed out the front door.

"Might as well get this over with," she muttered as enthusiastically as if she were heading to her yearly doctor's appointment.

She opened the door and plopped down next to Ruth. The happy chatter from the driver's seat kept Carolyn's mind off the looming evening of fun and festivities. As they pulled into the parking lot, Carolyn comforted herself with the thought that the hospital fund-raising set was usually fairly uninspired: *A couple of appetizers, Ruth's acceptance speech, and I'm out of here.*

Her speculations were rudely interrupted by the faint strains of music. "There must be another group celebrating here as well," Carolyn mentioned to Ruth. Ruth's unusual silence greeted her.

"Ruth?" Carolyn glanced at her friend for an explanation.

Ruth squirmed, looking uncomfortable. "Did I not mention there was square dancing at this event?" Unaccustomed to even a whisper of deception, Ruth's face screamed guilt.

Carolyn bristled. Remembering the importance of the evening for her friend kept her response in check but could not keep the annoyance from her voice. "No. You forgot that little detail."

Ruth looked sideways at her friend. "I'm sorry, Carolyn. When you said you'd come, I was so happy. I only found out yesterday that they were going to have square dancing, and I just couldn't bring myself to tell you. I knew you wouldn't come. Please forgive me." Her soft arms instantly wrapped around her beanpole of a friend.

Carolyn's reticent "You're forgiven" was followed by a spirited, "but don't expect me to dance."

Ruth's face showed she knew better than to push for that.

Carolyn provided a few cursory nods in the direction of the familiar faces she saw, obligingly watched as Ruth's honor was presented, then excused herself to the hall outside the dance floor. Old-fashioned country melodies and the caller's voice squeezed under the door and kept her company in her chair.

Even though she was annoyed, the vision of the hoity-toity, business-suited clan twirling about the floor to a country caller, touched Carolyn's funny bone. Her amusing visions were interrupted by the hall doors brusquely opening. Ruth, red-faced and teary-eyed, rushed past her into the women's restroom.

Carolyn bolted out of her seat and after her friend. Opening the restroom door, she saw Ruth sobbing in a corner chair. Carolyn quickly went to her side, and in an unusual display, wrapped her arms around her dear friend. She said nothing, waiting for her friend's sobs to abate.

After awhile, Ruth's shoulders stopped heaving, and her breathing slowed. "Oh, Carolyn. It was so humiliating. He was in the corner, looking lonely. I thought I'd cheer him up and ask him out on the floor to dance. He said he preferred a woman who made the effort to keep herself fit and would rather stay in the corner than dance with me. Everyone heard." The rendition of the story sent Ruth into a new fit of sobs. "I was just trying to be nice. It was just so humiliating."

Carolyn's ire rose faster than she did, as she stood bolt upright. "Which cad did this to you?"

"I don't know his name. I've never seen him before."

"What did he look like?" Carolyn demanded.

Ruth wiped her eyes. "Well, he was tall—probably six-one. He had that pure white hair. I'd say he was very distinguished-looking—especially in his dark suit. Why, Carolyn? What are you going to do?" Ruth paused, as if considering her own question. Her eyes widened at the determined look on Carolyn's face. "Oh, Carolyn, please. Don't make a scene. I can't bear to show my face out there as it is. I don't want any more attention."

Carolyn's jaw set determinedly. "Ruth, any man who would treat you in such a cruel and heartless way wouldn't hesitate to tread on the feelings of any woman. Maybe a bit of his own medicine will give him pause next time he is asked to dance. I'd say he needs a crash course in Civility 101—and I just happen to know a willing and able teacher." She winked at Ruth to alleviate her friend's fear. "Believe me, my dear, the attention will not be on *you.*"

With her parting words, Carolyn headed into the ballroom, armed only with the sketchy description of the offending party provided by her distraught friend. As she entered the dance floor, her gaze was immediately drawn to a tall, distinguished-looking white-haired gentleman who was deep in conversation across the room.

"Doesn't it figure—the best looks in the room wasted on an egoist," Carolyn whispered to herself. "Typical."

She squared her shoulders, straightened up to her full five-foot-two height, and marched across the room with unwavering purpose. Upon reaching the gentleman's elbow, Carolyn grabbed it, forcefully interrupting his conversation.

Surprise resonated on the white-haired man's face. "I'm sorry—do I know you?"

"After this conversation, you are going to wish you didn't," Carolyn responded loudly. "How dare you humiliate and ridicule my friend? You not only lost the opportunity to dance with the most wonderful woman here tonight, but you crushed and embarrassed her. You did not deserve the honor of having her invite you to dance—nor any other lady for that matter. In the future, however, if a lady *is* unfortunate enough to ask you to dance, I suggest you accept. If you choose not to dance with her again, that is your prerogative, but turn her down nicely, quietly, and without destroying her self-esteem. Do you understand? I can guarantee you this: No lady here tonight will be dancing with you if I have any say in the matter."

Carolyn turned abruptly and headed resolutely back across the floor. "Men," she mumbled. "It figures."

When she reached Ruth in the restroom, she managed to paste a smile on her still scorching-hot face. She helped her friend to her feet, wrapped her arm around her shoulders, and headed toward the beckoning exit doors. To Ruth's questioning gaze, Carolyn responded, "Let's just say I'm sure he's grateful that our paths will cross but once in this life." She paused, then punctuated her thought. "Good riddance."

13

Though Carolyn felt like a lamb being led to the Guild-party slaughter, she was forced to admit she was glad Ruth had pressed the issue. The unexpected value of the evening, the opportunity to dress down the debonair Mr. "I only dance with fit women," had ignited a pilot light she had not realized was out. Traces of the old Carolyn began periodically to show up, startling even her.

Carolyn admitted as much to Ruth over hot scones. "I caught a glimpse of my reflection last week in the produce mirror at the grocery. Not that the vegetable-and-fruit-aisle mirror is the most flattering, but I halted in shock and said out loud, "Who is that woman—and what has she done with my hair?"

She paused, looking at Ruth. "Do you realize I hadn't seen my beautician in over half a year? I don't care what the hair-care products promise, eight months of grow-out on this almost seventy-year-old head does *not* look natural."

Ruth clutched her stomach at her friend's comments and gasped. "Oh, Carolyn, stop. I can't laugh anymore. My stomach muscles won't take it." She converted her laugh into a wide smile. "It's so good to have you back, my dear. I've missed that irascible streak."

"Well, I'm not totally back to fighting strength, but I'd say I'm off bed rest. Maybe in time, I will recover." Carolyn paused, ruminating on her own words. "At least the hair's back to normal."

"Speaking of hair," Ruth awkwardly segued, "now that you've got your locks looking so good, wouldn't it be nice to show them off?" She smiled, guilt reverberating off her angelic pink cheeks.

"What now?" Carolyn snorted. "You got another square dance up your sleeve? No, thank you. As much as I appreciate it spurring me out of my blue funk, it was an experience I don't care to repeat in the near future."

Ruth smiled. "No, it's nothing like that. We're just really short on volunteers at the hospital. We could use some help."

"Sorry." Carolyn shook her head. "I don't have the legs for those candy-striper skirts."

Ruth stood and handed Carolyn a Community Memorial badge with her name and *Volunteer* emblazoned in black. "You can wear something from your closet—and this badge. Your first shift is Saturday. You are assigned to the geriatric ward with me. It will be good for you. Besides, you couldn't have a better partner.

"I've got to go deliver dinner to Henry Lamb," she continued. "You know he can't cook a lick, and since Rachel died, he's been thinning out. I'll pick you up Saturday at nine A.M." Ruth's eyes twinkled, and she bustled out the door.

Carolyn sat speechless, staring at the badge. As recognition of what her friend had roped her into dawned, she couldn't help but wryly grin. "Anyone who says that girl doesn't have a manipulative bone in her body doesn't know Ruth Welch like I do. Innocent, my foot. She may talk a sweet streak, but she's a sly one." Looking down at her name badge, she tried the words on for size. "Carolyn Sheffield, Volunteer." Just the thought made her chuckle. "Won't Emily get a kick out of this. I bet she will be as surprised as I am."

By Saturday, Carolyn's surprise had turned to determination. "If I could run a legal firm for decades, I certainly can volunteer at a hospital successfully." Carolyn walked through a two-hour orientation with Ruth and then headed out to take Geriatrics by storm. Even Ruth's questioning gaze couldn't shake Carolyn's confidence.

Carolyn turned down cold Ruth's "Are you sure you don't want me to stay with you for a couple of hours, until you've practiced a bit?"

"Ruth, if I could take orders from a bunch of legal eagles, I can certainly handle the over-seventy crowd's lunch orders. Don't worry, I'll be fine."

Carolyn resolutely marched to the first room and commenced her duties. "Ms. Smith, room 675. She requests meat-loaf and potatoes, hold the gravy; apple juice; and whatever the pudding was she had for dinner last night—it was yellow, but she doesn't have a clue what flavor it was. Mr. Johnson, room 652, would like a big bowl of green Jell-O—nothing else." The list proceeded smoothly, as did Carolyn's shift.

Ruth gave Carolyn a thumbs-up and a wink each time she saw her. Toward the end of the shift, Carolyn approached room 643 and knocked lightly. When no one responded, she cracked open the door to see a dark-haired, heavy man meander over to the television and turn it on. He then stretched, walked over and got a drink, and headed for the restroom. Carolyn shut the door and walked down the hall, deciding to return when Mr. Holland was finished.

About fifteen minutes later, she headed back to room 643. The door was slightly ajar and Mr. Holland's loud, demanding voice reverberated in the hallway. "How dare you ask me to move. Don't you know anything? What kind of a nurse are you anyway? I bet you don't even have a degree. I was in a car accident. Do I need to spell it for you? C-a-r a-c-c-i-d-e-n-t. I can't move anything. I can't walk—I'll probably be paralyzed for life. Bring me my blanket and my lunch. Now! Oh, and. find someone to rub my feet."

Carolyn's ire rose faster than the twenty-something nurse bolted from the room. She pushed open the door and marched resolutely across the floor.

Mr. Holland's gaze met hers. "You got my lunch yet? It better be hot. You the one who's going to feed me? Or are you the foot rubber?"

"Mr. Holland. Not only am I not going to feed you, I'm not going to get you a blanket, and I wouldn't touch your feet with a ten-foot pole."

"Excuse me?" the red-faced Holland sputtered.

Carolyn's voice dropped. "I know your kind. I saw scores of them throughout my long career. You aren't really hurt, but you will milk this for all it's worth. You'll lie and twist the truth to get money from the insurance company and the other driver. You'll lie and fake your injuries to make the hospital staff kowtow to your every whim. You'll lie and try to justify having your family wait on you hand and foot. But when everyone's not looking, you'll stand up and walk yourself over to the TV, pour yourself a drink, use the restroom, and not have an ache or a pain."

Carolyn paused, then pointed to her nameplate. "Well, buddy, not me. This sign may say 'Volunteer,' but it certainly doesn't say 'stupid' or 'doormat.' You want your feet rubbed? I suggest you get a cat!"

Mr. Holland's face froze with shock. A myriad of emotions visibly played across his large features, as if his brain were broadcasting his thoughts aloud: "How does she know? Could she have seen me? Nah, she can't know. She must be guessing." Finally, he spoke. "I don't know what you're talking about. I'm in terrible pain. I may never walk again. Someone will hear about this. My lawyer will hear about this. The hospital will hear about this. If it's the last thing I do, I will make sure you regret your words to me for the rest of your life."

Carolyn stared at him stonily. "Mister, I can guarantee you that of my regrets in life, you will not even be on the list. If I recall, the Scriptures say something about honesty and taking advantage of others. In the end, sir, if you do not change your ways and repent, I believe *you* might be the one with some eternal regrets. While you have all this spare time on bed rest due to your supposed injuries, you might want to think about that." With that her final declaration, Carolyn turned and marched out of his room.

Mr. Holland was true to his word. Before finishing her shift, Carolyn was informed she would no longer be welcome in Geriatrics but would be transferred to the Pediatric Unit. Riding home in the car, she railed, "Ruth, that man was crookeder than half the inmates at the county jail—and meaner than the other half. How could the hospital defend him?"

In classic Ruth style, her friend grabbed Carolyn's hand and responded, "Well, I for one couldn't care less what the hospital did. I think you have a heart of gold to defend that nurse the way you did and to put Mr. Holland in his place. I wish I had the courage to do it. I also thought it was admirable how you stood up and delivered that sermon."

"Sermon? That was a tirade, not a sermon."

"Carolyn, I know you don't often talk openly about God, but

when you stood up and told that man he needed to repent, I bet our heavenly Father was right proud of what you did. I know I was."

Carolyn shrugged Ruth's comments off but couldn't help revisiting them later when she was alone, snuggled up on her couch. Gazing out her window at the salmon-tinged clouds unnaturally suspended in the pretwilight sky, she wondered: Did she really not talk about God very much—even to Ruth, her dearest friend? Why was that? She believed. It just seemed she really hadn't needed Him all that much. With her career and busy life, she hadn't had much time for recreation, men, or God. Now she had lost everything. Did she blame Him? Did she need Him? Did she have the right to ask Him for help now, after all the years of ignoring Him? Carolyn went to bed with far more questions than answers.

Tuesday dawned bright and provided a marked contrast to Carolyn's outlook for the day. "Volunteer shmolunteer," she muttered as she put the finishing touches on her hair. "Demoted from sixth floor to fifth in one day. At this rate I'll only have five more shifts before I'm out of there. If the hospital kicks me out, even Ruth will have to admit that her rose-colored glasses, when it comes to my charitable personality traits, have to go." The thought of escaping Ruth's guilt trips once and for all spurred Carolyn out the front door to her friend's waiting vehicle.

The drive to the hospital consisted of a crash course in caring for children. Despite visiting her niece Emily and her young charges, and periodic visits to Ruth's house as her children were growing, Carolyn was not what one would call child-friendly. She certainly had no experience handling kids alone.

"Now how do you fasten a diaper again? Are there instructions on it?" Carolyn asked, rapidly jotting notes while they talked.

"Carolyn, relax. You'll do fine. It's a diaper, not a bag of microwave popcorn. There are no instructions on the package. You just affix the tabs. Somebody there will show you what to do." Ruth shook her head at her friend's unaccustomed lack of expertise.

Diapers turned out to be the least of Carolyn's worries. Storytime was her assignment, and she was elated. "Reading a book—right up my alley." She picked up her reading material and thumbed through the pages. "Twenty-five pages—not bad. Looks like a short day for Volunteer Sheffield."

Her confidence was short-lived. Opening the door to a room of over twenty active preschoolers stopped her in her tracks. Fortunately, Nurse Jana was on hand. "They are so wiggly. And noisy. How do I get their attention?" Carolyn asked, stress evident in her voice.

"Piece of cake. I've got you covered. Go sit over there in that chair." Jana pointed to a seat in the middle of the throng of three-footers. As soon as Carolyn was seated, Jana placed her fingers in her mouth and blew a whistle louder than any Carolyn had ever heard.

Apparently Carolyn wasn't the only one surprised. A hush fell over the curious crowd, all frozen in midactivity.

Jana addressed her audience. "Boys and girls, please find your seats. Our special reader today will be Ms. Sheffield. She has a wonderful story to share with you."

At the invitation to find a seat, Carolyn found a mass of five young but vigorous bodies competing for her lap. The victor, a blond, pig-tailed girl, straightened her garments messed in the battle and wiggled to find a comfortable spot.

She turned, looked at Carolyn, and announced, "You do *not* have a gramma's lap. It's not comfy or soft like it's supposed to be."

Carolyn wasn't in the mood for criticism, especially from a three year old, but she let it lie. "That's because I'm not a gramma."

A chorus of "Why?" arose, leading unsuspecting Carolyn down a path trickier than any she had seen in her legal career. Each answer she provided was countered by another "Why?"

When, after a half hour, Nurse Jana poked her head back in the room, the book still lay on Carolyn's lap unopened, and she was exhausted, inextricably entangled in the *why* web of the three-year-olds' world.

"This audience was tougher than any group of defense counsel I've seen. I'm worn out," Carolyn later explained to Jana, after admitting the book hadn't even been opened. "I am a fish out of water when trying to deal with these small children. I think they can smell that I'm a rookie. Ruth's the grandmotherly type. I'm not even sure I'm the mother type, much less a grandmother figure." She stared at Jana with pleading eyes and produced the best lost-puppy look she could muster. "Please, please get me out of here. I'll do anything."

Within a week, Carolyn found out what her "anything" would be. When she showed up for her shift early the next Saturday morning, she was ushered into the Transitional Care Unit.

"This is a rather unusual case," Ethel, the volunteers coordinator, explained. "We are experimenting with increasing the personal contact our comatose patients are receiving, to see if it has an effect on their recovery rates. We're asking people to talk with them, hold their hands, and communicate with them as if they were fully aware. We're not exactly sure what effect it will have, but we know it can't hurt." Ethel paused outside a door marked TCU 121, 122, 123 and ran her fingers through her large gray curls.

"We would like to assign you to be the one-on-one caregiver for Marti Thule. She's seventeen years old. She was in a car accident four weeks ago and has been in a coma ever since. It will be a big commitment and will take a lot of time, so I want you to see Marti and think about it before you decide." Ethel met Carolyn's gaze. "If you accept this assignment, it will be important for you to follow through. She's behind the first partition. I'll be at the nurses' station if you need me."

Carolyn pushed open the white curtain surrounding bed 121. Lying on the pillow, the flesh color of her face starkly contrasting with the sea of white about her, was a petite, auburn-haired teen. "So young and with so much life left to live," Carolyn mused. The face reminded her a bit of Emily at a much younger age. As Carolyn gazed down at the helpless girl, an indescribable feeling came over her. She immediately headed out of the room and down to the nurses' station. She wasn't sure why, but Carolyn knew exactly what she was supposed to do. Carolyn Sheffield, Volunteer, had a new assignment.

*S*eventy-one-year-old attorney and widower Michael Flannigan brushed a stray white lock away from his piercing blue eyes and stared at the five-two hurricane who was verbally assaulting him. Stunned from the attack, he speechlessly watched her spin on her heel and march across the dance floor. When he realized her irate dressing-down had brought the attention of the rest of his colleagues and friends, his silence turned to explanation. Not sure what had generated the rash of accusations, he joked with the very interested crowd, "Oh, apparently cousin Mary's forgotten to take her medication again. I'll have to get hold of her doctor."

A wave of laughter seemed to pacify their nosy curiosity but did nothing to quell Michael's own questions. Despite his lighthearted comment, this was not cousin Mary, and she was saner than any woman he'd seen in awhile. She was also angrier. Even after replaying the episode again and again in his head, Michael couldn't for the life of him figure out what he had done to set her off.

He returned to his spacious condominium overlooking Lake Union and headed for bed. After tossing and turning for forty minutes, Michael had to admit the futility of the exercise. Sleep was not coming. He went to the living room and leaned against the window, gazing at the reflection of the pumpkin moon in the purple-tinged water. A familiar thought crossed his mind, as it often did when he observed some of God's more glorious creations: *Are You finding as much pleasure in the beautiful work of Your hands as I am right now? Thank You. It is amazing.* The first thought was followed by a second, equally familiar: *Too bad Elise is not here to share it with me.*

Even absorbing the beauty of the night couldn't rid Michael's mind of the evening's events. What had he done to set the spitfire of a woman off? Why did he care so much? Michael was not one easily riled. In just fewer than fifty years of marriage to Elise, he could remember only a handful of occasions on which they had quarreled. Sweet Elise. How different she was from the little fireball who assailed him tonight. She *never* would have done anything like that. Tall and refined, she was more the "scrub the floor in silence" type when she was upset with him. Boy, he missed her. Even though it had been almost five years since he lost Elise, it seemed like she was with him constantly. No other woman had caught his attention or eye since. Until tonight. For some unexplainable reason, Michael felt drawn to the feisty woman who had whisked on and off the dance floor in a flurry of angry energy.

Staring at the stars dancing on the night waves, Michael wondered whether she would ever cross his path again. And if he'd ever find out what he, or whoever the cad she thought he was, had done to raise her ire.

Michael didn't have long to wait for an answer to his midnight reflections. Two-and-a-half weeks later, he headed to Community Memorial for some medical tests. After spending a good hour as a human pincushion, Michael emerged poked, pricked, and prodded.

"Doctors," he muttered. "What a job. They spend all day inflicting pain and discomfort, yet they are still revered and well paid. Maybe I should change professions."

His half-hearted comments were interrupted by a sweet voice calling his name.

"Michael Flannigan? Is that you?"

Michael turned to see the familiar white-haired owner of the honey voice. "Ruth Welch. How are you? It's been so long since I have talked with you. I thought I'd run into you at the hospital fund-raiser, but you must have escaped before I could snag a dance. What brings you here today?"

"You know me. Every chance I get to volunteer here at Community, I take." Ruth turned her head and scanned the halls. "Wait here.

There's someone I'd like you to meet." With a quick wave, the little woman hurried down the corridor.

Michael leaned against the wall and smiled. For Ruth Welch he'd do anything. The woman had a heart that rivaled Texas in size. When Ruth had heard of Elise's passing, she had provided him meals for a month. Often he'd come home to find a casserole on the porch and a "Made a little extra tonight" note attached. Any friend of that saintly woman had to be worth meeting. He closed his eyes and waited.

His reverie was interrupted by a familiar anger-tinged voice. "What are *you* doing here?"

He quickly opened his eyes to find a memorable glare affixed to the middle of his forehead. Looking past the steely glare, he met the gaze of a clearly perplexed Ruth.

"Carolyn? Have you met Michael?" Ruth asked.

"Met him? How soon you forget. I gave him the dressing-down of a lifetime. It was well-deserved, I might add." Carolyn's fixed stare dared Michael to move.

Ruth's love-lined face showed rare consternation. "I don't understand. Michael is my friend."

It was Carolyn's turn to look concerned. "Now I'm the confused one. I mean, forgive and forget is one thing, Ruth, but it's only been a couple of weeks since this cad humiliated you to tears. I know the Scriptures talk about turning the other cheek, but how can you deem him your friend?"

Ruth's face reddened until it matched Carolyn's coat. "*This* is the man you dressed-down? *This* is the man who received your wrath? Oh, Carolyn. This is my old friend Michael Flannigan whom I told you about. Don't you remember? He wasn't the man who rejected me at the dance."

Michael watched as recognition, then remorse, passed through Carolyn's eyes.

Extending her hand, she took his and grumbled out an apology. "So sorry. Looks like I got the wrong man."

Even in the obvious throes of embarrassment, this woman was formidable.

"It's all right," Michael assured. "If I'd heard the man reject my dear Ruth, I would have had a word or two for him myself. Although," he added with a wink at the shuffling Carolyn, "I don't think I could have produced a performance to equal yours."

Ruth wasted no time taking advantage of the lull in the apology-fest. "Michael, have you had lunch? Carolyn and I were about to get something to eat and would love a handsome male escort."

Michael knew better than to let that invitation pass him by. This was his chance to get to know a little about the woman who had occupied so much of his thoughts the last couple of weeks.

"You bet I'm in." He deviously smiled at Carolyn and added, "As long as your friend promises to treat me to dessert for the terrible way she spoke to me. We men have fragile egos, you know."

Carolyn snorted at his feigned hurt. "I worked with a bunch of male attorneys. You better try the fragile-ego line on someone other than this seasoned gal. I'm old enough to know better. Dessert, however, I will do."

The afternoon flew by as Michael and Carolyn parried with sarcasm under chaperone Ruth's watchful and obviously pleased eyes. Before parting, matchmaker Ruth invited Michael and Carolyn over to her house for dinner the next evening. Michael observed Carolyn's response very carefully.

"We'll see, Ruth. I'll have to get back with you about that when I have my schedule in front of me," Carolyn offered, her voice not giving Michael much hope she'd be anywhere near Ruth's house the following night.

When Ruth attempted to insist, Michael observed Carolyn's set jaw. *This woman is one to be reckoned with,* he wryly noted.

His afternoon with Carolyn served to raise many questions in his mind. She was highly intelligent. She was also fiercely loyal, as he had found out during their unfortunate first encounter. There was something else, however. She had a protective wall around her. Michael wondered if anyone had ever been able to penetrate it. What had put it there in the first place? Would she ever be willing to take it down?

Thoughts of Carolyn, along with the unanswered questions, accompanied him far into the night as Michael and the moon kept watch over Lake Union.

❧

Carolyn straightened the white silk collar on her button-down blouse and pulled on a tailored vest with her volunteer name badge affixed. Although she had only spent two afternoons with Marti Thule, she felt as if she knew the girl. Spending time with the young lady, poised on the brink of life's opportunities yet unable to take advantage of any of them, released a flood of Carolyn's own emotions. She fiddled for a few more seconds before the mirror, grabbed a bunch of radiant gerbera daisies in a vase, and headed for her much-anticipated visit with Marti.

When Carolyn arrived at the Transitional Care Unit, she went into Marti's room, placed the bright bouquet on her bedside table, and grabbed her hand. Speaking in hushed tones so as not to disturb the patron on the other side of the cloth divider, Carolyn addressed her new friend.

"Well, dear, I wish you could see the flowers, but let me tell you about them. Gerberas are my favorites, and these are glorious shades of jeweled purple, red, orange, and yellow. I had to go to a special florist to get them this time of year, but they are worth it. They bring an instant kaleidoscope of colored light to any room, even on the dreariest days. You know, I've never been a roses kind of gal. Funny thing is, not one of my would-be suitors over the last fifty or so years could tell you that. I guess none of them ever cared to know me well enough to ask. Have had more roses than I've ever cared to see, though. I'm sure there are a lot of folks at the local retirement home wondering where all those large rose bouquets came from."

Carolyn paused, still tightly gripping the girl's seemingly lifeless, tube-punctured hand. Fifty years of painful memories overwhelmed her. Safe in this room with a captive, albeit silent, audience, Carolyn allowed the feelings she normally would have banished to the deepest crevice in her mind to surface. She softly continued, "You know it's not that I wouldn't have loved a fresh flower bouquet, or someone who cared enough to figure out what I liked. In fact, I thought I had found love once. I was a young thing—barely older than you." Carolyn looked down at the unlined face of youth on the pillow.

"A handsome fellow. Magazine-cover handsome. Smart to boot. I was new at the law firm. A bit of a thing, naive and young. He worked three floors above and swept me off my feet. Dinner invitations. Flowers. The works. He was a smooth cookie, and I fell like an anvil—hard. Couldn't pass him in the elevator without my heart pounding like I had just completed the first half of the Boston Marathon. After a couple of dinners, I knew. He was the one. I couldn't believe God had found me such a great husband. The man gave me a ring and told me he wanted to marry me after six months. He asked me not to tell people at the firm about us, because there was a policy concerning colleagues becoming romantically involved." Carolyn's voice faltered.

"Funny. Seems like yesterday in some respects. I went up to his office one day to drop off some lunch. His secretary took the bag. She then took my heart when she said, 'I'll deliver it as soon as his wife leaves.' I took off my ring, put it in the lunch bag, and left. Never told a soul. Didn't even talk to God about it. Too humiliated and ashamed. Wasn't sure exactly how to approach it with Him. 'Please heal my heart that the married man I was in love with broke,' somehow didn't sound too good, so I just let it lie." Carolyn stopped her reminiscing and let the wave of pent-up emotion keep her company. Much later, she placed a kiss on Marti's cheek and silently walked the hallway toward the neon green Exit sign.

Carolyn numbly drove home, feeling strangely peaceful, despite the exhausting emotional battle she had waged this afternoon. *What would God have done if I had turned it over to Him? Would He have condemned me for my stupidity and relationship with a married man?* In the back of her head, a still, small voice asked, *Or would He have taken you in His loving arms, knowing you hadn't known, and healed your broken heart?*

Pulling into her driveway, Carolyn dragged herself from her vehicle and up the front steps of her home. A heavy Seattle mist bathed her in gray. Even in her exhaustion, she couldn't miss the brown box on her doorstep. Lifting the lid, Carolyn found the largest bouquet of wildflowers she had ever seen. When she took them into the light of her house, Carolyn gasped. Amidst the other flowers, three dozen gerbera daisies stood tall.

For the first time in as long as Carolyn Sheffield could remember, she allowed herself to cry.

$\mathcal{C}$arolyn's musings of the last week finally found a voice. "Three dozen gerberas, Marti. Can you believe it? Who could have sent them?"

As usual, her silent companion provided no answer. "You know," Carolyn's voice added in the silence, "I haven't even told Ruth about receiving them. With that ammunition she'd have me hooked, tied, and down the aisle with any one of her 'dashing and highly eligible' senior gentlemen before I could stop it. At least for now, I have to play this one close to the vest. I can't imagine any man who knows me well enough to know my weakness for those daisies. For that matter, I can't imagine any man who would make the effort and go to the expense of finding them this time of year!"

Carolyn sat quietly in the room, her mind running through the possibilities. Finally, her growling stomach broke her train of thought. She squeezed Marti's hand. "Well, dear. My stomach is calling. I'll be back in a few minutes, after I grab a bite to eat."

Carolyn shut the door to bed 121 and set off to find Ruth. *Wonder if she can break for lunch?* When she finally tracked Ruth down, her friend's hurried gait, pink cheeks, and harried smile answered Carolyn's question. Pediatrics, Ruth's work assignment this week, was hopping today. Carolyn would be dining alone.

She aimed her now starving body toward the cafeteria in search of lunch. Halfway down the hall, a vaguely familiar voice heralded her. "Carolyn?"

Turning abruptly, Carolyn was surprised to see the still dashingly handsome owner of the voice. Unwilling to let Michael believe she remembered his name, Carolyn smiled. "Fred, how have you been?"

Michael's slightly furrowed brow spoke louder than words. Carolyn wasn't sure whether this man bought that she was suffering from memory loss. His consternation turned to a large grin.

"You know, only my more formal acquaintances call me Fred. Close friends call me Michael. I know we'll become close friends, so please feel free to call me Michael. Let's go grab a bite to eat."

Carolyn, for once, was speechless. This man not only ignored her deliberate indifference but also had the courage to insist they'd become close friends and ask her to lunch. She didn't quite know what to make of him or the weird fluttering feeling she had in her stomach each time she saw him. *It's those dashing good looks,* she tried to convince herself. *If he were an average Joe, I'd have him wrapped, packaged, and sent on his way without a second thought.* But even as the words played through her head, they didn't quite ring true.

Suddenly realizing her thoughts had left her standing speechless in front of this man who was, with obvious enjoyment, awaiting her answer, Carolyn cleared her throat. "I'm on my way down to the cafeteria if you'd like to join me—Fred." She walked resolutely down the hall, not even pausing to see if he were following.

As she rounded the corner to the lunch line, Michael's much larger stride enabled him to catch up with her shorter but quick-paced stride. A bit out of breath, he joked, "I hope my wallet will hold out. The way you charged to the cafeteria, you must be hungry enough to eat an elephant."

Carolyn had to smile. Her efforts to ditch Michael seemed to not be working. Despite her apparent failure to shake him, Carolyn wasn't upset. In fact, she felt rather exhilarated. Maybe this fellow wasn't so bad after all. Not that she'd ever tell him, but deep down, Carolyn found herself enjoying the encounter.

Plate piled high, Carolyn headed for the register. She was hungry. If Michael wanted to foot the bill, he'd find out just *how* hungry. When she slid her tray next to his, he didn't even blink. "I love a woman with an appetite. I'm so glad you feel comfortable enough in my company to eat. I can't stand it when a woman picks around a plate trying to convince you she eats like a bird, and goes home hungry. Senseless."

Carolyn had said the same thing to Ruth many times but wasn't about to admit to Michael that she saw eye to eye with him on this, or anything else. "Hmm," was her noncommittal reply.

Carolyn had as much fun at lunch as she'd had in a long time. Long-dammed-up laughter escaped in uncontrollable bursts. Carolyn knew her best efforts couldn't hide the fact that she was having a marvelous time with her luncheon companion. She went to grab another soft drink and tried to get her schoolgirl enthusiasm under control. When she returned to the table, a second man was standing there.

Michael rose to his feet and introduced Carolyn. "Bob Marin. Carolyn Sheffield. Bob is one of my oldest friends. Carolyn . . ."—Michael turned with a deliberate wink in Bob's direction—"is one of my newest friends."

"Sheffield." Bob rubbed his hand over his hair-challenged scalp. "Do you come from the Boston Sheffields?"

Carolyn responded. "Oh, no. Not the Boston Sheffields. Didn't even know there were any. I'm from the much more auspicious Alderdale Sheffield clan."

"Alderdale?" Bob's furrow met his long, receding hairline. "Alderdale, Oregon?"

"That's the one," Carolyn proudly replied.

"One of my dearest friends lives in Alderdale. Absolute gem of a woman. Perhaps you know her." Bob shook his head as if he couldn't believe his faux pas. "What am I thinking? Of course you must know her. If that saint and gentlewoman resides in the town, her good works and fingerprints have made their way all over it. Alderdale—lucky home of Harriet Taylor."

The mention of Harriet's name with the glowing endorsement was too much for Carolyn. The drink she had so demurely sipped during his oration on Alderdale flew across the table, propelled by her shock. When it sprinkled Michael's plate like spring rain, his response set off her jangled nerves.

"Just what I needed. My food was a little dry." Michael winked and continued to eat his soft-drink speckled entree.

Carolyn erupted in gales of uncontrolled laughter. Tears coursed down her cheeks unheeded. Embarrassment at totally losing control in front of the two men did nothing to stop her. When she finally calmed down, she managed to say between remaining chuckles, "Harriet's fingerprints *are* all over the town, that's for sure. Her footprints are there, too." She left out the fact that the footprints were all over the backs of those Harriet had walked on.

Bob stared at Carolyn like she was an absolute loon, but Michael's face was tinged with obvious amusement. The men said their goodbyes. Yet even after Bob left the table, he continued to look over his shoulder as if he had severe questions regarding her sanity.

Carolyn resumed finishing her drink. She had been so amused by the image Bob had painted of her meddling cousin, she had overlooked a very disturbing possibility. Could Bob's involvement with Harriet and Michael be just coincidence? If Carolyn had learned anything over the years it was that "coincidence" and "Harriet Taylor" didn't normally fall in the same sentence. Carolyn's defense system, so recently let down, was instantly reactivated. Could this be one of Harriet's matchmaking ruses? As much as she didn't want to believe it, she couldn't dismiss the idea outright. She'd have to watch this fellow.

"Well, Fred, it's been fun, but I have to head back to my volunteer duties. See you around." Carolyn stood with her drink, and her new set of disturbing questions, and prepared to make a quick exit.

Michael rose to bid her farewell, confusion written all over his rugged face.

Carolyn headed to her car before returning to Marti's room armed with a sack. After bringing the girl up to date on the lunchroom dramatics, Carolyn reached into the bag and brought out a leather-bound journal. "I was going through some old boxes in my garage the other day and found this book." She opened the pages gingerly and turned to a black-and-white picture of a teenage girl.

"I knew you reminded me of my niece, Emily, but until I found this picture, I didn't realize how much you resembled her. It's amazing. You know, life dealt her some major blows, just like you. She thought she'd never be able to fulfill some of her dreams, but she held on. She found love and happiness, and just last spring, she was married at the ripe old age of forty-six. Marti, what I'm trying to say is, even though things look rough from where you are right now, hang on. God has a plan for you. I'm not sure what it is, but I promise: He does. Just like He had a plan for Emily." *And,* added a small voice in her head, *like He still has a plan for you, Carolyn Sheffield.*

Carolyn read from her journal the remainder of the afternoon. Visions of a much younger and much more vulnerable woman filled the corners of the room. Stories of rejection, pain, and heartache touched the mature woman who now remembered the events with a much more analytical eye. Editorial comments interspersed her reading. "Should have known better on that one." "Look, girl, can't you see him coming from a mile away?" "Good riddance to the cad."

Carolyn was surprised to find some prayer entries in her journal; the heartfelt petitions she had written to her heavenly Father she could now see had been answered. Some had taken years, but the benefit of time's passage now opened the much older woman's eyes. At what point had she stopped journaling? At what juncture had she decided she didn't have time to pray? Looking back through the journal pages, it was clear those decisions had been made long before the Lord answered many of her prayers.

"So," she quietly reflected, "even though I gave up on Him, He never gave up on me. He continued to answer my prayers from long ago, even when I no longer asked. He remembered." For the second time in as many weeks, tears followed the lines of Carolyn's face.

"Oh, bother. If I keep this up, it's going to become a habit," she muttered, wiping the stray droplets from her cheeks. "Good thing no one is around. They'd think I was a dotty old woman." Even for all her bluster, Carolyn Sheffield knew today was a day that would change her life.

After kissing her friend Marti on the forehead, Carolyn left the hospital. Instead of heading for home, she drove to West Seattle. She parked at Lincoln Park and headed across the grassy lawn. Peeling madrona trees beautifully framed Puget Sound's angry gray waves below. The blustery wind on the beach walk pushed at Carolyn's small body, daring her to try to walk. She tucked her head against the wind's power and propelled her body forward, despite the powerful gusts. Out in nature, battling the elements, Carolyn felt renewed. The spray of salty water carried on the wind stung her face but awakened her senses.

Though the inclement weather had chased off much of the human population, Carolyn braved the elements and found strength. Standing on a piling, she held up her arms and shouted, "I, Carolyn Sheffield, am alive!" Her words were swallowed by the hungry wind as soon as they were uttered. The almost-seventy-year-old woman continued, shouting into the wind, "I am sorry. Please forgive me."

The wind screamed louder.

"I'm sorry I forgot You. I love You. Please don't leave me!" The answering howl of the wind knocked Carolyn from her weathered piling. Sitting on the rocky, wet ground, she quietly added, "I can't do it without You."

As soon as the words left her lips, an unnatural calm fell over the beach. The wind's gyrations quelled. The leftover breezes skimmed waves and left them dancing. Peace filled Carolyn from head to toe. She felt as if warm, loving arms had encircled her in an embrace. The warmth had a familiar feel.

Carolyn stayed on the beach until the last rays of the brilliant sunset dimmed, then disappeared. Even after the sun's rays were gone, she did not feel the winter chill of the night air. The continued warmth of a heavenly embrace reminded Carolyn Sheffield that she had returned home.

16

I f I find out Harriet Taylor has stuck her meddling paws into my pot of honey, that woman will rue the day she was born," Carolyn threatened over the phone.

Her softer niece, Emily Carr Hamilton, replied in kind. "I know. I'm very familiar with those 'paws.' Remember, I was her 'cause of the month' for awhile."

"Emily, I really am relying on you. Track her. Spy on her. Follow her. Whatever you need to do. Just find out whether she has anything to do with sending a Mr. Michael Flannigan my way." Carolyn's normal control wavered slightly. "It's really important." After a pause, she added. "Of course, if that woman is involved, I'm sure it won't take much undercover work to find it out. She'll be announcing her 'charitable efforts' on my behalf all over Alderdale."

Emily assured Carolyn she would search out the truth. "Just tell me: Is he as bad as Herman Dobbs? I knew *I* couldn't control Harriet, but I thought for sure she'd leave *you* alone. I mean, you're so—formidable."

"If she is involved, Harriet will find out firsthand how formidable I can be. And no, I wouldn't say this fellow is of the Herman Dobbs ilk."

Carolyn gathered from Emily's silence that she knew better than to press the Michael Flannigan issue.

Carolyn found comfort in the knowledge she would soon have the answers to the questions that had plagued her since her meeting three weeks earlier with Michael and his staunch Harriet-supporting friend, Bob Marin. She sat down in her plush living room, armed with a grapefruit and a spoon, and contemplated the events of the last month.

The intensity of the turmoil she felt over the possibility that her relationship with Michael was of Harriet's making, surprised her. Either she was becoming soft in her old age or the fellow had worked his way under her shell far more effectively than she had believed. She had tried to peg the strong feelings in the "overflow from her deeply spiritual experience" column but knew instinctively that they didn't fit there. Funny, she was awaiting Emily's return call almost as much as a teenager awaits a call asking her out on a prom date. The fluttery feelings were back in her stomach, too.

The ringing of her doorbell interrupted Carolyn's contemplation. She grabbed a sweater and went to answer it. When she reached the front door, the disappearing UPS delivery truck caused her to glance down. A medium-sized package lay on her porch. *I didn't order anything,* Carolyn thought as she scanned the box for a nonexistent return address. Shutting the door and opening the box, Carolyn was shocked to see a beautiful, brand-new leather-bound journal. She was also amazed by the pound of See's chocolates, her absolute favorite. Her disbelief continued when, upon opening the box, she discovered that whoever ordered them knew her far better than she thought anyone did. Inside was a full pound of orange creams. No one, besides Ruth, knew of Carolyn's addiction to the orange-filled rounds of light chocolate. Her monthly trek to downtown Seattle to pick up a small stash was top secret.

"Who on earth?" Carolyn muttered aloud.

Later that night, Carolyn posed the same question, but to a higher source. "Heavenly Father, You obviously know who is doing this. I trust You. Please, just don't let me get hurt." Although she didn't receive an answer telling her who was delivering the gifts, Carolyn once again felt at peace.

A week later, armed with her new journal, Carolyn headed toward the hospital for a much-anticipated meeting with Marti. She couldn't wait to tell the girl her exciting news. It appeared that Michael Flannigan had been exonerated. Emily's call indicated Harriet hadn't seemed to know anything about Michael, although mention of his friend Bob had sent Harriet into a lengthy adoration-fest. According to Emily, no mention of Harriet's "good deeds" or Carolyn Sheffield had made their way around the Alderdale rumor circuit, either.

When Carolyn passed the hospital desk on her way to her friend's room, the now-familiar ladies at the nurses' station greeted her. "How are you doing this morning, Carolyn? What did you bring for Marti today?"

The peppery charge nurse, Denise, brushed her short gray hair behind her ear, and came around the desk. "I'll tell you, I don't care what the study says, I can attest that your visits with Marti have done wonders. Even though she hasn't come out of the coma, there is a peace about her that has developed in the months you have worked with her." She gave Carolyn a hug. "Thank you so much for spending so much time with her. You have been a godsend."

Carolyn nodded. If Denise only knew. God *had* sent her to Marti; she was sure of that. But Carolyn didn't think it was only for Marti's benefit. The blessings had been Carolyn's.

Working her way down the hall, Carolyn stopped when she heard voices emerging from Marti's room. The muffled conversation took shape as she drew closer to the slightly ajar door.

Dr. Duncan's recognizable voice drifted into the hall. "I can't give you any guarantees. We're not even sure how much brain activity is there. Sometimes miracles happen, even after months and months. I really don't know whether this will be one of those. It has to be your decision, though."

"I wish Mom and Dad were still alive," a young female voice lamented. "They'd know what to do for Marti."

A male voice piped in. "They aren't. As her brother and sister, we have to make a choice. Marti was full of life. You know that. She would have hated to see herself this way. She's not going to get better. There has been plenty of time for a miracle. You heard what Dr. Duncan said—she could stay on life-support for years and years and never come out of it. I say we disconnect her and let her go. She was always a free spirit. I say we let her fly."

The sister's voice acquiesced with relief that someone else was making the decision. "If you really think it's best . . . Anyway, she'll be with Mom and Dad."

Carolyn could hold back no longer. Bursting into the room, she addressed the shocked young people in front of her. "Miracles do happen. Sometimes it takes a lot longer than we think, but if there's any chance at all, don't you think Marti deserves to have that chance?" Carolyn's severe demeanor dissolved as she pleaded. "She's my friend. I know she's getting better. Even the nurses here see it. Ask them. Please. Let me work with her for a little longer. Let me have a little more time. I'll come every day. Please, just don't give up on her yet."

The brother's obviously harried face grew stern. "Who is this woman?" he asked a shocked-looking Dr. Jensen. He turned his wrath on Carolyn. "What do *you* know? You didn't live with her for almost twenty years. You didn't grow up with her. You didn't comfort her when our parents died. She's not *your* younger sister. She's ours. She was in a coma months ago. She is in a coma now. Time isn't going to change that. I suggest you attend to your own affairs." The man's veins bulged in anger. "And stay out of our business."

Realizing what she had done, Carolyn fled from the room and out of the hospital. Tears coursed down her cheeks with the realization that her dear friend Marti would not be on this earth for much longer. Carolyn locked herself in her home, unplugged the phones, and refused to answer the door. Pain coursed through her body and doubled her in half. She wondered if she'd ever be able to breathe again as sob after sob shook her body.

Around four in the morning, Carolyn realized she had to go back to the hospital. If she only had a little time left with Marti, she didn't want to waste a moment. She gathered a few belongings and headed back to the Transitional Care Unit. When she stepped into the night air, it robbed her of breath and flash froze her lungs. She wrapped her coat close and braved the late winter night's fury.

As she passed the hospital desk, Denise's familiar, but utterly weary, face greeted her. "Carolyn. I held over on the night shift hoping you might come back. I wanted to talk with you. The administration found out what happened this afternoon. They have officially removed you from your duties."

The pain in Carolyn's solar plexus intensified. "What do you mean? I can't visit Marti anymore?"

The lines in Denise's face showed deep emotion, and she nodded. "That's exactly what it means." She took Carolyn's hand and led her down the hall toward the room. "I'm not supposed to do this, and it might cost me my job if they find out, but say your good-byes. At five A.M., no administrator I know is going to have a clue."

Carolyn slowly opened the door leading to bed 121. The familiar rhythm of the machines was missing. Marti lay on the pillow, unhooked from tubes and needles. Carolyn resumed her place at Marti's side, grasped the girl's hand, and squeezed out, past the lump in her throat, "Well, my dear, it looks like this is the end of the road for us. I'm sure glad I got a chance to meet you. I can't tell you what you have done for me. You know, this wasn't a real easy time in either of our lives. You got me through my tough time. I just wish I could have returned the favor."

Glancing down, tears formed in Carolyn's eyes. "I can give you one thing. The place you're going—well, I've got a contact up there. I'm sure He'll take real good care of you. I'll tell Him you are coming, and I'll ask Him to keep a special watch out for you. He'll make sure you feel at home. I promise."

Carolyn laid her old journal by Marti's bedside. "I would like you to have this. Because of you, I don't need the book to remember who I was and *whose* I was." Carolyn pointed to her head and then her heart. "You see, now I remember. Here and here."

Leaving her beloved journal at Marti's bedside, Carolyn squeezed her hand, planted one last kiss on her forehead, and choked out, "Good-bye."

❦

Carolyn flipped over in bed, attempting to ignore the incessant ringing of the doorbell. *Go away. Can't a person get some sleep?* The turning of a key in her front door lock let her know it was Ruth. *That will teach me to give her a spare key to my house,* Carolyn grumbled. The sound of small footsteps marched up the stairs toward Carolyn's room. Ruth's bright smile poked around the corner.

"There you are. Up and at 'em." Ruth attempted to help her friend rise.

"I'm tired. I'm staying in bed," Carolyn growled back.

"Oh, no, you don't, Ms. Grumpy. No healthy person needs a week in bed. Let's get you a nutritious breakfast."

"I'm not hungry, Ruth." Carolyn toned down her anger-filled voice. "I'm sorry. I'm not trying to be a bear. But I really don't feel like eating. Please, I just need a little space."

"If this is about you losing your volunteer position, I'm sure I can get you another one. You did a great job with that girl." Ruth's smile reminded Carolyn of a puppy dog's wagging tail, the animal just begging for a positive response.

Unfortunately, Carolyn was running a little short in the positive response department. "You don't understand. I don't want another volunteer position. I don't think I ever want to go back to the hospital."

The confusion broadcast across Ruth's caring face clearly showed she didn't fully understand why Marti meant so much to Carolyn, but Carolyn was not up to a heart-to-heart explanation, even for Ruth.

After a half hour of futile cajoling, Ruth worriedly left her friend, vowing to return soon. Less than an hour later, the doorbell rang again.

"When she said soon, she meant *soon*," Carolyn mumbled. "Can't she take a hint?" Pulling herself out of bed in the hope that her friend might see her upright position as a sign she could leave, Carolyn went to answer the door.

When the door opened, Carolyn wished she were still snugly tucked underneath her covers. It was not Ruth who had come calling. It was a very dapper-looking Michael Flannigan.

Carolyn's hands went instinctively to the hairstyle her pillow had so painstakingly worked to create over the last three days. "Michael. So glad you could call. Do you always surprise your friends at the door, or do some warrant an advance phone call?" Carolyn's sarcasm was spurred by her embarrassment.

Michael appeared to ignore any unloving tone in Carolyn's voice. "I'm so glad you feel comfortable enough to call me by my real name. It's nice to know I've graduated from Fred to Michael."

Only after Michael mentioned it did Carolyn realize her slip. Not that it caused her much consternation. She was far more concerned about her sloppy attire and hairdo. Concentrating on the quickest way to the shower, Carolyn didn't object when Michael suggested that he walk around the block a couple of times while she got ready to go for a drive with him.

The cold pellets in the shower pierced the clouded thoughts that had kept Carolyn company since Marti's departure. Curiosity replaced numbness. Why did Michael want her to go for a ride with him? Where were they going?

It wasn't until hours later that Carolyn got her answers. Standing on a craggy rock high above Deception Pass, Michael finally broke the silence that the two had shared the entire drive up. "This is where I came when my wife, Elise, died. I thought you might find peace here, too."

Carolyn stared down the ragged, jutting slope. Waves sprayed the stark gray rocks as they passed through the narrow pass. Moss clung to the stone, as if daring to live and grow in an impossible environment. Caught in the harsh beauty of the place, Carolyn didn't even realize Michael had gone. How had he known this place would bring her comfort? How had he known she was in *need* of comfort? Carolyn forced her mind back into contemplating her natural surroundings. Today was a day for healing. The questions would wait for another day.

he trip home from Deception Pass was much livelier than the wordless trek up. Although still grieving for the loss of her friend, out in the raw elements of God's creation, Carolyn had found a surprising salve for her pain. She could relate to the exposed rocks, constantly battered by the powerful waves. In a way, their constancy, challenging whatever the churning waters had to bring, empowered her, Life's blows of late had been harsh ones: the loss of her career and life's ambition; her confidence and will to continue; and her dear friend Marti.

Yet even though she felt the pain of the last months, a small voice reminded her that it had also been a time for gains: a rekindled relationship with her heavenly Father; Michael; and of course, sharing her life with Marti.

While Michael and she gently bantered in the car, Carolyn couldn't help but feel a small ray of hope pierce the dark shroud that encircled her. Michael turned the car into a parking lot and brought it to rest at the base of a fifteen-foot-tall ice cream cone. There wasn't much question what they were doing there. Carolyn couldn't remember the last time she had desired a late March ice cream. Hot chocolate, maybe, but not ice cream. Funny, after the odd day they had shared, ice cream seemed perfectly fitting.

Armed with treats in hand, Michael led Carolyn down a small dirt path that snaked around behind the hand-dipped ice cream place. Fifty yards down the path was a two-person wooden bench. The remnants of the tree trunk next to it hinted of its yesteryear grandeur. Crocus poked small bright heads up and surveyed the land.

Once they were seated, Michael said, "Why don't you tell me something about yourself that I don't know?"

Carolyn mentally noted that, given her reserve of late, it might be a very long list. She responded, "I worked as a paralegal downtown for almost fifty years. Seems like I was there every spare minute of my life, slaving away for the attorneys. Went in early. Came home late. Let's just say I was offered a retirement package that I really couldn't refuse."

"A really great one, huh?" Michael questioned.

"No. One I *really* couldn't refuse."

Michael's answering wince showed that he knew exactly what she was saying.

"I'll tell you, though," Carolyn continued, "I've had a lot of time in the last year to develop a great repertoire of attorney jokes. You want an attorney taken out at the knees, I'm your woman."

Carolyn wasn't sure how to read Michael's second wince.

Their bench conversation continued well into the early evening. Carolyn regaled Michael with stories of her early Alderdale escapades. Michael returned the favor by inviting her into the escapades of his younger years. Laughing, the two headed for the car. Michael opened Carolyn's door, then paused. "Thank you, Carolyn Sheffield, for letting me get to know you a little bit better." He winked, then added, "I don't care what all those other folks say. Deep down, you're a pretty good cookie."

Pleased, but slightly embarrassed by Michael's comment, Carolyn quipped, "You're not a bad egg yourself." When Michael walked around the car, Carolyn softly added, "And you'll never know how much today has meant to me."

After her excessive sleep of late, the next morning, Carolyn rose with the sun. She fiddled around the house, tackling chores that had been recently neglected. She showered, dressed, and readied herself for an early morning walk. Chaotic noise in her front yard sparked her curiosity. "What in the world is going on?" she muttered, making her way downstairs.

When she opened the door, it was all she could do not to slam it again. Standing in her doorway, casting a long shadow in the early morning sunshine, was Mr. Herman Dobbs, hat in hand and all five of his children in tow.

Carolyn gathered every ounce of politeness she could muster. "Why, Mr. Dobbs, what are *you* doing here?"

Herman's reply caught her completely off-guard.

"Well, Ms. Sheffield." He shifted his hat in his hands. "See, ever since my poor wife took ill and left me and the children, it's been awfully lonely 'round our house. I can't cook a lick. And as you know, my kids need someone to care for them. A mother figure. Ms. Taylor was mentioning your singleness and how you might be looking for a man. Since I'm looking for a woman, she—I mean I—thought you might be interested in being the woman in my home. You know, getting hitched and all."

Carolyn's laughter was tinged with compassion. "Herman Dobbs, I'm old enough to be a grandmother to your children. I may even be old enough to be a grandmother to you." The nods of the motley group assembled in her front yard indicated that she wasn't the only one who felt that way.

Carolyn's amusement still tickled the corners of her mouth. "Herman, have you ever thought of enrolling in a cooking school? They have plenty of great classes at local community colleges and community centers. I'm sure they even have one in Alderdale. Seems to me that if you took all the time Harriet has you running around on these wild goose chases and spent it in a cooking class, your problem might be solved."

A glimmer of thought showed on Herman's face. "They have classes like that?"

His interest provided Carolyn hope that maybe she was getting through to the man. "You better believe they do. I think you would do great there."

The hope brought by Herman's answering nod disappeared when he opined, "I bet there are a lot of ladies there who will be right good cooks when they're finished. Maybe I can find my wife there."

"Maybe, Herman." Carolyn shook her head. "Maybe."

The encounter left Carolyn in gales of laughter all morning long. Herman's visit, coupled with Emily's report that Harriet didn't have anything to do with Michael, settled her doubts once and for all. Michael was definitely a man of his own making.

"Now what am I going to do today to keep myself busy?" Carolyn contemplated. Today was her former volunteer day at the hospital. Even though Michael's companionship was filling some of the void left by Marti's departure, twinges of pain still haunted her. "I guess it's just a matter of time," she said. She combed her hair, threw on a light coat, and headed out to enjoy the sunshine. "Pain or not," Carolyn Sheffield vowed, "I'm going to live my life."

If Michael Flannigan had thought Carolyn Sheffield was special at their initial meeting, he was hog-tied now. As much as he admired the woman's fire and indomitable spirit, he was equally, if not more, impressed by her tenderness and vulnerability. Not that she'd ever willingly let anyone see it, but circumstances had placed Michael in a position that he was able to see things he doubted many, if any, had seen before. Unfortunately, it seemed that as his love for her grew, the obstacles grew as well.

Why did it have to be a group of attorneys that had stung her? Why couldn't she have worked in a doctor's office or in a beauty shop? The thought of Carolyn in a beauty shop sent Michael into a fit of laughter. "With her forthrightness, I can just see the havoc she'd wreak with beauty shop clientele. I don't suppose she'd have much use for the gossip and minutia, and I somehow don't see her holding her tongue."

Even with his temporary amusing reprieve, Michael still worried. How was he going to break it to this woman that he was of the same stripe as those who had ripped her life's rug out from underneath her? Right now, the last thing Michael Flannigan wanted to be was an attorney.

The questions plagued him the remainder of his exhausting day. He had to tell Carolyn. The longer he waited, the more she'd believe he was trying to deceive her. He knew he was in for a tongue-lashing regardless. It was not the lashing he was concerned about, though; he just didn't want to lose her. Given the upheaval in her life lately, would this be the last straw?

Even the thought of that outcome made him shudder. After discovering Carolyn, he wasn't about to let her get away. What should he do? Late into the evening, he pondered the question. Finally, he knelt down beside his bed.

"Well, Father, You know I never thought I'd find anyone after Elise. She was my love and my life. I was so blessed to have her and wouldn't change my life with her for anything. But now, You've brought this new woman into my life. Her energy and spirit renew me. She makes me glory in each day. I can't imagine spending the rest of my life without her. I think of her each waking moment. Help me. It seems as if forces are conspiring to keep us apart. Guide me that I might know what to say. Help me to find a way to get through to her. Bless me as I try to find ways to communicate my love to her. And be with me, Lord, that I may have more time on this earth to spend with Carolyn Sheffield."

Michael concluded his prayer and peacefully headed to bed. He wasn't sure what the solution would be, but long experience told him that whatever the outcome, the problem was now in the right place. He knew his heavenly Father would have the solution.

18

*R*uth anxiously perched on the edge of her chair in Carolyn's tastefully arranged living room, awaiting the next far-from-sordid detail in the Carolyn Sheffield/Michael Flannigan saga. Pleasure resonated from her face. "He drove you to Deception Pass? You had ice cream? If that doesn't beat all. If I didn't know better, Carolyn, I'd say you had yourself a suitor. I can't believe you didn't tell me sooner!"

Carolyn shrugged, trying to mask the excitement that she felt. "Oh, Ruth, we're just friends. I'm sure he just felt sorry for me."

Ruth's snort spoke loudly. She obviously wasn't buying that line. "Well, if I were you, I'd make sure to hold on to this one. I thought he was totally unavailable. After Elise, I assumed there would be no other woman in his life. Mark my words. Had I known, Michael Flannigan would have been number one on my list of potential dates. He's a keeper. Though what he sees in you, 'Ms. Hard-to-Get,' is beyond me. If you let him go, be warned. I'm next in line."

Ruth's wink and forthrightness made Carolyn laugh. Joined by her friend's chuckles, Carolyn warily admitted, "Amazingly enough, he *is* kind of getting to me. I'm not quite sure why. At first I thought it was his good looks. On appearance alone, that man would attract the attention of most women. It isn't that, though. I really am starting to like him. A lot."

Ruth's "I knew it" look, coupled with the shock her face reflected at hearing Carolyn admit it, started Carolyn's chuckles afresh. "Yes, Ruth. Me. Carolyn Sheffield, virtually seventy years old, smitten. I know. You don't have to say it. You never thought you'd see the day."

She stood and made her way to the kitchen with their empty

472

lemonade glasses. As she turned the corner, she barely heard her friend's, "No, but I've always hoped and prayed I would."

❧

Carolyn found her admiration of Michael growing daily. Slowly, the all-consuming pain from losing Marti was replaced by anticipation of what the next day with Michael would hold. They trekked across the Northwest together, basking in the warm summer sun and observing the wonders of nature. Car rides were filled with laughter and poignant conversation about life and deity. Slowly, the woman who Carolyn had spent so much time concealing over the years, began to emerge.

Carolyn's seventieth birthday was spent with Michael, far from the reaches of Ruth's "likely to throw a surprise party" grasp. Michael picked her up early. After a long day's hike through the hills surrounding Leavenworth, Washington, Carolyn and Michael found a bit of needed shade under the lacy green leaves of a towering maple. "Boy, this is the life," Michael contentedly murmured.

"You said it," Carolyn responded. She took one of Michael's hands. "If I forget to tell you, thank you. The last few weeks have been wonderful, and even though I wasn't looking forward to the Big Seven-O, this has been one of the best birthdays I can remember. You really are a great guy."

Carolyn's unaccustomed journey into the sentimental seemed to startle Michael. He composed himself quickly. "You really deserve a great guy, but hold off on the compliments until you hear what I have to say."

Carolyn braced herself. This did not sound good.

Michael continued, his gaze fixed on the ground. "I've wanted to tell you for awhile; I just didn't want to risk losing the relationship we have developed." He took her hand. "Carolyn, I am head over heels for you. When I leave you at night, I think about you. When I rise in the morning, you are the first thing that pops into my mind. I didn't think I'd ever feel this way about another woman. You are as different from my Elise as night is from the day, but my feelings toward you are equally strong."

Carolyn's pleasure over hearing his feelings for her was tempered by her concern over what his bad news would be. "Michael," she softly interrupted, "just get to the unpleasant part. Remember, 'Forward and Direct' is my motto."

Michael looked at her. "I never meant to deceive you. I didn't even know until a few weeks ago what your career circumstances had been. You once told me you could take any attorney out at the knees; I'm just hoping you'll spare mine."

She shook her head in confusion. "I don't understand. What are you saying?"

"Carolyn, I'm an attorney. Lawyer. Counselor at law. A J.D. Whatever you want to call it. Right now, I wish I was anything else. I know we're not your favorite breed on the planet. I think what happened to you was awful, and I'm truly sorry."

The shock of the news silenced Carolyn. This man, Michael Flannigan, was an attorney? It couldn't be. Betrayal and hurt filled every pore in Carolyn's body. Looking at Michael—his eyes tightly shut, obviously braced for one of Carolyn's infamous tongue-lashings—Carolyn couldn't oblige. The words caught in her throat. Why hadn't he told her? How long had he meant to deceive her? For the first time that day, Carolyn felt all of her seventy years.

She couldn't bear to look up again when she quietly said, "Please take me home."

The pleasant intermittent silence that had kept them company on the drive over the mountains was replaced by an uncomfortable, brooding silence. Carolyn gazed stoically at the heat-scorched deciduous leaves. Their wilting appearance matched her mood. When Michael finally reached Carolyn's home, he went around and opened her car door. He awkwardly followed two paces behind her up to the front porch. "I'm sorry, Carolyn. I'm truly sorry. I should have told you earlier."

Carolyn said nothing. She marched inside and shut the door. Once on the other side of the closed front door, Carolyn allowed herself to feel the impact of what she had learned.

The doorbell interrupted her grief. Tempted to not answer it, Carolyn thought better of it and moved toward the door. Peeping through the hole, Carolyn was shocked to see her niece Emily. What was *she* doing here?

She didn't have to wait long to find out. After exchanging hugs and greetings, Emily exclaimed, "Happy birthday from Michael."

"Michael?" Even the sound of his name started the painful twinges. "What does he have to do with you?"

"He called me a month ago. He said he wanted to do something special for you for your birthday, and he thought you'd really enjoy a visit from me. He sent the plane ticket and arranged everything. I'm here for a week."

Carolyn was stunned. Michael had planned for Emily to come visit?

Emily continued, "I'll tell you, Aunt Carolyn, I don't know what Michael is like in person, but if his phone demeanor is even close to accurate, he is a wonderful man. And he is obviously very fond of you. How do you feel about him?"

Michael's recent confession, coupled with Emily's unanticipated question, was too much for Carolyn. The usually stoic aunt opened her heart to her niece and laid out the events of the last year. Carolyn talked for almost an hour. Emily, a born listener, quietly pondered what she was hearing. Finally, Carolyn's rendition stopped.

Emily remained silent for a long time. When she did speak, it was softly. "Do you think he loves you?"

Carolyn didn't want to answer the question. "I guess I'd say yes. But how can I trust him? How can I forgive him?"

Emily shook her head. "It may not be easy. I know that for a long time, every time I'd see Harriet Taylor, her nasty words would replay in my head. Every slight or sly comment or ugly thing she'd said about me would come to mind when I'd meet her. Given the size of Alderdale and Harriet's propensity to be out and about the town, I was feeling that way a lot. One day as I passed her, I realized my anger and hurt were hurting me but having no effect on her. She hadn't a clue I was upset with her." Emily paused and winked at Carolyn. "You know Harriet. She thought she'd been doing me favors all those years. I was the one still suffering."

Emily smiled softly. "I decided to do the thing I least wanted to do. I began to invite her to join Nathan and me for Sunday dinner. At first, I thought she'd refuse. You know, have much more important invitations for Sunday dinner. I was wrong. She accepted. She's been coming over to our house every Sunday. You know what I've learned? I think deep down, Harriet's meddling is a way she keeps herself busy. I don't think she is real fond of her own company. I know that since Amelia left, Harriet doesn't feel useful. She is a lonely woman. After I reached out and forgave her, I began to see her in a new light. She's still as meddlesome as can be, but she's kind of sad."

Emily's story reminded Carolyn of her recent visit with Herman Dobbs. Remembering her feelings of compassion for the desperate but highly annoying man, Carolyn said, "I see what you mean, but what does that have to do with Michael?"

Emily thought for a moment. "I guess what I'm trying to say is, if we are focused on our own hurt and pain, sometimes we miss out on what is really there. It wasn't until I forgave Harriet that I could see her pain. It may not be until you forgive Michael that you can see how great his love is for you. I believe there is a reason God asks us to forgive one another. Part of it is for the other person, but I think most of it is for us."

Throughout the day and the remainder of Emily's visit, Carolyn thought about what Emily had said. Slowly she began to recognize the lesson. She had to forgive Michael, but it didn't stop there. She had to forgive Marti's family; she had to forgive Harriet—Queen Matchmaker; and she had to forgive the attorneys who fired her, as well. It wasn't about what any of them had done. It was about her. It was about what her reaction to them was doing to her.

After Emily left, Carolyn knelt down by her bed. She began by thanking her heavenly Father for her many blessings. Then she asked for His help in learning to forgive and move on. When she concluded her prayer, Carolyn found peace. She knew all would be well. Now she needed to tell Michael.

Michael's relief at hearing her voice after more than a week of silence was readily apparent. "Carolyn, I'm so glad you called."

Carolyn swallowed hard. "Well, Michael, I've got to tell you, I'm not real happy about you not being honest with me in the first place.

You should have told me—regardless of what you thought my reaction would be." She paused, then continued. "However, I can understand how I may have made it a bit hard for you to tell me. I made it pretty clear what I thought about attorneys. I'm starting to work through that, though. I just wanted to let you know I forgive you."

Michael's joy leaked through the phone. "Hot dog! I thought I might have lost you. What changed your mind?"

"Your birthday present."

"I don't understand. . . ." Michael's voice echoed confusion.

"Emily. She reminded me what forgiveness was all about. Besides, how long could I stay mad at someone who sent my favorite niece to me on my seventieth birthday? I still can't figure out how you knew about her. I've only mentioned Emily to you once. How did you find her?"

Michael muttered something about trade secrets, then rapidly changed the subject. "Don't suppose you're up for some ice cream and a good walk. I'm in the mood to celebrate."

Carolyn replied, "I'm always up for ice cream, but what are we celebrating?"

Michael's response was soft. "I've just been reunited with the woman I love."

*C*arolyn's lesson in forgiveness did not end with Michael. She wrote a letter in care of the hospital to Marti's brother and sister, apologizing for her interference and expressing her gratitude for the time she'd spent with Marti. She visited the hospital administration. Her appearance, coupled with glowing recommendations from Ruth and the charge nurse, Denise, landed her back as a Community Memorial volunteer. She even signed and sent back the waiver of litigation form the law firm had tried to get her to sign when they issued her severance package. Holding the sealed, addressed envelope, she comforted herself.

"Even if I'd been able to take them to the cleaners, it would have been more years that I would have had to interact with them. At my age, every year counts. Besides, after spending the majority of my life working on lawsuits, why on earth would I want to waste the rest of it doing the same thing?" Her self-motivational speech did the trick. The envelope was deposited in a U.S. mailbox within the hour.

Getting back into the volunteer routine was just what Carolyn's spirit needed. Between her weekly hospital duties and Michael's planned adventures, Carolyn sometimes wondered if she weren't as busy as she had been before "retiring."

Back on the Transitional Care Unit, Carolyn had the chance to meet a lot of seniors preparing to make the journey from the hospital back to their homes. She was able to help those who weren't as lucky to cope with the realization they'd be going to a nursing facility. Carolyn found that given the events of the last year, she was more than capable of understanding the devastation a major life change could bring. Her experience, though far different from the experiences of the seniors she was counseling, proved remarkably helpful in allowing her to relate. She also enjoyed making follow-up visits outside of her volunteer duties to her friends' new assisted-living abodes. Somehow, her frank assurances that they would survive seemed to provide comfort. Perhaps her forthright demeanor made them feel they had no choice but to take her word for it. Whatever the reason, Carolyn Sheffield found a new calling.

Even the nurses recognized her valuable contribution. They began assigning her to all patients who would not be returning to their own homes. In the spare moments Carolyn had left, she was delegated the mind-enriching duty of chart filing. On one of the rare occasions she was filing charts, Carolyn came across a familiar name—Michael Flannigan. Carolyn was confused. Why would Michael have a recent Transitional Care Unit chart? He hadn't said anything. Maybe it was a different Michael Flannigan.

The moral twinges of her conscience couldn't stand a chance against the years of ingrained investigative instinct. As she "accidentally" dropped the chart to the floor, it "fell open." Carolyn couldn't lift her gaze from the pages. Her throat dropped to her stomach. She was no medical genius, but even she knew what the words R/O hepatic CA stood for; the doctors thought Michael had cancer. Liver cancer. Carolyn couldn't even say good-bye to the hospital staff. She picked the chart off the floor, set it on the counter, and left for home.

For a week, Carolyn wrestled with what to do. She diligently avoided answering the phone. The doorbell rang with no response. Memories of Marti flooded back. Carolyn's intense struggle permeated every aspect of her life. She didn't sleep. She couldn't eat. Her infamous postfiring hairdo threatened to make a curtain call. No matter how she played it out in her head, the solution seemed unavoidable. Much as she loved Michael Flannigan, and her restless nights had left no question that she did, she couldn't risk giving her heart to him if he was going to die. She couldn't face the hurt again. Finally resolute, but devastated in her decision, Carolyn made the call.

"Michael?"

His relief was instantly apparent. "Carolyn? Are you okay? I've been so worried. I've called. I've rung your doorbell. No one answered. Even Ruth didn't know where you were. Are you sick? Do you need help? I can't tell you how concerned I've been."

Michael's reaction made what Carolyn had to do even harder. "Michael, I know everything. I know about the cancer. I know you could die. I can't go through another death of someone I love. I lost Marti. Hard as that was, it wouldn't even start to compare with losing you. I'm sorry. I thought I was strong, but I'm not. I don't have a choice. I love you, but our relationship has to end."

Michael's silence spoke volumes. Finally, Carolyn heard his voice.

"I probably know better than anyone else, Carolyn, that when you set your mind to something, you aren't real open to changing it. I can tell you, however, that even though I felt like I'd died inside after I lost Elise, I wouldn't exchange the time I had with her for anything. There are no guarantees in this life, but I love you. Even if you don't want to listen to my pleadings, at least promise me you'll pray about it."

Willing to say anything to be released from the uncomfortable conversation, Carolyn gave her word.

The sad good-bye haunted Carolyn in the lonely autumn weeks that followed. Each twinge of regret was met with an equally strong twinge of relief that she would not risk the full emotional brunt of Michael's death. Despite her attempts to put on a strong front and re-claim her "terminally single and proud of it" mantra, Carolyn couldn't find the old gumption to put behind it.

Now that her days weren't filled with exciting adventure, Carolyn had more time to spend with Ruth. Despite the curiosity that oozed from Ruth's pores, she didn't say one word about Michael. Ruth's matchmaking prowess had its limits, and her silence showed she knew better than to touch her friend's freshly opened wounds. Carolyn found comfort in Ruth's presence. In lifelong friendship there was a constancy that soothed life's roughest spots.

"So how is your work going in the TCU? You still bringing your boot camp bedside manner to those seniors?" Ruth joked one day at lunch.

Carolyn ruefully rolled her eyes. "You know the funny thing? Those of us who have lived this many years seem to have an understanding. Even if we don't speak the same language, or in the same manner, there is something about a caring heart that seems to provide the translation. I think some of the younger folks feel that the only reason the older generation listens to me is because I'm an old battle-axe who won't take any guff. They're wrong. I believe they listen to me because the lines in my face show them my assurances that they will make it through these tough times are based on experience. And in this life there is nothing quite like having someone who has been there to hold your hand."

"Amen to that, sister," Ruth added. "I'll tell you, after my husband, Jim, died, I wouldn't have made it through without my support group. Sometimes one of us would start a sentence about how we were feeling, and the whole group could finish it. We had arrived from all different walks of life, but our one shared experience in losing a spouse provided an instant bond."

Carolyn couldn't help but ask, "Do you still miss him? Like burning, aching in your gut miss him?"

Ruth removed her glasses. "Oh, yes. He's been gone a decade, and I still wake up in the middle of the night and roll over to put my arms around him. A couple of times I've trailed old men around the grocery store believing they might be my Jim. Good thing I don't look more sinister, or I might have a couple of stalking charges around my neck. I miss him terribly. Sometimes so much that I pray I might just feel his presence for another minute. Every time I wish upon a star, I pray for one more day with my husband. I know it will never come true, but I can always hope."

"Would you wish for another day even if you knew you'd lose him and have to face the pain again after it ended?" Carolyn asked.

"You better believe it," Ruth insisted. "See, that's the thing about real love. Even a minute of it makes your life better."

Ruth and Carolyn finished their open-faced sandwiches and said their good-byes. Yet late into the night, Carolyn pondered her friend's words. Was love really that powerful? Was it really worth risking everything? Suddenly she remembered her vow to Michael. She had told him she'd pray about it. So it was a few weeks late—she could still live up to her promise.

She knelt and laid out her concerns to her heavenly Father. When she finished, a verse she had learned long ago in Sunday school, Proverbs 3:5–6, came into her head: "Trust in the LORD with all thine heart; and lean not unto thine own understanding. In all thy ways acknowledge him, and he shall direct thy paths."

Ruth didn't have any minutes left with Jim. Carolyn did have time left with Michael. She wasn't sure how long or what the outcome would be, but she knew however long it was, her life would be better because of it.

This phone call was much easier to make than the one she had made a few weeks earlier. "Michael?"

"Carolyn?" Michael spoke only her name.

"You know I'm not one who readily admits she's wrong. Of course, it's probably because I have to do it so infrequently." Carolyn chuckled in her nervousness.

This time it was Michael who came to the point. "Carolyn, break it to me. 'Forward and Direct,' that's my motto. Or at least it's the motto of a good friend of mine."

Michael's lighthearted reference to the words she so often muttered released Carolyn's voice. "I just realized that each day I don't see you is one less day I have to put you in your place. I don't know how long you'll have; maybe it'll turn out you don't even have cancer. Then again, I don't know how long I'll have. Given my emotional state this last year, I'm beginning to wonder if something is wrong with me, too. I guess I'm trying to say you're stuck with me. That is, if you still want me."

"Still want you?" Michael's voice shook. "Where else would I find someone who can conduct herself as admirably at a good old-fashioned, husband dressing-down? You better believe I still want you."

❧

December 1 brought a layer of snow to Seattle. Carolyn awoke and donned a cream-colored sweater set. It was going to be a cold day. She poured herself a mug of hot chocolate and relaxed back into the familiar grasp of her living-room couch. The sound of sleigh bells brought her to her feet. She moved toward the door to answer the knock. Standing clad in a long gray wool coat and cream scarf, Michael looked as dapper as a magazine advertisement. In the background Carolyn could see a carriage drawn by two horses and complete with driver.

"Get on your coat, my dear. We're going for a ride," Michael invited.

He didn't have to extend the invitation twice. Carolyn pulled on a long red wool coat, a. matching hat, and mittens. She was going on a sleigh ride. When she got in, she gasped. Gerbera daisies lined the carriage.

"How did you know? How did you get them at this time of year?" Carolyn queried.

Michael's response was a bit hesitant. "Well, the answer to the first question is kind of a long story."

"Go ahead," Carolyn urged.

"You see, when I was first going through all the tests to determine if I had cancer, they placed me in the Transitional Care Unit. Bed 122."

"Bed 122? That was right next to Marti. But I never saw you." Carolyn felt perplexed.

"I was pretty sick. And on the other side of the curtain. I didn't see you, either. But I heard you. I didn't put two and two together until you started talking about Marti. I realized the deeply intelligent, sensitive woman I was hearing was the same woman who gave me the biggest what-for I'd ever had coming to me." Michael paused, taking Carolyn's hand. "I wanted to tell you, but when you opened up with me on your own, there didn't seem to be a huge need. After I started spending time with you, I got to see the sensitive woman firsthand. I didn't just hear her through a sheet. I did, however, get a few interesting tidbits of information."

"The gerbera daisy bouquet." Carolyn suddenly remembered. "If you knew how many hours I spent trying to figure out who sent that! And the orange creams from See's. Nobody knew about them. So that's how you found out! The new journal! You must have seen mine in Marti's room. You wanted me to have one." One by one the pieces fell into place. "And *that's* how you knew about Emily. You heard me tell Marti about her."

Carolyn fell into shocked silence.

"All true, my dear." Michael took her other hand and knelt down on the narrow carriage floor. "But it was inadvertent and certainly not purposeful. Besides, didn't you get some great gifts out of it? Gerbera daisies. Orange creams. Emily at Christmas. I promise, no more secrets—but there's one condition."

Carolyn looked at him warily. "I am not fond of conditions."

Michael looked up from his kneeling position. "I think you might like this one. No more secrets, but you have to agree to be my wife."

Carolyn was shocked but recovered quickly. Uncharacteristically planting a kiss on his forehead, she responded, "You got it. But only as long as the See's orange creams and gerbera daisies keep coming."

As Michael smiled, Carolyn silently thanked God she had found "Christmas" in the winter of her life.

Epilogue

Alderdale, Oregon, December 30

*T*he whisper of furtive footsteps, the rustle of clothing, and the heavy scent of perfume accompanied the first guest to enter the evergreen wreathed, white-light-adorned reception hall of the small church in which Carolyn Sheffield had just become Mrs. Michael Flannigan.

Harriet Taylor slowly scanned the beautifully decorated room and smiled with satisfaction. No one could ever say Alderdale didn't care for its own. Although Carolyn Sheffield had left the village almost fifty years earlier, the townsfolk had turned out en masse for her wedding.

A murmur in the hall leading from the chapel replaced caution with haste. Straight to the front of the reception room she strode, the carpet mercifully muffling her steps. Once there, she carefully scrutinized the name cards on the head table. She had not been included among the most favored. Instead, a card bearing her name mocked her from an adjacent table.

Harriet glared at the last two cards at the end of the head table: *Ms. Denise Thornton, Mr. Bob Marin.* "Well!" she exclaimed. "I'll just see about that. As sure as my name is Harriet Taylor, Ms. Denise Thornton, whoever she is, is *not* going to sit at the head table. After all, I'm family."

The laughter and voices in the hall grew louder. In another moment, the wedding party would burst into the room. Harriet set her jaw and grimly snatched the offensive bit of pasteboard with one hand, her own name card with the other. A lightning exchange worthy of one skilled in the fine art of sleight of hand relegated the unknown woman to the place of lesser importance, leaving the last two cards at the end of the table to read *Mr. Bob Marin* and *Mrs. Harriet Taylor.*

With a purr of accomplishment, Harriet fled from the table just before the wedding party entered and planted herself in prime position to be first in the reception line.

❦

Carolyn Sheffield Flannigan glanced at the sleeve of the classic cream silk suit embroidered with pearls that she had chosen for her wedding day. The small pearls glistened, but not as brightly as the two pearls flanking the large diamond on her ring finger. She entwined her fingers with Michael's.

He glanced down at her. "Lovely wedding."

"Yes. It's a good thing. It's the only one I plan to have."

His hearty laugh rang out. "It better be. Besides, a man like me only comes along once every seventy years. You better hold on to me while you have the chance. Now smile and greet our well-wishers."

Carolyn grinned at him. "Look who's first. What a surprise." She gestured toward the tall, spare woman in a dark blue dress, obviously purchased for the occasion, who was sailing toward them full steam ahead, and beaming like a lighthouse. "Harriet Taylor, in person."

"Oh, the lady Bob Marin admires."

Carolyn bit her tongue to hold back a sharp reply. No way would she mar her wedding day with a recitation of all the reasons Bob should *not* admire Harriet.

After greeting Emily and Nathan Hamilton, Harriet reached her target. "Dear Carolyn," she gushed. "I am thrilled for you. I just knew someday you would find love and happiness." She shook the groom's hand as if it were a pump handle. "Mr. Flannigan. I hope you know just how lucky you are to capture our dear Carolyn's heart."

"I certainly do."

Carolyn heard the current of laughter just beneath the surface of Michael's heartfelt reply. She felt her lips twitch. Harriet was Harriet, and perhaps—as Emily had said—the woman's meddling came from loneliness.

Harriet leaned forward. For once in her life, she had the courtesy to lower her voice before saying, "Carolyn, I want to thank you so much for what you did for Herman."

Carolyn stiffened. "Herman? You mean Herman Dobbs?"

"Oh, yes." Harriet rushed on. "Herman took your advice and signed up for a cooking class." She smiled broadly. "It won't surprise me one bit if he finds himself a wife there. He says a couple of very eligible ladies are enrolled." She threw a smile at Bob Marin, who stood beside Michael. "So many weddings. Love is certainly in the Alderdale air; don't you agree, Mr. Marin?"

Carolyn lost Bob's reply in Emily's giggle. "Hush," she ordered her niece, whose face was as crimson, from trying to hold back laughter, as the floor length gown that so became her. "If you get me started, I'll never stop. Oh, Isaiah. Mrs. Gerard. Good to see you. Have you met my friend Ruth Welch?" She nodded toward the white-haired friend in the gorgeous scarlet gown who was vainly attempting to shepherd people through the reception line and to their places at the tables.

"We have," the attorney boomed. "Charming lady. Congratulations, Flannigan."

A tug on Carolyn's arm, followed by a gasp during a slight lull in the greetings, turned the bride's attention back to Emily. "Aunt Carolyn, did you change the cards on the head table? I thought you placed your nurse friend Denise, from the hospital where you volunteer, next to Bob Marin."

"I did. Why—what on earth . . . ?" Carolyn stared at the angular woman taking her place at the end of the table and smiling at Bob Marin as if her dearest wish had been granted. "Harriet at the head table? How? When?"

"Who knows?" A ripple of laughter from Emily subsided, and she said, "Let it go, Aunt Carolyn. In all the years I've known Harriet, I've never seen her look happier."

Carolyn's mounting irritation subsided. "I guess if it means that much to her to sit at the head table next to Bob Marin, it's all right, even if she did perform some hocus-pocus to get there."

She didn't realize Michael had overheard the conversation until he quietly said, "Boy, she is a bit of a manipulator, isn't she? But she does appear to be happy. And Bob is obviously enjoying your friend's company."

Carolyn rolled her eyes at Harriet's typical antics. In another hour or two, she would part company with Harriet. Even two more hours with Harriet Taylor didn't seem too daunting on her wedding day, especially with Michael by her side. In the meantime, a delicious meal catered by a high-end Portland deli awaited them.

❧

If Carolyn believed her wedding would be free from any further Harriet-style shenanigans, she was sorely mistaken.

The tasty meal and good wishes lasted long into the afternoon. All that remained was for Carolyn to throw her bouquet, then begin her new life as Carolyn Sheffield Flannigan. Mrs. Michael Flannigan.

"Throw your bouquet, my dear," Michael urged. "We need to be on our way."

The look of love and quick way he squeezed her hand warmed Carolyn. They stepped out of the church. A light snow the night before had frosted shrubs and trees, but roads and sidewalks soon dried. Now the late afternoon sunlight pouring down on Alderdale turned it into a wonderland as sparkling as the cider with which the wedding toasts had been given.

Carolyn paused on the steps, remembering Emily's wedding and the laughter that swept through the crowd when she caught her niece's bouquet. How inappropriate and unwanted it had seemed at the time. Yet God had known her future—and Michael's. A phrase from the wedding ceremony came to mind . . . *"as long as you both shall live."* She glanced at Michael and silently thanked her heavenly Father.

"Ready?" Michael prodded. "Close your eyes and let 'em fly."

Carolyn smiled and shut her eyes.

"Wait for me," a familiar voice called.

Carolyn's eyes popped back open. Face avid and flushed with exertion, Harriet Taylor pushed through the group of girls and women intent on catching the prize.

Carolyn choked back a laugh and flung the flowers. Up, up, then down they arched. With a triumphant cry, Harriet sharply elbowed aside three smaller women, outreached the others, and snatched the bouquet.

The joy in her face when she cradled the flowers in her bony arms and searched the crowd to find an applauding Bob Marin, actually brought a lump to Carolyn's throat. Filled with her own happiness, she quickly shot a prayer skyward, a prayer that Ms. Harriet Taylor, second cousin thrice removed—or whatever she was—might find some of the happiness God had bestowed on Michael and her.

Carolyn smiled at her husband and stepped into their car. She cast a farewell look at Ruth and Emily, and the radiance in their faces warmed her like a benediction. She raised her arm in farewell, then turned her gaze to the beckoning, ice-touched, tree-lined road. A road she knew from experience held many twists and bends. A road she and Michael would travel together, for as long as God in His wisdom permitted.

A Fairy-Tale Romance

by Melanie Panagiotopoulos

For my daughter, Sara, whose love of New York City inspired this story. Thanks for all your help and encouragement. You are the best!

Prologue

*H*e asked you to go to New York to become a model, Natalia? I don't know about this," said Martha Pappas, Natalia's much older sister.

Hopping up from the chair, Martha grabbed a sponge and began wiping the already immaculate kitchen table. She stopped, though, when their *baba* put out his hand to still her.

"Martha, sit down," he directed, his voice raspy but kind. He looked over the rim of his glasses at Natalia, his youngest child, and the only one of his six children who was adopted. "Tell us everything that happened. From the beginning."

Natalia nodded. Never had she been happier for the equilibrium of her father than at this moment. He was the clergy in the village of Kastro, so everyone referred to him as *Papouli*. But to his six children he was their beloved *baba,* and Natalia felt honored to be his daughter.

She reached for her glass of lemonade, took a sip, then started recounting the events that had brought her back unexpectedly to Kastro for the night. "Yesterday, feeling dissatisfied with the courses I'm following at school—" She paused and grimaced. "That's something else I have to talk to you about, *Baba.*"

"Tell me about the modeling first," he instructed her gently.

She pushed her shoulder-length hair behind her ears. She was glad for his leading. "I decided to go up to the Areopagus, your favorite place in Athens." She referred to the hilltop location where the apostle Paul was purported to have preached to the Athenians in Acts, chapter seventeen. Her father went there whenever he visited the capital. "I was questioning whether I was indeed following the path God had laid out for me when a man came up to me and in a very nice way—and in English—asked if he might speak to me."

"English?" Martha asked, her brown eyes as round as basketballs.

Natalia nodded. "His name is Jasper Howard, and he is the president of Smile Modeling Agency in New York City."

"How can you be sure of this?" Martha asked. Natalia wasn't surprised. Martha had always been protective of her.

"Not only did he give me his business card"—she pointed to it on the table before her father—"but he removed from his wallet his passport, driver's license, and social-security card so I could see for myself that his identification proclaimed him to be Jasper Howard."

"And he wanted to talk to you about becoming a model for his agency?" her father prompted.

Natalia shrugged her shoulders. "That's right."

"What sort of modeling?" her father asked.

"Tasteful, fashionable clothing, nothing I might consider at all compromising."

"I don't know," Martha said again, and Natalia could hear the anxiety in her tone. "I've seen fashion shows on TV. I usually have to change the channel. They are"—she searched for the correct words—"well, you know."

"I know." Natalia reached out to comfort her. Martha was thirty-two years her senior; since their mother had died when Natalia was only ten, Martha was in many ways more a mother to Natalia than a sister. "That's why I told him the only way I could consider such a thing would be for him to come here and meet both of you, along with Allie and Stavros, who are Americans and know how things are done there." She referred to the village doctor and schoolteacher; doing so brought smiles to all three of their faces.

For at that moment they knew Stavros had taken Allie, who loved fairy tales, up to the castle that sat above the village to ask her to marry him. Allie had come to the village about a month ago and had changed the lives of Stavros and his daughter, Jeannie. Natalia, Martha, *Papouli*, and, in fact, the entire village knew that, if it was God's will, a romance was about to come to that deserving couple, and they would live happily ever after.

"But tell us," Martha asked in her quick way, "what did this Jasper Howard say when you asked him to come here to meet us?"

"He agreed to do so," Natalia replied.

"He did?" Her father's eyebrows shot upward. That seemed both to surprise and impress him.

"Yes."

"When?" Martha asked, jumping up from her chair.

Natalia pulled her back down. "Tomorrow. So calm down, Martha."

"Tell me." Her father leaned forward as he always did when he was about to ask something very important. "How would you feel about moving to New York?"

"That's the part about this whole thing that surprises me the most, *Baba*. Not only do I want to go, but somehow I almost feel pulled to the city. It's as if it's the path God wants me to take—the path He has laid out for me."

"You said you aren't happy with your courses at the fine arts school you are attending in Athens?" her father asked.

Natalia held her hands out in front of her, then let them drop onto her lap. Her father had given so much to send her to school in Athens, and she hated to disappoint him, but she knew she had to be honest. "It's not at all what I was expecting, *Baba*. It's too general and too abstract. It's wonderful for people who like that kind of art," she qualified, "but I don't. None of my classes has anything to do with fashion design." Ever since her mother had showed her how to hold a pencil and sew a straight seam, Natalia's hobby had been to draw and design dresses and make them into garments she could wear.

Her father was quiet for a moment, as if he were thinking over the matter. Suddenly he said, "Then perhaps you are meant to go to America at this time. I have always known God would somehow lead you back there."

Natalia had no idea about this. *"Baba?"*

"As you know," he began, "I feel certain that your birth mother was from the United States. That is why I have insisted upon your learning to speak English so well." She knew that at a great expense he had made sure her English was as perfect as it could be. Even Jasper Howard had commented on how fluently she spoke.

"But why do you feel this way, *Baba*? Not even the American embassy would recognize that I might be from America."

"The letter that was pinned to you from your birth mother said you were American. Plus you were dressed in that American-flag suit when *Baba* and *Mamma* found you at the bus station," Martha said. Natalia knew her sister still had the infant sleeper she had worn then; it was carefully wrapped in tissue paper tucked away in her dresser drawer. "And the blanket you were wrapped in was emblazoned with the American flag."

"But that still doesn't prove my nationality is American. Anyone of any nationality could have written that letter or dressed me that way so I would be taken to America."

"True. That was the reasoning at the American embassy," her father admitted. "Plus, not a single American citizen had reported a missing baby." He sat back and settled his palms upon his skinny knees. "I don't know how to tell you why I feel as I do, Natalia. It's just something God has put into my heart." He looked at his daughter over the rim of his glasses. "And in the same way I have always known God would lead you back there someday, somehow, too." He lifted his hands then dropped them upon his knees again. "Maybe it is God's will that you search for your real parents."

"*Baba!*" She was aghast. "You and *Mamma* are my real parents!"

He smiled and patted her hand. "Yes, we are, and you have been such a blessing to us. I know your mother fought her illness and lived as long as she did only because she wanted to raise you—her beautiful and sweet-natured, fair-haired child—for as much time as she could."

"I loved her so much," Natalia whispered as she thought about the loving smiles and gentle voice of her mother. She would always remember her mother whenever the white jasmine flowers bloomed. That was her mother's scent.

"We all loved her," Martha said. "Still do."

"She was a very special woman," their *baba* agreed, and his eyes sparkled brightly with remembered happiness. It was a joyous look, but also the only time Natalia thought her father looked close to eighty years old. Even after eight years he missed his wife dearly.

He took a deep, settling breath. "Your mother was never angry at the woman who left you in the bus station. She always felt, as did I, that there must have been a reason, a good reason. Women do not give up their children without one. Maybe someday you will be led to her."

"That is not the reason why I want to go to America, *Baba*." Natalia wanted to make that clear. "I don't feel one way or the other about her, neither angry nor sad." She shrugged her shoulders. "I'm just glad I'm a part of *this* family."

"A very big part," Martha added quickly.

Natalia smiled over at her. "I don't know why I feel drawn to America—why something jumps in my soul at the idea of going—"

"God's leading, *agapi mou*—my love. God's leading." Her *baba* spoke with the authority of his calling. "Not only do you feel pulled to go, but also the way has been opened for you to go. I never would be able to afford the plane ticket for you, much less the other expenses involved with your living in New York City. If this *Jasper Howard*"—he spoke the unfamiliar name in a heavily accented tone which made Natalia smile—"is indeed the man he says he is, and if he can assure me you will be well taken care of, then I say go."

Six years later, New York City

$\mathcal{N}$oel Sheffield glanced at his watch as he dashed from Seventh Avenue up Thirty-fourth Street on his way over to Fifth Avenue. It was an overcast day, and one might consider it gloomy with dusk falling earlier than usual. But the excitement of Christmas left no room for dreariness in the air. People were smiling and chatting like high school students at pep rallies do.

Noel glanced up at the pine that adorned the windows of Macy's Department Store and took a deep breath. Not only was it beginning to *look* a lot like Christmas, but it was beginning to *smell* like it too. Who would have imagined that midtown Manhattan could smell like a pine forest?

This was Noel's favorite time of the year. Judging from the expressions of people wrapped in brightly colored scarves and with smiles as big as the state of Alaska on their faces, he felt certain he wasn't alone in liking the season.

Christmastime in New York. He took a deep breath of satisfaction as the city he loved danced and pulsated to its own special holiday melody all around him. *What could be better?* he wondered as he stood at the traffic light at Herald Square where Broadway and Sixth intersected Thirty-fourth Street.

He glanced at his watch, and a sobering sigh of annoyance whistled through his teeth.

Of all days to be running late.

He had planned to leave the high school, where he worked as a guidance counselor, earlier today to ensure that he didn't miss his yearly rendezvous. Then a problem with one of his students had arisen. He sighed. Sixteen-year-old Rachel was running in the fast lane and was going to find herself in big trouble if she didn't listen to reason. But Noel knew it would have been easier for him—for anyone—to reason with a mouse than to try to persuade the girl of that fact.

The light changed. As Noel dodged holiday-garbed people coming toward him, he wondered again how he could make the girl understand that her lifestyle would lead only to heartache.

He took his position as counselor to the students at Westwood High School seriously. He felt that if he could catch a problem in a person and solve it at the high school level, it would be one less individual who would need the other profession for which he had trained: criminal lawyer.

But Noel didn't know if he had succeeded this time with Rachel or if he ever would. The girl was in trouble from a lack of good judgment. *Humph,* he thought. *A lack of judgment, period.* She had gotten herself into circumstances that needed much more wisdom than Noel could offer.

He drew in a deep breath.

But he was the girl's only chance. Her parents had paid thousands of dollars to private clinics and therapists in order to help her.

Nothing had worked.

As Noel had seen too often in the fast-paced world in which people lived today, busy lives precluded parents from doing anything personally for their children. That was the challenge of the whole situation. Most kids longed for their parents—at least one of them—to be around. After two years of counseling problem kids, Noel had decided they wanted quantity time with some of the overlauded quality time.

But it was what so few received.

To have their mom or dad in another part of the house with them—to be there for the two or three minutes they wanted to ask a question or be with the person who had made the commitment to raise them—meant a lot to children.

Noel had to give Rachel his best shot. Since she seemed to listen to him more than to anyone else, her parents had begged him to do whatever he could. He didn't want to let them down.

As he neared the famous shopping street, Fifth Avenue, the throngs of people were growing thicker and thicker. Even though Noel normally didn't mind rush-hour crowds—he found it exhilarating to be among so many people all in one spot at one moment and somewhere entirely different the next—it annoyed him today. He might miss the young woman with the dog.

The Rockefeller Center tree had been delivered during the previous night. Noel had seen it leave on the first part of its journey from his parents' home in New Jersey. He now had a tryst to keep with the tree *and* the woman.

For the past three years she had come to the center with her dog—a gorgeous German shepherd—at dusk on the day the tree was delivered. She always sat on the same bench in the Channel Garden and gazed up at the tree with a look of both yearning and joy. She had captured Noel's attention the first time he'd seen her. Noel knew she came to visit the tree on this day because he had done so ever since he was a little boy. His father used to bring him and tell him how *their* tree would one day stand at that "blessed spot."

Noel didn't know the woman and had never talked to her. He hoped to change that today. As he picked up his pace, his trench coat flapped out behind him like a flag.

He would speak to her this time in honor of *his* tree—the one he had grown up with—finally being the one to stand at the center, to grace the city of New York.

New York.

He glanced up at the decorated lamppost and flashed a smile at the red bow and Christmas flowers suspended from it. This city was the greatest place on earth, to Noel's way of thinking.

Especially at Christmas.

❧

"City sidewalks, busy sidewalks, dressed in holiday style. In the air there's a feeling of Christmas!" Natalia sang the refrain from one of her favorite holiday melodies softly as she walked with joyous steps down Fifth Avenue. Her four-and-a-half-year-old German shepherd,

Prince, clipped by her side in perfect canine posture. With a plaid ribbon and bow of green and red tied around his neck, he was as well tailored in the Christmas way as the city of New York itself.

This was Natalia's favorite time of the year in the city. The hustle and bustle, the songs filling the atmosphere, the decorations, but mostly the way people seemed to smile at one another a little more as they passed each other brought warmth to her heart.

But as an arctic wind whipped around the corner of Central Park South and Fifth and caught her under her jaw, she gave a slight shiver and snuggled deeper into her down-filled ski parka.

"It's cold, Prince," she said.

He hunched his shoulders forward, looked up at her, and sent her his friendly, if lopsided, doggie grin.

Natalia laughed and wondered how anybody could be frightened of him. But people were, and she realized they had a right to be.

Prince would do anything for her, anything to protect her. He was as docile as a lamb—unless someone looked at her the wrong way. She smiled. She knew that fact made her *baba* and her sister Martha happy. Her *baba* might be a man of faith and trust God to look out for his youngest child in far-off New York, but he certainly didn't mind letting one of God's creatures help with the job.

She and Prince had returned the previous day from visiting her family in Kastro, Greece. As was her custom whenever she flew home, she had spent two glorious weeks there. She had moved away from the village six years ago, but not too much had changed, which of course was one of its main charms. Allie and Stavros, the village doctor and schoolteacher, had just added another child to their brood, making little Jeannie Andreas, who wasn't so little anymore, a very happy big sister. Jeannie loved her two brothers and her new baby sister to distraction. A smile curved Natalia's lips as she thought about Jeannie. The girl loved her stepmother, Allie, as dearly as any child could ever love a natural parent.

But that thought stole the rosiness the cold city day had put into Natalia's fair cheeks. Her *baba* had surprised her—shocked her even—on this trip home by almost insisting she search for her *own* natural mother. He hadn't said too much about it in the six years since she had left Kastro. But this time he had told her all that was in his heart; he felt that God wanted her to look for her biological mother or at least be open to finding her or to the possibility of her mother discovering her. The time was right, he said.

Natalia wasn't so sure.

She had done some research about people looking for biological parents; contrary to the stance of sentimentalists, it wasn't always so wonderful. Sometimes people didn't want to be found. Plus Natalia now had the added disadvantage of being what she called herself—a "genetic" celebrity. Because of the genes she had inherited from her unknown biological parents and the career she had chosen, her face was quite well known, at least in magazine layouts and on billboards.

Most models looked different in person than they did in magazines. Natalia was glad she was one of them. Further, she rarely wore makeup while going about the city, thus adding to her disguise. And one of the reasons she loved walking with Prince was because he was a good distraction. Most people looked at him more than they did her.

She smiled down at the dog.

Prince kept the tabloid photographers at bay too. They could snap pictures of other interesting people in New York, who didn't have a large dog with a mouth full of sharp teeth, rather than bother with her.

Jasper Howard had done more than make Natalia into a model. He had turned her into a modeling star. Not only was she famous in certain circles, but she had also made more money than she ever knew existed! And she gave large percentages of it away, something that made her feel happy. Her father had often preached that God required good stewardship of those He'd blessed materially. As Jesus taught in the parable of the talents, the more she gave, that much more she seemed to receive.

She wouldn't mind giving to her biological family should they be in need—she would be happy to do so. But she thought that she had to be careful because of the mystique behind being a model. Had her natural mother put her up for adoption it would have been different. But the woman had deserted her: She had left her in a bus station in a foreign land. If the woman had left her in an orphanage, at least Natalia would not have felt as uneasy about looking for her. But to be left in a bus station? What sort of woman did that?

"The desperate kind," a voice seemed to answer her. *"A woman desperate in a way you have never had to experience—because of her actions."*

Natalia sighed.

She didn't know what to do. The truth was, her birth mother might have deserted her, but no one could have asked for a better set of parents than the ones who had loved her for much longer than she could remember. Her adoptive mother died when Natalia was only ten, but that didn't take away the joy she had in being that lovely woman's daughter.

The sound of a Volunteer of America Santa ringing his Christmas bell drew her attention. He was a joyous figure in red splashed against the backdrop of the city. Natalia reached into her pocket for some bills.

"Merry Christmas!" she said as she dropped them into the bucket.

"Ho, ho, ho," he sang out and rang his bell loudly. "Merry Christmas to you too, young lady. And many thanks."

Nodding to him she walked on, a warm feeling of hope and good cheer washing over her. She looked up at the green lamppost above her. Its artful arrangement of bows and poinsettias made her smile widen.

She loved New York.

Loved it passionately.

She wouldn't want to live anywhere else.

But she knew that having the means to live in a nice area of the city meant she had a responsibility to give back the blessings.

That thought inevitably returned her to her father's views on searching for her biological mother. His opinion was too wise to ignore. She breathed a prayer into her plaid, cashmere scarf, adding to the many she had said while flying the previous day across the Atlantic. "Dear Lord, Your will be done in this matter, please. If You want my natural mother and me to find one another, so be it." She paused and smiled as a professional dog walker handling seven dogs passed her. "But if my natural mother could now be a Christian, that would really help." With that, she let go of the thoughts that had been plaguing her about her biological parentage. She wanted only to enjoy this very special moment of being back in New York City.

Natalia was heading for the tree at Rockefeller Center. She'd heard from her doorman, Roswell Lincoln, that it had been delivered during the night. It had become her personal tradition to see the tree before it was decorated. She loved the trees when five miles' worth of lights graced their branches, but there was something special about seeing them in their almost-natural state.

The Walk sign flashed on in yellow letters. She tightened her grip on Prince's lead, then motioned the dog forward and crossed the intersection. Glancing to her right, past the horse-drawn carriages and the Pulitzer Fountain ringed with twinkle lights, she saw the towers of the Plaza Hotel.

Natalia smiled as she remembered the first time she had walked into that building, which was styled after a French château. It hadn't been dressed and waiting for the arrival of Christmas as it was now, sparkling in holiday adornment, with lights aglow along its towers and bunting festively arrayed across its entrance awning. But it had still seemed like something out of a storybook to her. Jasper Howard had rented a suite of rooms for her there upon her arrival from Kastro.

She'd felt like a little girl who had just entered a fairyland castle. But it wasn't a fortress-type castle like the one of thick stones and buttressed walls she had played upon in Kastro; rather it was like a palace where kings and queens might live in splendor. With all that velvet and mahogany, crystal and gold, it was opulent and exquisite with rich detailing and an elegance that Natalia had never experienced before. She was thankful Jasper's wife, Janet, had come to meet her there. Taking one look at Natalia's tired and flabbergasted face, she had understood that the Plaza was not the place for a young woman fresh from a Greek mountain village to be staying in on her own.

Janet had immediately invited Natalia into their spacious apartment, where she had stayed like a beloved daughter for nearly a year. Natalia now had her own apartment in the same building on the Upper East Side and was still very close to Janet and Jasper. They were her mentors, her friends, but, most of all, her sister and brother in the Lord. They had wanted her to stay with them longer, but when the three-bedroom apartment came up for sale she knew it was time for her to move.

She loved her apartment. Although it was bigger than what she needed, it was the one area in her life where she had splurged and felt no guilt in doing so. Because of it, her numerous brothers and sisters—but mostly Martha, the sister she was closest to—and her father had often come to visit her. It never failed to amaze her father that he could look out the window and see a good portion of the trees that filled Central Park. He took daily walks in the park whenever he came. On her most recent trip home, Natalia was pleased to see that, at eighty-five years of age, he hadn't changed at all in the six months since she had last seen him. She felt certain the final verse in Psalm 91, "'With long life will I satisfy him and show him my salvation,'" applied to her dear *baba*. Even though he was semiretired, he was still the village clergy, still as strong as he had been ten years earlier, and still helping others, both physically and spiritually.

Prince looked up at her as he came to a stop at the corner of Fifth and Fifty-eighth. She reached down, adjusted his collar, and rubbed his neck beneath it.

"Good boy," she whispered to him and smiled. Prince was trained never to cross a street without first stopping to check for traffic. She gave the command for them to continue and looked up at the sophisticated decorations at Bergdorf Goodman. Holiday wreaths adorned every window of the building.

But it was the giant snowflake suspended high over Fifth and Fifty-seventh she was searching for now. She gave a light laugh when she saw it lit resplendently above the avenue, then spoke to her dog.

"I love snow, but I'm sure glad snowflakes aren't really that big." She patted the dog's thick woolly fur. "Even you would have a problem walking through the amount of snow such flakes would produce, dear Prince."

Crossing over Fifty-seventh Street, she pushed up her sleeve and glanced at her watch. It read 4:25. She increased her pace. If she didn't hurry, she wouldn't make it to Rockefeller Center until too late. It had been her tradition the last few years to see the newly arrived tree as day faded into night.

But even more important she wanted to get there in time to see the handsome man who had filled so many of her romantic thoughts during the last three years.

Because of her work and studies, but mainly because she hadn't met anyone she wanted to know better, Natalia had shied away from dating during the years she had been in New York. But something about that unknown stranger tugged at her.

She had first seen him three years ago.

He was tall and dark, with a ruggedly handsome appearance, and she had noticed him standing by the corner of the South Promenade that first year gazing at the tree with a sort of longing and thoughtfulness, which had touched her heart. The strangest thing, though she would never admit it to another living soul, was that he looked like the man she had dreamed about ever since she was a little girl, the man she knew God would someday bring into her life and with whom she would spend the rest of her life. It wasn't that he was so handsome—those kind of men could be found anywhere—rather, it was an illusive *something* that drew her to him.

She had found herself thinking about who he might be, what he did, and what he believed at strange times throughout the years. She supposed it was because she didn't want to date, and thoughts about him were safe.

But when she saw him again last year, not only on this day but also at the Macy's Thanksgiving Day parade and again at the Lincoln Center's annual performance of the *Nutcracker* ballet, she had thought she'd conjured him up. New York was a large city, and it was rare to meet the same people at various locations.

But with all the longing of a woman who loved fairy tales, she hoped she might see him again today. He could easily be her "Prince Charming."

She shook her head at the silly notion and, reaching down, rubbed her fingers across the velvety softness of her dog's ears. "You're my only Prince, aren't you, Boy?"

The dog looked up at her with that look in his eyes he sometimes got that made her think he understood her perfectly. Giving a little laugh, she said, "Never mind," and turned back to the avenue upon which they walked.

Even though it was barely mid-November the sounds of Christmas filled the air—bells, music, laughter. Some people said it was too early, too commercial. Natalia didn't agree.

Maybe it was commercial, and perhaps many people didn't allot enough time to think about the true meaning of Christmas. But Natalia saw it all as being in honor of the Babe who had been born so long ago. *Well, maybe not all,* she conceded as a street vendor called out to everyone to buy his "cheap, barking, 'dog' toy." But the Babe born in Bethlehem was the original idea behind the celebration of Christmas. Natalia felt that the so-called Christmas feeling or spirit so many people loved at this time drew many to look again at the birth of Jesus.

Maybe some of the people she passed on the busy street with their holiday bags and Christmas colors adorning them didn't have any insight into the "mystery that has been kept hidden for ages and generations," until Christ's arrival. But perhaps the celebration of Christmas appealed to so many because something stirred within them at this time, something that made each person somehow know a mystery had been made known to mankind upon Christ's birth. She wasn't sure, of course. But that's what she thought.

She looked around her as her steps carried her farther down the world-famous shopping avenue. It was festooned with red and green and lit in a Christmassy way. As she crossed one street after another she remembered how her father had taught her that Christmas, from the beginning of its observance in A.D. 354, was more for nonbelievers to draw close to Christ than for believers. With so many Christmas scenes all around her, she believed it was probably still so.

The Gothic spires of the cathedral on the next block down and across the street caught Natalia's gaze. As a structure built to honor the Prince of Peace, it was superb. When its construction was first considered back in the mid-1800s, no one could imagine how the city of New York would grow up around it. Until skyscrapers appeared in the 1930s, she had read that the 330-foot spires of St. Patrick's Cathedral had towered above the city and had been part of its skyline even then.

It was counted as one of the largest cathedrals in the world, and, throughout the last six years, Natalia had often found solace and peace within its welcoming walls. People representing the entire world might be passing by its huge bronze doors, but the peace and tranquillity she found in that Gothic structure made it one of her favorite places in the city. It didn't matter to her that it wasn't a church of her persuasion. What counted was who was honored and loved there: Jesus, God's Son.

She glanced up at the sky.

It was dusk now. *Perfect for seeing the tree,* she thought.

She walked onto the North Promenade and gasped.

It was like a fairy world.

In the dusky mistiness of the late autumn evening, the horn-blowing ensemble of wire-sculpted angels was aglow, reminiscent of those actual angels that had heralded the birth of Christ so long ago. The stars that twinkled around them made them seem as if they were part of the heavenly host.

And the tree . . .

Natalia stood in awe of the Norway spruce. It was bigger and fuller than any she had seen before. Framed by the seventy stories of the General Electric Building behind it, the ice rink and Channel Garden before it, the tree stood, majestic and beautiful, a monument to the wonder of God's work on the third day of creation.

She repeated softly the words in Genesis as she gazed at the tree's regal beauty: " 'Then God said, "Let the land produce vegetation: seed-bearing plants and trees on the land that bear fruit with seed in it, according to their various kind." ' "

In this city of concrete and steel, the tree was like an oasis, a small selection of nature that God, the bestower of everything good and wonderful, gives life to and shares with His creation on earth. The workmen who had built the center back in the early 1930s during the depression had brought the first Christmas tree here, starting a yearly tradition. Meant to gladden their spirits, as well as the spirits of all those who passed by and saw it, similar trees had done so for more than six decades.

Natalia inhaled a deep breath of air. The tree's limbs still held their natural clean fragrance. This was another reason she looked forward to seeing the tree upon its arrival. By tomorrow it would no longer smell so much like the country. Having grown up in the mountains of Greece, Natalia almost craved the fresh aroma.

She walked over to one of the benches situated beneath an angel and sat down.

She knew that once the tree was lit she wouldn't find a place to sit at this time of day. That was another reason she always came now. And she wanted to watch the faces of the people as they rushed along Fifth Avenue and see the childlike brightening that filled their faces when they spied the tree in its place.

A lovely representative of the Tree of Life and the redemptive work of Jesus Christ, the Christmas tree in its celebrated place would catch most by surprise. Young and old, rich and poor, people from all over the world would pause for a moment on their journey through life that day and look up at the tree. Without fail, a dreamy sort of smile would soften the lines of their faces, as if the sight of it would, for a moment, cause them to forget their worries and cares.

The tree proclaimed the arrival of the Christmas season in New York City. Christ's incarnate birth, which enabled all who believed to become children of God through adoption, would soon be celebrated once more.

And that made Christmas-loving Natalia very happy.

She scanned the Channel Garden. The only thing that would make her woman's heart happier would be to see the prince of her romantic daydreams.

$$2$$

oel turned the corner of the South Promenade next to the French Building. Before he even looked up at the tree, he searched for the woman he had hoped to see again this year.

He immediately spied her sitting on a bench opposite the fountains, looking like an angel in a forest of celestial beings. He skidded to a halt.

Her head was uncovered, and her hair, as golden as the radiant beings that surrounded her, glowed luminously in the cozy duskiness. She was gazing upward toward the ninety-foot tree, but to Noel it was as if she were looking at much more than the tree he had played upon and beneath as a child. The tilt of her profile made her seem as though she were trying to see into her future, contemplating what it might hold. He wished it to be one full of sunshine and beauty—and him.

Usually he would pause for a few minutes, wondering if the next year his tree would finally stand in this special place, and send covert glances in the girl's direction.

But this year everything was different.

This year *his* tree—one of the most beautiful, most symmetrical, and most cherished trees in the world—was in the place it had been marked to grace since Noel's grandfather had witnessed the first tree placed in Rockefeller Center in 1931. When six of the ten Norway spruces planted at the same time as this one had succumbed to last winter's severity, his parents decided to let this year be its turn at the center. The official gardener of the Rockefeller Center, who had kept his professional eye on the tree during the last twenty years, agreed it was the right decision. It was very old and might not make it through another hard New England winter.

And because of his tree Noel wasn't going to wonder about the girl any longer; he was going to go over and talk to her.

With long strides he let his feet carry him the short distance to the North Promenade.

The dog was the first to notice him. He turned his noble head with his finely chiseled jaw in Noel's direction. Noel casually looked into the dog's eyes. From growing up with German shepherds he sensed this one had to have been well treated and was probably one of the more gentle—unless his mistress had a need. Noel knew he didn't need to fear him. Seeming to come to the same decision about him, the dog's long, feathery tail started to brush softly against the ground, and Noel was glad to be recognized as a friend. Feeling the dog's movement, the girl turned.

She looked up at Noel.

Their gazes met.

Her blue eyes blinked.

His blue eyes blinked back.

Vitality and excitement seemed to flow through every line of her. He had thought she was beautiful when glancing at her from a distance. But from only about eight feet away and looking directly at her, with her soul seeming to shine through her eyes, she carried Noel's breath away on a cloud of enchanting white.

Golden and light, blue and bright, she fit in perfectly with the twelve sculpted Clarebout angels that surrounded her. If he didn't know better, he would say she was one too, of the highest order. He hoped she wasn't, though. He didn't want to fall in love with an angel.

He wanted to fall in love with a woman.

With this woman.

And as superficial as it might sound, even to him, he knew he was already in love with her, or at least he was the closest he had ever been to that elusive emotion. Something about her, something almost familiar in her eyes—a certain light—made him love her when their gazes came together in an embrace of mutual interest. At that moment their souls seemed to merge and sing like a celestial host proclaiming something wonderful and right. Noel felt an explosion within his head as bright with lights as his tree would soon be, and even more he felt as if he were the happy prince in a wonderful fairy tale.

As strange as it might sound for a healthy, red-blooded American male to admit, Noel loved fairy tales now as much as he did when he was a little boy, especially those in which the guy and the girl lived happily ever after. He only hoped he might soon be living one with this remarkably beautiful girl who caught his interest and wouldn't let go. Her beauty encompassed much more than the fine placement of her features upon the planes of her face; rather, it reached out and touched the core of him.

❧

When Natalia looked up and saw the man she had wondered about during the last few years before her, she blinked, thinking her recent thoughts about him had conjured him up.

His eyes were blue, something that surprised her. With such dark hair she had expected brown. But she wasn't disappointed. Who could be? They were the warm and restful blue of the Grecian sky in summertime. Besides, she didn't think that anything about him could disappoint her at this moment. His appearance was everything she could ever want in a man. A part of her almost didn't want to know him any further; he was perfect now.

As he nodded his head toward Prince, she knew he was going to speak. She braced herself for what he might say, for what might come out and shatter the illusion she'd built. She hoped he wouldn't say anything that might turn her prince into a toad.

❧

Noel, indifferent to the impression he created, pointed to the dog and said, "He's a magnificent beast."

Her head dipped slightly in response. Scratching behind her dog's ears, she said, "I'm glad you like him."

"What's his name?"

She smiled up at him, an almost self-conscious sort of smile. "Promise not to laugh."

His mouth quirked in a humorous line. She sounded like one of his students admitting to an embarrassing occurrence. "I promise."

"Prince Charming."

In light of his thoughts a moment earlier, Noel wouldn't have laughed even if she hadn't asked him not to. "I like it."

"Really?"

"I guess you must like fairy tales then."

"I grew up on them. Love them," she admitted quickly. "Romantic movies too."

"Is that why you come here to see the tree year after year on the day it arrives? Because it brings a little fairy-tale wonder to New York?" He could tell his observation had startled her from the way her eyes widened.

He felt bad for being so blunt. But now that he had finally talked to her, he wasn't going to play games. She didn't know him any more than she knew the millions of people walking the streets of New York, and she might think it strange if, after even a few minutes of talking, he told her he'd seen her before. He didn't want her to think he'd been stalking her.

After a short moment her pale brows lifted. Nodding in the direction of where he usually stood leaning against the French Building, she returned, "Is it why you come too?"

Now it was his turn to be taken aback. His mouth narrowed. He hadn't expected that. But the fact she admitted to it told him something about her character. She was honest. Not a game player.

He liked that—a lot.

Most of the women he had met during the last few years played the male-female game. That was the reason he hadn't formed a lasting relationship, even though it was something he desired.

"I love the holiday season," he answered. He was glad for his training that enabled him to think about several things while answering something entirely different. "Perhaps because the city does take on a fairy-tale type appearance during the Christmas season."

"I agree. Except I like to think of it as a God tale," she said.

Her description of the Christmas season stunned Noel. His parents often compared the season to being a God tale rather than a fairy tale. He had never heard anybody else describe it like that. It unnerved him.

"Christ's birth is proclaimed around the city, around the world," she continued, oblivious to the sensation her words brought to him, "in its decorations, lights, and pageantry. It's really nice."

Noel knew then why she had seemed familiar to him. The bright, open look in her eyes, one of wholesomeness, forthrightness, and an otherworldly sort of wisdom, was similar to what he often saw in his parents' eyes. She had to be a Christian as they were, making Christ the center of their lives. It had always bothered Noel a bit concerning his parents—he had a thing about fanatics of any kind—but he didn't mind the trait in this girl at all.

In fact, somehow, it made her seem even better to him.

Because of his parents he had a good idea what sort of character she would have and, as important, wouldn't have.

It was as if he held a secret knowledge about her.

He liked that.

He had rejected his parents' all-encompassing religious lifestyle, but he found he could accept it in her.

This was quite an ironic revelation for Noel.

❧

Natalia stopped speaking.

Sometime in their conversation she had lost him. She wondered if it was her description of the Christmas season in New York City being a God tale rather than a fairy tale. She felt sad to think this might prove a stumbling block to their getting to know each other better, but she didn't regret saying it. It broke her heart to see the beauty of the true story behind Christmas turned into a multitude of fairy tales. Loving fairy tales as she did, she believed they definitely had their place. Didn't she hope for her own Prince Charming someday? But he would have to know God personally and would have to believe that

Truth came into the world the day God came to earth as a human baby.

"I'm sorry," he said. Natalia noticed his strong, square-cut chin lift a fraction of an inch. "My parents have always described this season that way."

She felt her pulse pick up its rhythm. Could this man she had thought about so often during the last few years be a believer? Motioning to the bench, she did something she had never done before. "Would you like to sit down?" Her sister's teaching on safety in the big city had been deeply ingrained in her, and she had always been careful about strangers.

"Thanks," he said, lowering his tall frame with an easy grace onto the bench. She wasn't surprised when Prince stood, instinctively putting himself between her and the man.

"Hey, Prince Charming." The man slowly extended the back of his hand for the dog to sniff. "You're a handsome fellow."

The dog stood in perfect German-shepherd pose, with his hind legs stretched back, his chest out, and his head held high. Natalia laughed. "Careful—he's already too vain."

The man turned his head to get a good look at the dog's lines. "He must come from championship stock."

"Sit, Prince," she commanded the dog, who promptly obeyed. "Yes, his grandfather was the world champion a few years ago." She leaned down and nuzzled her nose against the velvety smoothness of her dog's ears. "But I don't show him. He was a gift and is champion enough for me without the ribbons. You know about German shepherds?"

"I grew up with them," he returned. "My parents still have two. Ten-year-old Laddie and his son, Harry."

Yes, we have a love of dogs in common, she thought. That was nice, especially if . . . they should get to know one another better. "I hope you don't mind my asking, but are your parents Christians?"

A smile tugged at the corners of his mouth. "I don't think anybody could be any more so."

She laughed, a merry musical sound that expressed how happy his response made her. "Well, I doubt they feel that way. Being a Christian is a work in progress. I don't think any Christian feels he or she is living the Christian life perfectly." She laughed again. "No one is perfect except Christ."

"I think they would agree with you."

"And you?" Her gaze narrowed. She wanted to know.

He took another deep breath. "I'm not sure. I guess I haven't wanted to give my parents' beliefs a chance because"—he flashed that endearing grin again, but with a touch of remorse to it—"it's what *they* believe."

She'd heard of that before. Janet and Jasper had had a similar experience with their oldest son—a man now in his forties—until he met a special woman of faith. Natalia decided it was better not to comment.

His response wasn't what she had hoped it would be, nor was it entirely negative. He might be open to learning *if,* like Janet and Jasper's oldest son, he had someone other than his parents to show him the way.

"So, tell me, do you believe in fairy tales?" he asked, obviously redirecting the conversation back to their original discussion.

"Sure, I do. I've seen them come true often enough."

Noel turned his head to the side. "You mean with real princes and princesses?"

"No. Between a doctor and a schoolteacher. Between the president of a modeling agency and a museum director. And, well, between my own father and mother." She shrugged her shoulders. "Simple people like that."

He chuckled. "I don't think there's anything simple about being a doctor or a schoolteacher or any of those things. And for a child to think of her parents' marriage as a fairy-tale romance must mean you have remarkable parents."

"Very."

"I do too," he quickly returned and smiled at her. She smiled back. It was as if he knew what a gift his parents had given him, as her parents had given her: a family unit in which a child could find that special place of peace and security and love.

In this age of divorce and light romantic flings, his words made Natalia's heart sing. They had something basic and important in common: parents who loved one another and who loved God. She nodded her head, but as the star on the top of the tree flicked on—the tree's only light—and caught the corner of her eye, she exclaimed, "Oh, look! Isn't it beautiful?"

❧

Noel turned his gaze toward the tree.

Seeing his tree at this famous plaza and finally meeting the young woman made him happy in a way he hadn't been since he was a child on Christmas morning and beheld the gifts under the tree for him. With her profile silhouetted before the Rockefeller tree he whispered out, "Beautiful."

Both the girl and the conifer were.

And no matter what the future might hold for them, this moment would be one of his most cherished memories.

"This night is almost more thrilling than the tree-lighting ceremony. We are mostly alone"—she waved her arm toward the heralding angels and laughed—"except for our heavenly host, of course, and we have the expectation of the coming holiday season before us."

"I like this time of the year more than any other," Noel admitted. He didn't know why, but the lights and happy music, the ringing bells and merry decorations, seemed to make something within him jump to life.

"I think hearts are more open to God's truth at this time of the year than at any other. Maybe"—she looked shyly toward him—"that's what you feel." She motioned toward the people rushing along the avenue in buses, taxis, and cars; on roller blades, scooters, and feet. "Perhaps everyone does."

"The spirit of Christmas," Noel whispered, thinking that explained what she described.

She looked at him in a sort of contemplative way, as if she wasn't sure she should speak her thoughts.

"Tell me," he prompted.

Her smile widened. "Are you sure? I have quite strong opinions about things, and once I get started—"

"I'd like to hear them," he interrupted. He wanted to know everything she thought, everything she believed. He'd like to spend a lifetime learning.

Amusement glinted in her eyes. "Okay," she said and twisted a strand of golden hair behind her ear. "Well, did you know that 'the spirit of Christmas' is actually an expression from the Middle Ages that describes a jovial medieval figure?"

"Really? I had no idea. If I had thought about it, I would have said it came from the pen of Charles Dickens."

"I know. But it was around long before he was. And there is a big difference between the 'spirit of Christmas' and that of God's Spirit touching people's hearts in a personal way. God is real. Not an invention of man."

His parents might have said the same thing to him in the past, but he hadn't paid attention. He found himself wanting to pay attention to this golden-haired woman with perfect features. "Go on." He motioned for her to continue. He liked watching her lips curve as she spoke.

"Are you sure? As I said, I have a lot of thoughts about these things." She laughed, a light tinkling sound that reminded Noel of fine crystal touched by the wind.

"I want to hear what you believe." He really did. She was a thinker. He was glad she was so much more than a pretty face. It didn't surprise him.

"Well, I think God's Holy Spirit can more easily touch the hearts of people now. Christmas makes people wonder a little more than they normally do about God coming to earth as a little baby." She pointed behind them to the statues of the heralding angels.

Could that be the reason I love Christmas so much? Noel wondered. It was an interesting thought, but he doubted that was it. To believe in the message of Christmas, a person had to believe God did, in fact, come to earth as a baby. He wasn't so sure about that. It seemed like a nice fairy tale. But that was all. He believed in God and thought Jesus had been a remarkable man.

But God born as a human baby?

He wasn't going to tell this young woman that now, though. It wasn't the time or the place. And more than anything he wanted to meet her again, and he doubted—

His thoughts ground to a halt as she reached for her dog's lead and stood. "You're going?" he asked.

Nodding, she motioned for Prince to take his correct place beside her left heel. She glanced at her watch. "I have to."

He jumped up. "Wait—I mean—" He looked down. The dog watched him carefully, without his tail wagging. Noel knew German shepherds well enough to know he'd stood too suddenly for the dog's liking. "I'd like to see you again."

The girl reached down and patted the dog between his ears, assuring him all was well. She flashed her bright and lovely smile. "I have a feeling we'll meet again next year right here."

"I'd like to see you before then." *And learn what you think about and believe,* he wanted to say. Instead he watched as her gaze roamed over his face; something in the way she looked at him told him she wanted to see him sooner too.

"I'll be at the Macy's Thanksgiving Day parade," she offered.

He grimaced. "You and several million others."

She smiled at the truth of that statement. "Well, I'll be at Herald Square." She went a step further and offered him her exact location before she looked up at the tree one more time. "It was special to talk to you finally." He wondered if she could hear his heart pound louder at her admission.

"Kind of like a fairy tale," he said.

She flashed him a high-wattage smile of agreement and, giving a command to Prince, turned and walked through the Channel Garden, around the corner, and out of sight. It was only as he watched the dog's feathery tale disappear around the edge of the building that Noel realized he hadn't asked her for her name.

He banged the heel of his hand against his forehead and laughed. There had to be poetic irony in that. The study of names was one of his favorite hobbies, and he'd even written a book titled *What's in a Name?* It had recently made the *New York Times* best-seller list. He turned and walked in the direction of his tree. For a few days more she would have to be the girl with the dog who visited the tree on the day of its arrival.

But that didn't matter. He had something more important than her name; he had a glimpse of the soul her beautiful exterior housed. And he was beginning to think it was more attractive than her appearance—he glanced in the direction she had walked—if that were possible.

He doubted that Cinderella or Sleeping Beauty could have had souls any nicer than his very own fairy-tale princess.

Princess, he mused, gazing at his tree. He wondered if her name might be Sara. It meant 'Princess.'

"Could very well be," he muttered to himself. He felt better than he had in a long time. He could almost break into Gene Kelly's rendition of "Singin' in the Rain" and click his heels at any moment. He bowed to a family of tourists who looked at him as if he were the perfect specimen of one of those "crazy" New Yorkers they had heard about, one who walked along the streets talking to himself.

But Noel knew he *was* crazy.

Crazy in love with a woman he had only talked to once, a woman he would meet at Herald Square in a little over a week.

Noel did click his heels.

And the tourists practically ran away from him.

3

*L*ess than a week later he turned from a side street onto Fifth Avenue and saw her. She was standing in line with Prince to see the Christmas windows unveiled at a famous department store. Noel felt as if he were living a fairy tale.

What were the chances of their running into one another like this in New York City? Slim to none, he knew. Noel didn't believe in chance or destiny or that New Age mumbo jumbo. Enough of what his parents believed had rubbed off on him to trust that God had a hand in directing the steps of people. Noel liked the way his steps had been pointed this day.

The woman who had occupied much of his thoughts was standing not far from the end of the line. He walked up to her. As at the Rockefeller Center, the dog noticed him first. Noel was glad to see her canine friend did his job so well.

"Hi, Prince," he greeted the dog, putting his hand out for him to sniff it. The woman turned to him. Pleasure covered the smooth lines of her face. He was glad to see it. He knew his own face had to be wearing the same emotion.

"Hi!" she exclaimed. Noel felt as if the joy of the season were expressed in the brightness of her gaze. "This is a nice surprise!"

"Nice surprise." Something jumped inside Noel at her words. "I couldn't agree more."

"What are you doing here?" she asked as if he were an old friend and not a person whose name she didn't know.

He motioned to his camera, then toward the decorated windows before them. "I understand each one resembles a Victorian-dollhouse set this year. My mother loves dollhouses and collects and makes them, so I wanted to take some shots for her."

The girl's mouth dropped open as she touched her chest. "I collect dollhouses too! That's why I've come today, even though"—she hiked up the sleeve of her coat to check her watch—"I don't have the time."

He wondered what she did to make her so pressed, but he only said, "I'll have to get you together with my mother. She has several scattered around her home. She's built Victorian homes herself—one from a kit and the other from scratch, plus another modeled after her own home, also from scratch."

"Really!" Her eyes widened in appreciation of the work that went into making three houses. "That's impressive. I've only just finished building my first Victorian. And that from a kit," she said. "I would love to see them. Does she live here in Manhattan?"

"She used to, but now my parents live in a big old home with lots of land around them in New Jersey." It was actually a mansion, one that had been in Noel's family for several generations. But he didn't tell the girl that.

"Hey, Buster," a man with a heavy Queens accent who had a little girl by his side called out to Noel from about three places behind them. "If you're goin' to see the windows you have to move to the back of the line. No line breakin' allowed."

Grimacing, Noel turned to the man. "Sorry. I just ran into—"

"Yeah, yeah. I've heard that story before," the man said without giving Noel the chance to explain.

Noel stiffened at the uncalled-for accusation, but sensing the woman's soft touch on his arm, he swallowed the retort he'd been about to make.

"Let's move to the end of the line," she urged him and, not waiting for his reply, motioned for Prince to turn around.

"But you said you were in a hurry—"

She shook her head. "It doesn't matter. We're only about"—she glanced toward the end—"thirty places from the rear anyway. If it makes that man happy, then why not? Maybe he's had a hard day. It's an easy way to show him people care about him, even people he doesn't know."

If Noel hadn't already thought she was a remarkable woman, he would now. She seemed to be wise in a way that was far beyond her years.

And—her appearance aside—he understood why he was already in love with her.

As they walked back, the belligerent man's gaze followed them in surprise. Noel noticed that his anger seemed to evaporate off his broad shoulders like snow under the shining sun. "Hey—thanks. If only more people were so fair."

The woman smiled over at him with a look that could have melted the largest iceberg in the arctic. It definitely warmed the man's disposition. He stared at her, with his mouth hanging open and his eyes as round as saucers, and Noel guessed he was probably falling in love with her as well.

"I wonder," Noel said as they took their place at the end of the line, "how much better that stranger's day will be because you agreed to move back." Her action wasn't too unusual for Noel. He had seen his parents do things like that many times. But never someone near his own age. "You didn't have to move back with me."

"I wanted to," she replied quickly. Noel felt gladness fill his heart over her admission. Did he dare suppose she wanted to know him as much as he wanted to know her?

She smiled. "I know we weren't in the wrong. I could have come early and saved a place in line for both of us." Noel liked the way that sounded. That would mean they were a couple, or at least friends. "But," she said, shrugging her slender shoulders, "my father always told me if I could do something to calm another person, especially with such a little cost as this, a place in a line"—she shrugged her shoulders again, a cute habit Noel was beginning to associate with her—"then why not? Who knows what's going on in that man's life?"

"Sounds as if you have a wise father."

"I do," she agreed as they took short steps forward to the display. "So tell me," she said, changing the subject, "where in New Jersey do your parents live?"

"Madison."

Her brows came together thoughtfully. "I'm not sure where that is.

I haven't seen much of New Jersey, but I hear it's beautiful." She flashed her smile and gave her tinkling little laugh. "Much more than the New Jersey Turnpike, that is."

He chuckled in agreement. Most people thought New Jersey looked like the industrial area that followed the turnpike across its length, not realizing the state was one of the prettiest on the East Coast. "That it is. But, shh," he said, leaning toward her. At her scent—clean and fresh like powder on a baby's skin—his senses reeled, and he took a hasty step back to clear his head. "It's one of the best-kept secrets in that area."

"Then I won't tell," she said in a conspiratorial way. Craning her neck toward the first window whose brightly lit display was becoming visible, she said, "Now you know one of my favorite hobbies is collecting and building dollhouses." She turned to him. "How about you? Do you have a hobby?" In the chill of the evening her frosted breath mingled with his like an enchanting cloud of togetherness. Snappy holiday songs piped out onto the street from the department store helped turn the moment into a great Christmassy one. *"It's that time of year, when the world seems to say . . . Merry Christmas!"* And Noel wanted to lean toward the woman who, because of the crowds, was standing as close to him as a girlfriend might and kiss her.

But, of course, he didn't. At even the slightest start Prince might grab his leg, but, even more importantly, Noel knew it wouldn't be right.

He stood up straight and fought to remember her question. His hobby? "Names," he managed to reply. He was pleased he could get the word past his throat. He felt as tense as the tightest setting on a windup toy.

She blinked back at him in confusion. "Names?"

He nodded his head. "I enjoy onomastics."

"Onoma—" She paused. Then, as if a light had suddenly switched on, she exclaimed, "You mean you like the study of names?"

Now he was the one to be surprised. "I'm impressed." He was. Most thought onomastics had something to do with gymnastics.

"Don't be." She laughed, a sound that to Noel sounded like the bells of Christmas ringing out over the wintry world. She shook her head and explained. "*Onoma* is the Greek word for 'name.' If you know elementary Greek, it's easy. *Onoma* is, of course, one of the first words a person learns. *Ti enia to onoma sou?*— 'What is your name?'"

To say he was astonished would be to put it mildly. He was flabbergasted. He was normally the one explaining the history of a word to another. "How do you know Greek?"

She touched her gloved hand to her heart and, in a way he could only describe as proud, replied, "I am from Hellas . . . from Greece."

"*You're* Greek?" That was the last thing he expected. He had met many Greek people or Americans of Greek ancestry. Most had fair, olive skin and straight, thick hair that was either light- or dark-brown. This woman was as blond as a towheaded toddler. And it was obvious from her pale lashes and skin that the color was natural.

A smile touched the corners of her mouth. "Yep."

"Do you have any more secrets to tell?"

"Oh, I have a few," she assured him with a mocking glance.

He was sure she must. He would enjoy getting to know each of them. If she would let him. "Well, how do you speak English so well?"

"Most people in Greece speak English—actually, several foreign languages. But, for personal reasons, it was important to my father that I learn to speak English well with as little accent as possible." Now, as he listened to her carefully, he could hear a slight difference to the way she pronounced words. She softened the English language. Not an accent exactly, but more a treat for his ears, a caress he rejoiced in hearing. "I had lessons from a very young age."

"Greece . . . that's neat. I went there once," he said, "when I was a little boy." It was shortly after his parents had married. The thought always brought a smile to Noel's lips. How many couples include a young boy on their honeymoon? But that's how it had always been for Noel and Jennifer, the woman his father had married. He considered Jennifer his mother in every sense of the word; she had included Noel in everything. He doubted a woman could love a child of her own body as much as Jennifer loved him, and he loved her. The three of them—Noel, his father, and his stepmother, Jennifer—had a very special relationship. Probably his parents' faith in God had a lot to do with it, he admitted to himself. "I don't remember too much about

Greece," he continued. "Just that I liked it. How long have you lived here?"

"More than six years."

"Alone?"

⤴

Natalia wasn't sure she liked that question. She didn't know much about this man, and she had made it her way never to be too open with anyone. People had preconceived notions about models—some of them arrived at correctly. But not where she was concerned. He didn't know she was a model—at least she didn't think he knew—but that possibility existed. So this was getting too personal for her. In case he did know—had, in fact, seen her picture and was using their "chance" meetings as an excuse to talk to her, though she didn't believe it—she wasn't going to give too much information away.

"Of course not." It wasn't a lie. She lived with Prince.

"Oh." She could tell from the way his face clouded over that he assumed she meant with a man. His disappointment was palpable. "You're married?"

"No."

"Oh," he said. She groaned inside. That "oh" meant he thought she lived with a man without being married. She couldn't let him think that, especially since he knew she was a Christian. "So you're in a relationship right now?"

She prayed that her thoughts about his being a decent person were true. "No. I don't live with a man. I would never live with a man who wasn't my husband. But I wasn't lying—I try never to do that either," she said, flashing a quick smile to relieve the self-righteous way it could be construed. "I live with Prince." She ruffled the dog's fur. "And I live in the same apartment building with my surrogate family here in New York."

The relief that crossed his face almost made her laugh and definitely made her thankful she'd been honest with him. "I'm glad," he admitted on a frosted breath that made his words seem to dance in delight around his head. She wasn't sure if he was glad because she didn't live with a man or because she hadn't altered his idea of how a Christian should behave. "It might sound funny in this day and age," he continued, "but it's nice to find a woman with old-fashioned values."

He was glad because of my second thought! That made her feel tingly down to her toes. But she wanted to clarify from where her standards originated. "I don't think my principles are really old-fashioned as much as God-fashioned." She lifted her brows and tilted her head toward him.

He nodded thoughtfully, something in itself that astounded her. Often such declarations on her part had been scoffed at. "Like my parents," he said.

She let out the breath she hadn't realized she'd been holding. "I think I'd like your parents," she admitted.

He chuckled. "I *know* they would like you."

The music, the sounds of happy shoppers on the street, taxis and buses and trucks passing them, faded as they looked deeply into one another's eyes, into one another's souls. What Natalia saw in the blueness of the man's eyes made her heart rejoice. That something very special was happening between them, an emotion deeper than time, was obvious. Natalia only prayed it was something God ordained. Somehow she felt that it was.

Tearing her gaze away from his, wanting to lighten a moment that was becoming too heavy, she turned toward the front of the line. She was relieved to see they were almost at the first window. She pointed to his camera. "You'd better get it ready." She glanced behind them. About a hundred people were there now. "With so many people wanting to see the windows, we can't stop for long."

She was relieved when, taking her cue to lighten the mood, he reached for his camera. She liked him and wanted to get to know him, but the emotions swirling within her needed to be tempered with time.

After a half hour of gazing together at the artistically recreated rooms in the store windows, all from the Victorian age and decorated for Christmas with garlands and tinsel, wreaths and ribbons, and greenery of every kind, Natalia glanced at her watch. "I really must go."

"Too bad. I was going to ask you to go to a little café and get a hot chocolate or something."

She gave a slight shiver, and for the first time since he had walked up to her side, she felt the cold. She fixed her scarf closer around her neck. "Perfect evening for it. I would have loved to. Maybe another time," she suggested.

"Definitely. But"—amusement glinted in his dark eyes—"if we're going to meet each other again, maybe we should exchange names."

She laughed. "For a person who loves onomastics I'm surprised that wasn't your first question."

"It normally is," he answered, his lips turning downward. "But with us nothing seems normal." The way he looked at her—with the gleam of a man who considers a woman special—made her forget about the cold again. "I like that."

"Me too," she heard herself whisper back.

She probably would have stood there gazing into his face for the next hour if he hadn't suddenly put out his hand and said, "Hi! I'm Noel Sheffield."

She extended her gloved hand to his waiting one. "Nice to meet you, Noel." She paused, then decided quickly to give him her real name, something she rarely did. "Natalia Pappas."

He whistled in appreciation of it. "Now that's some name. To be called Natalia, meaning 'of or relating to Christmas,' you must have been born around Christmas. And Pappas—well, you could most definitely be nothing other than Greek." His brows came together in a thoughtful question. "Isn't *pappas* what priests are called in Greek? I suppose there must be a long line of priests in your family."

"Very good." She was impressed. "And yes on both accounts. As a matter of fact, my father is a Greek Orthodox priest, as was his father, and his father before, and, well, I guess all the way back to the beginning of Christianity."

He whistled. "That's some lineage."

"It is kind of neat to know I was raised in a tradition that goes back almost two thousand years, practically to the Twelve Apostles and Christ, Himself. But—" She dipped her head and clamped her mouth shut. She could sometimes go on too much about history and her beliefs about things. She didn't want to do that with this man and risk alienating him from her.

"No, please continue," he encouraged her as he had at the tree the other day.

"Are you sure?" She grimaced slightly. "Once I start talking I don't seem to stop, and I have very strong beliefs and—"

"I want to hear them, Natalia," he whispered. "All of them."

All? She saw in his eyes an interest that went beyond the superficial. It was a heady feeling. Her father had always wanted to know everything her mother was thinking; anything important to her was important to him. Could this man feel the same way? And if he did, what did that say? That he cherished her? Cherished her thoughts? She still hesitated.

"Please go on." His eyebrows rose slightly, and he gave a quick, reassuring nod.

What else could I ask for? she thought. Taking a deep breath, she plunged in. "Well, the most important thing is that my father—my mother too when she was alive—has always made God the center of his life. Consequently God has always been the heart of our family's lives."

"I think that's as important to you as it is to my parents," he commented.

"It's the most important thing," she admitted and hoped he understood what she was trying to say. For them to have a future together, something she wished might be theirs, it would have to be the same for him. She hoped he understood that.

His right hand reached out toward her. When it settled on her left shoulder, heat enveloped her, and the noise, the bustle of the evening, seemed to slip away. It was as if they were the only two people on the avenue again as he smiled a crooked little smile down at her and said, "Well, we must meet for that cocoa sometime." He spoke softly with a husky, romantic sound to his voice that made her feel like the most valued woman alive. "Because I find I want to hear all about your beliefs, Natalia Pappas."

He looked away and squinted toward the bright lights. From the way his jaw clenched and unclenched, it seemed to Natalia as if he were considering something of importance.

"You might find it strange, but where I have never wanted to sit down and listen to my parents talk about their beliefs"—he looked back at her—"I want to with you. Very much."

She reached up and wrapped her gloved fingers around his. "It's not at all odd, Noel. How many children honestly ever want to pay attention to their parents?"

❧

As a counselor Noel knew that was true, but also as a counselor he felt convicted by her words. Was he ignoring the best advice his parents had to give? Since meeting this woman, he was beginning to think he was being as ornery as some of his high school students, even Rachel, whom he was so concerned about these days.

"Well, Noel." She let go of his hand and lowered hers to the dog's lead. The emptiness he felt over not holding it any longer was keen until she spoke her next words. "How about if we meet at the grandstand of the Thanksgiving Day parade? At seven in the morning. Perhaps we can go for cocoa afterward." She shivered slightly. "I heard the weather report last night, and it's supposed to keep getting colder and colder until Christmas. I think we'll have to thaw out after sitting outside for so long. I have tickets for the stands outside of Macy's, so we can enjoy the show up close."

"How do you have tickets?" he blurted out, then smiled sheepishly. "Sorry," he apologized. He knew grandstand tickets were hard to come by and much coveted. If he hadn't already realized there was something special about this woman, having grandstand tickets was one more indication.

"My surrogate parents, whom I mentioned earlier, receive them each year. But they won't be using them this year, so they've offered them to me." She patted Prince's head. "I was going to bring Prince as my date, but if you'd like to come . . . ?"

"As your date?"

If his tree at the center sparkled half as much as her eyes did right now—like soft blue diamonds reflecting the many-colored lights on the avenue—then he knew it would be the most beautiful tree ever.

"As a friend," she said with a smile that made her lips crinkle at their corners in such a cute way he wished he could touch them.

To be a friend was good. He would take that. For now. "I'd like that."

She nodded. "Me too."

$\mathcal{T}$t was fantastic to see the Macy's Thanksgiving Day parade arrive at Herald Square with its world-renowned performers, the huge balloons fashioned in whimsical characters, the marching bands, the clowns, the magical floats. But to Noel the best part of the morning was being with the girl and her dog and going for hot chocolate afterward to a little café off Broadway. The arctic bite in the air had combined with the wind to give them both rosy cheeks. The warmth of the café was a welcome change from the outdoor elements.

Soft Christmas music filled the café, continuing the sounds heard on the city streets. Ginger and cinnamon and sugary delights mixed with the scent of pine to please their sense of smell, as much as the parade had that of their hearing and sight. Evergreen and wood, windowpanes frosted naturally by the elements outside, and a stone fireplace running the full length of an inside wall with a tall Christmas tree to its side helped make the café cozy and festive. Each little marble-topped table came complete with its own miniature tree decorated with lights that softly winked and blinked too.

Noel and Natalia found a table near the fireplace. They laughed over some of the antics of the people trying to keep the huge helium balloons from taking off in the high winds.

"I thought one of the young girls holding the tin soldier was going to lift off just as Santa's sled was mounted to do!" Noel exclaimed. He mimicked the shock on the girl's face as her feet rose an inch off the ground, and they laughed until tears glistened in their eyes.

"Ah, Santa!" Natalia sighed as she wiped the corners of her eyes with her red holiday napkin. "Of course, the Santa Claus float is the best of all. His arrival into Herald Square officially opens the Christmas season in New York City and America."

That statement brought a quizzical frown to Noel's face. "You don't mind children believing in Santa Claus?" he asked, not waiting for a reply. He wanted to explain his question. "As Christians, my parents seem to be in a quandary about that. I was allowed to believe in him, though, when I was a young child." At the time his father hadn't seen any harm in letting Noel believe in Santa. But his father's views had changed through the years.

"That's a tough question," she replied. He watched her take a sip of her cocoa. "The Santa myth is such a delightful one for children to experience, especially here in America. It's become an American tradition, and I think Christians have to bear that in mind. But like many things surrounding the celebration of Christmas"—she pointed to the lights, the trees, the tinsel all around the room—"if we remember the reason behind it, then I think it's fine."

"Meaning?"

She shrugged. "Well, first of all, I think parents have to teach their children that Santa Claus was actually a man. He was a bishop in the church, and his name was Nicholas. He lived in Myra in Asia Minor and did much good, all in the name of the One he believed in and served his entire life—Jesus Christ. Even after Nicholas died, people remembered his life as an example of a wonderful Christian."

"You're talking about the man referred to as *Saint* Nicholas, right?"

She nodded. "Saint Nicholas of Myra. That's the one!"

"Okay, but what about children believing he lives forever?"

"Well . . ." She let the word roll off her lips in a hesitant way. "The truth is, as a Christian he *does* live forever. Bishop Nicholas was purported to have died on December 6, around the year A.D. 330. That day is celebrated as the first day of his life with Christ in paradise. In that manner, through his faith in Jesus, Nicholas of Myra, like all Christians, does indeed live on."

Noel knew his mouth dropped open at her words, but he couldn't have kept it from happening. She was saying things he had never heard before. "How do you know all this?"

She seemed to understand finally how much he enjoyed hearing her share her views, for excitement shone on her face, enchanting Noel with her eagerness. "Well, remember that my father is a priest—in the same tradition in which Nicholas of Myra was first a priest, then a bishop. Back in those days, Myra, the city in Asia Minor where Nicholas served as bishop, was a major part of the Greek world." She glanced toward the tree's lights and squinted in a way that almost seemed sad to him. "Until a few decades ago the city of Myra was Hellenic with mostly Greek Christians living there, even though the Turks from Asia had taken over the land politically during the Middle Ages."

Once again he realized there was more to her than outer beauty. Behind that golden hair, the blue eyes, and the features that looked like a master craftsman had sculpted them were brains. And she was knowledgeable about different things, things he had no idea about. As one who studied the etymology of names, he liked that. "I had no idea about any of this."

She sipped her cocoa, then said, "That's one of the nice things about cultures mixing with one another." She looked at him above the rim of her cup before replacing it on the table. "I'd never heard of some of the more current men and women of faith from this area of the world until coming to live here." She held up her hand and counted off a few people on her fingers. "D. L. Moody, Peter Marshall, and Billy Graham, for example. Those men and their walks through life should be remembered as much as the early Christians."

"I agree that history is very important. Does Myra still exist? I mean, are there still ruins from the time of Nicholas?"

"Oh, sure," she said, nodding. "Ancient Greek, Christian, and medieval Greek ruins are all over what is now modern Turkey. In Myra, the actual church where Nicholas taught, which was built during his lifetime, is still there. My father visited it when he was a young man. In fact, the church in our village is very similar in appearance."

"Wait a minute." Noel leaned forward. "He visited the exact church where Saint Nicholas preached?"

She nodded.

He whistled. "I never knew there was so much to the man who inspired the legend of Santa Claus."

"Not too many people in this part of the world seem to know

much about the early Christians, Saint Nicholas included. I've noticed since moving here that everyone knows about the apostles, and then there seems to be a break until about the time of Martin Luther. But we grew up learning about early Christians in Kastro, the village I come from. Rather than having our rock stars or football stars, we have those men and women who gave their lives so today we could have the same knowledge they had about Christ. Saint Nicholas, the real man, has always been one of the more important Christians to remember. Even today."

Noel shook his head. "So Santa actually was real?"

"Definitely," she said without hesitation. "And because he was a Christian, he still lives. So that's true too. A Christian's body might die but not the spirit. So to say Santa still lives is true in the same way that all Christians live even when our bodies die." She returned to her original thought. "When a person knows Santa Claus was actually a wealthy young man who became a priest in the church and gave in Jesus' name so generously his deeds were talked about for generations, then it's fine to enjoy that tradition. But a person should not believe in him, rather in the One whom Saint Nicholas believed in and followed—Jesus Christ. Otherwise I think a child is in for a great disappointment on learning Santa doesn't live at the North Pole or fly through the sky on a sled pulled by reindeer."

Noel heaved a deep sigh. "To be honest, that realization was one of the hardest for me to accept." He had learned it at about the same time his mother died, when he was six. The two losses coming together were— Another thought, an aggressive, almost angry one, intruded upon the first. For the first time Noel understood he was angry at God about both events: His mother had died, and as crazy as it sounded for a man nearly twenty-eight, Santa had died too.

Worse.

Santa, as such, had never really lived.

It was a startling thing for Noel to realize.

Maybe it was one of the reasons he never wanted to believe a baby born in a stable could be the God of the universe. If Santa was just a myth, then wasn't the idea of a baby born as fully God and fully Man also a myth?

But he knew enough to know there was a fallacy in his thinking.

There was a big difference between the two examples.

But not to a six-year-old child who had just lost his mother. To a grieving child it would be the same thing.

Worse even. For the baby who was God should have been able to save his mother for him. Noel remembered asking both Santa and Jesus to save her that year.

Neither had.

But he didn't want to get into this with Natalia now, so he kept the conversation on Santa Claus. "And I guess his name must have been derived somehow from the actual Nicholas."

"That's right. With your knowledge of names, can you figure it out?" she asked just before taking another sip of hot chocolate.

"Well, Nicholas is an ancient Greek name which means 'victory of the people.'"

She nodded. "Even today we say *nikisa* for victory. But more important we are certain Nicholas was Greek, of Hellenic heritage, by his name."

Now she was speaking on a subject with which he was familiar. "Absolutely. Back then names were never given lightly. They always told something about the person. Particularly from where they hailed. So let's see." He felt that thrill he always got when considering the history of names. It was like a tasty morsel to his mind. "How did his name go from being Nicholas, Greek bishop of Myra, to Santa Claus? There has to be an interesting etymology here."

"Want me to tell you?" She leaned forward and asked with all the eagerness of a child wanting to tell a secret.

He smiled and, sitting back, indicated with his hands to go ahead. He loved watching her talk, the way her mouth curved around each word as if it were a treasure and the way her eyes opened wide with an excitement similar to reading a good book.

"Well, the Dutch settlers of New Amsterdam"—she pointed out the window to the city by which it was first known to colonists—"brought with them their beloved *San Nicolaas*. Americans said it fast with a stress on the broad double *a* of the last syllable. A *t* slipped in after the first *n*, and we get *Santy Claus*. From there it was just a short step to Santa Claus. That's how American kids started calling the early Christian cleric from the Greek world Santa Claus!"

Noel shook his head in appreciation. "That's one of the more remarkable etymologies I've heard. But," he conceded, "it sounds correct."

"You're the expert in names, of course, but I think it is," she said with a bright smile. "Now enough about Santa." She glanced at her watch. "I have to get going soon or I'll miss Thanksgiving dinner. But how about telling me what you do?" She laughed. "We still seem to talk about everything but the normal things."

They hadn't had even one moment of boring "small talk" between them. "It's nice," he said. It was one of the things he liked about her.

She nodded and glanced at her watch again. "I agree, but if I'm going to tell my surrogate family about you at Thanksgiving dinner in about an hour, I should at least be able to tell them what you do."

He was pleased she was going to tell the people she was close to about him. It meant she must be beginning to care for him. Maybe even in more than just a friendly way.

He liked that. A lot.

"Okay." He sat up straight and wondered what he should tell her. He had told her about onomastics as a hobby. What he hadn't told her was that he was a writer and his current book was a huge success on the *New York Times* best-seller list.

He decided against enlightening her about it, though.

People always seemed to change toward him once they learned he was an author—particularly a successful one. He doubted she would, but he didn't want to take that chance. He didn't want her to act any differently than she had been. "I come from a very long line of lawyers, one that stretches back to revolutionary days."

"That's quite a lineage," she said, repeating his earlier words about her and her priestly ancestry.

"By American standards, it is. But I guess it kind of pales when compared to Greek ones."

She shook her head. "No. Don't say that. Everything is relative. America is new."

"Tell me something?" He leaned forward. "How old is the church in your village?"

Her gaze searched the ceiling, as though she might discover the answer there. "I don't know. It's from Byzantine times, so it must be at least five or six hundred years old, maybe older."

He held up his hands and smiled. "I rest my case."

She laughed. "You spoke just like a lawyer. Are you one too?"

"Only by degree."

Her brows came together. "What do you mean?"

"I studied criminal law, even graduated from Harvard Law School, but I'm a high school counselor." He shrugged his shoulders. This was what most women couldn't understand. Why he would be a high school counselor when he could be a high-powered, highly paid criminal lawyer with one of the oldest firms in the city. But she didn't know about his wealth—that he never had to work a day in his life if he didn't want to—and, for the moment, he would keep it that way.

He was shocked when he saw a look of wonder in her eyes. Just the opposite of what he normally saw in a woman's face when he told of his career choice. "Really. Well, a counselor is a counselor whether it is to direct people in the ways of the law or children in the way of life. I think, of the two, you chose the better."

He was taken aback. "You do?"

"Of course. You have the chance to shape young minds so that maybe they won't need the help of your other profession when they grow older."

She couldn't have shocked him more had she said she was going to walk across the Brooklyn Bridge. "That is exactly my reasoning. Precisely why I decided to counsel high school-age people."

"I know someone else who did something similar. Stavros Andreas is my village's schoolteacher. Because the village doesn't have too many children, he teaches all ages. But he left a career as a university professor here in the States—at Georgetown University, I think—and went to live in his ancestral village. That is my village of Kastro, and he did it so he could raise his daughter himself and, as he has often said, 'to help form young minds.' He has never regretted his decision. Especially since Allie Alexander, the village doctor, left New York and came to the village, and they fell in love—"

Noel held up his hand. "Wait a minute. Is this the fairytale romance between the teacher and the doctor you mentioned at the center the other day?"

Her face brightened more. "That's it!"

"They sound like interesting people."

Her smile deepened. "They are. Stavros's faith had been, well—let's just say he had been really hurt by his first wife—"

"He's divorced?"

"No. His wife died. But they had been separated. She had hurt him terribly. His wife hadn't wanted their little daughter, Jeannie." Natalia shrugged her shoulders. "From what I understand, the woman never wanted to be a mother. She was a lawyer who wanted a career, and she deserted both her little girl and her husband."

"That's tough."

"But it's another case of God taking something terrible and making something wonderful. Allie, Stavros, and their four children couldn't be happier. Stavros regained his faith and was given the family he had always yearned for as well." She looked down at Prince who was sleeping by their feet under the table. "Prince is from their dog's litter of puppies."

"Really?" He glanced down at the dog. Who would have thought such a handsome German shepherd would come from a Greek village? Leaning forward, he reached for Natalia's hand. It was warm and soft, so soft he felt as if he were holding a cotton puff. "Now. I've told you about me, and you've told me about Allie and Stavros, and even Prince." He smiled down at the dog. "How about telling me about what you do so I can tell my parents when they ask me about any special people in my life?"

When the pupils of her eyes seemed to expand and swallow up some of the crystal blue of her irises, he was afraid he had gone a bit too far in describing how he felt about her. But as her lips softly curved up at their corners, he knew she didn't mind. Maybe she even liked it.

"Well, I—" She paused, and he thought she was trying to decide what exactly she should tell him. He understood. She had to be careful. They had met several times now, but they didn't know anyone in common. And this was New York City. "I'm a fashion-design student at Fashion Institute of Technology."

"No kidding?" That meant she was an artist. "You mean you're one of those people who can sketch clothes super quick."

She laughed. "Believe me, Noel—sometimes I don't think quickly enough."

"I can't seem to draw a straight line, so people who can draw anything at all really impress me."

"I've always liked it a lot."

"How much longer do you have until you graduate?" Now that she was talking about herself, he was going to ask as much as he could.

"Next term."

"Fantastic. And then?"

She took a deep breath. "Then I hope to start my own line of clothes."

"And you have been going to school for six years?" That's how long she'd told him she'd been in New York. But he knew she must have been doing something more than just going to school. She had to support herself. New York was an expensive place to live. And he already knew what her father did.

"Yes, but part-time. I've been working too."

"Doing what?"

"A bit of modeling," she murmured.

That surprised him. Not that she was a model. She certainly could be. Just that he didn't expect a strong Christian to be in that industry. "What type of modeling do you do, if you don't mind my asking?"

"No, of course not." She tucked a long strand of hair behind her ear, and he had the impression this line of questioning had made her uncomfortable. Giving her the benefit of his own experience, he suspected it was for the same reason he didn't like telling people he was a writer. People treated him differently.

She flashed a self-conscious smile before continuing. "For some reason I'm often asked to model nurses' uniforms."

"Nurses' uniforms?" He had the feeling she had modeled more than nurses' uniforms, but he didn't push her.

Her mouth turned up in an amused way. "Tell me—do you think I look like a nurse?"

She was giving him the chance to look at her, really look at her, and it wasn't an opportunity he was going to pass up.

From her soft forehead to her full lips, he let his gaze roam over her face. Did she look like a nurse? He wasn't so sure about a nurse, but he thought the look of gentleness and wisdom in her eyes, plus her height, which must be close to five feet ten inches, probably got her jobs modeling the white nurses' uniforms. An aura of purity seemed to surround her like perfume. Other than being gorgeous to see, she had a look of capability about her. Yes, he could imagine her dressed as a nurse.

"Hey!" she exclaimed after a moment, reaching for Prince's lead. He knew he'd taken too much time and had made her feel uncomfortable.

He quickly leaned forward. "No, wait." He touched her hand. "Yes. I can see where you might make the perfect nurse. You give a feeling of competency."

She loosened her grip on the lead. "Thanks. That's a nice thing to say." She glanced at her watch. "But I have to go—"

"Me too." He had to catch the train out to New Jersey in fifteen minutes; otherwise, he would be late for Thanksgiving dinner at his parents'. And he didn't want to do that. "But look. Since we both love Christmas activities, how about if you and Prince, if you like, come with me to the tree-lighting ceremony at Rockefeller Center in three days? I have passes for the guest section."

Her pale brows rose. "The guest section? How?"

"I have a connection with the tree."

"With—the—tree?" she questioned in staccato.

"Don't worry. I'm not into any mysticism connected with trees. I have the passes because my parents donated the tree this year. It comes from their property in New Jersey."

He had the satisfaction of seeing her eyes widen. "It did?" But immediately they narrowed. "Oh, how could they part with it? That is the only thing about the trees at the center that has bothered me. They are cut down."

"No, it's okay," he assured her. "This tree has been marked for Rockefeller Plaza since, well, ever since my father was a little boy. Norway spruces have a life span of only 80 to 110 years. My great-grandfather planted this tree over 100 years ago. It wouldn't have been able to survive many more hard winters. Either that or it would have soon died of old age."

"I didn't realize their life span was that short. So your family wanted it to have a chance to show its beauty to the world?"

"That's right," Noel agreed and was glad she understood. "Please come with me to see it lit, Natalia. It would mean a great deal to me to have the woman by my side who loves and appreciates the center's trees so much she comes to welcome them upon their arrival every year." It would mean that and so much more. He wanted her to attend the special ceremony with him more than he could ever remember wanting anything in recent years.

Her lips curved up into that giving smile he was coming to expect from her. As her fingers squeezed his gently, Noel wondered at the way she made him feel, as if he wanted to hold her, protect her, never let her out of his sight. She was the mate of his soul, the woman his eyes yearned to see every day, forever. "I would be honored, Noel."

His heart seemed to bang louder inside his chest. A date. A real date. One that might end with his placing his lips on hers. "May I pick you up at your home?" he pushed out past his throat that had suddenly gone dry.

At first her eyes flashed with pleasure over the idea, but when they dulled and she shook her head, disappointment sliced through him. "No. Not at my home, but at my surrogate parents' home." She reached into her purse for a pen and, leaning over, wrote something on a napkin. "This is their address. I would like for you to meet them before we go out."

"On our *date*?" he asked, placing special emphasis on the word as he slipped the napkin into his pocket. He had to make sure she saw it that way too. It would change their relationship. He wanted it. But did she?

She flashed that million-dollar smile of hers, one that made her whole face shine like the sun. "Yes, on our date," she agreed, and Noel felt sure his smile had to be a reflection of hers.

Finally he would have a date with Natalia, a real one. Not just an outing as friends. As he paid and they walked out of the café together, it took every ounce of his self-control not to skip down the sidewalk.

$\mathcal{I}$t took a lot to impress Noel. But the apartment building did just that when a uniformed doorman let him inside on the afternoon of the day his tree was to be lit. He knew the prewar building was one of the great luxury apartment buildings in Manhattan. He rode the gilt elevator to the top floor.

"Welcome and come in," a woman greeted him, smiling warmly. She ushered him into the entrance hall. It had stone detailing on the walls and marble on the floors, reminding him of châteaus he had visited while in France. "You must be Noel. I'm Janet Howard, Natalia's, well—" She gave a light laugh that was full of good cheer. "I call myself her surrogate mother."

Noel shook Janet Howard's hand. "I've heard her refer to you in that way."

"My husband and I have been blessed with three sons." She guided him into the living room where the soothing strains of Christmas carols played softly in the background. "We are happy to count Natalia as a daughter. But please come in and sit down. Both my husband and Natalia will be out shortly," she said and motioned to a spacious room that made Noel feel more like he was in a Parisian apartment than one in Manhattan. Then he looked out the many windows at the panoramic view it had of Central Park and knew he could be nowhere but in his beloved New York City. The apartment sat just above tree level. The park was laid out below in its leafless, wintertime splendor.

"That's beautiful," he said, motioning to the view before he sat on the velvet sofa behind him.

Janet stood for a moment more and looked out the window at the

view. Noel thought she must have gazed upon it a thousand times before. To him, she seemed to be breathing it in as if for the very first
time.

"My husband and I have lived here for the last forty years, and
yet"—she shook her head at the wonder of it—"I never tire of looking
out these windows. It's one of God's greater blessings in our lives."
She sat in a chair adjacent to his. "I grew up on a farm in Connecti-
cut," she explained. "To have trees within my view is almost a must for
me." She turned and smiled at the older woman who brought in a silver tray laden with tea and coffee, cakes and sandwiches. "May I offer
you something?" she asked with a gracious wave of her hand over the
tray. "Juanita makes the best coffee in the world."

Noel leaned forward. That was of interest to him. He was a con-
noisseur of great coffee. He smiled at the older woman in the maid's
uniform. "In that case I'd like a cup. And a piece of that chocolate
confection too."

Though employer and employee, the two women were obviously
friends, and they shared a laugh of mutual delight. "Just what we like,
right, Juanita? A man who both appreciates and admits to wanting delicious food." Janet Howard waved the other woman aside as she
started to serve. "I'll take care of it, Dear. Thank you."

Noel nodded at the maid as she smiled and left the room.

Janet glanced up at the Charles X clock on the mantel. "Her favorite show is coming on TV," she whispered to him. "I hate for her to
miss it," she said, pouring the coffee. "Cream? Sugar?"

"No. Black is fine."

Janet nodded and handed it to him, then sliced the silver knife
through the luscious-looking cake. "Are you planning to go out anywhere after the tree-lighting ceremony?"

Noel looked at her in surprise. It had been years since a date's
parents, or even parent-type figures, had asked him what his plans
were for the evening.

Janet returned his gaze with a steady one, and he realized she was
serious. She passed him a plate with a slice of cake. Where Natalia
was concerned, he could understand the older woman's care and appreciate it. "I've made reservations at the Tavern on the Green for af-

terward." He referred to the famous restaurant located in Central Park.

"Oh! That's one of Natalia's favorite places, especially at this time of the year. It's decorated for Christmas. It has become our tradition to take her there for her birthday each year." She looked up, startled. "Oh, that's next week! I must remember to make reservations."

Noel paused in putting a forkful of cake in his mouth. "Her birthday is next week?" His own birthday was too. He wondered if it might fall on the same date.

"The first day of Advent. December the first. That's why she's named—"

"Natalia," Noel finished for her, and his eyes widened. They shared the same birthday.

Janet looked at him in surprise. "Why, yes."

"That's why I'm called Noel," he explained. "My birthday is the first day of Advent too."

"Oh!" Janet clapped her hands together at the coincidence of it. When Natalia and an older, distinguished-looking gentleman walked into the room arm in arm, she turned to them. "Natalia, you and Noel share the same birthday!"

Natalia's blue gaze met his. To Noel, as he stood up, it was as if the other two people weren't there. She had been beautiful the other times he had seen her, but now, dressed specifically for him and for their first real date, she looked like a modern-day, fairy princess should. She wore a burgundy cowl-neck sweater with a matching knee-length velvet skirt and high black boots that had ankle straps with antique brass buckles on them. But it was the look in her eyes that made all the finery fade almost beyond consequence. Her eyes shone like diamonds reflecting the light, and Noel had to remind himself to breathe.

"*Your* birthday is December the first?" There was that quality in her voice of a young girl pleased by the discovery.

He could only nod.

She moved forward. Actually she seemed to float toward him.

She extended her slim hands to him, her expression softening.

"Oh, Noel." She paused as the thought occurred to her. "*That's* why you're called 'Noel'?"

He nodded. "It means 'Christmas.'" The meaning behind his own name was one of the reasons he had started studying onomastics.

"And yours means the same," Janet Howard said. "How remarkable."

"Something else we have in common," he whispered to Natalia, and she nodded her golden head slightly before turning to the man who was standing behind her. "Jasper Howard, I'd like for you to meet Noel Sheffield." Extending the same honor to Noel she said, "Noel, Jasper Howard."

"It's good to meet you, Sir," Noel replied and shook hands.

"Sheffield?" The older man looked at him with the narrowed gaze of a man trying to place another. "Is your father Quincy Sheffield of Sheffield, Brokaw, and Thomas?"

Noel saw in the man's eyes that light of interest he was used to seeing when someone recognized his prestigious family. He stiffened but nodded. He didn't like having to be associated with his family's law firm in order to see that look in another's eye. He was actually disappointed to see it in this man whom Natalia thought of so highly. But since it had happened all his life he was used to it and answered truthfully. "Yes, Sir."

"But Natalia told us you don't work in your father's firm?"

"No, Sir, I don't. If I did, though, I would work with my father, who does mostly pro bono cases."

"Yes, I've heard that. Your father is a Christian, isn't he?"

That surprised Noel more than anything else the man could have asked. No one, with the exception of Natalia, had asked him that before. Noel stood a bit straighter as he answered, taking sudden pleasure from doing so. "Yes, he is."

Jasper shook his head and smiled. "I've heard many good things about your father. The world would be a much better place if there were more men like your father in positions of responsibility. You must be very proud to be the son of a man of such well-placed principles."

Noel hadn't realized how highly he esteemed his father until that moment. "Yes, I'm proud of both my father and my mother."

Noel saw Natalia flash a see-I-told-you-so smile at her surrogate parents before saying, "We must be going." While she gathered her coat and scarf, Noel realized he didn't feel the need to make a hasty retreat from these people as he had when he was a young adult wanting to get away from a girl's relatives. It was a strange but good feeling.

"It was nice to meet you both," Noel said and shook hands again with Jasper. To Janet he said, "Please tell Juanita her cake and coffee were delicious."

"Juanita must take credit for the coffee, but the cake was my creation."

Noel's brows lifted in surprise. Most women he knew who had full-time help didn't do much in the kitchen. "It was fantastic."

Jasper Howard put his arm around his wife's waist. "Everything my wife does is fantastic," he said in a loving, yet not boastful, way. Noel could feel the air around them radiating with the love they felt for one another, exactly as it did around his own parents. It was something wonderful and perfect and special. He only wished, as he helped Natalia on with her coat—a gray, double-faced, cashmere design that was soft to the touch—that he and this woman whose birthday he shared might find such a love someday.

The older couple walked with them to the door. "It must be very special to see *your* tree being lit," Janet Howard commented.

Noel looked over at Natalia. The boots she wore almost made her his height. "It's even more so by having Natalia with me," he admitted and looked back in time to catch Janet and Jasper Howard exchanging amused glances.

"Have a wonderful evening, you two," Jasper said while Natalia reached over and planted a quick kiss on first his cheek then Janet's.

"We will."

As they stepped out the door, Noel stopped suddenly. "Hey! Haven't you forgotten someone?"

The three looked at him in confusion.

"Where's Prince?"

Their faces settled into smiles, and Natalia slipped her left arm through his right one. Noel couldn't remember the last time anything had felt better. "I thought I would hold onto you tonight."

Noel looked over at her surrogate family and gave them a small wink. "I like the way that sounds."

❦

The tree-lighting ceremony was everything and more than Noel had thought it would be. The only thing that would have made it better would have been to have had his parents with them. They had planned on coming into the city for the occasion, but his mother had developed a cold. Having suffered from pneumonia the previous winter, they deemed it prudent to stay at home and watch the ceremony on TV.

Noel missed them but was glad he had Natalia with whom to enjoy it. When the giant TV screen at the center showed his tree being trussed, then cut down on his parents' property, Noel thought it had to be the most novel way to introduce a girl to his parents' affluent home.

When the Tudor-style mansion was shown, Natalia leaned toward him and whispered, "Your mother has made a model of *that* house?"

He nodded but braced himself for what would most likely follow—her understanding of his parents' wealth.

"Must be a beautiful dollhouse."

Noel turned to her. She was actually thinking about the difficulty in re-creating the mansion as a dollhouse rather than about what the historic home represented—generations of wealth.

That was a first for him.

By this time he would usually see dollar signs in the eyes of women. He saw none in Natalia's. They still sparkled like diamonds, but for the occasion and not for his wallet.

He quickly realized the fallacy of his jaded thinking. Her beliefs wouldn't allow her to be impressed by wealth except, like his parents, in the context of how it might help others. After seeing the Howards' luxury apartment, he should have known the stateliness of his parents' home wouldn't faze her. Her own apartment was located in the same building.

The show included famous singers performing Christmas songs,

Olympic champion skaters, the Radio City Rockettes, and even some- one dressed as Santa waving and dancing to a merry tune across the stage. Then the time for the lighting of the tree finally arrived.

"Noel." Natalia leaned over and spoke directly into his ear. With all the happy noises going on around them, that was the only way to be heard. Noel was glad; he liked the closeness, savored the way her perfume scented the air around them. "Do you know who is going to turn the switch that lights the tree this year?"

"I think the mayor will."

It was the mayor, and soon the countdown began. "Ten. Nine. Eight. Seven. Six. Five. Four. Three. Two. One!"

A gigantic shout erupted.

The switch was turned on.

Thousands of lights lit the tree. And everyone looked on it with childlike wonder, the multicolored lights illuminating each person.

"It's a fairyland of delight!" Natalia said among all the "oohs" and "aahs" and clapping around them.

Noel had to agree. It *was* like a fairyland: a beautiful land of won- der and enchantment, goodness and light. And *his* tree was at the cen- ter of it all.

"How do you feel?" Natalia asked into his ear.

He turned his head so their gazes met.

How *did* he feel? The word that came to him he had never used. But it was the only one that described what this moment meant to him. He leaned toward her and spoke it.

"Blessed," he said. Her eyes narrowed as if to ascertain she had heard correctly. He nodded and mouthed the word again. "Blessed."

She reached for his hand and patted it gently, and a feeling of blessedness that even he could recognize as coming from God in- creased within him. As everyone started singing "Joy to the World" and praising the One whom the tree was meant to glorify, Noel won- dered how he had ever lived without the feeling singing through his soul. And how he had ever lived without this remarkable girl.

❧

"That was one of the most wonderful things I've ever experienced," Natalia said after the host at the Tavern on the Green seated them at their table. "The tree couldn't have looked better. And what a surprise this is." She looked around the restaurant. "I usually come here only for my birthday."

"So Janet told me. That's how we found out you and I share the same one."

"I know! Why don't you come with us this year?"

"That would be great, but I always spend it with my parents—"

"Of course you do. How silly of me!" She felt the heat of embarrassment fill her face.

"But that's in the evening," he was quick to point out, apparently trying to relieve her discomfiture. She appreciated it.

"How about if we make a *date?*" He paused as he accentuated the word.

Understanding he meant it in its true form, as a romantic appointment, she smiled.

"Let's make a date," he repeated, "to come to the park first thing in the morning of December 1. To be here"—he waved his hand over a small section of the huge park—"before anybody else. That would be a fun way to celebrate our birthdays. And with this freezing weather we might even have snow that day."

She felt laughter bubble up inside her. This was one of the things she liked about Noel. He did different things. No movie and a dinner date for him. They did unusual and special things. "I'd like that. I've never come out very early because of safety reasons."

"Well, I'll come to your apartment and get you. Between Prince, me, and"—he pointed upward—"your faith in God, you'll have nothing to fear."

She liked the fact that he had included God in the list, although she wasn't quite sure whether it was in a mocking way or not. When his next words came out, they not only settled the question in her mind, but thrilled her.

"I must admit, I'm beginning to envy you, my parents, and the Howards for your faith in God."

She reached for his hand and gave it a gentle squeeze. "It's not something you have to envy, Noel. It's something that can be yours so easily. It's about your volition, your choice, as a human being to believe or not to believe Jesus is who the Bible says He is."

"I believe He was a great man, Natalia, a great politician, a great moral teacher. Probably even the most important person in history to have ever lived," he conceded. "But God's Son?" He sighed, and she heard the regret in his tone. "That I don't get."

Natalia felt her heart beat fast with the desire to hand this special man her faith. But she knew it didn't work that way. It went back to volition, that gift of choice from God that made humans . . . well . . . human. To decide whether Jesus was who He said He was, was something people had to choose for themselves.

But Noel was questioning now, probably things his parents had been praying he would for many years. Saying a quick prayer, she reached for the crystal goblet of water and took a sip before speaking. She knew she could speak her mind because Noel had encouraged her often enough to do so. "Noel, do you know that on many occasions Jesus declared Himself to be God?"

"God's Son," he corrected her.

"Yes, He said He was God's Son—one Person of the Trinity—but also that He's God."

His brows came together in a frown. "Where did He say that?"

She breathed out deeply and said a prayer that her father's teachings might come back to her. "Well, in the Book of John it's recorded that He said, ' "I and the Father are one." ' "

"So what does that mean? To my way of thinking, it means He's God's Son—'I *and* the Father'—not God."

"Actually it means both. With those few words He's telling us He is both God's Son and God. Listen: ' "I and the Father are one." ' My own father"—she touched her chest as she referred to her *baba*—"once gave a lesson on the fact that the term 'one' in Greek is neuter, meaning 'one thing,' not 'one person.' In other words the two—Jesus the Son of God and God the Father—are one in essence or nature, but They are not identical Persons."

He frowned. "So how many Gods are there?"

"One."

"But you just said"—he paused as he seemed to listen in his mind to exactly what she had said—" ' "one thing," not "one person." ' "

"That's right. The verb 'are' used here indicates the Father and the Son are two Persons. Distinct, but united in essence, will, and action. God is one Entity but made up of three Persons—the Father, the Son, and the Holy Spirit."

"The Trinity?" he asked.

She nodded, relieved he knew the concept and she didn't have to explain where the three Persons suddenly seemed to come from.

"Okay, so Jesus is saying He is God here in this one place—"

"And He says it elsewhere."

"Where?"

Natalia drew in a deep breath and was grateful the waiter chose that moment to take their order. She was glad she'd told Noel to order for her—anything but liver—so she could get her thoughts together. She had relied so long on her father to guide people that it was a bit strange for her to be the one to do it now. Even with her years in New York, no one had ever asked her point-blank so many questions of such deep import. *Dear Lord,* she prayed silently, *please give me the words, the words my* baba *might use.*

And it was as if a voice answered her. *"Just think about what your* baba *has taught people—you included—throughout the years. You have heard it often enough. Just think. And My Holy Spirit will guide you. Only trust."*

The waiter left, and Noel sat back and looked at her. "You look pale. I'm sorry. I probably shouldn't have asked so many questions—"

"No." She held up her hand. She wouldn't let this opportunity pass. "Your asking me makes me very happy, Noel." She cupped her hands together on the edge of the table. "Believe me—it's like a gift. What would hurt is if you didn't want to know."

"I really do want to learn. It's strange. My parents have been trying to teach me things for years, but until now, until meeting you"—he held his hands out in a shrugging way—"I had little real interest. But you intrigue me. And the fact that you believe so strongly makes me want to know why. Does that make sense?"

Her heart seemed to pick up its tempo. "It makes perfect sense. I would want to know if the situation were reversed."

"You would?"

Emotion threatened to clog her throat. "You are becoming very special to me, Noel. But the fact that you don't know Jesus . . . would prove"—she had to swallow—"to be a stumbling block to our forming any lasting relationship. So your asking is hope—for me, for us—that we might"—she paused and, holding her hands together against her chin as if she were praying, ventured to finish with—"have a future together."

"Natalia," he whispered. Rather than her words scaring him away, as she feared they might, they seemed to have done just the opposite—draw them together. "I so badly want that with you. I have from—"

"Shh." She touched her finger to her lips. "Let's not say anything else yet. It's too soon."

He nodded, but she didn't think it was in agreement to its being too soon. "So you said there are other places where Jesus declared He's God, not just God's Son?" he asked.

She took a deep breath and let it out slowly. "If I had my Bible with me, I could show you."

"That's okay. Whatever you remember." He surprised her with his encouragement. But she shouldn't have been. Wasn't he always encouraging her to speak her thoughts, her beliefs? How could she do otherwise?

"Okay. Well, in the Gospel of John, the fourteenth chapter, Jesus said some of His most forceful words about His deity. In the sixth verse He said, '"I am the way and the truth and the life. No one comes to the Father except through me."'"

"I've heard that before. How does that prove His divinity?"

"Well, '"the way and the truth and the life"' is a Person. It's another name for Jesus."

"You mean those are all His names?"

She had forgotten about his love of onomastics. "That's right. Well, some of His names anyway," she clarified. "He has a lot of them." *"Ask him to study My names."* The thought popped into her head. *Yes, Lord,* she answered. *Yes!* "Noel, you love to learn about names, right?"

"Yes," he answered slowly.

"Why?"

"Why what?"

"Why do you like to study names?"

"Because they're important. In older times a name identified a person. Among other things, like telling where a person came from—as we said the other day concerning Saint Nicholas—they were used to reflect personal experience or express or influence one's character."

"Exactly!" she exclaimed, but then she lowered her voice when she saw people from a nearby table glance in her direction. "And nowhere is that more true than in Bible times, both the Old and New Testaments." She opened her hands before her. "So why don't you study the Lord's names? Maybe you'll come to know who He is through learning about His names."

Noel sat back, and she could tell from the way his dark brows nearly touched that the thought intrigued him. "Hmm, might not be a bad idea." He leaned forward. "As a matter of fact, it's a good one."

"You know, I've heard of people—lawyers even—who started out to prove to the world that Jesus was a fraud only to fall at His feet in worship of His divinity. And all because of their studying about Him."

"Natalia," he said, his voice husky, "I would be very happy if the same thing happened to me."

"Me too, Noel." She blinked at the tears that had gathered in the corners of her eyes. *Dear God, please,* she implored. *Please give him Your understanding.*

"Do you remember any other places where Jesus says He's God?" he asked after a moment. Ducking her head down, she smiled. God seemed to be answering her prayer by Noel's persistence. He wanted to understand.

"Well, in the same chapter of John He said, ' "I am in the Father and the Father is in me." ' That means—"

"That He and the Father are one in essence and undivided."

She was impressed. Without a softened heart she thought it must be almost impossible for a person to grasp the concept even if that was precisely what it meant. "That's right."

He whistled softly. "That's quite a statement. Someone would either have to be a lunatic or, in truth, God to say such a thing."

"Precisely! That's why for you to say, as you did earlier, that you believe Jesus was a great man, a great politician, a great moral teacher, is an absurd declaration. On many occasions Jesus also declared Himself to be God."

A frown slashed across his face. "I see what you mean. The one crosses out the other, doesn't it?"

"How can a person be a great moral teacher if people don't believe all He said about Himself? Jesus said He was God. He said it so often the leaders and people of His day wanted to kill Him."

"And didn't they? Kill Him, I mean?"

"They didn't do anything to Him that He didn't allow, Noel." She lowered her voice. "When the time was right for Him, He allowed them to kill Him, after He had completed His ministry on earth. And with His resurrection He established His church, the rock upon which believers in Christ's redemptive work would flourish."

Noel repeated the words she had spoken a few minutes earlier: " ' "I am the way and the truth and the life. No one comes to the Father except through me." ' "

Natalia felt adrenaline flow through her body. To see Noel try to understand the Christian message was the most thrilling thing she had ever experienced. It was almost like watching a baby try to walk for the first time.

"That's right," she said. "And because of what Jesus did, if we choose to believe what He said about Himself—all His words, not just a select few—we will be resurrected as He was. We will be given brand-new bodies that will never perish, never get sick. And we will see loved ones who have gone on before us." From the way his gaze intensified and his blue eyes darkened to look like a midnight sky, she felt that was something very important to him. For the first time she wondered if perhaps he had lost someone close to him to death's sting. "Best of all, though," she continued, "we will be in complete fellowship with God for eternity."

She looked at the happy people around them and smiled. No one could say there wasn't something special about how people acted at this time of the year in America. In Greece it happened both at Christmas and at Easter time. "I like to think of this season, when goodwill seems to abound more than at any other time, as a glimpse of what heaven will be like, though it will be far more wonderful." Reaching over to the tree to her right, she detached a beautiful, handcrafted Christmas-tree ball from it. Moving the golden globe around in her hand so that all the colored lights from the room were reflected in its shiny glass, she said, "I think heaven will be so much more superior, though, like the sun in the sky is to this Christmas-tree ball."

"I wonder if that's why I've always liked this season most of all. Because it is a bit like everyone's idea of heaven."

She replaced the ornament and, taking his hand, lightly squeezed it. "It could be, Noel."

"Natalia, I *want* to believe. I really wish I could say, 'Okay I believe you.' It's just that—"

"Shh," she said. "I understand."

"You do?"

She sat back and took a sip of water before answering. "People come to the Lord in different ways, Noel. It's possible your way will be through the study of His names. Even then I can't be sure." She replaced her glass and, resting her palms on the linen tablecloth, said, "But I feel it will happen."

"I *want* it to happen, Natalia. It's the only thing that has stood between my parents and me. I feel somehow it's true. I just have to know it is in here." He touched his heart.

She couldn't agree with his reasoning more. "That's the only way God wants a person, Noel. Many have the wrong idea about God. But, you know, I think one of the reasons God gave us the ability to read and study is to learn about Him. Perhaps it's laziness and the traditions of ancestry that keep people from opening the Bible and learning."

"Funny, but that's something I often tell my students."

She could understand laziness but not the other. "Tradition has to do with their not learning?"

"You'd be surprised how many kids think an education should come to them by osmosis. Or because their parents learned or didn't learn and they did okay, so the kids think they shouldn't have to study, either. So many waste the marvelous education they have available to them at the school in which I work."

Growing up in the village of Kastro, Natalia had never seen that. And the competition for entrance into her university had been so tough that most felt privileged to be there. "I suppose you're right." Then another thought came to her. "Noel, do you have a Bible?"

"Sure. I even have a study Bible with a concordance. My parents gave it to me a few Christmases ago." He shrugged his broad shoulders. "I haven't read more than the Christmas story." He twisted his head to the side. "Guess I should study it, huh?"

The waiter came then and placed their artistically designed plates of scrumptious-looking food before them.

"It's your choice, Noel," Natalia said. "Either it can stay dusty, or you can brush it off and use it, and"—she smiled brightly, trying to give him hope—"you can learn."

6

*L*ater that night in his brownstone town house on the Upper West Side—ironically directly across the park from Natalia's apartment on the Upper East Side—Noel wondered about the things they had discussed. After searching his bookshelf, he found his Bible in a back corner. It was in such a forgotten location that not even his competent housekeeper's vacuuming had managed to keep the dust off its upper edge. Noel blew on it and coughed as the particles swirled around his head.

He opened the book. It seemed so foreign to him. Something his parents should be reading. Not him.

Walking over to his four-poster bed, he sat on the thick burgundy quilt. He was careful to move the ecru afghan his mother had made for him to the side. He'd told Natalia he would try to learn about Christ by studying His names. But how could he study Jesus' names when he didn't even know more than a couple?

He sighed. That was a cop-out. But he was too tired to reason it out. He put the Bible on his night table.

He would start tomorrow. Maybe.

~❧~

"I don't know, Prince," Natalia said to her dog about a half hour after Noel brought her back to her apartment. She sat on the thick white flocate, a rug from Greece made of sheep's wool, in front of the fireplace.

She glanced up at her dollhouse on the table to her side. Its windows were ablaze with the little electrical lights she had installed herself, and in honor of the season, wreaths hung on each door and a lighted tree stood in the bay window.

A gas fire burned in the apartment fireplace while Handel's *Messiah* played softly in the background. She was brushing the dog's shiny fur. It was a nightly winter ritual they both enjoyed. "I think Noel wants to learn, but the tradition of his not knowing and believing in his own brand of Christianity will be tough for him to break. And even though I suggested he start learning about Christ by studying His names, I doubt that's enough. I don't think he knows how to begin, Prince. I want to do more. But what?"

The dog turned his large head to her and nudged his nose against her hand. It was a comforting gesture he often gave her. Natalia put the brush down and, wrapping her arms around his back and chest, leaned her head against his clean fur and listened to the rhythmic *beat, beat, beat* of her beloved companion's heart. Steady and clear, it never failed to ease the worries of Natalia's own heart. "Dear Lord," Natalia prayed to her heavenly Father, "please show me what to do, how to help Noel."

The rest of their evening at the Tavern on the Green had progressed much the same, with him asking questions and her answering to the best of her ability. By the time dessert came they had moved on in conversation to talk about his work, and he had told her about the student, Rachel, with whom he was particularly concerned.

Natalia's heart reached out to the confused teenager. It amazed her how people went from being little kids to acting as grown-ups and dating so quickly in modern American culture. Teenagers here seemed in a big rush to become adults; it was not that way in Kastro. Natalia might be nearly ten years older than Noel's student, but she knew she was far younger in terms of the dating game, for which Natalia was very grateful.

Until Noel, no other man had truly interested Natalia as a possible life mate.

Growing up in Kastro, her friend Dimitri had hoped for more with her than the brotherly love she had always felt toward him, but even he had finally admitted to their not having that "special something" that should exist between a man and a woman. She was thankful he had finally turned to Maria, who had loved him all her life. From Martha's reports on the romance, Natalia was almost certain she would soon hear wedding bells pealing for Dimitri and Maria.

But Natalia knew everything was different with Noel. For the first time, she felt that "special something" for a man, and she knew Noel felt it for her too. If his beliefs could get into line with the precepts of Christianity Jesus had laid out, she would be very happy to spend her life with him.

As it was, she could hardly wait for their mutual birthday in three days' time. Their date for an early morning tryst at Central Park sounded like something out of a dream to Natalia. She wished she could see him sooner, but both her work and school precluded it. Not only did she have an intense modeling shoot in Harlem, but she had her demanding portfolio class to prepare for over the next three days too.

As her favorite part of *Messiah*—the choir singing Isaiah 9:6—started to play on the stereo, Natalia reached over for her remote control and turned it up. She could never hear those beautiful, prophetic words the prophet Isaiah penned several hundred years before Christ's birth without chills running up and down her spine.

"'For unto us a child is born, unto us a son is given,'" she sang along with the choir and wished her voice could do it justice.

"'And his name shall be called Wonderful, Counsellor, The mighty God, The everlasting Father, The Prince of Peace!'"

Natalia stopped singing as the words moved over and around her, and the Spirit within seemed to guide her in how to help Noel start his study of Jesus' names.

Isaiah 9:6. Handel's wonderful oratorio *Messiah*.

Scrambling to her feet, she ran over and picked up the newspaper. She flipped to the entertainment section. She was certain she'd seen it listed there. A special performance with opera stars was to be given one night soon at Carnegie Hall. But it was sold-out. That didn't deter Natalia. Picking up her phone, she dialed her agent's number. If anybody had spare tickets, it would be David. She glanced at her watch. It was late, but then he hardly ever slept.

When his cheery voice answered, she knew she was correct in calling him, even at such a late hour. "David, it's Natalia. I need a favor. . . ."

After talking with him for scarcely thirty seconds, she hung up the phone, then picked up a pillow and hugged it to her chest. It was done. As she'd expected, David had tickets, which he'd happily offered to her. He usually bought extra tickets for special events for his clients. Also, as she had expected, they were the best seats in the house.

Natalia knew now how she could help Noel in his search. She would let the wonder of the Christmas season and the wondrous truths heralded so perfectly in Handel's monumental work speak to Noel's heart. With God's Holy Spirit going about His holy business and the music filling Noel's being, it had to be a combination that would work.

It just had to!

Three days later, while the earth still slept in 4:00 A.M. slumber, and Natalia did too, the phone by her bed rang out shrilly.

Reaching over to her table, she fumbled around for the noisy contraption. "Happy birthday, sleepyhead!" Noel's voice sounded as cheery as a robin singing in the spring.

"Noel! Happy birthday to you too!" she croaked and, pushing her hair away from her eyes, tried to focus on the numbers displayed on her clock. When she saw what time it was, she gasped. "Noel!"

"I know—I know. I said I'd come and get you at six. But something has changed."

Alarm filled her. "You won't be able to make it?" She had been looking forward to this morning with the same anticipation she normally reserved for Christmas and Easter.

"Not at all—just the opposite. We need to leave earlier than planned if we're going to get the full benefit of the wonderful gift to us today, the anniversary of the day of our births."

She shook her head, trying to wake up. "What are you talking about?"

"Put your feet on the floor, walk over to your window, and look out."

Carrying the phone with her, she did as he instructed. She pulled back the curtains and was instantly wide-awake because of what she saw. "Noel!"

" 'The moon on the breast of the new-fallen snow gave a luster of midday to objects below . . . ,' " he quoted. She recognized part of the poem *The Night Before Christmas*.

"Oh, Noel," she whispered into the phone. Her eyes took in the beauty of the park covered in a glistening blanket of the purest white. "The first snow of the season . . ."

"And in time for our birthdays."

"Thank You, God." She whispered her thanks to the One she credited with this minor miracle.

"It is rather amazing, isn't it? Especially after our conversation the other night at the restaurant." But before she could reply he quickly said, "Tell me how it looks from your window."

She didn't hesitate. "Like a pristine world that's at once familiar and yet so utterly unfamiliar. I can see the tops of the buildings across the park, but they look as if they are floating above the trees, not connected to the ground at all." She squinted. "Almost as if they aren't really there." She gazed at the trees directly across from her window and placed her fingertips against the windowpane, not minding that it was freezing. "And the branches that seemed so bare yesterday are now covered by garments made to fit each of them perfectly. Like haute couture."

Her voice lowered to a whisper. "And it's so quiet, Noel. Even the light from the park lamps glowing among the branches seems to be hushed." She gave a little laugh. "As if light can be described as hushed. But it is." She paused. "There is no noise, Noel. No noise from the city at all. Everything is hushed with a serenity, a beauty, a solitude that is at once so humbling I feel as if I'm in the most beautiful cathedral in the world, and it makes me want to fall to my knees and pray. And yet"—she took a deep breath—"it is so thrilling too that I want to shout for joy. Oh, Noel! I've never seen the city look so perfect!"

"Few have, Natalia," he responded softly, and she could hear the smile in his voice. "Can you and Prince be ready in twenty minutes, birthday girl?"

She glanced down at Prince. He lifted his head from his mat and cocked it to the side in question. "Prince already has his coat on. We'll be ready and waiting for you, birthday boy!"

7

*E*xactly twenty minutes later, looking every inch the abominable snowman, Noel stood at the entrance to her building. He was covered from the top of his head to the toes of his boots in snow.

Natalia giggled at the sight of him.

When Roswell, the doorman, allowed him inside, an icy blast of air shot into the relative warmth of the hall. Without pausing, Noel reached out for her, picked her up, and twirled her around. She couldn't keep from squealing in delight.

"Happy birthday, birthday girl!" he said.

"Happy birthday, Noel," she returned softly in his ear. The smell of the snow on his shoulders was clean and fresh and cold.

She could have stayed in his arms forever, but Prince wasn't so certain about the situation. Noel as a "snowman" was not a familiar sight to him. When a soft growl emanated from the four-footed friend, Noel stopped twirling her and put her down.

"It's okay, Prince," she assured the dog. "He's a *friend*." He listened to her words, and she knew he understood the term "friend" from the way his head tilted to the side; but still it was obvious from his stance that he wasn't convinced. Only when Noel removed his glove and held out his hand so Prince could identify his scent did he relax. His tail started brushing back and forth in happiness over seeing Noel again too.

Natalia praised him. "Good boy, Prince. Good boy."

"That beast takes his job seriously," Roswell said from behind them.

"That he does," Natalia agreed, then turned to Noel to introduce the two men. "Noel, I'd like for you to meet the best doorman in New York City as well as a dear friend." Then to Roswell she said, "Noel is not only a very special person in my life—one you may let in whenever he comes calling—but it is his birthday today as well as my own."

"Oh!" the older man exclaimed. "That it is. The first day of Advent." He looked at Noel. "And it's your birthday too?"

"For the last twenty-eight years," Noel replied.

"Isn't that fine? You share the same day. Very special. And Advent too." He pointed to the snow that was swirling around the streetlights like a dancing troupe of white moths. "And you have the first snow of the season as a gift sent straight from God. A happy birthday to you both!"

"Thank you, Roswell." Then pointing to the key the older man held with uncertainty within his large hand, Natalia said, "You'd better do as I say and go up to my apartment and rest. Your wife doesn't need a sick husband for Christmas this year too."

Before Noel arrived, Natalia learned that Roswell had been unable to return home the previous night because of the snow, but his replacement had made it in. So she offered him the use of her apartment while she was gone. She could tell that reminding him of his illness the previous Christmas was all the encouragement the older man, who should have retired years ago, needed. He loved his wife dearly and never wanted to cause her distress.

"You are so right. Mary deserves me well this year," he said. "Thank you. I will take you up on your offer, Miss Natalia. But if I fall asleep, you must promise to wake me the minute you step through the door."

"I promise," she replied. She knew the older man had a code of ethics that would be disturbed at the thought of her being in the apartment while he slept. She understood it perfectly; it was how men in Kastro, her *baba* included, would feel.

"Now at least I know why it had to snow so hard last night," the older man continued as if a mystery had been solved. "The good Lord has blessed this, the anniversary of your birthdays. You two young people are about to enjoy New York as few do. My Mary and I once went to the park early in the morning on the first snowfall of the season. But that was when we were as young and strong as you," he said. A special gleam came into his eyes as he recalled that time. Then he continued. "Central Park will be more marvelous right now than you have ever seen it before." With a flourish, he opened the door so the three of them could go on their way. "Have a wonderful time! And a very, very happy birthday to both of you!"

Roswell's words about the park being "marvelous" were correct, Natalia thought. It was that and so much more.

They shuffled through half a foot of the fluffy crystals that had settled on the avenue's sidewalk and stuck out their tongues like children to catch the new flakes as they fell from the sky. Soon they walked through one of the park's many gates and found themselves in a winter wonderland of delight that took their breath away on puffs of joy.

Were they in the park she knew so well? Natalia wondered. They walked with hushed steps across terrain she at once recognized yet didn't. It was as if Someone were sprinkling a deep layer of powdered sugar over the park, reminding her of the Greek Christmas cookies *Kourabiedes.*

She'd gone out at the first snowfall in Kastro many times and trekked up to the castle with her father, Martha, and older brothers several mornings to watch the sun rise over the white world of rural wonder.

But this was different.

This was New York City.

They were standing in the middle of one of the biggest cities in the world, and yet it was as if no one else existed.

Noel, Prince, and she were alone in a landscape as unfamiliar with its white pearly covering as it was familiar in its layout. She looked around as if she'd never seen these surroundings before. *Perhaps I haven't,* she thought. *Not in this light.* The character of the land had been transformed, made more perfect somehow—cleaner, smoother, crisper. She could hardly believe she had been living above these same trees for six winters but had never seen them looking quite like this before.

"Oh, Noel," she whispered and watched her words float to him on a wisp of icy breath. "Have you ever seen anything more excellent?" she asked as her boots crunched through the snow. It felt like a crime to mar the smooth path with her footsteps, as if she were trampling on something holy.

They were standing so close they were almost touching. "It's as if the snow has created the perfect landscape," he said, pointing out different things to her. "Look at the branches of the trees, the earth, the little creek with its stones that look like powder puffs with the snow piled upon them." He swept his arm up to the tall, ghostlike buildings that rose above this "rural" scene. "Even those structures look as if they're an illusion and not places where thousands of people are sleeping." He paused. Natalia took her gaze off Central Park in the predawn, snow-painted day and turned to him. "But most of all," he said, glancing at her curiously, "it's as if the great Artist Himself has reached down from heaven and with a palette of pure white re-created the world exactly as He might wish it to be. Pure, without anything to mar it, nothing to blemish it."

Searching his eyes, she saw sincerity in their depth as well as a clear vibrancy that she thought must come to a person when he recognized Truth. She was almost certain God's creation was speaking to Noel's soul.

She spoke softly. " 'For since the creation of the world God's invisible qualities—his eternal power and divine nature—have been clearly seen, being understood from what has been made, so that men are without excuse.' "

"That's in the Bible?" Noel asked. She heard awe in his voice.

Slowly, reverently, she nodded. "The New Testament. The Book of Romans."

He took a deep breath, one that made his chest expand, before turning back to the vista of trees and fields and hills that stretched out before them like a silk painting. "Something about this moment, Natalia," he whispered, "makes me feel as if that and everything you said at the restaurant about Jesus being God couldn't be anything but real." He sighed. "It's as if all this were created for our eyes alone." He shrugged his shoulders. "But I know it wasn't. It's for any of the millions of people in this great city who make the choice to get up early and come out and see it. Come out and see how God, during the restful night, has painted this special spot of His earth."

He turned to her again, and his gaze searched her own, as if he were trying to pull knowledge, her knowledge, from her. Like at the restaurant, it was something she wished to give freely.

"Isn't that like what you said the other night about human beings' choice? This"—he waved his hand out but didn't remove his eyes from hers—"is here for all the people in this city. Not just us. It's perfect right now, the best I've ever seen it; and yet I've never bothered, never made the choice, to get up early enough to come and experience it."

"It's exactly like that, Noel." She paused and smiled. "Except God doesn't require us to lose sleep when we make the decision to believe Him."

"Natalia," he breathed out her name. Wrapping his gloved hand gently around the back of her head, he slowly, respectfully, leaned down and brushed his lips against hers.

She closed her eyes.

She didn't think anything she'd ever felt, not even the warmth of the Grecian sun upon her skin in the summertime, was better than that of Noel's lips on hers. It was right and good and brilliant in the way she had always thought the kiss from her "Prince Charming" should be. And she knew she would never want to join her lips with another man's again.

Seemingly of its own volition, her mouth moved against his, and the motion deepened into a dance like a ballet of warmth and love.

"Natalia," Noel whispered against her lips, "I love you. With all my heart I do."

"And I love you," she heard herself respond and knew, even as the declaration sent her pulse spinning, that it was true. She couldn't have kept the truth of it from him any more than she could have kept the snow from swirling like a perfect dream around their heads.

They stood with their foreheads and noses resting together, making a silhouette of a heart with their profiles—that complete heart that could only be made by a couple in love. It was a romantic picture often represented on greeting cards with a sunset behind the couple. Natalia liked the fact that they had a sunrise.

After a moment Noel took a half step back and smiled, that all-encompassing smile of a man content with his world. She knew her smile had to match his. Her pulse was beating so fast she was certain he could see it move in her temple. She was just beginning to wonder where they would go from here in their relationship when he suddenly grabbed hold of her hand and started running.

"Come on!"

"Where are we going?" she squealed out as their boots crunched over snow.

"Somewhere special," he said and laughed. "You'll see!"

Prince pranced all around them, first kicking up the snow, then plowing through it like a burrowing animal building a tunnel. Letting go of one another's hands, they reached down, scooped it up, and tossed it at one another as they frolicked down the cozy, lamplit path. But when they reached a certain point and were ready to drop from their merry-making, they sat for a moment. They were panting as hard as Prince.

When Noel removed his scarf from around his neck, she looked at him in question. "Are you hot?" Playing had warmed her but not enough to be without her scarf. Central Park this morning was as freezing as it was beautiful.

"I want you to see the place I'm taking you from a certain vantage point. And I don't want you to look at it until then. So I want to tie this around your eyes and guide you there."

She looked out over the park. Except for the tall buildings surrounding it in the distance, it looked like a wilderness. But she trusted Noel. This would make it more of an adventure and more fun. "Okay," she agreed and, turning slightly, let him fix it. "Umm, the scarf is warm from your neck." It felt good. Her skin was tingling from the cold bite of morning air. "But I want to hold Prince close to me. Prince!" she called to the dog, who immediately stopped his snow-plowing and came to her side. She attached his lead and wrapped her arm around him. "What a good boy you are," she cooed into his ear.

"And me?" she heard Noel ask from behind her as he secured the knot that held the scarf. "Am I a good boy?"

She reached out her arms and brought his face close to hers. "No. You aren't a good boy. You're a good man."

"Hmm." She could hear the pleasure in his voice and was sure his head had tilted to the side, as Prince's often did. "I like that. Come on." He reached for her right hand. "Let me show you the most perfect spot in all of Central Park."

They walked quietly down the path.

Seeing the white world was one thing, but feeling it and hearing it now that her eyes were blindfolded was another thing altogether. The snow crunched beneath their feet while her nose lifted and sniffed. She loved the way snow smelled. It was a clean, fresh scent, the same whether it fell in the wilds of Kastro or in the middle of this city of concrete and steel. But never had it smelled or felt better than it did now. She had never walked through the snow with the man she loved. She hugged Noel's arm closer to her.

He chuckled, and she knew he was looking at her when he asked, "Are you scared?"

"No, I just like the excuse to hold you close."

He paused. And she knew a moment before it happened that his lips were going to touch hers. She sensed them coming close. "I like it too." His voice was deep and husky. "But you don't ever need an excuse. That, dear Natalia, is something you are welcome to do for no reason at all."

Natalia placed her head on his shoulder. She hadn't known that to be so close to a man would feel so good. She was aware of the muscles beneath his coat as he moved, the way his breathing sounded, the soft scent of his aftershave, and even his height as he crunched along beside her. It made her feel warm and toasty and feminine.

"We're here," Noel said after a few minutes and situated her in a certain direction. "Stay like that," he said as he undid the scarf. "And keep your eyes closed until I tell you to open them."

"You're certainly full of orders," she teased.

"Not usually." She could hear the smile in his voice. "There—got it." As the scarf fell away, a sharp, sudden chill stung her skin, but she hardly noticed it as she concentrated on Noel and his surprise. "Not yet, not yet," he spoke slowly. She felt as if he were a cameraman telling her to hold a pose until the lighting was perfect.

"Now!"

She blinked her eyes.

"Oh!" She couldn't help the gasp that came from her at the vista before her. The little Gothic castle, Belvedere, which sat on a rocky outcropping to the west had always been one of her favorite places to visit—probably because of the castle in Kastro. But she had never seen it looking like this.

To the east and behind them, the dawning sun had found an opening in the clouds. It highlighted the castle with golden light even as snow still swirled around it like laughter falling from the sky. Natalia half expected to see a rainbow appear at any moment.

And one did!

Shafts of sunlight lit up the blanket of snow in the glen before the castle, and the snow sparkled like that of a rainbow in the sky.

"Oh, Noel," she breathed out. "It's enchanting."

"Perfect for our fairy-tale romance?" he asked.

Turning from the castle to him and with her heart thudding heavily in her chest, she wrapped her arms around his neck. "Absolutely perfect."

He reached out and tucked a strand of her hair that had come loose from her hat back under the fabric. "Happy birthday, Natalia."

"Happy birthday, Noel," she whispered back.

"It's been perfect."

"And it's not even six o'clock in the morning yet!"

He nodded toward a man walking from the opposite direction. "I'm glad we came out so early and got to see the castle like this. Now that the sun is coming up, the park will soon be filled with joggers, dog walkers, and even cross-country skiers out to practice their technique." Noel squinted toward the man who was cutting a wide arc so as not to disturb the pristine snowscape. "But I think that man is here to try to capture this moment forever for a book or a calendar."

Natalia looked at the man. The camera equipment he had strung across his shoulders told its own tale. "He might capture the scene," she agreed. "But one can only experience the moment, the enchantment, by coming here into God's world and feeling it. It is so special, so ethereal, so—"

"A part of God?"

That was exactly what it was. "Do you feel it, Noel?" she whispered. "Do you feel God speaking to your soul through this encounter with His creation?"

"I do, Natalia. It's something I feel here." He tapped his chest. "I know God exists. I just don't know Him as I'm realizing I should." He sighed. "I wanted to tell you today that I started my study of Jesus' names. But I didn't know where to begin, even though I've found my Bible and have it on my bedside table now."

"I thought that might happen," she said softly.

"You did?" His chin lifted a fraction of an inch in reaction to the news. "How?"

How can I explain it to him? she wondered. *"The way it actually is,"* a voice replied within her. So she did. "It's just something God put into my heart."

"Really?"

She nodded. "I think you'll soon see how He does that."

"Do you think so? I want that. I want what you have and my parents have . . ."

"That want is God knocking on the door of your heart, Noel. ' "Here I am!" ' Jesus says in His revelation to John. ' "I stand at the door and knock. If anyone hears my voice and opens the door, I will come in and eat with him, and he with me." ' " She gazed out over the beautiful park. "It's the way you hear His 'voice' here today."

"That's beautiful," Noel murmured. "I'm beginning to see the Bible is a very poetic book. Every line seems to contain music."

Her heart beat faster. "Do you like music, Noel?"

"Love it. Especially classical composers."

"Yippee!" she exclaimed and laughed.

Noel looked at her as if she had gone mad, but she couldn't help it. She was so happy. Reaching into her pocket, she pulled out an envelope she had decorated with a length of candy-cane-colored yam and gave it to him.

"Here," she said. "This is my birthday present to both of us."

"To *both* of us?" he countered, with an amused lift of his dark brow.

"They go together like the celebration of our birthdays does."

As the world slowly started filling with people—the joggers, dog walkers, and cross-country skiers Noel had anticipated—he removed the yarn from the envelope and pulled out two tickets. He turned them over, read them, then looked back at her. "Natalia . . . Handel's *Messiah* . . . I don't know what to say." So he didn't say anything else with words; rather, his face bent toward hers and touched his lips lightly to hers. She wrapped her arms around his neck and rested her head against his shoulder.

"I think you just 'said' everything perfectly, Noel," Natalia whispered.

8

With the first sounds of the orchestra, Noel knew he was in for an experience he'd never had before.

Normally he was a visual person. But this performance of Handel's *Messiah* was already making him use his sense of hearing unlike any time before. And that sense seemed to demand that another one was to be employed, different from the five physical senses he was so accustomed to relying upon.

As the notes filled the air around them, Noel glanced over at Natalia.

Her eyes were closed. Her lips were moving as if in prayer.

It was something Noel almost felt like doing.

When the tenor sang the first word, "Comfort," Noel smiled to himself. What a poignant way to start a work titled *Messiah*. Nearly everyone needed comfort in some form or another.

Noel sat back in his seat. But as the music combined with the wonderful words, he found himself leaning forward. The Word of God, which he hadn't known how to start reading a few nights earlier, was proclaimed so beautifully by some of the world's most highly trained voices. What struck Noel too was that they sung only the words written in the Bible.

Nothing else.

And those words did things to Noel.

They stirred him in a way he had never been moved before.

When the choir sang, "'And the glory of the LORD shall be revealed,'" it made Noel want to stand up and sing with them. A thrill went through him. It was as if a chorus of angels were on stage glorifying the Lord.

He didn't understand what they meant by "all flesh shall see together." But he wanted to find out.

The bass singer came in with the words, "'He will shake the heavens and the earth,'" like thunder giving an exclamation to what had been sung. "'The LORD, whom ye seek, shall suddenly come to his temple'" was like a wake-up call to Noel. Something like tears formed at the back of Noel's eyes when the bass singer asked, "'But who may abide the day of his coming? and who shall stand when he appeareth?'" Noel wondered if he would be able to. He suspected that, as he was now, he would neither abide nor stand when the "He" they referred to, Jesus the Christ, the Messiah, should appear.

"'He is like a refiner's fire'" sounded ominous to Noel.

"'But who may abide the day of his coming?'" the singer repeated the question, and Noel, like a child, wanted to shout out that he would. He would stand! But to do so he thought he had to learn how first, like a child learning to stand on his feet for the first time.

The choir came in singing so sweet and calming, like a rest after the bass's ominous question. But what was this angelic-type choir saying? Noel leaned forward to catch the words. "'He shall purify.'"

Whom shall he purify?

"'The sons of Levi,'" the choir seemed to answer him, "offer unto the LORD an offering in righteousness." Noel wondered who the sons of Levi were and what they had to do with him. It sounded like a glorious hope to him, though.

But wait! What was the alto proclaiming now?

"'Shall call his name'"—His *name*—"'Emmanuel: God with us.'"

Emmanuel. God with us! She sang it only once, and for a moment Noel wondered if he had heard correctly.

He glanced over at Natalia. Her face was glowing with a light that had nothing to do with that found in the dimly lit auditorium. It was a light shining from her face.

"'Behold your God!'" the alto sang. "'The glory of the LORD is risen upon thee.'" And Noel knew that was exactly what was upon Natalia. The glory of the Lord had risen upon her face. Noel looked around him. On so many faces—Caucasian faces, African faces, Oriental faces, Indian faces. And yet they all looked the same, almost as if light was upon them, and it in turn was shining out from their souls!

The choir sang the same words, "'The glory of the LORD is risen upon thee!'" It was joyously sung, and Noel's heart thumped to its glorious beat.

Then the bass sang again. A soulful sound of sadness. Noel listened to his words and realized he sounded so sad because the words he recited were sad. "'For, behold, darkness shall cover the earth, and gross darkness the people.'"

'Gross darkness?' Was that how he was? Was he living in gross darkness by not getting to know God the way his parents knew Him? He glanced over at the woman he loved. The way Natalia knew Him? He looked at others seated around him. The way so many people in this auditorium apparently knew Him?

The music changed again, and Noel felt expectation in the melody, though still sad, that now diffused throughout the room. "'The LORD shall arise upon thee. Upon thee, and his glory shall be seen upon thee! The people that walked in darkness have seen a great light! Have seen a great light!'"

Yes! Noel sang within himself.

Light!

That was it!

The people around me—Natalia, my parents—they have seen a great light, a light Noel was beginning to realize he wanted to see.

"'And they that dwell in the land of the shadow of death'"—Noel had heard his parents refer to that phrase often—"'upon them hath the light shined.'"

With shock Noel realized the Light referred to must be Christ, the Messiah, the Son of God, the Light of the World! He knew that was one of Jesus' names. People didn't have to be an expert on the names of Jesus to know that one.

The choir lifted up their many voices in song again with a part of this work Noel had heard many times but had never listened to before. It permeated every corner of the hall.

"'For unto us a child is born, unto us a son is given: and the government shall be upon his shoulder, and his name shall be called

Wonderful! Counsellor! The mighty God! The everlasting Father! The Prince of Peace!'"

Noel felt goose bumps break out over him.

Names!

Christ's glorious names filled the hall.

Names of the Man—the God—Natalia and his parents wanted him to understand. Amazing names. Descriptive names. Significant names. Names for him to study and help him know the character of the Man, the God, who meant so much to so many people he loved.

He glanced over at Natalia.

She turned her gold-crowned head to him and reached for his hand. "His names," she mouthed. He knew then why she had bought these tickets for them.

Nodding, he smiled. And chills of wonder, of hope, flowed through him because he knew the only barrier between this woman and him having the life together they both so desired was his faith. He was beginning to think that along with his lack of faith—though he had always believed in God—was a lack of knowledge about the nature of God, about who God is. He could read and study, and he had ignored probably the most important book ever given to the world. The Bible. The Word of God. The Word these beautiful voices were proclaiming a small portion of so magnificently and mightily.

The choir sang in allegro. As before, Noel wished he could sing with them. His soul yearned to sing the declaration, the praise, the acknowledgment.

"'Wonderful!'"

"'Counsellor!'"

"'The mighty God!'"

"'The everlasting Father!'"

"'The Prince of Peace!'"

Something inside him jumped to the fullness of the resounding sound. He wanted to hear it over and over again.

And yet, even when it ended, which seemed too soon, he found he couldn't be sad. For the pastoral symphony that followed the chorus was like a gentle caress on the excitement of his soul. One that gave him the chance to rest and listen to the remainder of the story.

Noel now had several names to study: Emmanuel, Light, Wonderful, Counsellor, the Mighty God, the Everlasting Father, and the Prince of Peace.

All names that described the Person of Christ.

He glanced over at Natalia, who was dressed in a sequined gown of soft, royal blue that winked and blinked with her movement. She turned and looked at him. He knew he didn't have to tell her how he felt. She could see it.

And he was certain it pleased her.

When the soprano started singing again, they turned their gazes toward the front, but their hands remained intertwined as the words flowed around them and through them.

"'There were shepherds abiding in the field, keeping watch over their flock by night.'" Noel knew this. It was the Christmas story. "'And the angel said unto them: Fear not: for, behold, I bring you good tidings of great joy, which shall be to all people. For unto you is born this day in the city of David a Saviour, which is Christ the Lord.'"

Savior! Christ the Lord! More names! Noel's mind reverberated with the belief that was supplanting the disbelief within him.

"'Glory to God in the highest!'" the female members of the choir sang. "'And peace on earth!'" the men returned. When they started singing in a round, exhilaration filled Noel. "'Good will to men!'" The many voices, both male and female in turn, overflowed into the room, with a joyful noise that seemed to seep into every pore of Noel's body. He felt himself break out into a light sweat, an amazing thing considering the snow that covered the ground outside.

"'Rejoice greatly,'" the soprano sang, sounding like bells chiming, like Natalia's laughter. "'Behold, thy King cometh unto thee . . . speak peace unto the heathen.'"

Heathen. The word stuck in Noel's brain. For the first time he realized belief in God was not enough. Belief in a Supreme Being made him little more than a heathen. There was much, much more to belief than believing in God.

The words *"Yes, belief in God's redemptive work through His Son"* marched through his brain. He wasn't sure when he had heard them, but he thought they were probably some of the many bits of knowledge he'd picked up from his parents through the years. Before this evening they were just words; now they were so much more. Now they were truth. A truth Noel was coming to accept.

" 'Then shall the eyes of the blind be opened, and the ears of the deaf unstopped; then shall the lame man leap as an hart, and the tongue of the dumb sing.' " That was what Noel was feeling at this moment, as if he were seeing and hearing and his heart was jumping in knowledge of God's greatness for the first time. And like a man who had never had the use of his tongue, he wanted to speak it out and sing it out too! The thought went through his mind that he had been dumb for years because he hadn't bothered to proclaim truth, the truth of God.

But what was the alto saying now? What truth was coming forth from the notes of her mouth? " 'He shall feed his flock like a shepherd: he shall gather the lambs with his arm.' " The imagery was beautiful.

And now the soprano sang, " 'He will give you rest!' " Noel wanted that. The choir was singing the best sermon he'd ever heard. The music was moving his heart in a direction he'd long yearned to travel but, at the same time, had long fought to go.

" 'And ye shall find rest unto your souls.' " Noel recognized that rest for his soul was something he'd never had. Oh, he didn't have any major problems—he wasn't an unhappy person at all—but there had always been an unease, as if he were missing out on something in his life, something great.

The choir came in now, singing words that sounded like a springtime dance of delight, reminding Noel of butterflies flittering around daisies. " 'His yoke is easy; his burden is light!' " And he smiled. Almost laughed.

" 'Behold the Lamb of God,' " the choir now sang in largo. Noel knew he was hearing another name of Christ's, one he'd heard as a child in Sunday school. *Jesus, the Lamb of God.* He recalled the lambs in his Sunday school coloring books, lambs with Jesus in the picture.

The next words filled Noel with sadness. "He is despised and rejected of men: a man of sorrows, and acquainted with grief." But when Noel realized he was one of those men who had rejected Him by simply ignoring Him, by not believing all His words, only a select few, the grief and sorrow and conviction that filled him were nearly overwhelming. The section was so long and slow he thought Handel had probably written it like that for a reason: to give each man and woman time to let the full import of the words sink into their souls.

They sunk deeply into Noel's. Very deeply.

Sadness filled him as he realized by his lack of interest in God's Son he had, in fact, rejected Him. He hadn't taken the time to get acquainted with Him or, as Natalia had pointed out that night at the restaurant, to learn all about what Jesus said while He was on earth as a Man.

Here he was, a counselor, always advising parents and children to get to know one another. God had given everything for people to do that, but Noel had spent the first twenty-eight years of his life practically ignoring Him.

As the sad, convicting words filled the glamorous hall, Noel remembered his father telling him once, "God has given us everything we need to know Him. He has given His Son, His Holy Spirit, His Word to hold in our hands and read, the testimony of men and women from the earliest days of Christianity to the present as witnesses and examples of true belief. All that plus the gift of volition. God, the Builder and Designer of the infinite universe and the smallest leaf on a tree, has left it up to us whether we puny, sinful humans want to know Him or not."

Noel felt a keen sense of conviction upon remembering his father's words and hearing the current ones sung in the auditorium.

He suspected that George Frideric Handel must have loved God very much to write such inspirational combinations of sounds to go to the arrangement of biblical words.

That was Noel's thought when the music stopped and the lights in the auditorium flicked on for intermission.

As people all around them arose from their seats, Noel and Natalia continued to sit in silence.

Finally, when he could speak, he admitted to her, "I am speechless." He squeezed her hand gently and whispered, "It is so wonderful, so convicting." He touched his free hand to his heart. "I have so much learning to do, so many decisions to make."

"Only one decision, dear Noel," she corrected him quietly.

He nodded slowly. "Yes," he agreed. "Only one."

After the intermission the music continued to wash over Noel. When the choir in magnificent allegro broke into singing, "'Hallelujah, for the Lord God omnipotent reigneth,'" Noel felt something sacred was happening.

He thought he'd been moved earlier when the choir had sung, "For unto us a son is given." But it was nothing compared to the emotions that filled him on hearing the voices of the men and women when they praised God in this refrain. He was not even surprised when everyone—like a giant wave—stood up for the words filling the airwaves of the room. The question would have been, how could anyone not stand in the face of such a magnificent sound of praise? It was the most heavenly sound Noel had ever heard, and he imagined angels taking part in the singing. It was too beautiful to belong only in the human realm.

As the glorious combination of words and music rose higher and higher, a majestic crescendo proclaiming glory to the one and only God of heaven and earth and to the Messiah, the Christ, who is One and the same God, Noel's unlearned heart cried out to believe in Jesus as God's one and only Son.

To the "'King of Kings, and Lord of Lords!'"

For these were not words composed by men but glorious truths God had given men of things to come. At that moment as the choir sang, "'The kingdoms of this world are become the kingdoms of our Lord, and of his Christ,'" Noel knew it was the truth. "'He shall reign for ever and ever! He shall reign for ever and ever! King of Kings, and Lord of Lords!'" Noel knew this to be true too, and he wanted to live under that rule. He didn't want to be left behind or not allowed to be present when the King of the universe reigned, simply because he hadn't taken the time to know God's Son now—while he had the chance.

The choir ended, again too soon for Noel, and the people sat down to experience the rest of the prophetic and inspired words Handel had set to music. Noel resolved not to tell Natalia about his decision yet. It was something personal between him and God and too new for him to share even with the woman he loved. He still wanted to learn about the names of Christ. Then he'd tell her he finally understood that, to be one of God's children, a person must believe in God as well as acknowledge that Jesus is the Christ, the Messiah.

He looked over at her as the chorus of amens was sung and smiled.

It was enough to know that because of his decision, his new and as yet unrevealed one, he and this most wonderful of women now had the prospect of a future together. Because second only to his new relationship with the Lord Jesus Christ—which he somehow knew must always hold first place in his heart, in the hearts of all humans—was his relationship with this woman. Next to God and his parents, she was becoming the most important person in his life.

And he prayed, yes, prayed, as she turned her sparkling blue eyes upon him, that they would be granted a long and lovely life together.

9

*I*t was snowing again—bright, fanciful flakes that flittered and danced around their heads—when they walked out the doors of the concert hall.

"It's wonderful!" Natalia laughed and held out her ungloved hand to the crystals. Surprisingly, for something so cold, they only seemed to add warmth to the ambience of the night. She felt Noel's arm go around her shoulder, and she gladly snuggled against his side.

"This has been one of the most wonderful nights of my life, if not the very best," he said. She didn't think she'd ever been happier.

"Me too, Noel. I'm so glad you enjoyed the oratorio."

"'Enjoyed' is not the word to describe what I was feeling in there," he admitted, and she said a silent prayer of thanks for his declaration. She thought it had moved him. She only wondered to what extent.

He guided her over to the line of people waiting for a taxi. He paused and looked up at the swirling snow falling from the nighttime sky. She waited without comment, allowing him the time to speak his thoughts, as he had so often allowed her. "It was almost as if . . . the door to my heart were somehow opened, as if those wonderful words somehow drew me near to God. I don't know. Here's yet another metaphor for you." He looked at her. "I felt almost as if God were embracing my soul as my father used to hug me when I was a little boy. Does that make any sense to you?"

"Perfect sense," she replied, watching their frosted breaths mingle together and wrap around their heads like a happy cloud. "Jesus said, '"But I, when I am lifted up from the earth, will draw all men to myself."'"

"That's it!" Noel exclaimed softly. "I feel as if I want to learn all about Him and that I can believe everything Jesus told us when He was here on earth, even that He is God."

She didn't say a word but wrapped her arms around him and squeezed the man she loved close to her. Their heavy wool coats were between them, but it didn't matter.

Wool was just material.

What had been between them before—Noel's lack of belief in Jesus as God's Son and as God—was something she could not have taken away herself. Only the anointing and urging of the Holy Spirit could do that. And faith.

The change she sensed in Noel was as pure and wonderful and refreshing as the snow that danced around them and settled upon their heads, their shoulders, the ground upon which they stood, as well as the lighted building tops that soared into the sky above the city of New York.

To say it was a magical moment would be to take something away from God.

There was no magic involved.

This was a God-sent moment, one of those special instances where eternity and time seem to make everything still and sweet and as similar to heaven as people on earth can come to it. It was a passionate moment but one that had nothing to do with the passions of the body, rather, everything to do with the passions of the spirits, the souls, of two of God's children. For although Noel didn't say it, Natalia was almost certain he had made the most important decision a person could ever make, the one about Jesus, during the soaring sounds proclaiming His prophecies, life, work, death, resurrection, and future reign. Natalia was certain Noel was God's child by conscious choice now.

The verse "No one who denies the Son has the Father; whoever acknowledges the Son has the Father also" went through Natalia's head. Somehow she could sense the change in Noel; his spirit was no longer denying the Son His glorious place in the Godhead.

As much as she might want to, Natalia wouldn't press him for any more information right now. Neither God, her heavenly Father, nor her earthly father, her *baba*—the wisest person she knew in the ways of God—ever pressed a person; rather, they both waited until the person was ready on his or her own to speak.

Natalia would wait.

It was enough to feel this change, this heaven-sent change in the man she loved.

He turned and, with his nose almost touching her nose, said, "This feeling of belonging, of being drawn to something so right and good as what those words in there"—he pointed to the concert hall—"proclaimed, is like coming home after a very long absence. Almost as if I'd been lost but now am found."

"Dear Noel," she said, reaching up and touching the snowflakes that made his dark hair shine as if with stardust, "do you know you repeated some famous words in the Bible almost verbatim?"

He tilted his head to the side, and she knew he was waiting for her to continue.

"In the story about the prodigal son—"

"Wait," he interrupted her. "I know this story. From Sunday school when I was a little guy. It's about a man who takes his half of his father's inheritance and squanders it on immoral living. When he runs out and sees the pigs where he's working are eating better than he is, he realizes he must go home and apologize to his father."

She nodded. "And when he returned his father said, ' "Let's have a feast and celebrate. For this son of mine was dead and is alive again; he was lost and is found." ' "

Noel clicked his cheek thoughtfully. "That's another good metaphor to describe how I felt while listening to that music—how I still feel. I feel as though I was dead before, as if the life I led before this evening was almost totally different from the one I want to lead now."

If their turn for a taxi hadn't arrived then, Natalia wasn't so sure she could have kept from asking Noel what had happened to him during the concert, about the decision he'd made. But as she bent down and scooted into the warm cab, taking care not to muss her gown, she knew it had to be God's timing. Noel would tell her everything at the right moment.

But for now he had told her enough.

The man she loved was coming to know God. That's all she needed to see.

Noel instructed the driver to take them to the General Electric Building where he'd made reservations for them at the Rainbow Room. Reaching into his breast pocket he asked, "Do you mind if I turn on my phone? I'm concerned about Rachel, that student I told you about."

"Of course. Turn it on."

"I think she's at an intersection in her life now. She can either go the right way or—" He let out a deep sigh and smiled. "She should hear the *Messiah*."

"Do you know how many people's lives have been touched by it during the last two hundred and fifty years?" she asked.

Noel looked at her in surprise. "That long? I didn't realize Handel lived two hundred and fifty years ago."

Enjoying history as much as she did, Natalia studied things she particularly liked, so she knew a little about the composer. "Handel was born in Germany in the late 1600s and moved to England in the early 1700s. Ludwig van Beethoven said he was the greatest composer to have ever lived."

Noel's brows rose. "Beethoven said that?"

She nodded. "And most people considered Beethoven the greatest."

"I think if anybody should know, he would."

She smiled. "When Handel composed *Messiah* he was fifty-seven years old. But just before its success he was depressed, plagued by rheumatism that didn't allow him to sleep and afraid to answer his door for fear he'd be hauled off to debtors' prison."

He looked at her curiously. "Are you serious?"

"It's sad, but so many people who have given the world such mighty works or used their talents in one way or another have had very difficult lives. But I've always thought it might be something like the apostle Paul and his thorn. It made these very gifted people realize His 'grace is sufficient' for them, and it was the thorns that made people strive for new heights. Heights in writing, like people living under persecution, and in music like Handel's *Messiah*. God's grace was sufficient for them."

"I've never thought about it like that."

"I read that while composing *Messiah* Handel was said to have seen visions about the subjects he was writing, especially during the 'Hallelujah Chorus.'"

Noel whistled. "Now that's something I can believe."

"You can?"

"It was"—he held his hands out before him—"as if angels were singing."

She nodded thoughtfully. "The amazing thing, though, is that it portrays not angels, but humans who have come out of the Great Tribulation and are proclaiming the 'Lord God Almighty reigns' and He is the 'King of Kings and Lord of Lords.' It's a prophecy for us today, who wait for Christ's second coming, as much as what was written hundreds of years before the birth of Christ in Isaiah, 'For to us a child is born, to us a son is given,' was for those at the time of Christ's first coming."

He looked at her with the same admiration in his eyes she remembered seeing in her father's eyes for her mother. It made Natalia feel warm and cherished and adored. "You amaze me. How do you know all this?"

She shrugged. "My parents and family have tried to live by the Word of God—"

"I have had that too, though," he interrupted her. She knew it was true. His parents were believers.

"Yes, but I didn't fight what my parents taught me by their wise counsel as you have fought yours, Noel." When his gaze seemed to glaze over, she felt heat rise to her face as embarrassment flooded her. She took his hand in hers. "I'm so sorry, Noel. That sounded so pompous, so self-righteous. . . ."

"No." He reached up and touched her cheek. "It sounded only like honesty to me. I don't mind that."

"I don't want to hurt you."

"Don't you think I know that?"

"I just want you—"

"To 'get it'?" he asked.

"Do you?" she whispered. They were in a taxi zipping through midtown Manhattan, but the world seemed to stand still as she waited for his answer. "Has everything changed tonight?" she asked in spite of her best intentions not to press him. She was almost certain of it, though. Her spirit could sense it.

In less than a heartbeat he covered the few inches that separated them. And just before his lips touched hers he whispered, "My darling, I think you might count on it. . . ."

The kisses they had shared in Central Park had been special because they had been the first ones and given with a declaration of love. But this kiss was like a merging of souls going in the same direction. Natalia wished the moment to last forever.

But the trill of Noel's phone in his pocket would not allow it.

He pulled away and reached for the phone. "I sure hope that's a wrong number."

Glancing at the name on the screen, Noel frowned. "It's Rachel—that girl I told you about." He put the phone to his ear. "Rachel—" Natalia watched him raise his hand. "Wait a minute. Start from the beginning." It was clear the girl had a problem. More than the usual. Natalia leaned forward and sent up a prayer on the girl's behalf—and on Noel's that he would know what to do. "Yes, of course I can come." He gave Natalia a questioning look, as if to ask for permission.

"Of course," she whispered. Their plans to go to the Rainbow Room could wait for another night.

"Okay, where are you?" He glanced at his watch. "Sit tight. I'll be there in ten minutes." Ending the call, he turned to Natalia.

"I'm so sorry—"

Natalia stopped him. "Don't be. Is there anything I can do?"

A sheepish grin crossed his face. "I was counting on your asking. Would you mind coming with me? I make it a practice never to meet students away from the school alone. In this situation I would normally ask another counselor to accompany me, but I don't want to waste time. The girl sounded very frightened, and I'm afraid—"

"You don't need to explain," Natalia said, smiling. "I would be very happy to come with you."

"You're amazing, you know that?"

It thrilled her that he thought so. Reaching up, she placed her hand against his cheek. "Since you're the one who's going to the rescue of a disturbed teenager, I think *you're* the amazing one."

⁓❧

Not ten minutes later they walked into the diner where Rachel sat slouched in the last booth in the corner. And Noel learned that Natalia was even more remarkable than he had thought.

Rachel looked up then and saw them approaching the table. The look of astonishment and pleasure that crossed her face on seeing Natalia was so out of character for the normally ill-tempered teenager that Noel thought she was a different girl. She seemed to change before him. She went from having eyes that resembled mud on a stormy day to ones that looked as bright as a travel brochure of Bali might.

"Oh! Oh! Oh!" The girl scrambled to her feet and stood before Natalia with barely constrained glee. "Mr. Sheffield, how did you know? How did you know?"

"Hello, Rachel," he heard Natalia say and was further surprised by the way she was unflustered by the girl's reaction to her, almost as if she were used to it.

"Audrey Shepherd!" the girl exclaimed. "You're my favorite! My absolutely favorite model! I want to be just like you. Oh, I know I don't look like you. I've got dark hair, and you're very blond. But, oh, I would love to be a model like you someday!"

"*A model like you someday?*" Noel heard the girl gush and knew she couldn't be referring to someone who modeled nurses' uniforms. That wasn't Rachel's style. The girl wore only the latest, most trendy, and expensive fashions on the market. For Rachel to react this way, Natalia had to do much more than "a bit of modeling." And much more than nurses' uniforms.

The way she carried herself, her expensive address, taking six years to complete the program at the university, her clothes. Yes, now that he thought about it, he should have known. There were other things too. The way people often looked at her, almost as if they knew her. It hadn't registered that they were looking at her that way because she was famous, rather than because of her lovely appearance.

But he couldn't be angry about her omission.

He understood it.

Hadn't he done the same thing by not telling her about his book that was now six weeks on the *New York Times* best-seller list?

Rachel stopped speaking and pressed her hand against her stomach. "I don't think that will ever happen now." She turned to Noel. "Mr. Sheffield, I think I might be pregnant."

Noel's eyes widened. He couldn't help it. He'd never had to deal with this area of counseling before. The female counselors at school took these cases. He'd known he might eventually confront it, but did it have to happen now, with Natalia present?

"Now calm down, Rachel," he said and motioned for the girl to be seated. "Are you sure you are? Have you seen a doctor?" He and Natalia sat down also. He was glad Natalia chose to sit next to the girl. In her gown of sequined jewels, which even the fluorescent lights in the diner caught flashing from between the folds of her cashmere coat, she might have looked out of place in the diner. But she didn't. She looked as wonderful as she had at the concert.

"No," Rachel mumbled, sounding like a six year old. He brought his attention back to the girl, rather than where he would prefer it to be, on Natalia.

"Then how can you be sure?" he heard himself ask.

"I'm not," she shot back sullenly. "But I'm late. And I'm never late." Her voice was hard, until she seemed to remember who was sitting next to her. She looked at Natalia and asked with a sugar-sweet voice, "What have you done when you've found yourself in this situation, Audrey?"

Audrey? Noel frowned then remembered. The girl had said Natalia's professional name. Audrey something—Audrey Shepherd. She must have chosen "Shepherd" for *German shepherd*.

He watched as Natalia took a breath. He wanted to hear the answer as much as the girl. Even though he knew Natalia, in light of her profession, he wondered how she *had* coped.

"Well, first of all, my real name is Natalia, and you may call me that," she said to the girl.

"Thanks." The girl looked down but not fast enough for Noel to miss seeing she was pleased by the honor.

"Second," Natalia continued, "I have *never* found myself in that situation, Rachel, because I have never been married."

"You've *never*—I mean—I didn't think models thought they had to be married before . . ."

Natalia smiled wryly. "Some, no, but as with all groups of people and professions, not all. Many are wise about their relationships. A few are not, and they are the ones by whom people judge all others."

"Wow! So you're—I mean—since you haven't been married before—that means you're a . . . ?" She let the last word trail off, but it was obvious what she was asking. Natalia smiled at the girl before she turned back to Noel.

"That's right," she responded. Noel was glad she answered him even if he hadn't asked—and would never have asked—such a thing.

He had known all along she was pure; he had sensed it the first time they spoke at the tree. But the way he felt upon hearing her words was as if she were handing him a gift.

"Wow!" Rachel repeated her earlier declaration. "That's amazing."

Natalia looked back at her. "Not really. What is, though, is that young men and women would do things that could forever alter their lives, either through illness or"—she paused and spoke more softly—"through bringing a child into the world."

Rachel moaned. "What am I going to do?"

"Have you talked to your parents about this?" Natalia asked.

"No way!" the girl exclaimed. "They'd tell me it was my fault, and they'd probably want me to get rid of it." Natalia cringed at her words. Noel could tell that Rachel saw her cringe too, because she was quick to assure Natalia. "But I couldn't. That's one thing I couldn't do. Even if being pregnant disfigured my body so I could never be a model, I would never do that."

"I'm glad." Natalia took the girl's hand in her own. "If you are pregnant, the Bible tells us God already knows your child and wouldn't want you to hurt him or her."

Rachel looked up at her with what Noel could only describe as awe. "Do you believe in God too?"

Natalia smiled and nodded her head. "Absolutely."

"If you believe in Him, He must be real. Would you teach me about Him? I think I need Him," the girl admitted.

Noel couldn't believe what he was hearing, but he knew it was true.

And he understood it.

It was simple really: Natalia's life was a witness to this young and impressionable girl.

He heard Natalia respond with an offer of friendship. "I would love to teach you about God." When a big smile spread across Rachel's face, Noel felt that, for the first time since meeting the troubled young student, she would be okay.

Where his counseling and talking had failed, Natalia and God would not. The witness of God in Natalia's life would turn the girl around.

Of that Noel was almost certain.

And it made him glad.

Two evenings later Noel stood gazing into the miniature house—a perfect, doll-sized re-creation of the home in which he had been raised. Even the tree—the one that now graced Rockefeller Center—was included in the model. The Sheffield family would never forget it, especially Noel, because it had brought him and Natalia together.

All the miniature lights were lit in the dollhouse, giving it the warm, cozy feeling of Christmas. His mother had made tiny wreaths for every window as identical wreaths hung in the windows of the actual house.

Noel leaned down and peered into the replica of the comfortable den in which his parents and he now sat. A tree—similar to the one that stood in the corner beside the hearth—was there. Even dolls that represented his parents, him, and the two German shepherds that were lounging by the side of the fireplace were in their proper place. A miniature woman with soft platinum hair was sitting on her sofa. A man with wings of distinguished silver around his temples was ensconced on his recliner watching television. And a young man in slacks and a polo shirt stood looking at the replica of the dollhouse, which was even represented in the dollhouse itself.

Noel breathed out a sigh and turned to his mother. "I don't know how you did this. It's fantastic."

She laughed, a light tinkling sound that reminded him of Natalia. It wasn't identical, just flavored with the same pitch of happy humor. He suspected it probably had to do with his mother's and Natalia's faith. "To be truthful, I'm rather amazed I did it too."

"It was a labor of love," his father declared and gazed over at his wife. His face had that special look he reserved for the woman he loved.

His mother glanced around the room. "This home has given me much joy since the day I came to live here. I guess the model is a small way of returning some of the love I've felt within these walls since you two welcomed me and made me a part of it and a part of your lives." She placed the afghan she was crocheting to the side and reached out for the older Sheffield's hand, which was never too far away. "As your wife." She looked at Noel and sent him that wonderful look of a mother's love he had so craved when she and his father had first married and one he still treasured seeing. "And as your mother."

"It's Noel and I who have been blessed by your being here with us," the elder Sheffield was quick to respond, and Noel nodded. "I don't know what we men would have done without you, Jennifer. We would have rattled around this big, old house and driven one another nuts." His eyes twinkled in humor.

All three smiled.

They all knew they'd gotten along much better than most fathers and sons could ever hope to.

After a moment Jennifer Sheffield turned to Noel. "What I'd like to know is why the sudden interest in my dollhouses? You've made the rounds of all three of them this evening."

Noel grinned. He should have known she'd notice. "Because, Mother, I've met a young woman who shares your love of the same hobby." He'd told Natalia at the café on Thanksgiving that he was going to tell his parents about her, but he hadn't. His feelings for her had been too new for him to share with someone else then.

Jennifer clapped her hands together, then reached for the remote control. She turned the volume down on the Christmas special until only the faint sounds of carols filled the room. "Is she the reason for that special gleam I've seen lurking in your eyes lately?"

"What gleam?" Noel was prepared to tell his parents about Natalia now. But he was going to enjoy watching their curiosity run rampant first.

"As if you have a secret, but one that is too wonderful for you to believe might be true," she replied without pause.

Noel laughed. "You know me too well, Mother. But it gets even better, especially from your standpoint."

"What do you mean?"

"She's a Christian. I mean a Christian like you and Dad are Christians."

"Hallelujah!" his mother sang out. Noel wasn't surprised when he saw tears fill her eyes. She was an emotional woman. "That's an answer to our prayers for you, Son."

Noel's father reached out and placed his hand on his wife's arm. "Now wait a minute, Dear," he said with the steadiness of his legal profession. "Noel didn't say he was marrying her."

"But I'd like to." Noel didn't want to leave any doubt in their minds concerning his intentions toward Natalia. He had the pleasure of seeing shock, unlike any other time before, cover his distinguished father's face. He chuckled. "Dad, I think I've finally gotten the last word." That was a joke between them. Quincy Sheffield was a brilliant man, and it was a rare moment when someone said anything that could close his mouth.

The older man, whose appearance was a good indication of how Noel would look in thirty years, chuckled back. "Most definitely," he conceded before his face turned serious. "But if she is, as you say, a Christian, who holds Christ as the center of her life, then I'm sorry, Son, but—" He paused and looked at his wife.

Her joy seemed to wilt like a flower left without water on a hot summer day, though with a nod she encouraged him to continue.

"What, Dad?"

His father turned back to him. "I'm sorry, Son, but I doubt she'll marry you without your being one as well."

Noel walked over to the dogs and, kneeling down, patted the head of the older German shepherd. Laddie responded with his happy-go-lucky doggie grin and his tail tapping happily against the floor. Noel smiled at the dog, then stood and faced his parents.

"She took me to see the oratorio *Messiah,* by George Handel, the other night. To say I was emotionally moved would be a gross understatement." He paused and looked up toward the star that twinkled on top of the tree. It made him remember the star it signified. The star that heralded the birth of God's Son on earth, the star that told the world that a whole new volume in the world's story was starting.

He looked back at his parents and smiled. "What I experienced," he said, "was something almost life changing. No." He corrected himself. "It *was* life changing. During that performance, I realized I wanted all the promises of those fantastic, prophetic words. I wanted to believe everything. And you know what, Mom?" He looked at his mother, then turned to his father. "Dad? I do. I might not know much, but I believe. I believe with all my heart that it's true—that Jesus is God's Son, that He is God."

"Hallelujah!" his father's voice sang out.

Noel saw tears come into his father's eyes, but he wasn't concerned. They weren't the sad ones of the only other time he had seen them in his strong father's eyes: the day they had buried the wonderful woman who had given Noel life. These tears were happy ones. And with his limited understanding Noel could grasp why his father felt so moved that tears would fill his eyes now.

"Tell us about her," his mother whispered, dabbing at the corners of her own eyes. "Tell us about this woman we've been praying for many years would enter your life."

"You've been praying for her?"

She nodded. "We suspected that only a woman you loved would be able to lead you to Christ."

"That's why we've been, well, leaving you alone," his father added.

"We always hoped that such a woman would come into your life and share her faith with you," his mother explained.

"That's the truth," his father agreed.

"Natalia is wonderful and—" He stopped speaking when he saw his parents' faces turn ashen. "What?"

"*Natalia* is the girl's name?" His father reached over and took his wife's hand.

The atmosphere in the room changed from joy to apprehension. Noel felt the muscles along his shoulders tense and forced himself to relax.

"Natalia Pappas—"

His mother gasped, and Noel stopped speaking. She seemed to wilt against his father while her slender white hands covered her face. His father cradled her against him.

Noel was at a loss. Then his mother lowered her hands from her face, and he saw a rapturous expression coloring her features.

"Has she . . . by any chance . . . mentioned to you whether she was adopted?" she asked.

Noel frowned. "Adopted?" An uneasy feeling ran through him. "No. She's never said anything to me about being adopted. The only thing I know is that she loves her family very much. Her father is a priest—"

His mother's gaze searched his face. "A Greek Orthodox priest? From Greece?"

"How—?" He held out his hands in question.

For a moment it was almost as if he weren't there. His mother turned to his father, and Noel heard the older man say, "All in God's timing, my dear. It's all in His hands."

She nodded, and her soft, platinum blond curls bobbed silkily against her shoulders. "That's what you've always told me, my dear, wise husband. And it seems you have been correct."

Ordinarily Noel wouldn't interrupt such a moment between his parents, but he had to know what they were talking about. It concerned Natalia. "What's 'all in God's timing'? What's 'in His hands'?"

The older Sheffield narrowed his eyes, silently asking his wife for permission to tell. She nodded slightly, and his father turned to him. "You recall we told you that before your adoptive mother and I met, she gave birth to a little girl. What we haven't told you is that she deserted the little girl in a bus station in a small city in Greece on Christmas Eve nearly twenty-five years ago. We've been praying for the little girl every day since we met. A Greek Orthodox priest and his wife adopted her. She was born on December 1, the same day as you, my son, three years later. That little girl, Natalia Pappas, grew into a young woman who models under the name Audrey Shepherd."

Except for the clock striking the hour of ten and the soft breathing of the dogs, silence reigned after his father stopped speaking.

Noel knew he was staring at his parents.

His mouth hung open.

But he couldn't help it.

Never in his wildest imaginings would he have considered such an amazing story as his father had just described. The fact that his adoptive mother had given up a baby, when she herself had been little more than a child, wasn't news to him. His parents had never made a secret of the life she had led before she met his father and, more importantly, before she met the Lord Jesus Christ. Both occurred at about the same time.

No.

What astonished Noel was that the little girl his father referred to, and the woman he had thought about since the first time he had seen her looking at the Rockefeller Center Christmas tree three years earlier, were one and the same. Natalia!

He smiled at his parents to ease their minds in case they were wondering how he felt. And the thought kept playing through his head: The Supreme Being had been orchestrating the events of their lives as much as the conductor had orchestrated the *Messiah*.

"Hallelujah!" Noel finally managed to whoop out. He reached for his parents and engulfed them in a gigantic hug.

The three stood together and laughed with relief, joy, and thanksgiving. Then, in the twinkling lights of the Christmas tree, with the soft strains of carols playing inside and the snow falling gently to the earth outside, they cried happy tears.

❧

Natalia looked away from the slow-burning fire to the Charles X clock on the mantel in the Howards' living room as it struck ten o'clock. She sighed. The sound of Christmas carols from the special the Howards were watching on TV and the softly falling snow lit by streetlights outside the huge window gave a cozy feeling to the night. It was a moment of family comfort, one Natalia treasured to have found in New York City. Kneeling down, she rubbed her fingers absently across Prince's velvety ears. The dog lifted his head, seemed to smile, yawned, then lowered his head to the carpet. Prince liked a warm place to lie down and a thick carpet beneath him.

Only one thing would make this moment more perfect, Natalia thought. And that would be to have Noel by her side. She sighed as she looked out the window again. That wouldn't happen for a few days. She had to go to Maine on a modeling shoot early the next morning and wouldn't return until the following week.

"You really like him, don't you?" Janet Howard asked from her place on the sofa.

Natalia looked over at her. "Who? Prince? Of course I do."

"Oh, darling girl! Don't you think I know you well enough to know when you sigh over your dog and when you sigh over the man you—love?" she asked. Her husband chuckled softly.

"She has a point," Jasper Howard agreed with his wife, tilting his recliner forward.

Natalia knew what that meant. He was ready for a serious discussion.

Her gaze went back and forth between the two people she loved as much as she did her own family. She knew they wouldn't be put off. She was glad. She wanted to tell them. "I do . . . love . . . him," she admitted. She let the smile in her soul shine out and laughed. "I do!"

Janet clapped her hands together. "It's like a fairy-tale romance."

"It is!" How many times had she herself used that expression? "Made even more wonderful because the prince of my dreams wants to welcome the Prince of Peace into his life."

"Oh, darling girl!" Janet exclaimed.

"That's wonderful," Jasper said.

"I was going to ask about that," Janet admitted. "But I trusted your judgment."

"Just pray for him," Natalia implored. "We haven't really had a chance to discuss it, but I'm certain he made a decision the other night at the *Messiah*." His answer, after she had asked him if everything had changed, *"My darling, I think you might count on it . . ."* had been going through her head like a glorious refrain for the last two days. "He hasn't said anything specifically," she continued, "but I don't think he will until his decision to believe can be justified by his knowledge of who Jesus is."

"Many people need to let their intellect catch up with their belief, especially when it's new and profound," Jasper pointed out. "Don't worry."

"Oh, I'm not," Natalia said, smiling. "I just can't wait for these next few days to pass so we can see each other again. He loves onomastics, the study of names, so I challenged him to discover who Jesus is by studying His names and—"

"That's it!" Janet exclaimed and jumped up, startling both Natalia and Prince. Prince jumped up suddenly too and stood at canine attention while Natalia gathered the pillows that Janet's sudden movement had scattered all over the floor.

"What's 'it'?" Natalia asked, looking at Jasper. His eyes crinkled at their corners. He was used to his wife's sudden movements.

"That's where I've seen him before!" Janet clicked her fingers together. "I *knew* he looked familiar."

Natalia frowned as she instructed Prince to lie back down. "What are you talking about?"

But Janet only waved at her as she dashed over to the bookshelf. "Here it is!" She pulled a book off the shelf. "*What's in a Name?* by Noel Sheffield."

"What?" She reached for the book Janet passed to her. She turned to the back jacket and gasped when Noel's smiling face stared up at her. Rubbing her fingertips over the beloved features, she whispered, "Noel."

"'Loves onomastics, the study of names,'" Janet repeated. "Darling girl, he's one of the foremost authorities on the meanings of names. Not only that, but this book has been on the *New York Times* best-seller list for weeks. And I think he's had other successful books as well."

"He never said a word."

"Does that bother you?"

Does it? Natalia wondered. She shook her head. "No, it really doesn't. I didn't tell him much about my modeling career. Probably for the same reason he didn't tell me about this. He didn't want me to judge him by it any more than I wanted him to judge me by my modeling." She held up the book. "Is it good?"

"Wonderful," Janet answered. "I bought it in case one of our sons ever decides to make us grandparents. I'll have it ready for them to search out names."

"Umm." Natalia wasn't thinking about Janet's words nor the Howards' married-but-childless sons. She had turned to the beginning of the book Noel had written. It was his thoughts, his words. That made it important to her.

"Why don't you read it?" Janet suggested.

"I think I've already started," she admitted wryly.

Janet and Jasper exchanged amused and knowing glances, then settled back and watched the Christmas special.

"Happy reading," Janet said.

Natalia gladly lowered her gaze to the book.

But out of the corners of her eyes, she saw Jasper wiggle his left ring finger with his wedding band glistening around it, then motion to her. Janet nodded and smiled. Natalia knew they thought wedding bells might soon be pealing for her.

Natalia hoped they were right.

❧

"I still don't see how you could have kept from going to her and telling her everything once you found out she was living here in New York," Noel said for about the tenth time to his parents.

The Christmas special had ended long ago, although, after his parents' revelations, no one had paid any attention to it. The three were sitting around the fireplace talking. They had a lot to talk about.

"I wanted to," his mother admitted. "Oh, how I yearned to. But after much prayer I didn't think it was right. Maybe if I'd put her in an orphanage, I would have gone to her. But, Noel, I had deserted her in a bus station and in a foreign country. It would be difficult for anyone to forgive another person for that, especially the person who had given you life." She shrugged her shoulders, reminding Noel of Natalia. "It goes against even the most primitive laws of how a mother is to act toward her child."

"Mom." Noel squeezed his mother's hand. "I know Natalia. She will forgive you. In fact, I'm sure she already has without knowing you."

"But, from what you've said, she hasn't even mentioned she was adopted."

"That's true. But I don't think it's a reflection on you as much as a reflection on how much she loves the family that raised her. She loves them dearly."

"I am so glad for that, so thankful," his mother said. Noel could feel the truth of that declaration. It radiated from her.

"Please let me handle introducing the two of you," he said.

His mother beamed at him. "Would you do that for me?"

"Of course, Mom. What do you think? I have no choice really. I love both of you. I now know something that concerns Natalia in a very personal way." He paused. "Other than that, would you understand me if I said it's something I feel led to do?"

His parents nodded.

"God's leading," his father said, his voice filled with emotion. "It's a wonderful gift God gives a believer in His Son, Jesus, by the Holy Spirit."

Noel nodded. "I have a lot to consider the next few days while Natalia is away on her photo shoot." He had already told them she would be in Maine for the next several days. "Not only do I have to consider how I will tell her what you've told me about her parentage, but I have an assignment from Natalia too. She's charged me with learning about Jesus through studying His names."

His mother gasped. "Oh!" She hopped up from her chair like a surprised cat and dashed over to the tree. Kneeling down, she rummaged through the gaily wrapped presents until she found one. Coming back to Noel, she held it against her chest for a moment. "I ordered this several weeks ago. It arrived today." She handed it to him. "Please open it now."

Noel glanced over at his father, who shrugged his shoulders.

He gave his attention to the Christmas gift paper that covered the book. The Christ child was depicted on it. He rubbed his fingers over the golden image. *"For he shall reign for ever and ever!"* He didn't think he would ever look at manger scenes again without the music from the *Messiah* going through his head and thrilling his soul. He removed the paper carefully. It was his turn to gasp when the title of the book was revealed to him.

The Names of Jesus.

He looked up at his mother and didn't try to hide the tears that had gathered in his eyes. "You . . . and your . . . daughter—" He paused. "You and Natalia are so much alike, Mother." He looked down at the book again. "What a coincidence."

"Son." His father rested his large hand upon Noel's shoulder. "You will soon find that with God"—the older man cleared his throat—"there are no coincidences."

Noel nodded. That was something he was fast learning.

11

atalia arrived at her apartment at 10:00 P.M. the following Tuesday night. The phone rang one minute later.

She answered it, and Noel's voice greeted her. "I'm glad you're back in town," he said.

She took off her coat, flipped on the tree-lights switch with her toe, and plopped down on the sofa to gaze out at the flurries of snow that danced among the trees in the park across the avenue.

"Me too," she responded. "I missed you."

"Not nearly as much as I missed you."

She pushed her hair behind her ear and smiled into the phone. "That's debatable."

"Well, how about we debate it tomorrow?"

"When and where?"

"Central Park. Noon. By the statue of Balto."

She laughed. "I think you've set me up."

"That's only the start. I have a very special Christmas surprise for you."

"But it's not Christmas yet." They still had a week to go before that blessed day arrived.

"Ah, dear Natalia, I'm beginning to think that Christmas, for those who believe, is an event to be celebrated every day."

"Noel—" she whispered then hesitated. "Does this mean—?"

"Tomorrow," he interrupted her. "You told me the first day we spoke that you believe in something similar to fairy tales, what you called 'God tales.'"

The delight she felt at his words made her weak. She was glad she was sitting.

"Well, let me organize tomorrow. Trust me and"—he paused and his voice lowered—"trust God. It will be a day you won't ever forget. I promise you. A day that will change your life, mine, and probably several others' forever."

She squeezed her eyes shut. She was sure he was going to tell her he believed, and then he was going to ask her to marry him. She knew what her answer would be. It was a fairy-tale romance, made perfect because her prince had finally discovered why he liked the Christmas season so much and let the Spirit of God—not just the Christmas spirit—work in his heart.

"Okay. Tomorrow. Noon. By the statue of Balto."

"Good night, my love," he whispered.

After they hung up she looked down at her dog. Why did Noel want to meet by the statue of Balto? It had been built to commemorate the brave dog that had led the last relay team of sled dogs over treacherous terrain in 1925 to bring antitoxin to the stricken people of Nome, Alaska.

She shrugged her shoulders. It might be a strange place for a man to propose marriage, but she didn't care.

Kneeling, she rubbed her hand through the soft fur of her tired dog. Prince loved traveling. But after being transported first by helicopter, then plane, then car, he was ready to rest. "Sleep well, Prince Charming, my boy!" Natalia sang out. "For tomorrow we're going to see Prince Charming, the man of my dreams!"

After being away from each other the last four days, Natalia was glad to see Noel waiting for her by the statue. Snow from the previous night still spotted the ground and clung to Balto's curly tail. She detached Prince's lead from his collar and watched her beloved canine friend dart over to Noel.

Feeling jealous, Natalia ran too. Noel lifted her off her feet and twirled her around in his arms. Crystal flakes of snow flittered around them as Noel's lips touched hers. Even though the day was cold, Noel's lips were warm and welcoming.

The kiss ended much too soon for Natalia. But sensing he would soon speak words that would enable them to have a life together, she stood back and looked up at him, leaving her hands locked around his neck.

"I've missed you, and I have so much to tell you," he said, his blue eyes vibrant with a clear light that seemed to originate in his soul.

"Tell! Tell!" She could hardly wait.

"You aren't curious, are you?" he asked and laughed, a deep, rich sound that reverberated around the bare trees, filling the air with joy and her with warmth.

"I am!" she admitted and laughed too. She felt as free and happy as she had when she was a child. "I want to know what happened to you the night of the performance of the *Messiah*. What did you mean when you told me I might count on everything having changed for you? And I want to know why you believe Christmas should be celebrated every day." She let go of him and climbed onto the rocky outcropping on which Balto's statue stood. She wrapped her arms around the statue as she had her own dog so many times. "And I want to know why you wanted to meet here." She stood up straight. "I love this spot and what this statue represents, canines who have given so much in service to humans." She looked at Prince, who was playing in the snow in the clearing to their right. He had served her on a daily basis by offering her unconditional protection, companionship, and love. "But I'm intrigued as to why you chose it. I know you have a good reason."

He stepped up beside her and laid his hand on the ears of the stone dog, worn smooth by children rubbing them for more than seventy-five years. Natalia had often thought people were trying to resurrect the dog, rubbing it like Aladdin's magic lamp, yearning for the same goodness. But if they had only known much more remarkable goodness and truth could be theirs simply by believing in the redemptive work of Jesus, the Man who was resurrected.

That thought brought all others to a stop.

She guessed, even before Noel spoke, that that was the reason he'd wanted to meet here.

He must have seen the resemblance between Balto and his teammates' heroic drive in the dead of an Alaskan winter to save the people of Nome and that of the much greater redemptive work of the Lord Jesus Christ who came to earth to save humanity with the medicine He brought for sin: His own death and resurrection.

"Did you know it took twenty mushers and that many teams of dogs to carry antitoxin to the people of Nome, Alaska, who were dying from diphtheria?" Noel began speaking without preamble. He patted the dog, who had been about the same size as Prince. "And that Balto was the lead dog who got them through, using his God-instilled instincts in the blizzard during those last crucial miles into town?"

She nodded. She knew but didn't want to interrupt what Noel was saying.

"I've known it too, since I was a little boy." He indicated the shiny ears. "I helped polish them by touching them so much when I was a boy. Whenever I could I came here." He sighed. "Like who Santa Claus represented, I loved this dog and what he symbolized." He jumped down and pointed to the plaque in front of the dog.

" 'Dedicated to the indomitable spirit of the sled dogs that relayed antitoxin six hundred miles over rough ice across treacherous waters through arctic blizzards from Nenana to the relief of stricken Nome in the winter of 1925.' "

He was silent for a moment; it seemed to Natalia as if the angels in God's heaven waited with her for Noel's next words.

"The night of the performance I finally started to realize that a rescue mission was exactly what Jesus did for the town of earth by coming to us as a baby. It was something much more grand than what God's creatures and the men who drove them did for the town of Nome all those years ago."

"Hallelujah," she whispered.

In the space between the snowflakes falling around them, she was certain she heard angels sing out the same word of praise.

"I used to think that if Jesus had been anything more than a good man or a prophet, He would have taken the misery and pain out of the world. But I finally realized that His coming to earth as fully Man and fully God, more than two thousand years ago, was just part of the story. A climax in the story of God's redemption of mankind, to be sure," he added, "but only part of the story."

He gazed into her eyes deeply, and Natalia saw the love of a man for a woman—for her—shining out of his eyes. It was a love she readily recognized because she had seen it often between people she cared a great deal about: her parents, Stavros and Allie, her married brothers and sister, Janet and Jasper. But to see it directed toward her, a true love—not one of infatuation or for the beauty of her outward self—was an experience that nearly took her breath away. His next words did that, however, for what he said had maturity to it, an unusual understanding for a new believer.

"I finally realized we are only partway through the Book—that the patriarchs, judges, kings, and prophets of the Old Testament, the birth of Christ, even the church, are part of the story. They are climaxes in the novel, but not *the* climax. That climax will be when Christ returns. That will be the 'happily ever after' of the story. Sickness and pain will be no more, and the heavenly choir of angels as well as believers will sing, ' "He will reign for ever and ever!" ' " His eyes widened in joy. "And you know what, Natalia? Both of our voices will now be part of that choir."

"Oh, Noel!" She pulled him to her. "I am so glad. So glad."

"Wait. There's more."

"What else could there be?"

"You'd be surprised," he replied in a way that perplexed her. "First, did you know there are more than a hundred names for Jesus? That's because not one name, or even three, can contain all of who He is."

"Noel! How did you start studying them? Using the *Messiah* as a guide?"

He moved over to the rock outcropping, sat down, and pulled her onto his lap. She felt warm and wonderful and cherished, everything a woman sitting upon a man's lap on a cold December day could want to feel. "Well, now, here's something amazing."

"Something else, you mean?"

He rubbed his nose against hers. "So many great things have happened the last few days."

"Tell me," she prompted. "I promise not to interrupt."

He laughed. "Is that possible?"

She laughed too.

"Well, when I told my mother about your having advised me to learn about Jesus by studying His names, she gave me a gift she had oddly bought for me this Christmas—a book called *The Names of Jesus*. I thought at first it was a coincidence."

Natalia was about to tell him she didn't believe in coincidences when he seemed to pull the words right out of her mouth.

"Of course, I now understand that nothing is happenstance. God had your advice and my mother's gift coordinated."

"Coordinated. Hmm. I like that." She had never heard it put that way, but she thought it perfect. She could see that Noel would add fantastic thoughts to a believer's efforts to understand God. Life with him would be an adventure.

She paused. If he ever offered to share his life with her.

But when would she hear the words from his mouth?

He leaned toward her until his forehead came down to touch hers, then moved his head back a fraction of an inch. "I still have more to tell you, things I've—recently—learned." He hesitated over the words, and she felt fingers of apprehension move up her spine.

"What things do you have to tell me?" She thought he was referring to his career as a writer. But he said things he'd recently learned.

He glanced at his watch. "I'll tell you on our way."

"On our way?" She looked at him, even more puzzled now. "On our way where?"

"To meet my parents."

12

*A*rm in arm, talking and laughing the entire way, Noel and Natalia walked across the park to the garage close to Noel's brownstone town house where he kept his cars: a Jeep and a red sports car. Since the weather was inclement and Prince was with them, he pulled out his Jeep. After awhile of Noel maneuvering the Jeep across Manhattan's busy streets, Natalia turned to him with a grin. "So when were you going to tell me about your publishing success?"

He grimaced. "How did you—?" he started to ask then stopped. "Actually I was going to tell you about it today." He glanced over at her as they drove onto the George Washington Bridge. "Are you upset?"

She offered him her hand, and he took it. "I hardly have the right, Noel, since I didn't tell you the extent of my modeling career, did I?"

"Being a writer isn't who I am—"

"Any more than being a model is who I am."

"Exactly."

She was glad they agreed.

"It's a wonderful book," she said as they crossed over the state line and into New Jersey.

The corners of his mouth turned up in surprise. "You've read it?"

"Uh-huh, a few nights ago. Janet Howard had a copy. That's how I found out."

"I think the next one will deal with the names of Jesus found in the *Messiah*."

"Noel!" she exclaimed. "That's wonderful."

"No," he corrected her. "*He's* wonderful."

She certainly wouldn't deny that. "But on a human level you are too, my love. You are a wonderful counselor. Look at what you've done for Rachel."

"Me?" His glance left the road for a second to meet her steady and open gaze. "Don't you mean *you?*" he corrected her.

"I haven't done much," she demurred. "Just talked to her by phone a couple of times."

" 'Haven't done—'? Natalia, giving the girl your personal number and allowing her to call you is—"

"Just trying to be a good steward with what God has given me, Noel," she finished for him. "If the profession in which I make my livelihood can help somebody simply by its nature and by the way I live my life within it"—she shrugged—"then that gives my work real worth."

"Well, the example of your life has turned Rachel's around. She doesn't wear skimpy clothes to school anymore, she's cleaned up her speech, and I don't think she'll lead a wild life any longer. Her parents don't think so either, and they couldn't be happier." He drew in a deep and satisfied breath. "They were so concerned about her and didn't know what else to do. That was why they asked me to help her as much as I could in my capacity as her high school counselor. It's so rewarding to see that family drawing together."

"I'm so glad for them. And of course you must know she's not pregnant. It was a false alarm."

"But one that God used in His plan for her."

Natalia let her gaze roam over his profile. He had chiseled male features that appeared to be cast in bronze as he concentrated on both the road and his thoughts. But she knew what warmth was there, that of a man who cared about a young high school student, about his own family, about her, and now about the things of God. The degree of his understanding amazed her. Seldom did a person come to believe and learn so quickly. But he had been around parents who believed all his life. That had to have made a difference. "You're absolutely correct," she agreed after a moment and turned her gaze forward as the jeep ate up the miles. She felt such contentment. Her world seemed to be falling into shape perfectly.

"If only *my* mother had had a role model like you to talk to when she was young," he continued after several minutes of companionable silence. "She might not have become wild."

Her glance slid to his face again. "Your mother was wild?" She knew from earlier conversations that his mother was a strong Christian.

"Well," he replied, "my biological mother was a very strong Christian. My father has laughingly told me in the past that she probably never did anything wrong in her entire life."

"Your *'biological*—'?" Her eyes widened. "You mean the woman you refer to as your mother is your *stepmother?*"

"No, she's actually my mother too," he stated. "She adopted me legally when I was nine."

"I had no idea." But as with his being a writer and her, a high-fashion model, she wondered what else they might have neglected to share with one another. She had never told him she had been adopted either, but only because the subject had never come up. And even though her father had encouraged her to be open to finding her biological mother, she had given the situation to God on her first day back in New York from Kastro, and she really didn't think about it. At some point she knew she must tell Noel. But right now he was telling her about himself. And there was no way she was going to interrupt that.

"It isn't something that's in my mind. I remember my biological mother with much fondness and love, but Jennifer *is* my mother."

"I can understand that." *Could she ever!*

"I imagine you can," he said evenly.

She looked at him sharply. Did he know about her having been adopted? Or was he simply referring to her being able to empathize with him? But as the car covered the miles across New Jersey on the way to his parents' home, he continued to talk about his family, so she decided to let it go. She had plenty of time to tell her story.

"My natural mother died when I was six. Remember the conversation we had about Santa Claus at the café the day of the parade?"

Surprise flickered across her face. Santa Claus? What did Santa have to do with this? "Yes?"

"Well, I finally figured out a few days ago that one reason I was so negative about letting my parents teach me about God was because I was angry about the death of both my mother and, as strange as it might sound, Santa. Finding out Santa wasn't real, he didn't live at the North Pole, and he didn't fly through the sky with a sleigh full of toys every Christmas Eve was very traumatic for me. It was almost as if he had died too."

Her heart went out to the hurting little boy Noel had been. In Kastro, little Jeannie Andreas had been wounded in a similar way by her mother's desertion of her. But at least Natalia had been able to hug the little girl close to her and do fun things with her to try to ease her pain. Then Jeannie's new mother, Allie, had come into her life and filled it with the mother's love the little girl had so craved. But Natalia couldn't do anything for the boy Noel had been. She could only be thankful for the new mother who had adopted him—the boy who had grown into the man she loved—when he was nine.

"That's one of the dangers associated with the secular myth about Santa." Her answer was soft but firm in its psychological affirmation of what had happened to him. "What concerns many is that kids are taught to believe in Santa and his powers, rather than being taught that the true Santa Claus was a Christian, who believed in Christ with his whole heart. Children are given a tarnished and untrue image of Christ to believe in, as a sort of Christmas spirit, rather than the real God. All these things would, I think, make that dear old clergyman Nicholas from the Greek world long ago very sad."

"You know, Natalia, I can remember crying out to both Jesus and Santa to save my mother." There was a steely quality to his voice as he thought back. She reached over and placed her hand over his. Instinctively his hand grasped hers. "When neither did, I decided they were both fake."

"But, Noel, just because Jesus didn't save your mother—"

His hand tightened on hers before he let go of it to take the exit ramp off the interstate. "I know that now. But try getting that into the head of an angry six year old who just lost the most important person in his life, as well as the Santa he thought could give him his wish for Christmas—his mother's health." He turned into a gated roadway and pulled the car to the side. He cut the engine, and peace enveloped the car. Only the sound of Prince's breathing could be heard in the hushed world that surrounded them.

Natalia gazed out on one of the most beautiful wintertime vistas she'd ever seen. A Currier and Ives print couldn't have painted the snow-covered world any better. Rolling hills, distant barns, stately homes, the bare branches of trees silhouetted against the horizon, and a few brave conifers holding out their needle-clothed arms, filled the white world of earth and sky. It was still and wearing its snow mantle, perfect and pure.

Noel turned to her and took her hand in his again. His fingers were warm, firm, sure. "I know I'll see my mother again because of what God, born as a baby, did for us all. And in Jennifer I was given a wonderful second mother."

"From how you've talked about her, it's obvious you love her very much."

"I do. She's a very special woman."

Natalia thought that now was the time to tell him about her own background. It wasn't important to her because she had always considered *Mamma* and *Baba* her very own parents, but she knew she had to tell Noel. Whether she wanted it or not, her biological parentage was part of who she was. She leaned toward him and placed her hand on his cheek.

"That's something I can understand, Noel." She was silent for a moment. "You see, I was adopted too, by both of my parents. I never knew my natural mother or father."

When he didn't respond, by word or even a flicker of emotion in his face, she felt apprehension slicing through her again.

Finally he admitted in a low and husky tone, "I know you were adopted, Natalia."

Then fear ran in to keep her apprehension company.

That was the last thing she'd expected. Her hand fell from his face, and she sat back. *How did he know?* "You know? Did the Howards tell you?" That would be the only way he could have known. Not even the tabloids had that information.

"No. My father told me a few days ago."

"Your father?" Now panic ran through her system like a fire alarm might a building.

"Until then I had no idea of what I'm about to tell you."

"Noel." She hugged herself, rubbing her hands against her arms. She could feel the goose bumps rising beneath her cashmere sweater. "You're scaring me. How could your father have known?" Then suspicion filled her. "Have you had me investigated?" She nearly choked on the word and reached for Prince who, picking up on her fear, had stuck his head into the front of the Jeep. His great head, with its mouth full of teeth, was between her and Noel. She was unexpectedly glad she had her trusted canine companion with her.

Dear Lord! Have I been wrong to trust Noel? To love him? She cried out to God, the One who would always be with her and could always be counted upon.

"No," a voice spoke calmingly within her. *"Everything is in My control. Just trust."*

"I know this seems strange to you—"

"Strange!" Her voice shook. "Noel, how do you know—?"

"I know because Jennifer, the woman my father married when I was nine, was a very wild teenager. More so than Rachel. And, unlike Rachel, when my adoptive mother was sixteen, she did become pregnant. Then, when she was seventeen, she was backpacking around Greece with her boyfriend—"

"Greece!" Natalia gasped. *I know! I know what Noel is about to say.*

She saw him reach for her, but she barely felt his arms as they wrapped around her. She went numb and had to force herself to hear his words through the pounding in her brain.

"—when she gave birth to a baby girl."

'Gave birth to a baby girl!'

As if a gigantic vacuum had pushed its way into her chest, Natalia's breath was sucked out of her. It would have been easier for her to understand if Noel had announced he was going to take a trip to the moon rather than grasp the words he'd just uttered.

"I—was—that—baby?" She finally managed to gulp enough air to ask against his shoulder. Tears flooded her eyes at the unexpected wave of euphoria that washed over her upon discovering her mother's whereabouts. She had always been so blasé about meeting her biological mother. Suddenly she realized her cool indifference had been a facade. Now it was melting like an ice sculpture under the warm rays of the sun. And she knew her *baba* had been right to encourage her to meet her natural mother someday.

She heard answering tears in Noel's voice. "Yes, you, my darling. My adoptive mother—is your biological mother. She gave birth to you in Greece—on December first—three years to the day—after I was born." Emotions clogged his throat, halting his speech.

For a moment they held one another, and Natalia knew the arms holding her were the ones she wanted around her—*"for better or for worse, for richer or for poorer, in sickness and in health"*—forever.

His clean masculine scent filled her senses. She was so glad Noel was the man she had thought he was. "My *baba* always encouraged me to find my biological mother, or at least be receptive to her finding me," she whispered.

He moved just far enough back from her on the leather seat so he could look into her eyes. "Really?"

She nodded.

"And are you, my darling? Receptive to her finding you?" She thought from the way the blue of his eyes became as deep and intense as a mountain lake in winter that it was something for which he fervently hoped.

She wiped the tears from her eyes as the miracle of God's timing swept through her. "It's something I prayed about and gave to God the afternoon we met, Noel. The only other thing I asked of Him—" She stopped speaking as the wonder of it filled her, and she turned her gaze to the pristine world of white that surrounded them.

"What, my darling?"

She turned back to him and, remembering her plea to God, repeated it. "I asked Him, if possible, that my biological mother might be a Christian now," she said softly.

Making a sound of joy, he pulled her close to him and, like leaves rustling on the ground, said, "She is, Natalia. Not only that but"—he spoke with more force—"she's been keeping an eye on you through your doorman Roswell for the last five years—ever since she realized the modeling superstar Audrey Shepherd was her daughter."

She blinked. "Roswell?"

He nodded. "She came to your apartment building, and after understanding what sort of man Roswell was, she confided in him. That's why the dear man hasn't retired. He's been staying on for my mother." He gave a small laugh and touched the tip of her nose. "Your mother."

"My mother . . ." *To have a mother again.* It was a gift, especially since she knew what sort of woman she was from hearing Noel talk about her so much.

"But now Roswell will retire and live in the beautiful carriage house on this estate with his wife and family for as long as they wish—now that he no longer needs to give her weekly reports about you. When he met me the morning of our birthdays, he didn't know I was Jennifer Sheffield's son. He just found out yesterday when I told him."

"And your mother—my natural mother—wants to meet me now?"

"With all her heart. And—to ask your forgiveness."

Natalia shook her head. That thought seemed almost absurd to her.

"I've had a wonderful life, Noel. I grew up in a land that seems like something out of a fairy tale with the most wonderful family imaginable. Then God brought me to America, and I've lived like a princess in a storybook. And now the man I love, the prince of my dreams"—she ran her hand over the fine contours of his face—"has not only discovered the Prince of Peace but has welcomed Him into his life." She shook her head. "No, Noel, I don't have to forgive my natural mother for anything. I only have to thank her. I would not ask for a different life."

"Natalia," he whispered and pulled her close to him. "Dear Natalia. That mind of yours keeps up with your heart in a way I wouldn't have believed possible"—he leaned back and held her face between his hands—"if I hadn't lived with Jennifer for nearly twenty years. She has filled my world with the same mature wisdom. You and she walked different paths—something unusual for mothers and daughters to do—and yet God has brought you both to the same blessed one. You are so much alike. It is—" He stopped what he was going to say. "Well, it *would* be unbelievable if I didn't understand how the Great Conductor works."

Natalia nodded. "Amazing, isn't it?"

"More like miraculous."

She laughed lightly, thrilled to hear Noel speak in such a godly way. "I'll agree with that."

His eyes narrowed. "Are you ready to meet your mother, my darling?"

She nodded slowly. "That is something for which my earthly *baba*, as well as my heavenly Father, have been preparing me for several years. Yes, Noel. I'm ready."

13

To say that Natalia was delighted with the woman who had given her life would be putting it mildly. God had ordained their reunion so there were only tears of joy and much laughter. Natalia felt more like a beloved child coming home after a long absence than a daughter who had been deserted so many years before. If she had been given a choice of any woman in the world to be her biological mother, it would have been Jennifer Sheffield. She loved her mother upon sight, and she knew her mother loved her too, as Jennifer held her and kissed her and explored her face, looking for the infant of so long ago. All the days of their lives they would cherish finding one another after so many years.

The tree lights twinkled, a new snowfall drifted down past the windows, and the three German shepherds lay happily near the fireplace, for Prince had become fast friends with Laddie and his son, Harry. And Noel and his father sat quietly while Natalia and Jennifer held hands and talked about everything—the far distant past and the more recent one.

"You must remember, Natalia, that I was a very foolish young woman," Jennifer said. "To put it succinctly, I was a spoiled brat. I had been given everything money could buy, and I spurned it and the lifestyle it bought for me. But, worst of all, I left you, my precious baby, in a bus station in a foreign land. The only right thing I did was to wait and make sure good people found you. When that wonderful man—that Greek Orthodox priest—and his wife held you, I knew they would love you and never let you go." She glanced at the older Sheffield and sent him a look of thankfulness. "Until I met Noel's father, I was a very lost, very nasty young woman. Quincy's faith and his love of God got through to me as nothing else could—not the doctors my parents took me to see or the rehab clinics from which I repeatedly escaped."

Natalia squeezed the long and slender hand that so resembled her own. "That's an amazing testimony . . . Mother." The title rolled easily off her lips. She had always called her adoptive mother *Mamma,* so calling her natural mother "Mother" did not conflict with the special relationship she'd had with her *mamma* at all. Natalia knew too that her *mamma* would have been glad.

"Mother?" The older woman squeezed her eyes together. "What have I done that you'd call me that wonderful name?"

"You gave me life," Natalia responded, "and it's a life I've liked very much. Thank you."

"But can you forgive me, dear daughter? Can you ever forgive me for being so immature, so wrong, to leave you behind?"

Natalia was slow to answer. She wanted to do so with care. "By giving me away, I think you gave me the best life you could at that time. To grow up in the loving family you found for me was a rare treasure. Not only is my family very special, but the village where I was raised is too."

"We went to Kastro once," Jennifer confessed and motioned to both Noel and her husband. "The three of us did."

"What?" Natalia and Noel asked in unison and looked at one another in disbelief.

Jennifer nodded and answered Noel. "That's where we went on our honeymoon."

"*Kastro* was where we went?" Noel turned to his father for confirmation.

The older man's smile widened. "That's it."

"I remember the village." Noel squinted, as he seemed to search through his memories. "It was a beautiful place. There was a castle on the top of the mountain and donkeys and chickens and kids. Lots of kids."

"Certainly sounds like Kastro," Natalia said, chuckling. She turned back to Jennifer. "But Noel went with you on your *honeymoon?*"

"I had already left one child behind me," Jennifer said quickly. "I wasn't going to leave another I was blessed to have come into my life."

"They took me with them everywhere," Noel interjected. "That's why I didn't remember Kastro at first. We went to so many places."

"Plus, you were just a little boy of nine," his father pointed out, sounding like a lawyer with a mind for details.

"Did you see me?" Natalia had to know.

A dreamy look came into Jennifer's eyes, and Natalia suspected she was recalling memories she often liked to contemplate. It made Natalia feel very special. "Yes, we saw you. We went to church service Sunday morning. You were there dressed in a little yellow sundress with white flowers and matching yellow ribbons that held your nearly translucent hair back in a ponytail."

"I remember that dress." She did, even though it was long ago. "My sister Martha made it for me. It was one of my favorites."

"You were so happy. So carefree. So loved. Your whole family was there." She laughed. "So many people."

"I have five brothers and sisters, and I think several of them were already married then."

"And your father was such a man of God. I knew that day as I watched you with your family that God had taken my bad actions and brought good out of them."

"Did you talk to my *baba?*"

"No. I couldn't do that to the dear man. I learned that his wife, your mother, was quite sick. You were the apple of his eye. I didn't want to chance scaring him. Plus, how would we have communicated without any misunderstandings? I didn't speak a word of Greek then."

Natalia caught the word "then." " 'Then'? You do now?"

"*Malista,*" Jennifer replied, surprising Natalia with a yes. Greek was not a language many people spoke. She listened as her mother continued to speak in perfect Greek. "I thought if I should ever be blessed to be reconciled to you, I wanted to be able to communicate with you. So I've been studying Greek for years. I didn't know, until you became Audrey Shepherd, that you had learned English so well."

A million words could never have conveyed to Natalia the depth of her biological mother's love for her as that act of learning Greek in the hope of their meeting did. It told its own tale and touched Natalia deeply.

"*Fharisto poli,* Mother," she said, thanking her mother.

"*Parakalo.*" The older woman responded with "you're welcome." "Your English is superb, Natalia. And with only the barest trace of an accent. Very lovely. How did you learn to speak so well?"

"My parents were certain I was American, even if the American authorities wouldn't acknowledge it."

"The little sleeper I dressed you in and the blanket I wrapped you in were emblazoned with the American flag. I wasn't thinking too clearly back then, but I remember I thought everyone would know from those things that you were American. I also wrote a letter saying you were. But I'm not sure exactly what I wrote. I'd started taking drugs by then."

"Drugs?" To see her, Natalia didn't think it was possible.

An almost haunted look entered Jennifer's eyes. "I was very confused, Natalia, and I did a stupid thing. A woman does not desert her child in a bus station without having major problems. I didn't know what else to do. I was desperate."

Natalia remembered the day she'd met Noel. On her walk to the Rockefeller Center Christmas tree she had been praying about her birth mother. She had wondered what kind of woman would leave her newborn baby in a bus station. And God had told her, "*The desperate kind.*" Exactly what her mother was admitting to having been—desperate.

She looked deeply into Jennifer's eyes and, seeing how sad recalling her past made her, decided now wasn't the time to question her further. She would sometime but not today. Those questions could be asked and answered in the days and weeks and years to come. They had time.

She went back to Jennifer's question about her learning to speak English. "In the event I ever searched for my roots, my parents wanted me to be able to speak English well."

"And did you?" Jennifer asked with a degree of yearning in her tone that almost made Natalia feel sad. Particularly since she knew her answer. "Ever want to find your roots, I mean?"

Natalia didn't want to hurt this woman who had been such a wonderful mother to Noel, but she had to be truthful. She spoke softly, tenderly. "Not really. I mean I always wanted to come to America, but—oh, please don't feel bad—I never really felt the need to find my biological parents. Even though it was something my *baba* always encouraged me to do."

"He is a very special man. A man of faith, who, I think, has a great understanding about human nature and need."

Natalia thought about her dear *baba* and all the good he had done for the people in Kastro throughout her life and more. "Yes, he does," she agreed. "I always knew I was adopted." She touched her blond hair. "I looked so different from my brothers and sisters, and my mother was too old to have had children when I came along. I assumed you had given me up for a good reason. That's what my parents told me too. Either you couldn't care for me, or I was an embarrassment to you because you were unmarried, or you were sick. Something." She quickly continued, "I've had a wonderful family. One I thank you for finding for me."

"It was God." Jennifer held her hand upward.

Natalia smiled her agreement. "But when Noel told me you were my natural mother, at that very moment I realized how important it was to have you in my life, how right my *baba* was to encourage me to find you or be open to your finding me. And even though it wasn't something I thought I needed, having you in my life is one of the most important things to me now. I'm so thankful to have met you after twenty-six years."

"Thank you, Natalia," she whispered. "I don't deserve your forgiveness, but I thank you from the very bottom of my heart." She dabbed at the corners of her eyes, then blinked and sent Natalia a bright smile. "I thank God He gave you wisdom not to question my motive in giving you up, as if it had been a reflection upon you. Never that! And I thank God for the wonderful people who raised you to be such a lovely young woman. But mostly, right now, I thank God He has brought us together again."

Leaning toward one another, they fell into a natural embrace. Natalia took a deep breath of the essence of the woman who had given her the gift of life. She smelled of peaches and freshly washed clothing, wholesome and clean. Natalia whispered a prayer of thanksgiving to God for protecting her mother through her wild years. "What about my biological father?" Natalia felt compelled to ask after a moment.

Her mother sat back but still held her hand. Natalia was glad. She didn't want to let go either. "He was as bad as I."

"Did he know about me?"

Jennifer nodded sadly. "He told me to get rid of you."

"So you did." Natalia didn't mean for the words to sound so harsh. She offered a thin smile to soften them.

"Yes, but after you were born. Thank God—and only Him—I at least gave you life. On the first day of Advent. I always loved Christmas." She looked at the tree sparkling from its place near the decorated hearth, and a pensive quality came into her tone. "Even when I was a terrible, disrespectful, immoral young woman, I loved the Christmas season, and I thought it was very special you were born then. That's why I left a note saying exactly when your birthday was. The first day of Advent." She looked over at Noel. "The same as my son's."

"The day my parents found me," Natalia explained, "was Christmas Eve, my *mamma*'s birthday. Her name was Natalia, but she was always called Talia. So I was named for both Christmas and my *mamma*."

Jennifer's mouth formed an O. "Your mother's name was Natalia?" She laughed. "What an amazing humor our God has to have orchestrated everything so perfectly. For your mother to find you on her birthday, for her name to be Natalia, for the Christmas season to be something that spoke to my hardened heart even then." She shook her head at the miracle of it all. "From reading Noel's book I know Natalia means 'of or relating to Christmas.'"

Noel nodded. "'She who is born at Christmas.' Just like my name means 'born at Christmas.'"

"It is the name I would have chosen for you, Natalia, had I been a responsible mother then."

There was a moment of silence in which Natalia lifted up her thoughts and prayers to God, and the other three people seemed to do the same.

Then Natalia, wanting to know one more thing, asked, "Where is my biological father now?"

A look of sadness crossed Jennifer's face.

"He never changed. He died of a drug overdose a couple of years after you were born. But his parents are still alive. I think meeting you, their granddaughter, would be one of the most wonderful gifts they could ever receive." She turned her head in a searching way. "You inherited your exceptional outward beauty from him." She let her fingertips slide across Natalia's face. "Your fine, high cheekbones, your sparkling blue eyes"—she touched the ends of Natalia's hair—"your true blond coloring. He was a handsome man."

"I always wondered who I looked like." Natalia thought most adopted children wondered that, whether they admitted it or not. It wasn't important, just nice to know.

"Your father. Totally." She sighed. "I don't have any pictures of him, but his parents do. It would do his parents good to meet you. After they saw how my life changed, they've been leaning toward Christianity." She shrugged. "But they haven't been able to let go of the bitterness even after all these years. He was their only child. Someday, when you feel ready, maybe we can invite them over."

"I would be honored."

She nodded. "Tell me about your *baba*. Is he well? And your brothers and sisters?"

That Jennifer should ask about her family cemented the love Natalia already felt for the woman who had given her life. Maybe she hadn't done much more than that in the beginning. But it was more than many received in these modern times. And that was something.

Natalia happily told her about her *baba* and Martha and her brothers and sisters. Jennifer asked if they might call and talk to her *baba*, and even though it was very early in the morning in Greece, Natalia didn't hesitate to call him. This was one phone call her *baba* had been waiting for a very long time.

As it was, he had just returned from church, where he had felt the desire to go and pray. Natalia told him what had just transpired, and the dear man understood.

"Ah." His deep gravelly voice spoke through the wire and satellite to his daughter so far away and yet so very close spiritually. "That's why *O Theos*—God—directed me to get on my knees this morning and pray extra hard for you, *Kali mou kori,* my dear daughter. He knew."

"*Malista, Baba,* He knew," Natalia agreed. And when she told him that Jennifer had learned Greek, and the reason why, the man was overjoyed to be able to speak to her. Smiling, Natalia handed the phone to Jennifer.

Her mother's first words, with tears of joy and thanksgiving, were, "*Papouli,* thank you so very much for raising Natalia in such a God-centered and wonderful way." Natalia took Noel's hand then and walked with him over to the picture window.

For a few moments they stood and looked out at the pristine world surrounding them. Snow still fell softly, a blanket of righteousness and protection for the winter's night.

"King of Kings and Lord of Lords," Natalia heard Noel whisper by her side.

She turned to him.

He turned to her.

They nodded their heads with a degree of oneness that could come only from an understanding of the words Noel had spoken.

Those words said it all.

Everything.

And using only two of the Lord's names.

But for the couple who believed, those two names were enough.

More than enough for them to build a lifetime of happiness and commitment in a continuing fairy-tale romance that would forever have God at its center.

❧

And, beside his tree at Rockefeller Center on Christmas Eve, on bended knee Noel asked Natalia to be his wife. All were present—

Jennifer and Quincy Sheffield, Janet and Jasper Howard, Mary and Roswell Lincoln, and Rachels and, through the amazing technology of cell phones and computers, Natalia's *baba* and sister Martha and a multitude of friends in Kastro; as well as Prince who, as was his job, watched everything carefully. And they clapped their hands in joy when Natalia, to the sound of church bells ringing and the singing of Christmas carols in New York City, said, "Yes!"

Well, not Prince. He thumped his tail against the pavement and smiled his big doggie grin.

Prince seemed to understand he was soon to see his canine family in Kastro again. By Natalia saying yes, a wedding would be planned. Probably for March. And since *Papouli* would officiate, they would all be flying to Kastro.

Prince thumped his tail harder against the pavement.

That was something that appeared to please him very much.